W9-ACO-501

HELL'S MARCH

HELL'S
MARCH

TAYLOR ANDERSON

ACE
NEW YORK

ACE
Published by Berkley
An imprint of Penguin Random House LLC
penguinrandomhouse.com

Copyright © 2022 by Taylor Anderson

Library of Congress Cataloging-in-Publication Data

Names: Anderson, Taylor, 1963– author.
Title: Hell's march / Taylor Anderson.
Description: New York: Ace, [2022] | Series: The Artillerymen series
Identifiers: LCCN 2022001453 (print) | LCCN 2022001454 (ebook) |
ISBN 9780593200742 (hardcover) | ISBN 9780593200766 (ebook)
Subjects: LCGFT: Novels. Classification: LCC PS3601.N5475 H45 2022 (print) |
LCC PS3601.N5475 (ebook) | DDC 813/.6—dc23
LC record available at https://lccn.loc.gov/2022001453
LC ebook record available at https://lccn.loc.gov/2022001454

Printed in the United States of America
1st Printing

Book design by Daniel Brount
Interior art: Smoke background © swp23/Shutterstock.com

To my dad, and that entire fast-dwindling generation of heroes who stood in the light to hold back the darkness and formed me in so many ways. One was to recognize the very stark difference between good and evil while understanding that no human endeavor can be all one or the other. But "mostly good" isn't just slightly better than "mostly evil."

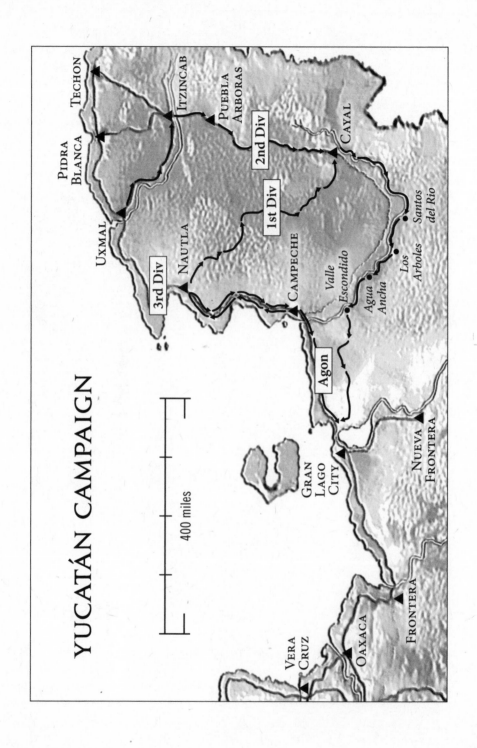

YUCATÁN CAMPAIGN

400 miles

VERA CRUZ

OAXACA

FRONTERA

NUEVA FRONTERA

GRAN LAGO CITY

Agon

CAMPECHE

Valle Escondido

Agua Ancha

Los Arboles

Santos del Rio

CAYAL

3rd Div

1st Div

2nd Div

NAUTLA

UXMAL

PIDRA BLANCA

TECHON

ITZINCAB

PUEBLA ARBORAS

BATTLE OF GRAN LAGO

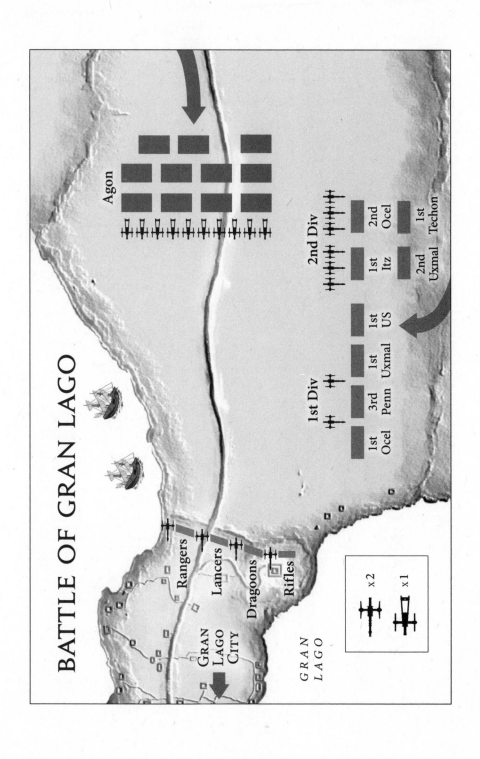

Agon

Rangers

Lancers

Dragoons

Rifles

GRAN LAGO CITY

GRAN LAGO

2nd Div

1st Div

1st Itz

2nd Ocel

2nd Uxmal

1st Techon

1st US

1st Uxmal

3rd Penn

1st Ocel

x2

x1

Still reeling from the traumatic "passage" from their Earth to this . . . very different one, the people we first referred to as "1847 Americans" (due to the year they arrived, since we knew little more about them) were even less prepared to comprehend their circumstances than we were when the decrepit US Asiatic Fleet destroyer USS Walker *was essentially chased to this world by the marauding Japanese in 1942. Still, in surprisingly short order, Lewis Cayce (formerly of the 3rd US Artillery) consolidated all the surviving artillerymen, infantrymen, dragoons, Mounted Rifles, and a handful of Texas Rangers—even a few Mexicans who'd been unluckily nearby onshore—from three appalling shipwrecks.*

Regardless of their confusion, the terrifying lethality of this world quickly convinced Cayce that they must all work together or die. Particularly after he discovered that the savage, unimaginable beasts all around them were the least of their concerns. Humans can be far more monstrous than the strangest, most ferocious animals, and the savage Holcano Indians, their few but shockingly Grik-like allies, and of course, the vile, blood-drenched "Holy Dominion" became a constant, looming menace.

In less than a year, Lewis Cayce and his capable companions had united various city-states on the oddly shaped Yucatán Peninsula against the long-feared Dominion and its Holcano proxies, built and trained an army, and repulsed a numerically superior but arrogant to the point of incompetence "Dom" army at the "Battle of the Washboard." It was a stunning victory that convinced the locals they had a chance to live free from fear of the most significant, diabolical power known to dwell in the "Americas" of this world.

But Lewis Cayce knew that wasn't the case. The Dominion was obsessed with conquest (and blood sacrifice) and would never allow "his" new people to live in peace. Any example of successful defiance would erode Dominion tyranny over its own people and had to be exterminated. Moreover, a purely defensive stance was ultimately doomed to failure. The Dominion had to be beaten, and the only way to do that was to attack. . . .

Excerpt from the foreword to Courtney Bradford's
Lands and Peoples—Destiny of the Damned, Vol. I,
Library of Alex-aandra Press, 1959

HELL'S MARCH

CHAPTER 1

The sun stood bright and hot over the "ruined" city of Nautla on the west coast of the Yucatán, which was being hacked back out of the dense surrounding forest even while other labor was under way to reclaim it. Like the larger, even more ancient Campeche to the south, it boasted finely fitted stone walls around impressive dwellings and other structures, as well as the seemingly ubiquitous central stepped pyramid that appeared to grace every city of any size in the region. Unlike distant Campeche, however, Nautla's condition wasn't a result of centuries of neglect. Right on the edge of the Contested Lands, or "La Tierra de Sangre," largely controlled by Holcano Indians and furry-feathery, extremely ferocious, "Grik-like" beings (these struck most as a terrifying cross between vultures and alligators with their upright physiques, raptor claws, and toothy jaws), Nautla had received too much attention over the last several decades. First conquered by Holcanos about fifty years earlier, it became almost a traditional battlefield for Holcanos and Ocelomeh Jaguar Warriors to trade back and forth. The Ocelomeh were never as numerous and used imaginative tactics, especially after the arrival of Har-Kaaska and his Mi-Anakka (vaguely catlike folk from an unnamed land shipwrecked there twenty years before). They finally made a serious attempt to permanently liberate the city a decade ago, but never induced enough people to return and make it prosper. They gave up. It had "belonged" to the Holcanos ever since, though its only real inhabitants were bands of wild "garaaches," essentially young feral Grik that hadn't joined a tribe. They were a menace to everyone, even their own species, and Grik and Holcanos both hunted and ate them.

Despite years of fighting in and around Nautla, the combatants hadn't possessed the means to seriously damage its durable structures, and it remained largely intact. Troops under the command of the Blood Cardinal Don Frutos of the "Holy Dominion"—a power based on a warped mix of centuries-old Spanish Catholic Christianity and Mayan-Aztecan blood ritual, dominating most of what should've been Mexico and Central America and bent on conquest and subjugation—had briefly bombarded it when they passed through. They'd only been exercising their gun's crews in preparation for knocking down the walls of the independent northern coastal city of Uxmal when they got there, so the damage hadn't been severe.

But Don Frutos had been stopped short of his objective at the "Battle of the Washboard" by a small army led by Major Lewis Cayce, composed of recognizably Christian natives of the Yucatán and their pagan Ocelomeh protectors and trained by American castaways from "another" earth who'd been bound for a different Vera Cruz to join Winfield Scott's campaign against the president of Mexico. And just like this different earth, the geography of war had changed very little. The ultimate enemy (besides the land itself and wildly ferocious predators) styled himself "His Supreme Holiness, Messiah of Mexico, and by the Grace of God, Emperor of the World," and ironically ruled from the same . . . but different . . . Valley of Mexico. Major Cayce's roughly seven hundred American survivors were no longer engaged in a political war, however—a spat between neighboring countries over past grievances and territory. They'd joined in a war of survival against an existential threat and had a cause they could all believe in: build a strong Union of threatened city-states, oppose the Dominion—and hopefully survive. The odds were very long indeed. Major Cayce followed his victory over the "Doms" by marching his still largely American Detached Expeditionary Force and the 1st Uxmal and 1st Ocelomeh Regiments down to fortify Nautla into an impassable strongpoint astride the Camino Militar. So far, the most difficult tasks had been rooting out garaaches, repairing the walls and backing them with earth to better resist Dom artillery, and cleaning out years of accumulated filth to make the place tolerably sanitary. The first priority in this respect had been to fill in the hopelessly fouled freshwater wells and dig new ones. Nautla was "alive" again in a sense, but as a formidable fort, not a city. It was in this light Lewis Cayce surveyed it now, standing on the south wall with a collection of his officers and some luminaries from Uxmal; friends, he hoped and believed.

"This isn't exactly what I meant when I urged you to take the war to the Doms," said Alcaldesa Sira Periz in a dissatisfied tone. Tiny, dark, and beautiful, she'd become the ruler of Uxmal when her husband was killed in a treacherous parley before the Battle of the Washboard began. Her suite of advisors included a shrewd, also beautiful Englishwoman named Samantha Wilde and the oddly inseparable Reverend Samuel Harkin—a tall, bearded, overweight Presbyterian—and Father Orno—a short, slight, Uxmalo priest from a vaguely Jesuit tradition. They'd been brought down by the wiry, craggy-faced Captain Eric Holland in HMS *Tiger*, an elderly, lightly armed, retired British man-o'-war that had been carrying European passengers like Samantha away from the "old" Vera Cruz after General Scott's invasion there. She'd only incidentally been close to the American *Mary Riggs*, *Xenophon*, and *Commissary*, and the sailing steamer *Isidra* (taking troops to join General Scott's campaign) when they were all so . . . bizarrely and cataclysmically swept to this world by an appalling—some said "supernatural"—storm. *Mary Riggs* and *Xenophon* actually "fell" to earth miles inland, and *Commissary* crashed down on the beach. All were hopelessly wrecked with great loss of life except *Isidra*, now in the hands of the Doms, and *Tiger*, which they'd repaired and put to use. Old and decrepit on the world she came from, *Tiger* was the fastest, most capable ship the Allied cities had at their disposal. Sadly, most of her passengers had been carried away to "safety" by *Isidra* and had likely been gruesomely sacrificed to the bloodthirsty underworld God of the Doms. At best, they still lived in slavery.

Sira Periz was dwarfed by most around her, standing near one of the new embrasures for cannon captured at the Washboard like a bronze-skinned pixie in a dark green dress covered by gold scale armor. As was customary for widows still in mourning, her long, jet-black hair hung loose around her shoulders. Uxmalo women accepting suitors gathered their hair behind their heads (to best display their pretty faces, believed most of the young American soldiers). Sira looked particularly small beside the tall, broad-shouldered Lewis Cayce. Instead of his usual dark blue shell jacket that all mounted forces now wore (distinguished only by red artillery trim in his case), he'd donned his fine, single-breasted frock coat and crimson sash under a white saber belt for the *alcaldesa*'s visit. Otherwise, he still wore the standard wheel hat and sky-blue trousers used by all the branches, but his trousers were tucked into knee-high boots, carefully blacked and polished by his scrawny, villainous-looking orderly, Corporal Willis, of the 1st Artillery. Lewis had apparently even allowed the man to closely trim his hair and thick brown beard. He was adamant that all the people in "his" army, Americans or not, maintain the highest degree of uniformity and hygiene—*particularly* under their strange circumstances—and demanded all the Allied cities provide proper uniforms for their people. Not only did he believe that men who looked like soldiers tended to act like them, he wanted all his troops, no matter where they were from or which regimental flags they flew (locals who hadn't joined "American" units fought under their city-state flags), to look and feel like one combined army, united by a common cause.

"I believe what the *alcaldesa* means," rumbled Reverend Harkin in his deep pulpit voice, "is that she hoped you might be able to do more than just come down and retake Nautla—and stop."

Lewis smiled. "I know. But that's already more than the enemy would've expected. Even their General Agon, a cut above the rest, I believe, probably thought we'd lick our wounds at Uxmal and wait for them to come at us again. He can't have any idea that King Har-Kaaska and Second Division have already driven down to relieve Itzincab in the east, and are pushing his Holcano allies back toward Puebla Arboras." Puebla Arboras had been the southernmost "Allied" city, but its *alcalde*, Don Discipo, had given it over to the enemy. "Agon will see this as an aggressive step," Lewis continued, "but still essentially defensive. More than he expected, like I said, and therefore as much as he'll think we're capable of. It'll focus his attention."

Another tall man, Captain Giles Anson, formerly of the Texas Mounted Rifles (or Rangers), chuckled lightly. He was lankier than Lewis, with a graying beard, and wore the plain blue jacket of a Ranger. Instead of a saber belt, he was burdened by a pair of huge Walker Colts in holsters on a waist-belt, suspended by braces, and a pair of smaller Paterson Colts in holsters attached to them high on his chest, almost under his arms. "You know how our Lewis is," he reminded with a combination of irony and fondness. The two men had known each other but hadn't been friends before they wound up here. Now they were. "Always focusin' the enemy on one thing . . ."

"While he does another!" burst out Varaa-Choon, clapping her hands. Varaa was a Mi-Anakka, one of only six known on this continent and the first the Americans ever met. Wearing silver scale armor over a reddish leather tunic covering dark tan fur—and with a long, fluffy tail that often seemed to have a mind of its own—she was also most emphatically not human. She claimed to be forty, but there was no white fur around her nose and mouth, only lighter and darker highlights around impossibly large blue eyes the color of the afternoon sky. She and her then more numerous companions were shipwrecked here twenty years before and taken for minions of a feline deity the Ocelomeh worshipped in their distant past. (This was particularly strange since, though Mi-Anakka did bear a certain resemblance to cats, as far as anyone knew, there were no Jaguars on this world.)

Their leader, now King Har-Kaaska, gradually corrected his follower's beliefs, but Mi-Anakka remained in positions of leadership among the Jaguar Warriors, more effectively guiding them in their apparently self-appointed, mutually beneficial role as protectors to the more peaceful and civilized peoples of the Yucatán. Varaa Choon was Har-Kaaska's female "Warmaster" and liaison to the Allied Army in the west. Devoted to her king and his interests, not to mention the Ocelomeh in the army, she'd also become a close friend to the Americans and was a trusted advisor and battlefield commander in her own right. Friend or not, there was only one subject she would never speak on, out of concern the Doms might eventually learn it too: where her people came from.

"Like last time," agreed Lieutenant Leonor Anson in a husky voice. The Ranger's daughter was almost as tall as him, having effectively passed as a young man in her father's Ranger company. Everyone knew she was a woman now, considered very pretty when she gave a rare smile instead of just boyishly handsome, and she no longer stuffed the shoulder-length black hair of her Mexican mother up in her hat. Nor did she tie it in back in the local style for a variety of reasons. She'd been . . . abused by straggling Mexican soldiers during the war for Texas's independence a decade before, and the "girl" she'd been was virtually extinguished, her mother and brothers killed. Her father had been with Houston's army, and she was all he had left. He couldn't leave her behind again, so she grew up fighting Comanches and

Mexican border incursions like a wildcat at his side. All that resulted in a somewhat . . . limited social development and an implacable hatred of Mexicans only now beginning to fade as she slowly befriended the young (newly promoted) Capitan Ramon Lara, also standing by. Lara was an agreeable young man, brave, resourceful, and funny, all of which earned Leonor's respect. He'd been in charge of a scouting force of Mexican soldiers onshore that was also . . . brought . . . wherever they were, by the same freak occurrence that dumped the Americans here. He now led the 1st Yucatán Lancers under Captain Anson's overall command, as were all the Rangers and dragoons.

Leonor still dressed and acted like a man in the field, even though she'd been taken under the wing of Samantha Wilde and her French friend, Angelique Mercure. Both ladies were abandoned by *Isidra* on the beach with *Commissary*'s survivors. Fortunate for them, as it turned out. But under their influence, Leonor had taken a few tentative steps toward becoming a "lady," when she deemed it appropriate. Still a fighter, however, she'd earned the men's respect as such with her own pair of Paterson Colts, often leading scouts. Otherwise, she stayed busy at her self-appointed task as aide and protector for her father—and now Lewis Cayce, whom she had secret, complicated feelings for.

Lewis smiled and nodded at her. "Like last time," he agreed. "The smaller force, and I expect we'll almost always be, must do the unexpected."

"I hope *Tiger*'ll have a bigger part in whatever you cook up this time," Captain Holland groused.

Lewis grinned at the old sailor, now in uniform as well, but still wearing his gray hair long and unbound. He looked eighty, but couldn't be. Even if he was only sixty, he was as strong and fit as a man half that age. He'd been master of the privately owned transport *Mary Riggs*, but spent time in the navy and knew how to fight a ship. Once referencing going through the grinder with Porter at Valparaiso back in 1814, he wasn't fond of the British and passionately hated carronades. He'd gone out to *Tiger*, lying helpless and dismasted at anchor offshore, and taken charge of her demoralized skeleton crew. Her owner and master had left with her passengers in *Isidra* to "get help." From what they'd learned of those people's fate, Holland figured *Tiger*'s skipper was the only one who deserved it. The ship was unquestionably "his" now, manned by the surviving sailors of all the wrecks and some Uxmalo fishermen.

"Stop complaining," Samantha Wilde told Holland, rolling her eyes and briskly waving her little folding fan. Like Sira Periz, she was dressed in green, a classy but sensible day dress complementing the curly blonde hair escaping from the wide-brimmed, low-crowned straw hat on her head. Like them all, she was perspiring, and the fan was useless against the heat, but it served as a—probably unconscious—manifestation of her moods. Impatience, in this instance. "You've had considerable excitement of late!" she exclaimed.

Tiger had all her heavier, lower-tier guns removed when she was sold out of service—she *was* sixty years old and couldn't bear their weight anymore—but her twenty upper-deck 12pdrs and ten 6pdrs had been more than a match for several Dom transports and now *two* armed enemy galleons snooping around the mouth of Uxmal Bay. There'd been no survivors from either one since Dom naval officers had been early converts to the even more radical "Blood Priests" who were gaining power in the Dominions and apparently had the same "victory or death" mindset as their upper-class hidalgo lancers. In the first instance, they'd murdered their surviving crew and then themselves after their ship was hopelessly bilged on coral heads inside the bay itself. In the second, after being disabled, they burnt the ship with everyone aboard. The horrifically voracious predators in the sea on this world quickly devoured those who jumped in the water.

The same wasn't true for the transports *Tiger* caught, loaded with supplies for Don Frutos's army. Their officers had been taken, too afraid to kill themselves, but then even more fearful of talking—at first. The fate of their souls was a factor, but they were more concerned what would happen to them if they were "rescued." Their crews were another matter. Nearly all were slaves, terrified and expecting to be murdered, eaten—who knew what—by demon and heretic captors. They were so pathetically grateful when treated well, Holland thought he could use them when their shock wore off. Granted, they'd been enslaved in conquered territories and were deemed "heretics" themselves, but Varaa said slaves often acted as rabid as Blood Priests to "prove" they'd converted. Lewis considered. *Either way, it's the first indication the perverted "True Faith" of the Holy Dominion isn't all-pervasive, even where it's been long-established.*

"I did, a little," Holland agreed, "an' the prize money for the cargoes was appreciated by the lads."

Sira Periz waved that away. "A small payment to your crew was cheaper than producing the goods and ships."

"*I'm* most thankful for the part of the cargo coming to *us*," asserted Captain Elijah Hudgens, commanding C Battery. His accent left no doubt that, like *Tiger*, he was born in Britain. Lewis suspected nearly half his six hundred or so surviving Americans had been immigrants to the United States—before they came here. *So many factions, so many rivalries! But maybe that's for the best. All those factions from that world and this have fused into a surprisingly cohesive "us" against the "them" of the Doms.* He shook his head and looked back at Hudgens, who was also responsible for emplacing ten of the twenty field guns they'd captured at the Battle of the Washboard.

"All that gunpowder and copper roundshot for these ugly buggers," Hudgens continued, gesturing at the nearest weapon. "The powder's not as good as the 'powder monks' are making at Uxmal now, but it'll do. And we needed more roundshot than we captured with the guns. It's all the wrong bloody size!" He elaborated, waving at the closest cannon again. The tube was bronze and reasonably well-made, but American guns (and the British ones on *Tiger*) were bored for six- and twelve-pound shot, a little more than 3.5 and 4.5 inches in diameter, respectively. Dom field guns were 8pdrs and required a ball just under four inches in diameter. A whole different size they'd have to make. The captured cargo gave them more time to do so. The "ugly" part Hudgens objected to most was the bright yellow–painted, split-trail, solid-wheel carriage. It was ridiculously heavy, bulky, and entirely un-suited to rapid movement around the battlefield. "Proper" carriages were under construction back in Uxmal and elsewhere for the captured cannon, even the giant siege guns they'd taken, but emplaced in the walls of Nautla, these didn't need them yet.

Looking back at Holland, Lewis asked, "There were charts in the transports you took?"

"Aye." Holland grinned. "Crude, ugly sketches showin' little more than the Caribbean, an' all lookin' like somethin' Magellan or Cabrillo would'a scribbled."

"I don't know who they are," Varaa said, "but remember, the shorelines on this world are not the same as yours. The charts may be quite accurate."

Holland frowned. "Don't see how. It gets *really* strange down past the Mosquito Kingdom . . . area. . . ." He shrugged. The Mosquito Kingdom didn't exist here, of course.

Lewis wasn't interested in south at the moment. "What about Vera Cruz?"

Holland dipped his head and sobered. "I was hopin' you'd ask about that. When the merchant officers we caught started talkin', they confirmed *Isidra*'s there. Maybe some o' her people." He scratched his bristly chin. "No idea if she's fit for sea or her engineerin' plant's in one piece—regular folks don't ask questions like that—but the stack's been down, then back up, an' there's been a lot o' comin' an' goin' aboard, aside from general repairs." He frowned. "Hafta assume they've drawn plans o' ever'thin' in her by now."

Varaa frowned and blinked rapidly, tail swishing behind her. Lewis knew she and King Har-Kaaska were concerned the Doms would develop steam-powered ships and eventually threaten their homeland. Wherever *that* was. Lewis didn't like it either, but without information, there'd been nothing they could do. *Now . . . ?*

"On the bright side . . . maybe," Holland continued, "they've replaced her masts an' crossed her yards. No sails hoisted last time our fellas saw, but they've had time to sew a suit an' get it up by now. Prob'ly won't risk actually *operatin'* her without backup. We might still cut her out before they do. Deprive 'em of experience if not a design." He paused. "Wouldn't want to try it if she can't make sail, mind. We'd never tow her clear. There's usually two or three warships like we already handled in Vera Cruz. Wouldn't concern me if we could maneuver," he said disdainfully, "but luggin' *Isidra*, they'd pick us apart. Them an' the shore batteries."

"Shore batteries?" Lewis asked.

"Aye. Big devils. 36pdrs like those siege guns you captured. Confirmed that by talkin' to the transport crews, though they don't hardly know *how* to tell us what we want to know, if you get my meanin'. Most'a the poor devils ain't allowed ashore an' some can hardly speak. More like dogs than men. Prob'ly been cooped up on ships since they was nippers, just doin' what they're told. Ask 'em about shoals an' some might know. Ask about shore batteries an' they know they're there, just nothin' about 'em. Hafta get the officers to draw things up better if they can." He chuckled. "It finally dawned on 'em their best chance o' livin' is if they *don't* get rescued, so one, at least, is bein' more cooperative." He paused and rubbed his stubble again. "I *did* get that the Doms don't have many warships in the Atlantic. Seems they're more worried about the Pacific." He glanced at Varaa. "Them 'New Britain Isles Imperials,' er whatever they are."

No one knew much about the "Empire of the New Britain Isles" except its people were—apparently—British, or descendants of British sailors who'd come to this world just like them at some point and were based out in the Pacific. Other than that, it was believed they were enemies of the Doms, but also traded with them—some said for slaves. It was rumored they'd established outposts or a colony in territory the Dominion claimed but didn't inhabit, up in the "Californias," and the Doms had spent years building a massive force called "La Gran Cruzada" to expel them. That was probably the only reason they hadn't sent more troops here.

"Damned Brits're always stirrin' things up wherever they are, even here," Holland groused, then hesitated, thinking aloud, "I guess the Doms could bring more ships 'round the Horn if we raise too much fuss."

Varaa blinked rapidly, thinking hard, eyes narrowed. "I don't *think* so. When my people came here twenty years ago—Mi-Anakka," she stressed, as opposed to her Ocelomeh, "we surveyed the coast as best we could. Exploration was our purpose, after all." She bowed slightly to Sira Periz. "I assure you the coastlines we contributed to the embroidered atlas in the map room of the Audience Hall in Uxmal are correct. We missed places," she confessed, glancing at Holland and blinking curiosity, "a long stretch to the south of what you call the 'Mosquito Kingdom,' in fact." She shook her head. "But we started as far south as possible. There *is* no passage around the 'Horn.' It's entirely choked with ice."

Anson shrugged as if none of that mattered. To him, it didn't. "So there's Brits in the Pacific. Good. If so, they've helped us this time whether they meant to or not. Remember what Don Frutos said about not givin' much of a damn about us right now, with somebody else pesterin' 'em somewhere else?" He nodded at Varaa. "Goes along with the rumors your people picked up, about most of the Dom army bein' drawn northwest."

"Which makes this the best possible time for us to press them *here*," Sira Periz insisted. "Destroy them," she added hotly, "so the shadow of the horror they bring no longer lingers over us!"

Lewis smiled at her again. "Oh, I agree entirely, though I don't think we'll do it *here*, exactly."

Sira was taken aback. So were most of the others. "Before I go on, let me ask a few questions," Lewis said to Sira. "First of all, can you tell me how negotiations are going to form a true Union of all the city-states on the Yucatán? We all agreed it's essential," he pressed.

Sira and Samantha both looked troubled. "We did and do," Sira confirmed, "but others are . . . less sure." She sighed. "I fear little has changed since our earlier efforts except I and King Har-Kaaska are now convinced as well. So are Alcalde Truro of Itzincab, Alcalde Ortiz of Pidra Blanca, even Alcaldesa Yolotli of Techon. All the leaders of the biggest cities. But the 'how' and 'to what extent' we'll unite remains undecided, so many smaller towns and cities stand and wait," she ended sadly. "They send supplies and volunteers to join us—all know what is necessary, that we must work together—but this 'Union' is too strange to them, too much like, pardon me," she apologized, "surrendering themselves to become one with the Dominion."

Leonor snorted. "Big difference is we won't kill 'em for not joinin', but the Doms'll kill 'em whether they do or not."

"And that's part of the problem, my dear," Samantha said. "Many of their leading citizens blame *us* for stirring the Doms against them!"

"Nonsense, of course," Father Orno assured, speaking for the first time. "The Doms would've had us already, just using the Holcanos, if God hadn't brought you here."

Captain Anson shook his head. Like Lewis, he was always uncomfortable with the idea that God—quite traumatically, in fact—brought them all here just to fight the Doms. *Harkin an' Orno are convinced, an' so are a lot of the men*, he thought. *Lewis never discourages the notion an' I wonder if he believes it himself, deep down?* He supposed it *was* easier to accept everything that'd happened to them if they thought there was a purpose behind it. "So where does that leave us?" he asked.

"Officially, essentially where we were," Sira confessed, "but unofficially, things are much closer than that. Uxmal, Techon, Pidra Blanca, and Itzincab—I'll include King Har-Kaaska and his Ocelomeh—remain independent, but as firmly allied as it's possible to be."

"Rather like your various states under the 'Articles of Confederation,'" Samantha supplied helpfully.

"That didn't work very well," Lewis reminded her.

Sira Periz shook her head. "Whatever *that* was, we're integrating our economies and everything we make, beyond what our people must have for themselves, to support the army"—she threw Holland a smile—"and navy." She looked back at Lewis. "All under *your* direction, Major Cayce. Even King Har-Kaaska will obey your commands."

"How do you keep all that sorted out?" Anson asked skeptically.

"As originally envisioned, Colonel De Russy mediates disputes between us and advises us what the Allied Quartermaster's Department under Mr. Finlay and Procurador Samarez requires, who must supply it, where it must go, how it will get there and who will use it."

"Watch that little villain Finlay." Holland chuckled. "Wasn't above linin' his pockets when he was my purser in *Mary Riggs*."

"He and Procurador Samerez both, then," Sira Periz said dryly, "but there's no evidence they're doing it now."

"Not while their lives are on the line," Holland said, nodding. "Both were made for the job an' neither wanted it. It's that or fight, though, an' die if we lose. I reckon they'll do fine till the war's over." He laughed. "After that, you better fire 'em both."

"The whole thing's working rather well," Samantha assured hopefully. "De Russy presides as manager over the Council of Alcaldes and makes final decisions. He can be outvoted," she admitted, "but it hasn't happened yet."

Lewis grunted, obviously less than pleased. Everyone knew he wanted a truly united nation, a "new United States" and rock-steady cause for his army to fight for. But the army was already united. It knew the stakes, and its cause was survival and freedom. *He'd* united it into a single, integrated force, already fighting for the cause he envisioned, whether its provincial leaders understood it or not. And after he led it to victory over the Doms at the Washboard—something no one ever imagined—Lewis Cayce would've been amazed, possibly horrified, to learn the army would go anywhere and fight anyone—for him.

"Does this affect your planning?" Sira Periz asked anxiously.

"Yes," Lewis murmured absently. "Well, no, not really. As you say, with Agon on his heels and most of the rest of the Dom army with this Gran Cruzada and heading as far away from us as it can go, we've a brief opportunity to beat the enemy soundly and decisively. We have to seize it." He looked at her. "Perhaps clear away that 'shadow' you spoke of forever. What's the strength of the Home Guard now?" he asked as if changing the subject. "And the Pidra Blanca Home Guard as well?"

Sira raised her eyebrows. "Guard losses at the Washboard weren't severe, but they were heavily depleted by transfers to line regiments that did suffer badly, to bring them up to strength. Particularly the 1st Uxmal and 3rd Pennsylvania," she added somberly. "But the victory has boosted enlistment to the point that I don't think we'll have to resort to conscription. At least not right away."

That was good news. Lewis hated the very idea of conscription, almost as much as he hated slavery. Ironically, slavery was as deeply entrenched on this world as the one he'd left, but it didn't have the impossible (for him)-to-defend racial component prevailing in his homeland—and his native state of Tennessee. Only captive enemy warriors—mostly Holcanos—were forced to labor by the Allied cities on the Yucatán, and having seen the savage aftermath of battle with that hated foe, he had to confess that well-fed servitude was more humane than slaughtering them all. *Far more humane than what the Holcanos—and Doms—mean to do to every living soul in this land*, he grimly rationalized. He still didn't like it. It had too much of the sense of Imperial Rome to suit his Whiggish leanings, but the only way to change it was to win.

Sira Periz was still talking. "And Major Wagley—much improved from his wound, by the way," she inserted a little smugly, knowing no one had expected the young Pennsylvanian to live, "is finding the new recruits more enthusiastic and willing to learn. As of now, the Home Guard at Uxmal stands at fifteen thousand including support—at various levels of readiness, of course—and a thousand are armed with captured Dom muskets. I'd ask for more of those, but I know it takes time to make the necessary alterations and most must go to 'line' units until we can make our own weapons." (As issued, Dom muskets were bulky and crude but reliable enough. The biggest deficiency was that their bore diameters ranged wildly from roughly .72 to .76 caliber, so the "standard" Dom ball was about .70 caliber and rattled erratically down the barrel when the weapon was fired, making it ridiculously inaccurate. All were being reamed true to .77 caliber, to fire a larger standard ball for better accuracy. Blacksmiths were also reforging the thousands of plug-style bayonets they'd recovered and fitting them with tubular sockets that could be fitted on the outside of the barrel, allowing soldiers to keep shooting with the blade affixed.)

"Even horse recruitment is up, in addition to the seventeen hundred sound Dom animals collected after the battle," Sira continued, "but I credit a new enthusiasm for the cause more than anything. Their owners no longer hide them. Loose or wild horses are getting harder to find."

Horses were indigenous to the Americas on this world, though they looked a little . . . odd. Generally shorter but broader and more powerful, they were usually tan or brown with dark contrasting stripes. The problem was, "this" Yucatán was covered by dense forest, and its people largely relied on smaller or much larger animals like burros or armabueys (basically two-ton armadillos) to haul burdens from place to place. Wild horses were rare in the forest, hard to catch, and extremely difficult to protect from predators after all the effort to domesticate them. Doms had plenty of horses, mostly bred from those their seventeenth-century ancestors brought, yet were happy to rely on placid, plodding armabueys to draw their army's guns and other heavy burdens. Lewis was convinced that only mobility gave them a chance in this war, and he demanded horses.

"As for the Pidra Blanca Guard, four thousand men, armed and trained with pikes, are marching from there to Uxmal now," Sira ended triumphantly. "These numbers don't count recruits from Uxmal, Pidra Blanca, and Techon already training for line regiments as well."

Lewis frowned. "Too many able-bodied men taken from fields and factories could kill us as quickly as not enough troops," he warned. The "Powder Monks" had established a great gunpowder factory on the banks of the Cipactli River, and a number of rotary tool machine shops had been built as well, supervised largely by Pennsylvania, Virginia, and Tennessee gunsmiths, blacksmiths from everywhere, and other men from the ranks who'd worked in such places before joining the army on another world. Still near the beginning of the "dry season," when it only rained once or twice a week but the Cipactli still ran high, they were making a lot of good gunpowder in the new mill, but the gunsmiths (and their numerous apprentices) were repairing, reaming, and sometimes shortening almost nine thousand captured muskets. The mines and foundries near Itzincab had been reopened, and smelters were casting copper roundshot, canister balls, and lead projectiles for rifles and muskets at a fantastic rate, sending much of it downriver on flatboats. Gun carriages, limbers, caissons, forge wagons, battery wagons—all were being made to precise plans taken directly from the manual, *Instruction for Field Artillery Horse and Foot—1845*, that Lewis had provided. Copies were made on improved paper (also good for making musket cartridges), and Colonel Ruberdeau De Russy and Major Andrew Reed had between them produced all three volumes of *Scott's Tactics*. Those manuals together had just about everything anyone needed to know about training and equipping a modern army, and even how to use it—to a degree.

"I can't stop them from volunteering for the guards *or* line regiments," Sira said a little wistfully. "Not when you need them so badly. I *can* make sure they train their replacements, and those replacements are available. People are swarming into the cities, often from those very towns and settlements not yet committed to the cause. Women"—she frowned, glancing at Leonor and Varaa—"whom *you* won't allow in the army, already outnumber men in the factories and shops. The very old and young are joining them now. You'll have all the troops and supplies we can give you," she added a little haughtily, "but what will you do with them?"

Lewis pursed his lips. "You need to keep five thousand guards in Uxmal to man the defenses in case the Doms try something from the sea, and to protect the people and production facilities from agents of the enemy." They'd already had trouble of that sort. "I want the other ten thousand, plus the four thousand Pidra Blanca Guards here at Nautla, manning these guns and fortifications. Their primary purpose, at first, is to convince Don Frutos and General Agon our whole army is here. Hopefully, they won't have much to do but continue to drill and train."

"The rest of the army *won't* be here?"

"No."

"That's a lot of troops just putting on a show," Harkin grumbled. "More than we had in the whole army at the Washboard."

"Yes," Lewis agreed, "the force we leave must be strong enough to fool Agon, but the guards won't just be for that. Like I said, they still need training, and pikes are better for defense than attack. They *will* have to defend Nautla if Agon mounts an assault." He paused. "And I'll need them for other things . . . when they're ready."

"So you *are* planning an attack of your own," Sira said, sounding a little confused. "But where?"

Instead of answering directly, Lewis gave the *alcaldesa* a reassuring grin, then looked at Captain Holland. "What's your opinion of the Dom transport galleons you captured? Are they fit for sea?"

Holland squinted, contemplating his response. "Aye, they weren't damaged, but they're shameful slow—an' dismal slugs beatin' into a wind. Freeboard's so high aft, they're the very devil ta tack an' the prize crews—fine sailors—missed stays bringin' 'em in. Thought we'd lose the masts outa one when she was taken aback." He fumed. "Damn things got less for forestays than any ship I ever seen. Don't even *use* staysails!"

"Can you alter the rig in any way—that wouldn't be too noticeable—to make them faster? Handle better?"

Holland chuckled mischievously. "If they was dismasted in a storm, I could *jury-rig* a better mast an' sail plan!"

Everyone laughed appreciatively at the sailor's confidence, but Lewis shook his head. "But would it be a rig the Doms would know? Best leave things as they are otherwise. In any event, I want you to take one of the prizes and have a look at Vera Cruz yourself. *Tiger* will accompany you, but stay out of sight." He paused, then pressed. "Your First Lieutenant, Mr. Semmes, he can handle her in your absence? Be counted on to take whatever action is necessary?"

Holland raised a brow. "Sounds to me like 'havin' a look' is the least you want, but aye, Billy Semmes is a good 'un for a Britisher. His old skipper left his guts a little sour, but he's perked right up." He considered. "I'll take Mr. Sessions with me in the slug. He ain't as good a seaman as Semmes, but was a privateersman once an' knows how ta use a cutlass."

Lewis held up a hand. "Obviously, I *do* want you to recapture *Isidra*, but only if it can be done with almost no risk. I've told you before, Captain Holland; we can't spare you. Nor can we spare *Tiger*."

Holland grinned. "An' I replied that I can't spare me neither. I'll get *Isidra* out for you, an' I'll be careful too."

Lewis nodded, then looked back at Sira Periz. "As for the army and the offensive I have in mind, whether the Blood Cardinal Don Frutos remains in overall command or not, I expect General Agon will be strongly reinforced in fairly short order."

"If they let *him* live," Anson inserted.

Lewis bowed his head. "True. We've all seen how little tolerance the enemy has for failure. But until our scouts tell us more, we'll proceed as if the enemy *can't* be stupid enough to execute the only commander they have who knows anything about us. That means we *have* to assume he'll fortify Campeche and have plenty of troops if we march down there."

"An attack there would be mighty tough," Leonor said. "We got a lot o' new troops ourselves, an' even our 'veterans' only been in one big fight. They did good," she conceded, "but throwin' 'em against a well-defended position would be bloody as hell." That was a long speech for Leonor in a discussion like this, but she, her father, Varaa, Hudgens, and probably Corporal Willis were the only ones who already knew what was cooking in Lewis's mind.

Lewis was nodding, looking steadily at Sira Periz. "Exactly what I've been thinking," he agreed, then added in a matter-of-fact tone, "so we'll rely on the local knowledge of Captain Anson's Rangers, dragoons, and lancers, and Varaa's Ocelomeh scouts, to find a way *around* General Agon."

There was silence for a moment until surprise overwhelmed the short, dark-haired, barrel-chested Captain Marvin Beck, commanding the 1st US Infantry. "You'd leave him in our rear?" he blurted. The other young infantry commanders shifted uneasily; Captain James Manley, in charge of the 1st Uxmal Infantry, Consul Koaar-Taak (the only other Mi-Anakka with the division) of the 1st Ocelomeh, and the newly promoted Captain John Ulrich, now leading the 3rd Pennsylvania with George Wagley gone. All trusted Lewis, but with Major Reed away in Uxmal, they felt a little adrift. Beck was the senior infantryman present—he'd been promoted an hour before the others—and probably considered it his duty to speak.

"I suppose he would be behind us eventually," Lewis conceded, then added vaguely, "but he won't be astride our line of supply."

Varaa clapped her hands, blue eyes bright. "It's a *lovely* plan," she exclaimed with a grin, tail whipping. "Lewis and I have *always* thought alike, you know." She *kakked* a laugh at the questioning looks. "And if you don't see it—you who already know us so well—I'm sure General Agon won't. After we take a rather lengthy stroll and help Har-Kaaska—and Major Reed when he joins him—finish our business with the Holcanos once and for all, First *and* Second Divisions"—she blinked amusement at Holland—"and our gallant little navy, of course, will end up astride the *enemy's* line of supply. And fourteen thousand highly motivated—and better trained by then— Home Guard troops will be in *General Agon's* rear!"

Lewis's expression turned somber. "That's the size of it. It won't be easy, and we'll have to move with care not only to elude the enemy's attention but to avoid—or deal with—the many monsters we'll encounter." He was looking at the dense, gloomy forest to the southeast. "About three hundred miles, I should think."

"Through *that*?" Captain Ulrich almost squeaked. The big former sergeant had a deep voice, and no one would've imagined he could make such a sound. He didn't either and continued more normally, embarrassed, "It's swarming with man-eating boogers, and there's not even roads!"

"But there are," Consul Koaar countered thoughtfully. "Nothing like the Camino Militar," he conceded, "and they'll be difficult to negotiate with artillery, but my people know them." His eyes narrowed. "As do the Holcanos.

After King Har-Kaaska finishes with those still around Itzincab, he'll press on toward Puebla Arboras."

Anson was nodding. "Drive 'em out of there an' there'll be nowhere for 'em to go but Cayal. We'll meet Har-Kaaska an' Major Reed there. Finish the Holcanos for good."

Consul Koaar blinked at Anson and grinned. "None must get past us to warn General Agon. Your Rangers will be very busy, Captain Anson."

Anson grinned back. "You too."

Samantha Wilde fluttered her fan. "There's that 'Captain' again. 'Captain, captain, captain!' 'Captains' everywhere now. Don't you all find it remarkably tedious? And all to keep from stepping on Colonel De Russy's toes! How absurd, and how do you keep it all straight?"

De Russy had come to this world in command of the 3rd Pennsylvania Volunteer Regiment. Appointed by the governor, he was a politician, not a soldier. Sadly, but fortunately, he recognized that early on. He wasn't a coward, but wasn't a leader either, so he put Lewis in charge until he was "fit" to take over. That would never happen. He did have a politician's gift for coercing compromise, however, and was perfect for his role as "Manager" of the Council of Alcaldes.

Samantha looked sternly at Lewis. "Colonel De Russy has decided you must accept a brevet promotion to lieutenant colonel. Andrew Reed will as well, though you'll retain a few moments' 'seniority.'" She chuckled. "Now at least everyone can *call* you 'colonel' and you can spread a few more 'majors' around. Surely there'll be less confusion."

"None of *us* are confused about who leads us," Consul Koaar pronounced.

Alcaldesa Sira Periz cleared her throat with an apologetic look and admitted in a small, vulnerable voice that only those she trusted completely would ever hear. "I am, sometimes. I *pray* it is the One God who leads us, as Father Orno and Reverend Harkin insist"—she looked again at Lewis—"but whether He does or not, it's up to you to do so on the battlefield, so I pray He guides your steps and your hand."

Lewis took a long, deep breath. "I do too."

CHAPTER 2

*P*oom-poom, poom-poom, poom-poom! roared the smoke and fire-tarnished bronze 6pdr guns of Justinian Olayne's A Battery of the 1st US Artillery, firing by sections of two. Each coughed a spear of orange-yellow flame shrouded in a gout of dingy white smoke as it recoiled back about seven feet, its crew leaping to the spokes to push it back into battery. As soon as the Number Three man rushed back between the right wheel and trail, stabbed a bristle brush down the vent, and shouted, "Clear!" the process of reloading commenced, all while ripping-canvas shrieks of roundshot tearing downrange were punctuated by hollow *crump*s when they hit the masonry wall surrounding the city of Puebla Arboras, five hundred yards away. Behind the wall (and as carefully avoided as possible, so far) were impressive buildings much like those in other cities on "this" Yucatán.

Almost all were shaped stone, like the burnt-out dwellings surrounding the city, but their roofs were mostly clay tiles instead of thatch, and many were quite large. Some were long, low, and narrow, while others stood two or three stories high, supporting broad roofs with columns. A stepped pyramid stood in the middle of everything, not quite as tall as the one in Uxmal. The most glaring difference seemed to be the number of sculpted trees among the buildings and groping green ivies with their profusion of flowers tastefully covering so much of the city. It would've been beautiful if not for the circumstances and the recent jarring places where greenery had been torn away to begin garish carvings depicting the gruesome blood rites of the "Holy" Dominion that sought a foothold here.

"Keep at it, lads, fast an' hot!" called the thin, almost wispy Captain Olayne atop his prancing, dark-striped "local" horse. His young and only slightly Irish voice was rough from use and smoke, but stronger and more mature than just a few months before. "The gate's down already, and it won't take much more!"

Olayne had good reason to believe that. Most of the inhabitants of Puebla Arboras would doubtless welcome them as liberators. The minority who wouldn't had converted to the twisted Dominion faith because that's the way the wind had blown. They'd get no support from neighbors they'd oppressed. The real enemy here were Holcanos: unusually savage, seminomadic woodland Indians that normally only raided the outskirts of towns or preyed on travelers between them. Stirred by promises of conquest and plunder by Dominion Blood Priests, their various bands had joined together under a chief calling himself "Kisin," and along with their even more savage "Grik" allies, had embarked on a campaign to seize vast swathes of the central and western Yucatán when Don Frutos's regular Dom army had marched on Uxmal. But Don Frutos was beaten, and so were Kisin's Holcanos besieging Itzincab. They'd retreated here, where things were currently going quite well for King Har-Kaska's advance brigade of 2nd Division.

Holcanos weren't used to cities and had no more idea how to defend one than the handful of local zealots who'd never been warriors to begin with. And the morale of these Holcanos had already suffered grievously at the hands of Har-Kaaska's Ocelomeh Jaguar Warriors, a sound force of hurriedly trained Itzincab militia, and the timely arrival of a thousand well-trained pike-armed troops from the cities of Pidra Blanca and Techon. Then, immediately after his victory at the Washboard, Major Lewis Cayce dispatched some of his mounted troops to join Har-Kaaska's push south. These included Olayne's A Battery of 6pdrs and a section of 12pdr howitzers from Emmel Dukane's B Battery, a company of (largely Ocelomeh) Rangers under the bearlike Lieutenant Bandy "Boogerbear" Beeryman, and two companies (J and L) of the 3rd Dragoons under Captains Coryon Burton and Hans Joffrion. All were technically under Olayne's command, but he knew better than to ignore "advice" from Boogerbear. In any event, with such a force after them, many Holcanos and almost all their Grik allies simply kept running past Puebla Arboras. It was believed that fewer than two thousand "defended" the city now, with very few firearms and certainly no cannon.

Poom, poom, poom, poom, poom, poom! went the guns, one after another, almost as if firing a salute, and the Pidra Blancos and Techonos arrayed behind them in sky-blue uniforms with pikes on their shoulders gave a cheer. Olayne turned his horse and bowed to them.

"Show-off," chuckled his short, burly, Scottish-born First Sergeant McNabb.

"That's 'show-off' *sir*," Olayne stressed with a haughty chuckle.

"Aye, it is. An' ye've earned it," McNabb agreed.

Olayne would've flushed if the sun hadn't already darkened his skin beyond it showing. "Thank you, First Sergeant, though I would've lost every gun in my battery at the Washboard if not for you."

"It wasnae *that* bad," McNabb deflected. It had been.

"All the horses dead in the traces, the damned Doms overrunning our *limbers*? Only you with the sense to pull the guns back by hand and keep loading them from the caissons!"

"You would'a thought of it," McNabb assured loyally.

"I did! I just didn't know how!" McNabb had called for wounded men, infantry—anyone at hand—to clap onto the prolong ropes and heave the guns back even as their crews kept loading and firing. Any pause at that moment would've doomed them all.

"Well . . . it was fine in the end."

The guns roared again, to more cheering, and Olayne opened his telescope to peer at the distant target as pulverized stone exploded in all directions and a long section of wall by the gate collapsed in a billowing cloud of dust. "It was never built to withstand artillery," he murmured.

"No sir," McNabb agreed with a touch of irony, "just hugeous man-eatin' beasties."

Olayne frowned. *Too true*, he thought. *By anyone's reckoning—whose mind I can understand—the . . . different enemy we've found on this strange and deadly world seems as starkly wicked as any soldier could hope that men he's ordered to kill could be. Their prisoners—combatants or not—are invariably tortured and murdered, even eaten by Holcanos and Grik. And bent on "holy" conquest by extermination, the Doms are just as cruel and ruthless to their own troops, enforcing mindless discipline with ghastly examples. For all that, however, their battlefield tactics are straightforward enough. Too straight-forward for their own good, so far. But as McNabb said, the land and creatures infesting it are terrible enemies in their own right, even more frightening and incomprehensible than the Doms. At least to those of us "new" here.*

They'd encountered no Holcanos on their ten-day dash down the Cipactli River road, or during the week it took to get here from Itzincab, but even their large, noisy, well-armed force couldn't discourage all the monsters, and they'd lost nine men. Four were killed in a single attack by what looked like a furry, ten-foot-tall . . . crow, with great toothy jaws instead of a beak, long arms with terrible claws on its fingers, and a rigid, whiplike tail under bright plumage that spread out toward the end. A fusillade of shots finally drove it off but didn't seem badly injured. Just possibly frightened and annoyed by its many wounds. The others—as many Ocelomeh as not, so even the woods-wise weren't immune—were lost to slashing attacks by similar, smaller beasts, usually at night. Without the wall they were battering down, no city could survive in this densely wooded wilderness, and that explained why even the surrounding homes were stoutly made.

McNabb nodded behind them. "Colonel's comin'."

Olayne turned again, muttering lightly, "And I was only just now contemplating 'strange creatures.'"

Colonel "King" Har-Kaaska drew near, surrounded by a small staff—mostly colorfully dressed civilian leaders from Pidra Blanca, Techon, and Itzincab—all human. Har-Kaaska wasn't. In fact, he looked like a man-size cross between some kind of wide-eyed cat and a burly, furry ape, complete with what seemed like a disproportionately long tail. Wearing gold scale armor over a black and brownish-gray brindled pelt, he rode a bipedal crea-ture that might've been a giant platypus . . . shaped more like a lizard . . . or a fat duck, complete with a broad protruding bill beneath smallish black eyes.

Still, as bizarre as all the Americans might still consider Har-Kaaska and his mount, all his Mi-Anakka, for that matter, they were ultimately just "another thing" on top of the multitude of *other* opium-dream phenomena they'd coped with as all their beliefs, worldviews, even prejudices came un-der unrelenting assault. After eight months of that, combined with actual bloody combat, a very few might still cling to old notions and bigotries, even teeter on the brink of madness, but most had accepted and adapted to their unexplainable situation. The portly Reverend Harkin's belief that God put them here specifically to confront the evil of the Holy Dominion was a comfort to some, but nearly all were inspired by their growing attachment to the natives and the cause of uniting and protecting them.

This offensive was a start; Har-Kaaska's brigade of 2nd Division was composed of the 2nd Ocelomeh (a thousand archers with big, powerful bows and heavy-shafted obsidian-tipped arrows), joined by a thousand uniformed pikemen from Pidra Blanca and Techon, and two thousand militia from Itzincab (some in uniform, some not). They'd come to liberate Puebla Arboras and secure the southeast approach to the Allied cities. *With a little help from us*, Olayne mused as his guns roared again, even though most of his roughly four hundred "American" troops were now either Ocelomeh or Uxmalos themselves. They were doing their part while Major Cayce completed refitting, reorganizing, and resupplying 1st Division in its new position at Nautla and prepared for whatever it was he meant to do next.

"Fine execution!" Har-Kaaska boomed at Olayne. "I do love your great guns—beautiful pieces—and it was good of Major Cayce to lend them to us."

"We're all in this together, Your Majes . . . I mean Colonel." Olayne would've flushed again and shook his head.

Har-Kaaska *kakked* a kind of laugh. "Don't be embarrassed. I'm not a real 'king,' you know. They just call me that. And I'm not really a colonel, since I'd outrank Major Cayce, and we all agreed he'd exercise supreme military command. I hear he's to be forced to accept a promotion, but . . ." He blinked that away and gestured forward through the smoke as another dust cloud drifted downwind from the rubbled wall, stark white against the deep green of the forest beyond the city. "Mustn't overdo it, though. That wall will have to be rebuilt to protect the innocent people remaining here"—he blinked something else Olayne knew held meaning but he had no idea what it was—"if there are any left," he added bleakly. "I believe it's about ripe," he continued decisively. "Your other guns—the twelve pounder howitzers—are in place, yes? And your Rangers and dragoons?"

"Yes sir," Olayne replied, glancing at a dragoon sergeant named Buisine who'd just reported.

"Very well. Cease firing, but you're welcome to advance your guns with the infantry. The enemy's heavy arrows won't carry past two hundred paces, and even if they have a few Dom muskets, they won't do any better."

"We'd be honored to accompany you, sir"—Olayne smiled—"especially if you'd be kind enough to detail half a dozen stout fellows to help us move each gun." He smiled wider. "We ordinarily pull them with horses, you know, and tired artillerymen make poor marksmen."

Har-Kaaska grinned back. "Of course! And I do appreciate it," he added. "Just because we don't *see* a great mob of defenders on the walls doesn't mean they aren't there. You can sweep them away with canister if they pop up."

"Gladly, sir." Olayne raised his voice. "Battery! Cease firing and secure implements. Prepare to advance by hand to the front! Caissons will remain here, but limbers will keep their spacing. Ensure there are at least ten rounds of canister in each chest."

A hundred Ocelomeh archers raced out ahead as skirmishers, followed by two ranks of five hundred pikemen in uniforms copied from the Americans and under the flags of their cities: what looked like a stylized feathery lizard of some sort on a red saltire crossing bright green for Pidra Blanca, and a red, white, and gold tricolor pennant for Techon. Olayne moved his 6pdrs forward under his own flags: a four-by-four-foot Stars and Stripes and a gold battery flag with crossed cannons on red-painted banners. There were no fifers, but Itzincab had supplied drummers aplenty, and they pounded their instruments in time with tramping feet, rolling louder as the bulk of the archers stepped off, followed by the Itzincabos themselves.

Olayne remained mounted near the center with Har-Kaaska's small entourage behind his spaced-out guns, watching the spectacle from above, as it were. The troops seemed determined enough, but then it wasn't the first time for them as it had been for the Uxmalos at the Washboard. These men had fought Holcanos already, and the terrifying, semireptilian Grik as well (even worse in Olayne's view). The closer they got to the looming wall and gaping gap his guns made, the more impressed he was with Har-Kaaska's little division. Of course, they weren't taking any fire yet. . . .

"There's smoke rising over the city!" Har-Kaaska suddenly exclaimed. "A lot of smoke." He looked questioningly at Olayne.

"We were careful, sir, and didn't even *bring* any exploding case shot. Haven't figured out how to make more, yet. Solid roundshot might scatter braziers or lanterns, but can't start fires on its own. Not like that." Even as they watched, the smoke spread and rose from other places.

"They're burning the city!" Har-Kaaska decided at once. "We must hurry! Major Klashi," he called to his human aide, who nodded and urged his horse toward the infantry commander. Moments later, the troops surged forward, and Olayne's cannoneers and their helpers were gasping to keep the guns with them. Then came the distant *Poom-poom!* of howitzers spewing canister on the other side of the city, followed by the rapid crackle of fire from the dragoons' breechloading Hall carbines.

"They're trying to escape out the south gate, just as expected," Olayne said, "and Boogerbear—I mean Lieutenant Beeryman—is giving them hell." The two 12pdr howitzers were mounted on the same carriages as Olayne's 6pdrs and were specifically designed to fire exploding case or shell—which they didn't have—at relatively low velocities and high trajectories. They were simply too light to fire solid shot on top of useful loads. If the thin-walled tubes didn't fail, the recoil would beat the carriages apart. They did just fine with canister at close range, however. They and all the mounted troops had secretly positioned themselves in the forest to the south, flanking the road, to catch the fleeing enemy in a crossfire. That seemed to be working, but the enemy was burning Puebla Arboras as they left.

"Very good, as we hoped," Har-Kaaska said distractedly, "but we must get inside the city."

Olayne nodded, chilled by the normally unflappable Mi-Anakka's tone.

There was no resistance as Har-Kaaska's troops swept through the shattered gap in the wall and started spreading out while the officers paused. "Get that debris cleared away so we can take a section of guns inside," Olayne told First Sergeant McNabb.

"Aye, sir. Bear a hand, you awkward buggers," McNabb tried to shout at some Itzincabos in terribly accented Spanya—what they called the odd mix of antiquated Spanish and Mayan the locals used. Olayne doubted they understood McNabb's words, but they took his meaning. Several dozen militia started clearing jagged stones from around the shattered gate as the rest of the troops surged through. "That'll do," McNabb yelled. "Sergeant Murphy, take yer section. I'm with ye. The rest of ye, stay here, but stay sharp an' ready ta come if called. Corporal Rosar, unhitch a limber an' bring it through by hand!"

Once the guns and limber were through, Har-Kaaska left Major Klashi and five hundred Itzincabos and two hundred Ocelomeh archers as a rear guard and reserve with the rest of the guns. His party entered the city as well. They were greeted by a terrible sight. Flames were leaping everywhere, most vigorously from thatch-roof stables and shops built against the inside of the wall, but heavy smoke poured from more impressive stone structures as their contents and framing burnt, shriveling the greenery covering the walls. Abandoned loot was everywhere, and all manner of livestock lay slaughtered in the street under blankets of swarming flies and feasting "lizardbirds." Goats, burrows, hundreds of "gallinas" (fat, vicious little semidomesticated types of lizardbirds the locals used like chickens), and even dozens of armabueys. Holcanos had little use for the giant, knobby-armored armadillos, but the fact all the other fine plunder had been left or wasted proved they were spooked and wouldn't carry anything to slow their retreat. It also sent Har-Kaaska into a near panic as he bolted forward on the heels of his troops, rushing through the smoke and littered street toward the plaza surrounding the looming pyramid.

"What is it?" Olayne called out, urging his horse to keep up.

"The people! Where are the *people*?" replied Alcalde Truro. The small, usually unassertive leader of Itzincab seemed consumed with a fearful rage. "If goats and gallinas were too much trouble to take—and they killed them rather than leave them—what of the people they'd consider their 'property' as well?"

They found them in the plaza, hundreds and hundreds of men, women, and children, all beheaded and dismembered with their bloody parts heaped in different piles. Hundreds more had been impaled on stakes and burnt, all around the base of the pyramid. From the condition of some of those remains, it looked like that had been going on for months, ever since Alcalde Don Discipo turned his city over to the Holcanos—and the Blood Priests of the Dominion. The latter had been "cleansing" their new acquisition of "heretics," no doubt.

The advancing troops stopped, frozen in shock and horror, and even though he'd almost expected it by then, the sight made Olayne take a sharp breath. He nearly retched from the stench. Whipping his neck cloth off and holding it over his face, he did retch when he saw fire-blackened cook pits with human bones strung around. Animal monsters aside, nothing in his previous life, not even lurid tales of Indian massacres, had prepared Justinian Olayne for the human barbarity displayed on this world. He'd fought Holcanos and Grik on the beach when they first arrived and had his first glimpse of it then, and he'd watched the Doms slaughter almost an entire regiment of their own men who retreated from the battle at the Washboard. He retained no illusions about their enemies and expected only depravity from them. But this . . . Nothing could more graphically reinforce the stakes they fought for, or more perfectly justify their cause.

Har-Kaaska was openly weeping, dark furry face wet with tears. "I failed," he said harshly. "I failed in my duty to protect these people. We should've moved on Puebla Arboras as soon as we suspected Don Discipo!"

"No," Olayne said softly, gathering himself. "What would you have done it with? Your Ocelomeh alone? You had no army yet, none of us did! You might've stopped Don Discipo, but we couldn't have stopped the Doms in the west without your Ocelomeh. Uxmal, Pidra Blanca, Techon, perhaps even Itzincab would already look like this as well."

There was movement in the smoke. Suspecting trapped Holcanos—the fighting to the south was still swelling—vengeful Jaguar Warriors raised their bows and blue-clad infantry surged forward with pikes. What they found were pitiful survivors: half-starved, ragged civilians, hopefully, tentatively emerging to greet their liberators. Olayne was surprised how many there were, their numbers quickly growing as they cried out in relief and thanksgiving at the distinctly familiar sight of Har-Kaaska.

"The tombs beneath the city," Alcalde Truro guessed, voice breaking with a kind of tragic relief. "Many look as though they've been there for months." Seeing Olayne's confusion, he explained, "The vile god of the Dominion dwells in the underworld and it's sacrilege for anyone but Priests to go down in the ground. Holcanos are afraid of such places for their own reasons," he snorted, "and Priests aren't warriors. Anyone who made it down in the tombs would've been safe enough, with sufficient provisions."

Evidently heartened by the fact he hadn't come too late for everyone, Har-Kaaska straightened in the saddle of his strange mount, tail whipping behind him. "There *are* more warriors to deal with, however," he snapped savagely, gazing toward the sound of battle. "Alcalde Truro, please see to the needs of these people and secure the rest of the city with your Itzincabos. I'll take my archers and the pikemen"—he blinked something that might've been a plea at Olayne—"and the artillery out the south gate. Judging by the volume of fire, Lieutenant Beeryman has likely pinned a sizable number of vermin in the depressions alongside the Cayal Road."

Armed with intimate knowledge of the ground he'd gained by personal scouting before Har-Kaaska arrived with the main force, Boogerbear and his Rangers and dragoons had done exactly that. A clot of mounted men, mostly Holcanos, escaped when he opened fire, bolting down the road as fast as their horses would carry them, but the bulk of Holcanos and few remaining Grik were afoot when lethal sprays of canister and murderous carbine fire and heavy-shafted arrows suddenly flew. Boogerbear's Rangers had their bows, of course, but most were also armed with captured Dom carbines, or "muske-toons." Instead of a single ball, they'd been loaded with handfuls of "drip shot" made by pouring molten lead through a copper bowl pierced with dozens of holes and letting it drop in a bucket of water. The individual projectiles looked like big teardrops, but hundreds of them discharged at once made the inaccurate musketoons much deadlier at close range.

And then there were the dragoon's breechloading Hall carbines, hated and loved by their owners. They leaked a lot of gas (and the force of their shot) and were prone to lock up with fouling when it was dry, but the high humidity actually helped with that and didn't affect their reliability as much as it did flintlocks. Relatively accurate and quick to load, they'd convinced the enemy they were surrounded by three times their number. Escape was impossible, a charge was broken, and some who tried to run back to the south gate of the city, for whatever good that would do, were shot down. The rest could only hunker in the ditches by the road and that's where Har-Kaaska found them when he poured out the gate with several hundred vengeful Ocelomeh archers, pikemen, and two 6pdrs loaded with canister.

Olayne never got to fire, and the 12pdr howitzers were silenced as well because Har-Kaaska immediately whipped his strange mount forward and led a screaming charge. It quickly turned into a desperate melee and even the dragoons had to stop shooting, but Olayne saw Boogerbear and his quickly mounted rangers dash from the woods and smash into what had been the enemy "front" and was suddenly its "rear." They fired musketoons from feet or inches and Boogerbear was doing the same with a Colt Paterson in each hand.

"Should we go amongst 'em as well?" First Sergeant McNabb breathlessly asked. All Major Cayce's artillerymen were trained as infantry and, except for the men in front of the gun (the Numbers One and Two), carried muskets slung across their backs. 1s and 2s could retrieve theirs from the limber.

Olayne grasped his M1840 saber as if to draw it, watching the furious fighting. Finally, he shook his head. "No, First Sergeant. Good artillerymen are hard to train, and we've already lost too many fighting like *that*." He nodded ahead. "Major Cayce and I agree we should avoid it when we can." He shrugged. "Besides," he added grimly, "I don't think we're needed."

He was right. The pikemen knew their business, plying their weapons like bayonets on the end of muskets, and after the initial wild flurry of slaughter, with shooting, stabbing, arrows whipping back and forth close and hard enough to pass completely through bodies, the fighting quickly began to taper off. Holcanos weren't Doms, and they *would* surrender when all hope was lost, even if the "rules of war" on this world were very "Old Testament" and their fate was uncertain at best. Many were killed unresisting before the blood of the victors cooled and they knew they just had to take it because continued resistance only prolonged the killing. *It'll be worse than usual this time, no matter what they do*, Olayne realized, *after what they did to the people of Puebla Arboras.* He was right about that as well, and the postbattle slaughter he'd seen only once before, thank God, went on for a frustratingly long time. Even Har-Kaaska was still killing men with his basket-hilt rapier after the fierce Boogerbear was already shouting for his Rangers to stop fighting and re-form. Har-Kaaska's Ocelomeh were busy taking heads, which Boogerbear wouldn't let *his* do anymore. Har-Kaaska's had been forbidden to *keep* them, but they did it out of spite, throwing them around with wild cries. Olayne felt dirty just watching. *Our friends can be savages too*, he knew, *but I understand how they feel.* That didn't make it less sickening.

"His spring's wound down at last," McNabb observed, and Olayne saw Har-Kaaska just sitting on his unusual mount, splashed with blood, looking around and blinking very fast.

"Take a detail and get him out of that," Olayne said, but Boogerbear was already shoving his big, tan-and-black-striped local horse named Dodger through the milling pikemen, shouting at them to pull themselves together and take charge of the captives. Unlike before this current war, with direct Dominion involvement, there'd be no occasional exchange of captives, and the Holcanos who'd been spared had only grim captivity and hard labor before them. *Better than dying*, Olayne supposed, *and perhaps more . . . ethical than the kind of slavery we had where we came from*, he considered uncomfortably. Now Boogerbear was leading the king of the Ocelomeh out of the mix. The big Ranger with his great black beard required his men to wear the standard mounted uniform—dark blue shell jacket and wheel hat and sky-blue trousers—the Rangers had no colored branch trim—but his only personal concessions to uniformity were the trousers tucked in his knee-high boots and a sky-blue vest. Otherwise he wore a wide straw hat, a yellow bandanna, and an "artillery red" shirt with blousy sleeves. He needed big sleeves to cover his bulging arms.

"Just come along over here, Colonel," he was saying in his deep, mild voice. "My boys'll sort that nasty mess out." He glanced over at Olayne. "Bad inside?" Olayne nodded. "Figured," Boogerbear simply said.

"I want to kill them all," Har-Kaaska said woodenly, large yellow eyes still blinking furiously.

"I know," Boogerbear soothed, "but you'll wish you hadn't, later." He considered. "Hang the chiefs," he suggested as a compromise. Holcanos would gladly die in battle, but were mortified by the thought of hanging, and they'd seen some evidence the prospect moderated their atrocities. These must've thought they'd get away clean—or were influenced by something else. . . . "Hang any locals collaboratin' with 'em too," he added.

"Yes," Har-Kaaska agreed.

The Rangers were sorting these out now while pikemen disarmed the remaining Holcanos and tied them together. A squad of dragoons with yellow trim on dark blue jackets cantered up from down the road where they'd been placed to catch "leakers." Captain Coryon Burton reined in, grinning at Olayne. "Look what we found," he said as a trooper dumped a figure in a dingy red robe off his horse. The man sprawled on the ground but quickly rose to his feet and disdainfully dusted himself off. He was youngish and almost pale, with a sparse brown beard and piercing brown eyes.

"A Blood Priest," Har-Kaaska said with surprise.

"He was skulking through the woods, trying to get past us by himself." Burton snorted. "Unfortunately for him, there was still a fair amount of sunlight filtering through the trees that close to the road, and red doesn't blend very well." He chuckled. "Didn't put up a fight, but menaced us with some extraordinary curses my Spanya can't do justice."

"You *are* cursed, all of you!" the priest spat at Burton. "How *dare* you handle me this way?" he demanded querulously, now addressing Olayne and ignoring the "animal" Har-Kaaska. "I'm Father Amistoso, worldly representative of God in this land. I speak with His very voice!"

As if on cue, Har-Kaaska's bizarre mount emitted a loud blatting sound under its tail and a series of massive, steaming brown turds plopped down into a large, pungent pile. One of the dragoons laughed out loud, and the Blood Priest glared at him.

"That's new," Boogerbear observed. "I thought you critters channeled the voice o' yer pope, er whatever he is—'His Supreme Holiness'—back in the City o' Mexico. Does he know yer jumpin' the chain o' command?"

Amistoso didn't reply.

"So . . . Blood Priests no longer even pretend to be ruled from the 'Holy City,'" Har-kaaska growled, wondering what that meant.

"I see the animal's mouth moving, but can't hear the speech of beasts or demons," the priest stated piously. Har-Kaaska seemed about to cut him down, or have his mount stomp him, but Alcalde Truro intervened. "If I may?"

The Mi-Anakka war leader jerked a nod.

"You're responsible for the slaughter in the city?" Truro asked, voice almost mild.

Father Amistoso visibly swelled with pride. "Despite my youth, I was directly tasked by Father Tranquilo with cleansing it of heretics, yes."

"*You* directed the impalements and burnings?"

Amistoso blinked surprise. "Over time," he conceded. "This being my first such assignment, I was perhaps overly judicious, extra careful to ensure only the most recalcitrant were brought to a state of grace in that fashion."

"There were *hundreds*!" Olayne blurted. "That was *restraint*?"

"My God," murmured Burton, who hadn't yet been inside.

"It's worse than you think," Olayne whispered to him, still looking at Amistoso.

"I showed a great deal. Too much," Amistoso stated crossly.

"I've already had enough o' him," Boogerbear rumbled. "Let's take him apart. He'll squeal what he knows."

"That won't be necessary," Truro said coldly. Perhaps only he and Har-Kaaska truly understood that Blood Priests had no fear of death and would actually welcome torture; their suffering earning them the "grace" they required for an afterlife in paradise. They also knew torture wasn't needed— yet. Amistoso wouldn't reveal details of an impending attack, of course, but had no compunction about telling the truth about anything they might discover for themselves. Lying is a sin, after all. And as for what he'd done in Puebla Arboras, his twisted faith left him no notion he'd done anything wrong. But Har-Kaaska was in no state to question the man, who'd pretend not to hear him in any event, so Truro continued. "Why did you murder the others?"

"I 'murdered' no one!" Amistoso rounded hotly. "You must see how it was. Chief Kisin, leading the Holcanos, and Don Discipo both agreed we couldn't hold the city."

"Discipo was *here*," Har-Kaaska blurted in shock, "while you . . . did what you did to his people?" Father Amistoso sent him a furtive glance but continued speaking to Truro. "Kisin and Discipo had a . . . disagreement some days ago, over the 'waste' of captives, as well as which of them was, in fact, in authority over all the Holcanos." He sneered. "The savages are . . . disappointed by the war, so far, and grow quarrelsome and divided. Chief Kisin no longer enjoys universal support and departed in a huff with only a few hundred warriors of his own band. Don Discipo left just this morning, obviously before you'd set your trap on the Cayal Road," he added as if they'd somehow cheated. "That left me alone to decide the fate of the people here. An unprecedented decision, I'll have you know! We couldn't take them with us, and the Dominion has never abandoned souls it's taken responsibility for. I *couldn't* leave uncleansed heretics behind, who'd never know God and paradise, so I took it upon myself to bring *everyone* I could find to Him." He glanced benevolently at the Holcano captives being led around the outside of the city walls. "*They* were most helpful, though I suspect it was more to secure last-minute rations than out of any real piety."

Olayne's mind's eye returned to the pile of legs in the plaza, and he realized it was smaller than it should've been. Then he remembered the ragged survivors emerging from the various tomb openings. "Well, thank God you didn't 'save' everyone," he murmured darkly.

"I did my best," Amistoso humbly replied and Har-Kaaska nearly killed him again.

This time it was Boogerbear who restrained the king of the Ocelomeh. "So, you were all headin' down to Cayal—what's that, two hunnerd an' fifty miles south?"

"Seventy-odd leagues, I believe," Burton provided for the others.

"Why leave? Why not send for more help? Lotsa Holcanos at Cayal, right?"

Amistoso hesitated. "As I said, and you must know, the Holcanos have suffered heavy losses and are . . . dissatisfied by the war in the Yucatán. Their reptile allies have suffered even worse and have practically abandoned them, their many bands splintering and fleeing into the forest. Only General Soor and his few hundred—you call them 'Grik'—still supported Kisin, and they weren't here. With the news of His Holiness Don Frutos and

General Agon's . . . reevaluation of your position astride the Camino Militar in the west, and redeployment back to Campeche—"

"You mean the news that we'd licked 'em," Boogerbear interjected.

The Blood Priest glared at him but continued. "Your appearance here in force convinced Discipo to fall back and fortify Cayal so it and Campeche might better support each other."

"That's more than I expected you to tell us," Truro conceded, surprised.

"Why?" Amistoso scoffed, gesturing at the surrounding Ocelomeh. Only those who'd joined "regular" units wore uniforms. The rest were still in buckskins and breechclouts. "You expect more from *your* savages?"

"As much as anyone else against the likes of you," Truro snapped angrily. "And they've defended us from the Holcanos for generations!"

Amistoso merely shrugged. "In any event, the fact of it should be obvious, even if the 'why' is not. I told you why so you'd understand the fact that, divided at present or not, virtually all the Holcanos left in the *world* are gathering at Cayal. You can't possibly meet them with the little army you brought. You've come as far as you can, and when His Holiness Don Frutos and General Agon rebuild their army and Don Discipo—or Chief Kisin—reestablishes control over the Holcanos, you'll *long* for the mercy I showed the people of Puebla Arboras when we erase you and your pathetic little cities to the north!"

"So Don Frutos still commands his army? And Agon too?" Coryon Burton asked. They might've found that out eventually, but it was still a surprise.

Amistoso hesitated, but it was unclear whether he was unsure or finally worried he'd revealed too much. "Of course," he eventually stated. "If a horse breaks its leg, you replace the animal, not the rider."

"Unless the rider broke the horse's leg by bein' a idiot," Boogerbear rumbled. "I don't know about Agon, but El Fruto's a idiot. Surprised they didn't cook his head or somethin'."

Amistoso thrust his thinly bearded chin out defiantly. "His Holiness is a *hero*. He stopped your larger force from pushing down to Campeche. He'll be heavily reinforced, I assure you!"

"Is that so?" Boogerbear asked, looking at Har-Kaaska.

"Yes! Now I demand you treat me with the courtesy due my position—or kill me. I've told you all I can or will, and torture will gain you nothing but my delight. My death agonies will shower me with grace, and God will take me straight to paradise!"

"We finished with him now?" Boogerbear asked Har-kaaska, who only nodded and said, "Don't give him the satisfaction. Make it quick."

Boogerbear drew one of his Paterson Colts and cocked it. "Funny," he said in his soft, gruff voice. "Never thought I'd meet a fella that hangin' really was too good for." With that, he shot Father Amistoso in the forehead.

Olayne flinched. Not in surprise exactly, but in spite of everything he'd been through and seen, the nature of war on this world—the remorseless, bloody-mindedness of it all, justified by the depravity of the enemy or not—was so different from anything he'd ever expected, it still startled him from time to time. He noted it didn't "startle" Boogerbear, but the big Ranger seemed born to a simpler, "protect friends, kill enemies" approach to war similar to that of the Ocelomeh. Olayne had been trained to respect "rules" of war, and taught that his honor depended as much on how he treated defeated enemies as whether he defeated them in the first place. But the enemy had no such notions. The Dominion meant to murder or enslave everyone on the peninsula, and the savage Holcanos were motivated only by age-old rivalry, plunder, and nebulous Dom promises of a free hand in the Yucatán. The irony was, with the cities allied against them gone, the Doms could eradicate the Holcanos at their leisure. That left Olayne to wonder, especially after what he'd seen in the city, how *his* honor could survive a war against enemies who had none.

"Now take him in the city and hang him up for the survivors to see," Har-Kaaska ordered a squad of his archers. "They'll want to watch us hang the neighbors who betrayed them as well. I'd hang every Holcano we caught," he added bitterly, "but some will still be watching, somewhere, and they have to know surrender remains an option"—he flicked his ears at the dead Blood Priest, tail whipping behind him—"and we'll kill every one of *those* we find."

CHAPTER 3

The coastal city of Campeche was believed to be the oldest, largest, perhaps once most populous in the region, and had obviously been a thriving, bustling place—a hub of land and sea commerce that had, like Nautla, been carved from the dense surrounding forest. Its stone buildings were more refined and ambitious in size and design than those of its distant neighbor to the north, indeed any other city on the Yucatán Peninsula. Its great central pyramidal temple rivaled even those in the Holy City in the Great Valley of Mexico, with entryways to vast interiors on every stepped level. But the whole place had been a dead ruin for generations, still impressive in scope and surviving architecture, but older than time on this world and virtually unoccupied in living memory.

One legend told how it was bombarded by great ships sailing into its fine harbor before being raided and razed by demons that left no survivors. Another recounted how the entire city came to this world as it was, enveloped in a ball of flame and utterly devoid of life. Both versions would account for the scorch marks touching every ruin, but not how the stories got started since neither left any witnesses. Regardless, they kept people away, and the city had been only sparsely populated by Holcano Indians, a few trappers, hunters, and hardy frontier traders the Holcanos suffered to live on "their" land until only recently. That's when Blood Cardinal Don Frutos del Gran Vale and General Agon's twenty-thousand-strong Eastern Army of God assembled there for a campaign up the coastal Camino Militar against the combined heretic cities of the Yucatán and their strange Americano friends. Now, less than half of that same battered army was back, but it constituted the first large-scale inhabitation of Campeche's crumbling buildings—or makeshift hovels the ragged troops built from rubble, since all their tents had been lost—in the near two-hundred-year history of the Holy Dominion.

Supplies were short since ships from Vera Cruz had naturally gone where the army was *supposed* to be, at first. Several hadn't been heard from since. No doubt they were taken or destroyed by the large, swift-sailing enemy ship that made an appearance offshore at the battle just a few *leguas* short of the principal heretic city of Uxmal. Its participation might've even been decisive since the galling barrage it had laid on the Dominion encampment, and General Agon's tightly packed formations of reserves landed a heavy blow on an army already badly bloodied, its confidence gravely shaken.

No one had been shaken as badly as the supremely arrogant Blood Cardinal Don Frutos, in overall command, and nothing had gone as he expected. An attempt to destroy the enemy leaders at a parley ended in disaster and his classically organized battle plan fell entirely apart. He even ordered General Agon to fire on his own retreating troops—before the bombardment and a surprise attack on the lightly defended camp caused him to flee himself. Left alone, Agon still outnumbered the heretics, but resuming the battle would've destroyed the Eastern Army of God even if it "won." He chose to preserve what was left, negotiating a withdrawal with the . . . disconcertingly capable Major Cayce, the enemy's Americano commander.

Supplies were finally coming to Campeche, and six big galleons were anchored in the bay, taking turns at the improvised pier to offload cargoes of rations, munitions, even uniforms. The food was most welcome, but clothes were needed by haggard men who'd marched four hundred miles through a terrifying wilderness to fight a battle, then straggled that same distance back. Three of the ships that arrived that morning weren't merchantmen, however. They were heavily armed warships, and one wore the red sails and bore the broad yellow pennant of Blood Cardinal Don Hurac el Bendito. He was considered "third" among the twelve "equal" Blood

Cardinals serving His Supreme Holiness, much more "equal" than Don Frutos had been, despite (or because of) his being a favorite of the tumultuous Blood Priests. Even now, Don Hurac was being rowed ashore in what amounted to a miniature, ornate galley, complete with a high, unstable-looking poop, upon which a gilded throne was perched. Naked women, all stunning, of course, sweat glistening on perfect brown skin, plied the oars. Reclining on the throne, affecting an expression of unconcern as the galley briskly wallowed on the choppy waves, was a heavy, youngish man with a pointed black beard, dressed in the fine, gold-braided red robes of his office. In contrast to the wide-brimmed white *galero* Don Frutos habitually wore, Don Hurac was topped by what looked like a tall, flat-topped conical red tube, adorned with braid matching his robe.

Capitan Ead Arevalo was wearing the best yellow-and-black officer's uniform that could be found for him as he waited to receive Don Hurac with a few soldiers and a large party of dingy Blood Priests. Standing almost six feet tall, he loomed over the others. In a land where the average was much shorter and "standing out"—for any reason—wasn't always wise, his height made him uncomfortable. That wasn't his only source of discomfort. An old, surprisingly small bullet wound high in his chest, inflicted by a beautiful young woman with a very strange pistol—and a startlingly savage expression on her face—still pained him and left him reflective every day. On top of that, it was like an oven with the sun overhead, the perfect white sand around the pier reflecting the heat back up and soaking his borrowed uniform with sweat. Still, discomfort had been a constant in his life, it seemed, and he was used to it. He was less accustomed to the uneasiness their visitor spawned in his chest, and what the visit might mean.

The Eastern Army of God was in trouble. *Never* had an army of the Holy Dominion failed to conquer territory for the empire once the decision was made to do so, and certainly none had been beaten in battle! Simply to *witness* any form of dominance by a rival over a Dominion endeavor was deathly dangerous because that witness might bear testimony to the possibility the Dominion could be bested at anything. It therefore went without saying that there'd be no admission of outright defeat, and despite a new seething, mutual hatred, Don Frutos and General Agon had agreed on an excuse. As Agon's personal aide, Arevalo knew it well, but regardless how they parsed the results of the campaign, it hadn't met its objective of subjugating all the cities and peoples of the Yucatán. That left the army's officers, particularly General Agon—and even Don Frutos himself—in danger of being impaled, boiled, or burnt alive.

Don Frutos might be loved by the zealous Blood Priests, always clambering for bloodier and more radical means of converting the world to the One Faith, but Arevalo had seen how fragile Don Frutos's own faith was. He wasn't only afraid to die, he was terrified of the suffering required to ensure his welcome in paradise. General Agon had no fear of death, but was a soldier who adhered to older traditions the Blood Priests scorned as cultish. He'd sworn to die on the *battlefield* for the Holy Dominion. Execution would deny him that and, he thought, the Dominion of the only general who knew how to fight Major Cayce. So Agon and Don Frutos, for different reasons, would project a united front to Don Hurac.

"Your Holiness," Arevalo said loudly, bowing low when the galley touched the dock. "Welcome to Campeche!"

"Indeed!" cried the scruffy Blood Priest at Arevalo's side, Father Descanco, searing Arevalo with a glare before prostrating himself on the rough-hewn planks. He'd declared that he wanted to be the first to greet Don Hurac. "Thanks be to God you've come to us in this uncertain time!" the priest wailed against the timber. "The Eastern Army of God has earned much grace, but must move again at once, to complete the victory!"

Arevalo gave a mental snort. Descanco was in charge of the Blood Priests here while Father Tranquilo was away doing who knew what. Tranquilo knew how weak Don Frutos was, and Arevalo wondered if the rest of his ilk did as well. It didn't matter. They'd hitched their cart to him, and his failure would be theirs. Don Hurac was assisted down from his chair and onto the dock by surprisingly solicitous oarswomen. *He must treat his slaves unusually well*, Arevalo mused.

"We'll see if you thank me for being here, priest," Don Hurac snapped in a deep, impatient voice. He waved at the ruined city. "And this is where the army *started* from, so I can't imagine your 'victory' is almost complete." He nodded benignly at Arevalo and asked, "You are?" After Arevalo saluted and introduced himself, Don Hurac continued in a softer tone, "Since Don Frutos isn't here to welcome me himself, I assume he hides—or means to receive me in a better place? My, how much hotter and steamy it seems now I'm off the water!"

"A better place, Your Holiness, out of the sun," Arevalo assured. "His Holiness Don Frutos hasn't been entirely well. If you'll please follow me?"

Don Frutos wasn't well. Always thin but energetic, he'd grown almost skeletal and weak, and one might assume he'd been touched by the same fever that afflicted many of his surviving troops during their grueling retreat. His ailment was rooted in apprehension more than anything, however, and he'd been staying in the center level of the ancient pyramid he'd caused to be cleaned and aired as much as possible. Unlike the levels above, nothing important had collapsed, and the lower levels were too big to make presentable. His officers stayed in them. This one was just right, genuinely cool and large enough to be impressive without seeming pretentious, and it was important he meet Don Hurac as the equal he technically was. That's also why he stood, a little feebly and ashen-faced, from an elaborate stone bench surrounded by several more officers and Blood Priests, and paced stiffly to meet his visitor.

"My dear Don Hurac!" he cried, opening his arms for an embrace. "How kind of you to come!"

Don Hurac stopped and eyed the other Blood Cardinal, who lowered his arms and gestured around, ignoring the snub. "I so wanted to greet you myself, but this wretched heat . . . My *cirujanos* absolutely forbade it. But it's much better in here, don't you think? And refreshments are already laid out." He nodded at a camp table piled with local fruit and several bottles. "The wine is disgraceful," he lamented. "It hasn't traveled well. The heat again, I'm sure."

"Most likely," Don Hurac agreed, "but I'll have some nonetheless." He frowned disapproval as more naked women—actually, young girls painted gold—scurried to open a bottle and pour several glasses. "And as you might imagine," he continued, tasting the wine and grimacing, "I'm not here out of kindness."

Don Frutos blinked. "Whatever do you mean?" He glanced at the short, dark, heavily built man in the yellow-and-black, silver-braided general officer's uniform. "Surely you dispatched your report, General Agon? There should've been nothing in it to raise concerns at the Holy Temple."

Capitan Arevalo watched Agon shift uneasily. One of the foundations of his warrior's version of the One Faith stressed truth in all things, aside from deceiving the enemy, of course. How can a commander make appropriate plans and decisions if he's only told what he wants to hear? Arevalo knew his general's report to the Holy City was essentially true—if somewhat misleading—and Agon was uncomfortable with it. "I did, Your Holiness," he said a little vaguely.

"And I have it here," said Don Hurac, removing a folded parchment from a pocket inside his robes. "A condensed version, covering the pertinent points." He looked at Don Frutos. "I also know the part *you* played before the campaign began. *You* took charge of the heretics taken from the remarkable Americano steam-powered ship *Isidra* when she appeared so suddenly off the coast of Vera Cruz. You and your Blood Priests sold all the female and many of the male passengers as slaves or sacrifices before even determining their status, or whether they might have knowledge of interest to His Supreme Holiness."

"They were mere civilians from several nations unassociated with those who controlled the ship," Don Frutos defended. "Even my best linguist could make no sense of what some of them said and they were of no use. Only the soldiers and sailors had value, and I extracted a great deal of information about the amazing ship itself, the Americano soldiers aboard it—and the others that Father Tranquilo reported had landed between Nautla and Uxmal in the Yucatán." He narrowed his sunken but still somewhat oversize eyes. "Most ironic that they were actually coming to fight a war in the 'Mexico' of the world they came from. Extraordinary! In any event, that's why I assumed command of the offensive against them. To destroy them before they could effectively aid our enemies there."

"Be that as it may, Vera Cruz is *mine*," Don Hurac countered, suddenly furious. "It's in *my* province, and the prisoners in your custody weren't *yours* to decide their fate. It's my understanding all but a handful were gracelessly sacrificed merely as examples to make the others more biddable—how well did that work?" he asked bitterly, already knowing Don Frutos and his Blood Priests had been too zealous by far. "And most of the rest were brutally 'cleansed' in the most invasive way that leaves obstinate minds as useless as an infant's. Some might've been turned with patience, given the chance." He glanced at Agon, then shifted his sharp gaze back to Don Frutos.

"And as for your campaign against the heretics and these . . . Americanos, just because I wasn't there is no excuse for such a *very* hasty assumption of command. Then, worst of all, you *didn't* 'destroy' them"—he took a long breath—"and left quite a mess for me. I'm currently trying to recover as many of those you sold as I can. I'm not very hopeful. It seems many were comparable to our *patricios* and hidalgos. *Not* well suited to servitude, by temperament or constitution. Most have likely been resold as sacrifices by now."

"I gave some of the sailors to the navy," Don Frutos defended in a sulky tone, "and *did* turn their commander, a Colonel Wicklow . . ."

"The sailors are useful," Don Hurac conceded, then angrily flared, "but you *lost* Wicklow on your campaign! Killed during your messy attempt to slaughter the enemy leaders!"

Now even Agon blinked surprise, and Don Hurac gave him a thin smile. "Not in your report, I know. Did you think I had no other? Clear the chamber!" he commanded suddenly. "I want only General Agon"—he paused and glanced at Arevalo—"and his aide to remain!"

"Do it," Don Frutos hissed at his other officers and Blood Priests, and the dozen or so of them filed out, the Blood Priests most reluctantly.

When they were alone, Don Hurac regarded Don Frutos. "You've been a great champion of Blood Priests, not only in their bid to increase their influence with His Supreme Holiness, but you've supported their attempts to establish one of their own as *patriarca* in every city with even more status and power than *obispos*. Worse, they clamber to *abolish* the hereditary step of *obispo* to the Blood Cardinalship and make a path for their vile, common selves!"

"They're very useful," Don Frutos hedged.

"It may change your mind to know my *other* report came from your senior Blood Priest here, Father Tranquilo! The same who first alerted us to the activities of the Americanos in the Yucatán."

Don Frutos looked surprised, betrayed. "But how?"

Don Hurac smirked. "You've heard of the experiments with small flying dragons that look like winged cousins to the demon allies of the Holcanos?"

"I've seen them!" Don Frutos declared. "They're trained, with great difficulty I imagine, to swiftly carry messages long distances. Very rare."

"Yes," Don Hurac agreed, "and Father Tranquilo has one—provided by yet *another* patron, I shouldn't wonder. Interesting that he should have one and you did not," he taunted. "In any event, after your failure to secure the Yucatán, he's decided to throw you to *los lagartos* before you discredit his cause. He clearly expected his report to result in your . . . replacement."

"Will it?" Don Frutos asked as steadily as he could. He wouldn't *just* be replaced.

"That's what I'm here to determine," Don Hurac stated simply. He took another sip of wine, grimaced again, then waved his condensed version of Agon's report and began to recite from memory: "As soon as the Camino Militar was dry enough to move wagons and artillery after the seasonal rains, you proceeded up through the abandoned city of Nautla almost to Uxmal itself. There you met a 'superior' enemy army on a rugged plain they referred to as the 'Washboard Glade.'" He looked at General Agon. "Tranquilo says your army numbered twenty thousand and the enemy had only six or seven thousand. Is this true?"

Agon sent a glance at Don Frutos but nodded. "Yes, Your Holiness."

Don Hurac blinked, surprised. "I've always respected your military . . . association, though some say it hearkens to the heretic 'Order of Calatrava,' even pagan Mithraism, but I know your devotion to truth. *How* could you honestly say the enemy was superior when you outnumbered them three to one?"

General Agon sighed. "Because they *were* superior in every way but numbers. They knew the terrain and every trail winding through the impassable forest. They stood on the defense, for the most part, on ground they chose before we arrived . . ." He paused with another glance at Don Frutos. ". . . and not only were they fighting to protect their homes, the Blood Priests had already stirred their fury. Those things alone would've made the battle difficult and costly to win outright, but others made it impossible. Their troops were better trained, far more flexible and mobile, and even slightly better armed. They had almost as many cannon as we did, but moved them with such rapid mobility and fired with such lethal precision, it was as if they had *five times* as many. And that was before their ship appeared and added its guns to the fight," he added darkly, then took a long breath. "Finally, and most important, their planning and leadership was *far* superior."

Don Frutos's pale face reddened, and he began to protest, but Agon carried on. "I mean no disrespect," he quickly added, "but it's true. We sought the battle, hoping for a real one. As you know, we've never had a *real* battle against a military peer. It was quite exciting," he wistfully confessed, darting another glance at Don Frutos. "But we deployed and marched against them just as we would against a gaggle of frontier rebels, drawn from their huts with farm implements and a few bows and spears they use against monsters in the wilderness. We were confident, as always, that the sheer size of our army, the precision of our movements, and the iron discipline of our men would overawe them, winning half the battle before a shot was fired." He shook his head. "It didn't work." He nodded at the notes in Don Hurac's hand. "I can add nothing to my report of the specifics of the action. Every word is true. We were outmaneuvered, drawn in, then assailed from all directions. We *profoundly* underestimated the enemy army, and its commander in particular."

"But you could've still destroyed him," Hurac pressed.

"It's possible," Agon agreed thoughtfully, "but it would've accomplished nothing but the utter destruction of the Eastern Army of God as well, unable to even threaten Uxmal, and leaving things just as they were to begin with." He straightened. "By that point, I considered a stalemate that preserved half the army—and the lessons it and its officers learned—a 'victory' in itself."

Hurac flapped the parchment. "So you reported." He sighed, then turned to Don Frutos. "Father Tranquilo also made some rather astonishing allegations of *cowardice* against you personally—frankly unbelievable—and I'll attribute them to his zeal to see you replaced and curry favor with others. In light of this, I'd advise you to tread carefully around him and the other priests and not move against him directly since we don't know who these 'others' are—besides myself, of course." He looked directly at Agon. "You should certainly appropriate his messenger beast, however. It's your right, and he can't object. Send it *only* to me at Vera Cruz, or Don Datu in the Holy City. It recognizes the yellow and red pennants."

"Am I"—Don Fruto gulped—"am I to infer this means you won't replace me?"

Hurac shook his head. "Not now. Not yet. There's wisdom in General Agon's definition of 'victory' under the circumstances. You're lucky to have him since we'll certainly need *him*." He perused the refreshments with disapproval. "I won't stay long, a few days at most, but while I'm here I may as well be comfortable. Send to my ship and have my servants bring a few things. Fresh wine, for one"—he smiled—"and my chef and proper food! You'll see he's accommodated, won't you? We'll dine together, of course."

"Of course," Don Frutos replied almost breathlessly. He'd been almost as worried about what he'd feed the other Blood Cardinal (there were no delicacies here) as he was about his fate.

Don Hurac turned to Agon. "General, if you please"—he eyed Arevalo—"and your aide as well, do escort me to my quarters, where I can freshen up." He looked dolefully around. "I hope they're not as dreary as this musty old place!"

"Take him to *my* personal quarters," Don Frutos instructed. "They're already prepared. Still quite humble," he apologized to Don Hurac, "but the best available."

Don Hurac bowed, and Agon and Arevalo led him away while Don Frutos summoned a messenger from the honor guard waiting outside and recalled the men he'd sent away. Outside the chamber in the sunlight again, and alone for the first time, Hurac stopped walking and looked at the two officers.

"I understand you met this Major Cayce," he said abruptly. "Both of you?"

"Yes, Your Holiness," said Agon. "Along with some of his equally remarkable officers." Arevalo absently touched his chest under his left collarbone. The small pistol ball was still in there, as were . . . other notions it might've carried inside him. He'd earned a great deal of grace from his pain, but something in the face of the woman who shot him might've had a stronger impact on his soul.

"How did he strike you?"

"Competent," Agon answered immediately, then after a pause, "confident. Whatever world he and his people are from, he's seen more *real* war than I."

"*Can* you beat him?"

Agon considered the condition of his troops. All needed more rest, a complete refit, and a lot more training. "How long do I have, and how many more troops and guns will I get?"

Don Hurac hesitated, considering. "That's the hard part. Most of the might of the Dominion has already marched from Tepic to Culiacán, the northwesternmost outpost of civilization. Soon La Gran Cruzada will begin, marching across the Desert of Terrible Monsters to the Californias, to expel the heretics from the Empire of the New Britain Isles who *dared* plant a flag and a colony on our sacred soil!"

Arevalo wisely refrained from pointing out that the threat from the Yucatán was much closer and they actually had no settlements anywhere near where the "Imperials" planted their flag. Only a few explorers had ever returned from there—after claiming it all for the Dominion, of course. But the Imperials were an old, acknowledged adversary, and the Gran Cruzada to kick them off the continent had been building for almost three years. At this point, sheer inertia would carry it forward whether the Imperials were still there when it got there or not.

"I can replace the men you lost fairly quickly, perhaps a bit more," Don Hurac mused. "They won't be the best troops, but it sounds like you'll want to retrain them in any event. That said, if Major Cayce is the man you say, I doubt he'll sit on his laurels. You must go after him as quick as you can."

"I agree, and that many men—properly prepared," Agon qualified, "should be sufficient." He rubbed his chin. "I still have perhaps a *batallón* of lancers. I don't need any more. They're poorly suited to action in the forests, and most we had were slaughtered. I'd rather have Holcano scouts if Don Frutos will abide them and we can peel them away from the operation in the east." He pursed his lips. "Mounted messengers brought word that's not going as well as hoped either. The last we heard, Don Discipo's siege of Itzincab had been broken and the enemy was preparing to move south against Puebla Arboras itself."

"I was not aware," said Don Hurac, face grim. "I have no dragons there. Others may, but why would they? Who cares about Holcanos? As for Don Frutos, he will abide whatever you recommend, and by all means do use any Holcanos you can persuade to help you." He waved airily. "Promise them whatever they want. What else do you need?"

"More cannon," Agon instantly replied, then shrugged. "The enemy took all of ours."

Don Hurac frowned. "That may be more difficult to arrange. I'll do what I can." He peered intently at General Agon. "Tell me the truth. Did Don Frutos really make you fire on your own men who fell back from the fight—in good order—and then flee the battle as Father Tranquilo said? Not that Tranquilo objected to shooting the men," he added grimly.

Agon stiffened, and his face became a mask. "Don Frutos ordered me to punish troops retiring from the action without orders, as any Dominion commander would," he said carefully, "and when we'd done all we could, he . . . led the army from the field."

Don Hurac grunted. "Just as I thought. Well, you'll have to make do with him. *I* can't lead the campaign, and I can't really get rid of him now that he's . . ." He snorted something like amusement. "Exposed himself so, already. Besides, who would I trust more in his place? All the best fighting

Blood Cardinals are off with La Gran Cruzada. They'll enjoy the adventure, I'm sure. The horror stories I've heard of the desert—it's not really a desert, you know. . . ." He smirked. "Besides, I don't know who put him in charge in the first place, and he wouldn't have taken it entirely upon himself. The fiasco with the prisoners in Vera Cruz, my own city . . ." He calmed himself before his fury could take him again. "*Someone* let him believe he could do what he wanted. I'll try to find out." He looked thoughtful. "Or maybe I won't. I'm only third in line, you know. If someone closer has set him and the Blood Priests up for a fall, I've already done too much." He shook his head. "But whatever happens, he may still lead the army, but *you'll* command. I'll make sure he understands that."

CHAPTER 4

"W elcome home, my dears!" cried a beefy, balding Colonel Ruberdeau De Russy when Sira Periz and Samantha Wilde stepped
down *Tiger*'s gangway onto the new, enlarged Uxmal city
dock. Handropes had been rigged, but Captain Holland and Father Orno
escorted the ladies, hands on their elbows, nevertheless. The *alcaldesa*'s entourage followed close behind, along with a handful of Ocelomeh Rangers
and dragoons under Captain Ixtla. Ranger Lieutenant Sal Hernandez and
Dragoon Sergeant Thomas Hayne looked particularly confused to be here
without their horses.

De Russy was in his finest uniform, cocked hat under his arm, more
hair sprouting from his bushy cheeks than his head. With him was his "intended," Angelique Mercure, clutching his elbow and bouncing excitedly
on the balls of her feet in a black-and-cream day dress that complemented
her dark hair and rosy complexion as she called out greetings in French.
Beside her, smiling gently, was De Russy's young black "servant" named
Barca, dressed simply in sky-blue infantry garb. Though not the only black
man to come to this world—there were quite a few sailors as well—everyone
now knew Barca was more De Russy's keeper, like a trusted and influential
aide, than servant. He was also a proven fighter, and Lewis Cayce had
offered him a place in any line unit he chose. He preferred to stay with De

Russy out of true loyalty, and everyone appreciated it. It was no secret the talented and intelligent but somewhat erratic colonel originally commanding the 3rd Pennsylvania Volunteers needed Barca's reasoned counsel from time to time.

The florid-faced but solid as a rock Lieutenant Colonel Andrew Reed was there, with a wan but determined-looking Major Wagley, as well as Captain Emmel Dukane (whose B Battery brought so many of the captured cannon to Uxmal for refit and sent a section of its own guns with Captain Olayne). There were also numerous prominent citizens and some of Father Orno's priests, and the Uxmalo Major Itzam (commanding the Home Guards) had brought a company of his sharpest-looking, musket-armed troops for an honor guard. All were at the head of a large, enthusiastic throng of welcomers that began assembling as soon as *Tiger* opened Uxmal Bay.

"And welcome to you, you old pirate," De Russy told Captain Holland with a grin before he smiled at Orno, bowed to Sira Periz, and kissed Samantha's hand.

Holland was looking askance at the large gathering. "Welcome or not, if I liked crowds, I never would'a gone to sea. I'll be glad to get back to it."

"As I understand, you'll have to linger long enough to make a few preparations," Sira said aside, then nodded and smiled at Major Itzam. "And you'll be making a few shorter trips first."

Holland looked at the captured Dom transports moored nearby, the men working on them also watching the *alcaldesa*'s arrival. "Aye" was all he said.

De Russy had been looking up the gangway. "You couldn't convince Colonel Cayce to return with you, even briefly?" he asked worriedly. "I'd so hoped he'd come." He glanced apologetically at Colonel Reed. "No offense, but the First Techon and Second Uxmal are almost ready to march, well equipped, and armed. I'd anticipated his opinion of them."

"Colonel Cayce has the utmost confidence in Colonel Reed," Samantha scolded lightly. "And Major Wagley as well," she added with a smile.

Wagley raised a brow. "I'm beginning to think I'm not going back to the Third Pennsylvania?"

"Not yet," Sira Periz temporized. "But this isn't the place to discuss such things. Please, someone find something I can stand on to address my people, then we'll reconvene in the map room of the Grand Audience Hall."

A couple thousand Uxmalos must've gathered by now, brightly colored dress and wide straw hats lending a festive air to the otherwise dingy and smelly dockyard under the loom of *Tiger*'s tall masts and tightly furled sails. Standing on a cask that Reed self-consciously picked her up and set her on as respectfully as he could, Sira Periz made a rousing speech reminding her people of their victory at the Washboard (the offhand, alien name had stuck), and thanking them for their efforts supporting the army that protected them from extinction at the hands of the evil Dominion. She ended with a promise that all their hard work and sacrifice wouldn't be for nothing and one day they'd breathe the air of the freedom they loved once again, without the fearful pall of the lurking Dominion and its Holcano pets, which had weighed on them for generations.

Sira Periz had always been beloved by her people, and her tragic ascension to power had touched their hearts. The fact she'd been present when they beat the Doms only made them love her more. Granted, few truly grasped the scope of the sacrifice they'd have to make to win this war, but her popularity and honesty with them would make it easier to bear. Now they cheered her loudly as she abruptly motioned Colonel Reed to help her down and then pressed him to lead her through the enthusiastic crush toward a string of carriages waiting to take them to the audience hall. Once she was in the lead carriage with De Russy, Reed, Itzam, Father Orno, Captain Ixtla, Samantha, and Angelique, De Russy was distressed to see tears streaming down her face.

"Whatever is the matter, my dear?"

"They cheered me," she stated simply.

"But surely that's a good thing?"

She smiled bleakly but shook her head. "I chastised Colonel Cayce because he didn't seem to have made as much progress against the enemy as I hoped. I suppose I imagined he'd simply chase General Agon down and destroy his remaining force." She sniffed wetly. "I know nothing of war. I thought his insistence on securing Nautla and waiting for reinforcements to make good his losses was squandering that opportunity, almost betraying the sacrifice of those already lost," she confessed. "But now I understand. Even battered as Agon was, he still outnumbered what Colonel Cayce had, and the ruins of Campeche would stiffen his defense. A direct assault would've shattered our army and left the road open for the Doms to return here. At best, our conflict would've come to resemble that of the Holcanos and Ocelomeh over Nautla—just shoving back and forth for years—but the

Dominion is vast, and we'd soon squander the cream of our lesser numbers." She hesitated. "I wronged Colonel Cayce badly—again. He's been preparing a bolder plan than I ever imagined. Frankly, bolder than I'm comfortable with, yet I gave him my wholehearted approval and promised every support. There's *great* risk involved." She sighed. "If he's successful, he might secure peace and security for all the Yucatán for generations. Perhaps forever," she added lowly, then gestured behind them with the handkerchief Samantha provided to wipe her tears. They could still hear cheering over the rumble of horse hooves and solid wheels on paving stones. "If he's not . . ." She paused. "Regardless of what happens, so many of those happy people will be mourning the sons and husbands Colonel Cayce marches into hell."

THE GRAND AUDIENCE Hall was a long, cut-stone structure with numerous entrances to its vast, airy interior. Access was gained by mounting wide steps up the sloping mound it was built on and passing under the shade of the high, heavy, pillar-supported, overhanging roof. To those from another world who'd actually visited or seen drawings, the result was that the second-largest building in Uxmal looked rather like an architectural cross between the Parthenon in Athens and a giant, rectangular mushroom. The largest building in the city was the Temple of the Lord Jesucristo, of course, standing in the center of its own manicured plaza adjacent to the one surrounding the Audience Hall. It was another of the apparently ubiquitous stepped pyramids that once had a darker purpose but was now the pulpit where Father Orno and his priests preached what had evolved over centuries into an amazingly direct, nondenominational form of Christianity that even the Presbyterian Reverend Harkin could find few arguments with. Most of the priests went directly there, but Father Orno, in his black version of the shell jacket, trousers, and wheel hat the Americans introduced, accompanied the others into the Audience Hall and through the door into a smaller, but still substantial chamber to one side. The space had none of the plaster carvings and decorations adorning the public room, and even great framing timbers and bare stone were visible. Its most striking features were a large wooden table surrounded by benches and an enormous embroidered atlas of the world known to the Uxmalos, from the sparsely populated Yucatán west to the Pacific Ocean, and up beyond the northern border of the Holy Dominion to a region known only as "El Desierto de Monstruos Terribles." The detail of the atlas was amazing, and it included every known road and town carefully sewn in fine thread, the forests and mountains actually sculpted in multicolored yarn to create the impression one was looking down on the earth from a great height. It was more like an intricate model than a map. They'd all seen it before, of course, and it drew only glances now as some of those present converted the distance they'd just traveled to their relative positions, or thought of people they cared for who might be "there," or "there."

Sira Periz hesitated slightly before sitting near the center of the table in what had been her husband's place. Samantha Wilde and Father Orno immediately sat on either side of her. De Russy, Barca, and Angelique sat opposite, flanked by Reed and Captain Holland. The rest found places wherever they cared to.

"Refreshments, anyone? No? Then let's proceed," said Sira Periz.

"You hinted that Colonel Cayce has a plan," De Russy immediately urged.

"Colonel Cayce always has plans, it seems," Samantha said airily, flipping her fan in mild irritation, "though he rarely shares them." She was referring to the way he'd kept his intentions and dispositions so secret before the Battle of the Washboard, but his caution had been justified. Tranquilo (and Don Discipo) had installed countless spies, saboteurs, even assassins in the city over time. Many had been rooted out, but they couldn't be sure they'd caught them all.

"Indeed," De Russy somberly agreed, "though I think you're being unfair."

"Of course I am," Samantha said, with a glance at Sira Periz. Even the *alcaldesa* hadn't been trusted at first, with good reason. Her husband had initially favored Lewis's plan for a union of the cities, but she'd been instrumental in turning him against it to the point he'd been tempted to seek a separate peace with the Doms. He hadn't, and it cost him his life, but even before then, Sira had begun to lean the other way. She was wholly committed now, actively advocating for a union and determined that the entire Dominion be ground into dust.

"I'm sure we don't know all of it, and that's probably best," Sira began.

"Then I suggest we stick to what we know—and what we're supposed to do," said Colonel Reed. He grinned. "With Colonel Cayce, there's no point speculating about the rest."

Sira nodded, then managed a real smile. "Very well. How is your Spanya coming along? Yours and Major Wagley's?" Spanya wasn't just the English word for the odd mix of Spanish and Mayan the locals spoke. Troops were learning English since it was easier for their American instructors, many of whom could barely understand one another, since they might've originally been English, Irish, Scottish, Swedish, French—the variety was astonishing— to train them that way. It was important they pick up some of the local lingo, however, for words that just didn't translate.

"Not as well as I'd like," Reed confessed guardedly.

"Pretty well," Wagley boasted, and Reed glared at him.

"Good," Sira said. "You'll take the First Techon and Second Uxmal, along with various companies of reinforcements, down the Cipactli River road to join King Har-Kaaska at Puebla Arboras or beyond, if he's begun his advance toward Cayal. You'll relieve King Har-Kaaska in command of what has become 'Second Division'—don't worry, Har-Kaaska will expect it—and"—she blinked something like skepticism in the Mi-Anakka way—"at some point, Colonel Cayce will make contact with you."

"Contact . . ." Reed said.

"Yes," she said simply and turned her attention to Major Itzam. "Using *Tiger*, the prize ships, and whatever other transport he can arrange, Captain Holland will begin carrying two-thirds of the Uxmal Home Guards— ten thousand men—down to Nautla. The four thousand Pidra Blanca Guards now en route here will join you, though they may have to march down the Camino Militar."

Major Itzam looked at Captain Holland. "Of course, Alcaldesa, but what will we *do* there?"

"Train, and continue fortifying the position in case General Agon attacks. Other than that, you'll *become* our army there, designated 'Third Division,' in Colonel Cayce's place while he leads 'First Division,' composed of the First US, Third Pennsylvania, First Uxmal, First Ocelomeh—and most of the Rangers, lancers, dragoons, and mobile field artillery"—she licked her lips—"across country to meet Colonel Reed in the vicinity of Cayal."

All eyes turned to the big atlas, judging the distance through the terrible forest. "My God," Wagley murmured. "He'll lose half his men."

"Warmaster Varaa-Choon assures me he won't," Sira said sharply.

Reed swallowed. "What then, Alcaldesa?"

"He'll tell you," she replied.

"They deserve a *little* more than that!" Samantha insisted. Even Captain Holland nodded. Sira gestured for Father Orno to continue.

"Obviously, *none* of this can leave this room," the little man began somberly, "but King Har-Kaaska reports that almost all the savage Holcanos and most of their remaining Grik allies have retreated to Cayal. I believe Colonel Cayce means to destroy them while they're consolidated, thus eliminating the threat they pose to us—and the rear of his further advance."

"*Further?*" De Russy almost gasped.

"Yes. The combined army will then strike west—still across La Tierra de Sangre—and take the Dominion city of Nueva Frontera before marching north to the coast"—he bowed to Captain Holland—"and resupplying."

"My God," Reed said, staring hard at the atlas. "That's a five-, six-hundred-mile march *after* we meet at Cayal, through the scariest country in the world, I hear!"

Captain Ixtla shook his head and spoke for the first time. He was older, very dark, with a perpetual brooding frown, but his voice held a tone of reassurance. "Cayal is at the base of the only mountains on the peninsula, and there's a substantial river. It ultimately leads directly to Campeche, but we can float men and equipment more than three hundred miles downstream on barges. Then it's not so far before the forest gives way to La Sabana . . . an open, grassy land. It's sometimes even cultivated by people like us who live beyond the borders of the Dominion. Travel, with all the supplies taken down from Cayal, will be easier there."

"Still," Reed murmured doubtfully, "even two or three hundred miles, with only what we can carry . . ."

"Will come as a complete surprise to the enemy," Samantha reassured, then laughed and gestured at Sira Periz. "It certainly came as a surprise to us! As for supplies, Warmaster Varaa-Choon and a number of Ocelomeh know that land and insist rations can be had on the march." She raised her brows. "Perhaps even recruits."

Major Wagley was frowning. "I can see how it might be done," he said slowly, "but what's the point? Obviously, Colonel Cayce wants to go around Campeche and Agon, but then"—he looked at Holland—"aside from relief by sea that I *hope* will be sufficient, that'll leave Agon, likely reinforced by all the troops in the region by then, sitting in our rear and firmly astride our only *real* line of supply."

"True, he should be stronger by then, but that's part of the plan," said Sira, eyes moving to Captain Holland. "We'll do everything we can to ensure it, in fact." Looking back at Wagley, she continued, "If it works, you should face little opposition to . . . the rest of Colonel Cayce's plan."

"Little opp . . ." De Russy cleared his throat. "Begging your pardon, my dear—I mean, Alcaldesa, but what's to stop General Agon from simply marching out of Campeche and chasing them down?"

Major Itzam laughed out loud. "I suspect that *I* will! The fourteen thousand Home Guard troops at Nautla—better trained and equipped by then, I'm certain, and probably reinforced, will be in *his* rear when he does. He'll be caught between two forces—with one of them threatening the Holy City! Oh, how the Blood Cardinals will howl! They'll insist that Agon pursue the greatest threat to their capital, and I'll pound him from behind. If he rounds on me, Colonel Cayce will hit him. It's brilliant!"

De Russy rubbed his closely shaved chin, then fluffed out his mutton chops. "Unless he catches either of you in the open before you can support one another and defeats you in detail," he grumbled unhappily. Or attacks Nautla before Colonel Cayce even draws near." He looked at Major Itzam. "Can you stop him alone if he does? If not, he might threaten Uxmal. *Our* 'Holy City.'"

"That's part of the 'risk' I spoke of," Sira Periz admitted darkly, "that Colonel Cayce warned me of." She turned to Captain Holland once more. "But *if* General Agon attacks Nautla and overwhelms the guards, it will hurt him badly. He can't come on to Uxmal without further reinforcements and supplies. In addition to its . . . other activities, our little navy will have to prevent that."

Holland snorted. "Well, I reckon I can't complain. I *did* ask Lewis to give *Tiger* a bigger job." He had a sudden thought and grinned. "Them 36pdr siege guns captured at the Washboard. Anybody decide what to do with 'em yet?"

Sira looked surprised. "A couple will be mounted here in the city, overlooking the bay. Others are having what Captain Dukane called 'proper carriages' made. I suppose Colonel Cayce may want them someday. There were four more. Why do you ask?"

Holland sniffed. "*Tiger* may be old an' her days o' supportin' the weight o' twenty-two 24pdrs on her gundeck are past, but I reckon her tired knees can manage just a pair o' those lovelies amidships, on either beam. On naval trucks, o' course. Can I have 'em?"

"What 'other activities' besides those we discussed?" Colonel De Russy asked Captain Holland.

Holland chuckled. "I promised Colonel Cayce, at some point durin' all this, I'll cut *Isidra* out o' Vera Cruz an' bring her home for him." He caught himself and blinked before slightly bowing his head in the direction of Sira Periz. "'Home' bein' Uxmal now, I reckon."

CHAPTER 5

Blood Cardinal Don Hurac el Bendito was exhausted and cross when he reached Vera Cruz, his pudgy frame battered, bruised, and uncomfortably empty after contrary winds and tumultuous seas tossed him about for eleven grueling days just to make the modest two-hundred-*legua* voyage from Campeche. If he'd suffered as much on his way to see Don Frutos, he would've impaled him on the spot. "Home" again at last, if he really had such a thing, there'd be no rest in his comfortable seaside villa north of the city. His secretary, Obispo El Consuelo, was waiting on the dock to present him with a politely worded note—waiting several days—from Blood Cardinal Don Datu el Humilde "requesting" the pleasure of his presence in the Holy City. There could be no delay. If Don Hurac was "third among equals," Don Datu was unquestionably first, tracing his lineage more than two hundred years with absolute certainty to an officer in the Sacred Manila/Acapulco Galleon that God brought to this land on this world to purify the Faith. Don Hurac's relations with Don Datu were excellent, but the hierarchy of equals was always in flux, and his "request" must be treated with the same gravity as a command from His Supreme Holiness Himself.

Boarding a carriage El Consuelo brought, Don Hurac dispatched the rest of his staff all over the city, to the garrison and fleet *comandantes*, the *maestro de puerto* and powerful *capitaz* of the dockyard slaves, the city arsenal, *avituallamiento*, and countless other *burocratas* before going to the *alcalde*'s palace to inform the puffy, grasping little man named Borac that he'd be directly responsible for ensuring the troops and other aid Don Hurac promised General Agon wasn't delayed. Then he went to his villa, quite late by then, for a meal prepared by the mothers of his sons, his *madres de hijos*—all former slaves like his small boat's crew and the only people in Vera Cruz he truly trusted to feed him—and managed a short night's sleep. By dawn he was on his way.

The roads were well tended, but the distance overland through hilly then mountainous country, west to Actopan, north to Puebla, then west again through ever larger mountains and towns to the Great Valley itself, was almost as far, as the dragon flies, as the distance from Campeche to Vera Cruz—and took just as long to travel. Don Hurac was still sore from near-constant retching and tumbling down a companionway in the ship, and no matter how soft the kidskin-covered cushions in his ornate coach, the leather springs jounced him abominably and the constant motion disturbed his stomach as much as the sea voyage had. Obispo El Consuelo was his only companion, aside from the coachmen and escort of lancers, of course. El Consuelo was a devoted secretary but, other than complaining that Don Hurac had brought no other servants, wasn't much for conversation. He was an aspirant to the Blood Cardinalship himself, of which there could only be twelve, but Don Hurac trusted him because another *obispo* with more direct blood ties to Los Santos—those first ancient arrivals—had been chosen to succeed him long ago and already performed most of his duties in the Holy City.

And that's the root of all this nonsense with the Blood Priests, Don Hurac fumed as the coach juddered and swayed. *The administration of our faith has always required a hard heart, even the display of bloody hearts from time to time. Blood and suffering pave the path to paradise, and God is never lenient in that respect, and never forgives. He's quite a terrible god, in fact, and expects terrible things of us. We must be rigid in regard to His requirements and frequently demonstrate that only Blood Cardinals—and His Supreme Holiness, of course—descendants of those who first found the path, can open the gate to others.* He frowned at a trio of red-robed Blood Priests watching over a sprinkle of slaves toiling in a field. Despite their obvious, fanatical zeal, most of Don Hurac's peers considered Blood Priests dangerous heretics themselves. Not only because they wanted their *patriarcas*, the abolition of *obispos*, and the elevation of *countless* low-born *patriarcas* to the cardinalship, but because they *didn't* see God as terrible and *gloried* in the spilling of blood. They believed it represented more than just a sacrifice to *honor* God and the salvation of His victims. Blood seeping into the ground actually *nourished* God in his underworld paradise!

That was their greatest heresy as far as Don Hurac was concerned. He wasn't squeamish; "traditional" priests and Blood Cardinals spilled plenty of blood themselves, but Blood Priests practically competed with one another to spill the most and attract the attention and favor of God! If they had their way, cardinals would no longer be "of the blood" of the founders, they'd be installed based on how much actual blood they'd bathed in. Eventually, even His Supreme Holiness would have to be chosen from among them, and holy bloodlines would lose their importance. And influence.

Over the days that followed, Don Hurac grew increasingly concerned by the number of red robes—as opposed to the black of traditional priests—he saw in Actopan, then Puebla, even little villages between. The . . . changes Blood Priests advocated had to be attractive to the others, and it probably shouldn't surprise him to see so many converts. He began to wonder if it was already too late to denounce them. They might simply turn it around. Even if all the Blood Cardinals stood against them (and they never would), they were only a dozen against hundreds, maybe thousands. Only His Supreme Holiness could stop them now.

Twenty long days after Don Hurac took his leave from General Agon and Don Frutos at Campeche, his coach and its escort passed through the affluent, mountainside town of Texcoco and began their descent into the Great Valley of Mexico. The road still went up and down—mostly down—but hardly a bump was felt since His Supreme Holiness Himself was known to frequent towns and cities in and around the valley. He'd grown more reclusive in recent years, and such excursions were rare, but the remainder of the road to the Holy City—another two days or so—would be swift and comfortable.

Don Hurac's spirits (and appetite) improved as the road switchbacked down between irrigated, terraced fields and protective, sharpened palisades surrounding vast grasslands full of herds of fine horses bred by crossing the old-world strain with the local variety for the best attributes of both. *Lagardos de patos*, smaller versions of the animal Har-Kaaska was said to ride, grazed with them. They were better known as *patos grandes*, and Doms used them like cattle. There were ordinary cattle as well, along with burros, goats, and pigs—all descended from livestock brought by that ancient galleon and other . . . arrivals over the years. Armabueys weren't particular what they ate and coexisted with stupendous beasts called "*serpientes gordas caminando*," or fat walking serpents. They were absolutely massive, with barrel-shaped bodies the size of a house and pillar-like legs rivaling the greatest architectural columns. Relatively tiny heads on the ends of ridiculously long necks, and tails tapering down to whips, gave them their serpent-like appearance. They lived on the low-lying plain speckled with clumps of trees the armabueys rooted among and were only domesticated enough to be harnessed to loads nothing else could pull, particularly enormous stone building blocks. Most simply called them "*serpientosas*," which was equally strange. Snakes still figured prominently in pagan lore but were only known to thrive on some Caribbean islands, and few ordinary people had ever seen one.

Ordinary people, mused Don Hurac. *What does that really mean? Everyone but sailors? I once saw a serpent on the Islas del Cielo, and I'm no sailor. Nor am I "ordinary."* The twelve Blood Cardinals served as apostles to His Supreme Holiness and answered only to Him and—in theory—a majority of one another. Their word was law wherever they went, but the Dominion essentially ruled itself on a day-to-day basis through *alcaldes* in cities and towns. Most *alcaldes* were "*aristocratas*" who could—sometimes torturously—trace their lineage to the founding era. Other *aristocratas* were lords over vast agricultural estates their eldest sons were groomed to inherit. Younger sons became army and naval officers, or *obispos* who might aspire to the Blood Cardinalship. Don Hurac had been the youngest of three boys himself. Sisters had value only for the lineage they added to the bloodline of whoever they were traded to in marriage, and marriage existed almost solely for the purpose of producing legitimate heirs.

Next in prominence were moneyed upper-class "*patricios*," who owned virtually every large industry from shipyards to weaveries and foundries or tanneries. *Patricios* also controlled most bureaucracies through the "hidalgo" middle class. Hidalgos were freemen of status who either worked for *patricios*, owned and operated smaller business concerns, or became merchants or priests or soldiers for hire. They might even become *patricios* themselves. Don Hurac's status would ensure his own "illegitimate" sons started life as hidalgos, at least. Below them, and working for everyone, were "*hombres libres*" (freemen), who might, theoretically, become hidalgos as well. More often they were driven by debt into the ranks of the countless slaves they worked beside.

Or the Blood Priests, Don Hurac brooded. Blood Priests had only existed for twenty or thirty years, their origin possibly connected to the arrival of yet another strange ship from a different world flying a three-colored flag. It was rumored that even as its people were converted to the One Faith, they'd done a little converting of their own. He remembered Father Tranquilo himself had been one of the founders of the Blood Priests and was painfully scolded to stop preaching absurd notions like "*libertad, igualdad,* and *fraternidad.*" But that was a time of prosperity, when fewer and fewer hidalgos were entering the traditional priesthood, and His Supreme Holiness, still young and concerned about lost souls on the frontiers, not only granted the order a charter, but allowed it to mimic Blood Cardinals in dress and take *anyone* into its fold—except slaves, of course. Don Hurac snorted. *An attractive alternative for* hombres libres *teetering on the brink, and possibly even accounting for its . . . particularly bloodthirsty zeal, not to mention growing ambition to upset the system that's worked so well for a hundred and fifty years! Blood priests are serpents in our midst for all to see,* he decided, *if they will only look.*

He gazed out the window at the Great Valley beginning to spread out before him and realized how much he'd missed it. The land, surrounded by distant high mountains, some even touched by snow, was the richest and most fertile in the Dominion. Don Hurac loved it dearly. Compared to the dense, menacing forest around Campeche and even the craggy mountains between Vera Cruz and here, it was almost like the sea in the sense that it seemed he could see forever. And it was so productive! Tiny dots toiled in all directions, accompanied by brutish armabueys pulling stone-pointed wooden plows. He supposed there were a thousand slaves in view at any one time. Perhaps dozens of armed hidalgos as well, mixed with a vast number of free workers. There were more of the latter two in the valley and the Holy City than anywhere else. He frowned. *But all the livestock is tended by slaves at night. Prohibited from bearing arms, even spears, they suffer as much at the teeth and claws of the great predators that hunt their flocks and herds.* There were always more slaves, however, the women less valuable than goats. *Do they count as "ordinary people"?* he thought. *Can they see the serpent? With its constant requirement for blood sacrifice, they're its most frequent victims. Then again, how is that different, any less brutal and arbitrary, than the life they already endure?*

Thoughts like that made Don Hurac uncomfortable because they made him wonder just how well the system really worked. *Not that Blood Priests will improve things for slaves,* he rationalized. *They slaughter more than the monsters.*

"You seem quite lost in thought, Holiness," said Obispo El Consuelo in a kindly tone. Don Hurac looked at the young man and forced a smile. "Just glad to see the Great Valley again after—three years, I believe. Vera Cruz is my home, but the scenery grows tedious." He straightened in his seat. "I'll be glad to see Don Datu—and the Holy City, of course."

"Do . . . do you think we may have an audience with His Supreme Holiness while we're here?" El Consuelo asked anxiously.

Don Hurac pursed his lips. No one he knew, except probably Don Datu, had actually *seen* His Supreme Holiness in some time. "It's to be fervently wished," he hedged. "I can think of nothing more pleasant than basking in His holy presence. I understand it would be your first time?"

El Consuelo looked down and nodded.

"Well. I pray we shall see Him."

They stopped only twice more, once to eat a large meal at the villa of an *aristocrata* Don Hurac knew well, and again to change horses at a small army garrison (even smaller now, with so many troops gone northwest to join the Gran Cruzada), but it still took the rest of the day and night to reach the Holy City. When they saw it glistening under the morning sunbeams piercing mountain valleys to the east, Don Hurac was struck by its gleaming splendor, as always. In some ways, its architecture was strikingly similar to the impressive ruins of Campeche, as if that lonely, forgotten place had been vastly enlarged in all dimensions and resurrected to its ancient glory, but in others it was unique. For one thing, the great, square, whitewashed wall of fitted stone encompassing the inner city was in perfect repair, each side extending exactly a *legua* (about two and a half miles) and standing six *vara* high (roughly sixteen and a half feet). Built to protect against the greater dragons of this world, none had tested it in decades. Few even ventured into the valley anymore. Those that did were content to snatch livestock—and slaves—at its fringe. The ballistae platforms atop the wall had been dismantled long ago, and it was never pierced for cannon. What humans would ever attack?

Inside the wall, in clustered but expansive villas, dwelled the highest percentage of *aristocratas* and *patricios* in the Dominion, since the Holy City was the center of power and prestige. Many were in business, peddling influence and ensuring their wider interests, clients or patrons, got the contracts or recognition they craved. They were tremendous consumers of art, the finest garments, wall hangings, frescoes, and furnishings that master artisans could produce, and the very finest food, wine, and delicacies from all over the Dominion. Some of all that made its way back out, going to those clients and patrons, but the only things actually produced there for export were the excess fruits of master artisans, their products gaining prestige and value the farther they went because of who made them and where they came from.

There were few government buildings, with most bureaucratic work being done in the villas of those responsible for it, but there were ornate offices adjacent to the thirteen most striking structures Don Hurac and Obispo El Consuelo could view from the long, narrow causeway between lakes Xaltocan to the north and Chalco to the south, still several *leguas* from the city walls. Twelve were stepped pyramids of equal size, thirteen stories high, including the temple at the top. Five were whitewashed the same color as the wall, though the roofs of all the temples were gold and topped with the same jagged, golden lightning bolt cross adorning the red Dominion flag. The rest were painted in pastel colors appropriate to the "number" they represented. The sixth was green, the seventh blue, and eight was a gray-black with oddly shaped silver lightning bolts carved and painted on it. The ninth pyramid was silver-white, and the tenth was the same yellow as the army uniform. The eleventh was red. The last two were naked stone, identical except for size. The thirteenth still had only thirteen levels but was twice as tall as the rest. That was appropriate since it represented the Son of God, and His Supreme Holiness dwelled inside. The others represented His apostles, now personified by the twelve Blood Cardinals, but Don Hurac thought there might've been another reason for the number when the structures were originally built. Every pyramid was the same in another respect; the many steps leading to the temples on top were all stained a dark brownish-black.

Apparently noting that as well, Obispo El Consuelo said, with some dis-appointment, "We missed the great sacrifice of captives last month. *Hun-dreds* of hearts torn out on the Great Temple itself, and *rivers* of blood to glorify God! Do you suppose we'll stay long enough for the next? It's just a small affair at one of the lesser temples—not yours," he hastened to add, "but it should be quite a spectacle compared to the rites we perform at Vera Cruz." Technically, Don Hurac's temple was the yellow one, but he hadn't presided over a sacrifice there, or even been in it, since his investiture eigh-teen years before. That wasn't unusual. Few Blood Cardinals actually lived in the capital, and their presumptive successors performed the rites in their absence. He'd done the same himself.

"Possibly," Don Hurac speculated noncommittally, "but I doubt it. Un-less Don Datu summoned me to perform some service and not just for con-sultations."

El Consuelo tried to hide his regret, and Don Hurac frowned. Human sacrifice was required by their faith and was the only path to paradise for pagans and heretics, but too many these days—including El Consuelo, it seemed—were more interested in the spectacle than the salvation it repre-sented. The next scheduled sacrifice would redeem more pagan captives from the frontiers, and most would be women, as always. Far more females survived infancy outside the cities in this terrible world, perhaps because so many males were killed during childhood while learning to hunt—Don Hurac didn't know. It might be that women were just hardier, healthier, and less accident-prone. Whatever the reason, the Dominion was overrun with them to the extent that it actually traded huge numbers to its sparsely pop-ulated arch enemy in the Pacific: the Empire of the New Britain Isles—which it was even now gathering the Gran Cruzada to eject from the Californias. It was a strange arrangement, beneficial and detrimental to both powers. The Imperials got more people they desperately needed, and the Dominion got better-quality manufactured goods—like musket barrels to kill Imperials with. But the upcoming event would also include a num-ber of *patricio* children, to show God that His chosen people could make real sacrifices of their own. *At least there'll be no fire at this one*, Don Hurac consoled himself. All offerings would be beheaded. Still, though he wouldn't question the necessity, he didn't enjoy watching children die.

The coach and lancers were taking them through the outer city now, and that part wasn't splendid at all. Ramshackle adobe structures sprawled in all directions, separated by an impossibly confusing network of streets and alleys filled with all the "freemen" and slaves required to cater to those in the city. Most of the women were slaves of their men, but all were inter-mingled indistinguishably in poverty amid squalling, running children, goats, myriad small two-legged furry reptiles called *lagardo gatos* that stole scraps and fought over them with piercing shrieks, and thousands of simi-lar, fatter creatures everyone just called *gallinas*. Only the Camino Sagrado, the Holy Road on which they'd traveled since Puebla, was straight and clear—left uncluttered on pain of death. The lancers would've speared any-one that got in their way, and they did kill a couple of staring goats before their owners could pull them aside.

Finally, the Great Gate stood before them, open during the day but guarded by a dozen smartly dressed infantry. The lancer *teniente* called something down in an imperious tone, and they all stepped aside and let the coach pass. As quickly as that, the rumble of the wheels grew quieter on even smoother paving stones, and their surroundings changed from squa-lor and chaos to opulence and order. The street was still lined with freemen and slaves and bright awning-covered tables laden with fresh meat and pro-duce, but only a cleaner, "better sort," wearing decent clothes, were allowed inside the gate.

"Should we stop and refresh ourselves?" asked Obispo El Consuelo.

Don Hurac considered but shook his head. "Don Datu begged me to come 'without delay.' We'll go directly to his office. Please instruct the drivers."

El Consuelo rose and squirmed through the coach window beside him to call to the men above. Satisfied they heard him, he returned to his seat, breathing heavily from the exertion. Don Hurac raised a brow. "You really should move about more," he gently chastised. "A small measure of grace can be earned even in the discomfort of exercise."

It wouldn't be long now. The first pair of temples, on each side of the road, were just ahead. All twelve Temples of the Apostles were arranged in a square around the Great Temple Plaza, and Don Datu's (naked stone) and the red one stood closest to the east to greet the rising sun. The lancers—they and their horses had to be tired!—trotted forward to form a line in front of Don Datu's columned "office," decorated in an ornate mudejar style, standing beside his soaring monument. The coach drew up and came to a stop. One of the coachmen jumped down, yellow army-like uniform dusty and rumpled, and opened the door. Mumbling about servants again, El Consuelo rose to help Don Hurac if necessary. The portly Blood Cardinal could use more exercise himself but managed to step stiffly down with just the coachman's hand to steady him. The guards in front of the office had announced their arrival, of course, and a stream of servant girls clothed in sheer white fabric belted around their waists and *not* covered in paint so harmful to their skin, arranged themselves welcomingly around Don Hurac and El Consuelo, a pair of them bearing tall mugs of cool nectar.

Don Hurac thankfully took a mug and drank, casting an approving eye at the girls. *One of the reasons I like Don Datu,* he thought. *Women are so plentiful, it's easy to disregard them when one doesn't need what only they can offer, but they* are *people, after all. Fallen and corrupted in the eyes of God, but still worthy of His grace.* And Don Hurac knew of nothing in nature more beautiful than the female form. It appalled him the way some Blood Cardinals, even *alcaldes* and *aristocratas,* defiled that beauty with paint. Don Datu felt the same. *And surrounding myself with their purest beauty constantly reminds me how they lured man away from perfect obedience to God. It keeps me forever on guard against them—and all things that would lead me astray,* he added piously to himself. *They must be more frequently sacrificed, of course; their numbers alone prove God has ordained they should still be punished for the original sin of their sex, but that doesn't mean He wants them wantonly mistreated.*

"Holiness," El Consuelo prodded, breaking his reverie. Some of the girls had heaved his baggage down from the back of the coach and were taking it inside while the rest stood almost at attention, making a lane for a tall, thin, heavy-browed young figure in a rich red robe striding briskly toward him.

"I am Obispo De Sachihiro, Your Holiness. You may remember me from your visit to the Techolotla Temple several years ago." He looked at Don Hurac's companion. "And you must be Obispo El Consuelo. On behalf of His Holiness Don Datu, please accept my warmest greetings." He looked back at Don Hurac. "My lord is most anxious to see you."

"Of course I remember you, and my stay at your temple was most pleasant." Don Hurac beamed. "I particularly enjoyed the wild boar hunting!" The only animals brought to this world two centuries before that not only survived but thrived in the wild were hogs that went feral. They fell prey to many things, but those that survived grew fierce enough to deter smaller predators and bred fast enough to more than keep up with the larger ones. "Congratulations on being chosen as Don Datu's successor, by the way." He waved at the baggage. "But what is this? Surely I can stay at my own office."

"Don Datu insisted you stay with us," De Sachihiro said a little lower. "It's been some time since you were in the Holy City, and things are . . . different. Some might even be surprisingly awkward if you're not expecting them. I believe he desires you not to be . . . inconvenienced or distressed by them."

In other words, I may not approve of activities—in my name—at the Yellow Temple and it's safer for me—and less likely I'll distress others—if I stay here, Don Hurac translated. "Very well, I gladly accept the hospitality of my dear friend Don Datu. Come, Obispo El Consuelo, let us go inside." He smiled and waved a buzzing insect away from his nose. "The weather here is quite pleasant most of the year, but the marshy lakes surrounding the capital support an astonishing number of mosquitoes. They quickly grow tiresome, particularly in the morning and evening."

"They do indeed, Your Holiness," De Sachihiro agreed, gesturing at the high, ornately carved door of the large office building. "Will you both come this way?"

The word "office" applied to Don Datu's official residence, or any of the other temple offices, for that matter, in the same way it would to an *aristocrata*'s villa. And the ornamental façade, mixing several old-world cultures with those they found here, actually was a façade: a high, stout wall enclosing an airy inner courtyard lined with decoratively trimmed trees and flowering plants. There was even a modest flowing fountain surrounded by stone benches in front of another entryway, smaller, but reminiscent of the outer one, opening into the residence proper. Don Hurac had been here before, but was again surprised by how cool it was despite a lack of wind, and the mosquitoes were entirely absent. Don Datu once told him the flowers he chose repelled them. And there was Don Datu himself, standing welcomingly in the open doors of his residence, a wide smile on his face, flanked by another pair of modestly dressed servant girls.

"Ah! Don Hurac! You've arrived at last!" Don Datu exclaimed. "I'd begun to fear for you."

Don Hurac smiled back, but took the opportunity to appraise his host. Don Datu had always been almost femininely slim, even slight, but kept himself fit and had only a few more than his own thirty-two years. But this man had quite a few extra, flaccid pounds hanging from a still-meager frame. Once-black hair was shot with silver, and his dark face was deeply lined. *The cost of being "first among equals" in this time of turmoil*, Don Hurac sadly assumed. "My dear Don Datu!" he cried. "It's been too long. My own fault, of course. I've grown too set and comfortable with my life away from the capital. And I apologize for taking so long to come after you asked for me. The voyage back from Campeche was most tedious, then the journey here . . . I came instantly upon receiving your request."

"Obviously." Don Datu's smile had turned sly. "Not even taking time to fill another coach with the delightful servants you're so well known for. Particularly the lovely Zyan." Don Hurac actually blushed. Zyan was his oldest and most senior *madre de hijos*, but she'd been a slave and was unsuitable for marriage to such as he. Don Hurac adored her and had never taken a wife. Don Datu waved around. "Never mind. My servants will see to your every need." The smile remained, but the eyes became more serious, settling on Don Hurac's aide. "And you must be Obispo El Consuelo. Welcome." He glanced back at Don Hurac. "I knew you'd go to Campeche at once, to learn what happened with Don Frutos's army, and I've had . . . some reports already, but I crave your views and begrudge only the time it took you to bring them. The precious *time*, my dear Hurac, not you! Come, let us take refreshment in private. You must be famished!" Was there a slight emphasis on the word "private"? Don Hurac wondered. "Obispo De Sachihiro, won't you show Obispo El Consuelo to the guest chambers? We'll gather again for a proper midday meal, and then our guests can have a well-earned rest."

"Of course, Your Holiness," De Sachahiro said, bowing. Don Hurac nodded at the questioning look from El Consuelo.

"Come, Don Hurac," Don Datu said, beckoning. "I'm so glad you're here!"

They ensconced themselves in an ornate little room on the second floor of the office villa with bright, multicolored lighting from a stained-glass window. Don Hurac remembered the chamber as Don Datu's "breakfast niche," and a large, much-appreciated breakfast awaited them. He also knew the walls were too thick for their words to pass through, and guards had stepped into place at the far end of the corridor behind them as soon as they passed. Their conversation couldn't be more private if they'd stood alone atop the distant mountains. They exchanged pleasantries as they ate an entire butter-and-garlic-seasoned loaf of the whitest bread Don Hurac had ever seen (garlic and tobacco had been among the first crops their ancient ancestors planted), a mountainous heap of fried eggs with brown yolks, layered with goat cheese, and sweet fried bread—*ensaimadas*. All this was washed down with the juice of something that looked like apples and were in fact called *manzanas*, but tasted like pears, as well as *chocolate caliente*. Unlike coffee, their ancestors had found a kind of native cocoa already here.

"Tell me," Don Datu finally said, "what did you really find at Campeche?"

Don Hurac sighed and wiped his mouth with a napkin. "Disaster. General Agon has done his best to pick up the pieces of the army, but needs supplies, reinforcements, and most especially the freedom to use them as he sees fit." He hastened to add, smoldering, "But any . . . setback by our arms anywhere in the Dominion can only be viewed as a disaster, no matter how Don Frutos frames the circumstances. He bungled everything from the start, from his disposition of the captives taken from the Americano steamship—I was never given access to them, nor were you, and I've no doubt that priceless information was lost—to his precipitous campaign up the Yucatán to crush an enemy he knew nothing about." He shook his head sadly. "The outcome was preordained. The army—under his control, not Agon's—was soundly beaten by a smaller, but better armed and more imaginative force. That's the truth, and *if* that truth was ever widely known . . ."

"It could be a disaster for us all," Don Datu grimly acknowledged. He hesitated. "For more reasons than you know." Don Hurac blinked, but he passed that over and continued, "Do you think General Agon is the man to retrieve the situation?"

Don Hurac shrugged. "Who else could we send? Virtually all our other generals are involved with the Gran Cruzada. Recalling one now wouldn't only draw attention to the necessity, but would introduce a dangerous delay in dealing with the Yucatán heretics. They've *beaten a Dominion army*," he stressed. "Their morale will be soaring, and they'll have time to prepare for our next move no matter what we do." He rubbed the black whiskers on his puffy chin. "General Agon is there already. He's met the enemy and knows them best . . . and it's my belief his remaining troops *appreciate* him. They'll fight for him better than any stranger inflicted on them." He rubbed his chin more vigorously. "You knew Agon's father. A valuable *aristocrata* ally against the Blood Priests after he retired from the army, and a strong supporter of blood succession to the cardinalship. Agon strikes me the same."

"What of Don Frutos?" Don Datu asked. "He supports the outrageous ambitions of the Blood Priests and they support him."

"No longer, I believe, except as an expedient. He didn't impress Father Tranquilo with his courage and is no longer seen as a suitable patron. I'm shocked to find grounds for agreement with such as Tranquilo. Don Frutos should be boiled alive," he added bitterly.

"We should've boiled *Father Tranquilo* years ago, instead of just tossing him out on the frontier, where he could continue to scheme," Don Datu seethed.

Don Hurac remembered something. "The messenger dragon I *thought* was carrying official dispatches to me and you was actually Tranquilo's. General Agon was unaware of it. Don Frutos might've known, but I've no idea who else it communicated with. I told General Agon to seize it and send it only to you or me."

"He did," Don Datu confirmed, "and it's been coming here. One reason I already knew much of what you've told me." He hesitated. "I also know who else it was going to before."

Don Hurac tilted his head in interest.

"All the Blood Cardinals *except* me," Don Datu said bleakly. "First to justify Don Frutos's actions, with the aid of the Blood Priests, of course, then to discredit Don Frutos and distance the Blood Priests from his failure. I learned this myself from Don Julio DeDivino Dicha only yesterday when he asked what news the dragon brought. He saw it fly in and was annoyed that it neglected to call at his temple. He apparently assumed it was carrying official dispatches as well, and had been coming to me all along." Don Julio was currently considered "second among equals" and was known to be the most sympathetic of the "top three" to the Blood Priest's cause and had personally sponsored Don Frutos's admission to the succession.

Don Datu paused and pursed his lips before taking a sip of his chocolate. It was cold, and he grimaced. "This brings us back to that particular disaster of which you have no knowledge. No one knows, in fact, and it must remain that way. There's far too much in motion—the Gran Cruzada against the Imperials, the reverse in the Yucatán, the Blood Priests seeking any advantage—to allow any further distraction."

Don Hurac politely tilted his head again, ready for anything—he thought.

Don Datu took a long breath. "His Supreme Holiness, messiah of Mexico and emperor of the world, is dead. Only I and my most trusted servants, and now you, are aware. All our beloved leader's closest servants have been . . . silenced." He gestured vaguely. "The great sacrifice mere days ago.

I know none of them could talk." (His Supreme Holiness's body servants and personal guards had their tongues removed so they could never reveal anything He said or did in private. A few were even ritually blinded and deafened.) "But His death was somewhat . . . ignominious." He frowned. "He was always given to communing with God through various intoxicants—even you must recall He was rarely fully present—and He spent more time in that state in recent years than not. For all practical purposes, I've ruled the Dominion in His name." Don Datu waved that away. "There's nothing unusual in that, and it's understandable that He'd spend as much time as He could in the spiritual presence of God in these troubled times, but there was no 'grace' in His end. He died on His chamber pot in a drugged stupor, and none who witnessed that could live." He pressed a hand against his breast. "Fortunately, I've been the only Blood Cardinal He would see for almost two years, and others are accustomed to that. Guards in the red-and-gold livery remain outside His temple, my own servants come and go, dressed as His, and I still go 'for guidance' from time to time. Obviously, however, along with the defeat in the Yucatán, not a word of this can reach the people!"

Don Hurac was shocked, but even more confused. "Dreadful news, of course, but why not simply step up yourself? It's long been expected you'd succeed Him. There'd be no dissent."

Don Datu raised an eyebrow at him. "You think not? Did you miss what I said about the messenger dragons? You think Tranquilo neglected me by accident? Tranquilo hates me even more than you for banishing him and keeping his order out of the Holy City as long as I could. They're all over now, of course, and have even taken over a number of temples." He eyed Don Hurac. "Yours, for example. That's why I insisted that you stay here. They might think they can reason with you, especially when you discover you've already been supplanted by your successor—one of *their* creatures, I'm afraid—but they don't know you like I do. Your very life will be in danger once they do." He shook his head. "They'll want Don Julio installed in the Great Temple as their tool. He's weak and lazy but ambitious and already sympathetic to them—constantly influenced by *his* successor, no doubt. If they learned of the demise of His Supreme Holiness, there'd be a crisis at the very top of the Dominion, a succession struggle that might even bring civil war right when most of our loyal army is away, embarking on its mission to the northwest, and the rest of our army is, or will soon be, occupied crushing the threat in the Yucatán. You see now why I worry so whether General Agon is the right man for that task?"

"Indeed," Don Hurac almost whispered, then cleared his throat. "His is now arguably the more important task, since war already wages in a weakened region of the Dominion and the Gran Cruzada is not yet engaged. Perhaps you should recall a portion of it, say fifty thousand, to help Agon deal with the heretics and their Americano allies."

Don Datu shook his head. "Impossible. The Gran Cruzada has been preparing for years, and it's the Blood Priests and their sympathizers who are most offended by the Imperial trespass in the Californias." His expression clouded. "It's so far away, filled with dragons and other monsters we don't even know, that we don't have a single outpost there!" he added angrily, frustrated. "I doubt the Imperials can maintain a presence either, supplied from their islands so far out at sea, but the Cruzada's taken on a life of its own, even supported by the hidalgos and freemen." He shook his head. "No, drawing forces from it now will be seen as weak, indecisive, even uncommitted. Worse, it will focus attention on where they go. It's known there's been fighting in the Yucatán," he conceded, "but there's always fighting against pagans and heretics on the frontier. No one can know there's been a reverse, and that's the main reason we mustn't boil Don Frutos just yet. Word of that would surely spread! Such a thing has never happened, the people would panic, the Blood Priests would stir them, and our dead Supreme Holiness will seem even weaker—possibly sparking the very civil war I fear," he added ironically. "No," he repeated, "sooner or later, His Supreme Holiness's . . . true condition must be revealed, and it would be better if the announcement—and my official ascension—was accompanied by news of a victory." He peered intently at Don Hurac once more. "*You* must ensure that happens. Do whatever you can to give General Agon what he needs; strip every garrison from here to the Grijalva River if you must and make sure Don Frutos, and especially Father Tranquilo, don't interfere with the general." He finally smiled. "Once the Yucatán is secure, we can also make the shocking announcement that Don Frutos, Tranquilo, and all his loathsome Blood Priests were defeated and had to be rescued by you." His face became a mask of bitterness. "Then we can publicly boil them all."

CHAPTER 6

Corporal Hannibal "Hanny" Cox of the 3rd Pennsylvania Volunteer Regiment was doing his best not to gasp in the heat under the weight of his musket, bayonet, double-loaded cartridge box (120 rounds of ammunition at fourteen balls to the pound weighed almost as much as his musket), knapsack, greatcoat (like he needed *that* then), plate, cup, toiletries, spare shirt, drawers, and socks, as well as a wool blanket wrapped in his half of a small canvas tent. In his case, almost all those things except the underwear (including the shirt) had come to this world with him, but even the new recruits were just as generously burdened with locally made equipment. Their jackets and trousers were lighter-weight material, better suited to the climate, but that was their only advantage. Wool probably kept him cooler as the sweat he soaked it with evaporated.

A heavy but precious canteen and haversack (filled with a week's worth of flat, folded, ground maize tortillas) brought the total to over sixty pounds. That was enough to make the tall but willowy towheaded youth just a year—and a world—away from the family farm along the Delaware River in Bucks County, Pennsylvania, believe he even detected the weight of his beltplate. Tortillas weren't all they ate, of course, but they gave the men something to munch on the march. Hanny guessed he had a hundred or more, just as hard as crackers or hardtack, but better tasting. They could also be eaten without softening in water if a man had good enough teeth.

He had to hide his exhaustion and discomfort, however, because now he had to set an example as the 3rd Pennsylvania led the long column of infantry down the surprisingly wide forest trace through these frightening woods. He and his best friend, an Uxmalo youth named Apo Tuin, had been honored to start the Battle of the Washboard as regimental color-bearers. Apo was knocked unconscious, which probably saved his life. All the other men who took up the regimental flag were killed. Hanny tied the Stars and Stripes to a shot-riddled caisson, grabbed a musket, and joined the desperate fight alongside Sergeant Visser and Private "Preacher Mac" McDonough. Visser made sure Hanny was elected corporal for his valor and spoke to the newly promoted Captain Currin when he replaced John Ulrich as company commander about awarding the honor of carrying the flags to other deserving youths. Hanny didn't think that was fair to the fellows because he hadn't fought any harder than anyone else in B Company, and it wasn't fair to him because he didn't *want* to be corporal, wasn't *ready* to be in charge of other men—especially the eight in his squad. Sergeant Visser thought different, still also impressed by the way Hanny stood up to the greatest bully in the army, a former sergeant (broken to the ranks of the 1st US over a far more serious affair) named Daniel Hahessy.

His squad felt the same even though half were Uxmalos, hadn't even been in the army at the time, and understood just enough English to follow commands in battle. Hanny's Spanya was improving but was still pretty bad. Apo already spoke good English and helped with that. But fair or not, Visser's and his squad's opinion meant a lot to Hanny, and he was determined to do his best. So he struggled along, pretending the weight of his gear and weapon and the thick heat and sugar sand dust swirling around the marching men didn't bother him at all.

"We're making good time," Sergeant Visser said, tone almost surprised. Hanny nearly jumped out of his skin. He'd been concentrating so hard on *appearing* fresh and alert while putting one sore foot in front of the other, he hadn't even noticed Visser's approach. Not good. One really had to *be* alert in this dangerous land.

"Seems so," he said after what he hoped his men and the sergeant mistook for a moment of reflection.

"We left Nautla the week before Christmas. . . ." Visser continued, then snorted. "Hard to imagine Christmas in this heat." He waved around at the tall, dense trees on either side of the trace. "An' wandering along through this."

"Feels like Christmas to *us*," Apo said with a laugh.

"Aye, an' ye go on aboot it fer half a bloody month," groused the Scottish-born Preacher Mac. "Biggest disputation 'tween Father Orno an' Reverend Harkin's been aboot yer popish 'Christ-mass.' An' even fer a 'New Light Covenanter' like him, Harkin's a wee bendy for me." McDonough sniffed.

"Father Orno isn't 'popish,'" Apo flared. To him the only pope was His Supreme Holiness of the Dominion. Catholics, mostly Irish among the Americans, still confused him.

Visser interceded. "Easy, lads. If Orno an' Harkin can get along, you damned well can." He chuckled. "An' as for Harkin bein' 'bendy' about Christmas, he's a Pennsylvania Presbyterian whose congregation was half Germans—like my people." He looked at Apo. "Doesn't mean he's settled with it. Some people figure if it isn't in the Bible, it's just flat wrong. An' Christmas *isn't* in the Bible." He shook his head and took on a stern expression. "I'm not even sayin' *he's* wrong. What makes him an' Father Orno *both right*, though, is that while we're all busy fightin' *real* evil together, they're willin' to let the little stuff be."

"It isnae 'little stuff,'" McDonough groused lowly.

Visser glared at him. "Compared to the *big stuff*, it is. An' you fellas will leave it be too, or you'll answer to me." He waved around again. "We've all had to 'bend' to cope with the mess we're in." Looking back at Hanny he continued as if there'd been no interruption. "As I was sayin', we've been on this track—Warmaster Varaa says Holcanos made it for movin' from Cayal to Campeche an' I'd call it a road whether it's on a map or not—for fourteen days. Best I can figure, we've made between thirteen an' fifteen miles a day—close to two hundred all told, more than two-thirds to our meet with King Har-Kaaska. Pretty good," he said, "considerin' how careful the Rangers have to scout our flanks, an' we can't outpace our supplies. Not near enough water on this stretch." He nodded down at Hanny's feet as they walked. "Still, a good enough pace to keep our trompers sore." He grinned and shifted the musket sling on his shoulder. "Hardly any sick or stragglers—which reminds me," he added darkly, raising his voice, "don't forget to replace those slivers of bark in your canteens every few days. I know it tastes nasty when it's fresh, but the Jaguaristas swear it keeps you from gettin' the fever. You get sick an' die because your water tastes funny, I'll have you on latrine duty forever—because I'll *bury* you in one, you hear?"

Local healers were convinced that mosquitoes, not the air or climate, spread many deadly fevers. Hanny didn't know how that could be or what a few slivers of foul-tasting bark did to prevent it, but between that and the smoky watch fires that kept mosquitoes away, the army had remained remarkably healthy. Apparently, mosquitoes also spread a far more serious illness called *el vomito rojo*, something like yellow fever, that the bark didn't stop. It was largely seasonal and controlled by smoke and natural mosquito repellants.

Visser's expression softened. "An' the Rangers an' lancers, even those prissy dragoons an' mounted riflemen, have kept most of the big, scary lizards off us."

"Most," Hanny had to agree, plain he meant "not all." That would've been asking the impossible, though, even now at the height of the dry season, when fewer predators roamed the woods. Some got through the protective screen their scouts maintained no matter how brave or diligent they were. One had attacked the rearguard battalion of the 1st Ocelomeh, killing six men before it was slain by a fusillade of heavy-shafted obsidian-headed arrows a lot of the Jaguar Warriors still carried. Hanny had been in the middle of another attack when one of the larger brutes suddenly charged in among the newly promoted Captain Felix Meder's mounted riflemen in front of the 3rd. It was the most frightening thing imaginable. The beast was thirty feet long from nose to tail and nine feet tall, its feathery fur blending with the dark woods around it. Only its rapid motion, horrible, ivory-colored teeth, and glaring red eyes gave any warning before it crashed into the scattering horsemen. One man was killed when his horse fell and rolled on him, but that saved others, because the screaming, writhing animal drew the beast's attention. Planting a huge foot with three hooked claws on the horse's head, it stooped and clamped terrible long jaws on its belly and tore out intestines like a tangle of bloody noodles. The riflemen managed to control their mounts and deliver a crackle of fire from their M1817 rifles and at least a dozen balls from the .54 caliber weapons slapped the creature in rapid succession. Few went deep enough to cause serious injury, but there was no question that they hurt. The monster's indignant, bloodcurdling shriek as it lunged at its tormenters proved that.

Almost in a daze, Hanny had reacted without thinking to Captain Cullin's shouted, "Third Platoon, make a line!" and he rushed forward, pushing men of his squad and others into position and shouting for them to "Load!" Fifty men, about half and half Americans and Uxmalos, scurried to their places, bunching up and overlapping the road into the trees even as they tore paper cartridges with their teeth, primed their pieces, and poured the rest of the powder down the barrels of .69 caliber M1816 Springfield muskets. Most were thumbing in the big lead balls, still wrapped in paper, as they found a place to stand, shoving them down with clattering iron rammers.

"Third Platoon, make ready!" Cullin had cried, echoed by First Lieutenant Eli Aiken, still mounted, who drew his sword and intentionally reared his horse to distract the monster from the reloading riflemen. It worked, but then the thing was focused on 3rd Platoon—and Hanny. Fifty men, wadded together, more than half with their muskets over the man's shoulder in front of him, delivered a near-perfect crashing volley when Captain Cullin roared, "Fire!"

Men shouted in pain when vent jets burnt their faces and necks or spat small fragments of flint or unburnt powder into their skin, but protests were overwhelmed by the agonized screech of the monster as a shattered leg gave way and it fell flailing to the ground. Fewer than thirty paces distant, virtually every shot must've hit. Even accounting for how soft lead flattened on impact with such a dense animal at its highest velocity, each ball weighed more than an ounce. The damage they did was much greater than the faster but smaller and lighter rifle bullets.

Colonel Cayce, Reverend Harkin, Leonor Anson, and Warmaster Varaa-Choon galloped back down the track from where they habitually rode with a platoon of Rangers and dragoons up ahead and reined in their horses in the standing white smoke. The monster saw them and struggled to rise, but crashed down with another bone-chilling shriek.

"Well done, Captain Cullin. Well done, Third Pennsylvania!" Cayce had called out, appraising the beast. "First time I've seen one this size incapacitated by musketry alone." He smiled at Cullin, who was almost panting with excitement. "You may as well finish it. Your men's weapons are already dirty. Give them each a crack at it, one at a time." He raised his voice. "A dollar to the man who finds a weak spot in that hard head and kills it instantly!" Perhaps unsurprisingly considering the most "modern" influence to their culture, Uxmalos—everyone they'd met in this world, even Doms— used *dolars* and *reales* (pieces of eight) for their currency, though the rate of exchange was somewhat disappointing to the Americans at first. Each private soldier, for example, was paid a *reale* a day, and Lewis had offered more than a week's pay as a prize. Grinning and talking among themselves as they reloaded and the monster rested, breath rasping, eyes glaring, the men's terror had turned to competitive revenge and Lewis had urged his big chestnut mare named Arete over to Captain Cullin. His companions followed. "That was close," Lewis had said lowly, but loud enough for Hanny and Apo. Neither was much interested in casually shooting a helpless beast, even if it would eat them if it could.

"Yes sir," Cullin had replied, removing his wheel hat and shakily wiping sweat from his forehead. "I'll try to do better next time."

"I don't see how you could," Lewis had said gently. "B Company's in fine hands."

Cullin had chuckled raggedly. "Thank you, sir. It's funny, though. I was still just a sergeant at the Washboard and only got elected to lieutenant after that. Next thing I know, I'm a captain, and the first combat order I give as an officer is to shoot a *lizard*!" He reflected. "Or demon. Whatever it is."

"Lots of promotions going around, Captain," Lewis had said wryly. "All deserved."

"That's no demon!" Reverend Harkin had declared loudly as the first musket cracked, the monster screeched, and soldiers jeered the shooter. "It's merely another of God's more unpleasant creatures that He moved from our world to this one."

Another shot, more jeers.

"Harkin thinks he has it all figured out," Hanny had whispered a little shakily to Apo. "He doesn't believe any whole species can die out completely, because that would mean God made something imperfect. He thinks everything that disappeared where we came from—who knows what: dragons, sea monsters, maybe even mermaids—all wound up here."

"What does 'species' mean? What's a 'mermaid'?" Apo had asked, and Hanny tried to explain while the shooting continued and he watched Colonel Cayce continue reassuring Captain Cullin. His eyes were on the riflemen extricating their fallen comrade from under his dead horse with touching care. The contrasts on display were almost too much for Hanny: sad, respectful riflemen; a captain unsure he'd done all he could; a solicitous and reassuring colonel alongside a preacher completely satisfied he'd solved a mystery assailing his faith—while a furry, catlike Warmaster

Choon sat on a horse beside him. Then there was a female . . . warrior, in Leonor Anson, whose eyes were always on their surroundings while soldiers who were terrified moments before were caught up completely in a bloodthirsty sport. Hanny had felt his legs start to shake as the stress of the moment bled off. Apo finally looked thoughtful. "You don't think that?"

Hanny shook his head. "I don't know what to think. I'm still not sure we aren't in hell," he'd answered darkly.

Apo puffed out his cheeks and glanced at the men still shooting when a ball ricocheted off thick bone and warbled away, *thwokking* into a tree. "You think *I* was born and grew up in hell? All my family before me? My mother? My *sister*?"

That shook Hanny out of his frightening train of thought, and even as his legs firmed up, he blushed. Apo's sister Izel was very pretty. "Maybe not Izel," he'd qualified with a tentative smile, "but your mother doesn't like me."

Apo grinned. "She likes you. She cooks for you when you come to her house! But you are a *extranjero*—a foreigner—so strange and so . . ." Apo laughed. "I've said before, you're too *white*! She thinks you're sick, and she sees how you look at Izel!"

"I can't help what color I am," Hanny grumbled.

"Don't worry," Apo had assured him, "Izel doesn't think you're sick."

Now Hanny pondered that again, along with the numerous grisly losses he knew the dragoons, Rangers, and scouts from the 1st Ocelomeh in particular had suffered to get them this far. *I've never been as frightened as I was during the Battle of the Washboard, but the thought of being attacked and torn apart by monsters is a constant, lingering fear,* he thought. *Not hell,* he decided with a shudder, *but close.*

"What was that?" Sergeant Visser demanded, listening over the tramp of feet and talking men. "Quiet, damn you!" he snapped at those nearby. Hanny heard it too, a kind of distant, muffled . . . *khoo*-like sound, followed by another and another. "That's carbine or musket fire ahead," Visser declared.

"Pretty far," someone said. "Building," he added.

"Not that far," Visser warned. "Trees deaden the sound. Scouts must've run into another booger."

Hanny had wondered how they'd steal a march on the enemy and sneak the whole army to Cayal if they had to shoot their way across the entire peninsula, but the report of gunfire really didn't travel far in these trees.

"There go the riflemen!" someone cried as the horsemen in front of the 3rd Pennsylvania thundered forward in a cloud of dust and dead ferny leaves. A rider without branch trim on his jacket—an Ocelomeh Ranger— came out of the cloud, galloping hard, throwing up more dust and debris in front of Major Ulrich as he violently slowed his mount. "Corporal Mirat, sir," he announced in near-perfect English except for the mixture of accents that influenced it. He saluted. "Colonel's compliments, an' please bring your men up on the double. Form line of battle to the left in a clearing ahead, but leave room for Captain Hudgens's battery to come out behind you." He started to bolt onward, but Ulrich stopped him.

"What's happening? What about our right?"

"I'm to tell Major Beck an' the First US to deploy on your right." Saluting again, the Ranger galloped down the line.

Major Ulrich turned his dark-striped local horse. "Pass the word for Captain Cullin. Take 'em forward at the double, Lieutenant Aiken," he said crisply. "Column into line. I'm sure someone will show you where. Captain Meder's riflemen and all the dragoons not scouting the flanks with the Rangers are already up there. So is Colonel Cayce." The firing ahead was almost continuous now. "Damned if I know what we've run into," he muttered.

"Why's it always us first?" grumbled Preacher Mac as Sergeant Visser repeated the "forward at the double time" command and Lieutenant Aiken spurred his horse to get ahead of them.

"Because we're leading the column," Apo replied with a grin. "You want to eat dust all day, every day? My friends in the First US and First Uxmal gripe about *that*!" Hanny figured that was true and the portion of the 1st Ocelomeh serving as a rear guard ate everybody's dust. Not many were back there, though. Several companies of Ocelomeh had been dispatched to follow scouts on lesser, parallel tracks on either flank. Those paths weren't much, but they had to keep them covered. Their biggest concern was that wandering Holcanos would detect them and get past to warn General Agon at Campeche. *And it must be Holcanos in front of us*, Hanny realized.

"We've run into a bunch of those cannibal Injins," said Sergeant Visser, coming to the same conclusion as Hanny. "This is their road, their country. Maybe some of those damned Griks too," he added darkly. The 3rd had been in a desperate action with both on the beach after they first arrived on this world and was lucky to survive. Many would remember that, and

Visser quickly added as the men around him started breathing hard from the pace the young drummers set, "But we were fresh fish the first time and thrashed 'em anyway. We'll thrash 'em again."

Hanny wondered how many remembered they would've all died if Colonel Cayce hadn't come to their aid. *Well, he's already with us, leading this time*, he consoled himself.

The shooting was louder ahead, and the dense forest fell away to reveal a brightly lit clearing full of tall grass and rotting, fire-blackened stumps. They'd come across places like this before, the result of lightning fires or native camp or village fires that got out of control. Some were relatively limited since, rainy season or not, it was always humid, and the big, armored, and short-tempered *sapos de hierro* (iron toads) the Americans called "horny turtles" shredded the deadfall that fed such fires in an insatiable search for insects. The result was nothing but porous debris that would've burnt readily if it didn't absorb so much moisture from the air. Like the carpet of dead leaves, it eventually decomposed into the sugar sand dust that bothered them all. This clearing was bigger than most, more than a mile across and stretching off to the southwest and northeast as far as Hanny could see as Company B peeled off to the left, forming two ranks behind a thin skirmish line of dismounted riflemen and dragoons kneeling in the grass. They were keeping up a steady fire at . . . Hanny gulped. He didn't see any of the terrifying, reptilian Grik, but hundreds of whooping, screeching Holcanos were coming at them the very same way, loosing flights of heavy-shafted arrows and whirling big spears and flint-studded clubs.

"Keep going, keep going!" Visser was shouting, "all the way down where Lieutenant Aiken is. He's marking the end of our line!" Captain Cullin was yelling for A and C Companies to push in behind them and get into line, but the loud jangle and rattle of a section of Captain Hudgens's C Battery almost drowned him out, along with Hudgens's swearing and First Sergeant Petty's demand that the infantry "move yourselves!"

"Hudgens is a hot one for action," Visser wheezed as B Company reached its mark and started dressing its ranks. Off to the right, the regimental flags had been uncased and flowed in the midmorning sun. "He jumped a two-gun section ahead of E Company—the next in line—and'll probably have another section up after them."

"Why's that, Sergeant?" Apo asked, gasping. "*We're* all bunched up to deliver massed fire—like you taught us. We don't have much artillery, so why spread it out?"

"Good artillerymen like Hudgens—and Colonel Cayce—know guns gotta have infantry support to survive, but we might need *their* support to live long enough to do it! Using Colonel Cayce's 'flying artillery' tactics with all their gunners mounted, they can bunch up or spread out as they need to. Now *load*, damn you!" he bellowed loudly, echoing Lieutenant Aiken's command. That jolted Hanny. He'd been focused on the big arrows with fluffy red fletching starting to bristle around the skirmishers and creeping back toward them. Hand shaking, he unclasped the strap holding his cartridge box shut and withdrew a coarse paper-wrapped ball and charge of powder. Biting off the end, he flipped the steel "frizzen" on the lock of his 1816 Springfield forward and dribbled a little powder in the pan before closing the frizzen again. Dropping the musket butt on his foot, he poured the rest of the powder down the barrel and shoved the paper-wrapped ball in after it. About the same time as the men all around him, he drew the gleaming rammer and shoved the ball down on the charge. Replacing the rammer, he raised the musket up.

The dismounted riflemen and dragoons were falling back, clearing the front, several helping others who'd been pierced by arrows that were falling among the men of Company B now. A scream came from the right, then another.

"Make ready!" cried Aiken, and Hanny thumbed the cock holding the flint back to the second notch, barely noticing a strange *qwok!* sound that he actually felt in the weapon. Without thinking about it, he twisted his wheel hat so the combination of the flat, pointed brim and high collar of his shell jacket would protect the left side of his face from the vent jet of Apo's musket. "Take aim!" Aiken shouted, finally spurring his horse clear of the front. Hundreds of polished musket barrels came down with a rippling flash to point at the rampaging enemy now less than seventy yards distant. Most of the Holcanos were naked, but few were decorated with the garish paint they'd worn before. Apparently, they hadn't had time to apply it. The arrows had almost stopped as well, but spears and clubs, dark faces contorted with rage, and high-pitched yipping and screeching were frightening enough.

"Front rank . . . fire!" bellowed Captain Cullin.

Hanny's front sight was dead center of the top of his rounded breech, hovering over the chest of a man running straight for him when he squeezed the trigger like hundreds around him. A sheeting volley roared out, yellow flame stabbing through white smoke. Hideous screams answered the crackling roar just as there came an earsplitting *poom-poom!* from the right and Hudgens's first section of 6pdrs sent lethal, yellow-smoke-wreathed swarms of canister whistling into the Holcanos.

The first rank was reloading when Lieutenant Aiken commanded the second rank to make ready. Hanny hadn't felt the recoil of his musket, but that wasn't unusual in situations like this. He never would've specifically *heard* it fire either. Now he realized it *hadn't* since the cock was still all the way back. Fiddling with it, he realized there was no tension on it at all.

"God damn it!" he shouted, the first time in his life he'd ever uttered something so foul. Even in the middle of battle, with a barbarous, cannibalistic enemy sweeping down, he felt the heat of his blush warm his face.

"What's the matter?" cried Apo, already ramming another load down his musket.

"My *mainspring* is broken!" Hanny railed.

"Terrible, terrible," Sergeant Visser lamented, returning his rammer to the groove under his barrel. "As hard up as we are for replacement springs— an', God help us, good spring steel—Lieutenant Aiken'll have you on a charge!"

"Fire!" roared Cullin, making even Visser flinch when a second-rank musket flared beside his head. That was followed immediately by the heavier roar of the two 12pdr guns farther down the line. Still, Visser continued as though he'd never stopped. "Some corporal you are," he admonished, looking at Preacher Mac and others in Hanny's squad. "Went into action at the Washboard with a dull flint and . . ."

"That wasn't my weapon!" Hanny said hotly.

"And now he's contrived to snap his mainspring," Visser continued seriously. "The lengths he'll go to to stay out of a fight . . . It's enough to make you weep."

"First rank, make ready!" came Aiken's shout, and everyone—except a furious Hanny—cocked their muskets and brought them up. "Take aim! Fire!" Another volley sheeted out, though few could see targets anymore for the smoke. One thing was clear: the arrows had stopped, and the enemy hadn't closed with them.

Hanny's face was burning with anger now, but Visser was grinning.

"Never fear, Corporal," he said. "No one here doubts your courage, just your luck. I think we've set 'em back on their heels or we'd be fixin' bayonets. Run get another weapon. I doubt we've taken many casualties, but there'll be a few." He nodded at the musket in Hanny's hands. "Get that to Mikey O'Roddy when we're done." With virtually all the others working in Uxmal, Ordnance Sergeant Michael "Mikey" O'Roddy, with the C Battery traveling forge, was one of the few real gunsmiths still with the army. "He'll fix it up like new," Visser assured. "He's a damned handy fellow, for an Irishman." Some of the Irish around them growled at that, and Sergeant Visser laughed.

CHAPTER 7

Ley're pullin' back," Anson told Lewis Cayce as he collapsed and lowered a small brass telescope. "All that can, anyway," he amended. Still mounted near the center of the line now including the entire 3rd Pennsylvania, 1st US, and C Battery spread out by sections, Colonel Cayce, Anson, Leonor, Varaa-Choon, Reverend Harkin, Felix Meder, and Lewis's orderly, Corporal Willis, could see farther than the infantrymen on the ground. Near the middle of the clearing in front of them were the widely scattered ruins of a truly ancient city and a surprisingly large camp of Holcanos, their hundreds of dome-shaped hide shelters intermingled with the rubble. Anson's scouts had been surprised to find them, but the Holcano warriors—burdened by women, children, and all their earthly possessions—must've been more surprised to be found by an army they had no idea was near.

"It certainly seems that way, Major Anson," Lewis observed.

"'Major,'" Anson huffed. "Wish you'd quit callin' me that. Don't sound right."

"Nevertheless," Lewis countered. "You've doubtless noticed that quite a few of us go by different ranks these days. Get used to it."

"That attack had less than half their fightin'-age men," Leonor said, still looking through her own glass, but her tone sounded amused by her father's discomfort. "Maybe six or seven hundred. Enough to swamp the riflemen an' dragoons we had close in front of us," she conceded, "but the infantry an' artillery comin' out smashed 'em back." She lowered the glass and removed her wheel hat, shaking out her short black hair. Then she shrugged and looked at Lewis with big, dark eyes. Once again Lewis caught himself unexpectedly captivated by the young woman; the unconscious grace infusing her movements—even shaking out sweaty hair—and the directness of her gaze when their eyes met. She reminded him of a predatory cat even more than the very catlike Mi-Anakka Varaa-Choon.

"Just boiled up out o' their camp an' at us," Anson agreed. "Like we'd kicked over an anthill. Surprised we caught 'em nappin', though."

"*I'm* surprised your Rangers—with so many of my Ocelomeh—were taken unaware by *them*," Varaa growled discontentedly.

"Me too," Anson conceded. "The fellas are pretty worn down, scoutin' all around, not just in front. Lancers too. No excuse, though."

"We had enough warning they were here," Lewis finally said. "Just not how many there were," he stressed with a glance at the Ranger.

Anson frowned. "Not much cover. They didn't have scouts out, but saw ours sneakin' up. That's what set 'em off. We could've halted the whole army an' waited for night, I guess. Scout 'em proper."

Lewis shook his head. "No, this is just as well. We're in something of a hurry after all and we'd have wasted a day waiting to fight them tomorrow. I think they would've noticed *us* by then and been more prepared." He watched another volley on the right chase the retreating Holcanos and called for his dragoon bugler to sound "cease firing."

A cannon belched a final blast of canister at extreme range, knocking several of the enemy down. Who knew how many bodies already hid under the tall grass and yellow-white smoke streaming out across the field? The rest of the Holcanos were running for their camp about eleven hundred yards away, where more warriors were gathering, but they didn't look anxious for more.

"What now?" Varaa asked.

"We have to go at 'em," Leonor said as if that was obvious.

"Perhaps," Lewis agreed, "but it's early yet. Barely nine o'clock. We'll wait for everyone to finish coming up." He gestured behind where the 1st Uxmal was beginning to emerge from the trees.

"We *have* to deal with 'em," Leonor insisted. "Can't just leave 'em."

"I'll remind you there are women and children over there," Reverend Harkin murmured warningly, but it came off as an obligatory remark. He knew as well as anyone they couldn't "leave" the Holcanos to run west and warn General Agon, but wanted them to consider the consequences of an all-out assault. Not only would they take significant casualties themselves—difficult to deal with on their isolated campaign—the Uxmalos and Ocelomeh might be hard to manage in the aftermath. They'd been fighting this enemy for generations, and the Holcanos committed atrocities without thought, often eating their victims. The Ocelomeh in particular likened them to dangerous vermin, and he expected a vengeful slaughter.

Lewis had more confidence in the growing discipline of the army's native troops. The peaceful (actually, rather spoiled by the Ocelomeh when it came to fighting) Uxmalos hadn't produced many senior officers yet, but they were learning. And their common soldiers had absorbed a lot from the example of the Americans in the Detached Expeditionary Force. Most of their new NCOs and junior officers had actually served in the ranks of the 1st US or 3rd Pennsylvania first. The Washboard, if nothing else, had changed them enough that he considered the 1st Uxmal as steady as his other regiments.

But Harkin had changed a great deal as well. Aside from losing a lot of weight and looking healthier (except for alarmingly baggy skin), the self-absorbed, comfortably complacent minister, who'd "followed the drum to Mexico" with his friend Ruberdeau De Russy to attend the souls of the 3rd Pennsylvania, had grown more thoughtful and (of necessity) more tolerant of notions challenging his prior beliefs. That left him concurrently more realistic about war in general, yet idealistic about their new cause. He'd been on the beach when the Holcanos and Grik attacked and seen their barbarity on display. He'd even fought in the Battle of the Washboard after a fashion, taking up a rifle himself, so he understood the nature of war with the Doms. But the greater cause of defeating the Dominion had become a holy crusade in his mind. The Doms weren't just *their* ultimate enemy, they were the chief enemies of God in this land that He had specifically brought them to confront. Why else were they here? The Holcanos were merely a gnarled finger on the malignant hand of the Devil, and if it wound up they had to kill every one to get on with their bigger business, he'd regret it terribly and feel very guilty, but he'd live with it.

Lewis, on the other hand, knew many of the American troops that came to this world simply wouldn't stand for that, even now. They seemed genuinely devoted to their new cause, but he was thankful that most still harbored a fundamental appreciation of the difference between right and wrong. *Not* making war on civilians—of whatever sort—remained the principal distinction between them and the enemy and convinced them their cause was right. He had to come up with a better way.

"All messengers to me," he called. "Yours as well, Captain Meder."

"What do you intend?" Varaa asked. She'd watched for signs of the ruthless obsession that came over Lewis in battle; almost a detachment from anything but the fight that both heartened and concerned his friends (especially her and Leonor, and maybe Giles Anson, Captain Hudgens, and Corporal Willis, who seemed to be the only ones aware of it). It heartened them because at times like that it was like Lewis could somehow see the whole battle from above and instinctively knew where the crisis would come or where he must mass his greatest strength. Sometimes he got that way when planning a battle, distant and thoughtful as if already knowing how it would go, but mostly it came in the thick of the fight, when musket balls and roundshot were tearing all around him. That's what concerned them; especially when the instant of decision seemed upon them and he whipped out his M1840 artillery saber and threw himself and his blade where he thought they were most needed. Varaa decided he hadn't been like that today, but of course there hadn't been time, or really even a battle. A quick survey had returned a report of six dead and eleven wounded. The Holcanos had certainly lost scores.

Lewis smiled at Varaa. "I'm not entirely sure." He gestured ahead. "I doubt the enemy will attack again and they can't retreat with their families." He raised an eyebrow. "To their credit, Holcanos do seem more attached to their wives and children than Doms. . . ."

"Only sons matter to Doms," Harkin agreed. "Wives and daughters are property that can be replaced."

"So we're given to understand," Lewis hedged. There was still so much they didn't know! "In any event, the enemy appears to be preparing what they must believe is their final defense. The only options they're likely to imagine are 'fight or run away.' We'll eliminate the second and give them a third to consider."

Mounted messengers had arrived as he spoke and he quickly detailed their instructions. "They must hurry," he told the men, "and cross the clearing far enough away that they're not detected." He pulled his watch from a pocket above his saber belt and glanced at it. "We'll advance in two hours and make the 'signal' shortly after." He glanced at Varaa. "If the detached battalions of the First Ocelomeh were where Consul Koaar-Taak's morning report placed them and they've managed to keep up on those parallel trails, that should be more than sufficient time." Koaar was the only other Mi-Anakka with the army, and he commanded the 1st Ocelomeh, but they were still "Varaa's" people.

"You're gonna surround 'em?" Leonor asked.

"That's the idea. Hopefully they'll see reason with three entire regiments in front of them and almost a thousand of their bitterest enemies blocking their retreat."

Varaa spat, flicking her tail. "Reason? With Holcanos? Bah!"

Anson chuckled, touching one of the massive Colt revolvers at his side. "You'd be amazed how easy it is to 'reason' with folks, even knowin' they'll be hanged, with one o' these pointed at 'em."

With the 1st US, 3rd Pennsylvania, 1st Uxmal, a battalion each of Rangers, dragoons, and the rest of Capitan Ramon Lara's Yucatán Lancers coming up from the rear, leaving only the rearguard Ocelomeh guarding their baggage train, Lewis's army spread out in a broad, impressive crescent with parade ground precision, flags snapping, drums rolling. And with that same daunting precision, the two sections of 6pdrs and one section of 12pdrs—a full battery of six guns—reassembled in front of Lewis and his "staff" in the center of the line. Glancing at his watch again, he straightened in the saddle and spoke to Majors Beck, Ulrich, and Manley, who commanded the 1st Uxmal. "We've given them an hour and a half to watch and think. Advance the infantry, gentlemen. Slowly, if you please, and why don't you strike up a tune? Advance your battery, Captain Hudgens. Unlimber your guns five hundred yards from the enemy. The infantry will stop there also."

Beck and Manley both nodded briskly and turned their horses to their troops. Ulrich hesitated only a moment but turned to his men as well. He was older than the other regimental commanders, almost thirty-eight—the same age as Lewis himself—but seemed the most unsure. Lewis understood. The man had been an NCO most of his life, joining the Pennsylvania Volunteers after twenty years in the regular army. He'd spent all that time taking orders and carrying them out, and it had to feel strange to give them to other officers.

The 1st US stepped off first, its musicians striking up "The Old 1812," followed immediately by the 1st Uxmal and 3rd Pennsylvania, which also took up the music. Four up teams of horses started pulling A Battery up by pairs, the two 12pdrs in the lead.

Anson was looking at his own watch. "A little early."

Varaa *kakked* a laugh. "It's a *pageant*, you old badger!" she said with great satisfaction when everyone laughed at his surprised reaction. Anson once called her a "possum" and wouldn't explain what it was. Leonor did later and suggested an animal that reflected not only her father's graying whiskers, but his temperament as well. Lewis smiled. He liked and relied on Varaa a lot and sensed King Har-Kaaska didn't fully approve of the casual, familiar friendship she returned. No doubt he was chiefly concerned she'd reveal where her strange people, stranded in this land by an ordinary ship-wreck twenty years before, originally came from. That was information he meant to keep from the Doms at any cost. Lewis understood and never pressed Varaa about it. Har-Kaaska needn't have worried. Aside from a few vague references regarding the background and culture of her people, she never even hinted where they were. "It's sure to focus the enemy's attention while the Ocelomeh get in place," Varaa now added triumphantly.

Lewis nodded at her. "A pageant, yes, but not much appreciated."

The Holcanos were already panicking. They had about the same num-bers as Lewis, but less than a third were warriors. Those were mostly al-ready on the defensive line they'd established, many having used the time Lewis gave them to paint themselves red and black. Others were tearing down shelters, however, or just running around in terror. Many doing that were old people, or bare-breasted women bearing infants. They had to know that even if their attackers only scattered them, there was little chance any would make it to Campeche. Even in the dry season (it was worse when it rained), only large, well-armed groups could defy the predators in this land—and they lost people too, as Lewis knew well. Men alone or in small groups were almost certainly doomed, and a woman with a squalling in-fant would only attract hungry predators. They were watching annihilation march slowly, remorselessly toward them in the shape of sharply uniformed men, brave flags, and cheerful music.

At a distance Lewis judged to be almost precisely five hundred and fifty yards, Captain Hudgens commanded, "Action front! Form line advancing— March!" Immediately, the chief of his section of 12pdrs cried, "Walk!" and the two others shouted, "Section into line right (or left) oblique!" The crews were well enough trained by now that there were no commands, while the men on the lead horses automatically separated their guns and limbers by the specified seventeen yards and halted until the gunners and other men sprang down from half the horses and ammunition chests atop the limbers, pulled keys from pintles, and raised the trails, and gunners cried, "Drive on!" to the men still on the horses. Even as animals and limbers pulled away to the left and rear, guns' crews spun the one-ton weapons around (almost a ton and a half for the 12pdrs and mostly achieved by the Numbers One and Two men pulling or pushing the sturdy spokes of fifty-seven-inch iron-shod wheels) and aligned them with the others on either side. Only then did the gunners and Number Five men lower the trails to the ground. Handspikes were unsecured from cheeks and locked in sockets at the rear of the trails while all the other artillerymen took implements and assumed their positions around the guns. The whole battery was now ready for action in seconds, with hardly a word, and Lewis was proud of the work Hudgens—who'd started as a foot artillery private—had done to turn these men into some of the best flying artillerymen he'd seen.

Then his eye caught the unremarkable, somewhat scruffy-whiskered First Sergeant Nevin Petty striding forward from the line where each limber and its team of horses had taken its place behind its respective weapon. He'd started here as a corporal, but like Captain Olayne's First Sergeant McNabb, Petty was a steady, knowledgeable artilleryman with long experience and had at least as much to do with C Battery's success as anyone. Some said he was a little intense and didn't talk much until he got to know you. Obviously, that made getting to know him somewhat tedious. Those few who made the effort reported that he talked quite a lot after that and had a good, dry sense of humor. *I should've sent him to Uxmal to form a battery of his own from captured guns,* Lewis thought.

Number Six men, as well as the Numbers Five and Seven men, were unlocking the chest and taking heavy leather haversacks to carry ammunition forward, and Lewis had turned to watch the infantry move up on either side of the line the artillery established when Captain Hudgens called back, "Shall we load, sir?"

"By all means. Load solid shot and hold," Lewis replied.

"Have you a specific target in mind, sir?"

Lewis pointed out a section of rubbled wall protruding from the distant tall grass, bleached white stone blocks harshly contrasting with the bluish green all around and the hazy forest beyond. "Destroy that structure, if you please."

"Why waste ammunition?" Leonor asked. "Those Holcano devils make a fine target."

"The 'pageant' isn't over," Lewis answered vaguely. "We're still slightly early, as Major Anson pointed out, and I'd rather intimidate the enemy a little longer than possibly send them running before Consul Koaar is ready."

"Couldn't have been much of a city if that's the most prominent ruin still stickin' up," Anson observed. "Doesn't look like there ever was a pyramid."

"We were wondering about that ourselves," said Capitan Lara, riding up with Captain Felix Meder of the Rifles and Lieutenant Fisher in charge of the dragoons. They'd be wondering what Lewis wanted his mounted men to do when the action started.

"Perhaps that's why it's such a desolate ruin," Reverend Harkin speculated darkly. He looked around at their questioning expressions. "No pyramid," he explained. "Judging by the condition of the ones we've seen and the ancient parts of the cities around them, the 'pyramid people' must've outlasted others. Perhaps they even wiped them out."

Leonor frowned. "Uxmalos have a pyramid. They call it the Temple of the Lord Jesus Christ."

Harkin was nodding. "But they didn't *build* it, my dear. And though they're aware it once hosted terrible rituals like the Doms still perform— Father Orno described the ghastly evidence they've uncovered—they've quite appropriately repurposed it. The Uxmalos—all the *civilized* nations of the Yucatán"—he raised a brow at Varaa, whose Ocelomeh remained largely pagan—"are recognizably Christian to a degree, but even though they've been here longer, they know little more than we do about the ancient history of this land."

Anson grunted. "Seems the Doms remember more, an' keep up the older ways. But by your reckonin', wouldn't the Doms themselves be sorta 'recognizably Christian'? Jesus is big to them too."

"Absolutely not!" Harkin flared. "Entirely aside from their . . . abominable practices, Jesus is *not* their savior. Only the pain and suffering He endured sets the example for their salvation. He's deemed a prophet at best, a weak, wayward son of their terrible god, full of silly notions of love, who was sent to die as an object lesson and example of the only path to heaven." Harkin was actually shaking with rage. "Their blasphemy is so profound, only the Devil could've inspired it!"

Leonor was quietly watching the Holcanos ahead, some standing silent, waiting for death, others working themselves into a frenzy. "What do *they* believe?"

"They're 'pagans,' like my Ocelomeh," Varaa answered sourly, blinking very fast and swishing her tail, "but the differences between them are as big as those between Uxmalos and Doms."

Each gunner (a corporal) had repeated the command to load solid shot when it was officially passed by his section chief and the Number Five men went forward with the fixed ammunition—new copper roundshot strapped to wooden sabots with woolen bags full of a pound and a quarter (two and a half pounds for the 12pdrs) of the finest new Uxmalo powder tied to the bottom of it—in their leather haversacks. They paused at the gunners who checked what they brought and nodded them on when the Number Three men cleared the vents and pressed firmly down with leather-covered thumbs to prevent air from sucking or blowing through them. This was particularly important when firing rapidly since rushing air could brighten lingering sparks. They did it every time so they'd never forget. Taking the worm staffs from the Number Two men, the Fives waited while they fished the ammunition out and brought it up close to their chests before sliding it along the bottom of the gun barrels and inserting it at the muzzles. The Number One men had been waiting, rammer staffs poised. Now they shoved the shot and charges down together, pulling as much as pushing as they stepped between barrels and wheels. Withdrawing the rammers, they stepped back around the wheels to their positions by the axle hubs. This was when the gunners stepped forward and placed vernier rear sights weighted on the bottom in brackets screwed to the back of the breech, crouching to rest cheeks on their left hands, now grasping the large, knob-shaped cascabels. Tapping one side of the trail or the other with their right hands—there were only hand signals now because voice commands would be lost in battle— gunners directed the Number Three men, gone to the end of the hand-spikes, in which direction to shift the trail. They adjusted elevation themselves, turning the four-spoke tops of large coarse-thread screws in front of them under the breech. When the gunners were satisfied their pieces were aimed at the target and the elevation was appropriate to the range, they stepped back and made a sign to their section chiefs, who informed Captain Hudgens. Again, with everyone working together, all this took only seconds.

"The battery's ready to fire, Colonel Cayce," Hudgens announced.

Lewis glanced at his watch once more. "Commence firing. Space them out."

Hudgens saluted and spun his horse around. "Battery! At the designated target"—he'd already told them what it was—"by the piece, from the left . . . commence firing!"

The section chief on the left drew his saber and roared, "Gun Number Six—fire!"

Gunmetal is more a kind of very slightly reddish brass than bronze and the artillerymen in C Battery were proud to keep their cannon barrels highly polished. The few rounds they'd already fired that day had tarnished the muzzles and areas at the breach around the vents, but the rest still glowed in the sunshine like fine reddish gold, incongruously set in black iron and dingy olive-painted carriages. With percussion primers for their Hidden's Patent locks running low and no idea when (or if) they'd get more, the Number Four men had been guarding smoldering lengths of slow match (tightly braided cotton rope infused with saltpeter), threaded through holes in the ends of yard-long wooden linstocks. The first of these arced his arm over the wheel and touched the glowing end of his "match" to a quill primer filled with finely ground powder that the Number Three man had inserted in the vent. An even brighter reddish yellow jetted upward in a mushroom of smoke before the gun roared, louder with solid shot than canister, and stabbed the smoke it billowed with a spear of fire as bright as the sun. The dazzling tube kicked down at the muzzle, slamming against the carriage, and the whole thing leaped back in the grass.

A shrieking, tearing-canvas sound accompanied the flight of the shot Lewis and those with him could see as a blurry black dot, rising high above the point of aim before falling again. They lost it for an instant just before it struck the crumbling wall, spraying shards of shattered stone from a cloud of white dust. The infantrymen cheered, and a moan of fear began to mount from some of the Holcanos just as the same section chief cried, "Number Five gun, fire!" The performance was repeated, the shot striking amazingly close to the first and throwing even more whizzing fragments of stone. The center section chief, gauging the cadence, commanded his left 12pdr, "Gun Number Four—fire!" The 12pdr was an order of magnitude louder, hurling a shot twice as heavy with double the powder at the same initial velocity. It struck quicker, though, since it wasn't twice the diameter and bucked less wind for the weight. It hit harder too, and a large section of the ruined wall no longer stood when the dust cloud cleared. The Number Three 12pdr blasted it again, but the round from the Number Two 6pdr was short, throwing up a geyser of dirt and grass more than a hundred yards in front of the target before bounding up and over the ruins. Hoots and jeers erupted from the infantry (though the Holcanos the shot barely missed weren't as derisive), and Captain Hudgens sent Lewis a furtive, rueful look. The right section chief, First Sergeant Petty, was clearly mortified. Five hundred yards really was rather undemanding, especially with no one shooting back. His next command, "Number One gun—fire!" sounded comparatively harsh. That last 6pdr redeemed its neighbor, breaking more stone and tumbling a disproportionately large section of the wall.

"That's enough for the moment, I believe," Lewis called.

"Sorry about Number Two, sir," Hudgens apologized, pausing as if deciding whether to explain.

"A creditable exercise," Lewis said louder so the gunners could hear. He'd been forced to leave experienced artillerymen to man the captured guns at Nautla and train their crews, and he'd sent even more back to Uxmal for the same purpose. For as many new recruits as they had, these artillerymen had indeed done well.

"Thank you, sir," Hudgens said, then called to the battery to cease firing. A few moments passed, and the Holcanos started shrieking and yipping and brandishing weapons defiantly once more, but not as loudly or unanimously as before.

"Wasted ammunition," Leonor murmured again. "What was the point o' that?"

Varaa blinked at her. "It showed what we *could* have done—and didn't, and they'll soon have another example."

It came very quickly, and they all noted a marked response among the enemy, whose belligerent cries and actions turned to shouts of alarm, a jostling and thinning of their numbers and even yips of panic. Anson grinned at Varaa. "Seems they finally noticed Koaar an' your Ocelomeh creepin' up behind 'em."

Varaa sniffed. "I assure you that Consul Koaar won't be 'creeping.'" She waved around. "Most Jaguaristas still carry bows, but ours are armed with muskets too. They'll use the same formations as everyone in the open." She *kakked* another chuckle. "There's a time and place for everything. The woods are for creeping about, and the Ocelomeh are very good at that, but in the open"—she shrugged and blinked philosophically—"we must all make great, huge targets of ourselves to mass our fire. Mi-Anakka have known this as long as you, Major Anson," she stated cryptically. "But with our captured weapons, the Ocelomeh may finally join you in a stand-up fight."

"I think he meant they crept into position to deploy," Lewis said dryly. They couldn't see all the way to the far end of the clearing because the rubble of the ancient city had created a grass-covered mound in the middle. But the enemy's behavior convinced Lewis that Varaa was right and it was time to make his next move. Holcanos didn't know what "flags of truce" were. Parleys among their own contentious bands were always arranged in advance. After the restrained artillery demonstration and the rapidly deteriorating situation they were bound to recognize, Lewis was willing to bet someone over there would accept an obvious opportunity to talk. "Captain Hudgens, have your battery stand by for signals. You know what I'll want?" Hudgens nodded, a little worriedly, it seemed. "Capitan Lara, please deploy your lancers and the Rangers on the left. Captain Meder, riflemen and dragoons on the right."

"Push ahead on the flanks an' try to look as scary as you can," Anson told the young officers. He was in overall command of mounted forces (aside from artillery) and still found it ironic that "his" Rangers, riflemen, and dragoons worked together with Lara's lancers so well. Of course, there was only a handful of "old-world" personnel among them. "But don't get close enough they can reach you with arrows," he cautioned. Both men saluted and turned their horses to go, Lara grinning and Meder looking grimly determined.

"Let's go," Lewis said. "You're in charge, Major Beck," he called to the commander of the 1st US. "If anything happens to us"—he paused and his expression turned grim—"destroy the enemy and press on to the rendezvous with Colonel Reed and King Har-Kaaska."

"This is stupid," Leonor grumbled, voice husky with disapproval as she joined Lewis, her father, Varaa, Reverend Harkin, and a dragoon bugler named Private Hannity who'd shadowed Lewis through most of the Battle of the Washboard (until he was wounded) as they cantered out on the grassy field in the direction of the enemy camp. Surprisingly, Corporal Willis kicked his horse and lurched along as well, muttering, "That's for sure."

Lewis looked at Anson, riding beside him on his big gelding, "Colonel Fannin." Like Arete, Colonel Fannin had somehow survived the wreck of the *Mary Riggs* when they arrived on this world and, unlike his namesake, was a bold and fearless warrior. "Do I detect a measure of insubordination in our party?" he asked pleasantly.

"Ain't insublimination," groused the clearly unhappy Willis. "Which we're goin' with you, ain't we? Just speakin' our thinkin'—an' we didn't do it 'round nobody else. Still a free country to think what we want, ain't it?"

Lewis chuckled. "The 'free country' you're speaking of doesn't exist on this world. Not yet. But that's what we're fighting for, isn't it? And I encourage free thinking in the army, and even free speaking—at the appropriate times."

"Which this ain't," Anson growled, guiding Colonel Fannin around a clump of Holcano corpses. "Why's he even here?"

"I take my orderly dooties serious!" Willis proclaimed. "Even if it means I gotta trust my life to this vicious nag"—the horse he was riding fluppered indignantly—"so's I can be near if the colonel needs me," he ended piously.

"You're just lookin' out for yourself," Leonor accused. "If somethin' happens to Colonel Cayce, nobody else'd have you for an orderly an' you'd be back on a gun crew or carryin' a musket!"

"*If* I lived through what happened!" Willis snapped at her angrily. He really had changed a lot after the Battle of the Washboard, and Leonor's accusation clearly cut him. "What're *you* always hangin' 'round him for?" he countered with a sneer. "Pertectin' yer old man? Sure." Instantly knowing he'd gone too far, Willis cringed when, despite her olive complexion, Leonor's face went red and twisted with fury.

"I appreciate you *both* looking after us," Lewis quickly interjected. He'd have to be blind—had *been* blind—not to see that Leonor had . . . feelings for him. And he had to confess, to himself at least, he was drawn to her subdued but genuine beauty, intelligence, straightforward personality, even her hot temper and lethality. But now wasn't the time for either of them to explore beyond the respectful, even companionable friendship that had developed between Lewis and most of his officers and advisors. That friendship didn't always extend to others, and a usually restrained dislike had evolved between Leonor and Willis. God alone knew how often Leonor shot someone drawing a bead on him, and Willis had probably saved his life the first time they parleyed with Doms. *Could* that *be the source of their rivalry?* he wondered, but shook his head. "It's a soldier's right to gripe, even to their superiors in the proper circumstances"—he grinned—"which I guess these are. We have a few moments. Tell me, Lieutenant Anson," he said to Leonor, "what's your primary objection to what we're doing?"

"The same as mine, I'm sure," Varaa groused, covering for the young woman—since she wasn't blind either. Her own face may not display complex emotions without the blinking that telegraphed them to those who could read it, but she recognized human expressions quite well and expected Leonor would embarrass herself if she answered now. "Holcanos are vermin, they're *scorpions*," she seethed, "and can't be trusted as much as Doms in a meeting like this." She glared at Lewis. "They won't imagine we'd be stupid enough to come out here with the *field commander of our whole war effort*, but they'll know we're offering up the highest-ranking officers in our army"—she blinked—"*me* included! They all know *me*, and hate me more than anybody! They're more likely to rush out and try to kill us than come out to talk!"

"I wouldn't worry about that," Reverend Harkin said, voice almost serene. "'Behold, I have given you authority to tread on serpents and scorpions, and over all the power of the enemy, and nothing shall hurt you,'" he quoted. "Luke, ten-nineteen," he added, nodding out to the sides, where Rangers and lancers paced their advance on one side, riflemen and dragoons on the other. They were some distance away, considerably farther than the enemy would be when Lewis called a halt (he'd told them they'd stop at the halfway point—about two hundred and fifty yards, the absolute maximum distance Holcano and Ocelomeh bows could hurl their heavy arrows), and the enemy had only a handful of horses.

Anson barked a laugh. "I was *gonna* ask what *you* were doin' here, Reverend," he said.

"Not just to pull scripture about stomping scorpions out of his hat," Lewis assured him. "Most of us have a fair amount of Spanya by now, which the Holcanos speak as well, but mine probably isn't any better than yours." He glanced speculatively at Leonor, knowing she'd picked up some, at least. Even Willis had, though his was atrocious. "But through his daily conversations with Father Orno, Reverend Harkin's is as good as Varaa's by now. Besides, he's a 'holy man.' From what I understand, Holcanos have fairly odd beliefs and think their priests are like wizards with supernatural powers. They figure other people's priests have powers too and avoid annoying them if they can." He looked around and reined in Arete. "About here, I think." The others dressed their horses on his and they formed a short, tight line with the dragoon bugler, Private Hannity (who'd wisely kept his thoughts to himself), stopping behind Lewis.

"Now what?" Varaa asked.

"Now we wait. With Consul Koaar still coming up—I see the new regimental flag," he added with a wink and nod at Varaa. The 1st Ocelomeh had adopted a green flag with a rampant black jaguar outlined in gold. As far as anyone knew, there were no *real* jaguars on this world, so the flag was as fanciful as one from their old world featuring a dragon or griffin. "And our flankers are still advancing, so they should get the idea fairly quickly."

He was right. Only moments later, what looked like every horse the Holcanos possessed—a total of nine—came galloping out in a gaggle through the milling defenders, thundering down upon them. The striped horses were painted with geometric red shapes, their bushy manes and tails stiffened and blacked. The riders were naked but for scanty breechclouts, red paint, and black tarred hair standing up stiff and straight like the crests of Grik. The biggest one wore a macabre necklace of what could only be dried eyes bouncing on his chest. All had huge bows and quivers full of arrows.

Anson's hands strayed to his big pistols, and Leonor actually drew one of her revolvers, but Lewis merely said, "Easy, now. They're scared to death and want to get even."

"He's right," Varaa said, averting her gaze to the sky as if intrigued by the shape of a cloud. "Stand fast. Don't even look at them. Pretend they're beneath our notice."

"Like hell," Willis hissed. "Buggers are comin' to kill us!"

"I'd say so too, if they were Comanches," Anson said through his teeth, "but I gotta trust Varaa with these devils. Remember, they let the lizard folks do the hard fightin' on the beach." He laughed out loud at Varaa as if she'd said something funny.

"I'll not avert *my* gaze from evil," Harkin said lowly, raising the small gold cross he habitually wore on a chain around his neck, holding it as if to menace the nearing Holcanos, who started whooping and yipping fiercely.

"Suit yourself, Reverend," Lewis said. "They'd probably expect *you* to look at them regardless—if they guess what you are." He turned in his Ringgold saddle to gaze at Private Hannity. "Lick your lips and keep that bugle handy."

"I . . . I'll try, sir," Hannity replied shakily, "but it's hard to conjure much spit right now."

"Just do your best, son," Lewis encouraged as the nine Holcanos arrived, yelling and shouting.

Even Willis managed to look disinterested as the garish enemy galloped around them in a big, ragged circle, hooting, screeching, even respectably imitating the roars of mighty monsters they'd seen. Through it all, for perhaps half a minute, only Reverend Harkin watched them, his searing gaze in no way diminished by his sagging skin and loose-fitting clothes. Eventually, the enemy representatives began to slow, their cries growing less strident, but Lewis caught movement in the distance to his left and saw a platoon of lancers cantering toward them. He cleared his throat.

"Reverend Harkin, you might introduce yourself and warn these fellows to stop their capering if they want to talk." He jerked his head toward the lancers. Lara was leading them, of course. "Before those men come and kill them."

Harkin did so, loudly and with admirable authority. The Holcanos bristled, but when they noticed the closing lancers for themselves, the biggest man among them—even bigger than Lewis—gave a shout, and the rest somewhat sullenly gathered themselves in front of Lewis's little line of officers.

"I know that guy," Anson said in surprise, referring to the giant Holcano, now glaring at him in recognition as well.

"Me too," agreed Leonor.

"How nice," Varaa said cheerfully, flipping her tail. "It seems I was mistaken. I believe he hates the two of you even more than me!"

Lewis understood the big man perfectly when he barked, "You stopped fighting to talk. We stopped fighting to talk. Tell the long-spear-men to go or we will fight again!"

Harkin began to respond, but Lewis beat him to it. "I'm Colonel Lewis Cayce, commanding all the Allied Armies of the Yucatán. I'll have them *stop* and we can talk, but if you still wanted a fight you wouldn't have already run from one, and you wouldn't be here now. You and all your people are surrounded, and you're still alive only because I allow it."

The big man's face contorted with rage. "I am Kisin! War chief of all the Holcanos! I could kill you all by myself right now and take your heads back for my wives to cook!"

"How'd that work the last time we met, El Apestoso?" Anson interjected fairly fluently, referring to another name for the God the big Holcano styled himself after. Varaa once told him it meant "the stinky one," or something like that.

If Kisin's tarred crest could've bristled more, it would have. "You do not fight fair!" he objected. "You use magical pistols!"

Anson patted the Walker Colts on his waist belt. "Still got 'em." He nodded at a huge, puckered scar on Kisin's thigh, the result of a bad compound fracture, and patted Colonel Fannin's neck. "Actually surprised you survived that. How do you get around on foot? But my pistols didn't do that, my horse did. Still got *him* too."

Kisin was seething, but managed to nod at Lewis. "Stop the long-spearmen *now* and we will talk," he grated.

"Sound 'halt,' Private Hannity," Lewis told the young dragoon, who quickly blew the short command, repeated twice. The Holcanos watched, surprised by how swiftly and uniformly the lancers stopped about a hundred yards away.

"I have heard sounds like that from your people before," Kisin confessed grudgingly. "You use the same 'horn magic' the Blood Priests give Dominion soldiers." He glanced at Harkin, sure that he—they'd identified him as a priest at once—had cast a spell on the shiny, flared instrument the young man blew into. "But their horns are bigger," he added with feigned dismissal.

"Bigger perhaps, but no better than ours—and they can't say as much," Lewis warned. "In fact, with a single word from me and a few short notes on that 'horn,' my army will destroy every living thing in this clearing where you so carelessly camped. 'War Chief' of all the Holcanos? You certainly don't have 'all' of them with you."

"I have enough to slaughter you when you come for us!" Kisin retorted sharply. "Enough of us will live to feast until we burst, cracking your cooked bones for the marrow!"

"A direct assault might be costly," Lewis conceded, "so I've no intention of making one." Kisin looked surprised, and some of the other warriors gabbled triumphantly, assuming they'd intimidated their enemy after all.

"No," Lewis continued softly, almost conversationally, "my troops now encircling you *won't* attack. Why should they? They'll merely kill each and every one of you, man, woman, and child, as they attempt to flee."

"We will never flee!" hissed another big warrior beside his chief.

"*You* won't," Anson agreed darkly, touching the plow-handle-shaped grip of one of his big revolvers again. "You'll be dead. Your people will, though, an' we'll kill 'em." He and Varaa, at least, already had an idea what Lewis intended, and now Varaa spoke up as well. "You Holcanos are so stupid," she jeered. "You let the Doms use you as their club until you break, now you've already forgotten the mauling you just had, not to mention our little demonstration!"

"Bugler, signal Captain Hudgens," Lewis said. Private Hannity blew another short series of notes, and firelit cotton balls flowered in front of all six of Hudgens's guns, the thunderclap roar coming just as five roundshot shrieked almost directly overhead and blasted more stone ruins into hurtling shards and billowing clouds of dust. Even Corporal Willis, hearing the order, had steeled himself for what was coming but still squawked, "Shit!" when a 6pdr shot skated along the ground, much too close, spewing a rooster tail of blue-green grass before striking and spraying a geyser of soil in the air and bounding up over the ruins again—toward the 1st Ocelomeh beyond. *Number Two's gunner still doesn't have the range*, Lewis reflected, but while he, Anson, Varaa and Leonor, Reverend Harkin, Private Hannity, and even Corporal Willis made do with tightening their muscles and clenching their teeth, the precision of the other shots made the near miss seem deliberate, and its effect on the Holcanos was profound. All cried out in panic, and most had difficulty controlling their mounts. Not natural horsemen, and without saddles or stirrups, three fell off.

Kisin was one of the first to regain control of his animal, but his foremost concern was his camp. The line of warriors had disintegrated to mingle in terror with women and children. The target had been the same as before, but it was clear these . . . *demonios* Americanos—as the Blood Priests now called them—and their friends could've put roundshot anywhere, possibly even hitting *individuals* at such a range. He already knew their men with the terrible . . . he thought the word was 'rifles' . . . could do it almost as far. As for the great guns, he didn't know if they themselves were deadlier than those of the Dominion, but the men who used them were. He'd seen the mangled wounded, most already dead and practically already butchered for roasting after the fighting on the beach, then seen the guns in action on the road from Itzincab to Puebla Arboras. He'd heard *these* Americanos—and this army in particular—had destroyed a Dom army of twenty thousand men. . . .

His heart seemed to settle somewhere between his hips, as heavy as a roundshot itself, and he feared his band—his clan—was doomed. *But if they can sweep us all away as easily as it seems, why do they want to talk?* he wondered. Then it came to him. *There are things they don't know! Things I can tell them. Things that will make us useful to them! Can they be useful to me as well?* He had no qualms about talking to Americanos. He didn't even hate them and only knew them as formidable warriors. He talked to the Dominion, and never liked or trusted them at all. It was always a matter of what they could do to help him against his traditional enemies: Ocelomeh, Uxmalos, Itzincabos, the rest. . . . *Not very much, as it turned out,* he decided bitterly. His eyes went to Varaa, and his blood ran hot. *But to help the Ocelomeh . . . On the other hand, what have they and city squatters ever done but honestly fight me? That's the natural way of things; we fight. They never promised something else and then stabbed me in the back! I owe nothing to the Dominion—or other bands of Holcanos!*

"Not many of you left at all," Lewis now continued relentlessly. "What does it look like to you, Major Anson? A thousand unsteady warriors? Three thousand noncombatants?"

"About that," Anson agreed. "Hard to tell with 'em all runnin' around like chickens with their heads cut off."

"You lost too often, El Apestoso," Varaa told Kisin, sure it was true. "You were thrown off as war chief by the rest of the Holcanos, and all you have left is your own band." She snorted derisively and blinked contempt. "You were going to Campeche for a handout from the Doms, hoping they'd feed you to scout for them."

Even through the drying, flaking paint on the big warrior's face, Lewis saw Varaa's words hit home, but got the sudden impression she needn't have even said them because the giant, fearsome warrior seemed almost to crumple into a big, petulant child.

"*I* was anointed 'Kisin' and given power over all the war bands!" he said, glaring at Varaa. "*I* was supposed to rule the Yucatán after we destroyed your Ocelomeh and the city squatters!" He looked accusingly back at Lewis.

"But I was *supposed* to get guns from the Dominion—and was never supposed to fight *you*! You just . . . came out of nowhere, and all my plans against the cities fell apart because my warriors wanted *your* guns." He glanced at several of the warriors beside him, a couple avoiding his gaze. "*They* thought it would be easy! We've plundered strange boats on our shores in the past, smaller, with fewer people," he qualified, "but their survivors were always confused, easily overcome, and great spoils were had." He glared hard at Anson and Leonor, unconsciously rubbing his leg. "It might have been the same again, but I got hurt and couldn't lead the attack."

"Mustn't discourage your followers from doing what they *want*," Varaa mocked. "I doubt your presence would've made a difference."

Lewis sent her a cautionary glance. Kisin seemed willing to talk, probably thinking it was all that might save his people. Lewis wanted to hear him.

Kisin didn't even argue except to say, "We wouldn't have been beaten as badly because I would've stopped the attacks sooner. I lost most of my Garrach'ka allies in one useless attack after another." He sighed. "They're monsters and barbarians, of course, but Garrach'ka—you call them 'Grik'— are very good fighters. All but General Soor's band left me, shattering a pact it took his whole life to build, and scattered into the wild. I was wounded," he reminded, "and carried to Campeche to join the Dominion army that was gathering to move against you. They still wouldn't give us guns," he complained, "and wouldn't even feed us! They told us to go fight for Don Discipo in the east. General Soor and a few score of his warriors were still with me, and I was still recognized as war chief of the Holcanos, but Discipo—the idiot of the world!—and his Blood Priests were war chiefs over all. No food or plunder if we didn't accept that." He spat. "Idiot!" he proclaimed again. "Discipo got us beaten back from Itzincab, then Puebla Arboras—I left before the end came there. The Blood Priest, Amistoso, had gone entirely mad, slaughtering all the captives he could find in the city"— that seemed to shock even him—"and I barely escaped with my life and my clan. I don't know what happened to Soor. Don Discipo escaped as well, and when he reached Cayal, declared *himself* war chief of *all* Holcanos, all the Yucatán! How could that be? Because he *fed* them, that's how—and the dragon told him if he held at Cayal, the Dominion would march another great army, bigger than the last, up to Uxmal and win the war. He—Don Discipo, not I—would rule the Yucatán!"

Kisin sneered at Varaa. "Yes, we were going to Campeche. To see my friend Capitan Arevalo," he said proudly. "He is aide to General Agon and would have set things right!"

"We've met Arevalo too," Leonor said dryly.

"She's the one who shot the hole in him," Anson reminded with a grin.

Kisin was looking at the tall, slender woman—almost as tall as him, in fact, if only half his size—but the intensity of her gaze left him no doubt she could and would kill him as quickly as anyone here. "I remember," he murmured.

Oddly enough, of all the people in front of him—including the "priest"—Colonel Cayce wore the least hostile expression. When he spoke, it was clear he'd been focusing on something else. "What did you mean when you said the 'dragon' told him?"

Kisin looked surprised, then suddenly apprehensive. "It didn't actually *tell* him, of course, but Father Tranquilo sometimes sent a messenger dragon from Campeche," he said as if it should be obvious to anyone.

"I don't believe it!" Varaa snapped, but all could see she did.

"What the hell's this?" Leonor demanded.

"King Har-Kaaska believes the Dominion has started training the flying dragons—those the size of garaaches—to carry messages from place to place. No doubt they're rewarded with something—or someone—to eat," Varaa added accusingly at Kisin, who blinked as if surprised that would bother her.

"Some captives are good for nothing else," he defended.

Varaa snorted and looked back at Lewis. "My king had no proof aside from 'coincidences' that the enemy always seemed better informed—more quickly—than they should about various things. The most recent being your arrival on this world."

Lewis shook his head. "They could've learned that from the people aboard *Isidra*. We *know* they did."

"But not that you were building an army so quickly," Varaa persisted. "That had to have come from Tranquilo and one of his beasts."

"She is right," Kisin conceded. "The one that came to Discipo's Blood Priest, Father Amistoso, was sent by Tranquilo at Campeche."

"A moment," Reverend Harkin said incredulously. "Are we talking about the same creatures?" He looked back and forth between the Holcano and the grimly blinking Varaa. "The things you call 'dragons' that behave like vultures, about the size . . ." He gasped. "You *are*!"

"I am," Varaa confirmed.

"When's the last time you saw one?" Leonor demanded of Kisin, Reverend Harkin somewhat dazedly repeating her question.

Kisin frowned, and dry red paint flaked and fell from his face. "Before we retreated from Puebla Arboras. The dragon came to Amistoso and Don Discipo suddenly sent all his favorites out of the city to bring 'reinforcements' to Cayal. I am not a fool. I sent my people away that night, though I was almost too late. Amistoso was certainly captured or killed, and I saw no other messenger dragon after that."

"So you had no idea we were on this road?" Lewis asked specifically.

"I still don't know how you got here!" Kisin almost exploded in frustration. "No one knows these roads but Holcanos!"

"Wrong," Varaa said a little smugly.

"Yes, I see," Kisin agreed impatiently, "but if I had known you were coming, I would have attacked you in a good place of my choosing and destroyed you!"

Lewis supposed that was even possible and felt some small relief, but the whole idea of flying couriers . . . No one—aside from Har-Kaaska apparently, he thought with a trace of bitterness—ever imagined such a thing. They could throw all his plans into jeopardy.

"Flyin' spies! Lordy!" Willis groaned.

"They can't . . . fly around an' tell people what they see, can they?" Leonor ventured.

Kisin actually laughed, and Leonor bristled. "No," he said more reservedly, noting her reaction, "they cannot talk. They only carry written words—and they are very rare."

"We have to spread this around, an' fast," Anson told Lewis. "God knows the enemy's got enough spies on us, especially back at the cities."

Lewis was nodding. "What's quicker? Couriers back the way we came—it'll take at least a platoon of mounted men for all to have a chance to get through safely—or press on and send word up the line behind Har-Kaaska?"

"Both," Anson pressed. Reverend Harkin, looking horrified, was nodding vigorously.

"I agree. Either way alone will take too long to inform the far end of the chain. Weeks, maybe." The now-permanent semaphore towers lining the Camino Militar back to Uxmal, and everywhere else past there, would pass the news very quickly, but it had to get back to Nautla first. He sighed. "What a headache. We'll have to assume any dragons flying between known enemy positions, around Allied cities, or even landing near our own troop concentrations are carrying dispatches. Our mounted troops will be run ragged investigating them, and most will just be lighting on carrion." He rubbed his face. "And every low-flying dragon will draw a fusillade of fire from now on! It'll drive people crazy."

"No, no!" Kisin objected, horrified. "The dragons are *sacred* to the Holcanos! You can't just kill them on sight!"

"Why should we care what's sacred to miserable, self-eating Holcanos?" Varaa ground out. "Soon there won't be any of you!" She looked at Lewis. "We should kill every dragon we see!"

Kisin sneered at Varaa, the first time they saw a flash of his old, belligerent self. "I used to respect your mind, Warmaster Varaa," he said with heavy sarcasm, "but you're as stupid as Don Discipo!" He looked back at Lewis. "I already told you: the ones that carry words are *very* rare and go only to places they know!" He frowned. "You *can* kill *them*, of course. Tamed by men, they no longer belong to the gods. But the Blood Priest Amistoso had to take one to Puebla Arboras for it to find its way there again. He brought it *through* Cayal in its crate, but it never flew to or from there. Don Discipo doesn't have another."

Lewis waved at his seething, tail-whipping Mi-Anakka friend and took a long breath, slightly reassured. Kisin was an enemy, but he wasn't lying. "Very well, we'll see. We'll get that platoon moving, though," he told Anson, then regarded Kisin and his warriors. "I appreciate all you've told me, and I'll have more to ask about Discipo's strength and posture at Cayal, but in the meantime I have to decide what to do with you." He pursed his lips. "Obviously, you aren't going to Campeche."

"Are you going to kill us?" demanded a short, stocky warrior who hadn't spoken yet.

Lewis looked at him. "That's up to you."

"You give us a choice to die or become captives and slaves?"

Lewis nodded. "In a sense. If you don't yield, you'll be killed," he said matter of factly. "Surrender, and you *will* be captives—but perhaps not for life," he added cryptically, and his voice hardened. "We're going to Cayal to destroy Don Discipo and the Holcanos who abandoned you to support him. I take it you wouldn't object to that. You might even join in the effort." Lewis saw Varaa bristle as Kisin leaned forward, interested, already calculating. "In the meantime, of course, your warriors will be disarmed and separated from their women and children. Anyone found with so much as a sharp stick without permission will be killed. Warriors will be formed into labor battalions, clearing the trail, gathering firewood, laying out camps, helping our scouts, and generally doing whatever they're told and proving they can behave."

Kisin frowned at the prospect of his warriors being required to work, but said nothing.

"In exchange," Lewis continued, "your people will be treated well and fed the same simple fare as my army." His lip curled, and he snapped, "You're *through* eating *people*. Even your own."

Kisin looked genuinely shocked. "A life lost that doesn't give life is wasted!" he exclaimed. "It's our way of honoring them. Even our enemies!"

"Unless you want to eat nothing *but* your people, you'll stop eating them at all," Lewis stated flatly. "Plenty of our troops will think every tortilla and piece of biscuit or salt meat we give you is wasted, so you better find another way to honor your dead." He looked at Varaa, who was already smoldering. She'd been fighting Holcanos for twenty years and leading Ocelomeh who'd been doing it for generations. *I'm about to really make her mad*, he thought. "And to make your labor battalions more effective, we'll organize them and start to train them as soldiers."

"You'd train them to *kill* us?" Varaa practically shouted, furious.

"We'll train them to help us at Cayal, possibly with engineering requirements or fighting positions, if we need them," Lewis told her firmly, "and to hold it when we move on." He looked back at Kisin. "You'll do it too, since as soon as we unite with King Har-Kaaska, your families will be sent to Itzincab as hostages against your good behavior. They'll be returned if you prove to be faithful, and you'll never trouble the people of the Yucatán again."

Varaa snorted incredulously, and even Kisin looked dumbfounded. "How can we do that? What else would we *do*?" He sounded honestly mystified. "We have fought Ocelomeh and city squatters across the Yucatán . . . forever. Even if we swore never to push north from Cayal again, how . . . how would we not? Who would we fight? Where would we raid? You'd turn *us* into city squatters too?"

"Peace is not so bad," Reverend Harkin said. "And in the meantime, you can always fight Doms—who'll certainly crush you as well, in time. I suppose you could explore as well"—he sniffed—"and raid if you must to the south and east. As I understand it, no one knows who or what inhabits that land."

Kisin considered that. He'd lost his gambit in the north because the Dominion hadn't supported him as promised, and he'd always known they'd turn on him. By supporting Discipo, they already had. He'd never trust them again. Going to Capitan Arevalo had seemed a desperate hope. Oddly, even though these people were his enemies, and especially the Ocelomeh, he already trusted them more to keep their bargains since they didn't *have* to make one. And they'd made no outrageous promises. Which reminded him he might as well ask; "Fighting the Dominion might be more fun than our endless war with the Ocelomeh," he mused aloud. "Especially if we learn to fight like you," he added. "You will give us muskets? Great guns?"

Varaa *kakked* loudly, bitterly, and Lewis shook his head. "Perhaps someday, *if* you earn them"—he gestured at Varaa—"as well as *her* trust, of course. For now, you should have no trouble holding Cayal behind us with your traditional weapons."

Kisin hadn't expected guns, but the fact none were promised actually reinforced his sense that the Americano Colonel would keep his word. He suddenly smiled and dry red paint showered off his cheeks. He'd expected to die, but now it seemed he might wind up leading all the Holcanos again, along with at least a brief period of peace to consolidate his position. He wasn't much worried about his women and children; even Ocelomeh were weak when it came to them, treating them well in captivity. His face suddenly fell. "But taking Cayal . . . You have enough warriors to destroy me," he confessed, "but Cayal is one of the 'Old Cities' of the Ancients, like Nautla and Campeche. It has strong walls, and virtually all the rest of the Holcanos are there. Thousands of warriors." He nodded at the distant battery. "You might batter them out from behind the walls, but they'll only attack and overwhelm you."

"They won't overwhelm us," Leonor said confidently.

"Perhaps," Kisin hedged. "Yes, especially if King Har-Kaaska and the army that chased us out of Puebla Arboras comes down, but then Don Discipo will just run away. All his warriors will flee to the woods. Discipo's a coward and a fool"—he glanced at Varaa—"but he betrayed all of you, even his own people at Puebla Arboras. He can't be foolish enough to expect to surrender and live so he won't. What good will it do me if I have no one to rule, and what good for you if Discipo returns when you leave and takes the city back?"

"Don't worry," Lewis said. "Don Discipo won't get out of Cayal." He tilted his head to the side, flicking a glance at Varaa. "You might even help ensure that. What better first step toward earning the trust and appreciation of our belligerent Mi-Anakka friend and her Ocelomeh? Now, why don't you send a few of your . . . officers back to your camp to instruct your people to lay down their arms. Be *very* specific," he warned. "No opposition will be tolerated. You'll remain here with me, of course." He then regarded Varaa sternly and said very formally, "Warmaster, if you please, kindly join Major Anson in riding around the Holcano camp to inform Consul Koaar that the *First Ocelomeh* will accept the surrender of the Holcanos." He could throw Varaa that bone, at least. "But they'll do so as . . . gently as possible," he warned. "They're free to defend themselves"—he shrugged—"and kill anyone who resists, but I'll rely on you to ensure there's no abuse or excess. Hopefully, the Holcanos will be our allies one day, and today will set the, ah, mood for that."

Varaa saluted just as formally, but muttered, "Allies indeed!" as she twisted her horse around and broke into a gallop that would take her to the riflemen on the right before heading around the Holcano camp.

Anson raised his eyebrows at Lewis, obviously just as surprised by how this turned out as Varaa, then urged Colonel Fannin after her.

"I hope you know what you're doin'," Leonor whispered at Lewis. "Havin' Varaa just stop fightin' Holcanos is like . . . havin' Father make friends with Comanches." She snorted. "Worse! Comanches don't"—she shook her head—"didn't *eat* people. They killed other injuns who did. And there *were* some who Father knew and respected, even if they'd kill each other on sight."

"Actually, I suspect it's the same with Varaa and Kisin, in some ways," Lewis murmured back. "Legitimate grievances aside—and we have our own with the Holcanos, God knows!—the main reason *they* fight is because they always have. We'll see."

CHAPTER 8

The army drew up and camped around the Holcanos amid the ruins with a heavy guard posted inside and out. The few Allied dead were promptly buried deep, but Holcano corpses, already starting to smell in the heat, were dragged to a pile downwind. Massive herbivores could be seen returning to the clearing in the distance, but night would bring multitudes of dangerous scavengers to the banquet Lewis's army had prepared for them. In the meantime, the 1st Ocelomeh sorted the captives and searched them for weapons, forming sullen, able-bodied warriors into "companies" of roughly a hundred men allowed only what clothing and bedding they could carry. These would remain under the possibly equally unhappy supervision of Ocelomeh and Uxmalo companies, who spoke the same language. They'd guard the prisoners on a rotating basis, setting them to labor and teaching them unarmed, close-order drill. Varaa came around on that, realizing it would make the Holcanos easier to move and control.

Their women and children and the very few old and infirm were placed in the custody of the baggage train guards and Ocelomeh rear guard, reinforced by another rotating company of Uxmalos, who'd have to eat the army's dust. Kisin requested that the women be allowed to drag their hide shelters and other belongings on travois, and Varaa—still angry but realistic—suggested Lewis agree. Just as Uxmalo and other "city" women held equal civic status with men, often owning shops and businesses and even many of the industries the army relied on, shelters, cooking implements, and other household goods traditionally belonged to Holcano women (men only owned their weapons, it seemed), and they were unlikely to abandon them. Burdening the women and children with their own possessions not only solved the problem of sheltering them, it made them less likely to lag behind or cause trouble.

All in all, though it took all day, Corporal Hanny Cox was surprised by how . . . well . . . *smoothly* it went. There was confusion and tension, of course, and the segregation and organization of almost four thousand Holcanos had looked like a frustrating nightmare from where he'd watched from a distance, but there was no violence. The previously savage warriors they'd fought only that morning, probably assured by Kisin, were clearly baffled by what was required of them and provoked a lot of exasperated shouting, but they were also amazingly docile, at least trying to do as they were told.

"Strange folk," groused Preacher Mac as he and Apo Tuin walked with Hanny in search of C Battery's traveling forge and Sergeant O'Roddy. Sergeant Visser had loaded them with half a dozen muskets—a depressing number considering how short the action was—and told them they'd find the blacksmith/armorer behind the gathered caissons. All the guns and their limbers still covered the Holcano camp, for now.

"Yes," Hanny said. "Remember how they just sat down and let themselves be captured or killed when they knew they'd lost on the beach?"

Mac nodded. "Aye. 'Twas a dreadful sight, watchin' our new Ocelomeh allies bashin' out their brains an' cuttin' off heads till Varaa an' Father Orno stopped it," he recalled.

"We've civilized the Ocelomeh and turned them into proper soldiers!" Apo cheerfully proclaimed.

Always the dour Scot, Mac glowered at him. "An' *you* were a 'proper soldier' then? Uxmalos weren't even there. Didn't much fight at all before then, I ken. Least the Cats were already bonny fighters!" McDonough, like many in the army, had started calling all the Ocelomeh "Cats." Not only did they owe their primary allegiance to a creature . . . person? who looked so much like one, their own name for themselves meant "Jaguar Warriors."

"I was at the Washboard," Apo countered grimly.

"Where Cats in their fine animal-skin 'uniforms' still took their share o' heads—even if they didnae keep 'em for trophies, for once. Aye, they've taken on a thin coat o' civilized paint, but it'll peel right off in the heat of a fight." He paused, considering, fingering the coarse wool of his sky-blue jacket. He had a newer, lighter-weight version made in Uxmal but, like many others, preferred the cooling properties evaporating sweat gave his tightly buttoned "honest wool." The fact the humidity didn't allow for much evaporation seemed lost on him. "As will the thicker coat these uniforms give our laddies—an' yers—come tae that," he continued, but then gifted Apo with one of his rare smiles and tousled his wheel hat until it fell off. "Och aye, who couldnae smile with wee Apo beside him, wavin' his banner an' roarin' 'confusion tae the Doms'! Only a 'civilized' man'd do that!"

Apo was carrying two other muskets besides his own and nearly dropped one stooping for his hat. "I honestly don't remember," he confessed.

"There are the caissons, past the baggage wagons—with the water butts," Hanny said with a touch of relief, nodding ahead. The baggage wagons were only now coming into the clearing. Relatively small as it was, the army had been stretched a great length along the track, and the sun wasn't far above the horizon of trees as the heavy, solid-wheel wagons creaked by. They'd crossed a meager, slow-moving stream just the day before, but because water was so scarce in the Yucatán this time of year, they had to carry it with them. It was the heaviest load in the wagons and taxed the poor horses pulling them.

"*Forfochen* beasties, those," McDonough said sadly, watching the bedraggled animals. "Not even fit tae pull a gun." He shouted out at one of the young Uxmalo teamsters: "Ye ken the one thing ye need tae learn about horses, laddie?" The youngster, wide-eyed, shook his head. "Slice 'em *across* the grain or ye'll break yer choppers when ye eat 'em!" He grinned at Hanny, exposing a couple of missing teeth.

Hanny rolled his eyes. "I've heard you say that to half the dragoons and mounted riflemen in the army. Sometimes they don't think it's funny," he added, looking back at the animals. "Still, short as we are on horses of any kind, we might as well have used armabueys to pull the freight."

"Colonel Cayce doesn't like them," Apo countered as if the colonel had personally told him. "That's what the Doms do. Even use them to pull their artillery and they move too slow. Those horses, poor as they are, move faster than armabueys."

McDonough was nodding. "Aye, there's that. An' I hear there's *nae* good way tae slice armabuey tae make it fit tae chew." He kicked through some grass with his left shoe and raised it up slightly. Copper hobnails on the soles had been polished bright by the sugar sand. "But they—er whatever they use—make fine, tough bootees!" Local-made footwear, patterned after the ankle-high shoes the Americans wore (requiring less leather and stitching than the knee-high moccasins fashionable in the cities on the peninsula) was comfortable and practically indestructible.

A squad of Lara's lancers thundered past on an errand and they trotted between the wagons, grateful the grass kept the dust down, and found a picket line of artillery horses, equally happy to munch fresh grass for a change. They'd all been taken from their limbers, but caissons remained hitched to the two-wheeled vehicles designed to pull everything in a battery.

"Still," McDonough concluded, dour once more, "I'll be glad when we're marchin' back *at* the Doms instead o' skulkin' off through these endless damned woods."

"Colonel Cayce knows what he's doing," Apo Tuin said loyally. "Sergeant Visser says we're dealing with the Holcanos behind us while we sweep around behind the Doms!"

"Little sweepin', if ye ask me," McDonough countered. "Jis ploddin' along, foot after foot—an' now we've fought Holcanos in the mornin', an' befriended 'em by evenin'!"

"I don't think we're exactly friends," Hanny retorted as they saw C Battery's traveling forge wagon set up by the trees, wheels blocked, post vise clamped to the tongue and support pole down, coals already glowing yellow-red in the firebox on the front while a young man in artillery uniform (probably from Techon by the shape of his wide, nonregulation straw hat) worked a long shaft to operate a leather bellows inside the round-topped box astride the vehicle above the axle. Another soldier, a scrawny American Hanny thought he'd seen on punishment parades more than once, was hanging hammers, tongs, and other mysterious tools in convenient places. That's when Sergeant O'Roddy appeared from behind the traveling forge wearing only sky-blue trousers, bootees, and a sweat- and scorch-stained brown leather apron. He was one of the biggest men in the army, probably second only to the bully, Hahessy, but even more powerfully built. Massive arm muscles bulged with the weight of an anvil he otherwise carried with no effort at all. Thick blond muttonchops covered most of his face except chin and upper lip, and his arms and shoulders were equally thick with fur. The only place hair didn't grow at all was on top of his shiny, sun-darkened head. He gave them a resentful glare as he set the anvil on a long-used stump of wood another assistant placed in the grass.

"Bringin' me more goddamn muskets to fix, I guess," he boomed in a voice with no trace of his Irish name and tilted his head toward the forge limber. The chest atop it, like all those on this campaign, was loaded with ammunition so the vehicle had been drawn a prudent distance from the sparks swirling around the forge. There were probably two dozen muskets already leaned against it.

"Yes, Sergeant," Hanny confessed.

O'Roddy sighed loudly. "Fix 'em yourselves. You know how to take 'em apart, don't you?"

Hanny hesitated. "Of course, Sergeant—but except for mine, we don't know what's wrong with them."

"What's about yours?"

"Broken mainspring."

"Shit, another one? Well, you know how to replace it. I still have a few. At least most of the spares we started with'll fit without too much filing. 'Perfect interchangeability' my baby-smooth arse! Don't toss the pieces, though," he warned and nodded at his disreputable-looking assistant. "Scoochy there'll take 'em. Spring steel's so rare, we save every scrap. I'll make frizzen or sear springs from the pieces." He looked at McDonough and Apo. "What's the matter with the others?"

"Don't know, Sergeant," Apo said. Hanny doubted any part of Sergeant O'Roddy was "baby smooth"—except his head.

"Then find out an' fix 'em, damn you!" O'Roddy snapped. "What would you do if I wasn't here? What would anybody do?" he added lower, then waved at the fire, smoldering almost as hot. "I got smithin' before anything else. Captain Hudgens needs new trace hooks, a worm, even a damned cap-square lock! Said his Number Two gun—the one plowin' dirt all mornin'—lost one. Probably fired every shot today without it an' it's a wonder they didn't dismount the tube or crack a trunnion. Anyway, captains come first." He glared back at them. "Fix all those other busted muskets while you're at it. Who knows? You might learn a trade."

"But . . ." Hanny began. O'Roddy cut him off. "I know you, Corporal Cox," he said to Hanny's surprise, who didn't remember ever speaking to O'Roddy. "First Sergeant McNabb, off with Olayne's battery, told me how you stood up to that damned Hahessy, an' Sergeant Visser said you ain't shy in a fight. There's . . . some who think well of you." His expression clouded. "So *don't* tell me Sergeant Visser wanted you back on the double. I know for a fact he'll loan you to me as long as I want." He relented slightly and actually chuckled. "He'll also make sure your tents are up an' save you somethin' to eat. Now, I got work an' so do you." He flicked his eyes at the limber. "Prob'ly nothin' even wrong with most'a those muskets, just fellas sayin' so to get out of the line this mornin'—or guard duty tonight. If you run into somethin' that stumps all three of you, ask. There's small arms tools in the box set down behind the forge. Drag it around an' lay out a gun tarp to work where I can keep an eye on you. Don't need to lose any goddamn screws. I *hate* makin' goddamn screws!"

They did as he said and soon had all the muskets laid out on the white, sun-bleached canvas. They settled into a division of labor; McDonough quickly dropping a rammer down each barrel to see if the weapon was loaded. If the rammer clanged and bounced off the breech face, it wasn't. If it didn't go all the way down and just kind of thumped, it was. On those that weren't, he blew down the barrel to check if the vent was clear. In several cases a badly clogged vent was all they found wrong, and they drew the loads with a special, heavy armorer's rod with a coarse-threaded screw on the end that they twisted into the soft lead ball.

"What should we do with these?" Apo asked.

"Scoochy" brought him a piece of chalk. "You learn to write?" he asked.

Apo hesitated. "I've learned some letters."

"Good. Write a big D on the stock for 'dirty.' The bastards that let 'em get that way can clean 'em. An' take the consequences too!" he added bitterly.

Hanny suspected Scoochy himself had been in trouble like that before. McDonough kept up the initial inspections, finding nothing wrong with some weapons, as O'Roddy predicted, and only a dull flint in most of the rest. That wasn't always a soldier's fault. A flint could *feel* sharp when tested with a thumb, but there might be the smallest rounded knob to keep it from scraping sparks. McDonough was unsympathetic. "Time to time, a frizzen'll have all the sparks scratched out—usually wasnae properly hardened—an' it must be hardened again. Flints jist dig in'tae the soft steel an' break. More likely by far there's a knob on the flint an' the doaty dobber shoulda jist hammered it off!"

Sergeant O'Roddy had started out slow, making a capsquare lock—little more than a tall, thin wedge with a hole for a small chain in a rounded end, but now he was swinging his hammer incessantly, ringing the anvil as he shaped glowing orange iron his helpers pulled from the fire. Occasionally he'd pause a moment to wipe his sweaty brow, but only until the next piece was hot enough and the tongs were handed to him. Hanny was mesmerized watching heavy iron spikes, probably salvaged from one of the ships, become long, slender rods. These in turn were twisted around the horn of the anvil, split and twisted again, before being cut to length. Each piece came back to O'Roddy only three times more before the intricate shape of a trace hook was born (something like a letter Q, but with its back-bent tail in the middle) and dropped to sizzle in a bucket of water. Hanny likened the big man's skill to magic, and Apo kept having to pull his attention back to his work.

The sun was behind the trees by the time they identified all the weapons with real problems, including Hanny's, and they'd have to work fast or get lanterns. With the aborted "battle" over so early and only part of the army dealing with the aftermath, Hanny had hoped for some real rest for a change, but that wasn't likely now. He had the lock off his musket and had just removed the broken mainspring—dutifully presenting the pieces to Scoochy—when First Sergeant Petty approached in the gathering gloom.

"Evenin', Mikey," said the scruffy-whiskered man, and Hanny looked at him more closely. Compared to the powerful O'Roddy, Petty's frame rather matched his beard: somewhat short and scruffy. Not that his uniform was untidy or anything, he just didn't wear it well. *He must know his business, though*, Hanny thought. He was the senior NCO in Captain Hudgens's C Battery and chief of a section of 6pdrs.

"If Captain Hudgens sent you, I've got his capsquare lock. *Your* cap-square lock," he corrected mischievously. "But I ain't done the worm an' I'm only half-finished with his hooks."

"Nah, I come for another reason," Petty said, glancing around, eyes landing on Hanny with recognition. He seemed about to speak again when thudding hooves heralded the arrival of Captain Felix Meder and several of his mounted riflemen. All wore the dark blue jackets of mounted troops, but they'd exchanged yellow trim for white to differentiate them from dragoons. Hanny admired Captain Meder. Barely older than himself, he (and his good friend Captain Hudgens) had both started on this world as private soldiers themselves. They'd also, along with First Sergeant McNabb, stood up for *him* when he stood up to Hahessy—and what seemed like half the army at the time. He was finally starting to warm to the idea of being a corporal, but that proved they were much more courageous than he and justly deserved quicker advancement.

Felix Meder saw Petty in the lengthening shadows and called out goodnaturedly, "Your section nearly took the colonel's head off today, First Sergeant! I'd say you need to reevaluate your choice of gunners."

Petty nodded, unsmiling. "They weren't none of 'em my choice. I just got put in charge of 'em. That bein' the case, I'm 'reevaluatin'' now. That's why I'm here."

O'Roddy spat a huge stream of tobacco juice he'd been hoarding. "You gonna put *me* on a gun now too?" He menaced Petty with a glowing trace hook that was almost complete. "On top o' ever'thin' else I gotta do?"

Petty shook his head. "No, not you . . ."

"Good." O'Roddy glared at Meder. "So what do you want . . . sir?"

Meder's men had their 1817 rifles slung crossways on their backs. Meder's own weapon was lying across his lap atop his Grimsley saddle. "The sling swivel on the back of my trigger guard broke, and I nearly dropped my rifle—the best-shooting rifle in the regiment," he reported without boasting. "It might've been destroyed or at least badly damaged. I'd have hated that. I hoped I might persuade you to give its repair your personal attention. . . ."

O'Roddy was waving the glowing hook. "*That* I'll do without complaint. Proper repair to honest damage to prevent worse to a weapon that does its duty is labor well spent," he said piously, nodding at where Hanny and his friends were working. "Not like pokin' out stopped vents an' hammerin' or replacin' broke flints. Any idiot can do that!"

"Thank you, Sergeant," Felix said, gently handing his rifle down to Scoochy. "I knew I could count on you." He looked back at Petty. "And you, First Sergeant. You expect to find your new gunner skulking among the fireflies?"

The sparks swirling up from the forge did look like swarms of demented fireflies in the deepening darkness. Apo was lighting a lantern to aid their gun repair, but O'Roddy hadn't asked for one. Hanny doubted he needed it.

"Maybe," Petty said in his usual short way and looked at Hanny again. "Sergeant Visser said Corporal Cox was here, most likely, an' there he is."

"Hanny Cox," Meder said, nodding satisfaction. "We know he's not shy," he added with a chuckle, "but can he shoot?"

"Me, sir?" Hanny almost squeaked, jumping up and saluting since he'd been "officially" noticed by an officer. Meder returned the salute and looked questioningly at Petty.

"I need a gunner for Number Two," Petty said simply. "Better if he's already a corporal since that crew ain't got a man fit to be one. They ain't *all* worthless an' can *move* their gun smart enough," he allowed, "but none's showed the talent for hittin' what he's aimin' at that Corporal Cox did durin' trainin'."

Artillery was the most lethal weapon on the battlefield and everyone, particularly infantrymen and mounted riflemen (often closest to the guns in battle), trained on them to some degree in case they were called to replace heavy casualties in action. Hanny had done fairly well, he thought, and even enjoyed it, but . . .

"I . . . I appreciate you thinking of me, First Sergeant," he stammered, "but I'm in the Third Pennsylvania. I *came* here (he meant to "this world") in the Third Pennsylvania. And what about my squad? They're counting on me." He didn't add that the men in his squad, from another world and this one, were his only friends.

Petty frowned. "I expect I'll be swapping half the gun detachment to Sergeant Visser. Let him make infantrymen out of 'em. You can bring your whole squad over if they want to come."

"Sergeant Visser . . . he said it was all right?" Hanny asked. "He wants rid of me?"

Petty seemed genuinely surprised. "No. Fact is, he says you've become a passable infantryman—when your musket goes off."

"Passable?" Hanny asked with a trace of bitterness.

Petty shrugged. "He also said you'll make a better-than-average artilleryman since you're the best corporal in the battalion, if not the whole Third Pennsylvania."

Hanny felt his face heat and knew only darkness hid a deep blush.

Petty snorted. "I can't credit that, o' course, so I'll only ask once an' move on. Look, Sergeant Visser's senior sergeant in Lieutenant Aiken's platoon an' has three other corporals. You got what, eight men in your squad? Countin' everybody, Captain Cullin's whole B Company has close to a hundred men who can point a musket at the enemy. Some o' your chums might miss you, even Sergeant Visser might, but nobody'll miss your shootin'. I need *one* man who can aim a big gun an' kill as many Doms as that whole company"—he glanced at Felix Meder—"an' who won't take the colonel's head off. What'll it be?"

Hanny looked at Apo, obviously thrilled with the idea. McDonough was frowning, as usual, but nodding. "I always admired the great guns," he confessed. "An' artillerymen don't walk everywhere," he added.

"One thing just occurred to me, I better tell you," Petty said, scratching his nose. "I got that damn Hahessy scoundrel in my section."

Hanny felt a chill. He'd seen the big man watching him from time to time, more so recently as the story of his defiance was revived after his promotion.

"He hates me," he murmured.

"He hates everybody," Petty countered. "The damn First US dropped him on Captain Hudgens unawares when he called for skilled artillerymen after the Washboard. I got him now an' can't get rid of him. *Nobody'll* take him." He raised an eyebrow at Hanny. "He's just a private now, o' course, an' I've heard you can handle him. Then again, if you're afraid . . ."

Hanny felt a hot, prickly, rushing sensation run down his back and took a deep breath. "All right, First Sergeant Petty. I'll do my best to justify your confidence in me." He looked at his friends. "In us."

Petty snorted. "Only things I'm 'confident' in is the Good Lord—an' that we'll all die in the end." He looked at Sergeant O'Roddy. "Find someone else to fix muskets. I'm takin' these boys with me."

CHAPTER 9

I 'm startin' to think this is gonna be a bigger show than we thought, at first," Ranger Lieutenant Sal Hernandez mused aloud, absently twisting one end of his huge black mustache as he stood on the big new dock at Uxmal and gazed out at the bay. Like all mounted troopers, he wore a dark blue shell and sky-blue trousers, but there wasn't any "branch trim" on either. Otherwise, he'd acquired a new, exceptionally well-made pair of knee-high boots and had a wide-brimmed natural tan-colored straw hat on his head. He pulled it down to shade his eyes from the glare reflecting off the water. A stiff breeze ruffled up waves and growing, glittering whitecaps threw up spray as a dozen or so broad-beamed, fore- and aft-rigged fishing boats plied back and forth carrying men to all *three* Dom transport prizes anchored a quarter mile out. (*Tiger* had taken another one.) All had been watered and provisioned before warping away from the dock days ago. Now, with yards crossed and anchors hove short, they looked ready for sea. They also looked dark and rather dumpy, with high forecastles and even higher poop decks compared to the even higher (because she was larger) but much sleeker lines of the old but much more "modern" *Tiger* anchored beyond them.

"Ye should'a known that all along, I'm thinkin'," scoffed the shorter man beside him. Sergeant Thomas Hayne of the 3rd Dragoons looked as different from Hernandez as was possible. He had light brown hair and huge side whiskers, his face tanned but not dark. In contrast to Hernandez's lanky frame, Hayne had the broad-shouldered, barrel-chested, bull-necked physique that almost seemed required of Irish-born NCOs in the army—on whatever world they were on. There was yellow trim on his uniforms and his saber belt was as white as snow, as was the wide sling and hook supporting his precious Hall carbine. Sal's belt and holsters for his pair of Paterson Colts were dark brown. "We *came* here with plenty o' fellas ta sneak in an' cut out *Isidra,* if that's all they meant us ta do," Hayne continued, "but they put us ta work, you, me, an' Cap'n Ixtla, trainin' two hundred men apiece." He stopped and looked around. The dock was empty for a good distance in every direction, the closest possible listeners a pack of old women and even older men mending fishing nets while small children tormented strange-looking crabs with sticks. The wall of the city was behind them, now pierced for numerous cannon taken from a Dom wreck in the bay, as well as two enormous 36pdrs captured at the Washboard. Beyond the wall was the barracks area for the Detached Expeditionary Force and whatever other "regulars" remained in the city. "An' not *all* that trainin' was fer things we knew much about," Hayne reminded. "Had ta teach *us* a bit for some o' it, didn't they?"

Sal Hernandez frowned. Hayne was right. Though most often employed as scouts, mounted dragoons and Rangers made excellent shock troops. Like cavalry, they were armed and trained to fight from the saddle and had the mobility to strike where least expected. Unlike cavalry, however, they were most effective at swooping in and dismounting to fight on foot, using brisk fire to block a column and force it to deploy before bolting, quickly adding mass to shaky infantry, or pressing a reeling enemy, even jumping on a flank left hanging in the air. When their job was done, they'd leap back on their horses and gallop wherever else they were needed. On the other hand, they weren't best at *getting around* on foot, and that's what they'd been practicing: learning to maneuver and keep together over long distances without their horses. They'd also been getting instruction from veteran Ocelomeh on sneaking around and using more brutal personal fighting techniques than most (besides Sal) were accustomed to. Sal actually supported all that and was pleased by the results. His battalion of two hundred new Rangers was more deadly than any so far, and he'd wished he could keep it all along.

He shrugged. "We came here expectin' immediate work," he reminded.

"We been here three months. Granted, Cap'n Holland an' *Tiger* been busy takin' reinforcements to Major Itzam at Nautla, but I figured they decided to hold off on goin' for *Isidra* just now." He twisted his mustache again. "Might as well use us to get some new fellas ready to join up with Colonel Reed."

"Then why just two hundred—six hundred total—when we could'a been workin' with three times that many? Or four. Others have been," Hayne reminded, waving vaguely around. "Other than the Ocelomeh, our raw material fer so-jers don't know shite about war, but they're sharp as paint." He paused. "An' what about the special trainin'?"

Sal shrugged again. "Maybe they're just tryin' it out, or maybe Colonel Reed's short o' horses an' wants fellas ready to run around with the infantry if they have to. *Quien sabe?*"

"I know, at last," said Captain Ixtla, stepping up from behind them and giving Hayne a start. The wind had covered his approach, and he looked around even more carefully than Hayne had, even peering down through the dock timbers looking for children playing in the low-tide mud. "I know *some*," he amended with his perpetual frown.

Sal respected the older man. He'd been fighting Holcanos all his life and took charge of some of their special training himself. He knew Hayne trusted the former Ocelomeh war leader as well, having accompanied him and Coryon Burton on the miserable, punishing, tragic scout all the way to Campeche before the "real" war began. They'd been among the few survivors.

Itxla pointed out at the boats full of troops going alongside the former Dom galleons. "I know, for example, as you must by now, those men *aren't* going to Colonel Reed." He lowered his gruff voice still further. "Nor are they going to Nautla. That's the story, of course; they're the final reinforcements for Colonel Cayce's command, waiting for General Agon's approach, and we're using the opportunity to work up the captured ships and their new crews." He sighed. "I hope the enemy believes that."

"You think there's still spies in the city?" Sal asked.

"I'm certain of it. The question is, can they still get information out?"

Hayne grimaced. "Not easy, prob'ly. Not on foot. But what about them flyin' spy lizards we been hearin' about?"

"Not as big a concern as we feared at first," Ixtla said with some relief. "New information from Colonel Cayce confirms they require skilled handlers and must have a base they know from which to operate. Mistress Samantha and Colonel De Russy liken their behavior to something they call 'post pigeons.' Do you know what they are?"

"Aye," Hayne grumbled, "but *these* post pigeons're considerable more frightenin'!"

Ixtla nodded out at the ships. "In any event, you may also have guessed that we'll be accompanying our new battalions to their destination because they are and always have been ours. I hope you've maintained good relations with your troops and NCOs."

"*I* already figgered that," Hayne said, flicking his eyes at Sal. "My question is, what'll we *do* with 'em?"

Ixtla glanced around again. "I have my suspicions, but all will soon be plain. I was sent to tell you to gather your kit, say your farewells—unhappy you're being sent to Nautla, mind—and repair aboard *Tiger* at dusk. She sails with the tide."

"*Tiger*?" Sal asked.

"Yes," Ixtla confirmed. "We'll be told"—he cracked the slightest smile at Hayne—"what we'll do before transferring to whatever ship bears our respective battalions. That'll be done when we're far out to sea, no doubt."

The little squadron sailed shortly after dark, clearing the treacherous crab claw shoals at the mouth of the bay by the light of the moon and steering straight out to sea. The wind was just forward of the galleons' starboard beam, and they crept along, leaning alarmingly and sagging disgracefully to leeward—nerve-rackingly close to the shoals—before they were clear. *Tiger* had only her topsails set so she didn't sprint too far ahead. The galleons—*Flor* had Ixtla's infantry aboard, *Viento Amistoso* carried Hayne's dragoons, and Hernandez's Rangers were in *Roble Fuerte*—would sail much easier with the wind abaft the beam, but with their shape and no staysails, Captain Holland considered them hopeless slugs. Still, he kept them on a northerly course while he held an informal dinner and met with Ixtla, Hernandez, Hayne, his own executive officer, Mr. Semmes, Second Lieutenant Randall Sessions, and a dark, round little man Holland introduced as "Capitan Razine" clustered around him at one end of the table in what would've once been the old ship's commodore's dining cabin. They'd use the larger great cabin the next day, when the other ship captains and junior troop officers came aboard for a more detailed briefing, but the current space was more than sufficient for this smaller group.

Sal ate quickly. He was hungry, and the food was good. Actual roast beef instead of the meat of some unidentifiable creature, and boiled, salty squash. There were also the ever-present frijoles of two different types, but he was used to that and liked them. A kind of sweet brown corn bread was available in baskets, kept warm by blankets and periodically renewed or replaced by a young Uxmalo sailor who acted as a waiter for them all. Holland didn't hold with any naval tradition of servants behind every diner. The men could refill their own glasses and carve their own meat.

Conversation was light, and Sal's eyes roved the room. It had been well-appointed, once, with carefully executed carving on high and low trim panels on the walls and around the doors. The exact shape of that carving was indistinguishable under half a century of haphazardly applied white paint, but the latest coat must be relatively fresh, because it reflected the glow of several gimballed lamps well enough to provide a bright, cheery light. Cheery only compared to the whitewashed walls of a jail cell, of course, since the only "window" was a square gunport open to the air, the gun itself under the table they ate on. Sal had painfully bumped his shin against the truck when he sat. To Captain Holland's enthusiastic approval, a caramelized gelatinous bread pudding arrived for dessert, sweet and slimy and full of dried fruit. Sal took a few bites, but each spoonful seemed to slide down his throat like a lump of phlegm and land with a thud in his stomach. He gave up, and the young waiter took his plate with a wink of understanding. Sal tried to cleanse his palate with a gulp of Uxmalo beer, but that didn't work too well.

"Now," Holland boomed, slapping the table after his own empty pudding plate was removed. He wasn't a big man and looked older than Moses, but could dominate a room a dozen times the size of the dining cabin with his personality and quarterdeck voice. "Let's get down to it, hey?" He gestured around at Ixtli, Sal, and Hayne. "You've all met my Mr. Semmes an' Mr. Sessions. I don't believe you know Capitan Razine. I expect you've guessed he was skipper o' one of our prizes. *Roble Fuerte*, in fact. He'll be goin' back to her with me an' Second Lieutenant Sessions." He paused and looked at Sal. "An' you, Lieutenant Hernandez, after we air things out tomorrow." He raised an eyebrow at the dark, rather nervous-looking man. Sal hadn't seen him eat much, come to that. "He don't talk a helluva lot, uninvited," Holland continued, "but don't get the wrong impression. I didn't *make* 'im come. After I told 'im what we mean to do, he volunteered. That took a hold full o' guts, as you'll see."

Captain Ixtli nodded. "I'm sure," he said dryly, then gestured at Sal and Hayne. "As I'm also sure my friends and I, and all our troops, are anxious to learn exactly what it is that *we did not* precisely volunteer for."

Holland looked at him a moment as if stunned, then burst out laughing. "I reckon it never occurred to anyone you fellas'd turn down a chance like this, so nobody asked! Ha! Course, you can always back out. Stay aboard *Tiger*, where it's liable ta be safe. . . ."

Sal and Hayne snorted simultaneously, and Ixtli rolled his eyes. "Captain Holland," he said with exaggerated patience. "*Will* you tell us the mission? We understood you meant to mount an expedition to steal *Isidra* back from the Doms at Vera Cruz and take her home." He shook his head. "But I'd imagine an operation like that would best be accomplished quietly, with a small force. Three ships and six hundred troops, not counting another hundred and fifty-odd crewmen, strikes me as . . . excessive, if you mean to employ stealth." His tone was still dry, but a little harsh as well.

Holland waved a hand as if dismissing his concerns. "Sure, we're goin' ta get *Isidra*. That's the priority." Then he grinned and his eyes glittered. "But we're also goin' on a raid. Vera Cruz is the biggest Dom port on this side o' the continent, the *only* one fit to supply forces goin' against Uxmal. There's shore batteries an' a few warships most likely, but Capitan Razine says there's nothin' on this side o' the world for 'em to guard against. Most of the troops've been pulled to join General Agon against us, or sent away for their Gran Cruzada against the New Brit Imperials. It's a empty shell right now, an' we're gonna smash it!"

Sal leaned forward, his predatory gaze mirroring Holland's now. "I volunteer," he said with a grin.

"I as well, of course," Ixtla said, then looked hard at Razine. "But what's he here for, and why do we need him?" He might as well have said, "He's a Dom. I don't trust him."

Holland raised both eyebrows. "Aye, he's a 'Dom,' by birth an' nationality, but even Varaa'll tell ye there's 'true believers' amongst 'em, an' then there's them as *has* ta believe, as it were. An' what they believe is startin' ta sag ta leeward as bad as them fat, primitive tubs out there." He tilted his head aft, indicating the galleons in their wake, then went on to briefly describe the class structure of the Dominion as Razine had explained it. Varaa and Har-Kaaska knew it existed, but even they hadn't had a complete understanding. The rising differences between the "traditional" Church and the Blood Priests seemed subtle and insignificant on the surface and didn't seem to make much difference to them, but it was starting to cause a rift in the upper classes. "It makes little difference a'tall to common soldiers, slaves, an' the lowest class of free folk either," Holland continued, "which ain't allowed ta even *think* about nothin' but servin' their betters er dyin' tryin'—though I expect some o' the Doms we licked at the Washboard might'a noted a crack er two in the dominance o' the Dominion." He bowed his head to Capitan Razine. "He's a hidalgo, a kind o' middle-class sort."

"Lower middle class, in effect," Capitan Razine corrected timidly, his English already fairly good after close to four months' practice. He looked at Holland, stricken. "My apologies," he quickly added. "I didn't mean to interrupt!"

"No, no! Go ahead!" Holland encouraged.

Razine looked at the others, obviously still nervous, and cleared his throat. "I'm a hidalgo, a status even *hombres libres*—the lowest class of freemen—might aspire to, though the likelihood of them ever reaching it is small. I was born to it, as the son of a *patricio* who set me up in the shipping business. *Roble Fuerte* is—*was*—my second ship. Perhaps, one day, I might've ascended to the rank of *patricio* myself," he said a little wistfully. "But as a man of property, who had to *think* to maintain and grow it, seeing to repairs, hiring crews, commissioning cargoes to pay for it all . . ."

"Ye *hired* yer crew, did ye?" Hayne asked, intrigued.

"Yes," Razine confirmed. "Slaves are expensive and not only often lose their will to live, they have little motivation to become better sailors. Why should they? How will it improve their lot? Freemen work cheaper than the purchase price of a slave, live longer, learn more, and ultimately become more valuable sailors. They might become ship's officers one day and save enough to buy a fishing boat. Perhaps become hidalgos themselves. In any event, I had to think, as I said, and at least vaguely recognized the oppressive nature of our system. . . ." He paused before whispering, "And our faith.

He looked at Holland. "I can't describe the terror I knew when *heretics* took my ship. I knew what the priests would do to me for allowing it, and what the *Blood* Priests would do. . . ." He shuddered. "So I imagined whatever *you* might do would have to be worse." He blinked and an expression of wonder crossed his face. "Therefore, when I and my crew were merely treated as men, detained but cared for and fed, questioned extensively but not abused, tortured, burnt, *eaten* . . ." Tears ran down his face. "Father Orno came to me many times and I learned a *new* history, a *different* gospel, that was purer, older . . . simply *felt* truer." He sniffed and wiped his eyes with a napkin. "I willingly became a heretic too, finally understanding the faith forced upon me, on all my poor people since time on this world began, is a cruel, twisted lie." He'd dropped his gaze to his hands on the table, still clutching the napkin between them. When he looked up, his expression was defiant. "I'm *in* your war now, in whatever capacity I can serve. Most of my crew as well. Win or lose, it's a fight worth making."

"Damned if I don't believe him," Sal murmured. Ixtla still looked suspicious, but Hayne was nodding.

"What about the crews of the other two ships?" Ixtla asked.

"Most were slaves," supplied First Lieutenant Semmes with a frown. "Some of those recently taken along the borders of the Dominion were enthusiastic to join us and even now help work the prizes. Those with a . . . longer tradition of servitude remain too afraid to do much of anything and are being cared for. One of the other captains went mad, I'm afraid, and the other contrived to, well, smother himself with the mattress in his cell before we could talk to him much."

"Damn," Sal said. "Fella'd have to really work at that, I bet."

"Still thought he was takin' the easy way out, most likely," Second Lieutenant Sessions agreed.

"Be that as it may," Holland interjected, "Capitan Razine has earned our trust. By his own admission, he's no expert on the layout o' the Dominion. His regular route took him to Cuba an' Hispaniola, usually from Vera Cruz, but sometimes as far north as Tampico. Not much there, he says. An' his voyage to supply the enemy—where they were supposed to be at Uxmal— was the first time he'd ever been to the Yucatán. His charts are pretty good for those areas. Don't go as far south as I'd like, beyond the Yucatán," he added with a furrowed brow, "an' that worries me a bit. We still don't know anything about what's past what we called the Mosquito Kingdom."

"What difference does it make?" Hayne asked.

"Only that Techolotla an' Vera Cruz are the only shipbuildin' centers he knows of, an' he's never seen 'em lay down a warship. Can't imagine why they'd need 'em in the Atlantic"—Holland grinned—"till *Tiger* got here.

But there was some. Still are a few, an' we don't know where they come from." He regarded Capitan Razine. "Anyway, he's along to help."

"What help can he be?" Ixtla asked, still unconvinced by the Dom sailor and refusing to talk directly to him.

Razine cleared his throat again. "We have been gone too long for anyone to expect these particular ships to return to Vera Cruz, and the unexpected arrival of three in company might cause . . . curiosity in the commander of whatever garrison remains. There will be *some* Dominion troops, and I may need to respond to signals. Just as important, not all the rocks and shallows appear on the charts and for those accustomed to sailing *this* wonderful vessel, our . . . transports can be difficult to manage in confined waters. It's best that I accompany Capitan Holland in *Roble Fuerte* to advise him on handling her and to respond to any challenge from shore. I strongly recommend the following ships watch us closely and do as we do. It would be unfortunate if we ran two aground just to bring one to anchor, and I doubt you can accomplish as much in your raid if two-thirds of your troops are lost."

Holland was looking around the table, examining Ixtla, Hayne, then Sal. Something about Sal's expression made him snort, and he focused back on Ixtla. "One thing you might've missed, Mr. Ixtla," he said a little frostily. "I even get it," he allowed in a slightly lighter tone. "All your life, the only good Dom's been a dead Dom, but the thing you might'a neglected ta consider is that some, like Capitan Razine, ain't necessarily *bad*, they just *do* bad for a culture enslavin' 'em through fear as much as any folk they conquer. They're misinformed—an' afraid o' them that's doin' all the informin'. Some might even be open ta the truth if we have a chance ta tell it." He nodded at Razine. "As good a reason as any ta bring our new friend along. We can yammer at folks till we're blue in the face an' they'll still just want ta kill us. They might listen to a word or two from one o' their own." He shrugged. "Worth a try."

"We won't be there long enough to *convert* anybody!" Sal objected, then paused. "Will we?"

Holland scratched the stubble on his chin. "Depends. Nothin' much within a hundred miles ta reinforce the city. Let's see how things go."

CHAPTER 10

Lewis Cayce, Giles Anson, and Varaa-Choon were riding with the short, dark-haired, generally cheerful badger of a man named Major Marvin Beck at the front of the column, now led by Beck's own 1st US Infantry. It was early morning, and sunlight filtered down through leaves of a far less confining forest than they'd been in for weeks. They'd curse the sun as the day wore on and its oppressive heat bore down, but 1st Division had been on the move for less than two hours, and many still marveled at the hint of a breeze like they hadn't felt since plunging into the woods at Nautla.

Varaa had just joined them, begrudgingly confessing that a remarkably cooperative Kisin (now riding unrestrained with Anson's Rangers) had confirmed they were within a day of their objective. Lewis didn't doubt it. Decaying evidence of the outskirts of Cayal was all around; old ruins, collapsed and choked with vines, showed where outlying settlements once stood. Reverend Harkin had asked why the Holcanos didn't restore and occupy them, but Varaa explained that, prior to their current unprecedented cooperation, the migratory Holcanos historically only used Cayal itself as a safe meeting place for their various bands (and Grik) to gather and consult, trade captives and daughters, or negotiate joint raids or brief alliances against one another. Kisin had also told her the Holcanos had started using

Cayal as a trading hub with the Dominion, sending timber in the form of rafts piled high with hides, dried fish, cured meat, and valuable plunder down the Usuma River flowing beside the ancient city. This in exchange for tools, Dominion assistance against their enemies, and promised weapons that never came.

In any event, the land was clearly changing, the forest more open at last (also revealing increasing numbers of bizarre, frightening creatures fleeing their advance through younger, sparser growth). The ground was more broken as well, crossed by streams tumbling from distant hills that sucked showers from the sky year-round. No doubt the streams—the best water they'd found—fed the Usuma River.

"And Kisin remains confident Don Discipo still holds sway over seven or eight thousand Holcanos?" Lewis asked Varaa.

"Warriors," Varaa stressed. "Likely three times that many women and younglings. The Maker knows how they've fed them so long, cooped in one place."

"Fish," Major Beck abruptly said, then explained more self-consciously than usual, "As you know, that damned Kisin wants his Holcanos back and doesn't know if they'll follow him. The ones we don't kill, that is. Especially if they can't eat people anymore. I overheard Reverend Harkin going on at him about throwing away sin and such, and gathering men to his cause. I know enough Spanya to catch his drift, but the reverend speaks it like a native."

"Well?" prodded Anson, interested.

"Harkin told Kisin about Peter, how Jesus told him to throw out his net again, even though Peter and his fellows hadn't caught anything all night. When they did as He told them, their net filled up smartly and liked to burst."

"What did Kisin say?" Lewis asked.

Beck shook his head. "Said Don Discipo had kept Holcano women busy with nets across the river, filling them every day, so he didn't see anything special in that."

"How did the reverend respond?"

Beck chuckled. "Pretty well. Asked Kisin if he ever thought of that. Kisin got huffy and said, 'Of course not.' Holcanos are hunters, not 'city-squatting fishermen.' That's when Harkin started in on pride, and how it was the worst sin of all and turned the Devil bad in the first place. Kisin got a little worried since his name kind of means 'Devil' to some, but Harkin assured him there's only *one* Devil and his name is Lucifer. Kisin allowed he might've heard of the fellow, and it was a relief to know he didn't *have* to be bad all the time. Figured being *the* Devil was more responsibility than he wanted."

Lewis laughed, and even Varaa *kakked* a Mi-Anakka chuckle.

"But Kisin asked how Don Discipo came up with the same notion for feeding folks that Jesus did. Harkin said the Devil—who's wholly in charge of the Dominion and started all this in the first place—can give people good ideas for bad reasons. Besides, Don Discipo's a 'city squatter' himself. There's no river by Puebla Arboras, but he'd seen them fish that way at Itzincab, on the Cipactli River." Beck was holding his reins in his left hand and held his right out, palm up. "Anyway," he said, "they're eating lots of fish."

There came a sudden low rumble in the distance, like thunder, but the open sky above held not a single cloud. The sound came again and again, still dull and distant, but Lewis knew what it was. "Artillery," he growled. "Kisin swore there was no artillery in Cayal. It must be ours. Second Division's," he clarified.

"A long slog for us an' them to both reach our objective so close to the same time," Anson said.

Lewis looked at him. "Who knows if we are? We've had no communication, and they might've been here a week or two already." He frowned at Varaa. "I hope your King Har-Kaaska hasn't gotten bored just sitting there and decided to storm the city. That could cause . . . problems." He paused, letting an unusual tone of annoyance creep into his voice. "Major Anson, go forward, if you please. If that's our artillery firing on the city, it's near enough that our scouts *should've* already found the place and reported its presence. Secure an early report from them—and find that villainous Kisin, if you can." He flicked a glance at Varaa when Anson urged Colonel Fannin ahead at a canter. "Unfamiliar wilderness or not, your Ocelomeh claim to know it to a degree and constitute the core of Anson's Rangers. On top of that, Kisin was just through here. I'm weary of stumbling upon enemies in the forest!" He raised his voice. "Major Beck? Let's pick up the pace, shall we?"

"Yes sir." Beck quickly passed the word to Captain Harris in front of his First Battalion. Harris shouted, "Battalion! Trail—*arms* (most of the men were already carrying their weapons that way), quick time—*march*!" NCOs repeated the orders, drums increasing the tempo, and the troops stretched their legs to take longer, quicker steps just short of a jog. They'd all heard the rumbling and knew what it was. Each battalion and regiment behind would do the same unless otherwise directed. Lewis, Beck, and Varaa loosened their reins to stay ahead of the infantry. The booming thunder of guns grew louder and more rapid as 1st Division almost flowed through the thinning forest like a stream on a suddenly steeper grade. It wouldn't take long for the men to tire, however, especially as the heat of the day began to mount.

"I don't like this," Lewis continued aside at Varaa, voice slightly jostled by Arete's gait. "Four hundred miles through country only vaguely known to any in this army, to a destination I've never seen—don't even have a *map* of, beyond some childish scribbles Kisin produced—and it sounds like we're arriving in the middle of a battle someone else has started!"

"Is that uncertainty I detect in your voice, Colonel Cayce?" Varaa retorted almost mockingly. "You showed no hesitation for your grand plan *before* we dove into the sea of trees!"

Lewis looked at her and snorted. "You know me well enough by now. I don't *show* a great deal of what I *feel*.

"Perhaps you should, sometimes," she retorted, then grinned. "Not now, of course."

"No." A moment later, he added, "But it does sound like Har-Kaaska has attacked. He wasn't supposed to do that until we could coordinate our efforts."

"He wouldn't act precipitously," Varaa defended loyally. "The Holcanos might've attacked *him*."

"Possibly."

Twenty minutes later, the forest had practically entirely given way to a broad, rolling savanna populated as usual by immense beasts of various sorts, all too big to be hunted. Even a large band might sustain casualties killing one of the long-horned, facially armored monsters. Holcanos didn't hunt from horseback, and the beasts *would* take a toll on such puny predators on foot, whirling and smashing them with their tails or catching and stomping them. It wasn't worth the risk. Besides, long before they took enough meat to justify such an effort, other predators would be drawn by the smell of blood and take it from them. In any event, they still couldn't see the city, and Lewis realized it must lay beyond a rise just ahead. That was the direction the artillery fire was coming from, at any rate. Sure enough, Anson and a cluster of riders were galloping back from where his

Rangers and riflemen were deploying along the low grassy crest about a quarter of a mile away.

"Slow the infantry to common time," Lewis told Major Beck. "We don't know what's ahead, and I want them rested when we do. Pass the word—no bugles—to send all the artillery and mounted troops forward."

"Yes sir."

Lewis gently kicked Arete with the round knobs of his spurs, and the mighty chestnut mare surged forward, followed by Varaa's smaller striped horse, and they met Anson and Leonor, four mounted riflemen, and an awkwardly riding Kisin about halfway to the crest. Kisin was wearing one of Sergeant O'Roddy's long white shirts (probably the only source for one that would fit him somewhat loosely) and a long red breechcloth belted around his waist. There still wasn't so much as a knife on the belt, but oddly enough, he looked even more powerful and intimidating in clothes and without spiked hair and red paint all over him.

"Sorry it took me so long," Anson apologized abruptly. "I was tryin' to figure out what the hell's goin' on."

"You can see the city?" Lewis demanded.

"Yeah, just over that rise, another half mile below."

"*Did* you discover what's happening?"

Dragoons and lancers were pounding along the column now, passing teams of horses pulling clattering limbers and guns, spokes blurred as they threw shredded grass like dust.

Anson glanced at Varaa. "Yeah, sorta. C'mon, I'll show you."

"Unlimber just this side of the crest," Lewis told Captain Hudgens, leading his guns.

"Aye, sir," Hudgens replied, his British accent always stronger when there was a prospect of action. "Battery!" he shouted behind him. "Unlimber on me when I stop, either side." That wasn't exactly a prescribed command, but the artillerymen knew what he meant.

"Orderly!" Lewis almost bellowed. "Oh, there you are, Corporal Willis. Have Major Beck halt his infantry, in column, about fifty yards behind."

"Yes sir," Willis replied in a long-suffering tone, having just galloped up, butt slapping his saddle. No one hated a horse or rode one as poorly as Corporal Denny Willis.

"And have Reverend Harkin join us if you see him," Lewis called after him before urging Arete after Giles Anson, Varaa, and Kisin. Leonor had waited, ready to stay by him as always in action if it came. Also as always, that gave him the same mix of gratitude and concern for her safety. He'd only seen her in passing over the last several days, and she looked weary, trail-worn, and dusty from her scouting, having been in charge of the squad of Rangers and riflemen—and Kisin—who first viewed Cayal. He wondered if Kisin had been any help and how he'd reacted to being under her supervision. She gave him a tired smile as they moved to join the others halting on the rise. He smiled back. "We seem to have arrived," he said, fishing his small brass telescope from its protective leather case.

"Yeah, but we're late to the party somebody threw early."

"You see," Kisin said grandly, with a guarded look at Leonor, "I brought you here just as I promised!"

"Did not," Leonor growled back. "We heard the fightin', same as everybody, an' stumbled across it." She looked at Lewis. "Then he says, 'Oh, there it is!'" She waved to the southwest. "We cut the Usuma River a couple miles that way, an he says, 'I wonder where the city went!'"

Kisin glowered at her, but there was fear as well as anger in his gaze. He clearly sensed—and remembered—how lethal Leonor was. "The closer one draws to the city, the more tracks are in the forest, spreading like fingers from both hands held together." That was true enough. Even the "main" track they'd followed had smaller trails converging on it from all directions over the last few days. "I may not have chosen the most direct path"—he glanced anxiously at Varaa—"that the sound of war brought you down, but they all look so much alike and across such a distance"—he blinked as if it couldn't matter—"a *legua* one way or other shouldn't be held against me."

"It *can*, you fool," Varaa snapped. "Either you deliberately led our scouts astray or you've no business even leading Holcanos!"

Kisin nervously waved that away. "City squatters may need to be where they want on certain mornings of certain days, but why should *real* forest warriors care about such things?" he haughtily proclaimed.

"*You* care," Varaa sneered. "Your plans against us in the past prove that!"

"Calm down, both of you," Lewis said mildly, surveying the scene ahead. The setting was actually rather beautiful, in a way. The ancient city of Cayal wasn't as large as Uxmal, but it looked like a crumbling, run-down version of it, complete with high stone walls surrounding the inner structures and a ragged, vine-covered step pyramid rising in the center. Bright green vines were everywhere, in fact, creeping all over the startlingly white masonry as if trying to pull it all down over time. Closely surrounding the city were countless dome-like leather shelters issuing a fog of woodsmoke that drifted east across the blue-green grass prairie and a broad, lustrous turquoise river bordering heavy forest on the other side. Colorful flying creatures, lizardbirds, or just regular birds of some sort, capered and wheeled above, but especially along the river. The only other "real" river Lewis had seen was the Cipactli, running alongside Uxmal to the sea, but it was always a muddy reddish brown. The water here looked like a ribbon of aquamarine emerald, sweeping down from distant hills, almost mountains to the northeast, winding southwest until it vanished once more in the forest.

Harshly intruding on the scene, a pitched battle was under way on the open plain north of the city. Musketry crackled, and storms of arrows flashed out from firm but disheveled lines of infantry looking as if they'd been rapidly formed on either side of a pair of 12pdr howitzers. They were coughing canister into a charging horde that outnumbered them considerably. Justinian Olayne's battery of 6pdrs was farther back (Lewis could see the gold artillery flag and Stars and Stripes beside it), still throwing round-shot over the heads of Har-Kaaska's forces and what had to be Colonel Reed's newly arriving regiments. Another battery, probably captured and recarriaged Dom 8pdrs, was unlimbering behind the infantry, preparing to push forward and add their canister to the howitzers. Other flags fluttered, but Lewis couldn't identify them from here. He hadn't seen the new regimental flags in any case.

He spoke to those around him. "While I'm sure the Holcanos are excellent woodsmen, I'm more inclined to believe Kisin himself is out of practice than that he deliberately delayed us. He couldn't know what was happening here, and while he may have taken our scouts slightly off course, he didn't delay the army. Besides," he added grimly, "he was right about something else: there are enough Holcanos down there to have overwhelmed us if they were properly armed and hit us on the march. At the same time, I don't know if Har-Kaaska started the fight or just got too close. Either way, he's in it now, and it might be bigger than he can handle."

Lewis turned piercing eyes on Kisin. "How big a reserve would Don Discipo keep back? How large a force would he leave in the city?"

Kisin looked bewildered. "Reserve? Oh! You mean extra warriors!" He shook his head. "Holcanos don't do things like that. Well," he corrected, "if we still had Garrach'ka allies, we'd be a 'reserve' for them, but I don't see any."

"*Nobody's* in the city? No warriors?" Anson demanded incredulously.

Kisin sounded defensive now. "Why would there be?" He pointed. "The enemy is *there*. Any who stayed out of the fight would be shunned as cowards. *They* would never again have a place among warriors—and would never be eaten when they die," he added a little resentfully.

Lewis looked at Leonor and saw her dark eyes already gleaming but was distracted by the arrival of Reverend Harkin and the regimental commanders of the 3rd Pennsylvania, 1st Uxmal, and 1st Ocelomeh, who'd joined Major Beck. Captain Meder, Capitan Lara, and Lieutenant Fisher of the dragoons had drawn near as well. Harkin may have lost a lot of weight, but he still didn't exercise and was puffing as loudly as if he'd been carrying his horse instead of the other way around. "Magnificent," he huffed, "and quite disconcerting. I thought you meant for us to combine our assault with our reinforcements from the north."

"I did, and we will. Gentlemen," Lewis said to the regimental commanders, "have your men drop their knapsacks, then shift from column into line. Four ranks deep for extra punch and to keep the lines compact. Each regiment will follow the other at first, and we'll leave no one here but the rear guard and baggage train—and those guarding the Holcanos, of course. The rest go forward together." He looked at Major Ulrich, then Consul Koaar and Major Manley. "The Third Pennsylvania will shift to the right and the First Uxmal to the left on my command." He nodded at Consul Koaar. "The first Ocelomeh will close up behind the First US, but be prepared to pass through to the front."

"Let my warriors join the attack!" Kisin pleaded. "Let us *lead* it!"

"Don't be ridiculous. They've barely begun training and aren't even armed." Lewis didn't need to add that whether he trusted Kisin to control them or not, no one else would.

"We'll find weapons in the fight!" Kisin pressed. "I have been among you"—he flicked his eyes disdainfully at Varaa—"even *that* one, long enough to know you were right. The Dominion is the true enemy, and I must help you fight them. I can't do that if I don't unite my people—and the only way to do that is to help you beat them! They won't accept me as their leader any other way."

Lewis stared at Kisin, measuring his sincerity.

"He's right," Varaa said, surprising them all. "Give him a token force and send him with the Ocelomeh."

"Varaa!" Consul Koaar objected.

"Take him—and two hundred of his warriors," Varaa ordered harshly. Koaar was still pledged to obey the commands of his warmaster in battle. She met Kisin's stare. "Today we'll find out how things will be. Your men will soak up arrows for mine, then fight beside them when they're close. If any of you betrays us, Consul Koaar will kill you all." She blinked defiantly at Lewis. She was stating a fact, not seeking his blessing.

"Very well." Lewis nodded, accepting it. "Corporal Willis, escort Mr. Kisin to his people"—they were just emerging from the woods—"and allow him to choose two hundred warriors. Bring them up on the double."

Willis murmured something under his breath but spurred away with Kisin behind him.

"And the mounted men?" Anson asked with raised eyebrows. Lewis pointed west. "Back in the woods, up on the enemy flank." He didn't have to caution Anson to avoid being discovered. Giving him and the others a lopsided grin, he then snorted a chuckle at Lara, still finding it ironic that a Ranger should fight alongside a Mexican lancer. Lara, equally amused, grinned back. All that was over, and they were firmly on the same side against *this* enemy, sure they would've been "back home" as well. "I'm confident you'll know the best moment to strike when you see it."

Lewis waited while Beck, Manley, Ulrich, and Koaar shook their men out, the latter reluctantly making room for the Holcanos Kisin quickly brought over, and Lara and Fisher assembled their riders, the scouts that had occupied the crest rushing to join their units. Lewis let none of his impatience show. These things couldn't be accomplished with a snap of the fingers, and he decided to use the few moments they had to good effect. Feeling a little awkward, he turned to Reverend Harkin. "Many of the men might appreciate a prayer. A short one," he stressed. "I know you've performed services for *our* men. . . ."

"Even Catholics!" Anson reminded archly, conjuring an irony perhaps even more profound than he and Lara fighting on the same side.

"Indeed," Lewis agreed. "In light of that, I hope you might broaden your . . . nondenominational message into a sentiment suitable for all: Uxmalos, Techonos, etc. . . ."

Harkin looked offended. "Of course." He stuck his bearded chin out at Varaa. "With only a few exceptions, as far as I know, since *some* are so notoriously tight-lipped, almost all of us worship the very same God and seek salvation through His son, Jesus Christ. Father Orno has influenced me to believe there's hope even for the Ocelomeh and that the various ways we come to know *our* God"—he clearly meant as opposed to the wicked God the Doms worshipped)—"are not as important as the fact that we do." He looked back at Lewis. "I'd be honored to lead the troops in a brief prayer. I doubt any will find it corrosive to their personal beliefs."

True to his word, Harkin's invocation was very short, couldn't have offended anyone in Lewis's estimation, and was even touchingly uplifting. Delivered in his loudest, strongest pulpit voice, it must've carried to most of the men. Lewis did not begrudge him the short time it took because the artillery had to limber up again, the mounted troops had to gather on the left, by battalions, and the leading infantry regiment, the 1st US, moved forward to the crest of the rise even as Harkin finished and heard a chorus of appreciative "amens." Then, with a nod from Lewis, Major Giles Anson nodded back and led his Rangers, lancers, dragoons, and riflemen back toward the trees on the left at a trot.

Now they were ready. Raising his telescope to view Har-Kaaska's battle once more, Lewis pursed his lips. The fighting was very close, the smoke obscuring the point of contact, but it looked like Don Discipo's numbers were starting to tell. Hopefully, anyone left in the ancient walled city was absorbed by the drama to the north and wouldn't think to look south. . . .

"Keep your musicians quiet for the moment, Major Beck. We'll try to remain unobserved as long as we can," Lewis said. "But take your men forward at the quick march again."

Varaa edged her horse close alongside Lewis's Arete and said, just above a whisper, "Where are your doubts, your 'hesitations' now, Colonel Cayce?" she asked.

"Now I know what must be done, they've all but vanished," he confessed. "Strange, isn't it?"

"You already know, with just a glance?" she asked, surprised.

"I think so, yes. And I personally find that even stranger, in a way."

EVEN WITH A compact front, a force composed of roughly three thousand men and six guns can't move quietly, especially when they're in something of a rush. Just the tramp of feet and horses' hooves makes a distinct rumble that can be heard at a considerable distance. Add the squeak and clatter of musket sling swivels, canteens, and tin cups tied to haversacks clanking against bayonets and cartridge boxes and muskets. Overriding it all was the creak and rattle and distinctive grumble of guns in motion, the pounding hooves and jangling traces hitched to horses pulling them. Nor is such a force invisible, of course. Anyone watching from Cayal's jagged-tooth walls would've seen the flash of bright-barreled muskets within the dense, surging, rectangular ranks of men in sky-blue uniforms, dark blue hats, and dingy white crossbelts, contrasting sharply against the distant, hazy trees and dark, blue-green grass. But anyone in a position to do anything about it, to form a defense or warn Don Discipo, must indeed have been focused on the battle under way, excited by the prospect of a crushing victory over the "city squatters" that repulsed them at Itzincab, drove them out of Puebla Arboras, and came to threaten them here.

CHAPTER 11

God help us!" swore Captain Justinian Olayne, still on his horse, bringing his battery up from behind the main south-facing line. His heart seemed to freeze as what looked like the whole 1st Itzincab began to collapse under the relentless weight of the Holcano assault on the left flank, down by the river. Men who'd been fighting desperately with pikes, shaky but determined against the whooping, shrieking horde, just seemed to snap and flee, streaming back through the 2nd Ocelomeh. That disrupted their volleys of arrows, and though they courageously tried to blunt the breakthrough with hand weapons, they couldn't hold a line like the pikemen. The fighting there degenerated into a shapeless melee, and the 2nd Ocelomeh would have to pull back or be overrun. Worst of all, Olayne had seen it coming, *known* it would happen, and there hadn't been a thing he could do.

King Har-Kaaska had resigned himself to falling under Colonel Cayce's command when they met, but still resented Colonel Andrew Reed "taking over" what he considered "his" campaign when Reed arrived at Itzincab weeks before with his smartly dressed, well-armed new brigade of Uxmalos and Techonos. It was an impressive force, joined by the rest of Captain Emmel Dukane's battery and two full batteries of captured Dom guns, all marching under crisp new regimental flags, the only things differentiating it at a distance from the still largely American 1st US and 3rd Pennsylvania. A long baggage train brought up the rear and the whole thing, without question, was the best-equipped, most professionally trained force the peninsular allies had yet assembled.

But "Colonel" King Har-Kaaska's crusade against the Holcanos was a personal fight. Fully aware it was merely a necessary prelude to their bigger business with the Dominion, he'd still been reluctant to subordinate himself to Reed. He would've—probably—submitted more easily to Colonel Cayce. He'd won a great battle, after all. But after two decades of fighting Holcanos, Har-Kaaska was the "expert" here, the only real "professional," his Ocelomeh the only true warriors. And the "city folk" soldiers and militia he led were the only other troops on this campaign who'd faced the enemy, and he was justly proud of how they'd driven the Holcanos from Itzincab and out of Puebla Arboras. He couldn't think much of more townsfolk in new uniforms, no matter how well they looked or marched. His troops were the veterans, and he'd insisted they lead the division's advance.

Colonel Reed, sensible to the logic in that—and Har-Kaaska's feelings—didn't press the issue. Now the somewhat loosely combined 2nd Division had advanced rapidly and fairly efficiently with few dangerous encounters with monsters and without meeting any serious resistance until Cayal itself finally loomed. Colonel Reed sent messengers urging Har-Kaaska to halt his brigade on the rocky, forested, ruin-covered high ground north of the city until the rest of the division came up, but Har-Kaaska pressed on, down to the plain, impatient to "chase" the Holcanos into the city from their surrounding camps as he'd done at Puebla Arboras. Once the enemy was trapped in its walls, they'd wait for Colonel Cayce to arrive. When they began their combined bombardment and assault, the Holcanos would know there'd be no escape, and Har-Kaaska rather hoped there'd be no surrender. The Holcanos would be eradicated once and for all.

But Don Discipo—or whoever commanded his warriors in battle—had learned his lesson at Puebla Arboras. Holcanos had no notion of defense, nor did they have the discipline for it. Besides, only in a stand-up fight could they bring their superior numbers to bear, and they'd prepared to take best advantage. They'd waited until Har-Kaaska's brigade was committed to the field and a significant gap opened between it and the rest of the division before erupting from concealment inside the city, pouring through the gateless entryways, surging over walls, sweeping down from the trees to the west, even leaping up from depressions or from behind scattered ruins to swarm Har-Kaaska's pike and bow-armed "veterans."

The problem unfolding now, that Olayne—and others—had foreseen, was even though Har-Kaaska's brigade reacted quickly, deployed as trained, and even fought with tenacity, they were really only veterans of *pursuing* the enemy and attacking relatively small groups they trapped. Now, beyond the simple horrifying surprise of it all, it seemed like the roles were reversed, and Olayne was frankly amazed they stood it as long as they did.

"Stay back, sir!" he shouted as Har-Kaaska himself thundered past on his great, improbable mount, waving a heavy-bladed sword with an ornate, almost delicate-looking guard and calling his staff, even the civilians still in his retinue, to follow him down to the cracking archers. He almost crashed into a galloping column of dragoons led by Coryon Burton and the recently (reluctantly) promoted Captain "Boogerbear" Beeryman, who bellowed, "Hold yer—whatever the hell that thing is—just a damn minute. You go down there, yer gonna get dead." Probably only the imposing size of the big Ranger and his unusually large local horse could've given the excited Har-Kaaska pause and he checked his charge, but only to yell, "My people are being slaughtered and those . . . *animals* are smashing our flank!"

Boogerbear looked behind him. "Yep," he agreed calmly. "Better pull your men back."

Har-Kaaska blinked amazed anger, tail whipping like a striking snake. "They'll destroy us all!" He gestured at Olayne's battery: six 6pdrs moving up by hand to join all six of Emmel Dukane's howitzers already in the wavering line of the rest of his Techonos, "Pidros," and Ocelomeh facing south. "They'll roll up our line!"

"They might," Boogerbear replied in his maddeningly even way, "but it'll take a spell longer an' cost 'em a heap more before they do. Lookie yonder," he added, nodding behind Har-Kaaska. The Mi-Anakka impatiently whirled his strange mount to see Captain Dukane himself urging both batteries of captured 8pdrs into line facing the collapsing flank. Behind them came the 2nd Uxmal arrayed in line of battle four ranks deep, marching to the rumbling thunder of their own drums while a pair of youngsters who'd mastered the fife played a rousing tune.

"'Araby's Daughter'!" Captain Olayne barked in amusement. "I wonder who taught them that?"

"I did," Boogerbear said, waving at Major Manley. "Had to hum it, though. Don't remember the words. Look behind you, Cap'n Olayne."

Olayne had been watching his men move the guns, First Sergeant McNabb giving all the commands for distracted lieutenants, and hadn't realized the 1st Techon was coming up behind *his* line in a longer formation two ranks deep with Colonel Reed and Father Orno riding in front, oblivious to sheeting arrows dropping men behind them. And the men themselves, who'd never tasted battle, looked grimly determined, admirably keeping their intervals and alignment even as men screamed and fell.

"I didn't want a battle today," Reed called out to Olayne with a dark glance at Har-Kaaska. "I certainly wasn't expecting one. But I'm glad you were supporting these men as they pressed so close to the city or they would've been routed, I fear."

Olayne bowed his head noncommittally. He'd been "supporting" Har-Kaaska ever since Lewis Cayce sent him to join the Ocelomeh king. He'd been uncomfortable with the polite rift in the division, understood Har-Kaaska's pride had been wounded and he chafed under Reed's command, was even leery of Har-Kaaska's push forward to "chase the enemy into the city" to re-create the advantage they'd enjoyed at Puebla Arboras. These were very different circumstances, however, and their scouts had reported more Holcanos than they'd ever seen. Olayne was no expert in war—God knew he was still learning!—but perhaps King Har-Kaaska would take today's lesson to heart. If he lived.

Olayne thought Reed should've confronted him, reined him in, but perhaps he'd feared a break? And the speed with which he brought up the rest of the trailing division made Olayne wonder if he hadn't expected exactly what was happening and planned for it all along. . . .

Reed beckoned King Har-Kaaska toward him. "Please join Father Orno and I. We'll give them a *real* battle now!"

"No," Har-Kaaska ground out, then modified his tone. "No thank you. I must rally my warriors as they pull back on the left."

"Of course," Reed agreed. "Are your guns loaded, Captain Olayne?"

"Double canister, Colonel Reed."

"Commence firing, if you please."

With four batteries directly in what was becoming an L-shaped line, twenty-four cannon coughing lethal spreads of canister as fast as they could, and now infantry armed with captured and improved Dom muskets firing sheeting volleys, the slaughter was indescribable. But these Holcanos fought more like Grik than men, disdaining casualties and surging into the bloody, corpse-choked crescents in front of the guns as quickly as they formed. Perhaps the Blood Priests that had been among them had inspired a new fanaticism, or Don Discipo convinced them that, as they'd sought to exterminate the other peoples of the Yucatán, their enemies had come to do the same to them. Or maybe it was just that they'd been driven far enough, once too often, by enemies they disdained as less than them, hardly "people" at all, and their initial success against Har-Kaaska's brigade gave them the sense they could crush their ancient enemy once and for all, made them insensible to losses, fear, even pain. To any who doubted, a quick glance behind them renewed their confidence.

They still had the numbers and surged tight enough against the thinning lines that guns had to be pulled back and musketry faltered, men now relying on pikes once more, or bayonets. The nearly broken "veterans" Har-Kaaska had rallied and thrown back in the lines helped take up the slack. Well equipped and trained as they were, Reed's new regiments had never used their modified bayonets in anger and the sand-filled sacks they'd practiced on weren't covered with garish paint, didn't scream and weave and leap and jump and try to stab them with spears or bash in their brains with flint-studded clubs.

"All guns are loaded, sir!" Olayne shouted back at Colonel Reed who still sat his horse by Father Orno. He wondered why they weren't dead. Then again, just as the musketry had dwindled to sporadic pops barely audible over the roar of hand-to-hand fighting, few arrows now flew. He noticed Har-Kaaska had finally joined them, his bizarre mount almost bristling with arrows and covered with blood. It seemed not to notice. He'd left the flank to Major Manley, who seemed to be holding well. It was here in the front where the enemy was focused.

"Fine, fine," Reed replied calmly. "Push them through and fire as soon as the muzzles are clear of our fellows. Try not to run anyone over. As soon as you've fired, pull them back and prepare to do it again, but wait until I give the word. Mr. Beeryman and Mr. Burton have taken half our mounted troops to the right and will attempt to annoy the enemy on his own left flank." Olayne was wondering why they took only half when Reed continued. "Cut any dead or injured horses out of your limber traces and prepare to withdraw by prolong. Mr. Joffrion's mounted men will assist you. They'll provide cover, and lend a hand pulling if they must." He nodded forward and frowned. "I *hope* Beeryman's attack and your sudden barrage will give the enemy pause enough for our lads to take a breath and reload their muskets at last, but either way we must be ready to attempt to disengage. Pull back to the trees and the slope behind us. . . ." He fastened his gaze on Olayne. "Under *no* circumstances will you allow any of your guns to be taken. Is that perfectly understood?"

"Of course, sir," Olayne replied indignantly.

Reed waved an apology. "Of course it is," he agreed. "I . . . wasn't expecting a fight today, you know. This is all my fault."

"What remains of *my* brigade will hold the enemy back while you save as much of yours as you can, Colonel Reed," Har-Kaaska said crisply, blinking determination. "This battle was *my* fault, as you well know. I've fought Holcanos most of my life and thought I knew what I was doing. But . . ." He waved around. "I've never fought a *battle*, not like this, and didn't have the first idea. If we survive, you won't find me dismissive of your orders again."

Even over the roar of the fighting, they felt as much as heard the deep *poom, poom, poom, poom, poom, poom!* of a battery of guns, and they all turned to look southwest to see a line of blossoming white flowers of smoke above the blue-green grass on the outskirts of the great collection of dome-like tents on the gentle slope west of the ruined city.

"*Dios salve a tus hijos!* I thought we were certain the enemy had no artillery here!" Father Orno exclaimed. It was the first thing Olayne had heard him say that day, but he wasn't looking. The roundshot arrived at about the time they heard the reports—and he watched it plow gory furrows through the right rear mass of Holcanos. Their paths of destruction were easy to trace by screams and flying debris and long spattering mists of blood that rose above them.

"Those aren't Holcano guns!" he shouted gleefully. "Even if they were, they couldn't *all* hit their own people at an angle that would miss us, even by accident!" Now he saw smoke rising above the city and darker smoke boiling from animal hide tents. "That's *Hudgens's battery!*" he shouted even louder. "Colonel Cayce's here!" Without waiting for Reed's order, he bellowed down the line, "A Battery, B Battery, push your guns forward and fire as you're clear!"

―――――

"Howdy, Cap'n," Captain Bandy Beeryman called out after he snapped at his men to lower their weapons and urged his horse, Dodger, out into a cut in the trees. Coryon Burton hadn't seen anything but followed the big Ranger without hesitation. Lizardbirds exploded from the far side of the cut, and Giles Anson, Capitan Lara, and Lieutenant Fisher trotted out to meet them.

"It's 'Major' now, you know," Anson mock-scolded.

"I heard," Boogerbear conceded. "An' they call *me* 'cap'n.'" He shrugged. "But that's the damn *name* I known you by for fifteen years or more. Ain't likely to change."

Anson laughed and motioned his men to follow him out of the woods. "If there was anything ahead to worry about, *Captain* Beeryman would've already chased it off." He grinned. "An' Captain Burton of the dragoons as well, of course. How are you, Coryon?"

"Fine, sir. Glad to see you." He smiled and nodded at Lara. "Never thought I'd be so glad to see a Mexican lancer!"

"Nor I an American dragoon!"

"We'll join forces and form up in this cut," Anson said, looking at Boogerbear. "I guess you're here for the same reason we are?"

Boogerbear nodded. "Hit 'em in the flank."

"Things look rough down there." Only a few steps by their horses would take them over the crest above the battle.

"Startin' to sting," Boogerbear conceded. "Colonel Reed was gonna stop an' fortify that high ground to the north while we skulked things out an' waited for you. Made good sense. Ol' Har-Kaaska got itchy, though, an' kicked over a anthill. Reed came down to support him, but there's a *lot* o' goddamn ants."

Anson was rubbing the graying whiskers on his chin. "That's what we thought. Well, that's the bad part. Good part is—" He was interrupted by a rolling battery fire from the south and grinned. "We got Hudgens's guns set up, an' Colonel Cayce's advancin' the whole division. Should be alongside the city by now. An' the 1st Ocelomeh should be *in* the city. Enemy was so focused on you, they left the back door open." He snorted. "Not sure there *was* a back door."

Boogerbear was grinning now too. "Soon as them Holcanos get worked up enough, pinched in the nutcracker 'tween First an' Second Divisions, we'll go gallopin' down an' push 'em in the river! Sounds fun." He glanced around. "That Joffrion kid is back yonder with more dragoons. Reed couldn't spare all his mounted fellas, so there's only a couple companies of us. Looks like you got twice as many. But where's little Leonor at?"

Leonor was almost as tall as her father but would always be "little" to her "Uncle Boogerbear."

Anson smirked. "Where do you think? Protectin' her heroic Colonel Cayce. Barely remembers her old man anymore."

"Just as well," Boogerbear declared. "Good for her to care about some-body 'sides us—long as Cayce don't break her heart."

Anson knitted his brows. "That's what I decided . . . once. They do seem to . . . fit in some sort of way. I know they like each other, but . . ." He looked at Lara and chuckled. "She an' Lara 'like' each other, but I don't think they'll ever get past"—he lowered his voice—"that one big, deep-down difference. But there's somethin' 'tween her an' Cayce too. Maybe they're too much alike; too much the killer, in different ways." He frowned. "Or maybe too broken or hurt. Cayce's got a dark side, you know."

Boogerbear nodded.

"Maybe Colonel Cayce rightly recognizes he's too old for her," Lara put in as neutrally as he dared, as if it was obvious.

"Barely ten years. That's just about right," Boogerbear retorted.

"Perhaps so, in a settled world, where a man takes a wife when he's made his fortune and can comfortably provide for her," Coryon Burton inter-jected, also overly casual.

Anson looked at him with wide eyes. "By God. You too? Does *every* man in this army have his sights on my wildcat daughter?"

Burton blushed under his tan. "Not me," he objected. "With respect," he quickly added. "But you might keep an eye on Mr. Meder and Mr. Hudgens."

Boogerbear rumbled a chuckle and rolled his eyes. "Little Leonor, the delicate flower, pinin' for a *man* ta provide for her. Won't do them other fel-las no good anyway. Leonor's full-grown, an' fixed on Colonel Cayce." He looked at Anson. "Like Miss Samantha Wilde's got her hooks in you. She's with Second Division, by the by."

"I thought she was advisin' Alcaldesa Periz. What the hell's she doin' here?" Anson growled.

"Helpin' Dr. Newlin, o' course. An' come to see you."

Dr. Francis Newlin, a somewhat scruffy, scrawny, and bespectacled civilian physician, had been engaged to look after the health of the 3rd Pennsylvania Volunteers so they wouldn't be entirely at the mercy of poorly trained army surgeons. As it turned out, on this world, there wasn't a lot he could teach the Ocelomeh and Uxmalo healers. They not only had a wealth of knowledge about terrible wounds (Newlin had never personally treated a man who'd had his leg *bitten off* and been thrown a fair distance) but had also developed some astonishing antisepsis medications (though sadly still not as effective as a hint of what the Mi-Anakka once had and couldn't replace). Newlin had seen men *shot through the body* already returned to active service, and far more had survived amputations than he ever would've imagined possible. Just as important, local healers understood how to treat or prevent various tropical fevers they insisted were transmitted by *mosquitoes*, of all things, and those sorts of ailments were almost unknown in the army. When heading to Mexico with the 3rd, Newlin had resigned himself to the fact that more men would die of disease than enemy bullets. That was just the way of things. Not here, at least not with *this* army, and that by itself almost doubled its combat power.

In any event, with his medical skills eclipsed by his Ocelomeh and Uxmalo colleagues, Newlin fell back on his training as a chemist, something the locals couldn't compete with. He'd helped organize the medical effort on a large scale, something the locals didn't have much experience with either, but focused on tinkering with less curative chemical compounds, like fulminate of mercury, that would aid the war effort in other ways.

Anson loosed an exasperated sigh, then cocked his head to the side as more cannon sounded and 2nd Division's musketry increased. "Won't be long now. Mr. Lara, you and Mr. Burton ease over the crest an' have a look. Captain Beeryman, let's finish combinin' our commands an' get ready for our little chore. Lancers first? That oughta scare hell out of 'em."

———

"Commence independent fire!" roared Captain Hudgens to his battery.

"You heard him," First Sergeant Petty growled loudly behind his section. "Let them devils have it!"

"Load solid shot!" shouted Corporal Hanny Cox, back at Private Apo Tuin, his Number Six behind the horses and ammunition limber. Another young Uxmalo named Kini Hau, the Number Five, had been standing by Hanny and now trotted back to repeat the command, while Apo—who heard it fine—opened the heavy, copper-covered lid of the chest in front of him and transferred the appropriate round to a large leather haversack carried by Billy Randall (Number Seven). He brought it briskly forward and stopped by Hanny's side. Hanny raised the flap and saw the shiny new six-pound copper roundshot strapped to a lathe-turned wooden sabot with a tightly woven woolen powder bag tied to its base. Seeing the tall Private McDonough raise his staff and rap the muzzle of the 6pdr with the rammer head, he put his hand on Billy's back and urged him forward before casting a quick glance back at Apo.

Ordinarily, a Six was a sergeant and "chief of the piece," but for reasons First Sergeant Petty hadn't made plain, the Number Two gun's sergeant went to the 3rd Pennsylvania, with his nearsighted gunner and a third of the crew. That let Hanny bring most of his infantry squad over with Sergeant Visser's blessing. He had friends around him, and that mattered a lot. Apo was diligent and made a fine Six from a supervisory standpoint, carefully guarding the ammunition and watching the crew like a hawk to prevent accidents. McDonough was a perfect Number One, whose duty in front of the gun, actually loading it while most exposed to an enemy, probably required a man with his brand of grouchy steadiness. Billy and Kini came with him as well, but the rest of his squad was still learning their jobs and were back with the caisson while the remnant of the gun's previous crew filled the other posts.

But as gunner *and* chief, Hanny had more responsibility than First Sergeant Petty led him to expect. Not only did he have to brush up on his duties as gunner, memorize the tables of fire, and in general get more comfortable with something he'd had only limited instruction in, he had to learn Colonel Cayce's modifications to the 1845 manual well enough to train his squad to work seamlessly with the others, some of whom were still somewhat demoralized. Worst of all, in a way, he was only an indifferent horseman to begin with. Normally, the chiefs of the piece and its caisson rode their own horses, and half the detachment rode replacement animals. Due to the shortage of horses and the long trek they'd embarked on with minimal forage, Hudgens's battery wasn't as well mounted as "proper" flying artillery. To Private McDonough's short-lived glee, the entire detachment did indeed ride something, but no one had a horse to himself. In

another departure from the manual, all six horses pulling the gun and limber, and indeed the following caisson carriage, had riders sitting on them.
Drivers—like Hanny had to learn to be, though he was on the rearmost
horse closest to the limber—still rode the lead, or left-hand horses, and
there were a lot of bashed knees and sore legs until the men and animals
learned to work as a team and anticipate one another's movements. Everyone else rode the limber (ammunition) chests, three on each one with arms
interlocked and only a folded canvas gun tarp to cushion their hips and
spines from the jarring, tooth-rattling ride. So there were nine men always
with a gun, theoretically ready to leap down and unlimber it and bring it
into action, and fifteen more on the caisson horses and carriage, their duty
to transfer ammunition forward if the primary limber ran low and serve as
replacements for casualties on the gun. There were no replacement animals,
however, except those that came from the same small herd all the other
mounted men drew from. That meant they got those already worn-out or
no one wanted to ride.

Hanny looked back to the front, saw McDonough seat the ammunition
down the bore, withdraw the rammer, and step outside the wheel. The
Number Three, an older man named Ricken originally from Baltimore, removed his leather-clad thumb from the vent and hurried to the handspike
protruding back from the trail. Hanny stepped forward, placed his sight in
the bracket screwed to the back of the breech, clapped his left hand on the
cascabel, crouched alongside the long wooden trail, and snugged his chin
into the gap between his thumb and fingers so he could align the front sight
with the notch on the adjustable slide, already set at the appropriate elevation for the six hundred yards between the battery and the surging horde of
Holcanos. He gently stroked the right side of the trail, and Private Ricken
used the leverage of the handspike to shift the trail ever so slightly that direction, aiming the gun a little more to the left. Hanny then gave the elevation screw half a turn clockwise to raise his point of aim—the gun had been
rolled back into battery in the deepening tracks the iron-shod wheels made
in the soft, grassy topsoil with the previous shots. He finally retrieved the
sight and stood straight, signaling to the rest of the crew he was satisfied.

Ricken returned to his place by the breech of the gun, pierced the powder bag inside it with a long brass "priming wire," inserted one of the new
paper "tubes" in the vent, and broke off the protruding end. They were very
low on percussion primers for their Hidden's Patent locks, and no one was

sure how to make the newfangled "friction primers" few of the regular artillerymen had even heard of and fewer had seen. About a dozen women
and children in Uxmal had been set to making "tubes" by treating coarse
paper with gummy sap, cutting it in long strips, pressing an edge in a tray
of finely ground gunpowder, then tightly rolling it into a tube a quarter
inch in diameter. These were then painted with a durable shellac, both to
stiffen and protect them from the elements. Breaking them exposed the
powder inside and rather splayed it out, making it easier for the Number
Four man to touch with the smoldering ember on the slow match inserted
in his linstock. After many drill sessions, both before and after a long day's
march, all this took about fifteen seconds.

Ricken stepped outside the right wheel and jerked a nod at Hanny—
who'd had *him* crying "ready" until Petty reminded him that was the gunner's job. That confused and alarmed Hanny, fearing he might get excited
and make the call before all the men were clear, but he did as he was told.
"Ready!" he shouted, for the benefit of his own crew alone, since they
were firing independently. Everyone assumed their positions, the Numbers
One and Two men even with the axles leaning slightly away and covering
their ears.

The Number One gun to their right suddenly fired, blowing smoke
across them. Hanny jumped slightly.

"Frightened poor Corporal Hanny, we did!" cawed a familiar voice full
of glee. No one was fooled by the lighthearted tone shrouding malevolent
amusement.

"Shut yer gob, Hahessy, an' clap onto them spokes," shouted Corporal
Dodd, but his voice lacked conviction. Dodd, a good gunner and chief of
piece for Gun Number One, was never anything but an artilleryman. No
doubt that's why First Sergeant Petty gave him Hahessy as a Number One
man. That made sense. Hahessy was big and suited the position. But though
Dodd was friendly enough and welcomed Hanny and his men to the section and the battery, even helping with their training, he knew Hanny and
the brutal former sergeant had a past that he didn't want to be involved in.
Most of the crew of Gun Number One seemed to feel the same, and that
was starting to build resentment among the crew of Gun Number Two,
even the older hands, already protective of their new gunner. It was a bad
situation. Rivalries between different batteries, even sections within them
was one thing, but crews of the two guns within any section had to be able

to rely on each other. "Back into battery, lads," Dodd called louder. "Swab her out an' we'll do 'er again!"

The smoke had largely cleared in front of Hanny now, not that it mattered. He'd simply aimed his piece into the mass of the enemy. He looked at his Number Four, Andrew Morris, an average-height, wiry man from New Jersey, gently blowing on the glowing end of his slow match. "Fire!" he called. Morris immediately arced his arm up and over the wheel, holding the linstock with the back of his hand forward, and expertly touched the slow match to the splayed end of the tube. Fire jetted up with a *fwoosh!* and the gun boomed and bucked, spewing orange fire and bright white smoke, the muzzle slamming down on the front of the trail between the ironbound wooden cheeks supporting the trunnions, the whole thing lurching back several yards with a clank and jangling rattle as the breech fell back on the elevation screw and brake chain jumped and swayed. The ripping-canvas sound of roundshot flying downrange was short, and Hanny didn't see where it fell through the smoke, but even over the booming of the big 12pdrs to his left and the rumble of distant battle, he heard shrill screams. Without a word, Hanny's crew was already rolling the gun back on the line. Once there, McDonough dipped the fouling-stained sheepskin wrapped around the opposite end of his rammer staff into the heavy iron sponge bucket on the ground under the muzzle. Deftly spinning the staff to throw off excess water, he ran it down the barrel while Ricken pressed his thumb on the vent.

"Missed the whole bunch, ye did. Seen it from here!" Hahessy taunted as he rammed a round down. "Shot plunked down in the river, most likely. Startled a fish er two."

"Reload solid shot!" Hanny called, trying to ignore the man and keep his voice level. McDonough couldn't do it and hoarsely shouted, "That's a god damned lie!" shocking everyone the confirmed Calvinist had chastised for cursing in the past. He seemed unaware.

"A *liar*, I am, am I?" Hahessy demanded darkly, stepping back outside his wheel. "I'll have satisfaction fer that." Dodd hesitated in stepping forward to aim his piece, caught in the middle of the exchange and unwilling to tamp Hahessy down.

"Aye," seethed McDonough. "Nothin'd satisfy *me* more!"

First Sergeant Petty strode up between the guns. "See to your duties, damn you! In case you haven't noticed, we're in action." He focused on

Hahessy and snapped, "*You're* the turd in the puddin' here, *Private*. If you don't leave off tormentin' better men, I'll see you never have another satisfyin' instant in yer' miserable life." Petty wasn't half the size of the big Irishman, but didn't show a trace of fear, deliberately emphasizing the fact Hahessy had been broken from sergeant.

Hahessy sneered at him. "You gonna have me flogged?" He shrugged. "Me back's been scratched before."

"You should'a been hanged. If any man in this section comes to harm because of you, I'll see that you are." He raised his voice to encompass them all. "An' that goes for the rest of you! Cap'n Hudgens is lookin' this way. If he comes an' asks why our rate o' fire is slippin', I'll tell him, by God, that your squabbles are more important than your duty. He was born a Brit, you know, an' came up from the ranks. You think that'll make him sympathetic? He'll more likely flog every man in the section!"

Hanny barely knew Captain Hudgens, but rather doubted that. Still, the 12pdrs to their left punctuated Petty's warning, and McDonough brutally seated the charge and shot the Number Two man had placed in the muzzle. Petty caught his eye as he stepped outside the wheel. "Am I clear, Private?"

"Aye, First Sergeant. Clear tae me an' mine, I ken. Corporal Cox'll see tae that." He flicked a resentful glare at Hahessy. "I'll not harm the blackguardly hurdie."

Hahessy snorted amusement, and Petty whirled to glare at him before stalking to the rear, past the gunners. "Tighten your grip on your men," he growled at them, "an' pick up the pace." He nodded down toward the city. 1st Division was almost up with them now, the regiments quickly deploying out from behind one another in their broad-fronted, densely packed rectangles that lengthened and thinned into battle lines with well-remembered fluidity. There was some confusion—how could there not be after such a long march? But the enemy wouldn't see it from the front. 1st Division would appear to them like a terrible wave rising up and expanding to sweep them away under a colorful spray of regimental and "national" flags, now uncased and streaming in the breeze. And it looked like some of the 1st Ocelomeh was beginning to form outside the north gate of the city, apparently having passed completely through. "We'll have to cease firing shortly, or move to get a better angle."

Even as he crouched to aim his piece again, it struck Hanny strange to see the whole division arrayed in the open once more. The sight of the disciplined ranks of men in blue, wherever they were from, and especially the Stars and Stripes flying over so many, stirred him and gave him heart. It also reinforced what Colonel Cayce had long implied: that everyone here on the field this day—*with some exceptions*, he thought with a final glance at Hahessy—whether they were Americans, Ocelomeh, Uxmalos, Techonos, Itzincabos, Pidros . . . All had come a very long way to fight for that flag, in a fashion. At least for the fundamental principles it represented. He wondered how many felt the same as he, and whether their allies had begun to realize it?

Stepping back from the gun, he waited while Ricken primed it, then called the men to "Ready" and gave the command to "Fire!"

CHAPTER 12

The artillery, both C Battery on the left, and the guns of 2nd Division were tearing the Holcanos up. Roundshot from the left was plowing great, long, diagonal furrows through their seething mass and canister, and point-blank musket fire to their front was literally hacking them apart. Some of that canister and a few warbling musket balls made it all the way to 1st Division, six hundred yards away, but most that had already passed through bodies or struck the ground and was largely spent. Those projectiles might still bruise, even crack a skull or shin, but the time had come to join the fight because the reason 2nd Division's fire had increased was that the Holcanos were finally aware of the danger behind them and were frantically turning to face it.

"Sound the advance!" Lewis Cayce said loudly to his dragoon bugler, Private Hannity, who quickly blew the notes. Drummers all along the line beat out the corresponding tattoos while Major Beck, Major Manley, and Major Ulrich shouted, "First US!" "First Uxmal!" "Third Pennsylvania!" all repeated by captains, lieutenants, then NCOs. "Advance!"

Drums thundered and settled into a common-time cadence as the various company commanders completed their order to "March!" and the long lines moved forward, brightly polished muskets with fixed bayonets riding high on men's shoulders. These regiments were all armed with 1816 and

1835 Springfields, and that glaring, lethal uniformity under the late-morning sun had to alarm the suddenly beleaguered and increasingly apprehensive Holcanos who'd felt on the brink of victory only to learn they were surrounded. Worse, they'd imagine their circumstances were the result of a carefully executed trap instead of the mere chance that brought both divisions upon them at roughly the same time.

"Music?" Major Beck called over to Lewis as he moved slightly away toward the center of the 1st US.

Lewis shook his head. "Drums only, for now."

"What're the odds, I wonder?" Leonor murmured as she walked her horse alongside Lewis's, Varaa-Choon's, and Reverend Harkin's, followed by Private Hannity, Corporal Willis, and half a dozen dragoon guards/messengers. Lewis and Harkin must've been thinking the same, because Lewis merely shook his head and Harkin grunted, clearing his throat, expression serious.

"There are no odds to calculate, my dear," he declared over the rumble of drums and *Poom-poom!* of a section on their left. The shot churned into the Holcanos, and an arm, clearly identifiable, twirled high in the air. "I believe Colonel Lewis remains . . . displeased that Second Division engaged without us. I'm sure there's an explanation. There can be no doubt, however, when one considers the very different paths we followed and the tremendous distances and difficulties we were both forced to overcome, that only divine providence could've brought our two forces here at the precise necessary moment to join"—he glanced at Lewis—"or rescue, if you prefer, Second Division in this battle." He gestured forward. What had been the rear of the Holcano assault was trying to sort itself into a sufficient force to attack them as well. "And His hand is certainly guiding events now. Even I—no military man!—can see that the enemy couldn't be better placed for destruction!" He nodded graciously at Varaa. "Consul Koaar must've already secured the strategic points in the city because some of his Ocelomeh are beginning to assemble outside the northern gate, closest to the Holcanos. The enemy will never get back inside, we won't have to root them out, and the bulk of Don Discipo's strength will be caught in the open and crushed between our two forces."

"*Four* forces, actually," Varaa told him, then grinned at Lewis. "I now understand your plan, my friend."

"Four?" Harkin asked, surprised.

"The river is the third."

"Ah. And that leaves the mounted detachment under Major Anson."

"Yes."

"Let's hope *his* timing's as good as the Almighty's," Lewis said dryly. "A lot of lives'll depend on it."

Leonor looked at him, slightly alarmed. They were going into a sizable action, but this wasn't the same man who commanded so confidently, almost . . . cheerfully at the Washboard. She wondered what the difference was. Looking to the front, she saw they'd narrowed the distance to about four hundred yards. More men would be getting hurt by their own people, firing into the enemy from the other side, but there was no help for that. And they'd soon risk hitting members of 2nd Division as well. *Maybe that's Lewis's problem?* she thought. *This plan was so simple—he cooked it all up on the fly—but it's also so damned . . . untidy. Unless it goes very wrong, he won't get in the thick of it, an' riskin' our own people to each other's fire is so wasteful that he can't take any pleasure in the plan.* It dawned on her then. *We've come all this way for this fight, and he's not going to get to* enjoy *it!*

"They're coming now," Varaa said quietly.

Roughly half the Holcanos, it was impossible to tell for certain, had turned to face them, working themselves into a frenzy. A few dozen arrows were already lofting their way but couldn't fly this far. Another pair of roundshot slashed through the warriors, and they seemed to convulse with fury before breaking into a mass sprint in their direction.

"Sound 'halt,' Private Hannity," Lewis told the bugler. "The regiments will engage at their discretion." He turned to a messenger as the notes cut through the drums and the rising, wailing fury of the enemy. "Ride to Captain Hudgens. Compliments, and have him cease firing and prepare his battery to follow our mounted assault."

The messenger saluted and bolted away. Leonor cringed as she always did when Lewis was saluted on the battlefield. His uniform was the same as any mounted trooper's at a glance, but salutes might single him out for disproportionate attention. If the young, excited dragoon had ridden past her, she might've struck him. They were effectively out of the battle at present, however. Everything was set in motion, and all they could do was watch. The bulk of the roaring horde seemed aimed at the middle right, at the juncture between the 1st Uxmal and 1st US, and independent or not, they echoed each other's commands to load and present their weapons, even as the 3rd Pennsylvania loaded and prepared to fire into them obliquely. Apparently, Lewis's commanders were concerned about the same things he was, shouting, "Front rank, ready! Aim straight at 'em! Don't hold high! Fire!"

Nearly the whole line, a quarter of a mile long, erupted in a sheeting wall of flame and smoke with the enemy still a hundred and fifty yards away. Aiming dead-on at that distance, most of the musket balls would strike the earth before they got there, but many would bound up and hit the enemy. Quite a few did, and the mass of Holcanos staggered. "Rear rank, Ready! Fire!"

After that, the volleys were more staggered as companies reloaded and made ready at different rates, but the fire was almost continuous. And the closer the wave of painted, screeching warriors came, the more brutally they mauled them, peeling whole layers off the leading edge.

"Terrible," Varaa said aloud, blue eyes wide, tail swishing.

"You feelin' *sorry* for them savages?" Leonor asked, amazed.

"*I* am," Harkin confessed lowly.

"Not sorry," denied Varaa, "but . . . I believe this division has killed more Holcanos in the last half minute than my Ocelomeh did by themselves in twenty years. I'm glad we're . . . ending their power, but that makes it no less terrible."

"You didn't feel that way about the Doms at the Washboard," Lewis pointed out.

Varaa blinked. "No. You might argue there's no difference between them; Doms and Holcanos are equally depraved. And you'd be right, in a way. But Holcanos are like cruel younglings, yes? They act as they do because they know no better, and in truth my Ocelomeh behaved little better toward them." Her expression seemed to harden. "But the Doms are arguably the most 'advanced' civilization on this continent, and they *do* know better, or should."

"Fire!" *Crash!*

The smoke was so thick, the volleys so fast, they could barely see through it. Men started screaming or dropping out of line as heavy arrows swept straight in. The enemy had to be close. Special details helped the wounded or dragged the dead from the ranks. The toll was mounting, but not quickly, and despite the weight of fire, Leonor knew some Holcanos would live to burst through no matter what. Sure enough, shapes appeared in the smoke, and she put her hand on the grip of one of the Paterson Colts at her side.

"Get that fellow, someone!" cried Captain "Mal" Harris, commanding Beck's 1st Battalion, when an enormous painted Holcano smashed roaring into the line, flailing from side to side with a huge club studded with jagged obsidian, bashing men down, the club quickly red. Bayonets jabbed, and a shot from the second rank turned the warrior's head into a gory, hollow bowl. He collapsed, bowling more men down. A wave of shapes now raced out of the smoke, but they were met by the whole second-rank volley, pitching them down in a glittering spray of flash-lit blood.

"Well done, lads!" Harris shouted. "Front rank, reload and fire at will. Rear rank will maintain volley fire—as convenient."

Lewis actually chuckled at the unorthodox command, but Leonor thought the order made sense and Lewis probably appreciated the young officer's initiative. They'd soon see if his notion had merit—or perhaps not, she realized, because that's when they heard another bugle some distance to the left, repeatedly sounding a series of notes. "Father's here," she told Varaa with a tone of satisfaction.

It was actually Capitan Ramon Lara and two hundred and eighty lancers, backed by Lieutenant Fisher's hundred strong company of carbine- and saber-armed dragoons who swept down on the disordered western flank of the Holcanos who'd turned on 1st Division. It wasn't a very large force, but the enemy only heard the thunder of hooves before the line of charging men, lances down, smashed into them out of the smoke. Piercing screams rent the air as clots of men were skewered and the lancers charged on through, leaving those they missed to the slashing sabers behind them. Holcanos farther on couldn't see what was happening, but the growing, panicked press took on a mind of its own. Faced with the withering fire of infantry to their front and an unknown terror on their right, Holcanos shattered like a clay jug dropped on a rocky slope, its fragments streaming away downhill toward the river.

Lewis stood as high as he could in his stirrups, telescope to his eye. The smoke was pushing east with the charge, and he saw Anson doing the same thing to the Holcanos in front of 2nd Division, peeling them off and away from the embattled troops with an even larger force of Ocelomeh Rangers, Burton's dragoons, and Felix Meder's saber-armed riflemen.

"Sound 'cease firing on the left,' Private Hannity, then sound . . ." Lewis paused and considered. The division hadn't performed any large maneuvers in a while. With so much confusion already, they didn't need more.

Besides, he remained an artilleryman at heart, not an infantryman, and it was possible his own orders would increase the confusion if he didn't state them plainly. "Messengers! Tell Major Ulrich to advance the Third Pennsylvania two hundred paces and perform a right wheel, continuing to press east toward the river. The First US will perform a right wheel in place and rejoin the line. The First Uxmal will . . . damn, I don't even know how to tell them what I want. I'll go to Major Manley myself." Without another word, he pulled Arete's head around and cantered off to the right.

"Shit!" Corporal Willis exclaimed as he, Leonor, Varaa, and Reverend Harkin, as well as a confused Private Hannity and the remaining cluster of dragoons, spurred after him. "You can't just be runnin' off like that, Colonel!" Willis called louder, surly.

"Hush, fool," Varaa scolded, sharing a look with Leonor. "Colonel Cayce isn't thoughtlessly impulsive, nor is he a man to just sit and view a fight. Now he has something to do, and we'll watch over him, yes?" Willis didn't respond, bouncing in his saddle behind them. There was still savage fighting in front of the 1st Uxmal, and Lewis was shouting for the men to take care since some of the lancers and dragoons had already bashed their way this far. So had an increasing mob of Holcanos, however, fighting with the renewed fury of terror to escape whatever unknown thing was pushing panicked comrades into them.

"Just hold them, lads, don't let them through!" Lewis shouted as he brought Arete to a stand by Major Manley, behind the Uxmalos. "They won't press you long!" he assured. "Are you all right, Major?" he asked a pale Manley, whose side was soaked with blood. An Uxmalo lieutenant was trying to get him off his horse.

"I'm fine, sir," Manley answered wanly. "An arrow went through the fat over my hip. I hardly feel it."

Leonor pursed her lips. Manley didn't have as much fat as a bird.

"All the same, you'd best step down and let your orderly have a look," Lewis said.

"Orderly's dead, I'm afraid. Another arrow," Manley added bitterly.

"See to it, Corporal," Lewis ordered Willis, who stepped down without complaint and helped the lieutenant get Manley off his horse. "Captain Suiz," Lewis called to the Uxmalo officer commanding Manley's 2nd Battalion. He was already jogging over. "The Third Pennsylvania and First US are forming a line at a right angle to yours, to the front. Maintain that relative position as they advance, shifting your line to the east. Contain the enemy in the box we're building. Do you understand?"

"I think so, sir," Suiz responded a little doubtfully, but shouted orders in rapid-fire Spanya that Leonor had difficulty following. Lewis seemed satisfied and glanced at Varaa. "Now we move the First Ocelomeh." He paused and a trace of a smile flashed across his face as he looked at the others. "Well, come on."

"You see?" Varaa told Leonor as they galloped behind him. "He only enjoys a battle when he's *in* it, moving *with* it."

"I ain't sure 'enjoy' is the right word," Leonor objected as across the field her father's Rangers and dragoons ignited a similar explosion of violence in front of 2nd Division. The cannon were silent, thank God, and Leonor was glad Lewis had men like Justinian Olayne, who could be trusted to assess the situation and act accordingly. "I don't know what the right word is, though," she confessed.

"He doesn't enjoy the killing," Varaa agreed, "and I know he hates what he calls the 'butcher's bill.' Quite an appropriate phrase. But never doubt he enjoys . . ." Varaa blinked rapidly and flicked her tail over the saddle cantle. "*Savors* living in the *moment* of battle, when every instant becomes an hour, a day, bursting with a thousand sights and sounds and doubts and certainties, overlaid by feelings of grief and fear and triumph and pride, even love and hate more intense than at any other time."

Leonor could only nod. She knew what that was like herself, to a degree—especially the hate part—though she'd never thought of it so. It explained many things. Her father must feel it as well, possibly as much or more than Lewis (with a slightly narrower focus). She'd seen him exhibit even greater exhilaration in the smallest skirmish. Obviously, in spite of her earlier comment about how "terrible" this war was, Varaa felt the same, or she couldn't have described it so well. She glanced at Reverend Harkin, huffing as hard as his horse, and saw the sweaty, righteous determination on his sagging face. *What about him?* she thought. *How did he feel when he fought in the Battle of the Washboard? He did seem awful cheerful. But he's savorin' his holy crusade, an' Lewis an' Father an' Varaa have the cause of beatin' the Holy Dominion. What do I have?* she asked herself. *The cause, sure. The Doms're worse than anything. But that ain't enough, is it? Am I really so busted I can't even spew all the hate in my soul at the Doms?* Watching Lewis Cayce rein in Arete beside Consul Koaar-Taak and the cluster of men around him, including that bizarre Holcano named Kisin, she hoped that watching over Lewis—and her father—would continue to be enough "cause" for her. Could love truly conquer hate?

―――――

With so many of its warriors still in the city, the 1st Ocelomeh was spread thin and didn't present much of an obstacle by the river at first. The Holcanos were more interested in disengaging, however, and by the time most reached the river, recognized their peril, and tried to get around along its banks, the shifting 1st Uxmal had doubled its lines. Just as devastating, as soon as he'd pushed as far as he could, Capitan Lara recalled his lancers and dragoons back behind the 1st US and 3rd Pennsylvania as they pressed remorselessly on, joined by Hudgens's battery in the line, advancing its guns by hand. All were free to deliver crisp volleys and devastating clouds of canister. Most important of all, Major Anson had communicated Lewis's intent to Colonel Reed, and with 2nd Division's own front now substantially clear, it was able to raggedly mirror 1st Division's movement. Within half an hour, the desperate battle had turned to a rout, and the dying, almost helpless Holcanos, most of their arrows spent, were pressed on all sides against the sluggish but deep Usuma River. There was no escape.

As was their custom when all hope was lost, nearly four thousand Holcanos spontaneously started casting down weapons and sitting on the ground, stoically awaiting their fate. Many would die, they were sure. The scope of the battle had been beyond anything in their experience and so must be the wrath of their foes. Those who weren't killed would face a life of captivity and menial labor. That was the way of things. When the firing finally stopped, however, there was no gleeful rush of shrieking Ocelomeh, wading among them and bashing out brains, cutting off heads or stabbing with obsidian or copper-bladed spears. There was only an eerie silence after a flurry of sharp commands as the smoke began to clear.

Lewis, Varaa, Leonor, Reverend Harkin, and Consul Koaar had moved out behind the 1st US to join Major Beck. Anson, Boogerbear, and Coryon Burton, each with a squad of their respective forces, escorted King Har-Kaaska, Alcalde Truro of Itzincab, Colonel Reed, and Father Orno out to meet them. Har-Kaaska's strange mount was studded with broken-off arrows and streaked with blood but didn't have any trouble keeping up with the horses. They were all blood-spattered too, as were their riders, and Har-

Kaaska had a red-soaked bandage on his shoulder, held by a complex web of dingy cloth strips. His pained grin at seeing the rest of them safe was replaced by a rigid-tailed, blinking stare of fury when one of Koaar's aides brought Kisin forward. The former Holcano war chief was covered in drying blood as well, enough to make him look painted again. The spear he'd seized during the fighting in the city had been taken by Koaar before he was allowed to approach. Har-Kaaska reached for his basket-hilt sword and winced at the pain in his shoulder. "Why is that murdering fiend still alive?" he demanded.

Varaa urged her mount toward him. "Because he's on our side."

Father Orno looked appalled, and Har-Kaaska glared at her, blinking astonishment. "What?" he roared. "He's been our chief enemy for *twenty years*, responsible for countless atrocities! Do you know what he did at Puebla Arboras? It was . . . unimaginable!"

Kisin wearily kicked his own horse forward. It was a different animal than he'd entered the city with. "You've committed no 'atrocities' against my people?" he asked lowly. "And they do know some of what *Don Discipo* and his vile Blood Priest did at his own city because I told them? I only heard the worst after returning here, however, when Don Discipo came and threw me off as war chief."

"So you *say*," Har-Kaaska hissed.

"So we *found* him," Varaa shot back, "wandering the wilderness with only his own band."

"He fought well in the city, my king," Koaar said begrudgingly, "and lost nearly all the warriors he took in there with us."

"So what?" Har-Kaaska demanded.

Now Lewis eased Arete forward. "Let's all take a breath, shall we? First, I'd like to say how happy I am to see you all. I wish our meeting had been . . . less chaotic and stressful," he added dryly, "but it seems to have turned out . . . if not for the best, then at least fairly well." He frowned. "At the moment. We'll know more when we learn the extent of our casualties. I fear yours must've been heavy."

Colonel Reed, face redder than usual, looked down, then met Lewis's gaze. "I fear so as well," he said. "The men fought splendidly, but we were badly outnumbered until your welcome arrival. Please accept my humblest apologies, Colonel Cayce."

Har-Kaaska expelled a long breath. "*You* have nothing to apologize for,

Colonel Reed. It was my fault," he confessed. "After Puebla Arboras—Colonel Cayce hasn't heard everything that happened there," he inserted with a narrow-eyed glare at Kisin, "and I suppose I let my enthusiasm for revenge get the better of me."

Lewis nodded. "Well, in the future, let's try to ensure our movements are better coordinated."

Leonor knew Lewis would never take his criticism further. Besides, it was apparent from Reed's expression and the Mi-Anakka's blinking, he probably wouldn't have to.

"As for Kisin," Lewis continued firmly, "he's our . . . provisional ally and will be treated as such as long as he acts like one." He gestured out at the surprisingly silent and docile Holcanos, then gazed intently at Kisin. After the roar of battle, the sudden almost quiet, broken only by orders and the moans and cries of wounded, was surreal. "*If* he can regain control of these warriors, of course. He already understands trust will take time and we can't have him *too* powerful, but he has to be strong enough to hold Cayal behind us and secure our line of supply or he won't be of any use."

"Allies," grumbled Father Orno. "They *eat* people!"

"My dear, dear friend!" Reverend Harkin exclaimed, moving his horse toward Orno's. "There's much you don't know either."

"They won't do that anymore," Lewis concurred firmly, still looking at Kisin. "Not ever. Not even ceremonially." Frowning behind at the body-strewn field, he continued. "Speaking of that, we need to finish this business quickly so we can get our wounded behind the walls of the city. We'll have more people injured or killed by predators soon."

"My people already in your . . . custody will help with that, if you allow it," Kisin offered, then snorted. "It isn't the nature of my people to be of use to others." He paused. "Yet we *have* been to the Dominion for too long and they used us up." He added bitterly, "I would rather be on the side of fellow warriors"—he glanced darkly at Har-Kaaska—"even bitter enemies I already trust to be *honest* enemies, than breathe the same air as a Blood Priest again." He looked back at Lewis and grimaced. "Shall we find out together if I can lead . . . that portion of my people you did not destroy?"

Lewis slightly bowed his head, scanning the faces of the others, looking almost challengingly at Har-Kaaska. "Why not? Consul Koaar, please return Mr. Kisin's spear." Har-Kaaska bridled at that, his tail whipping spastically, but Koaar tossed the spear to Kisin without hesitation.

It probably wasn't wise to go among the defeated enemy with the leadership of both divisions, filing on horseback through hundreds of exhausted, terrified warriors just sitting on the ground, but they'd been pushed into a large pocket right on the banks of the deadly river and *knew* they were defeated. There was no fight in them. In addition, almost immediately, Kisin started bellowing for Don Discipo to show himself.

"Come, Don Discipo, you cowardly filth! Eater of turds! Stop hiding!" he roared. "You abandoned your city and all your people to their doom—to a Blood Priest!—then dared denounce *me*, to throw *me* off as a bad war leader!" He looked at the men on the ground as his horse picked its way between them. It balked at the overwhelming smell of blood, but Kisin— poor horseman as he was—forced it to proceed. Lewis followed, straight in his saddle. So did the rest, but Leonor, Boogerbear, and Anson, at least, were intently alert with weapons in their hands. "Let me *see* you, Don Discipo!" Kisin cried in as close to the voice of a small girl as he could manage, and a few Holcanos actually barked amusement. "You are not *afraid*, are you?" Kisin screeked. "All these warriors trusted you to lead them to victory and half or more are dead! Due to interference from you and your Blood Priest master, I was defeated at Itzincab, but I faced my warriors afterward. Come out from whatever hole you've dug. Face *them* if not me!"

Lewis began to hear murmurs of agreement to that. A small cluster of warriors still stood by the riverside, and a number of faces had turned to them as Kisin continued to advance. He finally stopped in front of the standing men and raised his voice to carry. "I have an agreement with our ancient enemies," he declared. "Those who *beat* you here today and shamed the 'mighty' Don Discipo," he added scornfully. "I agreed to a peace that doesn't enslave us and does *not* deprive us of war! There must be changes and some will be hard," he prepared them, "but now we will fight for ourselves, for our future, against the treacherous Blood Priests and hateful Dominion! Through such as their creature Don Discipo, they lie and use us to their ends, while scheming to destroy us when their purpose is done!" He waved back at Lewis. "These, our enemies, *honored* enemies," he stressed, "have never been so false and would now have us with them. Who better to stand beside than those who fairly bested us?" His lips twisted into a sneer as he turned back to the clump of standing warriors. "Fight me, Don Discipo," he yelled. "Die like a man, not a worm. Then I will lead the Holcanos again, to glory and honor this time!"

Shouts of approval rose all around them, and Lewis saw someone actually pushed from the circle of warriors. As soon as he stood alone, all the others sat in the grass, signifying their acknowledgment of Kisin's restoration. Lewis was startled. Not by what happened, especially. He'd rather expected something like this. He was more surprised by the sight of Don Discipo. The former *alcalde* and Dom sympathizer wore fine golden armor over a long purple tunic bound by a golden sword belt. He clearly hadn't been in any fighting, because he was probably the only one among his former comrades not covered with dirt or blood. Only his hair was disheveled, from wearing the gold helmet now hanging from his fingers. Lewis had only seen him once, when the stranded Americans first arrived on this world and completed their march to Uxmal. He'd gotten the impression of a powerful man, somewhat overweight, but self-confident to the point of arrogance. Apparently only the Blood Priest Tranquilo had made him so because this . . . creature, while still robust, was unrecognizable in behavior and was actually shaking with terror, eyes wide and wild, scale armor dully clicking.

"Kisin is a barbarian!" he screeched. "I'm the *alcalde* of Puebla Arboras, brought here against my will. I don't *lead* here, I'm a captive! I beg you, Father Orno! Save me!"

Orno's face was twisted with disgust. "A captive in fine armor, wearing a sword," he practically hissed and turned his horse away.

"Father Orno!" Discipo choked, eyes even wider, more frantic. They settled on Lewis. "Captain Cayce!" he cried. "You remember me!"

Lewis leaned forward in his Ringgold saddle. "It's 'Colonel' now. We met once, and I *do* remember that very night there was an attack on my camp and the city. Good people died. You and Tranquilo were gone the next day."

"But . . . I had nothing to do with that! It was the Blood Priest!" He jerked his head at Kisin. "Whatever arrangement you have with that beast, I can serve you better!"

"How could you possibly do that?" Lewis asked, actually sickened by the display. He hadn't expected this at all. *How could the Holcanos have followed this man?* he asked himself. "You're clearly no leader, and I believe you've lost your army."

"King Har-Kaaska!" Don Discipo pleaded.

"You dare speak to me after what you did? To *beg* of me?" Sometimes it seemed Har-Kaaska's strange mount could actually read his mind, and it took a stride forward as if to stomp the quivering man, but Lewis pushed Arete in front of it.

"I believe Kisin has this in hand. Let's move away. Consul Koaar," he called louder as the Allied leaders began threading their way back through the defeated enemy. Hopefully, enemy no more.

"Sir?"

A wild scream came from behind them, probably when Don Discipo was seized.

"The same as before, if you please. Disarm the Holcanos and sort them out. Stand by to assist . . . Mr. Kisin with that, and remind him of our understanding if he omits any part of it when describing it to his men. Assure them their arms will be returned when we're sure they won't use them on us. Detail troops to help move their wounded who're likely to survive into the city. Identify their healers and bring them as well. The rest will go to the main Holcano camp. We'll protect them—and guard them—there." He paused, frowning. "And do make sure Mr. Kisin *promptly* explains that none of their dead or mortally wounded are to be eaten. Colonel Reed?"

A long, desperate scream arose by the river, and Lewis gritted his teeth but forced a smile. "I'm *glad* to see you, Colonel Reed, King Har-Kaaska— all of you. Honored to meet you again, Alcalde Truro," he said earnestly to the leader of Itzincab. "It's good to be back together, and we must prepare to move as soon as we're rested, resupplied, and reorganized. This campaign has still only just begun, and we have a long way to go. In the meantime, assemble burial parties from each company. The enemy and animal dead will be moved into piles convenient to firewood and burnt. Our dead must be buried, of course, and fires built over the graves."

"Yes sir. Thank you, sir," Colonel Reed replied, but Har-Kaaska was still smoldering. "Allied to Holcanos?" he hissed. "How can you trust them?"

Lewis sighed. "I don't, not really." His lips turned to a harsh slash in his beard. "But the only alternative is to kill them all, and we *will not* do that. If we manage this right, they might even be useful." He looked at Har-Kaaska, Truro, Father Orno, and Colonel Reed in particular. "As you may have caught from what was said earlier, the warriors will largely remain here to secure our line of supply when we advance." He quickly continued before Har-Kaaska could object. "The supply wagons we send back to Puebla Arboras—I assume you're already stockpiling things there?—will carry the

Holcano wounded. Their families on the other hand, all of them, will *walk* back to Itzincab, under guard. We've learned from experience they won't slow the wagons."

"My city? Why?" asked Alcalde Truro.

"Hostages," Leonor said.

"Insurance against the good behavior of the Holcanos," Lewis rephrased. "I don't know if we can build a lasting peace with them or not, but Holcanos do care about their children, even wives. They'll behave for a time at least. And it'll take fewer men to guard them at Itzincab as they plant their own crops and perform other reasonable tasks for the war effort than it would to more heavily guard our supply lines against Holcano raiders."

"I should go home, then," Truro said, frowning. "So many Holcanos, even women and children, will make people nervous." Truro was an unlikely warrior but seemed genuinely disappointed to abandon the campaign and the troops his city had supplied. "I suspect I'll have to protect them as much as guard them."

"I agree," Lewis said. "And frankly, I was surprised to find you here," he added with a smile to lessen the sting. "Your city is crucial to our ordnance production. But if it's possible to keep peace with the Holcanos, they should appreciate the good treatment of their families. They lost, after all, and it's more than they could ordinarily expect. With luck, they'll remember."

"So what's next?" Anson asked loudly as they passed through Hudgens's battery and a gaggle of mixed infantry trying to find their own units. NCOs shouted over the hubbub. Reorganizing troops after any battle was a chore, but there'd been no real plan for this one, besides what appeared fully formed in Lewis's head, and it had required some sudden and unexpected maneuvers. The regiments had gotten confusingly intermixed. They'd kept on fighting regardless, and Lewis was proud of them, but they needed more practice accomplishing large, combined movements without warning—*just as I still need practice directing them more succinctly*, he mused wryly. *Especially with the addition of Second Division. We'll have to keep practicing*, he decided. *It won't do to meet the Doms like this. Our troops may be better, man for man, and have a better cause, but the Doms maneuver with greater precision. If Agon still commands them, they* will *have learned to refuse a flank. Or pounce on one.*

All six guns of the battery were limbering up and tired men were securing implements and reclaiming jackets and accoutrements from limbers as others lifted heavy trails to drop on pintle hitches. Lewis returned Elijah Hudgens's salute and looked at Anson, then glanced at Leonor. As soon as he got his Rangers squared away, Anson would be looking for Samantha Wilde. Lewis wondered why she was here and who else would be with her, but he'd worry about that later. He had plenty of things to "square away" himself.

"We're about to begin the most difficult part of our campaign," Varaa told Anson. She'd spoken surprisingly little, said nothing to Har-Kaaska since their first tense exchange. Lewis wondered what she was thinking. "At least I suspect it will be," she continued. "Few of us have been where we're going." She grinned and whipped her tail. "But there'll be a fine battle at the end, no doubt. Something to look forward to."

"Most difficult part o' the campaign, she says," Preacher Mac McDonough murmured, leaning on the tall right wheel of the Number Two gun, gazing in the direction their leaders went, angling toward the near gate to the city.

"What's that?" asked Kini Hau, dumping soupy black water out of the riveted iron sponge bucket and making sure the wooden lid was locked firmly in place before securing the bucket to the carriage, directly under the tube. Everything about the gun was filthy, and they'd be cleaning and polishing the blackened bronze tube, washing the bucket and other implements as well as the carriage itself, and greasing the hubs, trunnions, and elevation screw as soon as Captain Hudgens told them where they'd camp. Other members of the crew would erect shelters and sort ammunition in the limber chest, replenishing what they'd used from the caisson. Still more, combined with other crews in the battery, would see to the needs of their horses. Even if it hadn't taken any damage and nothing broke from wear and tear, keeping a gun ready to fight took a lot of teamwork.

"I heard it too, God knows how," Hanny Cox said, working his jaw to pop his ears as he returned from the limber where he'd given the gun's pendulum hausse sight to Apo Tuin to stow. "Don't think we were supposed to, but that Warmaster Choon talks pretty loud."

"Aye," Preacher Mac agreed dolefully. "'Specially when her back's up."

Hanny chuckled, but then looked more closely at Mac. Like many, he called the Mi-Anakka "Cats" all the time, but the Scot wasn't known for his sense of humor, so Hanny had to wonder if the pun was intentional. "What're ye gawpin' at, Corp'ral Cox?"

"Nothing, Private McDonough."

"First Sergeant Petty," called Captain Hudgens, trotting up on his dark-striped horse.

"Sir!" Petty barked, stiffening.

"As you were, First Sergeant," Hudgens said, the strong accent that came to him in battle now subdued. He smiled. "Your section did you credit. We're moving the battery back to the other side of the Holcano camp. To 'protect' it. Your First Section and the Third Section'll face your guns outward, half loaded with canister and the other half with solid shot in case any of those big bloody lizards come to call. Second Section's twelve pounders'll both face inward toward the Holcano camp, loaded with canister." They'd already heard enough of the commands to the infantry and dragoons to know they were about to start herding the "prisoners" there. "We'll have riflemen in support and strong pickets, of course, and Captain Olayne's supposed to bring his battery over to watch"—Hudgens arched an eyebrow—"for threats from any direction on *this* side of camp." He frowned. "Dukane's battery had it rough. Lots of casualties, and they lost nearly all their animals. The new D and E Batteries'll form around them, along with much of the new Itzincab regiment. At least for the rest of today and tonight."

"Yes sir," First Sergeant Petty said. "Permission to leave off cleanin' the guns careful till tomorrow if we're just loadin' 'em again—an' might have to use 'em."

Hudgens considered that, then shook his head. "No, clean 'em good first. Hopefully we *won't* have to use 'em, an' can just draw the loads in the morning. I hate putting dirty charges back in limber chests. Fouling on the powder bags sucks too much wet from the air."

"Yes sir."

Hanny had known what the answer would be and stopped paying attention when he saw 3rd Section pull out of line, the Number Six gun in the lead. Beyond, however, a rider was coming: a young man he hadn't expected to see.

"Would ye look at that, now!" Preacher Mac said with something like gleeful surprise.

Apo Tuin had stepped back to tell them the chest was locked and they could climb on it or the horses as soon as the First Sergeant—and Hanny—gave the word. He was chief of the piece, after all.

"That's *Barca!*" Apo exclaimed. "And look! He's an officer now!" A lot of the men had already noticed, and Hanny heard a distinctive growl from the Number One gun. Hahessy. He clenched his teeth and ignored it as the young black man stopped his horse in front of Captain Hudgens and saluted.

Hudgens returned the salute, peering at the bright shoulder boards on the dark blue jacket. There still wasn't any branch trim. "Why, *Lieutenant* Barca! This is a fine surprise. Congratulations," he added, nodding at the shoulder boards.

"Thank you, sir. It's good to see you again. I'm looking for Colonel Cayce."

"Just missed him," Hudgens said, pointing toward the city. "Went that way with most of the brass." He paused, shaking his head, and couldn't stop a grin. "Just a minute, though. If you don't mind me askin', how'd you do it? How'd you get loose?"

Barca laughed out loud. "If you're asking how I came to leave Colonel De Russy's service, I didn't abandon him unattended. And he's certainly not as . . . needful of me as many seem to assume," he added protectively. "He's performed wonders managing the Council of Alcaldes. Whatever experience and judgment he may lack as a field commander is more than made up for by his political and diplomatic skills." Barca shrugged. "He's a born politician, and I wasn't much help in that respect." His smile faded a little. "Mistress Angelique Mercure—or I should say, the new 'Mrs. Ruberdeau De Russy,' is much better at that than I."

"They got married, then!"

"Yes sir." Barca's smile went away, and he continued carefully. "Unfortunately, and after everything that's happened I can't imagine how, Mrs. De Russy still labored under the misconception that my relationship with her new husband was of the more . . . conventional sort to be expected between our two races in the United States and her own homeland of France."

"Aye." Hudgens brooded. "Sometimes I forget. Slavery's only legal in half the United States, but it's still all over France an' her colonies." He blinked. "Was, at least, where we came from."

Barca nodded. "She knew I wasn't a slave. The colonel, even Mistress Samantha Wilde—her very oldest friend—made that quite clear, but she persisted in expecting me to behave . . . a certain way." He shook his head. "I can't and won't. Colonel De Russy became aware of this . . . friction,"

Barca continued, almost smiling again, "and his fury was so great that I heard him ranting about annulling their marriage, how it wasn't binding in any event since Reverend Harkin didn't perform the ceremony—no offense to Father Orno, I'm sure—and the colonel is actually already married on another world. I believe he won his point, and Mrs. De Russy became almost painfully respectful after that. But"—Barca sighed—"I reminded the colonel that Colonel Cayce had offered me any combat role I asked for and I'd very much like to accept. Perhaps in an effort to restore his newly found domestic bliss, Colonel De Russy agreed on the condition that I escort Dr. Newlin and, as it turned out, Mistress Samantha, to join Second Division at Puebla Arboras. He also insisted I accept a commission." Barca self-consciously fingered one of the shoulder boards.

Hudgens grinned. He'd been a mere artillery private when they came to this world. "Feels strange, doesn't it? Well, whatever you decide, I could sure use you in my battery. Everybody's doin' jobs above their rank."

"Thank you, Captain," Barca said, saluting. As soon as Hudgens returned it, he wheeled his horse toward the city. Then he stopped. "Hanny Cox," he said in surprise. "Apo Tuin. And Preacher Mac!" He grinned. "The last time I saw you—I recognize others as well—you were in the infantry! All of us drenched to the bone, pushing a gun out of the mud. Certainly *that* didn't induce you to transfer to the artillery!"

Apo had a big smile on his face. "No sir. First Sergeant Petty 'induced' us, if that means 'grabbed us up and made us.'"

"Close," Barca nodded. "And it's Corporal Cox now, I see," he added, tilting his visor toward the pair of red chevrons on Hanny's sleeves.

"Yes sir. We've all come a long way."

"By your leave, sir," Petty growled as the second section rumbled away behind them. "First Section, mount up! Gun Number One, you're in the lead."

"Yes, First Sergeant," said Corporal Dodd, repeating the command. That's when all of them heard the hulking Private Hahessy grumble, "Bad enough ta be in the army on a world full o' lizards big as houses, it is, but the shame of it all—we're expected ta trust heathen injuns in the army while makin' peace with savages that eat us! Now we've got darkie officers. It's a damned long way *down*, we've come!"

"Who said that?!" Dodd shouted, though everyone knew.

"I guess I was wrong, Lieutenant Barca," Hanny said, glowering at Dodd and then the big Irishman, climbing up on one of the Number One gun's lead horses. Hahessy didn't look back.

"Perhaps," Barca said thoughtfully. "But you've had the measure of that man since you met him. If anyone can do something with him, it's you."

Hanny could only shake his head at the ridiculousness of that as Barca spurred his horse and galloped toward the ancient city they'd taken that day. "What did he mean by that?" he asked Apo as they climbed on the limber and linked arms with Kini Hau between the chest handles. It was a very tight, uncomfortable squeeze, with only a threadbare gun tarp for padding between their bottoms and the hard, copper-sheathed limber chest lid. "I've got Hahessy's 'measure,' all right. He makes four of me. And he's not even on my gun. How am *I* supposed to handle him?"

Apo looked at him and cocked his head to the side. "You already do. Everybody hates him, and all his . . . *secuaces* . . . have abandoned him. Corporal Dodd is afraid of him. He only taunts and mocks you because he knows you are not. He tries to make you."

"That's a laugh!" Hanny almost shivered. "He scares me to death. He could break my back with his bare hands."

"Yet you always stand up to him. Why?"

Hanny cried, "Gun Number Two, walk on!" then thought about Apo's question as Preacher Mac spurred the lead horse and the gun and limber jolted forward. "I don't know. Because it's right, I guess. Doesn't mean I'm not afraid."

Apo nodded. "About the same way this whole army feels about the Doms, I bet. And because of *that*, your crew, probably Hahessy's, even the whole battery, would back you against him. And Hahessy is all alone."

Hanny hadn't thought of that. He wondered if it was true.

CHAPTER 13

T he last stretch of his tiresome journey back from the Holy City done, the roughest and longest being from Actopan to Vera Cruz, His Holiness Don Hurac el Bendito was battered and exhausted, almost stumbling as he stepped down from the coach in the courtyard of his villa by the sea. All his *madres de hijos* were gathered to greet him, dressed in silky yellow breechclouts suspended by gold-beaded belts. His legs were so shaky that two had to catch him before he fell, but the touch of their smooth naked skin revived him somewhat, and he breathed a great sigh of relief. Obispo El Consuelo, as tired as he, reflexes shot, never would've caught him. Consuelo required a little steadying by the coachman himself. Don Hurac smiled benevolently at all his "*madres*"—he really did love them and fancied they returned a fondness, at least, and managed to straighten under the low evening sun. "Thank you, my dears," he told them sincerely. "I've missed you all terribly, and it's *good* to be home!"

"We expected you days ago," gently scolded his beloved Zyan, the *matriarca* of the household.

"We should have been here," Consuelo grumped, surprising Don Hurac. He wondered if the *obispo* had actually condescended to speak to a woman or was still just obsessed with complaining. "We lost a wheel a *legua* out from Actopan and were forced to return and languish in that pest hole for *days* while another was fitted!"

Don Hurac gaped at Consuelo. He *had* responded to Zyan! Petulant as he remained, perhaps this trip had taught him something useful after all. Still unaware of the fate of His Supreme Holiness, of course, he'd witnessed the growing predominance of Blood Priests and their grudgingly respectful but very real occupation of Don Hurac's Yellow Temple. He'd heard Don Datu describe the growing fragility of pure blood succession within the True Faith, including the elimination of the step of *obispo* altogether. That threatened El Consuelo directly. And despite his former enthusiasm for the frequent blood rituals in the Holy City, he'd been appalled by the sheer wanton excess the Blood Priests engaged in. Unlike Don Hurac, he wasn't as disturbed by the imaginative cruelty as much as a sense that its frequency cheapened the "offerings." Regardless, his eyes had been opened to the threat the Blood Priests posed.

Don Hurac shook his head. "*Teniente!*" he called to the dusty commander of his escorting lancers. They'd wearily drawn up in the courtyard as if on parade. "Dismiss your men. Rest. My household guards are quite sufficient now."

"As you wish, Your Holiness," the *teniente* replied with a dry, croaking voice, before passing orders for his men to see to their mounts and equipment before leaving the barracks outside the villa compound. Don Hurac smiled. The escort had been on continuous duty ever since they left. Any who'd been found drunk or "misbehaving" in the Holy City would've been impaled. Now at liberty at last, he was sure they'd be drunk in a brothel in an hour.

"Help me to my favorite seat," he told his *madres*. "I just want to sit and look about for a moment before we go inside. I may fall asleep as I eat!"

Zyan sent two women for refreshments, and the others attended him as he mounted gentle steps to a platform in the courtyard topped by an ornately carved stone bench. "Do join me a moment, Obispo El Consuelo," he called behind. Consuelo sighed and did as he was told, tottering up the steps and settling on a wicker chair as the *madres* lowered Don Hurac to his bench. There he could see all of Vera Cruz: the lights of the city beginning to show, the setting sun glaring on the ramparts of the great fort on an island out in the harbor. At very low tide it was connected to the mainland by a slimy, slippery, cobbled causeway, but that access was invisible now. As usual, there was little activity in or around the fort, and he suddenly felt concerned by that. *There are too many enemies, within and without, to remain complacent anymore*, he mused. *I must have words with the* alcalde *and* comandante de la guardia. But all was blessedly peaceful at present, the breeze was pleasant, sea tranquil, sunset inspiring as always. His villa was far enough from the city center that all he could hear of it were feeble impressions of boisterous music in the *tabernas* and *salones*. The free sailors from ships at the docks would be celebrating the earth beneath their feet, and even the poorest free laborers always had money for cheap pulque to drown their woes. After the near-nightly mobs baying for blood at the various temples in the Holy City, he found the distant murmur of normality soothing.

Glancing at the fort brooding on the island, he saw two warships at anchor, still "guarding" the amazing heretic steam-powered vessel he'd had moved to the island's own dock under the guns of the fort. Those ships and guns couldn't deter a serious effort by a military peer to destroy or recapture the steamer, especially if an enemy knew how weakly and ineptly both were manned. All the best ships were needed in El Oceano Pacifico to support La Gran Cruzada, and the only "close" troops of note were with General Agon. But the heretic enemy on the Yucatán *wasn't* a military peer, and the single—reputedly formidable—ship they possessed didn't constitute a navy. Not yet.

Otherwise, the Holy Dominion had no external threat in El Oceano Atlantico. Not that it knew of, at least. There were huge, terrible *monsters* capable of smashing ships in the sea, but no real human or demon menace. Occasional pirates of unknown origin and the extremely infrequent "arrivals" from other worlds were the only reason warships stayed in the Atlantic at all. *The heretics are no threat to Vera Cruz*, Don Hurac decided. *But thanks to Don Frutos's stupidity—and those vile Blood Priests who distract Don Datu so—it's up to me and General Agon to ensure they never become one.*

He narrowed his eyes at the sight of three more ships, clearly merchantmen, just coming into the anchorage from the northeast. It was highly unusual for Dominion shipowners to risk the shoals and shallows of the harbor mouth with so little light. Their hidalgo status was often entirely dependent on the existence of their ships, and they could lose everything if they were wrecked. Worse, they'd be burnt alive if their debts surpassed what they could be sold for as slaves. Most captains would anchor offshore for the night and bring their ships in with the morning. The sight made him frown. He noted, however, that the leading ship was on an almost perfect heading to avoid any hazards (he watched often enough to know), and the others were carefully following its course. He harrumphed and gestured out at them for El Consuelo's benefit. "They must be returning from delivering supplies and troops to General Agon at Campeche. I've grown increasingly impatient for a report from him."

Their refreshments came, and they greedily drank the first cups of nectar before more was poured. Don Hurac smacked his lips. "That's better. Wine next, my dear Zyan?" he asked/commanded, a sure sign he wanted a moment in private with the *obispo*. When they were alone, he sighed. "I know how tired you are, but I'd ask that you perform a final service before you rest. Two, services, actually," he stressed apologetically. "First, go to the *alcalde*'s palace and announce our return. I expect him to wait on me in the morning. Not too early," he added with a wan smile, "but there's much to be done, and it's best to get started. Second, and even more important, I want you to see the Dragon Monk and collect any messages General Agon, or indeed, Don Datu has sent me in our absence." Unlike in the Holy City where the marvel of winged dragons coming and going from the temples had become commonplace, enhancing the divinity of His Supreme Holiness, messenger dragons weren't received or dispatched in Vera Cruz. Their very existence was denied or dismissed as exaggerations by travelers attempting to dupe the credulous on the "frontiers." Don Hurac knew that wouldn't hold up forever, especially as the very useful creatures increased in number. For now, however, he preferred they remain out of sight, their base some distance down the coast. A Dragon Monk posing as an ordinary priest, working in the office of the *maestro de puerto*, served as a courier for the dispatches. "You're free after that until I send for you," Don Hurac assured Obispo El Consuelo. "I can almost promise you several days of rest."

El Consuelo stifled a yawn, but bowed his head. "Of course, Your Holiness. It will be done. And thank you."

───────

It's never pitch dark on a clear night at sea, the stars see to that, but Captain Eric Holland and his six hundred raiders embarking by boats from the prize ships had the lights of a good-size city to contend with, not to mention the great navigation light in the tower in the fort, thankfully directed out to sea. At least there was no moon and it was late enough that many of those lights onshore had been extinguished. Otherwise, there were lamps on other ships, of course, and a couple burning braziers on the walls of the fort, but no activity was seen. Why should it be? Capitan Razine had told them as much of the history of Vera Cruz as he knew, explaining that, like most cities on the continent, the foundation and great central pyramid was older than time, but the permanent Dom presence only dated from the "Second Expansion" about a century before. In that time, the city had never been attacked, and no one imagined it could be. The guns in the fort were large and fairly new, but the garrison was mostly conscripted local freemen, and their officers felt exiled there. The same was likely true on the warships, though Razine had never spoken to their officers. They were probably hidalgos, like he, but the Blood Priests had been working on the navy longer than anyone and its officers were fanatics. Holland had seen that for himself. In any event, naval and merchant skippers didn't mingle. All that combined—aside from a potentially fatal misstep Holland himself should've foreseen and prevented—to make the grizzled old sailor feel pretty good about their chance for surprise.

Capitan Razine had proven his worth, guiding them past a tricky sandbar and a cluster of rocks not on the chart, straight through the shallows to the deep-water anchorage between the city and the island fort. They saw their objectives at once, even in the low light of dusk: the city waterfront, the two brooding warships, the fort, of course—and USS *Isidra* fastened securely beneath it. Then Razine almost panicked and even Holland feared they'd blown it when he gave the order to anchor *Roble Fuerte*—and *all three* ships smartly rounded into the wind together and dropped their anchors within moments of one another. Holland was proud the sailors he'd trained could perform in such a man-o'-war fashion, but cringed even before Capitan Razine stormed up demanding to know if he was trying to get them all killed. "Why—*how*—would three Dominion merchantmen ever do such a thing?" he'd practically screamed.

"Aye, my fault," Holland had admitted with a wince. "I should'a cautioned the fellas ta be a bit more lubberly about it. Pass the word ta be ready ta cut cables an' beat our way outa this sack, if we must," he called to Second Lieutenant Sessions. They were far enough out, and the wind was enough that Sessions could call over to the ship alongside with a speaking trumpet without danger. That done, they waited to see what would happen. Nothing did.

"When'll the harbormaster send someone out?" Holland finally asked Razine, who seemed to have calmed a bit.

"As I told you, smuggling is a fact of life, and the *maestro de puerto* will want any cargo viewed before it's unloaded so he can collect his bribe. If your bizarre arrival didn't pique his interest enough to send someone at once—with a dozen armed guards," he'd added darkly, "he'll surely wait until morning."

"Maybe it was dark enough; nobody saw," said Sal Hernandez. He was one of only a few Rangers on deck. The rest were crammed below, waiting for their part to begin.

Now it had.

"Quiet an' easy does it," Sal told the men on the oars in his boat. They'd been muffled with bundles of sailcloth in the oarlocks but still squeaked and plopped when the blades hit the water.

"We're not sailors, we're Rangers!" groused an Ocelomeh corporal named Ruaz. He was as good a shot with his shortened Dom musketoon as it was possible to be (he had a good chance of hitting a man at seventy-five yards) but was having more than his share of trouble with an oar.

"We're whatever Cap'n Anson—an' Major Cayce—tell us ta be, now shut yer damn yap!" Sal hissed, despite his sympathy. Of all the strange things they'd trained for, rowing (or steering, in his case) a boat wasn't one of them. They'd pulled around the ship a couple of times one day on the way down when the wind left them, but that was it. Now Sal's Rangers not only had the farthest to go, but arguably the most difficult and numerous tasks. It wasn't fair.

"*Que vaz hacer?*" he murmured to himself, looking ahead. Tightly furled sails dimly lit by glowing stern lanterns, both anchored warships were about two hundred yards ahead, a hundred yards apart, and bow on to them and the northeast wind. *Isidra*, even darker against the island dock, wasn't lit at all and lay another hundred yards beyond. Above loomed the fort—and Sal had to strike all the targets at once with only half his men.

Again, it was a question of boats. The ships that brought them could only carry four apiece. They were pretty big and held thirty men each, but some would have to row back for the rest of their force. Ixtla's infantry and Hayne's dragoons were going for the docks and merchantmen tied there. With the whole city full of thousands of people, they needed the most men. Razine had to show them around, and Captain Holland—who really wanted to come with Sal—went because he was in charge. Second Lieutenant Sessions was coming instead and would lead the boat boarding *Isidra* with a couple more sailors along. Not much resistance was expected there and hopefully most of the Rangers could join Sal's assault on the fort, leaving just the sailors behind. One was a black man named Daney Reese, a miraculous survivor of *Xenophon*'s upside-down crash on this world. Like a very few others, the Ocelomeh had rescued him and nursed him back to health. He'd been on *Tiger* ever since. One thing about Daney, he'd spent four years as an engineman on a riverboat, which meant he had more "steam" experience than just about anybody. He'd determine whether *Isidra*'s engine was operable and how long it would take to raise steam if it was.

Ultimately, though, it was the boat situation that left Sal with only twenty-four fighters to start securing each objective. Razine said the warships with their big—at least a hundred men—crews might be the toughest, even with most of their officers likely ashore. The officers would've taken their boats and the sailors were trapped on the ships. *Good way ta keep 'em from desertin', I guess*, Sal supposed. The water seethed with voracious predators, and nobody knew how to swim on this world. What would be the point? The very thought of falling in the water trying to board an unfriendly ship in the dark sent a shiver down Sal's spine. *Not my job, thank God*, he thought.

They were getting close, and Sal could see the warships better. His eyes had adjusted enough to make him worry his little flotilla would be seen as well, and he cringed with every stroke of the oars, expecting a bright cannon flash and spray of deadly grapeshot. Looking at the boat to his left, he waved to get Sergeant Tinez's attention and motioned him toward the warship on the right. Tinez nodded grimly back and leaned on the tiller, veering for his target. The boat behind immediately turned for the other. That went precisely according to plan, but "the plan" was almost exhausted except for what Holland, Ixtla, and Hayne would do. Razine knew the layout of the city, but no one knew the fort's internal arrangement. Sal expected a few sentries, but otherwise had to plan his attack there as he went.

As for the rest . . . Razine had told them there'd be more sentries on the city dock, but hadn't known how alert they'd be to an approach from the water. Their duty was to protect the ships and cargoes from thieves on land. No one had ever attacked a major Dominion city, and none had even been threatened on the Atlantic coast before. For that same reason, Razine hadn't *expected* vigilant watchers on the warships.

Sal could only pray as he eased his tiller over and aimed his boat for the dock under the new bowsprit the Doms installed on the dismasted *Isidra*. Sessions's boat, just astern, veered slightly left. There was a barge outboard of *Isidra*, snug alongside, apparently to assist with repairs. Sessions had seen it too and was steering straight for it. Sal shook his head. *Sailors'll have it easiest of all, gettin' aboard*. That was fine with him. The quicker they secured the steamer, the quicker some of them could help with the fort. The dock was just ahead.

"Slow down, damn you," he hissed, and Corporal Ruaz chuckled lightly. Sal didn't know what a real sailor would say, but his men eased up on their oars. Several toward the front stood and crouched with oars, ready to fend off as the boat glided gently into the deep darkness between *Isidra*'s bow and the dock with hardly a sound. Now, plan or not, Sal's Rangers fell back on training and experience. The men in the front of the boat, dark jackets and hats invisible, leaped up on the dock with a line. One held it securely while others drew long knives called "Bowie swords" and vanished in the darkness to the left and right. Intended for close work, Bowie swords had been made especially for Sal's Rangers, forged from the iron hoard salvaged from the wrecked transport ships, with hilts and guards like Bowie knives, but longer blades better shaped for stabbing—similar to the gladius-like short swords of the foot artillery. A second man pulled the back of the boat in with another line.

"Get the rest up, Ruaz," Sal whispered, "but keep 'em close till our boys come back."

The boat quickly emptied except for the men who'd return it to *Roble Fuerte* for reinforcements. Sal brought up the rear, still watching all around on the water behind them. "Cast off," he told the men holding the lines and thought he got that right. Two rowers pushed off with their oars as soon as he stood on the dock, and in spite of the prospect of imminent action, he released a sigh of relief. *At least now if I die, it'll be on land*, he told himself. He'd hated every instant on the terrifying water in such a little boat.

A strangled, muffled shout came from one of the warships. It was so quick, followed by silence, he almost thought he'd imagined it. He hadn't, of course.

"Now, sir?" Ruaz asked.

"A moment," Sal told him after a brief hesitation, as unaccustomed to being called "sir" as anything else on this world. A shape appeared from the left. The first man returning.

"One sentry," the young Ranger declared. "Died in his sleep," he added simply, with a trace of disgust.

"Could you see anything on *Isidra*?" Sal asked.

"Our sailors an' other Rangers climbing the rail. No other movement."

A second and third scout returned. All were Ocelomeh, chosen by Sal for their stealth and reputations as ruthless hunters of Holcanos.

"There was no one the direction I went," one said with a note of disappointment.

"More that way," murmured the third man. Now that *Isidra* wasn't blocking it from view, they could all see a large, heavy-timbered gate under an impressive stone archway at the base of the wall of the fort. Two burning braziers flanked the entrance, and a pair of bored-looking men in the yellow-and-black uniforms of Dominion troops sat against the wall, smoking long-stemmed pipes. They seemed to be relying on that and their conversation to keep them awake and couldn't possibly see anything beyond the glare of the braziers.

"*Madre de* Dios," Sal murmured. "The gate's just hangin' open. One side of it, anyway."

There was a low babble of excitement. "This is too easy," Ruaz objected.

"I'd agree," Sal said, shaking his head. "If I hadn't seen the arrogance of green Dom troops with my own eyes at the Washboard, I'd be *certain* of a trap. Even now . . . It's hard not to be suspicious." He nodded at the firelit figures. "But if those're just bored, lazy versions of the ones we fought before, just as arrogant an' never been attacked . . ." He shrugged. "Whatever fight there is, trap or not, we need that gate before a ruckus somewhere else makes 'em shut it. C'mon."

They were almost in position, half Sal's men in the shadows on either side of the smoking guards and the rest with him, waiting to burst through and surprise anyone beyond it—when shooting commenced almost simultaneously on the first ship to be boarded and the distant city dock.

"God damn it!" blared Captain Eric Holland in his best quarterdeck voice. "Push through, damn you. Make a line on the other side before the whole waterfront goes up!" Dragoon Brevet Lieutenant Tom Hayne sketched a salute and sent two companies down the streets on either side of the big, adobe-walled, timber-roofed warehouse that had suddenly become a raging inferno. "What kinda idiot stores so much o'—whatever's in there—in such a place?" Holland seethed at Capitan Razine. The former Dom sailor was still terrified by his part in all this, but that terror—and something else—had combined to make him almost giddy, somehow. "It's Alcalde Borac's pulque, Capitan!" He actually laughed. "All of it. A year's worth of bribes from every ship bringing it into port. It's easier and cheaper to guard it all in one place, not to mention convenient to the docks for taking it in and shipping it out. I fear he'll be quite distressed," he added with mock sympathy.

"What other mass store of 'bribes' do we need to worry about?" Holland demanded. "*Gunpowder?*"

"Oh yes. Who knows what else. And it isn't all bribes. The *patricios* who own nearly everything, even the men I carry cargoes for, did not get rich by being extravagant. They store their wares the same way. There's no external threat," he reminded. "The guards here are supposed to prevent theft"—he actually giggled—"and fires!"

"Gunpowder, by God," Holland seethed. "Now the whole place might blow up in our face. It ain't funny, damn you!"

"It is to me," Razine countered. "You *can't know* how amusing I find it."

Like every great endeavor or military adventure that goes awry, it was one of those little things that hurtled everything else out of control. Ixtla's infantry, mostly Ocelomeh and already experienced warriors, had been given the job of securing the moored merchant ships as they went ashore. This they did, almost entirely successfully and without notice—at least by anyone who lived long enough to sound an alarm. But if the ancients didn't have a terrible, two-faced god named "Almost," they certainly should have. A boat with a partial company of Uxmalo infantry had floundered to the left of the "line" on the way in, and the Ocelomeh infantry detailed to secure the smallest ship at the dock had been pushed inward where they doubled up on another one. The Uxmalos weren't supposed to board any ships and left the little one alone as well, assuring themselves the Ocelomeh would handle it. Hayne's dismounted dragoons, coming in behind the leftmost infantry, naturally assumed the small two-masted vessel was already secure. In the confusion, it wound up entirely ignored, *behind* the invading dragoons.

All might still have been well. Only merchant ships with free crews ever tied to the Vera Cruz dock, but they had to worry about thieves as well. If every freeman in the city had employment, none would sell themselves as slaves. Many wouldn't anyway and resorted to theft, possibly preferring impalement (if caught) to servitude. So the ships kept a watch. It was rarely big or even very diligent since "unprotected" thieves, meaning those not in gangs the *patricios* often supported to torment one another, usually worked alone. (The bounty offered to informers frequently tempted petty criminals to turn partners in.) In any event, that's why both "guards" aboard the little *La Bitcha* were sound asleep.

One old man wasn't asleep—a free crew member who never went ashore, preferring the safety the little ship afforded. At his age he wasn't worried about navy press gangs (most of its sailors died from mistreatment and malnutrition, not battle, and its ships were always shorthanded), and besides, he was a relatively rare "true believer" among the lowest class of freemen, and that earned him consideration by the relentlessly pious navy as well. No, he stayed aboard *La Bitcha* in port solely to protect himself from the terrible temptations of the flesh. He'd suffered dearly from his last transgression and still did. Worst of all, the Blood Priests said he accumulated no grace at all from that kind of misery. Best steer clear.

Thus it was that he was taking his ease, smoking his pipe and contemplating his piety while relieving himself at the ship's head when he saw shadows flitting about on the city dock. Armed shadows. Thieves didn't go armed. Most hired dock guards didn't go armed with anything other than clubs. Mere freemen weren't allowed arms unless on actual duty with *la milicia*. Hidalgos might wear swords and pistols, but only Dominion troops carried muskets—as these many, many men did. In a rising panic, he realized he wasn't watching Dominion soldiers, and he stood abruptly from the "seat of ease" and turned to bolt for the alarm bell. Unfortunately, he'd neglected to pull up his breeches.

Feet tangled, he fell against the headrail—and flipped over it. His scream was drenched by a splash, but then came the terrible, bloodcurdling screams of a man being eaten alive. One of the sleeping guards woke and ran to the alarm bell. Not because anyone could help the old man, but he saw the armed men as well. The bell alerted guards in the *alcalde*'s warehouse full of pulque, all of whom had been drinking as much as they could. Some were smoking pipes. Their sudden terror they'd be caught, drunk on the *alcalde*'s pulque, started a panicked, jostling stampede to flee and hide—which resulted in the inevitable. That's how "almost" nearly destroyed Holland's raid before it began.

The fire drew other guards, the curious and concerned, a fire brigade was quickly summoned—and so was a regiment of Dom troops quartered in the city, waiting for transport to join General Agon at Campeche. Musket fire erupted in front of Hayne's men as they pressed outward, killing one and wounding another, the yellow-and-black uniforms of Dom regulars illuminated by their weapon flashes. Hayne was a dragoon. He didn't know how many enemies he faced, but knew he had to hit them hard before they established a battle line. He charged half his men. Much the same was happening in front of Ixtla, Dom troops filtering forward as other people fled. Ixtla formed his men, fired a scathing volley, then advanced as well, bayonets flashing in the flames. Lit by the lurid, expanding fires on the dock, Captain Holland's raid on Vera Cruz turned into a battle.

The two Dom soldiers at the fort gate simultaneously saw the first gulp of flame on the distant docks and sudden flashes of musket fire on the warships much closer. They even had an instant to hear thumping reports of weapons before they were back on the ground, kicking in a spreading pool of blood.

"Go now!" Sal hissed. The "ruckus" they'd expected had set his flanking Rangers in motion, killing the distracted sentries with ease. He and his own men were already running for the gate. Anyone on top of the wall above was probably distracted as well, and a shout would only draw attention. That wouldn't be long in coming, regardless. There were more sentries *inside* the gate, probably keeping conscripts in. More alert at first or not, they were ready for *something* now. Or thought they were. Sal had his revolvers, and many of his Rangers carried surprisingly well-crafted single-shot pistols that once belonged to well-to-do Dom lancers. Most were collected after the Washboard, no longer of use to their former owners. The first to charge through and fall upon the inner sentries still wielded Bowie swords, however, and they slammed the sentries to the ground, stabbing, hacking, and slashing amid a chorus of anguished screams. Sal pushed through to join a panting Corporal Ruaz, catching his first sight of the inner layout.

The fort was a primitive design, little more than a great, thick-walled square with no overhead protection for guns or crews on the walls, or even the barracks and other buildings nestled in the center. The single tall tower stood on the eastern, seaward side of the fort, lit at the top by the strikingly bright navigation lamp. A man was silhouetted, looking down, before he quickly vanished and a bell began frantically sounding. Otherwise, men were running in all directions, more than Sal expected to find. Others in various states of undress were responding to the alarm, pouring from the barracks with their weapons and looking around in confusion. Someone must've seen them, and a man wearing nothing but yellow trousers and black boots pointed at them with his sword and shouted, "*Ahi ellos estan! Matalos!*" Sal was surprised to understand him perfectly, then remembered many Dom officers spoke what they called "High Spanish." There was a paltry, rushed fusillade of musket fire in their direction that did nothing but shower them with rock and lead fragments.

Sal raised his revolvers, and many of his Rangers wriggled out of the slings holding shortened Dom muskets secured across their backs. There was a commotion behind him, and Second Lieutenant Sessions rushed in, cutlass in hand, followed by at least half his men.

"*Isidra*'s secure," Sessions cried. "No one aboard except some poor, starving buggers, chained in the bilge. Part of her original crew, but of no use right now. Daney Reese is checkin' the engine, says it looks fine, but the Doms took her boiler apart an' put it back together. No tellin' if it'll hold pressure, an' there's little coal on board. Maybe enough ta raise steam an' get her out of the harbor—if nothin' flies apart—but never enough ta get her home."

"Then we'll hav'ta make sure there's no rush," Sal responded and raised his voice. "Sergeant Sana, take eight men up that stair to the right an' clear the wall above us. *Don't* spike the cannon unless you're pushed back!" He looked at the rest of his men, now almost thirty and spreading out in a line. "Quiet time's over, *mis muchachos*," he snapped, slipping further into his birth language as he always did in a fight. "Let's make 'em think we're *los propios asesinos del* Diablo!"

"Make ready!" roared Corporal Ruaz. "Take aim! Fire!" A ragged but lethal volley of buck and ball slashed at the forming Doms, blowing several to the ground and painfully wounding many more with the drop shot packed in around musket balls.

"At 'em!" Sal roared. "Kill 'em!"

To their credit, even confused, in pain, or still half-asleep, few of the Doms broke and ran, but even fewer had the self-control or time to reload—

even if they'd thought to bring more ammunition—and none had their plug bayonets. They fought like frenzies, using muskets as clubs, but were no match for the murderous Rangers who stabbed, shot, hacked, or beat them down. Sal shot several before coming face-to-face with the shirtless, wild-eyed officer. "*Rendición!*" he rasped, aiming a Colt at an unflinching eye.

"*Nunca!*" the man shrieked and lunged with his sword.

Sal shot him. "Didn't think so," he growled. "*Stupido.*" He looked at Sessions, standing with a bloody cutlass, white teeth gleaming in his dark, lined face.

"Haven't had this much fun in thirty years!" crowed Sessions.

Sal nodded. He'd forgotten Sessions was a privateersman in his youth, essentially a legal pirate. "More 'fun' ta be had in the barracks an' other buildings, I expect. Clear 'em out—but secure the magazine first!" He pointed at a reinforced mound of earth and fitted stones with a copper-sheathed door at the end of a barracks. "That looks like the entrance. Be *careful!* Even if there ain't a suicidal maniac already in there fixin' a fuse, one shot from a pistol'll do it just as well."

"You don't say?" Sessions barked ironically before calling some of the men he brought and dashing toward the apparent magazine.

"Yeah, well. *Lo siento,*" Sal grumbled to himself. Few men were as paranoid about fire—and magazines—as sailors. He looked around. There was still a lot of shooting. Mostly on the other side of the barracks and up on the wall. More men had reinforced Sergeant Sana, and they had a cluster of Doms cornered behind one of the great guns on the wall where it butted up to the tower. Sal had no idea if there was an entrance there, but it was time to check. He'd never been "in charge" of so many men before and felt a little overwhelmed. Everyone seemed to be doing what they were supposed to, however, with virtually no direction from him. He wondered if that meant he'd trained them well or they just didn't need him. "Corporal Ruaz!" he called, and the Ocelomeh NCO ran up with a small squad of men. "Sir!"

Sal pointed at the tower. "Time for that. Shut the back door ta those men on the wall an' stop whoever's up top from sendin' any signals. That light's gotta be visible for miles, up an' down the coast."

Someone had already tried to take the tower, and bodies were scattered by the doorway, some lying halfway in. Sal was saddened to see two of his own, but whether they'd succeeded or not, they'd kept the door open. This time, revolvers freshly loaded, he led the way. More bodies cluttered the ground floor of the tower, and there were even a few at the base of the stone spiral stairs. Two were wounded, still moving, and a pair of Rangers quickly checked them. One that looked like he might survive was tightly trussed. The other, shot through the chest, was still screaming rage and terror, blood spraying from his lips as he feebly fought to reload his musket. A Ranger almost gently took the weapon and slit his throat. Sal was impressed that his men, so ruthlessly trained to fight and kill and conditioned by a lifetime of hatred and fear of the evil Dominion, could still show such compassion. *Our cause is just, we are good, and I'm proud to fight with such men,* he thought. *Time to be worthy of 'em.* "Follow me!" he shouted, taking the steps two at a time.

As suspected, there was a "back door" to the rampart and the next level was full of Doms. They must've thought the lower door was secure because all their attention was outward, on Sergeant Sana's men. Most were loading muskets and passing them through the door to the fighters behind the great gun outside. Sal quickly shot two before he was noticed, then emptied his Colt into the first men to turn. Corporal Ruaz rushed past with two Rangers, Bowie swords flashing in guttering lamplight, stabbing and slashing. Men screamed in terror and pain as others turned to face them and were cut down or shot with pistols. It became hard to breathe in the chamber filled with smoke and the hot copper smell of blood. Sal heard boots chuffing on steps and shot two more men rushing down from above with his second pistol. Underpowered as they were, his Colt Patersons were deadly in his trained hands, and the first Dom fell bonelessly with a small hole in his forehead. The second shot was rushed, exploding the side of the Dom trooper's face in a shower of gore and teeth. Screaming, he fired his musket even as Sal shot him again. He fell facedown and slid to the bottom of the stairs, kicked aside by a Ranger behind Sal. Another Ranger had fallen back, however, face clenched in pain, arm a shattered, blood-spraying ruin. The big Dom musket ball had hit bone.

"Help that man!" Sal shouted, glancing around. All the enemies on this level were dead, and he had seven or eight more Rangers now. One slammed the parapet door and latched it in the face of a Dom outside. Two shots remained in his revolver, and Sal gestured for their fallen man's Bowie sword. His only other weapon was a short knife on his pistol belt. Sword in his left hand, Paterson in his right, Sal pushed up the stairs.

The fight in the tower seemed over, however, and Sal met no one on the next two levels, though he noted a trail of blood spatters on the steps. Only at the top, in the glare and tremendous heat of a large, bright flame backed by polished silver panels and encased in glass to protect the huge "lamp" from the wind, did he encounter a final Dom soldier. This one was an officer, shot or stabbed in the belly. One hand pressed a red-soaked rag against his wound, and the other supported a finely made brass-barreled pistol, its impressively large muzzle weaving slightly but generally pointing at Sal's face. "Stay back, muchachos," Sal called below. "The tower's ours, but I'd like a moment ta . . . reason with a fella up here."

"*Razón?*" the man gasped hotly, young face beaded with sweat and squeezed by a grimace of pain. "*Razonar conmigo?*" he scoffed.

"*Si es posible*," Sal replied calmly, nodding at the pistol and continuing in Spanish, "Do you command here? Put that down and we'll tend your wound."

"You would have me *surrender*? To *you*?" the Dom demanded with a rasping laugh. "I don't even know who you are! But to attack a city of the Holy Dominion, you must be crazed heretics, pagan animals . . . who knows? And what does it matter, after all? I will stop you!"

"By yourself?" Sal asked. The sound of fighting in the fort was fading. There was more fighting elsewhere, he could hear it, but he hadn't had an opportunity to look around. "Your fort has fallen," he said. "You might kill me, but you won't stop us."

The Dom shifted his aim to an enormous copper drum below the great lamp. "I'll shoot that."

Sal didn't know what was in the drum—some kind of animal or vegetable oil, he guessed, and it must burn like hell to light the great lamp so brightly. "So you'll burn us up—you an' me. What'll that accomplish?"

"I'll go to heaven, enshrouded in purifying grace!" the Dom officer exclaimed. "*You* will go to hell, of course, but more important, the flare of the flaming tower will be seen for a dozen *leguas*. Even if no one sees that, the later darkness will bring loyal troops from all over!"

Sal sighed. "Maybe so," he agreed absently, vaguely saddened he had no choice but to kill this young man, suddenly likening his delusions—and those of all his people—to those of intensely cruel children. Still, he'd already begun narrowing all his focus on the T-shaped target formed by the bridge of the man's nose and brow ridge. That's where his bullet would hit. An instant before he would've fired, however, the Dom surprised him and pulled his trigger.

Time seemed to slow, and Sal watched the ornate pistol's cock leap forward, the flint in its jaws striking the frizzen and kicking it back with a shower of sparks. He clenched his teeth, waiting for the flash of priming powder, the blast of the charge that would spit a large ball to blow an even bigger hole in the tank. It would only be a matter of moments before the splattering stream found the flames.

But there was no flash, no blast. Either the weapon was empty or had lost its prime. The Dom officer looked at his pistol, enraged, and Sal didn't shoot.

"Guess you ain't goin' to heaven just now," Sal said in English. The Dom didn't understand the words, but the irony in Sal's tone was clear. He snarled in fury and hurled the pistol at Sal's head. He missed, and the pistol clattered down the steps even as Sal raised his own weapon again. But the Dom didn't attack. Instead of drawing his sword, as Sal expected, he just turned . . . and jumped out the opening behind him. "*Vaya!*" Sal hissed and blinked. He thought he heard a thud below, but there'd been no scream. Some of his men were behind him now, and Corporal Ruaz handed Sal the pistol. It was a nice piece and, aside from a few new dents in the inlaid stock and engraved barrel, didn't seem damaged.

"Don't know why it didn't go off. It must be loaded. Powder fell out the vent," Ruaz said softly. He must've seen it all.

"Lucky," Sal whispered.

Ruaz nodded briskly and said, "Looks like we *do* have the fort, but only God knows what's happening elsewhere."

Stuffing the pistol in his belt, Sal finally took a moment to look around. In front of the lamp, it was hard to see anything beyond the roof support columns of the tower, but easing back behind the silver reflector he looked again. There was still a glare, and he couldn't have seen stars, but burning buildings along the city waterfront and flash of many muskets were unmistakable. So was the flaring shape of the first Dom galleon Sergeant Tinez boarded. The forward half of the ship seemed fully engulfed in flames, and boats full of men were pulling away—the boats intended to bring their reinforcements, no doubt. Just then, the Dom ship exploded with a yellow-red flash that seared Sal's vision, and he barely saw the flaming debris shower down for hundreds of yards in the periphery of the afterimage. A huge *boooom!* rumbled over them and echoed around the anchorage.

Sal clenched his eyes shut while Ruaz and others excitedly jabbered about what they'd seen or worried aloud about friends. When Sal finally opened his eyes, his vision was still dominated by a ghost of the blast, but he thought the fighting on the second ship had ceased, at least long enough for men to throw flaming wreckage over the side. Rising steam shrouded the ship like gunsmoke. Only a huge cloud of orange smoke, lit by floating, burning debris, marked where the first ship had been.

"Look at the city docks!" one of the Rangers cried. Sal squinted. It seemed like the fighting there was spreading out, going farther from shore, but there were obviously more troops—or people willing to fight—in Vera Cruz than Capitan Razine had expected. Sal looked at the light. "You've still got the flag, Ruaz?" he asked.

"I do," the corporal answered, requiring some effort to pull a tightly folded flag that once flew over the wrecked USS *Commissary* from his haversack.

"Tie it up there, in front of the light," Sal told him, pointing at an iron arrangement over the seaward opening in the tower. The devices were above and below every opening and must've been intended to hold shutters or heavy panels to protect the big lamp in bad storms. Minutes later, an oversize American flag was hanging down, the Stars and Stripes brightly lit by the light behind, rippling quite visibly in the gentle night breeze. "Be interestin' ta see what the Doms in the city do when they take notice o' that," Sal said.

Second Lieutenant Sessions huffed up the stairs, splattered with blood and still gripping his cutlass. "Fort an' *Isidra* are both secure," he reported officially. "So's the ship that didn't blow up. Got a few prisoners in her." He frowned. "Slaves, poor bastards. The navy Doms our lads didn't kill all jumped over the side." He had to repress a shudder.

"Casualties?" Sal asked.

"Seven o' our lads—your Rangers—killed. Eleven hurt. I've no count from the ships yet, but the boats are landin' your men that boarded 'em over here. I expect the cost was higher for those lads," he predicted bleakly. "Surprise or not, they had a stiff fight. Worst of all . . ." He lowered his voice. "One of the boats was swamped by the blast. Still," he continued, "your Rangers took or destroyed every objective they were given. Not bad for their first action together, I'd say."

"What about the reinforcements?"

"Got diverted to the city. I saw the signal," Sessions replied. "Those boats'll bring more sailors over to *Isidra* when they return."

Sal was looking toward the city. It seemed like the fighting was starting to fade a little, *or is it just still spreadin' out*? "What's goin' on over there?"

Sessions shook his head. "No idea. My job's *Isidra*. Yours was the warships an' fort. We did our part. The city's up to Cap'n Holland."

Suddenly decisive, Sal shook his head. "*Your* job is now *Isidra* an' the fort. I'll leave half my men with you, under Sergeant Sana." He nodded across the water. "But some o' my Rangers're still in the fight an' I'm takin' the rest over there. I'll use the boats bringin' your sailors."

Sessions wiped blood and gushing sweat off his face with his sleeve. The heat on the lamp platform was unbearable. "Fine. If the boats don't bring one, see if Holland'll send us a healer. Ours got knocked on the head."

"Go down an' catch all the boats, Corporal. Don't let any leave unless they're full of wounded an' headin' for the ships."

To Sal's mortification, Ruaz actually saluted, but then hesitated a moment. "You think we're really doing it?" he almost whispered, asking for himself and his men as he glanced at the city, then the fluttering flag. "You think maybe we're . . . *taking* Vera Cruz? A DOM city?" His voice was growing louder with excitement.

"*Quién sabe?*" Sal replied. "Seems we've got a chunk of it. For now, anyway. Long enough to get *Isidra* out." He gazed out to sea, wondering if *Tiger* would come in now or stay out of sight, on watch. He'd prefer the latter. Looking back at Ruaz, he let a smile spread under his huge, black mustache. "That's what we came for, ain't it? Any more is molasses on the flapjacks— an' I never turned that down. C'mon, Corporal," he added brusquely, heading for the stairs. "As long as we've got *any* Rangers in the fight, our chore ain't done. Maybe Cap'n Holland's found us some horses. I *hate* fightin' on foot!"

CHAPTER 14

D on Hurac had taken a long, luxuriant bath (awakened by one of his *madres* before possibly drowning), drowsily eaten a small meal with several glasses of his favorite wine, and was half carried into his bedchamber. He remembered nothing more. That made him feel even more fuzzy and muddled when . . . *something* snatched him from the depths of a blissfully dreamless sleep. *What a time for someone to clean in my room!* was his first muddled thought. *They're not even using a lamp! Probably don't want to wake me*, he imagined tolerantly, *but they've dropped a large book on the floor.* That was the only explanation that came at once for the loud thump he thought he heard. But it seemed he'd *felt* it as well.

"Please don't trouble yourself now, my dear," he murmured into his pillow. There was no response, and he found that odd but was already drifting back down when he became aware of excited, garbled voices in another part of the villa, accompanied by a strange sort of . . . crackling sound he thought he should know. Then there *was* a lamp, its meager light dwarfed in the expanse of the chamber, and the fine, gauzy netting surrounding his bed was pushed aside. His bleary eyes slitted, then widened at once when he saw Zyan and two more of his *madres* all fully dressed in practical, lightweight "working" robes, belted around their waists. He couldn't remember the last time they'd entered his bedchamber wearing anything at all, and he felt vaguely disappointed.

Zyan held forth a steaming cup of honey-sweetened chocolate. "Drink that," she commanded. She alone dared speak to him so. "Your Holiness must rise at once. There have been . . . alarming events." Don Hurac sat up with a groan and took the cup while one of the *madres* fetched him a clean robe, identical to those he always wore. "Bring another of the sort we keep for guests," Zyan told her. "As plain as possible."

Intrigued and growing worried, Don Hurac gulped his chocolate and allowed himself to be dressed. There was no more heavy "thumping," but the distant "crackle" was near continuous, along with a strange whooshing roar. "What's happening? What part of the night is it?" he asked as Zyan pushed shoes on his feet and helped him stand.

"Not yet midnight," Zyan replied. "I don't know what's happening. Come and see."

Outside in the courtyard, on the raised platform where he and Obispo El Consuelo spoke only hours ago, Blood Cardinal Don Hurac el Bendito, a large percentage of his *madres*, and half a dozen household guards beheld a sight none ever imagined in their nightmares. The great "thump" that awakened Don Hurac was immediately obvious; one of the warships between the city and the island fort had exploded, leaving only burning debris on the water. The other ship's smoldering, misshapen outline had moved, now in danger of crashing into the dock at the base of the fort. Something about that didn't seem right. . . . *The wind is wrong, is it not?* At least the fort seemed fully awake and a signal flag of some sort was streaming from the light tower.

Don Hurac's gaze was drawn to the glare of the Vera Cruz waterfront, and he saw that it was burning. Worse, the flames were spreading, uncontrolled. He supposed at first the exploding ship caused the fire, casting burning bits all about, but then he *saw* the "crackling" sound, the unmistakable flashes of muskets. Clear *volleys* slashed back and forth in the city, where dozens, perhaps hundreds of troops exchanged them, but some of the flashes were scattered, almost as far as the base of the mountains on the Actopan Road he'd descended that day, and he thought he saw more on the Camino Militar leading southeast to Oaxaca. There was nothing on the road north to Tecolotla as yet, but it came very near his villa. It would make a fine bastion for defenders—or whoever their attackers might be. He whipped his gaze back to the distant light tower standing over the fort. "Zyan, my dear, you have better eyes than I do. Can you describe the signal flying in front of the great lamp?"

"Of course, Your Holiness. A portion of it appears blue or black—the light behind makes it difficult to tell—but there are red and yellow—perhaps white?—stripes as well." She paused. "I've seen nothing like it."

"Nor I," Don Hurac replied grimly, "but I've heard it described." He turned to the commander of his household guards. "Call out your men and any of the lancers that might be in barracks." He nodded at the city. "I suspect most are in the middle of *that*, however. Drunk and helpless, no doubt."

"What's happening?" Zyan asked nervously, instinctively clutching his arm. A sense of wretchedness descended on Don Hurac as he realized he *should* have Zyan punished for such a display in front of others. He never would. After his long journey, as much philosophical as physical, he had to admit, he wondered how many other things he'd never be able to do again.

"Riders approach!" called a guard on the wall. If they'd been enemies, they couldn't have stopped them. The gate wasn't even closed. "It's Obispo El Consuelo!" cried the guard in relief. "Heading a column of lancers and two coaches," he added.

El Consuelo was a terrible horseman and nearly fell off his animal when it stopped in the courtyard. The carriages entered the gates as well, amid a clatter of hooves and creaking wheels, but the lancers remained outside, on guard.

"My dear Consuelo!" Don Hurac said, steadying the younger man. He seemed about to drop. "You've had no rest at all!"

"No, Your Holiness," El Consuelo confessed. "There's been no time." His heavy-lidded eyes widened. "We're under attack. By the *demonios Americanos*!"

"And others as well, no doubt. I gathered as much," Don Hurac managed not to add "of course."

"They've taken the fort, all the ships in the harbor, and are ashore in *force*," El Consuelo said. "I . . . I've seen them *myself*! They *fired* at me!" His voice was rising, outrage mixed with panic.

"Perhaps they were only shooting at the lancers you brought," Don Hurac soothed, knowing El Consuelo had never been in physical danger in his life. "Thank you for that. I presume you brought the coaches to evacuate my *madres* and *hijos*?" It dawned on him then that he hadn't seen any of his children in a great while, and he felt a tinge of loss. They would've been presented to him in the morning. . . .

"Indeed, Your Holiness! Those wicked heretics *cannot* lay hands on such as you or your offspring!"

"How very thoughtful, Consuelo. Zyan? See that all your sisters and the children are loaded at once. No baggage, and there's not a moment to lose." He pointed southeast. "I've seen fighting on all the other roads in or out of the city. They'll want to close this one as well."

"I believe the ones who shot at us were coming to do just that," El Consuelo said urgently. "Only a few were mounted. I doubt they brought horses ashore, but they'll take enough in the city."

"Indeed," Don Hurac observed ironically. "How fortunate for *them* we stopped sending lancers to General Agon. Oh, we've been *sending* them— dismounted and armed as infantry—while we kept their animals here!" He sighed. "Quickly now, Zyan, do as I said. No baggage," he reminded. "You'll be well cared for in Techolotla."

When Zyan left to herd all the women and children into the coaches, Don Hurac turned to Consuelo once more. "What was the news from the Dragon Monk?"

"Nothing of consequence, either from General Agon or His Holiness Don Datu. All continues as before, but both are waiting upon *your* latest thoughts."

Don Hurac nodded, then, after a glance around to make sure no one else was close enough to hear, spoke quickly. "I was wrong not to champion you as my successor," he confessed. "You are a good man and loyal." He frowned. "Far more so than that . . . creature of the Blood Priests who defiles my temple in the Holy City! I'll try to right that wrong, somehow. In the meantime, I have another request. You know where the Dragon Monks accommodate their animals, do you not?"

"I . . . Not exactly, Your Holiness. I can find it."

"Go and dispatch a message to *Don Datu only* and report what's happening here, in my name." He paused, thinking fast. "When—if—the dragon returns, it must *not* land unless it sees the yellow pennant. Is that understood?"

"Not land?"

"No." Don Hurac looked at the city again and saw the perimeter of musket flashes still widening. "This does not feel like a mere raid, somehow. In any event, once you accomplish that, make your way to Techolotla as best you can. My *madres* and *hijos* will need you."

"But . . . you . . . ?"

Don Hurac sighed. "I'm simply too tired to flee and I confess a . . . curiosity. I'll remain here to learn what I may. The only ones who know these Americanos are Don Frutos and Tranquilo on the one hand, who *know* absolutely nothing but what their twisted views inform them or they tell each other. General Agon respects them but knows them only as adversaries."

"Are they not?" El Consuelo asked.

"Of course! But what *kind*?" He nodded at the calamity engulfing Vera Cruz. "They're clearly competent and . . . imaginative. But they fight—they've done *this*—because we made them. How dangerous would they be if we simply left them alone? I *must* know that for the good of the Holy Dominion. I'm not yet certain they *must* be as great a peril to the existence of the Dominion and our whole way of life as Tranquilo and his Blood Priests are becoming. What the Blood Priests would *make* of the Americanos, for their own ends," he added darkly.

El Consuelo only stared, mouth agape.

"Will you do as I ask?" Don Hurac pressed.

"Of . . . of course."

"Very well. Half the lancers and all my mounted guards will escort my family to safety. Take the rest of the lancers with you, and stay safe as well!"

"I . . . Thank you, Your Holiness. I shall." He paused. "What will you do?"

Don Hurac was staring at the city, hearing the clatter of hooves as the two coaches pulled out of the courtyard. He couldn't watch. There was still a lot of shooting in the city, but the heavy fighting at its center had reached a crescendo and was tapering off, the apparent "defending" fire dying out. The peripheral shooting was dying as well, even as it spread. He felt a profound sadness, sure that whatever he did, the "way of life" he'd hoped to protect was doomed. Wrapping his robe of office tightly around him and tying the sash around his waist, he looked at El Consuelo. "I'll go down and meet the enemy—before they come and take me. The appearance of that may be important. Farewell, Obispo El Consuelo!"

El Consuelo looked close to tears as he took his horse's reins from the guard holding them and climbed painfully back in the saddle. At times like this, Don Hurac almost envied the heretics' belief in a God who cared about the welfare of His creatures, not just how much misery they'd endure to glorify Him. It was a strange sensation, wanting to ask God to *protect* his young assistant and others he cared for rather than merely accepting them into His realm if they suffered enough to earn it. Just as strange, he found himself wishing that God would watch over *him* as he went down to meet this new enemy they'd made.

All alone, Don Hurac thought, except for the guards and lancers defending his villa, he watched the city a while longer. He didn't know what he was looking for; perhaps a sign his people had turned the tide, or the enemy was satisfied with the destruction they'd wrought and were starting to leave? They'd spread out too thoroughly, and he didn't get that sense. A great flash silently lit the waterfront, and a massive orange cloud full of flaming debris roiled into the sky. A moment later, he was buffeted by a thunderous boom that whipped his robe and shattered glass and crockery throughout the villa. *A sign? No. Only that fool* alcalde's *store of gunpowder bribes he hoped to sell back to the army. There's no fighting nearby, and the enemy has had plenty of time to identify the contents of all the dockside warehouses.* He shook his head and turned, only to see Zyan standing there. Firelit tears streaked her face, and she wore a look of determination like he'd never seen.

"What are you doing here? Why didn't you do as I told you?"

She held up a basket, covered with folded linen. "Here's food," she said simply. "Someone must look out for you."

"But . . ." He blinked. "I'm going down *there*." He pointed. "We know nothing of how the heretics will behave in situations like this! How they will . . . treat women!" He knew what his own people would do in their place and shuddered.

"I'm not afraid, Your Holiness," she stated with finality. "If they treat me—*us*—harshly, perhaps I'll earn enough grace to enter paradise at your side."

Tears welled in his own eyes, and before he could stop, he damned himself to hell for eternity by sending a quick mental prayer to the Heretic God on her behalf. "That . . . that will not happen, my dear," he said. "I don't deserve your devotion, but if you're determined to join me, we'll go down to the sea together." Looking at the still-exhausted *teniente* who'd led his escort of lancers, he gave what he expected to be his final orders in this world. "I'm going to treat with the enemy. I understand they're prone to stop fighting to talk, on occasion. If I'm allowed to live, I may come away with information critical to the survival of the Dominion. I require two of your men to protect us from refugees fleeing the city, but they must be prepared to surrender their arms when we meet an enemy force," he warned. "You'll remain and guard my home from pillagers, but *not* the enemy. Do you understand?"

The *teniente* looked shocked. "Uh, no, Your Holiness, I *don't* understand!"

"You needn't," Don Hurac told him brusquely. "Just do as you're told." He considered. "You may attempt to *bluff* the enemy to keep them out, but under no circumstances fire on them. It may be of the utmost importance to our cause."

"Yes, Your Holiness," the trooper agreed doubtfully.

Don Hurac put his hand on Zyan's back and aimed her toward the gate. "Come, my dear."

"Jesus! What was that?" Captain Eric Holland demanded, working his jaw, trying to pop his ears as he looked back toward the burning dock and rising mushroom of firelit smoke.

"The warehouse full of gunpowder—and other naval stores," Capitan Razine reminded shakily. He was hunkered down by Holland and Ixtla by a heavy freight cart the enemy had overturned to fight behind, and he'd made no secret of his displeasure at being dragged along in the thick of things. Oddly, the stupid cart—still attached to a maddened armabuey and actually being *dragged* down the cobbled street for a time—had served as a moving rally point for the stiffest resistance they'd met so far. The armabuey finally broke free, lumbering and gurgling into the night and half the Doms stayed with it, using the armored beast for protection. Ixtla's infantry killed or drove off the rest of the cart's defenders. Now, despite a few potshots from the gloom, they'd been deploying to press forward once more when the great blast sent everyone instinctively diving for cover.

"Good thing that night watchman was scareder o' what was in them buildings than he was o' us an' told us about 'em," Holland agreed. "Would'a been nice to roll some o' them powder kegs outa there too, but the place was already catchin'."

"Back on your feet! Let's go!" Ixtla roared, a musket ball throwing splinters from the cart at him. He hardly flinched. Hooves clattered toward them, and a squad of Hayne's dragoons skidded to a stop. They'd found *hundreds* of horses in pens behind the burning warehouses, and Ixtla and some of Hayne's men had swept forward to secure the walled plaza around the *alcalde*'s palace to hold the animals. There wasn't any tack, but the mounted troopers quickly fashioned bridles and took their pick, riding bareback. No one had even cleared the *alcalde*'s palace yet. Half a dozen men were watching it and the horses, and no one had shot at them. The *alcalde* himself was either still there or he wasn't. They'd find out later.

Holland looked at Ixtla's men. He had about a company with him: nearly a hundred, and they hadn't taken many casualties. The rest were pushing forward to the west. "Don't let me hold you fellas up," he told the rough-faced Ocelomeh. "I'll be here, for now." He grinned. "This cart makes a good headquarters, an' ever'body knows where it is—now that it ain't movin' anymore."

Ixtla jerked a nod. "Forward!" he bellowed.

"Sir," cried an Uxmalo dragoon. "Lieutenant Hayne's Comp'mets an' he's stopped all the roads but the one runnin' north. We're headin' that way to reinforce Sergeant Zuir, who we ain't heard back from." He shrugged. "Just because the roads're stopped don't mean nobody'll get out, but we ain't seen many slippin' around."

"People think only the roads are safe," Razine explained. "Perhaps they *are* safer since predators often meet armed resistance there. Few people will travel elsewhere. Certainly unarmed. And unless they're *milicia* or hidalgos or higher, you'll find no armed civilians. Those won't have any idea what's happening," he continued, "and few will even think to flee. They will very sensibly *hide*."

"Roadblocks're more pickets than anything," Holland explained. "Keep us from gettin' surprised by troops comin' *in*. You said this is where most of the soldiers goin' to Agon start from. That's who we been fightin'. Don't want more that were almost here sneakin' up on us." He looked back at the dragoon. "That said, *remind* Hayne his men're just pickets, not there to fight anybody off. Just warn us. That'll free up men to join the fight here. We're pushin', not squeezin', hear? Any Dom soldiers *want* to run, that's fine. Take 'em days to walk anywhere to raise an alarm—if they don't get ate."

The dragoon looked surprised. "You think they *will* run?" he asked, then quickly added, "Sir."

Holland frowned. "Some already have. Ain't seen *any* fightin' to the last. Maybe they're all militia."

Razine shook his head. "Militia uniforms have no black cuffs or fac-ings," he reminded. They'd run into some of those, mostly spilling out of brothels, unarmed. They'd simply rounded them up and put them under guard with the horses.

"Then maybe these ain't frontline troops, er they don't fight as hard—or crazy—in smaller groups, which we've busted 'em into," Holland specu-lated.

"I think, more important, they have no overall command, or Blood Priests among them, watching everything they do."

"Could be." Holland looked back at the squad of dragoons. "Carry on." Even as the sound of their horses' hooves began to fade, there came a heavier clatter from the direction of the *alcalde*'s palace. Perhaps forty mounted Rangers came around a corner, lit from behind by the towering flames. Holland was suddenly torn between watching them come and try-ing to distinguish what the wind was doing. It was swirling down in the street, but the higher, heavier smoke was tending in an ominous direction. "'Hoy there, Mr. Hernandez," he greeted Sal. "I take it the fort an' *Isidra* are secure?"

Sal nodded. "Heard you swiped some o' my men. Figured I'd come an' make sure you didn't turn 'em into sailors."

"Small chance o' that," Holland retorted. "Yer welcome to the horses, by the way."

Sal grinned. "First fellas we came across said you were at the 'palace.' You weren't, but we found all these horses just standin' around with nothin' to do. Fellas there said to look for you this way." The grin faded, and Sal gestured behind him. "Things're gonna get bad. Wind's pickin' up, fixin' ta spread the fire. Liable ta burn half the city."

"That's what I'm thinkin'," Holland agreed. "Our little raid might turn into a rescue, if we can ever stop fightin' long enough."

"Rescue?" Sal asked, surprised. "What the hell?"

"You might say we started this damn fire," Holland grumbled. "Can't just let people burn."

Sal waved around. There were Dom bodies around the cart but no one else in view. "Who's to save? Everybody's gone."

"Everyone's *hiding*," Razine said through clenched teeth. "Without a warning they *believe*, they'll most certainly burn."

"*Madre de* Dios," Sal hissed, then added, "Shit." None of them had come here to slaughter civilians, Doms or not. He pointed at Razine. "Can you help us shout 'em out before they do?" Before Razine could reply, he thought of something and told Holland, "There was a commotion back where we got the horses, some dragoons comin' in from the north with important-lookin' prisoners. Two Dom soldiers with a man an' a woman." He paused and arched an eyebrow. "The man's wearin' a fancy robe like that damn Don Frutos had."

"You've caught Don Hurac!" Razine exclaimed in amazement.

"Who's he?" Holland demanded.

"The Blood Cardinal responsible for this *entire* province!" Razine told him with what sounded like a mix of joy and terror. "He's a prize beyond anything else we've accomplished! Beyond your steaming ship, beyond Vera Cruz itself! With him . . . You must keep him safe!"

Sal shook his head when Holland sent him a look. "Nobody was whuppin' on him. Seemed fine to me."

"Don Hurac will help you get people away from the fire," Razine said with complete confidence.

"Why would he?" Sal asked, surprised. "I thought Blood Cardinals were *pendejos*, so far above everybody they don't care who burns. Hell, *they* burn folks all the time."

"That's true for many," Razine agreed, "but Don Hurac is . . . different. He presides over the traditional sacrifices prescribed by the faith, but doesn't add more for his . . . amusement, as some do. He's perhaps more 'of the people' than any of his kind, and the people have real affection for him." He frowned. "Not the *patricios* and some of the other Blood Cardinals, perhaps, and the *alcalde* here resents his intrusions into city affairs, but the people will *listen* to him!"

Holland growled. He wasn't a diplomat. Wasn't a soldier, for that matter. He was just an old and very tired sailor who'd wound up in charge of a minor battle—and an escalating disaster. But he wouldn't let hundreds, perhaps thousands of people—enemies or not—burn alive if he could help it. He'd tell the devil himself to carry a water bucket at the moment. "Give me ten o' your Rangers, Mr. Hernandez. One o' you fellas hoist me on your horse. I'll go have a word with this 'Don Hurac.' You take Razine an' get started roustin' people out," he told Sal. Musketry echoed back from the direction Ixtla went, and Holland spat. "Right in the middle of a god damn fight."

But the fight was essentially over. The combination of Ixtla's then Hayne's aggressive advances (the defenders had no idea how few troops they had) and the growing, obvious menace of the spreading fire eventually generated a kind of very basic "I won't shoot at you if you don't shoot at me" understanding between the combatants, if not an actual truce. Razine was probably right; it never could've happened if the Doms had a unified senior command or Blood Priests attached to their units, but without those things the regular, largely conscripted Dom soldiers quickly concluded their priority must be to evacuate terrified civilians. Seeing Sal's Rangers and more and more of Ixtla's and Hayne's men doing the same, they actually worked together in several instances, including trying to control and direct the fire, if not actually stop it. When Captain Holland arrived with a stunningly compliant Don Hurac—each with speaking trumpets to loudly *order* cooperation—the rescue effort and channeling of confused and frightened people to safety and shelter turned chaos to something resembling order amazingly quickly. Particularly when—and Holland hadn't even asked him to—Don Hurac commanded the Doms to lay down their weapons in favor of buckets. It may not have registered to some, but Eric Holland perfectly understood that Don Hurac—for the first time in history—had *surrendered* a Dom city to an invader.

But the battle to *save* Vera Cruz raged on through the night. Fortunately, like Uxmal, most of the buildings were stone. Even some of the larger ones, faced with adobe, had stone underneath, and many had roofs covered with tiles. Other roofs and nearly all balcony and street vendor awnings were wood or thatched grasses and had to be constantly doused with water. A continuous stream of armabuey carts carried casks of water from public fountains and up from the smoldering harbor front, the buildings there entirely collapsed, flames burning out. Dawn broke through the pall of dark smoke and found Captain Holland in the *alcalde*'s palace, where he'd finally established a proper headquarters west of the path of devastation. Alcalde Borac, a short, puffy little man in gold-threaded clothes, was apparently incapable of understanding what was happening and strenuously objected to the "outrageous imposition" before being locked in the servant's quarters.

Now Holland leaned back in an ornately carved but creaky wooden chair on the ivy-covered veranda of the palace, black soot-muddy boots propped on another chair like he sat on, soiling the intricately embroidered cushion. Pipe dangling limply from his lips, he was staring through red, slitted eyes at the even more impressive herd of horses milling in the court-yard, munching the manicured grass. *Hadn't much thought about it before,* he mused tiredly. *Now I gotta decide what to* do *with this place. Never fig-ured on taking it.*

He glanced to the side, where a beautiful woman, probably midthirties, sat stiffly upright and rigid on yet another of the fancy chairs, staring at small hands clasped in her lap. *Don Hurac's . . . lady, wife, whatever,* he thought. *Name's Zyan,* he remembered. *Little fella seemed mighty protective of her too. I thought women were nothin' but property to these devils.*

"I need a drink," he growled at a dragoon guard standing a discreet dis-tance away. "Pass the word, wilya? Somthin' ta eat too. Then a bath an' some sleep." He nodded at Zyan. "Reckon the lady could do with the same—soon as I've had a real chance ta talk to El Jefe." He heard a shuffle of boots and the distinctive jangle of Sal Hernandez's spur rowels approach.

"Ain't you had enough smoke for a while?" Sal asked. His tone was tired but oddly playful.

"It's out," Holland said, taking the pipe from his lips and shifting his hat back on his head. Sal, Capitan Razine, and Brevet Lieutenant Hayne were escorting the short, rather roundish form of "His Holiness" Don Hurac. All looked worse for wear, with sweat streaked soot on their faces and grimy hands. Don Hurac's brilliant red-and-gold robe was likely ruined, not that Holland cared. To his surprise, however, the Blood Cardinal's first very solicitous-sounding words were addressed to the woman.

"*Está bien, mi querida?*"

"*Estoy bien, y tu?*" the woman replied, still stiff but clearly relieved.

Holland was pretty good with Spanya now. Always had been, in a way, with a number of Mayan sailors in his crew, but this was straight Spanish. He knew he had an atrocious accent but decided to stick with that.

"So, Don Hurac. We didn't have time to visit last night. You know who I am, an' I gathered you're the Blood Cardinal o' these parts. Pretty much in charge of a good-size chunk of territory."

"Yes," Don Hurac agreed. If it bothered him that Holland didn't stand to address him—or he wasn't offered a seat—he made no sign. "My author-ity is somewhat universal, but my direct responsibility extends to and somewhat overlaps with other Blood Cardinals—it's difficult to explain—as far as Techolotla in the north, Puebla to the northwest, Actopan to the southwest, and Oaxaca to the southeast. Vera Cruz is my home."

"He does actually seem to care about the people here," Sal conceded. "Yelled himself hoarse callin' for 'em to quit their homes an' such"—he paused—"an' told his troops to drop their muskets so we'd . . . work together better."

"I saw," Holland agreed, looking back at Don Hurac. "An' I appreciate your helpin' us save your people," he said with a touch of irony. "Never meant no harm to 'em, an' that fire wasn't our doin'. Not on purpose, anyway. Damn sure didn't expect you ta tell your troops ta quit fightin' an' lay down their arms, though. What's with that? We thought you Doms didn't surrender. Fact is, the only experience we have with Blood Cardinals is they *shoot* their men just for retreatin' a bit."

A guard and some frightened servants brought food and drink and set pitchers and plates on a table. Holland snorted and motioned for Don Hurac to sit. Sal and Razine also found chairs, but Sal deliberately put himself between Don Hurac and the woman. One of the servants, dressed only in a loincloth, shakily filled mugs and placed them in reach. He almost dropped the pitcher when he filled one for Don Hurac, and the Blood Cardinal seemed saddened by that. "Doms," he ruminated aloud. "Your name for us could be more insulting, I suppose." He nodded at the servant, who quickly retreated, then leveled his gaze at Holland. "As I understand it, the only Blood Cardinal you've met is Don Frutos. His . . . motivations and mine are quite different." He looked thoughtful. "From your perspective, those differences might be subtle, but I assure you they're profound. Traditionally, I'm one of twelve equal protectors of the True Faith in the Holy Dominion, under the guidance of His Supreme Holiness, and the principal guardian of this province. I take my duty quite seriously wherever I am"—he glanced past Sal at Zyan—"but feel a . . . special responsibility here."

"Torturin' an' murderin' yer people into paradise," Hayne snapped, speaking for the first time. Don Hurac's face reddened under the sweat-streaked soot. "Bringing them to a state of grace," he countered hotly, then sighed. "We can't reconcile our religious differences in an instant, certainly not in the bitter aftermath of our attack upon you and your attack here"—he raised his mug—"over a single cool drink of . . . whatever this is." He took a sip. "Pulque. Just what I needed. And *reconciliation* has never been the way of the Dominion in any event," he continued. "Our way has always been to spread our word, *our* faith, and bring others into the fold."

"Join or die," Holland said.

Don Hurac nodded. "Yes. It is"—he hesitated—"*has* been believed to be the only way. The Holy Dominion is a fragile, flickering light of civilization surrounded by horrors in the darkness of this terrible world of extremes. Before the current . . . unpleasantness, I gave little thought to the Uxmalos, Ocelomeh, and other members of your Yucatán alliance. Upon reflection, I suppose they consider themselves to be that 'flickering light.' But now . . . After hearing what General Agon had to say about them—how they fought!— you Americanos; your war leader, Cayce; your genuine horror over Don Frutos's treatment of his own troops who attempted to retreat just a bit; and finally your efforts to save the helpless here, it strikes me that the Dominion has grown too accustomed to defending the beliefs that support and feed that fragile light with such extremes."

Holland was surprised to hear that—almost—confession, but was equally interested to hear it confirmed that General Agon still lived.

Don Hurac frowned. "And extremes beget extremes," he continued. "No doubt you're aware of the increasing influence of the Blood Priests among us? There's no point debating the merits and heresies separating our faiths, particularly when it's obvious the Blood Priests have built on the foundation of mine," he conceded, "but they go to . . . outrageous extremes." He took a deep breath and blew it out. "I've just returned from a very long trip. First, as I alluded, to see General Agon." He blinked. "Even now he readies his next campaign against you."

Holland nodded. "We suspected as much."

"I then returned here, but immediately went to the Holy City to confer with"—he paused—"my superior. The war between us was much discussed, as were other . . . matters, but so was our shared concern over the rise of the Blood Priests. They've grown very powerful and have taken over many of the untended temples in the Holy City. Mine included. I won't enumerate the excesses they engage in or why I find them so repugnant. To you they would seem only differences of degree. But it should suffice that if the Blood Priests prevail and the True Faith is turned to the full extreme they'd take it to, you'll find the Holy Dominion an even more deadly, implacable foe." He shrugged somewhat vaguely. "I'd find it so as well, since their agenda would fundamentally change the status of Blood Cardinals in the Dominion. Even I wouldn't be safe. Worst of all, to me, would be the effect upon the people in my province, accustomed to my more . . . benevolent protection and *infinitely* less voracious appetite for the effusion of sacrificial blood, which the Blood Priests require as a matter of course."

Holland was trying to absorb Don Hurac's bizarre argument that he was "better" than the Blood Priests because he didn't murder as many people as they would when the holy man pressed on.

"Last night, just back from my journey and still tormented by what I'd seen and learned, I was awakened by your assault. I could have fled. The road to Techolotla remained open. Instead, I had an epiphany." He leaned earnestly forward. "Suffering is the price of Grace and the toll required to enter paradise, but unlike the Blood Priests, I suspect the daily existence of most in this world is suffering enough. Nor does whatever joy one manages to seize from time to time diminish that accumulated grace, and one needn't live in perpetual misery to earn it! Perhaps I even *hope* that God is more like you envision him—capable of compassion and mercy!" He glanced almost shyly at Zyan as if wondering what she'd think of his revelation, then shook his head. "I don't really know anymore. But we have a common enemy, and I'd oppose them if I could. The Blood Priests are a menace to us both!"

"What?" Holland snorted incredulously. "You want an *alliance*? That ain't gonna happen. I'm just a sailor, an' don't rightly know how *I* 'envision' God. An' the weather He's thrown at me over the years leaves me wonderin' how 'merciful' He is. Hell, He might be just as bloody-minded as *you* think." Holland's weather-worn lip curled in anger. "But evil's evil, an' free will is real. *People* decide what's right or wrong—ta be evil or not—an' whether to torture an' murder one another. At some point you Doms *decided* to do that shit, an' we're fightin' ya, Blood Priests an' all. You been after the Uxmalos an' the rest long before any Blood Priests came along, an' any differences you have with 'em *are* only 'degrees' ta us. Maybe you're *less* evil, but you're still evil as hell. If you don't like the Blood Priests, sort 'em out yourself, but we're gonna lick you both."

Don Hurac glanced at Zyan again then looked down. "No. I didn't expect an alliance, per se. As you say, as things stand, I don't see how that's possible." He looked up. "But it is also not possible for us to surrender to heretics in battle. We never have, and I did not *precisely* surrender to you."

"I reckon you did, by God!" Holland countered darkly. "We took everything we came here for an' then some. Don't even know what all that is, yet. An' we were whippin' your soldiers ta pieces before you had 'em quit. *You* had 'em quit," he stressed. "Now, we'll feed 'em an' treat 'em good, but if you stir 'em up, we'll kill every damn one."

Don Hurac sat straighter in his chair, double chin coming up. "I see it differently. Consider it a truce such as that which was held between General Agon and your leader, Cayce, after their great battle. I didn't surrender, certainly not to *you*. I made an . . . accommodation with the fire. Fire is an elemental thing, made by God." He suddenly seemed to wilt. "At least that is what I will *say*. Not that it will do any good."

Sal was shaking his head. "What the *hell* are you goin' on about? *Estás loco!*"

Capitan Razine cleared his throat. "You really *don't* understand, do you?"

Holland glared at him. "What? If you know somethin' you didn't tell me . . ."

Razine nodded toward Don Hurac. "I believe he's beginning to suspect you don't mean to remain here—as am I. He tries to put his defeat in the best light to protect his people from Blood Priest reprisals, but it *won't* make any difference."

Holland was taken aback. "What kind o' reprisals? Sure, I got a little ambitious with my 'cuttin' out raid' an' built a bigger force to do it because we *need* a force like this. An' aye, I thought it'd be a hoot to take the town for a while. Rub the Dom's nose in it. But I never meant to stay! We *can't!*" He looked at Sal. "Your boys an' Ixtla's took the worst beatin'. Most'a yours dead when that boat got swamped. Between wounded an' killed, we got what left? A little over five hundred men to hold a city with four different roads runnin' through it? Ha!"

"Then I did not surrender," Don Hurac said simply. "You came, recaptured *Isidra*, we fought, you left. That's what I'll say. I can only beg you to stay long enough to help find every Blood Priest and their spies in the city— and kill them." He sighed and shook his head. "Even that won't work. Some will have already escaped, bearing eyewitness accounts of our . . . cooperation. And the mere fact no Blood Priests remain will prove me a liar."

"What'll happen?" Hayne asked quietly.

Don Hurac looked at Zyan, wishing he could grasp her hand. "An army will come in a few weeks. It'll take that long to raise one in the closest cities. It won't be a large army, since most of the troops in this region have already gone to join General Agon." His expression hardened. "But after word of what happened here spreads, I've no doubt the army will be led, at least strongly advised, by Blood Priests." He absently rubbed his chin whiskers. "That actually matters little, as far as the people here are concerned." He looked back at Holland. "There's a *reason* Dominion troops don't surrender. What happened to General Agon was bad enough; he lost a battle, but there were mitigating circumstances. Even then, I couldn't have saved him and retained him in command if large numbers of his troops surrendered, or especially if he lost on Holy Dominion soil. Were he to yield *sacred* soil . . ."

"He'd be killed, right?" Holland grumbled. "Good motivation not to lose, that." He shrugged at Don Hurac. "So we'll take you off with us. I meant to do that anyway an' squeeze you for information."

"He still doesn't understand," Razine pronounced flatly, then gazed back at Holland. "Every man, woman, and child in this city would've been expected to die defending it from heretics. Having seen them prevail"—he shrugged—"they can't be allowed to live and pass word that such a thing is even possible."

"By yielding to you for humanity's sake, as *we* all know I did," Don Hurac admitted, "I effectively yielded responsibility for my city—and the nineteen or twenty thousand people within or around it. If you leave, all will die. Rather horribly, in fact. Now that you know *that*, what will you do?"

"*Estás loco!*" Sal snapped again.

Holland rubbed his eyes and suddenly yawned hugely—a result of horror heaped on exhaustion, not indifference. "Shit," he said. "Wish I'd had some sleep before you hit me with this. While I'm at it, I wish I was thirty years younger." He took a deep breath. "All right, we stay. We'll *try* to stay," he qualified. "Lots of 'ifs' involved." His red eyes narrowed. "But we won't fight for no Doms. We'll fight *with* people we *liberated* from Doms, understand? I mean that, an' them words make a difference. I start gettin' the feelin' they don't, we're gone. In other words, we ain't on *your* side, you're on ours. All the damn way. You better start makin' us believe it." He looked critically at Don Hurac's red robe. "An' I'd swap preacher suits if I were you, because you're gonna have to convince your people why you switched sides.

Why they're gonna be fightin' for their lives. An' they will be. Everybody we can trust, arm an' train. That's gonna be interestin' ta see, an' you better get on it quick. *We* don't have an army we can whistle up to come here. Gotta build our own."

He looked up at Hayne. The dragoon was as tired as he was, shifting from foot to foot. "I'm gonna need messengers to the fort, the ships, an' all the fellas combin' the city. I want Ixtla here too. Gonna be fun explainin' this to *him*, I bet," he grumbled with heavy irony. "Sal, you designate some detachments to scout up the roads. *Just* scout," he stressed. "Nobody gets stuck in with anybody without support, got it?" He raised his voice. "Somebody fetch that idiot *alcalde*. I gotta know where all the powder, shot, an' armories are, an' whatever else he's squirreled away we can use." He gestured at the table and raised his voice. "An' *somebody* get me somethin' ta eat besides these puffy little sacks o' air!"

Don Hurac coughed gently into his hand and cleared his throat. "That may not be altogether true."

Holland blinked. "What? Which part?"

"You have a large army at Nautla, I believe."

Holland frowned. "Sure. An' it ain't doin' much. Just keepin' General Agon from gallopin' up the coast an' takin' Uxmal," he said sarcastically. "I don't trust you as far as I can piss against the wind, an' if you think I'm gonna ask Colonel Cayce to weaken any of our forces for your sake, you're crazy." He wasn't about to even hint where Colonel Cayce really was.

"How colorful. But that's not what I meant. There's a . . . slight possibility I may still arrange it so General Agon is no longer a threat to Uxmal." He held up a hand. "I alluded to this before. I can't imagine General Agon and his army ever allying itself to yours. He's devoted to the Dominion. But few men hate the Blood Priests more, and he might be willing to engage in a . . . joint campaign against a common enemy."

"Huh," Holland grunted doubtfully. "I think you're scratchin' a backstay. Wouldn't *joinin'* 'heretics' be even worse than losin' a battle to 'em?"

"Oh, yes, indeed," Don Hurac confirmed. "But that depends upon what the definition of 'heretic' is after all is said and done," he added cryptically.

"I'm too tired for word games," Holland groused. "I thought I made that plain. Besides, what happened here won't stay secret long. How the hell would you 'arrange' anything with Agon?" He stopped, sleepy eyes gone wide. "I'll be. *You* have one o' those flyin' lizards, don't you?"

If Don Hurac was surprised that Holland knew about the things, he didn't show it. He only shook his head. "No. I'm quite sure it's gone by now, carrying word of your attack to the Holy City. The 'secret' will be out even quicker than you thought. But the dragon *should* return, and we might yet make use of it."

CHAPTER 15

MARCH 1848
CAYAL / LA TIERRA DE SANGRE

1st and 2nd Divisions had been in the vicinity of Cayal for ten days, but there'd been little rest for anyone. The arrival of the little army of camp followers, complete with "sutlers" who mostly sold beer, good food, and a few luxury items to off-duty troops, helped with morale. Particularly since their helpers were almost all young women with their hair bound up in white ribbons, signifying their availability to provide . . . recreation. That only after the men availed themselves of the baths also offered, of course. Since one couldn't safely just jump in the river to wash, the baths were popular with everyone. Lewis made it known he'd tolerate the sutlers only as long as beer was the strongest thing they sold and they were scrupulous about quantity. Other women among the "followers," mostly Itzincabos attached to men in the army, made money washing and mending uniforms.

Kisin's warriors stoically accepted the new reality and watched more and more of their families start the long march north, dragging all their belongings. Lewis wondered how such rugged, even savage, but evidently sentimental folk took the enforced separation so well and seemed to trust that their families wouldn't be mistreated. It had been Kisin himself, divested of all barbaric symbols and even his loathsome necklace of dried eyes, who answered.

"You could've killed us. Killed us all. We would've killed *you*," he said simply. "Those we didn't enslave," he continued, expression darkening, "or give to the Blood Priests." He suddenly grinned happily, and his hard, angular face transformed remarkably, as if eased of a terrible burden. "But it didn't happen, and now that I know I don't *have* to be bad, I feel a . . . lightness. A relief. As if the gods never meant me to be bad and I didn't know it." His expression turned serious. "It will still be hard," he admitted. "There are many complaints about . . . the treatment of our dead, the suppression of our culture and traditions. Just not killing Ocelomeh after fighting them so long! Many are confused." He waved his hand in the air. "I'm less so, the more I get used to it—and the more time I spend with them. We're really not so different, and we all hate the Doms. Hatred between our peoples will take time to pass. Perhaps it never will. But as I said before, there's a *kind* of trust between us, and I'm determined to remain hopeful." He eyed Lewis closely. "It doesn't hurt that *your* word enforces our agreement. We're not . . . natural enemies, and my people have taken their defeat by you somewhat better than if we'd been beaten by Ocelomeh alone. And the . . . surprise at our treatment has influenced a willingness to accept your promise that our families will also fare well. That'll change, of course, if they don't, but for now"—Kisin shrugged, perhaps startled by his own admission—"the Holcanos under my control will gratefully do their part, perhaps forever, as long as you do yours."

He seemed to be right. Slaves or not, Kisin's warriors labored like them under the supervision of the Allied cities' nascent Engineer Corps to improve the city's defenses, rebuilding ancient walls and fighting steps. More repaired the gates and improved shelter for supplies and people, while constructing extensive dock facilities to replace those that had virtually disintegrated over ages of neglect. Large parties of increasingly unsupervised Holcanos felled mighty trees in the surrounding forest while armabueys mooed and groaned and grumbled, dragging the woodland giants to the waterfront. There they were trimmed and split with wedges down their length and cut to the dimensions necessary to build scores of stout barges to carry the army downriver. Rotating army details under the supervision of experienced men, Americans and natives, took time from the drill and maneuvers Lewis wanted in order to perform most of the actual construction. It seemed everyone was building something: a "new" Cayal, in more ways than one, robust transports to carry heavy loads down a river the locals said could be . . . vigorous at times, and an army that was rebuilding and reorganizing around reinforcements and supplies that came forward as soon as the city was secure.

Lewis had been out of contact so long he hadn't really known what to expect in that regard. There could've been schisms in the alliance or squabbles over who should send what, so he was slightly surprised and deeply impressed by the sheer scope of the supply effort. Everything they could possibly want—replacement troops, new uniforms, tents, shoes, knapsacks, rations in abundance, good ammunition, more and more horses, tools, spare cannon implements and wheels . . . all was evidence of close cooperation between the Allied cities. Dr. Newlin even brought the first fruits of his chemical experimentation, having successfully—carefully—compounded a respectable quantity of fulminate of mercury. With sufficient copper formed into thin sheets, and stamps and dies made by the blacksmith/gunsmiths in Uxmal, he'd manufactured thousands of percussion caps for the dragoons' Hall carbines, smaller caps for the scattering of revolvers, and the much larger primers for the Hidden's Patent artillery locks. Lewis had fretted that the dragoons in particular were in danger of losing their "secret weapon": the quick-firing Hall breechloaders that made them so lethal. Granted, some of the caps Newlin made tended to explode more vigorously than the men were accustomed to, throwing sharp shards of copper rather painfully about, but they were reliable and well-sealed against moisture with a kind of shellac. One less thing for Lewis to worry about.

Lewis, Anson, Newlin, Olayne, Boogerbear, and Leonor were riding along the riverside southeast of the city inspecting completed barges and observing the preloading of those dedicated to supplies. Lieutenant Barca, Corporal Willis, and Sergeant Buisine rode discreetly behind at the head of a squad of dragoons. Lewis urged Arete onward and spoke to his companions. "Colonel De Russy and the"—he paused and smiled—"rather reluctant quartermaster department he assembled have certainly worked wonders. Our allies have denied us nothing they had the power to send, and organizing and prioritizing it all as well as they have . . ." He shook his head in admiration.

"Never seen anything like it," Anson agreed. "Stuff is still comin' in through Puebla Arboras every day an' we've already got more stuff stockpiled than General Scott ever had for his whole army, I bet."

"We can't take it all with us either. All the more reason Cayal must remain secure—and the Holcanos continue to behave," Newlin pointed out, pushing his spectacles up higher on his nose.

"True," said Lewis. "Let's hope we've provided for that."

"I'm appreciative for all the largesse," said Captain Olayne, "but particularly the artillery ammunition, of course. For the very first time, there's been more than enough for my gunners to practice until their gun tubes are too hot to touch." He chuckled. "And the infantrymen all have sore, throbbing shoulders when they crawl in their tents at night."

"Colonel Reed wants to work with them even more than he has," Barca supplied. "Second Division is still very green, and after the losses it suffered, it's been getting the lion's share of even greener replacements. The problem is, Colonel Reed is probably best qualified to apportion our allies' generosity in preparation for the rest of our campaign. King Har-Kaaska has taken up much of the slack, particularly when it comes to coordinating local labor. Getting the army ready to move, however"—he bowed in the saddle to the bespectacled physician—"has largely fallen to Dr. Newlin once again. And Mistress Samantha Wilde as well."

Samantha had started by helping Newlin with medical logistics back in Uxmal, but both discovered a talent for the art in general and expanded their efforts in all respects. Lewis was concerned about Samantha's presence, no longer because she was a woman (the number of women now following the army made that argument pointless) but because he'd come to rely on her as an advisor to Alcaldesa Periz. He worried the beautiful but headstrong ruler of Uxmal might do something rash without Samantha's calming influence. Anson's reaction to her arrival confused him most, however. Lewis assumed his Ranger friend returned the fine Englishwoman's obvious esteem, but instead of going to find her after the battle—as everyone expected—he'd avoided her entirely. Samantha feigned indifference, of course, but Lewis knew she was startled and hurt. She'd even sent him a note of greeting, indirectly asking him to inform the Ranger that she'd be pleased to see him. Lewis had done so, but Anson merely nodded—and proceeded to make himself scarce around the temporary army HQ in the city. Lewis didn't understand it. Anson was busy—they all were—but he could've found time to say hello. Now Lewis saw Samantha almost every day, but she hadn't even mentioned Anson's name.

"Don't sell yourself short, young man," Newlin told Barca and explained to the others. "He's been more responsible for the hands-on side of our organizational preparations than anyone."

Lewis stopped his horse to remark on that when all of them were probably equally surprised to encounter Samantha Wilde herself approaching them, rigidly but easily mounted sidesaddle atop a magnificent captured Dom officer's horse that looked almost pure Arabian. Wearing an emerald-green dress (a color that always complemented her lightly tanned but otherwise perfect complexion), and with golden blonde hair and—at the moment—searing green eyes, Mistress Samantha Wilde was prettily fuming. The delicate ivory-framed fan she always carried was practically a blur in her hand. Two escorts were with her, a very uncomfortable-looking Hans Joffrion, twisting the side whiskers on his cheek and pointedly avoiding Anson's gaze, and Captain Felix Meder, his boyish face red, expression harassed.

Leonor cleared her throat. "Surprise attack, Father. You mean to run, or charge straight through?" she needled with enough amusement that Anson turned to give her a glare.

"What're you talkin' about?" he growled.

"Yes, *Mr.* Anson," Samantha said coldly. "I'm also curious what tactic you'll employ to evade a direct confrontation. I can't imagine you'd avoid an *enemy* with such determination, so I must conclude that we're still friends, but friends simply *do not* use each other so."

Dr. Newlin coughed into his hand.

Lewis shifted in his saddle to regard the Ranger with wide eyes. "A very astute observation, Mistress Samantha. Positively profound, in fact. I've personally seen him flee from something only once—along with the rest of us—the first time we met one of those large predatory reptiles in the dark. I can't believe he'd equate you with one of those."

"Shut up," Anson snapped. "Sir," he added.

"Primordial fear," Dr. Newlin pronounced, nodding and peering over his spectacles at the increasingly uncomfortable Ranger. "Or perhaps he perceives you as both friend *and* enemy, my dear, and can't form a coherent response." Newlin straightened decisively in his saddle. "In my professional opinion, the subject has retreated to a position of moral, if not physical cowardice."

"Why, you little runt," Anson hissed. "Nobody's *ever* called me a coward, not even for a joke."

"Oh, good heavens," Samantha snapped. "Then call Dr. Newlin a liar—and prove him one. You can make up or duel to the death later, but as the principally aggrieved party, I demand satisfaction at once!"

Anson looked at her. "Of what sort?" he asked warily. Corporal Willis had edged his horse forward and now sniggered. Leonor punched him savagely in the arm, and he squeaked.

"I require an escort for a ride," she replied haughtily, gesturing at Joffrion and Felix with her fan. "These gentlemen were kind enough to convey me this far, but they have other duties, and frankly, I find their monosyllabic responses to my attempts at conversation most tedious. *You* may request to conduct me further, but I *insist* on more animate dialogue."

"You may have rendered him entirely speechless." Lewis chuckled and Anson gave him a forlorn "*Et tu?*" look before letting out a breath.

"I ain't no coward," he said darkly at Newlin. "I just like to think about things that confuse me on my own," he confessed. Spurring Colonel Fannin forward, he removed his hat and bowed in the saddle. "Mistress Samantha, please accept my sincerest apologies for neglectin' you so. Might I have the pleasure of your company for a conversational horseback stroll?"

Samantha touched her fan to her lips and regarded him with an arched brow. "I really shouldn't relent so easily, but I sought you out—quite publicly, in fact—and I detest inconsistency." She glanced at Lewis. "On the other hand, it occurs to me that I might be intruding on plans and schemes of genuine importance." Lewis shook his head, smiling. Samantha sighed. "Very well. Captain Joffrion, Captain Meder, you may consider yourselves detached from your odious detail. Mr. Anson, if you'd be so kind, I've seen nothing of the environs of this isolated outpost. No doubt you've uncovered many wonders over these last several days—while you grappled with your confusion."

"Some interestin' ruins," he acknowledged a little lamely.

"How fascinating!" Samantha said dryly. "Lead on!"

"Shouldn't somebody oughta go with 'em?" Boogerbear rumbled as the two rode away.

"No," said Leonor.

"But them ruins . . . He's a tad flustered an' there's dangerous boogers holed up in some of 'em."

Leonor shook her head. "He'll be lookin' for an excuse to change the subject from time to time, I expect. Prob'ly wantin' ta kill somethin' too."

"Like somebody *else* around here always is," Willis muttered in an aggrieved tone, rubbing his arm.

"You really need to learn when to keep your stupid mouth shut," Barca whispered, leaning close to him. For some inexplicable reason, Willis and the young black officer had actually become friends.

Lewis pulled Arete's head around to lead the group back the way they came. The only difficulty he'd seen was in actually launching the heavy barges once they were complete, and he wanted to talk to Har-Kaaska about getting Kisin to detail more warriors to help with that. The two old enemies would never like each other, but the strange respect he'd always suspected existed between them at least let them work together fairly well. He was thinking about that when Captain Meder suddenly said, "Riders coming, sir. Fast."

Lewis stopped his horse, and the group came to a halt around him. "One is quite clearly Warmaster Varaa. The other's a dragoon. Can you tell who it is, Captain Meder?"

"It's Cap'n Burton hisself, sir," Sergeant Buisine interrupted. "Beggin' yer pardon." Lewis only nodded. Buisine had phenomenal eyesight, almost as good as Varaa's.

"Well," Lewis said unhappily, "they're in a hurry."

It took only moments for Varaa and Coryon Burton to cross the remaining quarter mile and pull their blowing horses up. Corwin saluted. "We may have a problem, sir."

Lewis almost laughed. "Another one?" Normally, Varaa would've *kakked* at that, but she only solemnly blinked and said, "We just got the semaphore relay set up all the way here, and before we could even test it back to Itzincab, this came through." She fished in the leather shooting pouch hanging at her side and handed over a rough, folded piece of the new paper 2nd Division had brought down from Uxmal. It still looked more like parchment than paper but was easier to make and worked well for musket cartridges. Lewis unfolded the page and looked at the words scrawled on it.

The semaphore system still relied on flashing lights in towers or high trees. They had to be in line of sight but might be miles apart, depending on visibility. Obviously, such a long and vulnerable chain of signal posts as Colonel Reed established as he advanced would've been impossible for Lewis to leave on the far more dangerous track to Nautla, but it was still much improved over the simple system they'd used before the Battle of the Washboard because they could send more detailed messages. They had no means of re-creating the fascinating new technology of Morse's electrical telegraph at present, but they did have two men who'd worked with the sets in Philadelphia and New York and learned Morse's tedious but efficient code before the war. That same code could be sent by flashing lights at night and mirrors by day, and a crash course to train semaphore operators to use it had been instigated at once. The beauty of it was, for now, they didn't even have to know English to do it. They just had to record the long and short flashes, the "dots and dashes" they received, and pass them on. Mistakes were made and even wildly compounded at times, but the operators were conscientious, and the essence of the messages could usually be untangled in context.

Lewis didn't know the code either and couldn't have made heads or tails of it, but someone on Colonel Reed's staff had translated it. There was no punctuation, and the grammar was deplorable, but the translator had inserted gaps in appropriate places to help clarify the message, and Lewis was grateful for that.

TO COLONEL LEWIS CAYCE
   COMMANDING THE ALLIED ARMY IN THE SOUTH
   GREETINGS AND CONGRATULATIONS FROM COLONEL RUBERDEAU DE RUSSY AND SIRA PERIZ ALCALDE OF UXMAL FOR SUCCESS OF YOUR CAMPAIGN TO DATE
   ALL ARE ECSATIC WITH NEWS THAT GRIK HOLCANO THREAT IS DIMINISHED AND WE CAN BETTER FOCUS ON BIGGER BUSINESS
   REPORT RETURNED BY SHIP FROM VERA CRUZ TO NAUTLA AND SEMAPHORE FROM NAUTLA TO UXMAL
   CAPTAIN ERIC HOLLAND VERA CRUZ RAIDING FORCE RECAPTURED STEAMSHIP USS ISIDRA AND TAKEN A DOMINION WARSHIP INTACT
   NEITHER SHIP CAN SAIL AT ONCE BUT HOLLAND EXPECTS NO DIFFICULTY COMPLETING REPAIRS BECAUSE IN THE COURSE OF RAID HE XXXACCIDENTALLYXXX CAPTURED THE CITY

Lewis blinked. "My God," he muttered. "That crazy old salt—Holland," he added for those around him, "has *taken* Vera Cruz!"

There were surprised, excited murmurs, but Leonor cut to the chase. "What the hell's he gonna do with it? He can't *keep* it," she said.

Lewis shook the page. "Still reading."

PEOPLE THERE ARE DOMS BUT HOLLAND IS INFORMED BY XXXIMPORTANTXXX DOM OFFICIALTHAT BY LOSING THE CITY TO HERETICS ALL INHABITANTS WILL BE TREATED WORSE THAN HERETICS AND EXTERMINATED

"Jesus wept," Lewis said.

HOLLAND FEELS RESPONSIBLE FOR FATE OF INNOCENT IF MISGUIDED CIVILIANS AND WILL NOT ABANDON THOSE WILLING TO DEFEND THEIR OWN AGAINST THEIR OWN AND REPORTS DESPERATELY AGREEABLE SENTIMENT AMONG THEM TO HOLD THE CITY AGAINST RELATIVELY SMALL FORCES THAT MIGHT SWIFTLY RESPOND

WE CONCUR THERE IS VALUE IN HOLDING VERA CRUZ NOT ONLY AS IMPORTANT SUPPLY ROUTE TO YOU SHOULD OUR HOPES FOR YOUR CAMPAIGN BE FULFILLED BUT AS EXAMPLE THE DOMINION CAN BE DEFIED AND WE PROTECT ITS PEOPLE AGAINST IT AS MUCH THE VICTIMS OF ITS BLOODY TYRANNY

AT THE SAME TIME WE ARE HESITANT TO DIRECTLY REINFORCE VERA CRUZ

HOLLAND CONVINCED GENERAL AGON HAS THE ONLY ORGANIZED FORCE IN THE REGION SUFFICIENT TO DISLODGE HIM BUT WE FEAR AGON MIGHT BREAK THROUGH TO UXMAL IF WE WEAKEN MAJOR ITZAMS FORCE DESIGNATED THIRD DIVISION AT NAUTLA

ITZAM SHOULD KNOW IF AGON TURNS TO RESECURE VERA CRUZ BUT SHIPPING IS KEY AND OURS IS LIMITED

QUESTIONS

DOES AGON HAVE SHIPPING TO SEND SIGNIFICANT FORCE OR MUST HE MARCH

CAN ITZAM SEND SIGNIFICANT AID BEFORE AGON REACHES VERA CRUZ AND AID WINDS UP IN TRANSIT AND UNUSEFUL IN EITHER PLACE IT IS NEEDED

OUR CONCLUSIONS FOLLOW

HOLLAND CANNOT HOLD VERA CRUZ AGAINST A FRACTION OF FORCE AGON COMMANDS

IF HOLLAND MUST EVACUATE VERA CRUZ HE INTENDS TO RE-MOVE AS MANY CIVILIANS AS POSSIBLE

WE CONCUR IN THIS ALSO SINCE THERE COULD BE NO BETTER WAY TO DIFFRENTIATE US FROM THE DOMS FOR ALL THE WORLD TO SEE BUT WE HAVE INSUFFICIENT SHIPPING TO REINFORCE HOL-LAND AND EVACUATE HIM AND OTHERS AT THE SAME TIME

FRANKLY ALL HERE REMAIN UNSURE IF HOLLAND HAS CRE-ATED AN OPPORTUNITY OR PREDICAMENT AND CRAVE YOUR THOUGHTS

Lewis shook the page again. "Damn," he said. "You know what this says?" he asked Varaa and Burton. They both nodded. "When did it hap-pen?" he demanded, handing the message to Dr. Newlin to read and pass along. "They really need to start dating these things." He glowered.

"Good God. What was he thinking?" Newlin barked, clearly getting to the pertinent part.

Varaa glanced at him and blinked thoughtfully. "The message we re-ceived originated in Uxmal, of course, and I'm sure they contemplated Hol-land's naked report for a day, at least, before composing that one." She indicated the page Leonor was now reading. "As swift as semaphore mes-sages fly, it could've been sent as recently as yesterday morning, to arrive here so early today. Perhaps a five-day voyage from Vera Cruz to Nautla, depending on the ship that carried the news . . . Another two days from there to Uxmal." She shrugged. "The action . . . and whatever events oc-curred to influence Captain Holland's decision may have taken place as little as a week ago, or twice that long."

"Enough time for General Agon to have learned of it, particularly if a flying dragon informed him," Lewis said, frowning.

Leonor passed the sheet to Boogerbear. "Reads like De Russy expects *us* to do something about it," she said crossly, "besides figure out what to do next ourselves, now that that loco sailor's tossed a wrench in the works. We're *twice* as far as Agon from Vera Cruz."

"Not quite," Lewis said absently and was tempted to curse Holland as well. His entire carefully laid plan and tediously constructed strategy had just crashed off a cliff. *Or have they?* he wondered. 1st and 2nd Divisions were going to be hard-pressed to get near Agon's southern flank as it was. They'd already come almost four hundred miles through some of the worst country imaginable and still had even farther to go, albeit through easier country. But Vera Cruz was a thousand miles away, much of it through the heart of the Dominion. They'd never get there before the enemy. Lewis pursed his lips in thought. *And we don't have to, of course.* The crusty old mariner was one of only a handful of people, most represented right here, who fully grasped Lewis's entire ambitious scheme for the war, not just the current campaign. The distances were greater, the enemy more ruthless and unimaginably more wicked, and the land itself more hostile, but Lewis's plan to win the war wasn't all that dissimilar from the one General Winfield Scott had intended to employ against Santa Anna to take Mexico City. Neither had the forces or resources to just march up and repeatedly hammer the enemy, toe-to-toe. They could've simply attacked Agon at Campeche if that were the case instead of expending such effort to go so far around him. They might've even won at Campeche, and at the next battle and the next, but Lewis's fine army would've eventually died far short of his ultimate objective, and Uxmal and all the cities of the Yucatán would've been doomed in the end. So aside from retaking the steamer *Isidra*, Holland's raid had been designed to sow as much confusion and uncertainty behind Agon as possible, to heap him with doubt and hound him with conflicting orders and imperatives from his masters, distracting him from what Lewis was trying to do. At some point, he would know, but the longer that took and the more confused and strung out he was when it happened, the better. Lewis suspected Agon would see Holland's raid as a deliberate distraction and try to ignore it, but with Holland *in possession* of such a major city, Agon would be forced to do something. Word would spread, and his masters would insist he make an example and he'd *have* to send troops, by land or sea. That's the only way a society like the Dom's could exist. The fear and terror of the masses bred complacency in its rulers, but when that complacency was threatened, they doubled down on fear and terror. It was all they knew to do.

"Our enemy is likely to be even more rabid after this," he finally said aloud, "but I expect they'll be more fragile as well, over time. I'm sure Captain Holland is aware. His 'capture' of Vera Cruz might've been an 'accident,' but he knows we'll do our utmost to take advantage of it." He looked at Coryon Burton. "We'll reply to De Russy's and the *alcalde's* message in more detail shortly, but have Colonel Reed respond with this at once: 'If there's been no increase in enemy naval activity, I recommend we reinforce Captain Holland at once. At least two thousand infantry from Major Itzam. More, if they're available at Uxmal. And make sure General Agon *knows*. *Let* his spies see. He might try to force his way past Major Itzam at Nautla—hopefully he still thinks we're all there—but that would be chancy and too costly to attempt without major preparations *our* spies should see. If it looks like he'll try it, we'll think of something else. On the other hand, I expect he'll be getting panicky orders to send men to Vera Cruz too." He shook his head. "I don't think he'd care, ordinarily, and may not even believe it, but he'll have to report that it *seems* we're sending men, and I doubt he'd be allowed to refuse to do the same." Stepping down from his horse, he motioned the others close as he raked dead leaves away from the base of a towering tree with his boot to expose the soil underneath. Seizing a stick, he drew for a moment until all could see he was making a map of Cayal and the Usuma River. He poked the stick in the sand. "We were going to follow the river to *here* and march across country to the Grijalva River and take the town of Nueva Frontera. Dig in there with, hopefully, a secure line of supply intact and 'invite' General Agon to come throw us out." He chuckled. "He would've had to come for much the same reason he'll have to send troops to Vera Cruz"—he glanced up at Varaa—"and from descriptions I've had of the ground, we would've smashed any assault he could've made." He followed the river with his stick a little farther before looking up at Leonor. "Instead, we'll proceed to *here*, landing and making straight for the city of Gran Lago, just on the north side of this big lake near the coast. As far as I know, not even any of our Mi-Anakka friends have ever been there, but some of Holland's captured Dom sailors say there's a harbor. Not a good one, and the city's not heavily populated, but it's there. And the Camino Militar crosses a bridge over a swampy river *here*"— he stabbed the dirt again, between the big lake and the sea.

"A natural choke point," Barca observed.

"And not another crossing for a hundred miles to the south," Lewis agreed. "As envisioned before—I hope, since we don't know the ground— we'll dig in and fortify the town and the crossing. We'll be between Agon and his capital city, and Major Itzam's Third Division will be nipping at his heels. More important, we can stay there as long as we have supply from the sea."

"What if Agon gets wise an' brings his whole army?" Leonor asked. "What if he's already through Gran Lago, heading for Vera Cruz?"

"Then we'll fortify Gran Lago behind him, having leapfrogged our defensive line past Campeche without the head-on battle he wants. Holland will probably have to abandon Vera Cruz then, however." Lewis stood and dusted off his hands. "But I hope Agon doesn't have the ships to send troops to Vera Cruz and starts sending penny packets up the Camino Militar to satisfy his masters. We'll crush those at El Lago and *force* Agon to bring his army to us. He won't like it when he does," he added grimly, then sighed. "*If* we get there first, of course. It all depends on that." He frowned. "Which means we'll have to move fast, and our mounted troops may be very busy. You'll recall your father and I didn't get along very well, in the 'old' war, largely because I disagreed with the . . ." He paused, thoughtful. "The word 'uncivilized' seems to pale to insignificance when comparing what he did to what the Doms are capable of. But I want the bulk of our mounted troops slaughtering or slowing any real Dom advance. We *can't* let them press our backs to the lake or the sea, and both our divisions must be firmly lodged at Gran Lago before Agon's main force arrives. And while I want our Rangers, lancers, and dragoons to behave like saints to civilians they meet, to help and even defend them any way they can"—his lip curled—"I want the *Doms* afraid of what'll happen to them for a change, and think they've run into the devil's meat grinder." He looked steadily at Leonor, Boogerbear, then Coryon Burton and Felix Meder. "Pass the word. Those are the directions all our mounted forces will abide by from this moment on."

Varaa snorted and shook her head. "Kisin will want to come when he hears."

"That's up to Har-Kaaska and your Ocelomeh," Lewis said. "As long as Cayal is secure, I'd be happy to see him display his dedication to our cause. And the idea of unleashing Holcanos on Doms for a change, instead of the other way around, appeals to my sense of justice."

"Reverend Harkin and Father Orno may object," said Captain Olayne.

"There's that," Leonor agreed. "We stomped all over Holcano religion, makin' 'em quit eatin' folks an' such. The good reverends've been scamperin' to turn 'em all into peaceable Christians."

"I'm a peaceable Christian," Lewis said flatly. "So are most of our men and the Uxmalos, Itzincabos, Techonos . . . God grant we *find* peace again, someday." He paused and took a deep breath. "But in the meantime, 'Blessed be the Lord my rock, who trains my hands for war, and my fingers for battle.'"

"Amen," Barca said with such conviction, even Leonor was surprised by his intensity.

CHAPTER 16

General Agon's Army of God's Vengeance (Blood Cardinal Don
Frutos's lofty name for it) had actually topped thirty-two thousand
men (including over twenty thousand raw conscripts) and thirty-
five new-made 8pdr field guns before the supply and troop shipments from
Vera Cruz to Campeche abruptly ceased. Word was that with Don Hurac
gone to the Holy City, the *alcalde* of Vera Cruz had found endless excuses
not to send more. It mattered little. The army had already grown as large as
Agon, and his trusted subordinates could reasonably train to the "new
standard" in the time they thought they had, or even really handle in the
claustrophobic confines of this dense forest wilderness. As for supplies,
they'd greedily stockpiled rations and ammunition from the start, and
some of that still trickled in from other sources. As the troops' advanced
training progressed, focusing on lessons Agon learned from the enemy at
the Washboard, such as rapid maneuvers and more effective musketry, he
grew more and more anxious to *use* them.

Don Frutos had been impatient from the start, still stinging from their
previous defeat and unsure of his personal prospects regardless of the result
of the campaign. As it stood, Agon would likely reap the rewards for success, but Don Frutos was still positioned to face the consequences for failure. At the urging of his small army of Blood Priests—who'd inexplicably

warmed to him once again—he'd been emboldened to assert more authority over Agon and constantly railed at him to hurl his sheer numbers at the enemy at Nautla. A quick victory there, commanded by him—even in absentia, since he wouldn't leave Campeche—might still reverse his fortunes. Agon was having none of that. They'd tried that before, essentially marching into battle with brave but inexperienced troops better trained for the parade ground than combat. That worked well enough to overawe rebellious tribesmen and villagers on the near frontiers but was disastrous against a professionally trained foe. Worse, the "Washboard," as the enemy called the battle, had been a "meeting engagement" of sorts, where the terrain shouldn't have particularly favored either side and Dominion numbers should've been decisive.

Don Frutos had exercised direct command that time, and sheer numbers still ought to have worked, but his comparatively amateurish tactics allowed the enemy to use the ground better and maneuver at will. This time, by all accounts, Lewis Cayce already had the best "ground" imaginable, and the heretic force had erected formidable defenses in the ruins of Nautla. Better tactics or not, the coming confrontation would be bloody indeed. Raw conscripts would've been pointlessly slaughtered.

Still, Agon couldn't wait forever and didn't want to, truly believing his army was as ready as he could make it when he finally began his ponderous march up the Camino Militar to the enemy stronghold, crossing land he'd been forced to abandon just months before. A densely wooded land still spotted with the bones and rotting, cast-off equipment of that hungry, grueling retreat. The first sight of those grisly, depressing artifacts enraged General Agon, and he ordered details to follow the scouts ahead of his force and clear them from the trail. Without Blood Priests embedded in his army to—in his view—torment and terrify his men, their morale had been surprisingly good. Even soldiers who'd survived the previous retreat had seemed confident this time would be different. Reminders of what they'd endured, and what might await the new men, undermined that. Agon wanted them out of the way. It helped, no doubt, but then the harassing attacks began.

The Dominion had never used cavalry, per se, since cavalry didn't inspire the same dread in their enemies as lancers. Lancers were the elite, highest-born shock troops in the army, and their glittering armor, feather-plumed helmets, and long, red-pennant-festooned lances struck terror in all who faced them. The problem was, their unwieldy primary weapons were almost worse than useless in the dense forests of the Yucatán. Only twice during the preceding campaign had they even been able to deploy in their long, formidable ranks as intended, and in both cases they'd been smashed. The first time they were slaughtered by infantry and artillery, and the second they'd been taken from a rear flank by Lewis Cayce's own lancers, Rangers, and dragoons. Agon considered them a waste of men, horses, and equipment and only had a token force of about five hundred with him. Another problem with lancers is that they'd traditionally been arrogantly "above" such mundane, even impious and spiritually insecure tasks as scouting ahead and screening mere infantry, so Dominion armies normally relied on local sources for that. The only such in the Yucatán had been the Holcanos, and there were almost none of them now. Agon himself had sent them away, figuring they'd be of more use at Cayal and the fighting in the east than providing handy heretics to satiate the wanton cruelty of Don Frutos's Blood Priests, likely turning their own scouts against them in any event.

So, like it or not, Agon's few lancers had to be scouts. Fortunately, those he'd retained were veterans who'd literally been down this road before and knew they had to adjust their tactics, attitudes, and traditions to survive, even to the point of—gasp—discarding their lances and dismounting to fight with musketoons! Agon's final and most pressing problem was, as long and strung out as his column must be to snake its way up this eons-long neglected portion of the ancient Camino Militar, he simply didn't have enough of them.

Enemy Rangers and dragoons, largely composed of Ocelomeh "Indios," were led by men who'd fought Holcanos all their lives and knew every track and trail in the forest and fell on Agon's scouts and pickets, his "burial details," even his main, lumbering column almost at will. They'd strike like lightning out of the forest like the terrible monsters whose bloodcurdling cries they imitated so well, or erupt out of ambush and kill half a dozen before galloping back up the road or vanishing in the shadowy woods. Sometimes they even drove forest monsters to viciously crash into Agon's ranks, tearing handfuls of men to pieces and generally causing havoc before (much-improved) musketry killed them or drove them off.

The whole advance had been like that, step by bloody step, all the way up until his reinforced scouts and a regiment of infantry pushed a small but tenacious group of skirmishers out of their path and across an eerily denuded plain—enemy engineers had been very busy—south of Nautla. A few long-range cannon shots kept Agon's lancers back as he hurried to the front of the column with Capitan Arevalo and his personal staff and guards to emerge from the tree line and view the first objective of his new campaign at last.

Oddly, what initially struck him was that the ancient central pyramid of the city had been somewhat repaired and painted a brilliant white, glaring brightly in the late-morning sun. Equally jarring, high atop the small structure at its peak was a tall, plain, wooden cross, quite different from the jagged symbol of agonizing grace that God forced His son to endure as an example to His people. More concerning from a military perspective, the ancient city was hardly recognizable in less spiritual ways and barely resembled the ruin Agon remembered. First, it looked more like a "living," if extremely utilitarian city, than any other closer than El Lago, its walls almost seething with human movement. And those once shattered walls had been repaired, reinforced, and surrounded by wide trenches that would be mud pits at least, and possibly flooded this close to the sea. Sharpened stakes bristled everywhere, along with split-rail fences and other entanglements that provided little cover but would channel and slow an attacker to a crawl. Perhaps worst of all, as he'd seen at once, the ground had been meticulously cleared for at least a thousand paces in every direction of everything except countless jagged stumps and a lush new carpet of blue-green grass. The sheer extent of the fortifications and malevolent imagination of the killing field stirred a growing, sick anxiety in General Agon's gut, almost a portent of doom.

"Colonel Cayce isn't here," he said with blooming certainty, lowering his spyglass and resting it across his thighs.

Captain Arevalo looked at him, amazed. "My general . . . With all respect, how can you know that after a single glance? What makes you think that?"

"Simple," Agon murmured darkly, pointing all around, then at the distant walls. The army was still coming out behind him, spreading to either side of the track by two-thousand-man regiments. (He'd decided the traditional three-thousand-man regiments were too big and unwieldy and might even make them smaller. Enemy regiments might be seven hundred to a thousand men and lacked the power of larger formations but were much easier to move.) Now, even as his grand new army emerged, he had a nagging impulse to pull it back. His artillerymen had improved considerably, but a thousand paces remained an outrageous distance for them. The enemy had already proven that wasn't the case for theirs, and he suspected they'd only limited the expanse of the killing field for the precise purpose of having him deploy under fire. The enemy artillery was silent, at present, but he wondered if they were just waiting for the largest, densest target, or simply to lull him. That made no sense, of course. Nothing he saw could possibly "lull" anyone.

"This position is a nightmare for us, and those defenses *seem* quite impossible. We'd shatter our army against them even if we brought our big siege guns again. Look through your glass; you'll note that two of those very monstrous weapons we so considerately 'gifted' the enemy when we left them behind now gape at us from that closest wall." He shook his head. "There are a number of other guns as well, *more* than we lost to them. I wonder if all are real?" He shook his head. "Enough of them are."

"What are you saying, my general? That we've lost before we even try?"

"Of course not," Agon snapped. "But we'll have to give this some thought."

"But what makes you think Cayce isn't here? And why should that trouble you so?"

Agon pointed at the defenses again. "Simply because this *looks* so impossible. I'm not saying it is," he added hastily, "and . . . it may in fact be less formidable than it seems at a glance. We'll know when we test the army against it—which we must. But if *Cayce* built a defense he was sure would be impossible to overcome, he'd make it *look* easy to draw us into a massacre as he did before. He would *invite* the battle we both crave," he added with assurance. "This . . ." He waved. "This is a *deterrent*. Therefore, I don't believe he's here."

"And that troubles you because . . ?" Arevalo probed.

Agon sighed. "Lewis Cayce is a simple creature at heart, at least in the affairs of empire. I'm sure he must deal with many of the same problems we do when it comes to support and supply, even meddling from above. But he needn't fear he'll be replaced—or knifed in the back by a Blood Priest assassin." He paused, considering. "Well, he *should* probably worry about that as much as I do. Nevertheless, his is the mind that guides the army of our enemy—as I've been given leave to do for this one, for now, but he's earned a freer hand and many more options. As loose as my leash is at present, I'm still constrained to do the expected. I could only march up the Camino

Militar to face that"—he pointed once more—"and Cayce knew it. Simple creature in some ways or not, he's a bold and aggressive soldier, with a mind free to focus on battle while others he trusts prepare and send him the tools"—he frowned—"or protect his back from the knife. He's made an army that's an extension of his mind, that he can do with as he will. I can't believe he'd just pile it up and sit on it like this. What . . . troubles me, deeply concerns me in fact, is that if Lewis Cayce isn't *here*, he's very probably somewhere else, doing something . . . our way of war doesn't equip us to predict. Or stop."

Arevalo's brows came together as he rubbed the pointed whiskers on his chin. "So . . . what should we do, my general?"

"Coronel Uza," Agon called loudly aside, and his lancer commander moved closer.

"My general?" replied the tall, wiry lancer.

"Find me a way around that," he said, pointing at the city again. "A trail in the forest to the east. "I'm sure it won't be easy—or close—but it must exist. We can't cut the enemy off from supplies; they have a port, after all. But if we can get between them and their principal cities—at least threaten to do so, since then *we'd* have no supplies!—it might force them to come after us on ground of *our* choosing."

"Do you think that'll work, my general?" Arevalo asked.

Agon shook his head but said nothing.

"What will we do in the meantime?" asked General Tun. One of Agon's oldest friends, he'd been at the Washboard and met Lewis Cayce himself. Now he commanded the 1st Brigada, issuing from the trees.

"Continue to deploy, for now," Agon said simply. "If the enemy commences a dangerous fire, you'll merely melt straight back into the trees. Pass the word to the following *brigadas* to begin cutting and clearing space for our camps to the rear, but leave a wall of trees between them and the field to prevent observation. Erect our own fortifications with the timber they cut," he added dismally, then straightened in the saddle. "In the meantime, I'll attempt yet another parley with Lewis Cayce—or whoever commands over there. Perhaps I can learn something."

"That's much too dangerous, my general!" Tun and Arevalo both chorused.

Agon sighed. "I think not. It seems the enemy still recognizes the code of honor among soldiers that the more militant founders of our faith once observed. That . . . aspect of our faith has been deplorably subverted, but I've been careful to ensure the senior commanders of *this* army still believe 'grace' for a soldier can only be won in battle. The enemy can't be aware of that, or possibly even sure they're dealing with me—with the same philosophy—again, but it might be best if they were."

"They came to the first parley we offered, and Don Frutos betrayed them," Arevalo reminded.

"But they came to the next one as well," Agon countered.

"Maybe they're stupid," Arevalo said bitterly.

"We both know they're not," Agon soothed. "But they were desperate then. As desperate as we were, and they learned the difference between Don Frutos and I. The cease-fire we arranged saved both of our armies."

"And here we are again," said General Tun.

"Yes." Agon nodded. "And they'll be as curious about us as we are them." He looked at Coronel Uza. "I want those scouts probing the right immediately, but you'll also send a squad of lancers to advance halfway across the field at a walk."

"What shall they do when they get there?" Uza asked nervously.

"Stop and wait for a signal from the enemy. We'll know what it is when we see it, I'm sure." Agon hesitated. "Assure them they may return here at once if they're fired upon."

THE STRANGE LITTLE dance that ultimately resulted in the parley between 3rd Division's Colonel Itzam and General Agon had numerous awkward steps, all actually foreseen by Lewis Cayce and prescribed by him for this occasion. After much apparent confusion on the walls, the six lancers were eventually met in the center of the killing field by an equal number of Ocelomeh dragoons, as resplendent as their enemy in dark blue jackets and sky-blue trousers, yellow herringbone trim, bright brass buttons and belt-plates, and startlingly white leather belts and carbine slings. They weren't as garish as their counterparts, but looked just as fine. Speaking largely the same language, the dragoons communicated to the lancers that one of each of them would retire, pair by pair, until only a single trooper remained from either side. Only then would their principals emerge and meet, accompanied by a single attendant. Without such instructions, the Doms were at a loss for how to deal with this, and it was agreed among them there that a single pair would first retire to "consult," before returning simultaneously to confirm the arrangements. This, of course, so no one would ever be outnumbered.

Even after agreement was reached, the dance remained a stately affair, with each pair of troopers slowly retiring to their respective lines—at the plodding pace set by the dragoons—before the next pair turned to do the same. Finally, with only one dragoon and one lancer still sitting on their horses about ten yards apart, sullenly staring and saying nothing at all, Colonel Itzam and his young aide, an Itzincabo named Raul Uo, finally mounted their horses and trotted out through the massive, reinforced south gate of Nautla. There they waited until General Agon and Capitan Arevalo were seen to emerge from the ranks of troops still spreading out from the cut in the distant forest.

"Sir, may I ask what all is about?" Lieutenant Uo asked as they rode out into the killing ground, his tone slightly flustered.

Colonel Itzam chuckled. "It's been expected all along that the enemy commander—likely General Agon, Colonel Cayce believed—would want another meeting. As twisted as his cause might be, he imagines himself a proper soldier even as the Americans reckon such things and yearns to 'do things right.' Obviously, there's a big difference between 'doing things right' and 'doing the right thing,'" Itzam said more somberly, "but Agon and his . . . subsect of 'holy warriors,' as they perceive themselves, seem taken with the correct forms and ceremonies of war. Unfortunately for them, having never dealt with a military equal, they don't know exactly what those forms entail."

"So we could just make them up as we go and they'd be none the wiser."

Itzam chuckled again. "To a degree, we are. Not that it matters. Niceties between soldiers on the battlefield don't extend to Dom behavior toward conquered peoples," he continued more darkly. "And the . . . hobby manners of semisecret societies of Dom soldiers don't matter at all to Blood Cardinals or Blood Priests. But Colonel Cayce believes that starting a tradition of meetings before battle might be very useful. I don't know about that," he hedged, "but he hoped for this 'run around,' as Colonel De Russy described it to me, and now that we've got it, I'll put some of his ideas to the test. The form we followed is designed to accomplish several things; first, safety for ourselves. The Doms already betrayed one parley, after all. Second, I'm to drag the meeting out a while, get to know Agon and let him think he knows me, without spilling any truly important information. Not being a 'proper' soldier until recently myself, that's the part that worries me the most."

"You were Alcalde Periz's Home Guard captain. You may be better equipped for this sort of thing than Colonel Cayce."

"Could be. I'm sure I'm better at telling different city officials the very same thing—and having them all swear I didn't," he agreed wryly. "And I couldn't care less what they say about me." He brightened. "So I may be even better at Colonel Cayce's third instruction as well—the main reason he wanted me to meet with General Agon, if given the chance. I thought it was a good idea at the time. We'll see."

"What was it?"

"To 'rub his nose' in his previous defeat. To politely antagonize and provoke him. I'm told I can be *very* insulting."

They stopped beside the dragoon private, just as General Agon and Capitan Arevalo reined in next to the last lancer. There was an awkward moment while they all just sat there as if waiting for salutes, but none were forthcoming. Finally, General Agon broke the silence.

"I remember you. From the great battle west of Uxmal. You are Capitan Itzam of the Uxmal Home Guards Regiment. You helped arrange our . . . final dispositions there, after the fighting."

Itzam bowed. "It's Colonel Itzam now. Of the Third Division. My aide, Lieutenant Uo." He looked at Arevalo. "I remember you as well."

It was Arevalo's turn to bow. "I'm honored."

"I'd hoped to renew my acquaintance with Colonel Cayce," Agon said, "not that I mean any offense to you," he quickly added. "But I am, after all, the commander of the entire great host that will soon invest your works. It seems appropriate that I should be met by your overall commander. If he is present," he probed.

Itzam shrugged. "Oh, rest assured, Colonel Cayce's here. He's merely somewhat . . . indisposed this morning. I was available."

"Indisposed?" Agon exclaimed in mock alarm. "I do hope he isn't ill. I'd hate to test myself against him if he isn't at his best. I pray he's not afflicted with *el vomito rojo!*"

Itzam casually waved that away. "No, he isn't sick, and our healers have medicine for that in any case. Don't yours?" Itzam knew perfectly well the Doms had no defense against mosquito-borne disease. "Forgive me if I gave you that impression," he continued, then paused. "Let's just say he's 'indisposed' to spending valuable time speaking with you again. Time better used contemplating shattering your 'great host' as he's done before. He said you'd both made your positions quite clear the last time you met: you'd return to renew the battle to subjugate the Yucatán, and he'd destroy you if you did." Itzam smiled. "You're back, and he's getting ready to wreck you. Colonel Cayce always means what he says and *does* what he says." Itzam lowered his voice as if revealing a secret. "I have it on authority that he actually respects you as a soldier, and may even vaguely regret destroying you. He can't respect your cause, however, and detests those you stoop to serve. False courtesy would make him feel hypocritical, so there's nothing more for him to say to you."

Lieutenant Uo had struck a light to a long-stemmed clay pipe while Itzam spoke and had it drawing nicely. Now he handed it to the colonel, who took a satisfied puff and said, "I, on the other hand, am something of a . . . public soldier, in a sense. At least I was. As the Home Guard commander of Uxmal, I learned to spew false courtesies to all manner of self-important officials and mercantile luminaries." He gestured behind at the fortified city. "As you can surely see, there's little more I can do to prepare for your visit." He grinned engagingly. "That leaves me perfectly free to visit all day, if you like."

Arevalo's face was generally paler than Agon's, but now it flushed with fury. Agon raised a calming hand before his aide could speak. "I should feel complimented, then, that Coronel Cayce still imagines there's more *he* might do to receive me."

"That's *one* way of looking at it." Itzam nodded genially in a cloud of pipe smoke.

"Yes. Well." Agon straightened in his saddle. "Since Coronel Cayce is unavailable, perhaps we *should* stop wasting each other's time."

"To the formalities, then," Itzam agreed. "I'm just as new at this as you are, I believe, but since you're the aggressor, I understand it's traditional for you to go first."

"Very well." Agon took a long breath. "My Army of God's Vengeance is far larger and much better than the army I brought here before. I'm unconstrained by higher authority and may employ it as I will. You are doomed. Sadly, I don't have the discretion to offer you your lives, but I entreat you to surrender so I can be merciful in regard to the *manner* of your deaths. Your heresy doesn't celebrate the cleansing power and grace of pain, so should you yield, you have my word all your people will die as quickly and painlessly as possible." He grimaced. "You also have my word of honor that none will be delivered to the Blood Priests for their . . . amusement." He paused again before adding quickly, "Believe it or not, your deaths will grieve me more than I can say. The warrior tradition observed by our military officer class remains touched by ancient ideals from a gentler time when our respective faiths were not so different. That very similarity is what makes them so profoundly incompatible now. Regardless of that, I feel drawn to the notion that proper soldiers serve a higher calling and shouldn't have to slaughter others who can no longer resist—but I have no latitude in this. I've been charged with eradicating the heresy on this peninsula and must do so."

Itzam blew out a stream of smoke and nodded. "I appreciate your . . . gracious offer," he said, tone very dry. "I must refuse, of course. On the other hand, if you and your army will lay down your arms and approach the south gate of Nautla in an orderly, nonthreatening manner, you have *my* word that all will be treated firmly but well, with the utmost respect due fellow soldiers. Officers may even keep their swords or other personal weapons as long as they give their parole. That means *their* word of honor they won't try to escape, harm anyone, or damage our war effort in any way. They'll be treated as honored guests of this army, but any who break their word will be hanged. Enlisted personnel will be formed into labor battalions for the remainder of our conflict unless they choose to join us—that offer is sincere—but they won't be slaves. They'll be fed and sheltered, and none will be abused."

Arevalo could only stare, openmouthed.

"You can't be serious," Agon objected.

"I'm perfectly serious," Itzam countered harshly. "*We* don't make war on the innocent or murder the helpless. Prisoners of war are both, in their way."

A stutter of gunfire erupted in the woods far to the east, rising to a strident thumping sound before gradually tapering off. Itzam managed an amused glance at Lieutenant Uo. "Ah," he said. "It seems General Agon has already sent scouts to find our forest flank." He grinned at Agon. "They'll have discovered that we really don't *have* one." He gestured around at the countless stumps. "All these trees—thousands of them—have been dragged into the forest for *leguas*. There are impassable obstacles and breastworks *woven* into the very forest. Beyond even that is a convenient escarpment you'll never drag your guns up on. I only tell you to save some time so we can get down to business, but by all means, see for yourself. You won't like it a bit." His grin turned predatory. "I'm afraid Colonel Cayce has designed this defense in such a way that you'll be obliged to come right at us. Ponder *that*, while you consider my *very* generous offer."

"THAT . . . ENTIRE EXCHANGE was quite extraordinary, my general," Arevalo observed to his stony-faced commander as they rode back to their developing line. Two more regiments had spread out from the road, backs to the trees, and at least half of Agon's field guns had been deployed. Three five-gun batteries and around six thousand men arrayed in deep, disciplined ranks, garish red-and-gold flags popping in the offshore breeze. "What do you think about it all?" Arevalo almost pleaded. "He can't be as confident as he seemed . . . can he? And his offer . . . ridiculous! No one would be so generous!"

"I think I'm even more convinced that Colonel Cayce is elsewhere," Agon replied with a snort. "If that's the case, he'll have taken the cream of his army away. We must discover where he's gone, and the quickest way to do that is to defeat this former guardsman, this Colonel Itzam." He frowned. "Once we do, we can question him and his men as vigorously as we must."

"So we attack?" Arevalo asked.

Agon looked at him. "Of course, and at once. Particularly with Cayce's forces away, the defenses here *can't* be as formidable as they seem."

If anything, the defenses at Nautla were stronger than they looked, more so than Agon could've imagined. He began with a long-range cannonade, eventually bringing twenty guns online. They roared and bellowed and filled the stump-studded plain with choking white smoke while he watched their effect with his spyglass. *Lack* of effect, to be more precise, in spite of better accuracy than he'd really expected to see. Either his new artillery officers or the survivors of the previous campaign had seen the need for profound improvement. Still, the 8pdr roundshot that struck the enemy fortifications only geysered earth from the hard-packed berm heaped in front of the ancient stone wall and bounded ineffectually over it. Those, and the rounds missing high, might've created some injury and damage in the city, but didn't much bother the defenders on the walls—or the enemy cannon that finally replied.

The first to fire were the two great siege guns, 36pdr monsters that blanketed the field with smoke by themselves, the heavy shot roaring in and crashing right down the road that much of Agon's army still densely packed. Screams echoed down the cut for a depressing distance as countless men were spattered into flying, bony gobbets by the seemingly unstoppable spheres.

"Those *fiends!*" Arevalo cried, his voice edged with shock. "They did that on purpose!"

"Of course they did, you fool!" Agon snapped back. "They've had all the time in the world to lay those guns, and we obligingly walked right into them. Messenger! Go to Coronel Gonzals at once and have him *get those men off the road!*"

The captured enemy 8pdrs spoke next, about ten of them—which seemed to prove they didn't have as many as they'd made emplacements for—but these were aimed at the forming troops in the open, scything whole files of them down the depth of their deep ranks, before bounding up and crashing through the trees. And unlike the bigger guns, which took longer to load, these fired again before Agon's own gunners were ready to respond. *They don't* need *twice as many guns if they fire them twice as fast!* Agon seethed.

"I apologize for my outburst, my general," Arevala said. "I wasn't shocked as much by what they did as by the fact they could. Such weapons aren't known for their precision."

"Yet they make the most of what they have, somehow. I already doubted their superiority in most things has as much to do with their tools as it does how they use them. I'd be most intrigued to learn how they push a loose projectile down a barrel—any barrel—and manage to . . . tighten it on the way out. That's the only way they could do it." His twenty cannons fired again, one after the other, for the same small return as far as he could see, but their puny thunders were drowned by the 36pdrs once more, bounding down the Camino Militar and slaughtering men only now scrambling off it. The trees there were exceptionally dense, and so—Agon now realized—was the mass of entangling brush *deliberately* heaped among them. *They planned this very well indeed,* he growled in his mind. He couldn't see how far the awful confusion extended, but doubted his follow-on regiments could be reorganized quickly enough to do much.

"General Tun!" he called to his increasingly agitated friend.

"Attack?"

Another storm of 8pdr shot slashed into Agon's men among a spray of blood and a chorus of screams.

"Yes," Agon confirmed, rapidly assessing. "Advance your *brigada*. Advance *everything* already in the open being slaughtered to no purpose. All their guns will focus on you, but it'll be better than just standing and taking it. I'll try to untangle another *brigada* to strengthen your push." He paused, still thinking furiously. "They'll be expecting our usual, ponderous advance, so hurry your men. *Run* them, General! Don't stop to fire. Our cannon will try to suppress them. Get under the enemy's guns and drive up over the walls!"

"It will be done!" General Tun replied savagely. "God will revel in the suffering this day, but I cannot—until we inflict some on the enemy!" Whipping his lovely white stallion with the flat of his sword, General Tun galloped to the left, shouting at officers to keep their men firm—and prepare to charge. Tun was much like Agon in every way but looks. Where Agon was short and dark and built like one of the stumps on the field, Tun was tall, almost willowy, with shockingly light brown hair. But his background was the same. A third son who'd never inherit his father's wealth or position, he hadn't been drawn to the priesthood or obispado and the elusive track to the Blood Cardinalship, so he'd made a place in the army. A true friend, he shared Agon's devotion to the old ways of worship and the army and cordially (in public) hated the Blood Priests for what he saw as their impious power grab and self-serving, bloody-handed changes they sought to press on the Dominion. Even if those day-to-day changes were subtle, for now, like most of his and Agon's generation, he feared the extent to which Blood Priests would take things if their power was unchecked.

Nearing the very center of the line, in front of the better part of two *brigadas*—almost eight thousand men—he stopped and stood in his stirrups as another pair of 36pdrs shrieked by overhead. One struck a great tree by the edge of the road not very far back, and an explosion of bright splinters slashed into the backs of some of the men facing him before the tree groaned heavily and began to fall, accelerating rapidly to crash down across the road in a welter of expanding dust and ferny leaves. He didn't think many soldiers were crushed, but now the reserves were blocked. *Could the damned heretics have done that on purpose too?* he wondered. *At a thousand paces? How?*

"First Brigade!" he roared, and the frustrated men matched his feral shout. "First of the Second Brigada!" he added. (He must leave some men to guard the gun line and Agon, after all.) "At the sound of the horns we'll cross that field in a holy charge against the heretics such as this world has never seen! Affix your bayonets now and fire not a shot. Let nothing distract you from sweeping over their defenses and into their rear. You're the Army of God's Vengeance, and God will have His reckoning! *You* will enjoy the spoils and pleasures of victory before God takes their chastened, heretic souls."

A cheer welled up. That was another tradition the Blood Priests would undermine: demanding all the spoils of conquest, material and "spiritual," including all enemy survivors, for the Church. That meant for the Blood Priests themselves, of course—loot and unsullied young captives to use as they wanted before they were sacrificed. Like Agon, Tun would've been happy to humble an enemy—and not only was sacking a city or enemy camp consistent with that, it helped motivate his soldiers—but he disagreed with the whole notion of massacre. Not only was it . . . disrespectful to "honest" enemies, he was sure it made them fight harder. The "old traditions" often allowed truly excellent enemy warriors to be spared as slaves, sometimes in the benevolent service of their conquerors.

As the war horns sounded over the bleak, broken-tooth plain south of Nautla, General Tun had few illusions regarding who'd slaughter whom as he rushed some of what he considered the Dominion's finest troops across the vast killing ground the enemy so fiendishly prepared. There was nothing for it, however. The army couldn't yield to its fears and the confusion thrust upon it, just meekly turning away. Even a bloody nose was preferable to that—and Tun suspected the army's nose was about to get very bloody. "Charge!" he bellowed.

———

"Colonel Cayce was right," murmured Lieutenant Uo in something like shock when the tightly ordered Dom ranks suddenly surged forward, quickly losing the geometric precision they'd maintained throughout the brief bombardment and turning into a running, yelling, mob. Colonel Itzam nodded. "Yes. They'll be exhausted by the time they get here—and some of them will, mark my words—no matter how many we kill on the way. Heavenly Father, I really didn't think they'd do it, but they are." He cleared his voice and raised it. "Very well. All batteries except the section of siege guns will target the advance, switching to grapeshot at five hundred paces and canister at three. The siege guns will start throwing grapeshot at the enemy artillery."

The Allied Army had just about exhausted its exploding case shot from another world at the Washboard and hadn't yet managed to make any more. With examples to look at, the wooden fuses were actually the easy part, though getting the kinks out of timed powder trains so the shells would burst when desired was harder than expected. Powder had to be mealed and measured, wet and poured and dried just right, and no one had ever done it before. A lot of trial and error was required. Casting hollow iron or copper balls was still the biggest hang-up, though, and no one knew how to do that either. Experiments were ongoing. In the meantime, stands of grapeshot had been reintroduced. Grapeshot was like canister in that it turned a cannon into a giant shotgun. There were fewer pieces of shot in a stand of grape (just nine 2-inch one-pound lead balls in Itzam's 8pdrs as opposed to the new standard fifty .69 caliber musket balls in a tin of canister), so theoretically it wasn't as effective. But being considerably larger and carrying farther with lethal results against massed targets—easily shattering several men in a row beyond the lethal effect of canister—the results were not dissimilar to what might be expected from exploding case at those reduced ranges.

Screaming, steaming gaps started opening in the charging horde, all nine rounds from each stand of grape having difficulty not hitting *something* in the press, often many somethings, arriving before the boom of the guns and squall of whirring balls. These sounds joined the screams to make them even more unearthly and appalling to General Tun, who trotted forward gesturing with his sword, fully exposed on his magnificent horse and leaning into the howling storm of death as he encouraged his men to close with the heretics.

"Halfway there! Halfway there!" he shouted. "Keep going, keep moving! Soon you'll be under the guns, and mere *men* can't stand against you! God is watching. The joys of victory or heaven await!"

Clouds of earth still rocketed up from the enemy works as Agon's artillery pounded them, but even that was diminishing. A stand of grape for the 36pdrs contained thirty-six 2-inch balls that had more than sufficient energy to kill at one thousand paces. The pattern was badly dispersed by then, so death was highly random, but several—at least—balls from each blast slashed among the Dom gun's crews the distant siege pieces targeted, killing men and even damaging cannon carriages.

Tun didn't know what was happening behind him. He was surrounded by carnage enough and entirely preoccupied with shouting and exhorting men forward, almost *willing* the charge to hold together, keeping it moving at its brisk, exhausting pace. He'd learned at the Washboard and was being brutally reminded that nothing exhausts like terror—and he *was* mortally terrified, sure he'd be struck any instant. But he'd also learned that the failure at the Washboard had been one of leadership, not the men, and he'd *lead* these men, by his conspicuous presence alone if he must, as long as they'd conquer their own panting terror and keep pressing onward. "Three hundred paces, no more! Almost there!" he roared hoarsely.

"Commence firing canister!" called Colonel Itzam, and the drums rolled.

"Look at that fool on the horse!" cried Lieutenant Uo. In all the charging thousands, there was only one "fool" on a horse, his yellow-and-black uniform festooned with the silver lace of a high-ranking officer, his animal very distinctive as well. "Someone get that fellow!"

"No!" shouted Itzam. "Pass the word quickly; do *not* target the officer on the horse!"

Too late. An 8pdr roared close beside them, canister spraying out. The bottom of the pattern kicked up dust and shredded grass before skating up and smashing knees, shins, pelvises. Slowed and distorted projectiles slashed bellies open. The rest slammed into the gasping front of the enemy or fell on men behind. The horse reared up, red blotches on white fur clearly visible at a little more than two hundred paces, and it crashed down in the press. Troops seemed to waver in the vicinity, but almost immediately, Itzam was sure he saw the sun-burnished glint of the officer's sword rise above the heads of men, shouts lost in the din, and the Doms came on.

Poom! Poom! Ppoom! Pppoooom! All the guns fired canister now, and the Doms went down like stalks of maize in a whirlwind. Infantry was lining the walls, starting to fire muskets or launch heavy arrows.

"Why didn't you want that one dead?" Uo asked over the noise. "He's giving them more backbone than I like. Look to the left; they're getting awfully close."

They weren't, really. They'd been stopped by the fences and other obstacles that either slowed them too much to bear or funneled them into the fire. They'd also discovered the reinforced walls of Nautla weren't exactly as straight as they seemed from a distance. The added berm bulged with subtle lunettes that allowed men and guns to fire down the length of the wall instead of just straight outward. No, the Doms were in a meat grinder, and Itzam doubted any would live to crest the wall. They had no chance of taking it. "Two reasons," Itzam shouted back over the growing musketry. "First, they probably would've broken already if it wasn't for him. We get to kill more of them," he said simply. "Second . . . I hope he lives to see what we do when they *do* break."

Despite the best efforts of the dismounted officer, that didn't take much longer. Agon had known that affixing the wicked, swordlike bayonets in the muzzles of his men's weapons would leave them at a terrible disadvantage in a situation like this; stalled by blowing canister and a withering fusillade of arrows and musketry, his troops couldn't even shoot back. He'd gambled it all on the unexpected speed of his charge surprising, perhaps even panicking his enemy. He'd doubted the latter would happen, and as it turned out, Colonel Itzam hadn't been surprised either. Now the grand charge had degenerated into a futile, one-sided slaughter, and even before Agon ordered the battle horns to call the men back, General Tun had started sending runners to the flanks to deliver the very same message. "Pull back, retreat, but do not let them see you flee! Keep your intervals and retire like men!" And they did. The whole swarming mob shook its packed lines out under the galling fire, flags whipping—many falling—and turned the disorganized mass into a disciplined army again before finally beginning to back away. They were still helpless and would be for a while (Itzam suspected the Doms had left fifteen hundred to two thousand of the roughly six-thousand-man charge lying in the tall bloody grass among the jagged stumps, and he might even double that before they retired out of range, probably to the safety of the forest this time). It was *so* tempting to keep killing. The Doms had come to kill him and his family, after all . . . but that wasn't part of the plan.

"Cease firing!" he barked abruptly. Uo and several nearby officers gaped. A fine harvest still remained to be gathered. "Cease firing, damn you!" Colonel Itzam shouted loud, spittle flying from his lips. He understood what Colonel Cayce wanted, but didn't much like it either. "Sound it," he told the bugler, who still hesitated for an instant. "I said sound 'cease fire'! Drummers as well!" He pointed at the withdrawing enemy, still dropping, bleeding, suffering. "Agon's turned those men into proper soldiers, and we'll treat them as such—this once. They can't do anything to us. Maybe a demonstration of respect—and any man who doesn't respect what they just endured is a fool—will get them *thinking* like proper soldiers too, as Colonel Cayce taught us to do. How can that not get them thinking about other things as well? We'll try it—this once, like I said—and see what we see. Now, as God is my witness, if I don't hear 'cease fire' being sounded in one second, I'll have you all on a charge!"

The Allied forces in Nautla didn't cease firing completely; the great 36pdrs continued spraying grapeshot at Agon's artillery until he ordered it withdrawn. Two guns had been dismounted by roundshot, and one had its carriage shattered under it, and those were abandoned, for now. As soon as he left or removed his only means of harming anyone in the city, the Allied cannon fell silent. Stunned by the disaster, but even more astonished by the enemy's behavior, General Agon personally rode out on the field to meet General Tun and the soldiers marching back. After a couple hundred paces moving backward, Tun finally realized the enemy wouldn't just kill them from behind and ordered an about-face, constantly redressing his lines as his battered *brigada* limped to the woods.

"I'm so sorry about your lovely horse, General Tun," Agon said when he saw his bedraggled, blood-spattered friend, lightly supported by a bloody-faced trooper. More blood soaked his fine yellow breeches below a wound in his thigh, and his knee-high black boot squelched as he walked. Looking around, Agon decided there weren't many men without some blood on them. *Quite enough misery here to satisfy even a Blood Priest*, he reflected darkly. "A litter for the general!" he called. "Take him to my command tent!" Even as the assault was mounted, slaves had been erecting tents for the officers and healers in the woods between the field, where the main camp was already going up.

"Thank you, but I'll walk," Tun said. His face was pale and streaked with grimy sweat, but he was determined. He managed a wry grin. "Unless you have another horse at hand."

"Of course! Capitan Arevalo, your horse for the general. Fetch another and rejoin us as quickly as you can."

Riding together now, surrounded by a cluster of guards and other officers, Agon said, "My apologies, General Tun. I'd hoped a bold stroke might overwhelm the enemy and set a new standard of victory for this army. I should've known Cayce—or whoever commands over there—had goaded us into precisely that. We lost many men, killed and wounded, and you hurt as well." He snorted. "I wonder if we even scratched one of theirs?"

"It is I who should apologize, my general," Tun replied, but he didn't sound very sorry. There was . . . something else in his tone. "I should've pressed harder, got there sooner. There were more entanglements than we could see from here," he conceded, "but . . ." He stopped. "Those are just excuses and you're right. We did exactly what they wanted and paid for it in blood. But that blood also paid for a 'new standard' of courage and discipline for this entire force. My *brigada* set that standard," he continued proudly, "marching into the fiery teeth of hell, enduring it as long as they were asked, then pulling back in good order. We *couldn't* win the day, but didn't really lose it in the sense that an army that can do that was born."

Agon shifted uncomfortably in his saddle. "Indeed," he observed guardedly. "Something the enemy had to be aware of when they *let* you pull back 'in good order.'" He'd finally touched on the uncomfortable subject that had them both confused. "Colonel Cayce 'let us go' once before, but that was to preserve his own army. Not out of any sense of . . ." He frowned. "Some misguided notion of mercy. Yet I can think of nothing but mercy that might've motivated him here today, and—no offense to your gallant *brigada*, my friend—allowed it and you to *survive* to set a new standard. I watched it all. They *allowed* you—us—to fall back unmolested. If they'd done . . . what I would've done . . . you would've been fortunate to straggle back with half your force alive. And it wouldn't have been the standard-setting beacon of courage and discipline because half the survivors would've been wounded in body or mind and of no further use. It was my fault, but they could've *crushed* your entire *brigada* if they chose. Why not?"

General Tun frowned as they arrived at the shady fly extending out from the command marquee beneath the trees. There was no firing now, but the sound of axes attacking trees farther back was almost as loud and frequent as the rattle of musketry. Slaves rushed up to help Tun out of the saddle and he grimaced as they half carried him to a chair, propping his boot on a crate. Agon's personal physician was waiting, arranging tools on a clean piece of canvas while his assistants poured generous mugs of wine. "Don't cut that boot, healer," Tun warned. "The pair cost a month's pay, and

I can't replace them out here." He looked at Agon and tilted his head dismissively. "Perhaps they're low on ammunition."

Agon snorted. "Don't be ridiculous. Their industry's sufficient to dress their peasant troops, even Indio auxiliaries, in fine uniforms, and supply them with all the tents and accoutrements they need. Do you think Cayce would skimp on even more necessary things? We know they've built at least one large powder mill, and there's no questioning the quality of its produce. I'm sure they made good use of the small arms and 8pdr projectiles they captured from us, but we've never used the smaller tins of balls they call 'canister,' so they must've made many of those to fit our guns." He held his hands out to his sides as Tun gulped wine. "Now, most likely tonight, they'll retrieve another thousand or so muskets our wounded and slain dropped on that bloody damned field. Don't believe they haven't been free to make munitions of their own, since we've largely supplied them ourselves!"

"We should stop them from recovering our equipment." Tun smoldered as Agon's physician took a long gulp of wine as well and began cutting the breeches away from his wound.

"The carrion eaters will make that difficult enough for them," Agon said with a grimace, imagining the fate of the wounded out there. "Besides," he began hesitantly, but was interrupted by Capitan Arevalo galloping up on a borrowed horse, hooves throwing dry leaves and a drifting cloud of the sugar sand. Dismounting quickly, he strode under the fly and saluted.

"You seem in a hurry, Capitan," Agon noted. "And your eyes are quite wide. What else has happened today to surprise you?"

"The enemy sent a message, my general. A pair of their dragoons approached, and I took it on myself to prevent any firing."

"Quite right," said Agon, with an arched-brow glance at Tun. "This war grows more civilized by the moment. Next we'll be joining our enemy for *bailes* in the evening before slaughtering one another at dawn. Do they desire another parley?"

"No. Just a short truce. They have no wounded on the battlefield, but mean to comb it for equipment—weapons, of course—but say they won't fire on us if we send men to retrieve our wounded. . . ."

"Of which there are hundreds, no doubt," Agon murmured wonderingly.

"No doubt," Arevalo confirmed. "You can hear many calling . . ."

"Agreed," Agon snapped before Tun could object. Then he shrugged. "As you said, they'll get all they want later. And even if only a few of the wounded are saved to fight again, it may improve morale after this terrible day if the rest of the army sees we care about them—and they don't have to listen to the screams of hurt comrades being eaten all night. That alone will be worth it," he added grimly.

"How can you trust them?" Tun asked with a hiss when the physician started probing the large hole in the fleshy right side of his thigh.

Agon actually chuckled. "You already trusted them not to shoot you in the back."

If General Agon thought he'd had enough earth-shattering surprises for one day, he was mistaken. There was no more fighting, and the "truce" proceeded without incident, but not long after the physician finished with General Tun and the man was dozing under a net in Agon's own tent, Capitan Arevalo came again, accompanied by a pair of tired, trail-stained lancers. Agon had left a single regiment of recently arrived and therefore relatively undertrained troops at Campeche to guard Don Frutos and his growing entourage of Blood Priests under the control of the loathsome "Father" Tranquilo. That force had a mere eighty lancers to cast about in the vicinity, and carry dispatches to Agon, but they were veterans detached from Coronel Uza's loyal battalion. "They came from Campeche," Arevalo simply said, unnecessarily. "A messenger dragon arrived with a dispatch from the Holy City. The beast must've stopped at Vera Cruz, as usual, so Don Hurac or his representative could include an addendum."

Agon looked at him curiously. "You act as if you know what they say."

"I do," Arevalo confessed, then waved at the lancers. "So do they. So do Don Frutos and Tranquilo. Everyone we left at Campeche knows the contents of the *first* message. At Don Frutos's orders, the Blood Priests . . . reasserted their control over the messenger dragons." He nodded thankfully at the lancers. "*They* secured the discarded addendum from Don Hurac and brought it to you as well. No copies were made. All together, it's . . . interesting and troubling reading, my general, but I suggest you look at the message from the Holy City first."

"Hmm," Agon murmured, accepting the wooden tube the lancers had brought. When he tapped it lightly in his hand, a small roll of bright, perfectly cut paper tied by a golden ribbon dropped out. Untying the ribbon, he unrolled the pages. Glancing at the first, he recognized the strong, leaning penmanship and set it aside. "That's the one from Don Hurac," he said, then looked at the next. It was written in "high Spanish," as expected, and headed by a single oversize word: *Alegrarse.* The flowery, grandiose text that followed explained *why* the people of the Holy Dominion should "rejoice," but General Agon only felt sicker the more he read. Finally, he looked up to see General Tun had awakened and was watching him closely. "It seems," he began in a tone devoid of exultation, "that His Supreme Holiness has gone to His reward and now abides at the right hand of God, where He will stand foremost among those who have gone before Him in continuing His earthly labors to light our path to grace, et cetera, et cetera, until His own worthy successor ascends to relieve Him. Et cetera." His expression turned grave. "And that 'successor' is the Blood Cardinal Don Julio DeDivino Dicha."

There was a gasp, and even General Tun looked worried. "Not Don Datu, then."

"No."

Tun frowned. "Then Don Datu is dead. A 'presumptive successor' and 'actual successor' can't both exist at once," he said dryly. It was a profound understatement affecting them all, perhaps *especially* the Army of God's Vengeance, primarily led by Agon's picked men, who clung to fundamental tenants of an ancient and fragmented society they simply called La Fraternidad de Guerreros Fieles among themselves. It had no official members or secret handshakes and held no meetings. It was more a philosophy than anything else, that a true soldier could only find grace by dying in battle. They hated Blood Priests and Blood Priests desperately hated them. With the Blood Priests' principal advocate, Don Julio DeDivino Dicha, in absolute power—and likely beholden to them, Agon assumed—creatures like Tranquilo could rise unopposed to supplant the traditional (and vaguely more moderate) priests of the Faith. They'd get all they wanted in regard to *obispos* and blood lineage as well, and purge the army of anyone they suspected of belonging to any brotherhood of warriors.

"What of Don Hurac, I wonder?" Agon passed the proclamation of ascension to an orderly, who handed it to General Tun before looking at the page he'd set aside. "God!" he exclaimed, scanning what was written.

"What?" Tun asked, though everyone was keenly interested.

"Vera Cruz has fallen to the enemy, and Don Hurac is *there*! Did Don Frutos and Tranquilo see this?" he demanded of the lancers.

"Yes, my general," one said. "They control the flying beasts now. How could they not have seen it?"

"And they didn't want *you* to know it, General," Arevalo pointed out. "Nor did they want you to know they've abandoned Campeche, marching overland toward Gran Lago and eventually Vera Cruz itself with two thousand troops and five-hundred-odd Blood Priests they've been gathering. Incidentally leaving *us* stranded, with no more supplies or support from the rear. I'm sure they would've taken ships if they were available, but nothing's arrived from Vera Cruz. Presumably since it fell."

"*Cabrones!*" Tun hissed. "What else did Don Hurac say? There must be more. Is Vera Cruz where Coronel Cayce *really* is?"

Agon bit his lower lip. "It seems not," he said, proceeding to relate the Blood Cardinal's account of the "raid" that captured the city.

"A raid? A couple of ships? A *handful* of men?" General Tun exclaimed incredulously.

"There was a fire," Agon supplied loyally. "The raiders helped extinguish it, saving many lives."

"They saved *nothing!*" Tun snarled. "Do you think anyone there will be spared if the Blood Priests have their way? I'll wager anything that exterminating them is the primary reason Don Frutos and his creatures are heading there." He paused. "That, and concern over how *you'll* react, of course."

Agon left that aside, for now. "They'll all most likely be killed," he conceded, but added with heavy irony, "unless . . . our *enemies* hold the city."

"Or we pursue Don Frutos, my general," Arevalo interjected. "Pardon me for speaking, but if one carefully reads Don Hurac's addendum, it's plain he's greatly concerned about the . . . future of the Dominion under what would essentially be Blood Priest rule." He sighed. "And he was very close to Don Datu. He can't be happy about his removal, nor can Don Julio DeDivino Dicha be comfortable with Don Hurac running loose, so to speak. One might even say it's likely he would've already been assassinated if he hadn't fallen into the hands of the enemy."

"Who can't possibly be happier when they learn all of this?" Agon sighed. He thought for a moment, then finally said, "What's the state of our supplies? I have a general notion, of course, but how long could we sustain a campaign—*any* campaign?"

A *coronel* on Agon's staff piped up. "Thanks to your prescient stockpiling (he'd actually considered it paranoid at the time, but hadn't experienced the previous retreat or had to share the meat of his own beloved horse with starving troops), we have sufficient provisions in the baggage train for three months, and . . . lost only a small fraction of our small arms ammunition today," he added nervously, without reminding anyone almost none of it was fired and now languished on bodies the enemy would plunder, "but we've only enough ammunition for the artillery to match today's expenditures three, perhaps four times."

Agon tugged on his chin whiskers. "A most desultory and abbreviated barrage. Not enough, without resupply, to press our campaign against the heretics. Besides," he said more forcefully, "we now have *two* enemies intent on destroying the soul of our country." He gestured to the north. "And I consider *them* the lesser threat, at present."

Such a statement was outright, damnable treason, punishable by the most horrific death imaginable. Just hearing him voice it, all around him could share the same fate. None even blinked, and Agon congratulated himself on choosing his staff so well. "So, artillery ammunition aside, we can't proceed against the heretics without sustaining crippling losses that won't be made good, and I think the Dominion needs this army intact. I wish I could speak to Don Hurac. He obviously has a plan to *use* the heretics to our advantage against the usurper, so our first priority must be to relieve him. At least prevent Don Frutos from destroying him."

"We can't just leave," General Tun pointed out. "Even if the enemy doesn't learn about our . . . situation for some time, they'll pursue us. That would expose them to destruction, and in the open I think we could smash them, but we don't have the time—or, frankly now, recourses—to turn on them."

"We'll have to leave a credible blocking force," Agon agreed. "But the rest of us must chase Don Frutos and his Blood Priests, relieve Don Hurac—he's next in line for elevation, as you know—and secure Vera Cruz for ourselves." He massaged his brow with his fingers. "We came to destroy the heretics, but they must wait. They may even be content to do so. All they really want is to be left alone, after all. The Blood Priests won't leave anyone alone, least of all those of us who adhere to an older, purer version of the Faith. And could you imagine anything worse than *Don Frutos* in command of our armies? No. The Holy Dominion, in any form, would fall."

"I don't disagree," said General Tun, "but it must be said; we're contemplating civil war—in the middle of a war against heretics here, while the bulk of our national forces are embarked on the Gran Cruzada against the heretics in the Californias!"

Agon gave him a sad smile and nodded. "Precisely. And oddly enough, that's the only reason we have a chance. As I chose all of you for this army, the Blood Priests or their sympathizers like Don Julio appointed most of the commanders of the Gran Cruzada. Some are quite competent, but all will be constrained to act as the Blood Priests direct, as I did during our first campaign here, whether they truly support the Blood Priests or not. No doubt sufficient . . . examples will be made to ensure their cooperation," he added grimly. "But that's why we must race to secure Vera Cruz, and ultimately the Holy City, before substantial elements of the Gran Cruzada can be recalled. Only a quick victory, a 'countercoup' to reestablish the proper order, can undermine the Blood Priests now. If we lose that race, all is lost. It's as simple as that."

Coronel Uza's brows turned downward, and he pursed his lips. "If you think the heretic enemy will be content to be 'left alone' and watch from afar while the Dominion fights itself, why not have another parley with their commander? *Tell* him what we know and why we must leave?"

Agon sipped his wine, thinking. Finally, he set the mug down. "Can your lancers discover his *exact* strength and disposition in a matter of days?" he asked.

Somewhat surprised by the question, Uza shook his head. "Without Holcano scouts, and if his left flank truly is secured all the way to the *escarpa*—which seems likely after our probe was repulsed—it may take many days to work our way behind him and learn what we need to know."

"Then no. Whether Cayce is in Nautla or not, we really have no way of knowing how many troops are there, *or how many might be moving to join them*," Agon stressed. "They very bloodily demonstrated that their position is impregnable to a frontal assault with a narrow focus, and that's the only thing we're capable of without learning more or extensive engineering." He held his hands out to his sides. "The same may be true for them, all along the track to Campeche, but if they know we're leaving, they may be tempted to strike. They beat us today—no decisive blow, but an encouragement. They might not beat us as we march away, but every time we turn to blunt an assault, they'll cost us time and troops. Neither of which we can spare. Besides, with the run of the forest, they've already proven they can nibble us to death at their leisure. And frankly, why wouldn't they? We can't promise we'll never come back. The last campaign may have been inspired by the very man we'll chase, but it was under the authority we wish to restore. They see only differences of degree between us and the Blood Priests." He frowned as if contemplating that for the first time. "And perhaps they're right to do so." He vigorously rubbed his chin whiskers and continued. "In any event, as convenient as it might be, I doubt they'd stand quietly by if we said, 'Our apologies for attacking you, but we have a little trouble to sort out at home before we resume our engagement here. No, no! Don't trouble yourselves to stir from your impressive fortifications, we'll be back as soon as we can.'"

Uza looked sheepish, and General Tun chuckled.

"So," Agon continued after a long, indrawn breath, "we'll march the bulk of this army back the way it came, as fast as possible, leaving a sufficient force to make it *look* like the whole thing is performing all those tedious, time-consuming tasks we spoke of earlier; scouting flanks, clearing forest for camps and assembly areas, even preparing works the heretics can see beyond the trees. They'll figure things out before long, no doubt, but perhaps they won't believe it. Still, just a few days—a week—will allow the rest of us to get far enough to keep our distance from any dangerous pursuit."

"One momentous variable remains, my general," Arevalo reminded.

"I know," Agon conceded uncomfortably. "Lewis Cayce. If he was in Vera Cruz, he'd have a more powerful force than Don Hurac implied. And even if his"—he snorted—"'Allied captors' didn't want him to tell me, the Don Hurac I know would've found a way to plant hints in his message. I still don't believe Cayce is in Nautla either, so he must be elsewhere, with his very finest troops. I suspect he'll appear when it's least convenient."

CHAPTER 17

Parts of the Usuma River were relatively narrow and swift, even somewhat dangerously so, especially where it wound through the rocky foothills of some low mountains to the southeast and veered abruptly from a southwesterly direction to the west, northwest, about a hundred and fifty miles from Cayal. The long, broad, raft-like barges, averaging twenty-four by twenty-eight to thirty feet, and their passengers—many of whom were last on the water when they were shipwrecked on this world—had an adventurous time of it there. Even guided by steering sweeps, some of them swirled out of control and struck dangerous obstructions. The barges were tough, with strong decks deeply spiked to the massive tree trunks floating them, and heavy hawsers, often tightened, prevented twisting and warping, and loosening of the spikes. Their loads helped keep them rigid as well, to a degree. On barges carrying cannon, the gun's limber was snugged up tight over the trail, wheels overlapping and touching (and roped together), the limber pole lashed to the cannon axle. All was made fast to ringbolts in the deck timbers by a spiderweb of cables. The guns were then surrounded by heavy freight wagons and caissons, loaded and balanced and secured the same way, while literally forming walls around the irreplaceable weapons. The only men on those barges, among the heaviest, were the gun's crew, wagoneers, and those of Kisin's trusted

Holcanos, who'd not only volunteered to accompany him (he'd convinced Lewis and even Har-Kaaska he'd be useful as a guide and intermediary to certain groups and was allowed to come after all), but were experienced at exactly this sort of thing: navigating barges down to the sea.

Infantry barges carried troops and their equipment, with more freight wagons in the center. Everything was loaded like that, with the men and things they needed together. And these—like the ones built to transport horses, were equipped with strong railings. That turned out to be a wise design feature since all the barges that actually truck something were laden with men or animals. Their excitable (and movable) cargoes made them harder to handle and most likely to crash. None were destroyed, not a single horse was lost, and the railings prevented all but a few men from falling in the water when their barge smacked a rock. Sadly, though the river wasn't deemed as deadly as the sea in terms of predators, five men were pulled under by unseen things in plain view of their comrades. Only one was fished out alive, possibly because he'd been knocked unconscious and hadn't thrashed or screamed in the water.

That stretch of the river was behind the long flotilla now, the turbulence-muddied waters broader and slower. Terror of the not-quite-rapids had been replaced by equal parts terror and wonder at the sights. Gradually, the forests became slightly less dense and occasional clearings were revealed. Farmers among the soldiers, Americans and natives, marveled at the black richness of the soil practically oozing into the water, held in place only by roots of lush grasses and wild maize standing six or eight feet high. And the only things harvesting the bounty were stupendous beasts of every imaginable shape, larger than anything the city-born Indios in the army had ever seen. Ocelomeh encountered them on occasion, as had Holcanos, of course, but the creatures were a source of constant amazement—as long as they stayed out of the river. Most did. Whatever voracious predators prowled its depths must have annoyed them as well. Speaking of predators, however, the local variety tended to dwarf the dryer land, denser forest sorts as well, and these were generally seen in small packs of adults with a scatter of younger, smaller animals, stalking self-importantly about (the consensus was that they had every right to feel that way) in search of prey. They looked fully capable of taking down all but the very largest herbivores, but didn't seem interested in those. No attacks were ever seen, but the troops viewed the occasional aftermath with macabre fascination, pointing and chattering loudly as great, bipedal predators gathered around a kill—never the largest or healthiest specimens—their mighty jaws tearing at flesh and audibly splintering bone. Those bloody-mouthed monsters sometimes looked up to peer speculatively at the passing barges, even condescending to utter half-hearted, gobbling challenges—resulting in quite sudden silence among the spectators—but none ever deigned to so much as dampen its massive footclaws in the stream.

Thus days of placid floating passed, the river-borne troops moving at a brisk walking pace amid the sole inconvenience of swarms of voracious mosquitoes. Even despite the necessity of avoiding monsters on land, the mounted Ranger, lancer, and dragoon scouts screening the force from human enemies were never hard-pressed to keep up, or select night camps far in advance, strung along the south shore in areas chosen for ease of access, visibility, and defensibility from marauding beasts. There was no perfect safety in that regard because by their very nature, relatively clear campsites were habitual thoroughfares for large herbivores seeking water, as well as the creatures that hunted them. Large fires, tended through the night, generally kept them (and the mosquitoes) discouraged. So did the music the soldiers often made.

The locals hadn't possessed any string instruments before the Americans came, and now they absolutely loved them. Fiddles were most esteemed, but banjos were all the rage, being simplest to make and well suited to the rigors of a campaign. They were also comparatively easy to learn and perfect for the livelier tunes everyone liked the best. As an added benefit, their loud, twangy sound seemed most out of place (and possibly alarming to nearby fauna) in the deep wilderness. Most nights passed without incident, and with each dawn, surprisingly well rested, the mounted men resumed their scouting duties, and the foot soldiers and support personnel returned to the barges.

"We're making good time," Warmaster Varaa-Choon declared as she led her striped horse onto the "Command Barge" under the clear, gold-streaked, morning sky and secured the animal to the rail. Lewis did the same with Arete while Corporal Willis came grumbling aboard with his commander's bedding folded atop the canvas of a small wedge tent—all Lewis claimed he needed at present. As they often did, they'd spent the previous day with Anson's Rangers, looking for villages or roads. They had no plans to join any scouts today, but their horses would remain saddled, just in case.

"It seems so," Lewis agreed, but couldn't keep a measure of dissatisfaction from his tone. In spite of everything, the campaign was going much as he'd hoped, and even the changes hadn't disrupted it much, but now he was just as cut off from information as during his initial trek through the forest from Nautla—they were moving too fast to set up semaphore stations, couldn't safely man them in any case, and the same dangers prevented courier contact with Cayal. He was starting to get the sense events could be leaving him behind, and not only was his army *not* where it was most needed, but it wouldn't reach its objective in time. Worst of all, he'd begun to wonder if the whole arduous undertaking from start to finish might've just been a costly waste of time and men.

He rarely questioned himself so. He'd embarked on this expedition based on a reasonable strategy, he thought, but also a "hunch" of a sort, and those had rarely let him down. This one likely saved 2nd Division at Cayal, after all. But he harbored no illusions that his hunches were mystical things, in any way based on presentiment. They were intuitive evaluations, founded on current information and the situation as he knew it. That foundation was getting older each day, and his "feeling" was starting to taste stale.

"It *is* so," Reverend Harkin strongly declared, making way for his friend Father Orno, who, along with Captain Felix Meder and Lieutenant Barca, was escorting Mistress Samantha Wilde aboard. Following Har-Kaaska and several other officers (Har-Kaaska's strange mount, both larger and heavier than any horse, was secured in the center of the barge) was a full squad of Meder's riflemen, who joined them before the call, "Take in lines an' cast off" was heard. Meder's men, with their excellent M1817 rifles, were unquestionably the finest marksmen in the known world. All had horses now as well, but they weren't being used for scouting. Instead, they were spread among the barges to protect the people on them. Their .54 caliber weapons weren't as powerful as the .69 caliber M1816-M1835 American muskets many of the infantry carried, or even the re-bored .77 caliber Dom muskets most of the rest now had, but Felix Meder set a rigid standard. If his riflemen wanted to *remain* riflemen, they would, by God, demonstrate the ability to consistently hit a man-size target at three hundred paces *at least* twice a minute. Anyone unable to do that had his precious weapon taken away and given to someone who could. The unfortunate ex-rifleman then found himself in the artillery, or the infantry with a musket. But for protecting the barges under these circumstances, just hitting one of the huge monsters with a rifle *or* musket would be pointless if a surprising number of Meder's men hadn't shown they could hit one in the *eye* with their 1817s.

"I think we've made quite extraordinary time," Harkin continued as the men on the stern sweep worked vigorously and others heaved against the river bottom with long, dripping poles, easing the barge out in the channel to join others already moving more quickly there. Lewis was watching them, still impressed by the sight. Any kind of formation, or order of march—float?—was impossible to maintain, and less than half the barges had left the shore from where he and the others camped the previous night, but scores more were already floating down from other campsites upriver. Lewis hated splitting his force, especially leaving the various portions out of sight of one another, but there was only forest between them, and communication was quickly established. Besides, the whole was simply too large to camp in any clearing the scouts had yet found, and the confusion of getting an entire army under way from such a place every morning would've been a nightmare. *It would bother me more in "hostile" country*—he mentally snorted—*as if anywhere with giant, murderous beasts can be considered anything but hostile, but even in proximity to the enemy, we may have to advance in separate columns to mass efficiently. Hopefully our scouts will provide a good understanding of where the enemy is by then.*

Harkin was still talking. "By Varaa's best calculations, we've averaged between fifteen and twenty miles a day since reaching this less . . . vigorous stretch of river, and have come around three hundred miles—translating miles from *leguas*, of course—in less than twenty days! That's not far short of the entire distance we originally intended to use the river! How could you not be satisfied with that?"

Lewis looked at the tall, bearded preacher, who'd changed so profoundly, possibly even adapting more readily than anyone to their current reality. He'd lost all the excess weight he'd brought to this world, and the alarmingly loose skin was finally tightening up. He'd dropped a lot of other . . . baggage as well, including all vestiges of self-assured pious superiority and the notion his version of Christianity was more pleasing to God than that of the natives they'd befriended. He might still believe he was . . . better informed in some cases, with more enlightened interpretations, but the locals had the advantage of him in others. Particularly when it came to the conditions that formed their faith. One example was the aggressive fascination he now displayed as he drew their attention to another small clearing, just beyond where they'd camped. Large, fat-bodied, but otherwise shockingly serpentine creatures had halted their plodding approach to the river, heads high on great, long necks, peering at the passing barges with evident dismay.

"Just look at those things!" Harkin enthused. "Magnificent!"

"Look like cows that found a turd in their water trough, to me," Willis grumped.

Harkin ignored him. "Uxmalos don't have a name for them, and the Ocelomeh and Holcanos call them *serpientosas*. Descriptive enough, but it simply won't do. Still, I've no better name in mind." He seemed to concentrate. "A mere four or five years ago, the eminent Sir Richard Owen referred to the few fossil specimens known of possibly related creatures as, collectively, 'fearfully great reptiles,' or 'dinosauria.'" He pointed again. "But 'fearfully great' or not, those don't look like 'reptiles' to me." He smiled at Har-Kaaska. "Your devoted mount is no 'reptile,' and just yesterday, while most of you were riding ashore, I beheld a *whole herd* of other creatures. They were larger," he allowed, "but more like what I'd imagine our old friend 'Iguanodon,' on our home world, must've looked like!"

Har-Kaaska and Father Orno smiled indulgently, fully aware one of the things that made Reverend Harkin more . . . malleable on Church doctrine, and perhaps his own strict Presbyterianism in particular, was his enraptured certainty he'd crushed the scientific theory of extinction, which—as a man interested in comparative anatomy who kept up with all the latest sensational fossil discoveries back home—had most assailed his fundamental certainties. Now he felt free to wallow in his "scientific hobby" because it was clear to him that nothing ever *had* gone extinct; it merely came *here*, as they had. Beyond even that, of course, was his enthusiasm for the cause, and the holy crusade of destroying the Dominion that cloaked its depravity in the perverted vestments of his and Father Orno's faith. He had a true purpose, a real mission in life, and it made him a new man.

Followed by Lieutenant Barca, and Willis, of course, Lewis moved away from the discussion to stand by Varaa and Samantha. They were clutching the rail and staring ahead, ignoring the creatures under debate. Lewis could see a small dust cloud as a strengthening breeze blew it across the water.

"Mr. Anson is pressing farther forward today," Samantha observed, the dust likely rising from his scouting force.

"Yes. I asked him to."

Samantha glanced around, then looked at him. "And it seems dear Leonor has joined him."

Lewis sighed, knowing where this was going. "I won't pretend I don't enjoy her company. I do quite a lot. But as convinced as she is to the contrary, I don't need her protection. I'm fully capable of looking out for myself."

Samantha giggled and waved her fan. "She's not the only one who feels that way, you know."

"True," Varaa said, blinking amusement, but her tone was quite serious. "Your safety is important to the army. It trusts you to use it well and give it victory." She lowered her voice. "Not even the great Har-Kaaska enjoys that kind of confidence anymore," she confessed. "So just imagine how fearful the troops would be, *all of them* on this great expedition, if something happened to you. Do you think Har-Kaaska could pull them through? Colonel Reed?" She shook her head.

"They could, with the help of you and Anson," Lewis countered.

Varaa mulled that. "Perhaps. But they wouldn't have the same confidence when we meet the Doms. Only you've ever beaten them." She grinned. "So the *whole army* appreciates the . . . attention the lovely, lethal Leonor Anson heaps upon you. You should not send her away."

"She's used to protecting her father too, you know," Lewis said dryly. "I thought she might enjoy the opportunity to do that for a change."

"And I'm sure she does," Samantha agreed. "But there may not be anyone who's *perceived* by most to need that protection less."

"Do you think that?" Lewis pressed.

Samantha sighed. "No. Giles is a very capable warrior. I'm not sure one could properly define him as a 'soldier,' like you or my father, but he's also the most horrible, frustrating man, given to taking outrageous chances. I *personally* feel better with Leonor at his side, to temper his . . . immoderate impulses. But we're not talking about me."

"I am," Lewis denied, then gently smiled. "I'm not generally one to ask personal questions. I could say I wasn't raised that way, but that isn't true," he added with the usual trace of bitterness that came with any reference to his upbringing. "It's just the way I am."

"Always polite," Samantha agreed with an eye roll.

"Not to *me*," Willis mumbled, barely audible. Of course he was eavesdropping—he always did, just as he always made little comments.

Deciding to change the subject for a moment, Lewis turned to Barca. "And what of you, Lieutenant? Have you decided to join Mr. Hudgens's battery? You excelled in training, and he genuinely wants you as a section chief. First Sergeant Petty has been doing a good job, but his other duties have fallen to others. In addition, he's not interested in becoming an officer, nor would the battery be best served if he did. Good first sergeants don't grow on trees, you know."

"And lieutenants do." Barca chuckled.

"Not good ones."

Barca hesitated. "I'd *like* to join the artillery," he confessed. "I actually feel drawn to it. On the other hand, if my work's been acceptable, I'm almost equally drawn to remain on your staff."

"More than 'acceptable,'" Lewis assured, "and I'd miss you. But I want you to do what *you* want. You've earned it."

"You know the composition of Hudgens's First Section," Barca temporized, "so you know my leaderships may cause problems, right when we need their best performance."

Lewis nodded grimly. "Gun Number One—and its crew. As I understand it, however, you're well-liked by Gun Number Two." There were no secrets of that sort in the army. "Good men and bad."

"Perhaps," Barca conceded, "but all good artillerymen. I'll give it more thought, if I may."

"Please do. Still," Lewis continued, looking back at Samantha, "while we're discussing the organization and opinions of the army, I'll point out that the consensus is that you and Mr. Anson have come to an understanding." Samantha Wilde was a formidable woman in many ways, and her beauty and bold personality even intimidated Lewis when they first met. On one hand, that was understandable. His experiences with women had largely been unfortunate. The ones from "acceptable" families his brutal father insisted he court had been, as a rule, either weak-willed and vapid or capricious and conniving, determined to dominate him to their ends. As a result, with a few exceptions, he'd grown to disapprove of them all. Then, here, on another world, he met Samantha and Leonor, not to mention Sira Periz and countless Uxmalo and Ocelomeh women unlike any he'd met: strong-willed but sensible, full of life and interesting, honest, forthright, and formidable in other ways he admired. And the fact that two of them came from the same world he did proved not all the ones "back home" were "bad." It was as if he'd discovered *real* women for the very first time. Many of his men had Uxmalo sweethearts, even wives by now, but there hadn't been time for *him* to explore that discovery very far as yet. . . . In any event, he'd become close friends with Samantha and learned early on that she had her eye on the indomitable Ranger—and she believed Leonor had her eye on *him*.

"That's true," Samantha revealed without hesitation, then flashed a smile. "I *told* you we would. I never expected the lengths I'd have to go to secure it from him, however. And I didn't just come out here for that," she defended. "My work in Uxmal was done, and Sira Periz is quite capable of standing on her own. I actually began to suspect she *preferred* that I come out here so her people would see that themselves." She waved her fan. "I was no use to anyone there and thought I'd be a help to Dr. Newlin."

"Well, you were right about that. The two of you together have done more to untangle our logistics concerns than any dozen before you," Lewis confirmed. "But, if you don't mind my asking, what's the nature of your understanding with Mr. Anson?"

Samantha rolled her eyes again. Lewis suspected she did that better, with more meaning, than anyone alive. "We'll be married"—she held up a hand—"when the war is over." She snorted. "My God, that may be *years*! I'm close to thirty, you know. *He's* in his late forties! I'm quite sure there will never be children," she fumed. "How he can ever expect me to wait . . ." She stopped and looked at Lewis with a long-suffering sigh. "But I shall, of course, and so you see why I'm satisfied that your lethal little bodyguard should guard *his* body from time to time."

"She's not my . . ." Lewis began, and Samantha fluttered her fan at him.

"Oh, please. You may not have claimed her, but she belongs to you, body and soul. I'd get used to that if I were you and stop pretending otherwise. Doing so only tortures you both—and everyone around you."

"Up ahead," Leonor said, rising slightly in the saddle on the back of her local horse, named "Sparky," and tilting her hat to the front. "Group movement in the brush at the edge o' the clearin'. Could be predators puttin' the sneak on those big devils over there." She tilted her head to the left, where a herd of long-horned, bony-frilled beasts grazed contentedly, seemingly oblivious to their column of mounted Rangers and lancers. "Or maybe they saw us an' skedaddled," she allowed. "Could be somethin' else, though. I thought I caught a flash o' somethin' shiny."

As they had every day, Anson's Rangers and Lara's lancers were scouting the riverbank ahead of the plodding barges while Burton's dragoons stayed roughly even with them a bit farther out. Nobody was much worried about the north side of the river, since very few people lived over there. At least there weren't any villages or towns on that side between Cayal and Campeche. Small scouting parties of Kisin's Holcanos kept pace to the north just in case. The arrangement allowed the various groups, even the barges, to observe the widest area while remaining within reach to support one another if they ran into trouble. The screen's task was simpler and safer than it would've been if the army were on foot, and they all moved as quickly as if everyone was mounted.

"Seen it already," Giles Anson replied, squinting slightly at the brush she'd indicated, barely two hundred yards ahead. The forest beyond had thickened again, and the rising sun flooded it with shadows. "Might just be more o' those poky-faced boogers fixin' to come out for breakfast too. We'll check it out." He paused and turned to look at his daughter. "Not that I'm complainin', girl, but why're you doggin' me, today?" He grinned. "Colonel Cayce get fed up with your jabberin'?"

Only long exposure to the sun (and her Mexican mother) kept Leonor's face from reddening under the sweat already sheening it. It was going to be another hot, humid day. Besides, both of them knew that if anything about her company bothered Lewis, it wasn't that she talked too much. She'd come a long way since they wound up on this world but still felt . . . uncomfortable with casual conversation. Especially around someone like Samantha Wilde, who could talk so easily about anything. Compared to her, Leonor was practically mute unless she had something important to say. She wasn't the least bit shy about speaking up then, but she certainly didn't "jabber." "Matter o' fact, I'm 'doggin'' you for Mistress Samantha's sake," she replied a bit defiantly. "She worries when you go off castin' about by yourself."

Anson snorted. With the arrival of 2nd Division, his three mounted regiments, not counting the Rifles, were stronger than ever. Their baggage and support was on the river with everyone else's, but he had six hundred dragoons, nearly seven hundred lancers, and almost a thousand "Rangers" (still largely Ocelomeh, but now with a few Holcanos attached), to "protect" him, not to mention Boogerbear, Ramon Lara, and another score or so of the toughest, most experienced mounted fighters he'd ever known. Even Coryon Burton and a number of his dragoons were in that category now, regardless that almost half carried the same captured Dom muskets cut down to "musketoons" as the bulk of his Rangers and Lara's lancers.

He frowned slightly, thinking of that. *Burton's a good 'un, an' turned the dragoons*—a branch many, especially Rangers, held in low esteem before the old war—*into hard-ridin', thoughtful, frontier fighters. But the "new" percussion caps for their Hall carbines are a mixed blessin'.* Sure, they'd fire the weapons, but apparently the women and kids who made them back in Uxmal thought, "If a little of the explosive compound in the little copper cap is good, a touch more must be better." The result was a growing fear among some dragoons to use their quick-firing Halls because of the distracting, sometimes painful little bombs that went off in their faces when they did, often sending sharp shards of copper into their supporting hands, or even their cheeks. The cup in the hammer face generally protected their aiming eyes, but their marksmanship had been so degraded, Anson suspected most just closed their eyes to shoot. *Even Burton can't do much about that*, he thought. Fortunately, they'd discovered the problem while integrating and training all the dragoons at Cayal, and the complaint went back up the semaphore line. The next batch of caps should be better. In the meantime, though . . .

He returned his thoughts to Leonor—and Samantha. "I guess she'd worry, some. Doesn't know me like you do. Boogerbear!" he called out louder. "Detail a squad—better make it a platoon—to swing in behind the edge o' them trees ahead. Somethin's in there. Flush it out." Boogerbear merely nodded and spun his large, striped horse named Dodger before galloping back along the twin column of twos. Nearing the distant rear, he called out for a platoon of Teniente Espinoza's lancers to peel off and follow him. (Boogerbear never "detailed" someone else to fight.) The lancers did as they were told without hesitation, pausing only to hand their lances off to men riding beside them. "Halt the column, Capitan Lara," Anson called. Lara passed the command to the bugler.

The huge, somewhat round-backed beasts in the clearing weren't happy about that. Large heads with intimidating lances of their own over bony eye ridges looked up in annoyance when the bugle sounded, and their apparent displeasure increased as the long line of men and horses, possibly just single, strange-looking creatures to their nearsighted vision, came to a halt. The closest in the herd were about sixty yards away, however, and their impressive array of weaponry was principally defensive. The things only became aggressive—quite suddenly and astonishingly so—when an imaginary line, about thirty or forty yards away, was crossed. Otherwise, they avoided confrontations. That didn't stop the bulls from grumbling and hooting loudly in tones much like the bugle, but they started to edge away.

Anson pursed his lips and glanced at his daughter. "I s'pose Samantha told you we agreed to get married when the war's over. Sorry. Meant to tell you myself. What do you think?"

Leonor sighed, a little angrily. "You're a grown-up man, Father. Don't matter what I think—"

"But it *does*," he interrupted. "It's just been the two of us so long—well, Boogerbear an' Sal too, I guess—but after losin' your momma the way you did—"

"You can't just keep livin' for *me*, Father. I'm grown-up too," Leonor interrupted in turn. She lifted her chin. "I *miss* Momma every day, though hard as I try, I can only conjure the slightest notion what she looked like in my mind. I still feel her in my heart, but can't hardly see her anymore."

"I see her every day, in you," Anson said simply.

"An' that prob'ly makes it even harder for you," Leonor agreed. "Puts me a little in her place, so to speak, an' makes it harder for you to move on. Makes it *feel* like she's still sorta here. But I *ain't* Momma. We lost her a decade ago for you, a lifetime for me, an' it happened on a whole 'nother world." She shook her head. "Long an' far enough for you to leave your hurt behind, an' me to bury my hate. I been workin' on that part," she added when she looked back to see Ramon Lara—whom she'd once hated simply because he was a Mexican soldier—and Kisin—who'd, until recently, been an even worse enemy—moving forward to join them and lowered her voice. "An' it's helpin'. Can't hardly raise any o' the same feelin's I once had. Don't mean they're gone; they might never be. But I've found that carin' for somebody, even the . . . careful way I do, helps bury old hurts an' hates. I'm *glad* Mistress Samantha helps you with that." She grinned a little crookedly. "Even if she ain't like anybody I ever figured could. As for me . . . Like I said, I'm a grown woman, free to give my heart to whoever I want—whether they want it or not." She took a long breath. "I expect you know how I feel about Colonel Cayce. . . ."

"Everybody knows *that*—except maybe *him*," Anson retorted.

"You don't approve?" Leonor asked. "Not that it matters," she added. "I've had my own mind a long time."

"That's a fact," her father agreed dryly. "But let's see: aside from him bein' older than you, near ten years, an' not exactly showin' much interest, he's got his army an' duty an' cause, all more important to him than you. 'When the war's over' is the *least* you'll have to wait."

Leonor nodded. "I know, an' don't care. An' he does show interest, even if he fights it mighty hard. But after all the years I spent broke up an' empty, jus' carin' about somebody feels pretty good. Good enough that I ain't sure I want to risk findin' out how he really feels about me. Does that make sense? I reckon you have it better, with someone like Samantha prob'ly carin' more about you than the other way 'round, but I'm better off than I was, an' *for now*, that's good enough."

Anson frowned and shook his head, preparing to say how *he* saw things; Lewis Cayce was a fine man, and in spite of what he said, much too smart not to have a good idea how Leonor felt. And Anson suspected Lewis returned those feelings to the extent he'd allow himself, which probably made him a *much* finer man than Anson because he hadn't encouraged the girl. Anson, Leonor, Sira Periz, Har-Kaaska, Samantha, Varaa, Captain Holland, probably Colonel Reed, and maybe a dozen others were the only ones who knew Cayce's ultimate "war aims," and there was little chance they'd all make it through. Small chance for any of *them*. So who's more honest, more honorable? He chided himself. *The man pretendin' the strong but vulnerable woman he loves is just a friend, a companion an' fellow soldier in the cause he's set himself, or the one promisin' marriage when the "war's over," while never expectin' to see it?*

But Lara and Kisin were with them now, so that conversation, if it ever happened, would have to wait. Lara was peering at the slowly retreating herbivores, perhaps most dangerous when they felt only vaguely threatened—that thirty- or forty-yard invisible line growing closer to fifty. "You want me to deploy the lancers?" he asked.

Anson shook his head. "Too much chance one o' them boogers'll gore a horse an' tromp a man. Besides, all we seen was a little brush rustlin'. Might be nothin."

"I doubt it was 'nothing.'" Kisin disagreed. His hair was spiked into a kind of crest on top of his head, and he still wore only a breechclout over his lower body, the terrible scars of a healed compound fracture of his thigh still puckered and rough. He seemed proud of the old wound. But he'd thrown away the necklace of eyes, no longer painted himself, and, like the rest of his men, now wore the dark blue jacket of mounted troops—though he'd insisted on officer's shoulder boards. The jacket hung unbuttoned and open over his dark-skinned chest because there simply wasn't one available that would stretch across his massive shoulders and still fasten in front. The one custom-made for Boogerbear would, and he usually only wore a vest, but he hadn't offered it. "We're less than a hundred *leguas*—three hundred of your miles—from Campeche," Kisin continued, "and getting close to a cluster of villages our people rafting down to trade with the Doms have stopped at on the way in the past. People there are not Holcanos, but enough like us we could stop and stay with them. Trade with them."

"So you didn't kill or enslave them. Or eat them," Lara said. He didn't dislike Kisin as much as Har-Kaaska or Consul Koaar (neither trusted him at all), but still tended to bait him on occasion.

"No," Kisin replied mildly. "We only did that to enemies. These people were not enemies. They had their own, and . . ." He shrugged. "We didn't think enough of them to make them enemies."

Lara arched a brow. "I suppose we should feel flattered."

"Yes," Kisin agreed. "And for that reason, we didn't eat them either. Unless we're starving, we only eat honored enemies—and our own, of course. They're the only ones worthy of living on in us. . . ." He looked around. "Not that we eat *anyone* anymore," he stated emphatically. "But in any event, I'd not be surprised if you've found some of them. I'm only surprised it has taken this long."

"Will they fight?" Leonor asked.

Kisin seemed surprised. "Of course! They don't know you, so you're enemies."

"Does that mean they'll eat us?" Lara goaded.

Kisin snorted. "No. They're not as refined as Holcanos."

"Screwiest damn people," Anson muttered, then raised his voice. "Boogerbear'll be in position soon. Let's see what happens."

Almost immediately, there were sharp, yipping cries in the trees and a few popping shots from musketoons. Lizardbirds exploded from the treetops and swirled, squawking, as a loud yell and more shots reached them. Twenty or thirty men, dressed in a mixture of cloth and leather, much like the Ocelomeh once were, raced out in the clearing, sleeting heavy-shafted arrows back the way they came. The horned beasts trumpeted and stirred, trotting away in a zigzag pattern so they could watch behind them.

"Now you can deploy your lancers, Mr. Lara," Anson said. "A company or two should do." The bugle sounded again, and a portion of the left twin column peeled away before forming a staggered, double line of two hundred men. Their *teniente* gave a shout, and two hundred lances came down. Men were shooting from the trees now, dropping a few screaming archers who'd started lofting arrows at the lancers and the head of the column as well. Some of the lethal shafts fluttered down to stick in the ground quite close to Anson and the others. A scatter of Boogerbear's Rangers emerged, quickly joined by enough to start forming a line of their own in front of the woods. The strange warriors were surrounded now, with nowhere to run. Unlike Holcanos, who often surrendered in situations like that, these men only redoubled their shooting. A few of the closer Rangers' horses were hit, shrieking and rearing. One fell and rolled.

"Should I send my lancers forward?" Lara asked. "It seems such a shame to kill them all before we even know who they are."

"True," Anson agreed. "Would they know you?" he asked Kisin.

"*Everyone* knows Kisin!" the Holcano replied haughtily.

"Then why don't you go have a word with 'em?"

Kisin hesitated only an instant before whipping off his jacket and barking for a couple of his men to do the same, obviously so they'd be more easily recognized as Holcanos. Then, without another word, they galloped ahead of the column, yipping and shouting themselves, in the direction of the surrounded archers.

"Well." Lara chuckled. "That *ridiculo salvaje* is still brave enough. We'll soon either be rid of him, or . . . well . . ." An arrow took one of Kisin's companions high in the chest, and he tumbled from his horse. Instead of wheeling and running, however, Kisin merely halted and started shouting at the archers, who'd at least stopped shooting to hear.

"Well," Anson echoed, grudgingly impressed. "What's the damned cannibal sayin' to 'em?"

"He identified himself first, but mostly, he's calling them cowards and women," Lara replied.

"I caught some o' that. Doesn't look like they believe him, though, or care."

"Oh. Now he's going on about what'll happen to their village, their wives and children, after we slaughter them. Keeps insisting he *is* Kisin, war leader of all the Holcanos."

"I guess he is, what's left of 'em," Anson conceded. "Even the ones back at Cayal will stick to that—long as we have troops there, their families stay in Itzincab—an' we feed 'em, I expect."

Lara was frowning. "One's shouting back. Keeps yelling that Kisin is dead, killed by Don Discipo, an' the 'blue coats' who fight the 'yellow coats' would never let Kisin live either. He's adding that he wants no fight with the blue coats who fight the yellows."

"'Blue coats,'" Leonor said, glancing at her sleeve. "Makes sense. That's prob'ly all they know about us down here."

"Sounds like Kisin's getting to that," Lara agreed. "Still *insisting* he's who he says he is, that *he* killed Don Discipo—true enough—and the 'blue coats' aren't only his friends, they've whipped the 'yellow coats' out of the Tierra de Sangre—South Yucatán—and won't harm anybody but Doms." He laughed. "Swears we won't eat them! Ha! That did the trick. Look, they're lowering their bows."

"Doesn't much matter who you are, nobody wants to get ate," Leonor said with conviction.

———

There were Doms in front of them. Blood Priests, at least, according to the headman of the warriors they'd encountered, who, along with a couple of companions, was brought to the camp the army made that night and presented to Lewis and the rest of the command staff. By that time, the headman, Rau Kimichin, whose name, if not appearance (he was thin like all his men, but also unusually tall), was strikingly similar to an Ocelomeh word for "mouse," had spent most of the day with the Rangers and lancers. He was respectful of Kisin, but not deferential when he realized the Holcano wasn't in charge, and he gradually became fairly well convinced he wouldn't be eaten. That made him more cheerful and talkative.

"He looks a lot like your people," Samantha said aside to Har-Kaaska, where they sat in camp chairs in a lantern-lit circle in front of Lewis's command tent, erected for this meeting. Samantha referred to Har-Kaaska's Ocelomeh, of course, not Mi-Anakka. Kimichin had no tail or fur. "And I mean that as a compliment to you both," she quickly added. Unlike Holcanos, Kimichin and his people wore a lot of colorful cloth, their leather garments were well-made, and they were no dirtier than a few days in the wild would've made them. It was still difficult to get Kisin to bathe, and of course the sweat-soaked uniforms of the soldiers always stank.

"He's a Tikalo," Har-Kaaska told her. "A cousin tribe to the Ocelomeh from long ago, but they've forgotten the jaguar. Unless he's embraced the twisted Dom faith, his is probably closer to Father Orno's and the Uxmalos."

The latter seemed to be the case because Father Orno stood to join Kimichin, if any translation was needed, as he reported on the local conditions.

"My village, Santos del Rio, is just a few *leguas* to the northwest," Kimichin solemnly began. "Other villages are this far, even farther from 'civilization,' but lie on hidden tributaries of the Usuma River"—he looked at Kisin, who was standing by Varaa—"the better to avoid the notice of the Dominion and Holcanos." He shook his head. "That's no longer possible." Looking back at Father Orno, he continued, "The legends say my people—almost everyone in this land—were part of the Gran Exodo from the growing power and heresy of the Dominion from the time it was founded at Acapulco, even before it spread to the Great Valley of Mexico and became the abomination it is. Unlike the Uxmalos, Itzincabos, and others we know of but no longer know, we thought we'd fled far enough. Perhaps that was so, since our villages remained small and unnoticed while larger, more settled places, even farther away, always drew the evil eye of the Dominion. We even maintained peace with the Holcanos. . . ."

"While they ravaged us in the north," Varaa said cuttingly.

Kimichin gave her a look that seemed to ask, *What would you have done?* "Yes," he admitted. "And for a time, we lived simply but well. Now great and terrible change is coming. We've known the Blood Priests, horrible, cruel creatures, who stopped among us on their way to Cayal. They warned us our time was coming, that no heresy could exist in their land. In the *world*. We worried, but couldn't see that time approaching. Then the Holcanos told us of you," he said, looking at Lewis, "and a great battle in the north that threw the Dominion back. Another was brewing at Cayal." Now he looked at Kisin. "Nothing has come from Cayal before you and we believed the Holcanos were broken as well."

"Not broken," Kisin denied hotly, then seemed to consider, "but . . . chastised. Yes, 'chastised' into the light we should've seen for ourselves long ago. Whatever the Holcanos become in the future, we'll no longer be tools of the Dominion."

Samantha Wilde clapped her hands with a "Bravo!" and even Har-Kaaska managed to summon a blink of respect as his tail slashed the air behind his chair. Reverend Harkin bowed his head to the savage warrior with a slight surprised smile.

Kimichin continued, looking at Lewis and Anson. "None of us expected to see you here, nor will the Blood Priests. Not from this direction," he added cryptically. "I don't know the how or why of any of this," he forewarned, "but I've gathered much from those running from them, coming to Santos del Rio from villages to the west. They say perhaps five hundred Blood Priests and two thousand yellow soldiers crossed the Usuma River west of Campeche. Most of the soldiers and some of the Blood Priests continued down the Camino Militar." He looked genuinely perplexed. "I don't know why, but it's rumored they march to Vera Cruz. I've heard that's a coast city, very far away."

Colonel Reed frowned tremendously, ruddy face darkening in the gloom, but Lewis only raised an eyebrow to Varaa, standing across the fire from him. Anson growled, "That silly old sailor."

"Not all have gone toward that place," Kimichin went on, "and that's why people flee. Some of the soldiers—enough, I'm afraid, since more were summoned from El Lago, where they'd been preparing to move to Campeche—and many of the Blood Priests now rampage along the Usuma, razing villages as they come, burning them and murdering the 'heretics' they find. In this distant place, so long and far removed from their attention, that's *everyone*," Kimichin ended grimly.

"But . . . what on earth for?!" Samantha demanded in horror. "Why . . ." She shuddered. "Why even take the *time*? You said they don't know we're coming."

Kimichin looked at her after Orno told him what she said. If he was surprised to hear a woman speak in a setting like this, he didn't show it. "Again, I only guess," he said, "but I think they expect to be followed by others who might not approve and are determined not to leave any 'heretics' behind them. Even more strangely, since there's been no word of another great battle in the north, I don't think they're running from you."

"I'll be damned," Anson muttered.

"What in the *devil* is going on?" Reed said. "I wish we had news from Nautla!"

Lewis sat silent, pondering what he knew of General Agon, and what little he knew of the political situation in the Dominion. *Did Holland's raid on Vera Cruz spark an open break between men such as Agon and the Blood Priests? Do they have civil war? How can we use that?*

"How far away is this murdering band of Blood Priests?" Lewis asked.

Kimichin looked uncertain. "The most recent refugees were from a very small village called Las Vides. Fifteen *leguas*? Perhaps a bit more."

"Very well," Lewis said with a nod, then looked at his various commanders, his friends. "We'd have to deal with them anyway. We can't have them stuck behind us, or worse, running in front of us spreading the word." He smiled at Reed. "And that's the best and quickest way I know to find out what in the devil's going on." His smile went away, and he looked back at Kimichin. "If you don't mind me asking, with a threat so close from the other direction, why did we find you on *this* side of your village?"

Kimichin only blinked surprise. "We were scouting a route for our people to escape!" he exclaimed.

"Why not fight?" asked Leonor harshly.

"Fight . . . Dominion soldiers? *Blood Priests?*" The man seemed horrified by the thought.

"Yeah," Leonor snapped, eyes flashing. "It *has* been done," she added sarcastically, "and the worst they can do is kill you."

Kimichin shook his head. "Oh, no. That is not the *worst* they can do, by any means."

Leonor rubbed her chin. Kimichin was right, of course. She already knew that. But still, apparently Kimichin and his little band of warriors had been fully prepared to fight a column of . . . what, fifteen, sixteen hundred men? Not even counting the nearby dragoons. Yet were scared to death of a few hundred Dom priests. *Reputations can be worth more than armies*, she thought. *Distasteful as it is, maybe Lewis is right. Time to build one for the Rangers on this world.* "Then we'll just have to make 'em scareder of us than we are of them, won't we?" she said.

"I'm afraid so," Lewis agreed, then looked at Kimichin again. "And you're going to help."

CHAPTER 18

The army continued on much as it had the next day, the infantry, artillery, and all their supplies and support by river, the mounted troops screening by land. The only difference was that Anson's Rangers galloped ahead under Kimichin's direction, a number of remounts at the disposal of the villagers' men. That slowed them considerably since none were accustomed to riding. Still, by midday, they'd covered the distance Kimichin's band had managed on foot and appeared on the outskirts of Santos del Rio. To Anson's surprise, instead of mud huts and *jacales* he'd probably unreasonably expected, Santos del Rio was quite "homey" in the sense the buildings were made of pit-sawn planks and timbers and even shake-shingle roofs. It looked more like a similarly small East Texas town, nestled in the piney woods, than anything else. *Of course it does*, he reflected, as Kimichin and his men went forward, shouting to subdue the panic that exploded over their unexpected arrival. *They've got the same abundant building material here, an' the soggy, humid nature of this frontier ain't so very different. Maybe the houses an' such are built on higher pilings*, he judged, *probably for when the river floods, or maybe to discourage a few forest pests.* They'd never seen a snake, but there were other things. And lots of annoying rodents. It was different in another respect, of which he was reminded when he saw the outward-leaning, sharpened-stake palisade sur-rounding the center of town.

It took a while for Kimichin to calm his people and assure them the strang-ers were friends, all while the "strangers" did nothing more threatening than sit on their horses and smile. When they finally understood the Rangers were there to help, to destroy the approaching Blood Priests, it was easy to get them to cooperate with the second reason for the visit: the preparation of a camp for the approaching infantry. All of it. A cleared field was set aside and water and firewood gathered. Even food was prepared, though it was probably impossi-ble to explain to a village of fifteen or sixteen hundred what would be required by roughly eight thousand men. As relatively prosperous as these people were, it was pointless to expect them to supply it either. Perhaps that's why they did what they could, though. Some must've grasped the sheer numbers. Maybe they thought if they freely gave the strangers what they were able, they wouldn't just take what they wanted. Anson tried to assure them that wouldn't happen, but even Kimichin seemed unconvinced. Especially when the barges began to arrive that evening and troops started to land.

"Why are we takin' the bloody guns off the barges?" asked Preacher Mac, 1st Section of Elijah Hudgens's C Battery. Their barge had been warped into shore, "nose" on, and heavy timber ramps were being rigged to the riverbank. More teamsters had scrambled aboard to help move one of the freight wagons and a caisson off. "Folk here seem friendly enough."

"Jus' yer one section o' six pounders," growled the short, pugnacious First Sergeant McNabb, of Olayne's A Battery, peering up at them as he squelched through the mud under the overhanging grass. "If yer other damn gun ever gets here," he fumed, looking out at the barges stacking up on the river. "Don't want yer goddamn twelve pounders. Too goddamn heavy." He looked up at Hanny Cox, who was actually the senior man on the barge. "Aye, an' the Preacher's right, Corp'ral. Folk here're friendly as kittens an' ye wilnae abuse 'em. But yer section's tae be attached tae us fer a bit, while we take a wee stroll on the blessed dry land."

"First Sergeant Petty knows about this?" Hanny asked, scanning the confusion onshore, even worse than on the water, as both divisions un-loaded to camp in one place for the first time. There was nothing that wouldn't normally go ashore, just men and tents and mess equipment, as well as crates and casks of rations, but with so many landing and trying to sort themselves out in such a small area, it looked like a kind of bedlam.

"He should, but nae matter fer now. I'll tell the hackit ol' divil."

"But . . . what about our horses, and where do we go?"

"Aboot haffa A Battery's guns're landed an' we're campin' with the Rangers. See yon limber comin' this way? It'll pull ye off an' take ye there. Yer horses'll be sent along."

Hanny hesitated a moment longer. "Why us?" he blurted.

McNabb scowled. "Why indeed, says I, if this is how ye act." He shrugged. "If it makes ye feel better an' gets ye on the move, we'll be nosin' aboot with the Rangers as a heavy battery. Might hafta move fast an' be away fer a while. Twelve pounders're too heavy, like I said, an so're the captured eight pounders, even on their lovely new carriages." Those guns were actually very well-made. The tubes, at least. But they were almost as big as 12pdrs and had smaller bores. That made them just about as heavy. "Twelve pounder *howitzers* might be best," McNabb conceded, "but we'll soon be in more open country an' might need longer range."

"Thanks, First Sergeant, but again, why us specifically?"

Mcnabb hesitated, torn between rude dismissal and relaying a genuine compliment. "Because Cap'n Hudgens offered ye up, that's why," he snarled, but relented. "Bein' that yer his best section, that basturt Hahessy aside, an' yer equipment's in the best order fer a long march. First Sergeant Petty's doin, no doubt. Now get yerselves an' that goddamn equipment ashore! Yer jammin' up the landin'!"

By the time they got the gun and limber unstrapped and hitched, the A Battery limber had already hauled off their caisson and returned. Now they rigged a long prolong rope to the ring on the end of the limber pole and a full six-up team pulled the whole thing ashore, the gun's crew guiding the wheels by pushing or grabbing spokes to act as brakes. And even as the limbered gun crept down the ramps, teamsters shifted the other freight wagons to balance the load on the barge. It all struck Hanny Cox as very well organized and chaotic at once: men splashing down in the river up to their knees (not without urging), while still trying to keep the heavy weapon on the ramps. Horses straining, men shouting—some in fear as the limber wheels nearly fell off the ramp, likely crushing the men beside it. Finally, with a creaking rumble and a spray of grassy clods from the horse's hooves, the Number Two gun bounced away on dry land, spokes blurring.

"What about us?" shouted Apo Tuin after them.

"I reckon 'us' hafta walk," grumbled Preacher Mac.

"They'll come get the battery wagon, won't they?" Ap asked, still put out. "All our tents and things are in there."

"Aye, they'll be back," McNabb assured, then grinned evilly. "By which time they'll be here fer yer *other* gun." He nodded down the bank, where the barge with the Number One gun was being pulled in. "Cheer up, lads," he called behind with a wave, "there's always the man harness!" That was a hated collection of leather straps that allowed *men* to be hitched to a vehicle.

"'Man harness,' my ass," spat Private Ricken. Originally from Baltimore, the Number Three was the oldest man in the section.

"My ass!" cried Kini Hau from Uxmal. He was the youngest.

"I'm hungry, and that always makes me miss my mother more," Apo complained.

"I'm hungry too," Hanny agreed, then smiled a little shyly. "And I miss your sister!"

"Ha!" Apo exclaimed triumphantly. "I will write her and tell her that, after all these miles and months, you finally confess! I can even write some English now—not that she can read it. Why would she? I only learn because I'll be an officer someday."

Hanny blushed red, and Apo laughed at him. "Don't worry, from where we are, you'll probably see Izel again before she ever gets my letter—and if you were that color all the time, my mother wouldn't think you are sick!"

Fortunately, four of the A Battery limbers, all they had ashore as yet themselves, had been hitched to horses and came and got the section's battery wagon, Sergeant "Mikey" O'Roddy's forge wagon, and the Number One gun's caisson—all of which came off the next barge before the gun and limber could—and pulled them up through the swelling camp toward where the Rangers and lancers had already erected tents inside the picket line thick with horses. Hanny's crew climbed on the various vehicles. Looking around through a growing haze of soggy woodsmoke, Hanny was encouraged to see the chaos that dismayed him before he was almost entirely restricted to the riverside landing. There was still shouting and frustration as company streets were laid out and infantry came up in disorganized companies, but there was no longer the look of *incurable* disarray. Even that, in fact, seemed to be curing itself rather swiftly, and Hanny felt a growing pride in these men, most of whom had been townspeople, farmers, shopkeepers, and fishermen—practically peasant laborers—not long ago. Strikingly similar to his old comrades in the 3rd Pennsylvania, in that respect. And as Apo said, aside from the jumble at the constricted landing area, they'd all been doing this for months and countless miles. Once through that initial bottleneck, the men knew what to do. Hanny was only mystified by the reason for that. Why gather the whole army here, for the first time since they left Cayal? Preacher Mac answered as if he'd asked out loud.

"Colonel Cayce's throwin' the fear o' the Lord into the natives. In a good way."

"What do you mean?" Apo asked.

"While you was on the wheels an' wadin' in the river, I was on a tagline, dry on the barge, talkin' tae First Sergeant McNabb—God pity his heathen soul. He told me these people were set tae run from a pack o' them despicable Blood Priests, murderin' their way up the river." He waved around. "With all this—us—between 'em an' evil, Colonel Cayce's givin' 'em back their spines, is he nae? Recruitin' as well. Warriors here, an' from as far around as they'll spread the word, can fall right in, get trained on the march like we trained the Uxmalos in the 3rd Pennsylvania, an' fight for their own selves. That's important," he added somberly.

"Why . . . sure. The more the merrier," said Billy Randall, the Number Seven man.

"T'ain't only numbers," Mac scolded him. "We . . . us Americans're so far from home, the only cause we got is 'the cause': doin' right, an' fightin' for each other. Our 'clan,' as it were." He nodded at Apo. "An' that clan's a'growin'. But fer some like young Apo, the farther we get from their homes, the less it might *feel* like we're fightin' tae save 'em. They get tae wonderin' why, if we can lick the Doms when they come fer us, don't we just stay home tae do it? They dinna ken ye can't *win* on yer arse, an' if that's where ye stay, ye lose. Folk from here joinin' up'll remind 'em, an' make nae mistake; Colonel Cayce means tae *win*."

THE ARTILLERYMEN DETACHED to accompany Olayne's battery, as well as Olayne's own late arrivals, didn't get much sleep that night. Hanny was still chief of the piece, and responsible for necessary maintenance on his gun and its supporting limbers and caisson, whether they needed it or not. Harness had to be checked and repaired (and added to, since Lieutenant Fitch, Olayne's executive officer, told him they'd be given full six-up teams). That meant they'd be moving fast and their equipment would take a beating.

Wheels were pulled and greased, which required four men, two on each end of the handspike lifting the axle one side at a time, while two more pulled the heavy, fifty-seven-inch wheel nearly off. They could rest for a moment then, with the end of the axle still supported just inside the knave box in the hub, while another man slathered on grease. The men on the handspike heaved up again while the wheel was spun into place and the washer and linchpin reinstalled. That was the easy part, for more reasons than one, and while they worked, the sun went down, sliding behind the trees and plunging them into darkness.

The most dangerous part was performed by the pitiful light of a ring of lanterns. Several men lifted the heavy trail high in the air and stood the gun tube "on its nose," the muzzle sinking several inches in the soft black earth. It was preferred to lash the tube to a stout tree at this point, but they were camped in a cleared field, and the closest trees were inconvenient. Cap squares were loosed, and four men (always nervously) ringed the tube to support it, each pressing harder all the time and fighting the sense it was about to fall on them. Grunting and tightly embracing it, they looked like fervent pagan worshippers of some bronze phallic totem. The rest of the crew eased the carriage back to grease the cheek irons where the trunnions rested, as well as the coarse-threaded elevation screw. Only then was the carriage pushed back to the tube, trail high like a scorpion's tail, until the trunnions *cloncked* back in the cheek irons and the cap squares were re-placed. Finally, the trail was lowered, and the men were allowed a short break. Of course, then the gun tube had to be cleaned again and all excess grease wiped off.

Other chores continued. Implements like the worm and rammer staff were checked and repaired, if necessary, the sponge bucket filled with water and inspected for leaks, and all leather items—gunners' haversacks, thumb-stalls, etc.—were oiled and waxed. Apo Tuin, the Number Six man and only one with "dedicated" assistants (Numbers Five and Seven, Kini Hau and Billy Randall), inventoried the contents of the chests on the limbers and the two others on the caisson. This was done as much by feel as lantern light because no one wanted a flame too near. They oiled the locks and tested the key, counted ammunition (all four chests were full, with an un-usually high percentage of canister), and made sure each was equipped with the necessary tools, like brass vent pricks, brushes, pliers, gimlets, lan-yards, and any number of things. Apo then delved into his small, personal tool kit in the primary chest. In addition to duplicate tools, there were wrenches, a file, a folding knife, turnscrews, the all-important pendulum hausse sight for the gun, and the Hidden's patent lock. They had more primers for it now, and unlike the problem faced—quite literally—by dragoons with their Hall carbines, it didn't matter if artillery primers were more robust than necessary. A fiercer explosion might cut lanyards more often than usual, but lanyards could be quickly retied, and they had spares.

When Apo was finished and returned his tool kit and relocked the chest, he helped Hanny coordinate with Gun Number One's Corporal Dodd to ensure the battery and forge wagons were properly maintained. This required only a few of each crew, and the rest were allowed to eat and relax. It was while this detail was under way that First Sergeant Petty joined them.

"Captain Hudgens an' me were with Captain Olayne all day," he said, as apologetically as he was capable of, which meant hardly anyone noticed. "Got our order of march. We're 'fourth section' now, and'll be spaced out by sections 'mongst the Rangers an' lancers. Mostly guardin' against rampagin' monsters, I expect. Word is, the land opens up a fair bit ahead. There ain't much of a road along the river, but we'll follow it a ways before strikin' out to the south an' sorta followin' it from out o' sight, where we can pounce on them damn Blood Priests when we catch 'em." He looked thoughtful. "Though I reckon Colonel Cayce wants ta get around *behind* 'em before we do any pouncin'. Don't want none gettin' away."

"Colonel Cayce will be with us?" Hanny asked, surprised.

"Why, sure. Not much fightin' to do, floatin' down the river. Case you hadn't noticed, our colonel *does* love a fight. Colonel Reed'll be in charge o' the barges. He's 'sposed to come ashore at a little town about a hundred an' fifty miles northwest, called Valle Escondido. About the size o' this burg. We'll meet him. There's a couple more villages along the way." Petty paused and concentrated. "Los Arboles an' Agua Ancha. That's them." His expression darkened. "Blood Priests already been to at least one of 'em." He looked around and nodded, then frowned. "Seems like you fellas have this sorted out, but where's that damn Hahessy?"

Corporal Dodd wouldn't meet his gaze. "I, uh . . . He knocked off with the other fellas we sent to eat and rest."

"Did you specifically give him leave? Did he overwork his big stupid self? Get hurt? Pinch a finger?"

"No, First Sergeant."

"So he just took off with the rest on his own," Petty snarled. "Like he'll do when them fellas pull extra duty to make up to these." He motioned at the men still working.

"Probably so, First Sergeant," Dodd confessed miserably.

Petty stood silent in the darkness awhile, and when he spoke, his voice was strangely gentle. "What is it with you, Dodd? You ain't no coward. Why can't you control that big Irish bastard?"

Still looking down, Dodd only shrugged. "He's a good artilleryman—in action. Not many better. He's strong and fearless, and good for the lads around him."

"In action," Petty stressed. "But he's pure poison the rest of the time."

"Yes." Dodd agreed. "I just . . . can't make him mind. If I put him on report every time he doesn't, the rest of the crew'll think I'm an ass. If I try to *force* him to mind, if I *fight* him, I'll lose. Even if he doesn't kill me, nobody'll ever do what I say again."

Hanny rather doubted that, suspecting Dodd would have more help than he thought. Then again, maybe not. Dodd had already let Hahessy abuse the rest of his crew too much.

"If you ain't in control o' yer crew, you ain't the right chief fer it," Petty growled. "May as well put Hahessy in charge. You already have, in a way."

"I'd have to agree with you, First Sergeant"—Dodd sighed—"if any of the men were behind him. They don't like him either. This is your section. Why can't you just get rid of him?"

Petty shook his head. "Maybe I could have, once. Probably should have, when we cleaned out Gun Number Two. Now, it won't do *you* any good. Igettin' rid o' him gonna make your crew respect you more? You *need* ta beat the shit out of 'im."

"I can't," Dodd admitted.

Petty sighed. "So you said. Reckon I'll have ta do it. Still won't do you any good." For some reason no one doubted the relatively short, even somewhat scrawny first sergeant could find a way to best the Irish giant. "Still won't help you none." Petty glowered.

"What if I do it?" Hanny suddenly blurted. The others looked at him and blinked. "I don't mean *fight* him," he quickly assured. "He'd fold me in half and tear up the pieces. But I *have* gotten the better of him a time or two, so to speak, and I think he respects that." He smiled slightly. "I might at least survive a try at talking to him." He glanced at the other chief. "And not on Corporal Dodd's behalf, but the whole section. It's my section too."

"Put it that way, I prob'ly should deal with him myself," Petty countered resignedly. "I hear Lieutenant Barca's leanin' toward takin' the section—fine by me, I'm first sergeant for the whole damn battery, and I got other shit to do—but it's my section for now, an' Hahessy'll just get worse if Mr. Barca takes over."

"That's for sure," Hanny agreed. "Hahessy seems to hate everybody, and black men are close to the top of his list. But you can't do it. *Authority* is at the very top, and I don't have enough to matter to him." He actually chuckled. "If *you* try to reason with him, you'll have to kill him."

Petty shrugged. "Fine. Give it a go. But make sure you got plenty of help you can trust in earshot when you do." He glared at Dodd. "I can't lose *both* my gunners to that maniac."

Word began to spread that the infantry would remain in the vicinity of Santos del Rio for another whole day and night, recuperating from their long float and, more important, sorting the various regiments out a little better. They'd stagger their departure by as much as a day as well, allowing more spacing between divisions so 2nd Division could use the same site 1st Division abandoned ahead of it. No one believed there was a large Dom force in the vicinity, and that probably made the most sense. Indeed, they probably should've been doing it all along. But this kind of "advance" was new to everyone—even Colonel Cayce was essentially making it up as he went.

Near midnight, the moon was coming up and the camp was finally settling down, with nearly everyone ashore who'd camp there. Quite a few, especially late arrivals from 2nd Division, had simply given up, choosing to sleep on the barges. The new order of march would give them at least one day of rest ashore, possibly two. Tired himself, instead of rolling up in his blanket, more to keep the bugs off than to keep warm, Hanny Cox set out alone, looking for Private Daniel Hahessy. Apo, Mac, and Andrew Morris had told him to wake them if he did, but he decided to let them sleep. Besides, Hanny half expected Hahessy would know if anyone was around when they talked. That wouldn't work.

Nobody in the section had erected tents and most just wadded up under gun tarps rigged as flies to protect them from the falling damp around the guns and limbers. Hanny thought he'd find the big Irishman snoring away with the rest of the crew of Gun Number One, but he didn't. Even his bedroll was absent. No one was awake to ask, so Hanny continued his search. Campfires sputtered all around like orange reflections of the silvery stars, but there was little movement. There'd be pickets on and beyond the perimeter, of course, but there was little more than a fire watch otherwise: one or two men from each company lounging near the fires, smoking pipes and talking low, occasionally feeding sticks to the embers.

Hanny looked at them, sometimes exchanging a few quiet words, even asking if they'd seen Hahessy from time to time. No one liked the big man anymore, even in the infantry where he came from, but pretty much everyone knew who he was. After a while, Hanny began to fear he might've gone into the village, seeking amusement of the sort that caused him so much trouble in the past, getting him demoted and nearly hung. Following him there was impossible. Colonel Cayce had declared Santos del Rio off-limits and Hanny would only be suspected of evil intent himself, if caught. He'd just about given up when, down near the landing, a pair of watchmen allowed they'd seen a "big, hulking brute" with a blanket roll heading down toward the water. Hanny went to the river.

A short distance from where some barges remained tied and the ground had been churned to a muddy morass, the shoreline rose too high and steep to lay ramps. There the grass was thick and deep and Hanny found a lone figure sitting up, hat cocked back, arms crossed over his chest. The shape was distinct enough that he didn't need the better light from the much higher moon to tell he'd found Hahessy. Climbing the slope, he stopped behind the big man, sitting on his blanket in the grass.

"Away wi' ye, er I'll throw ye in the water fer the fishes, I will," Hahessy rumbled without turning.

Hanny hesitated, wondering how to respond. He considered saying something sarcastic or just sitting down himself, but the tall grass was full of biting insects, and the mosquitoes caused him enough misery. Finally, he just sighed and looked out at the river. "I couldn't sleep either," he said.

Hahessy turned his head slightly. "Young Corp'ral Hanny, is it? Aye. Well, I've slept all I care to already, an' couldn't care less about ye."

"Don't much care about anyone, do you, Hahessy?" Hanny countered. "Anyone or anything."

"Little er none a'tall," Hahessy cheerfully agreed. "Now off wi' ye, er I *will* toss ye to the fish!"

"Don't care much for yourself either," Hanny persisted.

Hahessy said nothing for a long while after that, just sitting and staring at the water. Finally, he *whooshed* out a long breath. "Ye've got guts, Corp'ral Hanny, I'll give ye that. Always have. An' ye've the right of it too: I care little more what happens to me'sef than to you. Neither of us has much of a chance, I'm thinkin'."

Hanny crouched down beside the big man. "Maybe not," he said. "I try not to think about the fix we're in. A rabid enemy that wants to wipe us out, monsters that want to eat us." He chuckled. "It's not what I thought it would be like to be a soldier." Hahessy made no response to his weak joke, and he went on. "Anyone alone on this world wouldn't have a chance at all. But we *are* soldiers. Colonel Cayce saw to that—that we'd stay soldiers and stay together. That *gives* us a chance, don't you see? Working together with our fellows and the troops we've helped train, we *do* have a chance to live, even win. . . ." He gestured around. "Sitting alone, out in the weeds, even the blasted chiggers can eat us up."

"Ha!" Hahessy barked. "So ye think all it takes is an army, all workin' together, do ye? Well, an army's made up o' men, each as different from the other as can be." When he continued, it was like a different man talking. His tone was as harsh as usual, but his signature Irish accent somewhat faded. "I've been a soldier nearly all me life. Why, ye might ask? Because I'm Irish. If yer the son of a tenant farmer, a Son of the Shamrock too, not born ta some contrived pet peerage bribed with land stolen from better folk—an' ye want ta eat—why, there's little real choice but ta take the king's shilling. Ta fight for a king an' parliament that thinks you're no better than an animal. Less valuable than a horse."

Hahessy smoldered over that for a moment, then said, "Still, I took the damned shilling an' fought men of every color all over the world, whoever the damned king pointed me at. Black Asantis in West Africa, bloody brown Marri tribesmen—do ye even know who Asantis an' Marris are? I didn't. An' I never did know *why*. Usually kicked our arses too, an' our useless, senseless, *gentlemen* officers respected 'em more than their own soldiers." He spat. "I got ta thinkin' maybe it's because, unlike the Irish, they *did* kick their arses."

He pulled some grass and wadded it into a ball. "Me enlistment up—oh, no, I wouldn't run, an' where to, I ask ye, in those hellish places?—I took me discharge. I would've gone home, but then where would I be? Ireland was even hungrier than when I left." He finally turned to look straight at Hanny. "I went to America instead. There, I thought, things'd be different. Men from all over go there. The 'land o' opportunity'!" he mocked. "The British hate ye, but ye whipped 'em so they respect ye." He shook his head. "But the *Irish* have it no better there than at home. No work, no respect, no *opportunities* if ye haven't the money ta leave the city. An' no money without resortin' ta crimes that'll get ye hung." He shrugged almost imperceptibly. "I went back in the army. Irish're still animals ta the 'gentlemen' officers in the American army. 'Unfit fer anything under heaven' is the oft-quoted line, er 'not a bad fellow, though an Irishman.' Still, an Irish soldier who knows *how* ta soldier can get promotion in time. It took me, a fightin' man already, *five years* ta make sergeant." He briefly glanced at his sleeve where his stripes used to be. "One drunken night ta be a private again."

"You could've been hung. Other men were," Hanny reminded.

"Aye," Hahessy agreed. "An' I likely deserved it. I did no killin', an' tried ta help stop it," Hanny was there and remembered, "but I did start it all, didn't I? Those fellas were just followin' my lead. Behavior *you* started by standin' up ta me, Corp'ral Hanny."

Hanny was taken aback and felt a surge of anger. "You're blaming your troubles on *me*?" he demanded.

Hahessy shook his head. "I did at first, aye. No more. Me main trouble was, after finally makin' sergeant—an' a mean one at that—I had almost no truck with officers. *No one* stood up ta me anymore. For the first time in me life I was *above* other men. Better. Not only better than darkies an' injuns, but white men as well. First Germans an' Swedes an' bloody *British* immigrants, then other branches, like artillery an' dragoons, an' you damn Volunteers. Even other Irishmen," he actually seemed to lament. "Long as it don't reflect poorly on 'em, officers don't give a shite what happens in the ranks. That meant *no one* who mattered looked down on me anymore, so I started lookin' down on others. Treatin' 'em like I'd been treated. Like I *hated* bein' treated. I had power. Too much," he lowly admitted.

His gaze had wandered off, but returned to Hanny. "I know why yer here. Come ta *reason* with me, have ye?" He sighed. "An' I reckon, like the goddamn British, I've come ta respect ye a mite since ye licked me, in a sense, an' I'll hear what ye have ta say."

Hanny was chilled somewhat to learn Hahessy saw it the same way others did. He watched him put his hands behind him on the blanket and lean back on his arms.

"All the same, I'll warn ye, just between us: I don't give a shite about you, nor anyone else. I don't *want* a goddamn 'friend,' an' I ain't gonna change. I'll keep on like I have and to the devil with the rest."

Hanny pondered that a moment. A simple statement of fact. "Well," he began thoughtfully, "I really don't care how you *feel*, or if you have any friends. I *do* care about *my* friends, the section and the battery. You're a broken spoke, Hahessy, a danger to the rest. And if you keep on like you have, you'll get people killed who I like. Corporal Dodd's had enough of you, so has the first sergeant, but for some reason they've left what happens to you up to me. I don't know why—or why I give a damn. Maybe it's because I saw a *glimpse* of a good soldier in you, once. Just once," he stressed. "If I was smart, I'd be asleep now, tell First Sergeant Petty you're not worth the effort. Or leave it to Lieutenant Barca to decide, if he takes the section. He's a *good* man, but I suspect if you call him a 'darkie,' you'll wish you were never born. He's had further to climb than you."

Hanny pursed his lips and slapped at a mosquito buzzing his ear. "The thing is, though, I *volunteered* to talk to you, so now you're *my* responsibility. If you won't change, you're too dangerous to leave where you are." He let Hahessy contemplate that. "Nobody else wants you, and if First Sergeant Petty throws you out, which he'll do *before* we set out in the morning if I say, you couldn't even get assigned to guarding prisoners in Itzincab. You could run"—he gestured around at the forest wilderness surrounding the camp clearing—"but you'd have to be suicidal. Big and tough as you are, out here alone you're just a snack. Seems to me, this is your last chance to *try* to be a good soldier again. Not for a king who hates you or a country that might not appreciate you, but for an army that needs you and good people who don't *care* you're Irish and are relying on you to fight a *real* enemy as bad as or worse than any you've faced." He sighed and stood. "We'll be moving in just a few hours, to go find that enemy. You've got a real opportunity to *prove* you're a better man than others, stripes or not, no matter where you're from." He actually chuckled. "In Colonel Cayce's army, that might get you more stripes than you want. Look at Lieutenant Barca—or Captain Hudgens! He was a private, remember."

Hahessy was looking at the water again, hunched somewhat forward now. Hanny just stood and waited. "What?" Hahessy finally snapped. "What're ye standin' there for? Be off with ye!"

"I want your answer," Hanny replied just as harshly. "I said what happens to you is up to me, but it's really up to you. What'll it be?"

"Oh, I hate yer livin' guts, Corp'ral Hanny," the big man seethed, "but ye have me word I'll *try*."

"Fair enough. That's all any of us can do," Hanny said firmly, but he was shaking slightly. He didn't know why. He wasn't physically afraid of Hahessy anymore, but it dawned on him this had been his first real test as an NCO—making a man do something he didn't want to do for the good of the rest—and he felt like he had the first time he dealt with a misfire on a cannon. The first time he was *in charge* of dealing with it. He knew his crew was rapidly coming to . . . love their gun, in some indefinable way. It was their collective weapon that required a team effort to tend and maintain and send each round downrange. It was becoming part of their identity. But they'd had a misfire while training outside Cayal, and their beloved "Number Two gun" had suddenly become an insanely dangerous, utterly unpredictable, monstrous *thing* that might go off any instant. He had to stand by and supervise while his *friends* gathered closely—too closely—around it to re-pierce the charge through the vent and re-prime the weapon. There was a very specific drill for that, to minimize risk, but if the gun went off during the process, at least two of his friends might be crushed or maimed by the sudden recoil, or lose a hand to the concentrated jet of flame from the vent. Hahessy reminded him of the potential menace of that misfired gun. He had to be dealt with, and Hanny was shaking with the same relief he'd felt before. At least Hahessy couldn't see it.

But nobody loves Hahessy, he thought, *and he might be even more dangerous and unpredictable than a misfire. Probably safer in the long run to transfer him, after all. Get rid of him.* A suitable metaphor came to mind. *Flood the tube with the sponge bucket, kill the powder, and draw and discard the round. I hope I've done the right thing.* Turning, he walked away.

CHAPTER 19

Bugles and drums sounded reveille shortly before dawn, and tired artillerymen, Rangers, and lancers stirred and began preparations to move while cooks labored to feed them. The temporarily desig-nated "Fourth Section" horses were finally led up by a squad of dragoons who wouldn't be joining them. All were "new," good-looking animals and totaled enough to hitch six to each gun and vehicle and still have some spares. That alone should've convinced any doubters they'd be pressing hard. Lewis and Warmaster Choon, along with Kimichin and Kisin and a small clot of warriors to "protect" them (though none would've been any use on horseback), joined Anson and Leonor at the head of A Company, 1st Rangers. A Company was, as usual, the first ready to move. Or so they thought. Together, they led the coalescing column through the trees to a rutted, overgrown trace of a road. There they found that Olayne's First Sec-tion of artillery had actually been ready *before* A Company and was waiting to fall in behind. The next company of Rangers would follow. And that's how the column proceeded: Rangers first, because they were better at rapid deployment and fighting in close confines, with three sections of guns in-terspersed among them, followed by the lancers, which were more intimi-dating if given the opportunity to deploy and attack en masse. The new Fourth Section was with them.

Scouts were already coming back down the road as the first rays of the sun filtered through thinning trees.

"Nothing, sir," an Ocelomeh Ranger reported to Anson. "No people, yet," he clarified, "but only a fool—or an army—would be up and moving at the favorite feeding time for *los monstruos*. We saw some of *them*"—he scowled—"some *very* big ones moving together, but we didn't tempt them."

"The beasts will get bigger as we move onto the plain," Kimichin explained through Kisin, though his Spanya wasn't much different from what most of the army spoke. "And there'll be more of them."

"More grass," guessed Varaa. "More and bigger grass eaters, so bigger eaters of them."

Lewis nodded, brows turned down in concern. "Our scouts must be extra vigilant, not only choosing the best route to avoid detection by the enemy, but to avoid the larger predators. The only thing we have that can truly discourage them is our artillery, and it can be heard for miles."

"Keep the column bunched up tight an' let the fellas sing," Anson suggested. "Looks like one big, loud, critter to the boogers an' they don't like it. It's worked before, an' the fellas enjoy it." He arched a brow. "Besides, singin' ain't as loud as cannon fire. Damn sure don't carry as far."

"We'll do it, but not yet," Lewis reluctantly agreed. "Thank God for *chocolate caliente*, but it isn't coffee, and I *really* miss coffee this morning. We'll wait until we need it before we strike up the choir."

The trees continued to thin as the morning wore on and a vast, flowery prairie opened to the west, covered with herds of great creatures, many like none they'd seen. Eventually, the forest barely extended beyond the road and only grew thick by the river. Far to the southwest, purple mountains loomed, their shapes, size, and even distance obscured by haze. Scouts returned regularly, beginning to report people, plodding along in caravans of a dozen to a hundred.

"Do you trade much with other cities?" Lewis asked Kimichin. "Los Arboles is next, is it not? Maybe forty miles . . . roughly eleven and a half *leguas*?"

"We trade some," Kimichin allowed, "but most of what's been seen will be . . . *refugiados*, fleeing from the Blood Priests."

"Could there be Blood Priests among them?" Varaa asked.

"They couldn't pass themselves as the same people they're with, but might pose as *refugiados* from villages farther along."

"Makes sense," Lewis said, then turned to Anson. "Time to leave the road and pick up the pace."

Anson gazed at the prairie. "Not much to conceal us out there," he warned, "an' we're liable to stampede any o' those critters that don't want to fight us or eat us," he added.

Lewis smiled. "That's why we brought Mr. Kimichin. He knows the low places and washes. As flat as it looks from here, it's really not."

"If you say so, Lewis," Anson agreed doubtfully, calling for the column to veer out to the left, diving into the knee-high grass. "Scouts ahead," he ordered. "Keep your eyes peeled for leg an' wheel breakers, an' low-slung predators."

Oddly, for the most part, the open ground was smoother than the road, and the ride in the saddles—and atop hard limber chests—was easier on bottoms grown tender after so long on the river. It was dusty, of course, and that might become a problem that bandannas couldn't solve, from a visibility standpoint, but Kimichin assured them they'd be hidden from view long before they reached the horizon. Anson remained skeptical until the village headman was somewhat startlingly proven right. Barely a mile and a half from the road was a dry, shallow river bed that seemed to parallel the much deeper Usuma behind them. It was rocky in places, but mostly fine sand with only the occasional muddy puddle.

"We couldn't go this way in the rainy season," Kimichin explained, "but now it's almost better than the old road. We must have a care, however," he warned. "*Los monstruos* don't graze here, but come to the waterholes—and they travel along it, of course." He hesitated. "And big eaters of grass eaters"— he glanced at Varaa—"are smarter than their prey. They use it to get close to them . . . so we may see more of them."

"I knew there'd be a catch," Anson grumbled. "Captain Olayne!" he called behind. "Bring one of your sections to the front." He looked at Lewis. "You up for a concert yet?"

"By all means."

The Rangers and lancers began to sing, some even managing to play along, with banjos, fifes, even drums slung alongside them on horseback. They started, as usual, with a few Uxmalo favorites with complicated if repetitive melodies, actually vaguely familiar to Ramon Lara and his handful of companions from a more modern Yucatán. But even the Uxmalos and Ocelomeh had begun to favor the more energetic and generally (though not always) more buoyant American songs. And seeing as those were often derived from older, Celtic tunes, the latter were popular as well.

As the day wore on, troopers sang the slightly modified and perhaps even more appropriate "Strike for Your Rights, Avenge Your Wrongs" set to the jaunty tune of "The Rose of Alabama." That led to more versions of the original song with "Roses" from different places. The "Rose of Allendale" wasn't from Allendale anymore either. Next came the "Enniskillen Dragoon," though the subject was no longer a dragoon, nor was he from Enniskillen. "Old Rosin the Beau" went quite long, incorporating old and new lyrics, but "Old Dan Tucker" was rendered without any changes, as was the apparently universal favorite "Blue Juniata."

The strange, fearless sounds must've done some good because, other than a few large, toothy creatures that peered over the edge of the bank into the dry riverbed from time to time, in more apparent curiosity than anything, they saw nothing overtly dangerous. Other beasts, usually only glimpsed, clawed and scurried up the bank and away from their approach. There were no other obvious dangers. That didn't mean they weren't there. The riverbed deepened and turned into mud, surrounding a thick, greenish-brown slurry swarming with insects. And all around the putrid, standing water were dozens of what looked like little caves—like giant crawfish holes.

"Keep the horses moving," Anson said. "Don't let 'em drink that nasty shit."

"Even as thirsty as they must be getting, I doubt they would," Leonor said. "Anyway, it's thick enough, they'd have to eat it."

"What's in those holes?" Lewis asked Kimichin. The Indio headman shuddered slightly. "*Tortugas de garra*," he said darkly but matter-of-factly. "Stay away from them." He glanced at the hot sun overhead. "They won't come out in the middle of the day."

Lewis glanced at Varaa and she shrugged, flicking her tail. She didn't know what had made the holes either.

"Hey, get away from that," Boogerbear called. He hadn't even had a chance to pass Kimichin's advice down the column, and a pair of Rangers had paused beside one of the larger, eerie-looking holes to peer inside. Very much like a crawfish hole indeed, there was a mound of what looked like regurgitated mud rimming the lower edge of the hole as if to hold water.

"Something's in there!" one exclaimed.

Who knows what he saw—perhaps the muddy swirl above a moving shape—but an instant later, mud and water—and a *thing*—exploded from the hole.

Combined with the appearance of the holes, the first impression of those around it was of a giant crawfish, of sorts. It had a long body, bigger than a wolf's, with segmented armor covering it from what must've been the head, to a flared and very crawfish-looking tail. And there were great gnashing pincers on the ends of powerful, armored "arms," but short, pebbly skinned, web-footed feet, as well as its tail, most likely, were what propelled it at its victims with such energetic force. The closest Ranger screamed in terror and agony as two-foot-long pincers with spike-serrated edges closed on his arm and torso. The horse bolted from under him, and man and monster fell to the ground.

"Shit!" Anson hissed, drawing one of his Walker Colts and wheeling Colonel Fannin around. Varaa already had her musket off her shoulder and up, but wasn't pointing it yet. A fusillade of carbine fire erupted at the thing, heavy lead balls skating off the natural armor and warbling away, leaving deep, lead-smeared gouges. Some punched through and made big, jagged holes, but they only showed the armor was an inch or more thick and the balls must've been spent before bringing blood. The thing never slowed, scrabbling back toward its lair with the screaming, blood-spraying, struggling man in its claws.

"Kill it!" shrieked the man's companion, jumping off his own horse and ineffectually pummeling the thing with his carbine butt.

"Get away, you idiot!" roared Boogerbear, he and Anson both trying to draw a bead with their revolvers. That's when they realized the monster's "head," the pointed end of the segmented carapace, wasn't its head at all. The real one, a beaked monstrosity the size of a 24pdr roundshot but resembling an oversize snapping turtle's, lunged out on a powerful, leathery neck like a striking snake and sank deep in its attacker's belly. That man screamed even more horribly than the first when he tried to push away while the head pulled out a wad of intestines.

Anson and Boogerbear both fired, blowing a bulging, lazy-lidded eye into a bloody crater, spraying the mud beneath it with red fragments of bone and gobbets of flesh. The thing flailed convulsively, further shredding the men in its grasp, pulling the guts out of one and nearly scissoring the other in two. Both finished kicking before their murderer did.

"My God," murmured Lewis.

"Keep yer damn eyes on them holes!" shouted a Ranger sergeant. "An' that nasty water too. Might be more in there!"

Someone must've glimpsed one in the water, or thought he did, because a carbine thumped loudly and a geyser of mud vomited up from the puddle, spraying everyone at the front of the column with reeking droplets.

"Cease firing, damn you!" Anson barked.

"We supposed to just let 'em get us?" someone objected.

"You actually *see* one?" Anson demanded. "Seems like they're layin' low, so wait till you got somethin' more than a swamp fart to point yer weapons at. Chances are, you stay away from the holes an' the water, an' nothin'll get nobody. I hope," he added in a whisper. "Shit!"

"Language," Lewis said mildly, equally low, now beside the Ranger. "Contrary to conventional wisdom, some of the smartest men I know use the worst language, but profanity can betray a degree of nervousness." He raised his voice. "Carry on, Captain Beeryman. Take the men through. We'll join you ahead where the riverbed rises."

"What'll we do with these poor fellas?" Boogerbear asked, waving at the corpses.

"Can't bury 'em here," Leonor agreed.

"No," said Lewis, dismounting to look at what got them. "It *is* some kind of turtle," he declared. "Not a crustacean at all, but a reptile. Reverend Harkin would be amazed." He glared up at Kisin and Kimichin. "A little more warning would've helped."

Wide-eyed, Kisin shook his head. "Lotsa bad monsters wake up in the forest when it's wet, but I never seen anything like that! It could've got *me*!"

"I've seen . . . smaller ones, I suppose," Varaa confessed, blinking hard. "Actually quite tasty. I never imagined they got so big. I'm sorry."

Kimichin shook his head unhappily. "We're used to them. I thought you were too."

"Well, we ain't," Leonor snapped at him. "We ain't used to much at all in these parts, not even those of us from . . . closer places. So if you want us to save you from the Blood Priests, you better not take stuff like that for granted."

Lewis gave Leonor a slight, approving nod before addressing Boogerbear. "You're right. We can't bury them here. Perhaps we'll find a place tonight, or can bury them by the cookfire and then move it on top of their graves when we're finished with it in the morning. Have a detail stay and wrap them in their own blankets and oilskins and put them in one of the supply wagons when it comes up."

They made good time for the rest of the day, avoiding further incidents with monsters. The only difficulty came when they had to cross a field of large, eroded boulders that would've made treacherous rapids if the river was running. Rangers and lancers took turns dismounting to help heave guns, limbers, caissons, and wagons over these impressive obstacles. They'd brought spare wheels for just about everything, but couldn't do much for sprung or broken axles, and they had a long way to go. They finally made camp at what might've been one of the widest, shallowest points of the river, had it been flowing, and drew all eight guns in the battery up around the area set aside for the men and horses. The perimeter was strengthened by long, sharp spikes they'd brought in the wagons, driven into the sandy silt at an angle, backed by a large, alert guard. Even their vigilance would be reinforced by spoons and tinned plates hanging on lines farther out. They'd have a fire and a hot meal, likely the last one for days. The banks of the riverbed would shield the flames from view, but the glow in the night haze might give them away. They knew this because they could see the glow of Los Arboles themselves, just a few miles northeast. They'd scout the village and observe, of course, but wouldn't visit. Kimichin had said Blood Priests weren't embraced there, but elements of the "traditional" Dominion faith had been to some extent.

"Probably why they haven't fled to Santos del Rio already. They think their relative piety will protect them," Ramon Lara said doubtfully. "Some will warn the enemy if they see us."

Lewis agreed and warned the scouts to avoid detection at all costs. He was counting on surprise when they fell upon the Blood Priests at last. That's why there'd only be cold camps after this, and the men were told to cook three days of rations to augment their marching fare of tortillas, dried fish, and jerked meat.

The spoons clattered on plates a few times in the night but might've been enough by themselves to frighten inquisitive creatures away. Guards saw nothing, no shots were fired, and an hour before dawn, the column made ready to push on. Not long after daylight, Alferez Rini of the 1st Yucatán Lancers—one of Lara's few remaining companions from that other world—returned from watching Los Arboles, galloping down the riverbed ahead with half a dozen Uxmalos. (Ocelomeh still didn't like lances.) Lara himself was waiting with Lewis at the head of the column, leaving Teniente Espinoza in charge at the rear.

"Sir!" Rini said, saluting. "Sirs," he quickly added. Including Lewis and Anson, and probably Varaa. "Beg to report."

"By all means," Lara said.

"What did you see?" Anson demanded.

"We watched the town all night, and returned when we were relieved by a squad of B Company Rangers. They took our positions and *should* still be there—if they followed my orders. . . ."

"What orders? An' why wouldn't they stay put?" Leonor asked. Anson made a "hurry up" gesture.

Rini took a breath. "The enemy—Blood Priests—about three hundred of them, and maybe that many Dom infantry, probably a dozen mounted men. All look ragged, even the priests. They arrived at first light and started rounding up everyone in the village."

"Artillery?" asked Captain Olayne, walking up to join them. Lieutenant Barca was with him. He remained part of Lewis's "staff" but spent more time with the young artillery officer. Lewis suspected he'd made his decision and was letting the men, particularly of the so-called fourth section, get used to having him around as much as he was "learning the ropes" from Captain Olayne.

"None we saw, sir," Rini told him.

"*Everyone?*" Lara asked.

"*Sí, señor. Todos allí. Hombres, mujeres, y niños.* They were not gentle about it either, and seemed in a great hurry," Rini added to Lewis.

"Obviously," Lewis agreed with a glance at Kimichin. "We never expected them to make it this far, so quickly. What were they doing?"

"At first, only collecting everyone. Some fled, and the mounted men chased them and brought them back. Most of them. These"—he paused and gulped—"these went on impaling stakes at once. We could hear the screams from where we were hidden, five or six hundred paces away."

"God a'mighty," Anson growled. "No wonder you had to order the Rangers not to interfere!"

"They would've been killed as well," Rini agreed.

"What about the rest?" Lewis asked.

"The soldiers put them to work gathering timbers, even tearing down buildings for them, constructing crosses."

"How many?" Lewis had a sinking feeling.

"Many," Rini told them. "Probably . . . enough for everyone in Los Arboles."

"They'll crucify them," Kimichin dismally stated. "Crucify and burn them, so they may 'earn' the grace to enter heaven. We're too late," he almost moaned. "And if they're here, they've already been to Agua Ancha and are just days from my own Santos del Rio!"

Lewis sat on his horse in silence a moment, thinking. As usual at times like this, his plan exploded fully formed in his mind, and he quickly described it. "We can't undo what they've already done, but we can stop them and make them pay. I only hope there's time." He turned to Anson. "Take four companies of Rangers and all but the extra section of Olayne's battery wide around to the left, avoiding discovery as best you can, and cut the road behind the enemy. Send a strong scout back down it to snap up any stragglers." He looked at Boogerbear. "Captain Beeryman will backtrack a short distance with the rest of the Rangers and the other section of guns"—he paused ever so slightly—"under Lieutenant Barca, to cut the road in front of the enemy." He pulled his watch from his vest and consulted it before looking back at the Rangers. "You have one hour to get in position."

"What about you, Colonel Cayce?" Varaa asked.

"I'll remain with Mr. Lara. We'll deploy his lancers as frighteningly as possible and smash the enemy in the village. That shouldn't be hard, with almost seven hundred disciplined men. Doms or not, I expect the enemy to scatter." He raised a brow at Anson and Boogerbear. "*Your* jobs will be to tighten the noose as soon as we strike and prevent them from getting away. Pay special attention to the forest along the riverbank beyond the village. *No one* escapes," he stressed, "and aside from enough prisoners to question, there'll be no quarter." Even with all he'd heard about Blood Priests, he disliked giving that order. But he wouldn't weaken his force by leaving men to guard prisoners, and certainly wouldn't drag them along. He glanced at Kimichin. The only alternative was to leave them with their victims. Killing them in battle was probably more humane. He cleared his throat. "You'll know when it's time to advance."

Anson was sure of that. "Fine. But Leonor stays with you, along with a company of Rangers." He grinned. "What with all the cannon, an' the only Doms comin' at us already panicked, it ain't like me an' Boogerbear are gonna be shorthanded. With another company, you'll be startin' the fight with as many men as the enemy, for once!" His grin went away. "Still, you're gonna have the hard part. Not your attack," he added for Lara's benefit when the young Mexican officer seemed to bridle, "I mean the waitin', with nothin' to do but think about what's happenin' over there"—he tilted his head toward the village—"while we get in place. It's gonna *seem* way longer than an hour before you charge."

Anson was right. Even though an hour was little enough time for the two prongs of the "ambush" to move about a mile and a half in one case, and the better part of two in the other, it seemed to a crawl at a snail's pace. Especially when Lewis, Leonor, Varaa, and Capitan Lara, joined by Kimichin and Kisin, and Corporal Willis, of course, moved up out of the riverbed to view the events under way in the village about fifteen hundred paces away. First, Lewis ensured that his detachments were moving undetected. *He* could occasionally see swatches of dark blue cresting the topped-out grass, or catch little swirls of rising dust, but even the dust was subdued by the morning damp, and no one in the village noticed. Especially since there were quite a few large creatures grazing along in a perfectly normal fashion. Then he saw Boogerbear's whole column erupt into the open more than half a mile behind, moving at a ground-eating trot back in the direction of the road, but the angle was such that it still shouldn't have been visible from the village. Anson's larger party had to cross a more open area between the dry riverbed and the trees extending beyond the road to the northwest, but the gap was fairly narrow, and they weren't exposed for long.

Not that they would've been noticed in any event, because the enemy's attention was firmly fixed on what they were doing. Lewis had only seen a few Blood Priests, and the mere proximity of "Father Tranquilo" was enough to make his skin instinctively crawl, but other than the psychotic sacrifice they'd—mostly—interrupted, which essentially started the terrible battle that ended the next day at the Washboard, he'd never really seen with his very own eyes what put the depravity of the Blood Priests on an entirely different level than that on which "ordinary" Doms routinely wallowed. Now, when Lewis turned his small brass telescope onto the village, he saw that there genuinely were quite distinct degrees of evil.

Nearly every building in the village was burning, the roofs (a mixture of shake shingles and grass thatch) largely fully involved, and a massive gray-white column of smoke towered into the morning sky. Hundreds of people, many as naked as they'd been dragged from their beds, were tightly huddled together, crying and wailing under the fixed bayonets of yellow-and-black-clad guards. More Dom soldiers were deployed around them, and there was another, wider ring around the village. Red-robed Blood Priests were busy in other ways. Perhaps a score of long stakes had been erected near where they would've entered the village, and these were topped with the *impaled* corpses of men and women. At least Lewis *hoped* they were corpses by now. . . . Nearer the center of the village, dozens of crosses had been erected, with more going up as he watched. Men and women were nailed up on them, and terrible screeches of agony, accompanied by mauls striking spikes, were audible even from here.

Lewis was silently horrified, and despite all he'd seen in his career as a soldier, it was all he could do to keep his breakfast down. Slightly adjusting the focus on his glass, he found a young woman centered in his view, writhing in agony on one of the crosses, ankles and wrists spiked to the wood. Streamers of blood spilled down from the spikes, and the woman's mouth was wide in a scream Lewis couldn't hear over crackling flames and general lowing of misery and terror. Even as he watched, several Blood Priests arranged kindling at the base of the cross and another brought a flaming brand from a cookfire. Only then did Lewis remember he'd heard of this before, possibly even dismissed it as exaggeration. Deep down, he couldn't believe anyone could be so cruel.

"They're crucifying people over there," he almost whispered, "and lighting small fires beneath them to *add* to their misery!"

"They'll do that to everyone," Kimichin said just as lowly.

"Even the ones who *support* them?" Lara asked in a tone of dazed horror.

"Yes," Kimichin said. "Those who don't must be 'cleansed' and earn their entry to heaven with pain. Those who do . . ." He paused. "Are expected to *welcome* this opportunity to do the same."

"But more important to *them*," Leonor snarled, clearly referring to the Blood Priests, "they won't leave any fence-sitters behind. Kill 'em all an' you don't have to worry about their loyalty."

"That's likely the main reason for their entire 'campaign' upriver," Varaa said, tail whipping.

Lewis collapsed his glass and looked at his watch. Every moment they waited allowed the Blood Priests to murder more people.

"Father was right, wasn't he?" Leonor asked grimly, her pretty face contorted into a furious, impatient grimace. "This is the hard part."

"Yes," Lewis agreed, looking back at his watch. "And so was I, to order 'no quarter.' Well," he continued, "I'm sure Mr. Anson and Mr. Beeryman know me well enough by now to understand when I say 'an hour,' I really mean 'forty-five minutes,' and they've had plenty of time. Deploy your lancers, if you please, Mr. Lara."

"With pleasure, Coronel Cayce!" Lara barked, whirling his horse around. "Teniente Espinoza! *Desplegar el regimiento!*"

The 1st Yucatán Lancers, nearly seven hundred men, surged up on the plain and peeled out to the sides to form four lines, nearly four hundred yards long. A few family groups of smaller herbivores bolted. Only about twice the size of a cow, they looked something like Har-Kaaska's strange mount going primarily on four legs instead of two. Even before the command to do so, troopers were whipping leather covers off razor-sharp lance heads and tucking them in valises. Many of those lance heads were iron, captured from the Doms, and despite daily polishing, wore a dusty red layer of rust from dew-damp covers. The rest were a kind of bronze, made from the same alloy that would hopefully make cannon one day, and they gleamed a bright reddish gold. All were quickly returned to an upright position, and those with carbines swiftly loaded and primed them. Those without them checked their swords. Leonor called on the Company H Rangers Boogerbear left to deploy behind the lancers, near the center. As quickly as this occurred, and despite the bushy-headed grass standing as tall as the stripey horses' bellies, at some point the Doms took notice.

Pandemonium erupted in the village and red-robed Blood Priests surged back and forth like chickens chasing bugs, possibly hearing conflicting orders from surprised leaders. Dom soldiers looked just as confused at first before attempting to form a line, but then prisoners broke through the thinning cordon and attacked them or tried to run. At the same time the Blood Priests were shrieking for the soldiers to defend them, others were screaming at them to stop the prisoners. Muskets flashed and thumped.

"Uncase the colors!" Lewis roared, his order repeated down the lines. There were some Itzincabos and Techonos in the ranks, but most were still Uxmalos and Ocelomeh. In addition to company guidons, the Uxmal saltire was joined by the new "Jaguar Banner," and the red, white, and green tricolor pennant, reminiscent of the Republic of Mexico, standing for Lara's 1st Yucatán. The Rangers used the Stars and Stripes, like other American regiments in the army, and Lewis was struck by its proximity to one representing enemies on another world, side by side on this one.

"Advance your regiment, Mr. Lara," Lewis said.

The Doms in the village grew more frantic when the lines of horses began to move at a purposeful, rippling trot, but there was very little they could do. Few were experienced soldiers. Those who were likely already knew they were doomed. About half the four hundred or so generally rear-area "city" troops the Blood Priests had collected formed a ragged line, but it immediately started melting when the men realized how few they were. "Senior" Blood Priests, as best they could be determined—most often by the bizarre hats they habitually wore, or staffs they carried topped with jagged crosses—were screaming for their own to join the line. Almost all Blood Priests were armed with short swords, but few had any idea how to use them against anything but cowering victims, so they started grabbing local hunting spears or farm implements, even a few dropped muskets they probably didn't know how to use. When the relentlessly approaching lancers leveled their weapons and charged—one of the most terrifying things even seasoned soldiers can stand and face—most of them fled as well. An embarrassingly ragged and ill-aimed volley from less than two hundred muskets met the lancers as they drove their charge home, killing several horses and wounding a score or so more, while emptying half as many saddles. Just enough to further infuriate the men who'd come to kill them. And they did.

Lewis, Leonor, and Varaa had edged forward as they charged, leading a small wedge of Rangers in among the lancers and up around Capitan Lara. Lara would've preferred that Lewis stay back, but wasn't in a position to suggest it since he was leading from the front as well. So it was that the four of them, surprised to be joined by the Holcano "war leader" Kisin, were galloping side by side at the center of the charge when it slammed into the crumbling Dom line. Lances bowed as blades struck home in chests (or backs) of screaming men and the lancers merely loosened their grip, letting their weapons slide in their hands as their horses pounded past, then pulled them from fallen bodies to bring them forward again. Some slowed among the scrambling enemy, stabbing downward, overhand, while carbines flashed and boomed.

Swords and sabers came out slashing, including the basket hilt "backsword," or partially double-edged rapier, Varaa carried. She'd never even bothered with her musket, and it remained slung across her back. She fought like the demon the Doms thought she was, and her sword moved like a striking snake.

Leonor's little Paterson Colts barked sharply, over and over, dropping the more fanatical Doms still trying to pull the leadership down. In less skilled hands, the .36 caliber weapons were underpowered for this kind of fight. They'd wound their victims, even kill them—eventually—but rarely *stopped* them at once. Leonor *was* very skilled, however, blowing bloody holes in heads and faces and chests without even aiming.

Lewis had drawn his prized, engraved M1840 artillery officer's saber, and was hacking down about him on either side, the heavy blade striking deep to flay heads and shoulders and necks and backs. His mare, Arete, did her part, stomping and kicking and bowling men down with practiced ease.

Leonor could only watch in admiration. Her little "native" horse, Sparky, had learned not to jump or buck when her pistols fired, even right by his head, but he only endured the fight, didn't actively join it. She absolutely adored Arete—the horse had surely once saved her life—and imagined the blood of some famous warhorse coursing through the mare's veins. Her father's gelding, Colonel Fannin, could participate in a fight as well (despite his name), and she wondered what it took, besides experience, to make them do that. A musket ball whizzed past her, and she refocused. Cocking her Paterson, she snapped a shot at a running Blood Priest. The back of his head seemed to explode, and his conical hat twirled away as he slammed down in the bloody village dirt, face-first.

Leonor's might've been the last nearby shot. Most everyone else's firearms were empty, and their desperate stand shattered, the defending Doms were streaming away just as Lewis predicted. There was still screaming, from wounded on the ground and people on crosses. Others joined them briefly when patrolling lancers stabbed down at crawling or squirming men, or chased those few who jumped up to run and took them from behind. Not a single Dom soldier or Blood Priest had tried to surrender—yet. Leonor figured some might before long, when they realized there was no escape.

Then Lewis was beside her, breathing hard and sweating, a kind of savage grin on his face. Bright white teeth gleamed in his brown, blood-spattered beard. His saber, already drying and crusted red, was in his hand and would remain there until he could clean it. "Short and sharp," he said of the fight. "They've had quite enough, here." He looked at her. "Most ran back the way they came, where your father will entertain them." His expression clouded as he looked past her. "Stop that at once, *Mr.* Kisin! I thought you meant to set an example for your people, and all the others here." He waved toward a fairly large number of villagers, still huddled where the Doms put them. They looked shocked, numbed, and had to be wondering what, if anything, had changed for them. Who were these fierce "blue" people? What kind of demon was the bloodstained *furry* one with a *tail*? But Kisin had jumped from his horse, dropped his bloody, flint-studded club, and been hooting loudly as he labored to sever a Blood Priest's head with a dull copper knife. Now he stood, looking contrite.

"My apologies, Colonel. It's just been so long since I enjoyed such a sweeping victory. . . . Even the fight at Cayal brought little joy. I wasn't *really* one of you then, and not only was I fighting my own people, it didn't end like this. I'm . . . afraid I let the moment move me too much."

"I understand, but don't do it again," Lewis scolded. "Besides, this isn't over. Where's Mr. Kimichin? Ah, there he is, with more of the villagers. Go with him and help take those poor people down." He pointed at a moaning form on a cross with his saber.

"What do you mean, not over?"

They felt a disconcerting pressure, and a deep *poom-poom, poom-poom, poom-poom* roared over them from the forest around the road to the north-west. Canister crackled through the woods toward the river, and more screams echoed in the trees. Then came the booming clatter of heavy car-bine fire. Obviously, Anson and Captain Olayne had arranged their recep-tion at a slight angle from the village so it wouldn't be directly downrange.

"I thought you, of all people, understood," Lewis replied. "Just as your Holcanos had to join us or die, this isn't a war for glory—chasing the enemy from the field. Kill a few, take trophies and captives, and scatter the rest, only to fight them again. This *isn't* a game. Look around you!" He pointed at the crosses with his saber again. "There can't be *peace* with people who do that!" He scowled with distaste. "You may have eaten your enemies, but you ate your own dead as well. Disgusting? Yes. Savage? Yes. Unacceptable to the rest of us you chose to join? Absolutely. Evil? Not necessarily. It's just the way you were. Some might say, 'different cultures, different ways,' and let you do as you want." He shook his head. "But this is *my* army, and you'll behave as I require if you want to be part of it. Your people will do the same if they wish to remain in the Alliance." He frowned back at the traumatized villagers while Kimichin led others to help them. "Causing such suffering, *heaping* it on solely for the sake of it and to achieve more power through terror—and despite what they say, that's the real reason for those behind it all—is pure satanic evil and must be destroyed. You can't reason with it, play war with it, or hope it'll leave you alone. You have to kill it."

The firing in the woods was lg louder, closer, and Lewis looked up. "And as I said, there's still work to do. Many of those who ran away are about to be back." The section of guns with Boogerbear, under Lieutenant Barca, roared as well. "From just about everywhere," Lewis added wryly.

"Then I shall fight!" Kisin exclaimed, dashing back toward his horse.

"No, you'll set the 'example' of doing what I told you," Lewis countered more harshly. "Mr. Lara! Dismount your lancers and assemble across that road." He pointed. "And detail half a company or so to search the village for Doms who've gone to ground. If there are locals sufficiently recovered from their ordeal to suggest likely hiding places, that'll help." He paused. "And remember: I want prisoners—but not many."

Then he looked at Leonor, and her heart did a kind of double thump when she saw the grim expression his face had assumed suddenly brighten with a depth of fondness, directed at her, that she'd seen only a very few times. "Take your company of Rangers and block the road from the other direction, if you please, Lieutenant Anson."

Leonor smiled back. Holstering the Paterson in her hand, she saluted. "Of course, Colonel Cayce."

Varaa was grinning, blue eyes wide and bright as she watched the by-play between them. *Everyone else knows. I think they're finally starting to figure it out for themselves,* she thought. *Good. They need each other. I wish that I . . .* She sighed. "I'll remain with you, if you don't mind."

Lewis smiled at her as well. A different smile. "I appreciate it, as always."

There was no more cannon fire after those first, thunderous rounds, but firing intensified in the woods to either side and down by the river as both detachments of Rangers converged on the village. Lewis expected a pan-icked surge of Doms and Blood Priests to lap back against the dismounted lancers, now reinforced by irate, almost frantically furious villagers who, if they had no idea who their saviors were, could clearly recognize them as such. As it turned out, only a few wounded, terrified Dom survivors filtered back, and at the insistent urging of the villagers and in accordance with Lewis's orders, these were shot on sight. Eventually, a little after noon, the bulk of the Rangers came in, roughly leading a short string of yellow-and-black-clothed Doms and a few red-robed priests all roped together. They were followed by the clanking, creaking rumble of limbered guns. Consulting his watch, Lewis frowned and called for the supply wagons and their escorts to approach the village. More shots were still thumping and popping down by the river as Anson reported.

"You *said* you didn't want many prisoners," he said with a trace of irony, tilting his head toward the few they had. One of the biggest hurdles Anson and Lewis had had to overcome to become true friends dated to their old war against Mexico and Anson's disinclination to bring in prisoners then. "Actually kinda knotty gettin' as many as I did, after the fellas saw what was happening here. Hard to miss when we crossed in the open, and them that didn't see for themselves heard it from others. Then again, though they were keen to get away, not many of the bastards wanted to surrender." He shrugged. "Fair enough, an' glad to oblige." Another short flurry of shots echoed in the woods. "Boogerbear sent scouts to cast about as far as the ruckus should've carried, and he's beatin' the bushes for any we might'a missed. Not many." He snorted. "Bright yellow an' red is hard to hide."

Lewis was aware of the irony and might even consider his own change of position hypocritical—he hated hypocrisy with a passion—but hated what he'd seen happening here even more. "Mr. Lara," he barked, "see to your wounded and combine any prisoners you took with those Mr. Anson secured. Then bring Mr. Olayne and join Mr. Anson and myself with Mr. Kimichin over there. He seems to have collected some local representatives."

Lara, Anson, and Olayne turned their commands over to their deputies, telling the men to refresh themselves and fall out in the shade but stay with their companies. No one knew if they'd be stopping.

"What about them?" Anson tilted his head toward the prisoners again. There were fourteen Dom soldiers and eleven priests, most with some wound or other. Lewis found it hard to believe there were so few, considering there might've been six to eight hundred of the enemy and the latest count of their own dead and wounded was twenty-six and forty-one respectively. Sure, there were plenty of Dom bodies scattered through the village, and there'd been a lot of shooting in the woods, but it was difficult to accept that their victory had been so one-sided and complete.

"Bring them," Lewis replied, pulling Arete's head around and urging her toward the growing group of villagers encircling Kimichin and Kisin.

All those who'd been crucified had been taken down, and army healers, mostly women in the same uniforms as men but without any branch trim, were attending the ones still alive, as well as several wounded lancers. The impaling poles were coming down now.

"What're you gonna do with 'em?" Leonor asked about the prisoners. Lewis didn't answer as he, Varaa, and Leonor finally stepped down from their mounts. Varaa whispered aside to her, "I doubt *he* will do anything, except ask questions." Leonor suspected she knew what the Mi-Anakka meant.

Tearfully grateful people surged around them, welcoming them as saviors and liberators. This was the first time that had happened. There'd been celebrations in Uxmal after the victory at the Washboard, and those who'd gone through Itzincab were welcomed with relief, but the Holcanos had received them with fire and death and even Kimichin's people were reserved and afraid. These people knew they'd all be dead if not for the Allied Army.

"Just smile," Lewis said as Corporal Willis shoved his way through the crowd of *very* smelly villagers. The soldiers were smelly in different ways, but all were clothed. Many of the villagers were still entirely naked, clutching at them, caressing and hugging them. Those wearing clothes dressed much like Kimichin's people: in hides mixed with bright fabrics. Willis finally secured Lewis's saber and started wiping it down with a grungy rag dampened in hot water.

"An' keep yer hands on yer weapons," Anson said, "to keep 'em from hurtin' themselves," he quickly added, gently slapping hands away from his revolvers. These folk were no deliberate threat.

A strained voice called for the people to part, and they quickly did so, revealing a tall, handsome older woman draped in a Blood Priest's robe. Like many others, she'd been dragged from her home, where she'd been sleeping in the nude. Her long gray hair was clotted with blood, so she'd probably been bludgeoned as well.

"This is . . . You'd call her Alcaldesa Consela. She's the . . . head woman here," Kimichin advised.

"You saved us," the woman said in strongly accented but understandable Spanya. "I owe you . . . everything," she added simply.

Lewis, Anson, Lara, and Olayne all swept their hats from their heads and bowed. "It was our pleasure, ma'am," Lewis replied. "We're at war with the Dominion, and benefitting others by destroying some of them is reward enough for us."

Consela bowed in return. "In that case . . . what will you do with the ones who still live?"

"I'll question them," said Lewis, "and deal with the soldiers in our own way. The Blood Priests will face *your* justice, of course."

"Oh yes. I see," Consela murmured, almost hungrily. "Then I beg you to question them quickly—so they can be mine."

"You place her even more in your debt," Kimichin whispered. "Her oldest son was one of the first to encounter the invaders and tried to raise the alarm." He nodded almost imperceptibly toward one of the last impaling poles to be lowered.

"Damn," Leonor hissed.

The prisoners heard the exchange and weren't much interested in talking. They might've felt the same in any case. Lewis considered that briefly. Despite everything, he wouldn't torture anyone. And the Blood Priests might only thank him for that in their perverted way. The soldiers, however . . . "The priests won't talk," he finally declared, after speaking with each and receiving no response. "Give them to the people they harmed." The eleven Blood Priests were dragged away, squirming but not really objecting. In their belief, they were about to go to heaven. The fourteen soldiers looked less eager for that, or at least the means of getting there. Their anxiety increased exponentially when the villagers used some of the very crosses they'd prepared to start crucifying priests who, whatever they believed, couldn't keep from screeching in agony as spikes were pounded through their bodies and into heavy timbers. And the screams only intensified when the crosses were raised, dropped into holes prepared for them, and wedges were driven down in the holes to hold them up.

Lewis saw some of his troops crossing themselves in the near distance, and his own guts twisted inside, but he kept his face and voice firm when addressing a young-looking Dom soldier with a bullet-smashed shoulder. The kid was in terrible pain already, and Lewis hated to torment him further, but he had to. Lara stood by to translate if necessary, but Lewis's Spanya had much improved.

"Let's see now, where was I? Ah yes. Ordinarily, we treat prisoners very well. But what you did here, what you were *part* of . . ." He shook his head. "That puts you beyond protections afforded legitimate soldiers by any civilized laws and usages of war. That leaves me no choice but to execute you all. I have no discretion in that regard." He paused while they listened to the shrill justice of the village of Los Arboles being meted out.

"On the other hand, if you'll tell me what I want to know, just *one* of you, I give you my word that *all* will die as soldiers, executed *by* soldiers forming a firing party. You will *not* be turned over to the people you helped torture so cruelly. This is the quickest, most humane, most *honorable* death I can offer." He paused a moment more while screams chorused loud from several throats, and his expression, carefully neutral till now, twisted with fury. "But if *none* of you speak, so help me God, I'll give you to the locals and tell them to take their time."

All the Dom soldiers started talking at once.

As it turned out, they'd only just arrived at Campeche, perhaps three thousand in all, as the final reinforcements for General Agon. But Agon had already marched up the Camino Militar against the heretics at Nautla. Rumor had it that a courier had brought news of various disasters: Vera Cruz had fallen, and the old Supreme Holiness had died of shame that such a thing could happen to a principal city of the Dominion. A new Supreme Holiness, Don Julio DeDivino Dicha, more sympathetic to the Blood Priests, was installed. Father Tranquilo, now calling himself *patriarca* of the province, persuaded the Blood Cardinal Don Frutos to abandon Campeche (and General Agon's campaign) to "cleanse" Vera Cruz. Unfortunately, more heretics were preying on Dominion shipping so they'd march the roughly three hundred *leguas* (around eight hundred miles) to their destination. Tranquilo meant to conscript more troops on the way, from frontier and eventually city garrisons. The soldiers were skeptical about that. They'd been one of those "frontier garrisons" and left very few troops behind, little more than required for policing.

From Campeche, they'd been sent with this large contingent of Blood Priests—vile, loathsome creatures, and heretics themselves they all proclaimed bitterly—to "cleanse" whatever inhabitants of La Tierra de Sangre they could reach so there'd be no potentially hostile force in Tranquilo's rear. All disliked the duty (of course) and would've been crucified themselves if they refused. Besides, it was pointless because General Agon would certainly be "hostile" to Patriarca Tranquilo and Don Frutos after they abandoned him, and would certainly pursue them with all his might. They expected the regular soldiers to flock to Agon's banner, and civil war would ensue.

Lewis motioned at the others to move away with him. "What do you think?" he asked when no one could hear them.

Anson scratched his chin through the tangled thatch of whiskers. "Everything they said is consistent with what little we know. Explains a lot of that too. Most important, seems they've confirmed a lot of our other guesses—with most o' their professional army off on its Gran Cruzada against those Britishers in California, Agon's the only real obstacle 'tween us an' their vulnerable interior."

"An' now Agon's runnin', hell for leather, chasin' Don Frutos," Leonor reminded. "That's a change. But can we use it?"

"The only thing it 'changes' as far as the 'big plan' is concerned"—Varaa blinked at Lewis—"is whether we can still get into position to block General Agon."

"Varaa's right," Lewis conceded. "We've succeeded in getting around Agon, perhaps a little too far, in fact, and I doubt we have a chance of catching this . . . advance force under Don Frutos. I hope Captain Holland and our friends at Vera Cruz can deal with it or escape." He rubbed the whiskers on his own chin. "I wanted to wait until we reached the coast, but we have no choice but to send word back to Cayal, where the semaphore can relay it to Uxmal and carry it by ship to Vera Cruz. . . ." He sighed. "Our communications are *much* too indirect."

"An' that 'word' will have to pass through hundreds o' miles o' monster-infested forest. Take a good-size party to carry it safe," Leonor pointed out.

"At the same time, we're in a tighter race to reach Gran Lago before General Agon does," Lewis agreed. "If he gets there first and learns we're coming, our roles will be reversed. We'll have to attack him on ground of *his* choosing."

Captain Olayne nodded at the prisoners. "So . . . are we going to shoot them?"

Lewis shook his head. "If we can differentiate them from the Blood Priests in the eyes of the locals, I'd rather not. As they said, they were just following orders, and have no moral foundation for disobeying them. Certainly no protection from being tortured to death themselves if they do. That's something they have to be taught."

"You always got aggravated at me for exceeding my orders," Anson grumped.

"Those were different circumstances," Lewis reminded, annoyed, "and when—if—I 'turn you loose' here, you won't be doing what Blood Priests do."

"Except maybe to Blood Priests," Leonor warned.

Lewis pretended to ignore her, but realized he didn't have a problem with that. When the time came, he *wanted* the Rangers to inspire terror in the enemy. He looked at Olayne. "But regarding the prisoners, I'd just as soon send them back to Cayal as well. Those we took after the Battle of the Washboard, wounded, mostly, have had time to learn a better way. They're still watched, but many are working in our industries at Uxmal. Sailors Captain Holland captured constitute part of his ship's crews. They aren't necessarily any more evil than Kisin is. They've just been conditioned to *do* evil all their lives, and many might be . . ." He shook his head. "Cured, I suppose. I'll try to convince Alcaldesa Consela of that."

"And if she doesn't agree?" Varaa asked.

Lewis's voice hardened. "We'll shoot them."

Ironically, the head woman of Los Arboles chose that moment to approach. With her were Kimichin, Kisin, and several fighting-age villagers, all now armed. Consela herself had discarded the red robe and dressed herself in a light blue tunic, bound around her waist with a silver-studded belt. She wore a lot of silver, in fact, which complemented her silver-gray hair. For the first time, Lewis realized what a handsome woman she was, not nearly as old as her hair (and circumstances) had made her seem at first.

Lewis hadn't realized how long he'd been questioning the prisoners and discussing what they'd learned, pushing the screaming Blood Priests and surrounding activity in the village to the periphery of his concentration. Now he noted the screaming was over (the villagers were more merciful than their former tormenters), corpses had been moved out of sight, and people were salvaging what they could from the wreckage of their dwellings. Lara's lancers and Boogerbear's Rangers were helping. It all looked very well organized. Quickly glancing at his watch, he noted they'd essentially lost a day in the "race" because by the time he reassembled his column and pressed on, they couldn't get far before they had to stop for the night.

"Alcaldesa Consela," he greeted with a respectful bow, then nodded at Kimichin before returning his gaze to the head woman. Her face still reflected her grief, but the blood and tears and grime were gone, and she'd even bound her hair like Uxmalo women who wished to advertise they were available for courting. Lewis wondered if it meant the same thing here.

"Colonel Cayce," Consela returned, bowing as well. "Forgive me for greeting you so . . . abruptly before. I was not myself."

"Who would be?" Leonor asked, almost in the "man voice" she sometimes still used. The crucified Blood Priests were festooned with arrows and hanging limply from their crosses. "They got off easy," she murmured lower.

"Yes," Consela said simply, then returned her attention to Lewis, gesturing at the Dom prisoners. "Have you decided what to do with these?"

Lewis nodded. "If you've no objection, I'll spare them—unless any can be identified by your people as having carried out the terrible orders they were forced to obey with any degree of enjoyment. Those will be shot. They answered my questions, and I gave my word."

"I have no objection," Consela replied. "I can't imagine what you'll do with them, but I've no doubt the chief responsibility for what happened here lies with those we already punished."

The Dom soldiers understood and almost collapsed with relief. Some were sobbing. Observing how grateful they were, Lewis said, "The first taste of mercy they've had in their lives. You might be surprised how useful they'll be."

Consela gestured behind her. "As you can see, my people are very busy, but food is being prepared. I hope you and your men accept our meager hospitality."

"Grateful to," Lewis told her.

"I'm glad. We haven't much food left—most was burnt—but there's more than we can carry."

"Carry?" Varaa enquired.

"Yes," Consela confirmed with a lingering look at the Mi-Anakka. She wasn't afraid of what many would regard as a demon, so Varaa's people must've been known to her, at least by reputation. "Los Arboles is dead," she said flatly. "Half our people will go back to Santos del Rio with Kimichin. At least until they can return to rebuild."

"We're losing you, Mr. Kimichin?" Olayne asked.

"Yes. You don't need me, but I'll be needed at home to help settle so many."

Lewis looked doubtful, but before he could speak, Consela said, "You'll have me to guide you now, and the aid of over three hundred strong warriors with a thirst for revenge."

"Well . . ." He considered. "That's excellent news. I'll be glad for your assistance, and the additional troops are most welcome. They'll have to learn our ways of fighting, however," he warned.

"Of course."

"What about the rest?" Anson asked. "Three hundred ain't 'half.'"

Consela blinked, as if the answer was obvious. "They will come as well. No old or lame or very young. Just those who can carry their burdens. They'll cook for you, make your camps, mend things that break or tear."

Jesus, more camp followers, Lewis inwardly groaned. *Enough of those are coming down the river after the infantry.* Virtually every army in his old world still used them, and they were handy for the things Consela described, but they tended to slow an army down, and Lewis's whole strategy was based on rapid movement. Consela seemed to realize this. "They'll keep up, at least until you meet the foot soldiers Kimichin said are following you on the river."

Lewis sighed and spread his hands. "Very well. Thank you."

"No," Consela said, that hungry gleam returning to her eyes. "Thank *you* for what you've already done, and for the chance to destroy those who murdered my son—and tried to destroy us all."

CHAPTER 20

The following morning, the shattered village of Los Arboles was abandoned and Lewis's detachment of Rangers, lancers, and artillery proceeded up the road once more. They had no reason to expect another sizable force until after they met Colonel Reed and the rest of the army and turned west toward Gran Lago, and their scouts should have the advantage over any Dom stragglers they found. Besides, the road was better here than before and easier on the guns and wagons. Not to mention the long tail of dismounted villagers they'd picked up. Anxious to hurry, Lewis was annoyed by that at first, before Varaa pointed out how well they were keeping up and that they couldn't have pulled the wagons much faster without frequent breakdowns in any event. Worse, if they hadn't already met the enemy at Los Arboles, and, yes, picked up a pack of people who'd slow their pace, they'd still be creeping along even slower in the dried-up riverbed. How much longer would that have taken?

Lewis hoped it would even out in the end, but for a while he wasn't sure *anything* would. He may have gained three hundred strong warriors, as Alcaldesa Consela promised, but also nearly *seven* hundred women, older children, and men a little past their prime. And aside from the astonishingly light combat casualties and various other injuries and illnesses that had chipped away at his force along the way, he'd lost fifty lancers and as many Rangers—a hundred men to escort those casualties and the people of Los Arboles to Santos del Rio, then carry dispatches back to Cayal. Their numbers should allow them to do the latter in relative safety. He began to modify his views over the next few days, however. The warriors Consela provided *were* very strong and at their physical peak. They had to be to survive in this land where the monsters were bigger than any Lewis had seen and most of their 'warfare' involved hunting them with bows and spears. Creatures that often hunted them back, with equally sharp objects. Even the least offensive and aggressive of their herbivorous prey could (and often did) kill or maim half a dozen hunter/warriors before the rest brought it down.

Compared to that, however, quite a few older youngsters and men who'd semiretired from hunting to focus on skills requiring brains and experience over brawn and agility were perfectly capable of engaging in modern war against mere men, and Alcaldesa Consela insisted at least a hundred more would find places in the infantry when it joined them. More, if Lewis would let women fight. Lewis demurred, explaining it wasn't their way—right in front of Leonor and Varaa. That restarted a long-simmering debate among multiple participants with different perspectives.

"It really isn't the 'way' of my people either," Consela said, now awkwardly riding a borrowed horse beside Lewis, Anson, Leonor, and Barca. (Barca reported no problems with "his" section under his command, and seemed more torn than ever between committing fully to it or remaining at Lewis's side.) Kisin was nearby as well, oddly fascinated by the *alcaldesa*, whose strength of character powerfully complemented her mature beauty. "But many of my women are eager," Consela continued. "They may be short" (as noted before, Consela was remarkably tall for indigenous females), "but they're strong, and I'd compare their endurance and motivation favorably with any man's. I don't see why they wouldn't be capable."

Varaa seemed to hesitate before speaking. "You all know I can fight," she said simply, not bragging, "and though it isn't exactly encouraged, females of . . . every species . . . in my faraway land can take up arms in its defense in whatever capacity their generally smaller statures don't make them a liability." She rarely spoke of her homeland, and Lewis never pressed her, but this wasn't the first time she'd hinted that the Mi-Anakka weren't the only ones who lived there. "And the same is true of the Ocelomeh," she continued. "There are relatively few female warriors among them, but they do exist." She blinked frustrated amusement at Lewis. "There are even some among your Rangers, as you know."

"I think he tries to pretend not to notice 'em," Anson quipped.

"Like me?" Leonor asked, her tone somewhat belligerent.

"Oh, no," her father told her. "You really had him fooled in the old days, thinkin' you were my son or nephew, if he thought about you at all. Ever since he figured you out—as much as that's possible"—he added wryly, "it ain't as if he's tried to keep you from the fightin'."

"I would if I could," Lewis blurted, immediately regretting it when he saw the hurt/betrayed/angry look Leonor threw him.

"Well," she exclaimed. "I guess I'll just keep myself away from *Colonel Cayce* for a while. You too, Father!" With that, she kicked Sparky in the flanks, and the little horse galloped forward until she joined Boogerbear and a troop of Rangers a short distance ahead.

"Now you've done it," Anson scolded. He looked at Consela. "Things are different in more . . . settled places. They're a *lot* different where we come from. Uxmalos, for example, didn't used to hardly fight at all, leavin' it to the Ocelomeh for the most part. They don't have any choice now, an' we've made respectable troops of 'em. Still no women, though, even if women run the place more than we're used to." He gestured at Lewis, Barca, and himself. "But Uxmalo, Techono, and Itzincabo women do all the things back home that *let* men go off an' fight: raisin' crops, sewin' uniforms, makin' gunpowder, castin' bullets, rollin' cartridges . . . Hell, they're even workin' in the mines an' foundries now, I hear, all while raisin' babies—which they *can't* do while they're fightin', by the way. Without them makin' an' sendin' on all the things the army needs to fight, we couldn't put *half* as many men in the field as we have.

"Where we come from"—he gestured at the other Americans again—"*much* farther away than Uxmal, or even wherever Varaa's from," he added enigmatically, "we fight wars all the time, but there hasn't been one where the consequences for losin' were so high for everybody—men, women, an' children." He glanced at Lewis and shrugged. "Maybe since the Mongols. And they at least gave you a choice to surrender. The Doms'll kill or enslave you whatever you do. Resistance just makes it worse." He looked back at Consela. "Sorry. Mongols were a long time ago. But women in our society are kinda, well, insulated in a way. At least that's the effect. Oh, sure, there's exceptions, though most o' those are frowned on. Others on the frontiers, like you are, I guess, have to scratch an' claw for a livin' alongside their men, maybe even fight, ah, raiders from other tribes from time to time. But that ain't what we *want* for 'em. What our *culture* wants for 'em. I expect a big dose o' that comes down through time as a means o' controllin' women, even ownin' 'em in a sense, but most who were raised like me were taught that there ain't no culture, no civilization, without women, an' it's a man's duty to take care of 'em an' give 'em the easiest life he can. An' above all else, *protect* 'em from harm. I know how it feels to fail at *that*," he brooded. "I was off fightin' another war once, when my wife an' boys were murdered." He nodded in the direction Leonor had gone. "She's all I have."

Consela looked thoughtful. "I'm sorry to hear that. But isn't it then possible that the women of Uxmal may be in danger as well, with their men at war and them unable to fight?"

Lewis and Anson looked at each other, but Barca said, "A portion of our force remains there. We can't imagine how an enemy would approach, but our defenses there should be sufficient." Anson, in particular, looked uncomfortable with that answer.

"But that brings us back to my suggestion. Any protection for the female 'camp followers,' I've heard you call them, would diminish your power in battle. It only makes sense they should be trained and have the means to protect themselves."

"Unnecessary," Barca answered again. "The supply train must be protected in any event."

Consela smiled. "But wouldn't it be more efficient if those who are now helpless be taught and allowed to do that for you?"

"Damn," Anson said. "She's got a point, Lewis. Did you put her up to this, Varaa?"

"She did not, and of course I do." Consela indicated Anson's daughter. "Especially since it's so evident that female warriors do in fact exist, even among your people."

"That wasn't my idea," Anson grumbled.

"But you could've stopped her," Lewis suddenly said, voice full of frustration. "You're her father."

Anson looked at his friend, surprised and angry. "When do you think was the last time that girl did *anything* just because 'I said so'? Never, that's when. Hell, even when she was little, I had to come up with good reasons to get her to wear *clothes*! Thank God for cactus an' thorns. Give her a *reason*

besides 'you're a girl,' an' she might stay out of a fight, but what am I supposed to say after lettin' her do it so long? Especially since she's the deadli-
est thing I ever saw, an' she knows it. I hoped by now, if anyone could
change her mind, it'd be you!"

Lewis looked stunned. "Me? Why?"

Anson rolled his eyes. "Oh, don't be an idiot, Lewis."

Varaa and Barca were grinning, but Consela seemed concerned. "I suppose I shouldn't have spoken," she said. "Not yet. I feel responsible for
this . . . argument."

"You are," said Varaa cheerfully. "For fanning the flames, at least. Come,
let's go talk to the 'girl' and leave these ridiculous *males* to stew!"

The tension lingered throughout the day and into the following morning, with Leonor avoiding both Lewis and her father, but then the scout
returned with the news they'd reached the next village where the Doms
had already been: Agua Ancha. Boogerbear came back and told them to
come up slowly. "We're downwind," he warned, "which ain't gonna be
pleasant, but it's a good thing we are," he added cryptically. His first warning was unnecessary. The reeking stench already surrounded them, long
before the village was in view. As soon as it was, they recognized the source
at once—and were gladder than ever they'd intervened at Los Arboles. At
Agua Ancha, the Blood Priests had been free to carry what they'd started at
Los Arboles to its final conclusion.

The village had been burnt to the ground, of course, and every single
thing that might've been of use to anyone—fishnets, meat- or hide-drying
racks, farming tools, bows and spears, even bedding—had been destroyed
or burnt. Nothing but charred ruin remained, and except for the horrific
activity of countless scavengers, primarily lizardbirds and their larger cousins, perhaps a few garaaches, nothing was alive there either.

"My God," Captain Olayne murmured quietly, so as not to alarm the
feasters, a couple in particular, "it looks like the wreck of *Xenophon*, as Mr.
Hudgens and Mr. Meder discovered her."

"It's very much the same," Varaa whispered. Many forgot she'd seen
that shattered, overturned wreck herself, and if it hadn't been for her and
her small war band, there wouldn't have been any survivors at all. "This is
worse," she continued, "because many more died here, and it was done on
purpose."

There were *hundreds* of crosses and impaling poles within the perimeter of the village. All the poles had been stripped by carrion eaters of various sizes, and they saw only black bloodstains on bright, fresh-cut wood. The majority of the bloodstained and fire-scorched crosses had been stripped as well, and the rest were being almost literally licked clean as they watched. That was why they were talking so low. Two of the largest bipedal predators they'd ever seen, easily fifty feet long from jagged-tooth jaws to whiplike tails, were almost delicately pulling portions of half-cooked corpses off the crosses and gulping them down. Neither had evident "arms" of any sort, making them seem like gigantic walking heads, and both were a kind of mottled gray-black and greenish-yellowish-tan (the colors blended very efficiently).

"Damn them," Olayne seethed. "They've even got ready-made picks for their teeth! Let me bring my battery up. We'll deal with them!"

"What are those things?" Lewis asked Varaa, glad Consela had stayed back. She'd see eventually, with the forest getting dense along the river again it might take half a day to go around, and she'd be reminded of what happened to her son and many of her people. They'd detail parties to bury what remains they could find. Regardless, he expected the argument over letting her women fight to flare again.

"*Lagartos gigantes*," Ramon Lara said with a shiver.

"Close, and descriptive enough," Varaa conceded. "Some call them *Dragones mayores*. Greater dragons. Call them what you want. I don't suppose anyone really cares."

"They're magnificent beasts, in a horrifying way," Lewis said. "I wish we didn't have to kill them."

"Well, it's kill 'em or hope we can get around 'em," Leonor said.

"If we go 'round, they'll be *behind* us an' catch our scent," Corporal Willis almost chirped. "I say kill 'em now."

As usual, everyone seemed to ignore the scrawny orderly, but some probably agreed with him.

"Are we sure we *can* kill 'em?" Anson asked. "They're so big, wouldn't shootin' one, even with a six pounder, be like shootin' a grizzled bear with a musket ball?"

Lewis considered that a moment, contemplating the fairly new science of comparative estimated velocities and energies, as well as observed penetration through pine boards. "While the relative sizes of animals and projectiles would seem to bear that out, there really is no comparison between a sixty-nine caliber lead ball and a six-*pound* iron or copper shot at roughly the same velocity and distance. The latter is roughly a hundred times more powerful but only five times the diameter. Even aside from the fact the roundshot would deform very little, if at all, it would penetrate a great deal deeper. No, I'm confident we can kill them, I just don't know if we should."

"Then let's scare them off," Olayne suggested. "Deploy my battery and fire blank charges at them."

As good as Olayne's battery had become, Lewis doubted it could deploy this close without making enough noise to draw attention. Moving guns in silence wasn't something they practiced, and the guns themselves—and horses!—were noisy. "No," he decided. "We can't be sure they would 'scare off,' and we'd end up killing them anyway—if we could. I doubt they'd calmly stand and make easy targets of themselves at that point. We're better off going around. It won't take that long." He pointed at the monsters. "Probably less than engaging *those* things ultimately would. And remember, this isn't a hunting trip, and they aren't the enemy."

They went around Agua Ancha, and it was just as well, Lewis thought. While killing a pair of the giant monsters that so plagued his men's dreams might've been good for morale, particularly the Americans that still made up the bulk of his artillerymen, seeing what had started at Alcaldesa Consela's village taken as far as it had been here wouldn't have been, for anyone. And what they'd already seen was bad enough. Riding along the column later, after it returned to the road, Lewis joined Barca for a brief visit with "his" 4th section and heard the hitherto incorrigible Private Hahessy remark; "Aye, an' I *am* a 'heretic,' Corporal Dodd, by any reckonin', fit ta drive poor Preacher Mac, er even Reverend Harkin ta tears! A waste o' yer breath, proslytizin' ta me, it is! But proud I am ta be a 'heretic' in the eyes o' them Blood Priest buggers. All you lads're safe from me, long as we have them ta kill!"

"Quite a reversal," Lewis said quietly aside to Barca.

"A slight modification, at least," Barca answered cautiously. "We'll see how long it lasts. First Sergeant Petty says Hahessy had 'words' with Corporal Cox again, and Cox apparently painted a bleak picture of a future in which Hahessy refused to reform. At least enough to do his duty. And I haven't heard him make any racial slurs over the last several days." He smiled. "*Ethnic* slurs, yes—against Scots and British and Germans and Poles, God knows who else—but nothing overtly racial, even directed at

Uxmalos and other, ah, 'Indios' seems to be the common term, in the battery."

Looking at young Hanny Cox, riding the lead horse pulling his Number Two gun, Lewis appraised him again. It was possible Hanny was eighteen, though he doubted it, but he was starting to fill out a little—no longer just knees and elbows. "A remarkable young man," he said.

"He'll go far, if he lives," Barca agreed. "And if I have anything to say about it." He looked at Lewis. "I like the artillery, and with the possible exception of Hahessy, I like these men. I'd like to stay. They do need a section chief, and I think I've learned enough to do the job."

Lewis grinned. "Good. I expect you'll 'go far' as well, Mr. Barca."

Two days later, on a bright, clear, muggy morning, Lewis's mounted detachment rode into the barren ground campsite being established where the village of Valle Escondido once stood. 1st and 2nd Divisions had clearly made better time on the river, but the infantry and the rest of the artillery was still coming ashore when Lewis met Colonel Reed, Captain Hudgens, King Har-Kaaska, Coryon Burton, and Samantha Wilde. All were glad to see them, but wore somewhat haunted expressions. Reed explained by describing what they found when they arrived: essentially the same thing Lewis saw at Agua Ancha, though a little more "cleaned up" by scavengers. Reed made the decision to erase the village entirely before establishing a camp, and that had taken a couple of days.

"How soon can you march?" Lewis asked.

"A day or two more, I should think," Reed said. "We still have to land the rest of the wagons and the bulk of supplies that'll have to remain here." He wiped his brow. "Not to mention our own 'camp followers.'" He'd seen the large number of villagers accompanying Lewis's force. "Most of those will be employed establishing a secure depot here."

"Very well. Mr. Anson! Mr. Lara!" Lewis called, and waited for them to join him. Anson tipped his sweat-soggy hat at Samantha with a grin but made no move to join her. "From this point forward, the possibility of a major action increases with each day that passes and mile we progress, so I'll stay with the bulk of our force. You have one day to rest and refit, and remount if necessary, before striking out westward for Gran Lago. You'll have the same composition as before, including the fourth section of artillery attached to Olayne's battery." Lewis saw Captain Hudgens and Coryon Burton frown unhappily, for different reasons. "We'll still need the dragoons and Rifles for our own security," he said for Coryon's benefit, then returned his gaze to Anson and Lara. "Your mission is to get to Gran Lago before General Agon, and keep the path clear for us. Avoid contact if possible, but if you can't, or it becomes necessary to slow Agon down, I expect you to strike his scouts and leading elements as savagely as possible." He looked meaningfully at the Ranger. "Is that understood?"

Anson didn't even blink. "Perfectly."

"Mr. Lara?"

"I believe so, sir," the young Mexican officer agreed with a troubled expression.

"I'm not telling you to emulate the Doms and kill everyone without mercy," Lewis quickly explained. "Quite the opposite. Show mercy when you can. On the other hand, I want your attacks brutal and unexpected. Make the enemy fear you." He paused. "And if you catch any Blood Priests, hang them."

"If our prisoners were right, there won't be many of those devils with Agon," Anson pointed out.

"With him or running from him, I want them dead," Lewis said coldly, "and left dangling where Agon will find them." He paused a moment, eyes resting on Barca, who'd trotted up to join them, then looked back at Anson. "You're now officially 'on the loose,' but be careful and keep us informed by courier. We'll be as close behind you as soon as we can."

CHAPTER 21

I t was early afternoon, and a line of heavy gray clouds was building across the water beyond the light tower in the fort when HMS *Tiger* swept in on a stiff breeze and anchored offshore of Vera Cruz. At the moment, she was the only large ship in port, aside from *Isidra*—still undergoing repairs to her boiler. It had been more thoroughly taken apart than Daney Reese realized at first, and the seven half-starved prisoners found in her bilge, mostly enginemen and stokers themselves, had improperly reassembled it. Every attempt to raise steam since had resulted in leaks and other issues. This had partly been to preserve their usefulness and extend their lives, of course, but also to ensure that if the Doms forced the issue, they could cause the boiler to burst and kill them all. Their enemy had the design already, but they could at least deny them the use of *Isidra*—and even the horrible death they'd endure was better than what they'd seen happen to some of their shipmates to get them to cooperate in the first place.

The rest of the ships captured at the dock had been sent to Uxmal and Pidra Blanca long ago, carrying Captain Eric Holland's initial dispatch and some heavy guns found in the city, too big to be put on field carriages. It was hoped they'd be used to turn some of their prizes into warships if that was deemed practicable. The ships used in the raid, *Roble Fuerte*, *Flor*, and *Viente Amistoso*, had been lightly armed here, and along with the Dom warship they'd captured and named *Libertad*, were either on station guarding against an enemy approach from the sea, or on errands back to Nautla or Uxmal. *Tiger* had just returned from Uxmal, in fact, being their fastest ship by far, and First Lieutenant William "Billy" Semmes, still in command in Holland's absence, immediately came ashore. Now he stood in the broad, mosaic-tiled receiving room of the *alcalde*'s palace, which served as Holland's command headquarters, while Holland himself squinted to read the dispatch he'd brought from Colonel De Russy.

Most of his command staff was there, having seen *Tiger*'s approach and quickly come from all over the city. Sal Hernandez, Tom Hayne, and Captain Ixtla were all standing, as was Capitan Razine a little to the side, almost between where Holland stood and Don Hurac el Bendito sat in an ornate chair, attended as always by his striking *madre de hijos*, Zyan. He was never seen without her, in fact, as if he drew the strength he needed to do the unusual things he must directly from her. One of those things was a quite obvious change in his personal appearance. Instead of the virtually obligatory bloodred robe, trimmed in gold, he'd always worn, he now had a white one, ever so minimally trimmed in red.

The newly appointed Capitan de la Milicia Don Roderigo and several of his lieutenants were present as well. Captain Roderigo, as he was called by the invaders-turned-protectors, was a well-known and generally well-liked local hidalgo "adventurer" who'd spent time in the Dominion army on the southeastern frontier several years earlier but resigned after a duel with another officer closely aligned with Blood Priest ideology even then. He'd become a friend of Don Hurac's and a frequent visitor to his compound. Now he eagerly absorbed the tactics Captain Ixtla taught him so he could pass them to his growing *milicia*. That wasn't a simple task.

Just as the Americans had found it difficult to turn Uxmalos and others (who'd historically left their protection to the more warlike Ocelomeh) into soldiers, Capitan Roderigo had similar issues with the now-former slaves and lower-class freemen in Vera Cruz. He could deal with that. The Dominion army acquired its conscripts from the same source, and like the Uxmalos, his "raw material" had a cause: self-preservation and the protection of their homes and families. The upper classes were more difficult. They were under the same threat of extermination as everyone, but hidalgos like himself ordinarily sought direct commissions as junior officers, while martially inclined *patricios* purchased higher rank. As often as not, this was to gain prestige and certain advantages high army rank brought to their everyday concerns. (*Alcaldes* were traditionally *coronels*, after all, and it was clear how the *alcalde* of Vera Cruz had used his military position.) Those inclined to actually serve and who took their duties seriously—like General Agon apparently did—became *"profesionales."* They learned on the job and were advanced (or punished) according to a different social order that most didn't understand and preferred to stay out of. Usually, only those with reputations for being *profesionales* were given real commands—and there weren't many of those in Vera Cruz. In any event, Roderigo needed officers, but he needed *real* ones, and the traditional system wouldn't supply them. More to the point, hidalgos and *patricios* were certainly never drafted as common soldiers, and that was causing Capitan Roderigo endless headaches.

Now, like the rest, he was waiting to hear what news First Lieutenant Semmes brought, but Holland took his time, reading the dispatch twice, occasionally glancing at Don Hurac and Captain Roderigo as if wondering how much to tell them. He trusted them more than he'd ever expected to, at least to look out for their own interests and those of their people, but it was possible they'd spill something he said. They couldn't have rounded up every Blood Priest in the city. Some had been hiding already, as spies.

"So," Holland said at last, whacking his leg with the two pages of thick paper, still looking at Don Hurac. "We wondered if Agon got the message you added to the note proclaiming the 'elevation' of Don Julio an' the power play by the Blood Priests when that flyin' lizard landed here." That had been rather nerve-racking. All the usual handlers had fled, and though Don Hurac told them they must fly the yellow pennant to attract the frightening beast, he had only the vaguest notion how to catch it, remove the message it already bore, add another, and send it on its way. A squad of Ixtla's Ocelomeh infantry drew the memorable detail and managed it only by stuffing the thing with food. One trooper lost a finger to its ravening jaws. When the time came to release it, it could barely get off the ground. In any event, they'd never known for sure if Agon got either message, because the dragon didn't return. Don Frutos or Father Tranquilo must've controlled it by then and simply sent it back to the capital.

Holland waved the pages. "We still don't know if he got yours, but I reckon he got the one about Don Julio takin' over instead o' your friend Don Datu. Probably a little late, accordin' to this, since he attacked Colonel

Itzam at Nautla an' got licked. The more I think about it, that musta been when he learned that Frutos an' Tranquilo stole a chunk of his army back at Campeche an' ran off. Why even attack Nautla if he already knew?"

"Does it say what Don Frutos and Father Tranquilo have done with those men?" asked Don Hurac.

"Yeah," Holland acknowledged. "Set off in this direction, overland. No ships to come straight at us. We must've taken 'em all."

That remained a source of contention because Don Hurac was insistent that the Dominion was mightier at sea than he, or even Capitan Razine, were aware. Holland didn't think so. If the Dom navy was so big, where was it? Why did it allow them to harass shipping with impunity? Still, that was why he wanted their captures turned into warships. Just in case. "Anyway, Colonel Itzam figures Agon lit out after 'em because he never renewed his attack. After awhile, Itzam's scouts figured he was gone, leavin' only a token force to fool everybody. Which it did, for too long," Holland grumbled. "Itzam's comin' down the Camino Militar now, but Agon's got a fair lead."

"I'd so hoped we could enlist General Agon's aid against the Blood Priests," Don Hurac said miserably. "They're his chief enemies now as well. What about your Colonel Cayce?" he suddenly asked in an urgent tone.

"He's . . . comin' too," Holland hedged. "He hopes to catch Agon near a place called Gran Lago. Still close to five hundred miles from here. Not much chance he'll catch Frutos an' Tranquilo, though, so we'll have to deal with 'em ourselves, an' whatever they scrape up on the way."

Don Hurac was nodding grimly. "Our two best commanders, leading our strongest available forces, will destroy each other when they should be working together."

"Stow that shit, Hurac," Holland growled. "I told you before: I can see 'em both fightin' the same enemy, but not exactly workin' together! The enemy o' my enemy ain't always my friend." He paused thoughtfully. "Still. Too bad we couldn't get 'em talkin' again."

"Ain't we workin' together, with the people here in Vera Cruz?" Sal asked.

"That's different," Holland insisted.

"How?"

Holland waved outside, past the arched entrance at the plaza beyond. The horses had been moved, and the grass was returning to life. "Because those're just *people* out there, who never came against us. They don't care if we believe the same way they do, an' don't deserve ta *die* just because we came. That's how!"

"But . . ." Don Hurac sputtered, "can't you at least tell Colonel Cayce the *possibility* for—call it a 'cooperative campaign'—exists? Isn't he with Colonel Itzam? He was just at Nautla and will soon be at Campeche. Can't you communicate with him?"

"It's . . . not that simple," Holland said, unwilling even to imply that Cayce had another entire column, much less where it was coming from. "Colonel Cayce moves fast when he's a mind to, and I expect he's already past Campeche. With this wind, it'll take even *Tiger* at least a week to beat down the coast. Where will he be by then? We could try to catch him somewhere else," he qualified, "but I'm afraid, no matter what we do, there'll be a fight before we can get a message to him."

"I see," said Don Hurac, rising with a groan. Zyan quickly helped him stand. He wasn't an old man, but a life of ease and recent stress had left him weak. "Well, as you say, we must see to our own defenses. Come, Don Roderigo, I'll join you in inspecting your newest recruits."

"They will be inspired, Your Holiness," Capitan Roderigo replied. There was obviously more in the dispatch that Holland wanted to discuss with his own people, and like Don Hurac, Roderigo was no fool. He and his lieutenants escorted Don Hurac and Zyan out the front entrance.

"What else does it say?" Hayne immediately asked.

Holland grunted. "Some o' this is pretty old news. The latest is that Itzam's Third Division has already reached Campeche. The rearguard prisoners he took—yep, they surrendered, an' willingly told him Frutos an' Tranquilo left with two or three thousand men. Agon's tryin' to catch 'em, but he won't."

Sal furrowed his brow. "If they volunteered that information, it means Agon *does* know Don Hurac hopes he and Colonel Cayce can cooperate."

"Could be," Holland agreed. "Doesn't mean they *should*, though." He sighed. "We been around these people a while, an' they *are* just people. Maybe we think they're kinda silly for puttin' up with their crazy system, an' Don Hurac's bent over backward ta help ease 'em into some different thinkin'. Still squirrelly, but he ain't sacrificin' folks on a whim. By all accounts, he never did." He frowned. "Only when he 'had' to." He shook his head. "But the Doms in general, meanin' the ones in power, buildin' armies, the sort Agon hopes to restore, ain't enough different from the Blood Priests to matter. It ain't just the Blood Priests that'll come here an' wipe out every-body that ever seen us. It's the *Dom way*! You think Don Hurac himself could ever be accepted back by what he's tryin' to save? Even if he succeeds, he'd have to lead his own revolution to change the Doms enough to let his people live.

"Shit!" he snapped in frustration. "I've been all over the world—the 'old' world—an' seen some really weird cults an' cultures. Some maybe weirder than this," he confessed, "but I never got caught in the middle of 'em!" He looked back at Sal. "So Colonel Itzam's keepin' the *possibility* o' cooperatin' in mind, even while he chases Agon as fast as his supplies can keep up. That's the most recent thing we know. Trouble is, we got *no way* to tell Col-onel Cayce an' let him decide what to do. Before his last report started out on horseback to Cayal, then by semaphore from there to Uxmal, an' finally here by ship, we only knew First and Second Divisions met up at Cayal an' licked the Holcanos. Now they've moved down the Usuma River, by land an' raft. Made good time, an' destroyed a 'detachment' o' Blood Priests an' Dom soldiers split off from Tranquilo an' Frutos. They was runnin' wild up an' down the river, murderin' everybody they came across! *That's* what's in Colonel Cayce's mind while he chases General Agon, an' if I know him, he's got blood in his eye."

He was silent while they considered that, then finally spoke again. "So far, we've had two little 'armies' come against us here, to 'eradicate the heretics an' punish the people who "allowed" us to land on their sacred soil.' First, there was those three hundred men that marched down from Techolotla"—he nodded at Hayne—"that the dragoons chased off with a couple o' cannon and their rapid-fire Halls." Even aside from the huge 36pdrs in the fort, they'd found quite a few cannon in the city, a total of twenty-two, either waiting to go forward to join General Agon or more likely hidden by the *alcalde* to "find" and sell back to the army. They were all 8pdrs, on vastly inferior "local" carriages, but carriages hardly mattered in a defensive position when they didn't have to move the heavy things around. "Didn't even have to send anyone to help you," Holland went on with a smile at Hayne. They'd been lucky with that, the Doms arriving boldly in the middle of the day amid a thunder of drums and a dirgelike melody played on their horns. With no experience fighting the American-led alliance from the Yucatán, or anyone, for that matter, they'd expected their mere appearance to dissolve all opposition. It hadn't, and they'd been ravaged by fire before they even deployed from their column. The survivors were allowed to straggle away.

"The second bunch was a little tougher," he conceded. Nearly a thousand men had come from the west, from Actopan, likely with the same expectation that no one would resist them. Wrong again. Still, this force deployed more professionally, under fire, and it took all of Ixtla's infantry, the Rangers and half the dragoons, as well as the three-hundred-odd *milicia* Don Roderigo thought competent by then to see them off. That was an eye-opener for everyone in the city, who finally realized not only that the rest of their country wanted them dead, but that it could still send troops who'd fight. Most important, they'd begun to accept that the lethal strangers they still feared but desperately needed couldn't defend them alone. Trepidation increased dramatically, but so had recruitment, and the ranks of Don Roderigo's *milicia* expanded to over three thousand almost overnight.

They needed more, and could still arm more, since a surprising number of the *alcalde*'s "hidden armories" had been found. They needed crews for all the field guns as well, but could only train so many troops at a time while maintaining a labor force sufficient to build defenses around the city. They did what they could. Like the army had done elsewhere, it formed all the civilians into labor battalions who'd receive basic military training even as they worked.

"So, what's next?" Holland asked, shoving the dispatch into his coat pocket and belatedly offering Semmes a seat. Everyone took that as an excuse to find chairs and the *alcalde*'s old servants used the opportunity to sweep in and provide more refreshments. "I may be 'in charge' of . . . whatever we've wound up doing here, but I'm just a sailor. I *ain't* no general!"

Captain Ixtla allowed a pretty young girl in a belted white tunic to pour him a cup of juice. "Well, the defenses we're building remain problematic. As you know, Vera Cruz isn't only a large city—much bigger that Uxmal!—it's a crossroads. The enemy can approach from four different directions, not counting the sea. And despite the impressive nearby mountains, the plain around it is broad enough that they can deploy and attack from just about anywhere. The roads in the city are good and the avenues wide, so troops—if not guns—can quickly move from place to place, but the overall perimeter is too big."

Sal was nodding. "Yeah, even with most of the Dominion's first-line troops a long way off with their 'Cruzada' against the 'Empire of the New Britain Isles'—whoever that is—we have to count on Tranquilo and Don Frutos, with three thousand men already, probably gatherin' that many more as they pass through some other good-size cities on their way here." At least they had access to excellent, up-to-date maps of the Dominion now, though they'd found nothing showing the rest of the world beyond its borders. Not even on the ships they'd captured, which had apparently only been used for coastal trade or protection within the bounds of the Caribbean. They didn't need charts of other places. And perhaps no one *wanted* people to know the Dominion wasn't the center of everything, and how vast the world beyond it was.

Sal continued, "As much as we need to keep up recruitment an' trainin', we need a smaller perimeter to defend."

"Yeah, I know," Holland agreed tiredly. They'd discussed this before. "An' I still don't know what to do about it." It turned out the most influential, indeed generally helpful "Vera Cruz Patriots" lived in impressive homes and villas on the outskirts of town. Those buildings not only made good fighting positions themselves, they obstructed fields of fire. They really needed to be demolished. "I've talked to a bunch of 'em, an' so's Don Hurac. They're all, 'Oh, of course! Those buildings must be demolished! Just don't tear *mine* down!'"

"Might change their minds if we stand a bloody impalin' pole outside their front doors!" Hayne grumbled.

Holland looked at him with widening eyes. "Damn. It just might at that! Who wants the detail?"

"My dragoons, by God." Hayne grinned, rubbing his hands together. "Who else? It was my idea!"

Sal laughed, but then sobered. "Well, the way I see it, we have some time. On top of that, we should know if Colonel Cayce met General Agon in battle before Don Frutos an' that damned Tranquilo get here. If Colonel Cayce wins, we might get some help. Send ships for some of his men, or Colonel Itzam's." He paused and glanced around, making sure none of the servants could hear. "Somethin' we need to think about, though. If we hear General Agon whipped Colonel Cayce, Colonel Itzam"—he pursed his lips under his big mustache—"an' Cap'n Anson, o' course, is there any point in us stayin' here? The Doms'll retake this place whether we're here or not. Seems that would be the time to get the hell out."

"Just leave these people?" Holland asked softly.

Semmes shifted uncomfortably in his chair.

Sal simply nodded. "Sure. Go defend *ours*. I know you feel kinda responsible for the way things turned out, but if nobody ever told you what would happen after we left—like we planned—they'd all be dead anyway. And that's their fault, not yours, that they didn't rise up against the *maníacos* who rule them a long time ago."

"I have to agree with Lieutenant Hernandez," said Captain Ixtla. "*If* we can still get out by then," he emphasized.

"There's that," Sal agreed, then looked back at Holland. "You're right, you're in charge, an' I know holdin' Vera Cruz'll help if our army ever gets here. But if it can't . . . this *ain't* the pass at Thermopylae or the Alamo, an' us dyin' here won't do our people an' our cause any good at all."

Holland sighed, then snorted. "An' I *damn* sure ain't Leonidas or William Travis. I guess we'll just have to wait an' see what happens somewhere else before we make up our minds. But that means the final decision for us to stay or go is up to Colonel Cayce, in a sense, an' I can't say I don't prefer it that way." His expression hardened. "But in the meantime, we need eyes of our own down around Gran Lago." He looked speculatively at Sal. "So we'll send some, as soon as a couple of our prize ships get back. The rest of us'll do our best to get ready for . . . whatever we have to do."

CHAPTER 22

ARMY OF GOD'S VENGEANCE

Not quite seventeen years old, Sonez Rinco was a mere *soldado de Dios*, the second-lowest rank in the army, just above *recluta*, or "recruit." And the only advantage he had over the very newest recruits was that he'd arrived at Campeche and embarked on General Agon's campaign up the Camino Militar against Nautla in a real uniform of yellow and black with durable leather boots instead of the coarse white linen shirt, trousers, straw hat, and sandals that fresh conscripts received. He'd also been issued a proper musket, bayonet, and all the accompanying accoutrements instead of a simple pike. Pikes were primarily for training, so the new men would get used to carrying weapons, particularly when engaging in close order drill and learning the new bayonet techniques General Agon insisted everyone acquire. It hadn't been intended that anyone actually march to war with them. A few didn't have any choice. Though everyone's training had been complete before they set out to the north, there still hadn't been enough weapons and uniforms to properly equip the whole army. Most said it was because the all-important Gran Cruzada had soaked such things up, but even as young and inexperienced as Sonez Rinco knew he was, all the young freemen where he was raised in Oaxaca understood what really happened. Of all the military equipment sent to *alcaldes* of cities where recruits were mustered, barely half ever got to the troops.

He didn't much care as long as he was fed and clothed. Freemen of the lowest class, such as he and most others in the army, were hideously executed for petty crimes more often than anyone else because there was little "honest" work to be had. Slaves did it all. So, in terms of food and clothing, slaves often had it better than freemen in the Dominion. That left those such as Sonez Rinco with roughly three choices: sell themselves into slavery, turn to crime and live short, brutal lives—and if you did that, you better join a gang or your life would be even shorter—or join the army or navy. He joined the army as soon as he was big enough. Recruiters didn't care about age. Now he was starting to wonder if he'd made the right choice.

He'd missed General Agon's previous campaign up the Camino Militar, but there were plenty of veterans in his regiment who loved to tell tales of the misery they'd endured on that long, hungry retreat back to Campeche after the Washboard. And no matter what the priests and officers said, there was no doubt in the ranks they'd been beaten. Still, they trusted General Agon. He'd shared their hardships, restructured and rebuilt the army with lessons learned, instituting hard new training that nevertheless made sense, and practically forbade the Blood Cardinal Don Frutos—derided as the "army killer" in the ranks—from even appearing in front of his troops. What most endeared him to the men, even the newest recruits, was he never allowed the Blood Priests to pester them—and most especially, "cull" them for the unusually harsh sacrifices they craved. Blood Priests may represent the rising power in the Dominion, but they were only loved in the oldest and largest cities, and perhaps along the Costa del Pacifico from whence they apparently sprang. In any event, less than perfectly equipped or not, the army had been confident when it marched north again.

That's when everything started going wrong. The march was a nightmare, and the enemy (and monsters) plagued them all the way. Then came the bloody repulse in front of Nautla. The army was far from shattered, and though none were pleased by what it would cost, the men still expected to win. Suddenly, however, General Agon turned most of the army around, twenty-four thousand of the twenty-six thousand remaining after the costly attack, and set a grueling pace south. The men were confused until word leaked—on purpose and actually largely true—that His Supreme Holiness had descended to heaven and Don Frutos (under the influence of Blood Priests) had abandoned them yet again. He was a traitor to the Dominion and posed a threat to the rightful succession. They must catch him and destroy him. Despite the killing pace they maintained, most of the army was heartened by that. "Most" because there were some Blood Priest adherents, but the rest understood "restoring things to rights"—imperfect as they were—in their own country better than conquering unknown lands. Aside from the perks of pillage (uncertain against this enemy, at best), the troops got fed and paid the same whatever they did.

Until they didn't.

There was almost nothing left at Campeche, and not a soul to meet them. All the stores Don Frutos couldn't take had been burnt, and the single ship left in port, not nearly large enough to take his little army anywhere, had been scuttled. After what had already wound up being almost a 170-*legua* march, the men were in a sorry state. Uniforms were ragged, boots worn-out, and food was running dangerously low. But the whole army was enraged at Don Frutos, and it didn't take as much urging to get it after him again as Sonez Rinco would've thought. He was as ready as the rest. Besides, the closest place they could resupply was in the direction they were already going—west, toward the town of Gran Lago, another sixty *leguas* away. All they could hope was they'd catch Don Frutos, or at least get to Gran Lago before he left it a wasteland.

Now the Army of God's Vengeance was almost halfway there and had made camp after another exhausting day. Despite the efforts of the army's better officers and NCOs, the camp was a sadly straggly affair. They'd long ago outpaced the heretic army, and the beasts roaming the moderately wooded, rolling coastal prairie were seen more as food than a threat. The ten 8pdrs they'd brought along (Agon left half his guns at Nautla to bang away, a few shots each day, until the enemy got wise or their ammunition ran out) could at least feed his men. Most went to their badly worn tents and collapsed as the sun plunged down in the west, and that was Sonez Rinco's intent when he got off watch and went to join his sleeping tent mate under their two-man shelter. He'd just worked his loaded weapon (he'd been on guard, after all) into the conical arrangement of half a dozen muskets near the company firepit and draped the protective canvas covering back over them all when a harsh voice stopped him.

"Get more wood for the fire, *pendejo*," said Cabo Estez, sitting by the little fire and roasting another hunk of one of the many beasts the *artierros* killed that day. Virtually an entire small herd of medium-large, four-legged, duck-faced things had been blasted down at the edge of a coastal marsh.

Cowering from what they must've thought was terrible thunder in a low, gray sky, they'd been easily slaughtered and dragged onshore by artillery armabueys to provide more than enough meat for Agon's troops. The extra was supposed to be cooked and carried, but many, like Cabo Estez, seemed intent on eating until they burst. Estez hadn't moved since Sonez went on watch as far as the young *soldado* could tell.

Sonez stifled an angry retort. Estez was only a *cabo*, just one step above Sonez himself, but even with things somewhat . . . disordered, at present, discipline for insubordination remained swift, harsh, and even somewhat arbitrary. "*Sí*, Cabo," Sonez groaned instead, turning to trudge back toward the thick stand of nearby trees his company had practically sprawled up against. That's where he'd been just shortly before, and should've thought to carry wood back. "*Hola*, Artin," he called to the youngster who'd relieved him. "It's only me, back for wood."

"You should've taken some with you," Artin scolded.

Sonez sighed. "I know." Then he stiffened. "Did you hear that?"

Artin considered, then shrugged. "Sounded like a horse snort to me. Maybe in the woods ahead. Might've been something else, but the big monsters usually stay away from our large camps."

"No, it was a horse," Sonez confirmed, "but what's it doing out here? We don't have many lancers, you know." They had far more lancers than horses to carry them, and most had been formed as infantry with their carbines replaced with muskets. Moving out of the heavy woods and into a more open-field campaign than he'd expected, Agon managed to find mounts for more lancers, but still had less than a thousand. Most were scouting ahead, seeking signs of Don Frutos and Tranquilo. The rest were in the rear, on the watch for pursuing heretics. Few ranged out on the flanks, even in daylight, and wouldn't be risked to monsters and nervous troops with itchy trigger fingers at night.

"Could be a courier," Artin suggested tensely, "bearing orders forward from General Agon."

Sonez shook his head when he heard the sound again. It was definitely a horse. But a courier would move amid the safety of the troops—and courier or lancers, there'd be other sounds of jingling bits, clanking sabers and canteens, not to mention the *thud* of hooves. They wouldn't just stand out in the trees in the dark, like this one seemed to be doing. Sonez suddenly grinned. "It must be a *loose* horse!" he exclaimed. "We'll be rewarded if we catch it."

"You're right!" Artin agreed, suddenly enthusiastic. "And it sounded very close." Together, they crept forward. They'd just reached the edge of the trees when they heard the rush of *many* hooves in the soft ground cover where grass wouldn't grow, and glimpsed the unmistakable forms of horsemen, even blacker than the surrounding night. Before that could register, there was an instant of swift movement in which Artin's musket was snatched from loose fingers and both boys were clasped in iron grips from behind. In seconds, it seemed, they'd also been securely bound and gagged. A huge horseman appeared directly in front of them, speaking badly accented Spanya.

"Just relax, fellas," the voice said in a low, deep, reasonable tone. "I reckon y'all'd get a helluva reward for catchin' *me*, but if you make the slightest peep, them boys behind y'all're gonna hafta cut yer throats to the neckbone. I'd rather they didn't, 'cause I'd like somebody ta pass my regards ta yer gen'ral." The dark shape of a wide-brimmed hat came off. "Cap'n Bandy Beeryman, First Rangers, at yer service. Don't forget that. An' I'm here ta pay a call with Cap'n—I mean 'Major'—Giles Anson. Agon'll remember him better'n me." The hat was pulled back in place. "Now you two just sit an' watch an' take yer ease—an' tell Gen'ral Agon what ya see. Shift 'em over yonder to the edge of the trees an' tie 'em up where they can get a good look," he said slightly louder.

Artin and Sonez were quickly secured, sitting on the ground and facing the camp. Only then could they tell there were dozens, maybe hundreds of horses in the dense trees behind them, milling and moving into line. That's when Sonez realized how unlucky (or was it lucky?) he'd been to hear the one horse of so many. Everything on them that might've made a sound had been carefully muffled or left behind. Glancing back at the tired, sleepy camp, illuminated only by lingering cook fires like Cabo Estez's, and a few candles burning in tents, he knew that if that unpleasant cabo hadn't sent him for a few measly sticks of wood, he'd probably be dead in a few minutes.

Suddenly, the one calling himself "Beeryman" gave a terrifying, savage whoop, echoed by a rising roar of spine-tingling cries as the horsemen thundered out of the woods and down on the camp. Sonez could only estimate their number at three or four hundred. Almost instantly, they were shooting men by the fires—Sonez saw a rising Cabo Estez tumble face-first into the coals, throwing up a swirl of sparks, and others fell screaming or tried to run. Most of those were shot down from behind, and based on the high percentage of hits, Sonez suspected the attacker's carbines—mostly cut-down Dominion muskets, it seemed—were loaded with handfuls of small shot instead of a single ball. Some riders fired down through the tents, and wails rose up inside them. Then the first tent caught fire. Within minutes, dozens were burning as whooping Rangers arced flaming arrows at them. Tents set fire to tents, and a burning cart was pulled on its side. Through much of the initial attack, Sonez saw the one called "Beeryman," huge beard backlit by flames, firing again and again from a single pistol, each shot taking a toll. Then his horse reared, and he and many others pulled sabers from what appeared to be heavy cloth or leather scabbards— another reason they'd been so quiet!—and dashed deeper into the camp.

Probably confined to mere minutes, ten or fifteen at most, the mayhem seemed to last forever, with stabbing orange jets and thumps of muskets and tents erupting in flames much deeper in the camp than Sonez would've imagined, but eventually the bulk of destruction appeared to veer south again, back toward the same side of the camp the attack began. Soon Sonez decided most of the shooting came from his own panicked people, finally "ready" but only shooting at shadows—or each other. Then, long after the firing died away, it seemed half the army was busy fighting fires. Eventually, exhausted by their own trauma, what they'd seen, and fear of what might still happen to them, Sonez and Artin must've fallen asleep. The next thing they knew, the sky was turning red with dawn and an angry-looking *sargento* was glaring down at them in contempt while other men cut their bonds.

"You'll be *impaled* for this, you miserable *comedores de mierda*! You'll wish the heretics killed you instead of just tying you up after falling asleep on guard! We have *three hundred* dead! Who knows how many hurt."

At the first mention of "impaling," Artin went white with terror, but Sonez spoke up angrily. "I wasn't on guard, Sargento, but Artin and I heard something and went to investigate. We were surprised from behind. We saw who did it, and they gave us a message for General Agon. I'm sure that's the only reason we're alive."

"A message for the general," the sargento murmured doubtfully.

"Yes," Sonez snapped. "And he'll want to hear it."

"Major Anson," Agon mused dourly to his assembled staff after the two young *soldados* were returned to their ravaged company. He'd considered having them impaled after all, as a warning against further negligence to the rest of the army—which *had* grown quite lax, he knew. But executing honestly innocent men was something Blood Priests would do, and he rebelled against the notion. Besides, it would only add to the terror and disgruntlement in the army—which he was sure was the primary purpose of the raid in the first place, and even he was somewhat stunned by the ruthlessness in which it was carried out. So many helpless, unarmed men, shot down! And yet the two young *soldados* bound and unhurt. That was as much a message as anything they could tell him. Then again, he was equally certain he was more responsible for the success of the raid than any other. With no previous evidence of close pursuit by the heretics, he'd grown complacent, and it was *his job* to maintain the standards he'd set before marching against Nautla, regardless of their privations and fatigue.

Well, they'll get some rest today while we pick up the pieces, he supposed. With so much to be salvaged and tended to, particularly wounded men and morale, not to mention righting overturned wagons—whether they were really damaged or not—tent repair, scattered stands of arms to be inspected and fixed or replaced, and draft animals gathered. Scattered armabueys, rampaging about, had done more actual damage to all the above than the raiders. In any event, they hadn't moved the army that day. Agon *had* ordered that it be better situated and protected, however, along with an increase in scouts and guards. "I believe I remember this 'Beeryman,'" he added. "A very large, intimidating character, as young Sonez described."

"Indeed. A difficult man to forget," murmured Capitan Arevalo.

"But," objected General Tun, now leaning on a cane when he wasn't mounted, "why should Coronel Cayce dispatch his mounted forces to harass us here, now? I should think he'd be pleased to have us gone from Nautla, believing he ran us off. Could it be simply a 'chase' reflex. To pursue what he thinks is wounded prey?" He suddenly glared at Coronel Uza, in charge of their scouts and small force of lancers. "And why were *you* not aware of their approach?"

Uza frowned. "My general, we already knew Coronel Cayce's mounted forces were . . . formidable. His Ranger, lancers, and dragoons—though I'm not sure why he maintains them as separate units. Each has its strengths, I suppose. As to why . . . There must be several reasons, but one was to show us he could. To frighten soldiers unaccustomed to attack by *anyone* in their sleep! Never has a Dominion army been treated so . . . brazenly as it was on the road up to Nautla, and again now, of course. As to why we didn't detect them, I must point out we have only what amounts to a single *batallón* of horse while Cayce has three, at least. Possibly more. Even if only one came against us, they can remain concentrated while ours are scattered all over, in front and behind us, and off to the sides when we can manage it. A careful approach from *any* direction could avoid detection."

He looked thoughtful. "Of course, even as we've reduced the size of our *regimientos* from three to two thousand, it seems their *regimientos*—horse and foot—have always numbered a thousand, often less. So each of their mounted 'branches' constitutes a *regimiento* in itself. I *can* see an advantage to that, both from an organizational and tactical standpoint."

"And Cayce has unleashed his Ranger regiment against us. Again, why—and how—if he's still so far behind that your scouts can't see him?"

"They see *him*, my general," Uza objected, clearly annoyed. "He comes down the Camino Militar directly behind us with an unequal but—as we know—quite formidable force. More than we can tangle with and still catch Don Frutos," he reminded. "But all reports agree he's still at least thirty *leguas* back. He can't *possibly* catch us if we maintain our pace."

"Obviously, his *Rangers* can," Agon snapped back.

"Well . . . yes. Not only are they mounted, but absent artillery and supply wagons, they're not tied to the Camino Militar."

"*Are* they absent artillery?" General Tun asked very meaningfully. It was known the American artillery was much more mobile than their own. They'd never captured any to examine, but it *looked* considerably lighter and the carriages more ingeniously made in other ways to facilitate agility. Not to mention the fact it was drawn by horses instead of plodding armabueys.

Colonel Uza looked around. "I fervently hope so. But the *other* 'why' is obvious. The Rangers try to slow us so Coronel Cayce can catch up." He gestured around at the unmoving, healing camp. "Which they have done. We cannot allow this again."

"No, Coronel Uza," Tun said harshly. "I suggest that *you* cannot allow it!"

Uza bridled and gathered a retort.

"Gentlemen, please," Agon said, pressing fingers hard against his temples. "We must all do our part." He looked at his old friend General Tun. "You'll make sure the camp is as well protected as possible each night when we stop. Field fortifications, extra pickets and observers, even strong parties farther out on any reasonable avenue of approach." He looked at Uza.

"You'll leave only a token force of lancers behind us, watching the approach of the main enemy army. You'll do the same with those scouting ahead. As long as we don't lose contact with them, all should be well."

"And if we do?" Uza asked.

Agon shrugged. "Then we'll know they've been attacked and destroyed and you'll have a better idea where the attackers *are*. A force that size, 'all together,' as you say, can't be difficult to track. You can then lead the bulk of your *batallón* against it and destroy it. In fact, for the time being, that'll be your primary duty. I'll no longer spread our lancers about in little, easily avoided or gobbled-up packets. Wherever and whenever the enemy is encountered, you must have the strength to strike him decisively." He stood from his chair. "Tomorrow, we press on. We *must* stop Don Frutos and Tranquilo, and we can't let Coronel Cayce slow us again."

CHAPTER 23

Anson and Boogerbear had a field day at first, and the raid on the unsuspecting infantry camp wasn't even their first action against Agon's army. But the earlier strokes were either carefully planned to wipe out small scouting parties and generally blind the enemy, or block longer-ranged efforts to discover Colonel Cayce's approach with 1st Division—and almost as important, the existence of Lara's 1st Yucatán Lancers (and nearly all their artillery), which Anson insisted must maintain its integrity as it pressed beyond Agon in the direction of Gran Lago. The enemy remained ignorant of that, or apparently any notion of any large force other than Itzam's 3rd Division, dogging them from behind. Scouts in that direction weren't molested—yet. But even before the "big raid," the mere presence of the Rangers had caused a significant contraction of those scouts, even if the enemy didn't know why. They probably just got the distinct impression that if they went out too far, they wouldn't come back.

Still, even if the raid made it harder to get close, and possible repeats more costly, it forced the enemy to consolidate his mounted troops. Anson was weary of picking at Dom lancers in penny packets. He wanted them all, and just thirty miles or so from Gran Lago and the bottleneck the great lake created along the coastline, Boogerbear galloped back up one of the broad, brushy arroyos the terrain hereabouts had given over to and rode up to join him.

"I think you may get your chance, Cap'n," he said by way of greeting, pointing north, still using Anson's old rank like a first name. "Looks like more than half the Dom lancers, minus those still scoutin' ahead an' behind—maybe three hundred an' fifty or so—are all together in a column a couple miles that way. Followin' right along the big trail we left 'em yesterday, matter o' fact."

"Do we have time to get in position?" Anson asked. Considering how many scouts he had out, the numbers were nearly equal. Boogerbear grinned in his huge beard and nodded. "All right, we'll get set. Give us"—he glanced at the hot, clear sky overhead and then at his watch—"Give us an hour an' a half an' then bring 'em to us!" He turned in the saddle and called out, "Lieutenant Barca!"

"Sir!" replied the young, black section chief. More used to operating on its own, "4th Section" had been attached to the Rangers while the rest of Olayne's battery was now with the lancers.

"I hope your boys're ready for a break in the monotony."

"They are to a man," Barca stated firmly, "and the axles freshly greased this morning."

"Good, because it'll take a short run. Pass the word to your men."

"Yes sir."

Anson slapped Boogerbear's massive shoulder. "Go. Be careful."

"Where's the fun in that?"

―――――――

"Where the devil are we going in such a rush?!" Apo Tuin cried, the juddering ammunition chest he sat on, atop the limber hitched to the Number Two gun, bouncing and jarring his guts behind the galloping six-up team and turning his voice to a warble.

"We're going to trap the enemy lancers!" Lieutenant Barca called back. Riding beside Gun Number One's foremost lead horse fifty yards ahead, they barely heard him over the thunder of hooves (theirs and the Ranger's) and the creak, jangle, groan, and pop of their own laboring gun and limber.

"About goddamn time it is too," grumbled Hahessy from the back of the lead horse just in front of Apo on the left side of the limber pole. "Harder ta stay on me best behavior, it is, ever' day passin' without a fight!"

"Watch yer tongue, ye filthy beast! I'll nae hae ye takin' the Lord's name in vain!" Preacher Mac sharply scolded from the horse in front of him.

"Don't get started now," Hanny Cox chastised them both from the back of the front lead horse. "Save your arguments for the enemy!" After his talk with Hahessy, and particularly after the big man's behavior up to the action at Los Arboles, he'd seen Hahessy was trying, but Corporal Dodd still deferred to him. It was just a matter of time before he backslid. So Hanny exchanged his Number Two man for Hahessy and put him at Number One, which he was used to. That had been Mac's position, but he didn't object because ramming projectile after heavy projectile used muscles rarely exercised otherwise and made his right arm and shoulder ache all the time. He went over to Number Two. Close to the same height, he and Hahessy made a good pair in front of the gun and worked together well in drill. They still hated each other's guts. *But that might be a good thing*, Hanny mused. Nobody on his gun *liked* Daniel Hahessy, and they certainly didn't "defer" to him, but he was big and strong and knew his job and hadn't—yet—shirked a duty, so he was accepted. Perhaps most important, the crew was tight and united, so they weren't afraid of him either. It was probably the first time in the Irishman's life that he'd been on a "team" of equals and treated as such.

The Rangers leading the way disappeared down a slope ahead, and the guns followed without slowing. Apo squawked when he bounced in the air, and only the handles on the ammunition chest kept him and the other two seated beside him from tumbling under the wheels of the gun. Not for the first time, Hanny was glad he rode one of the animals pulling their weapon into battle. He might fall off too, of course, and be trampled even *before* the gun ran over him, but there was more to hang on to, and the saddle was more comfortable than the hard lid of the ammunition chest, even with a tarp folded on it.

Ahead, he could already see what the plan was: a deep arroyo, almost a broad, shallow canyon topped with a brushy ridge, opened onto a wide, flat area where Rangers were already dragging up brush and emplacing themselves. Others were urging their horses up on the ridges and tying their animals off before easing up to the edge. As Barca led his guns on the line and they performed the wide turn that would leave them pointing forward, Hanny took a quick look down the arroyo and saw that it abruptly veered to the right. Anyone approaching inside it would be funneled directly at them and have no clue what awaited them until they were, essentially, doomed. That was only if the bait worked, of course. If the enemy came from any other direction, they'd have the Rangers—and Hanny's crew—at a distinct disadvantage.

Piling off the horses, Hahessy, Preacher Mac, Private Ricken, and Andy Morris unlimbered the gun and called, "Drive on!" Hanny urged the front lead horse forward and brought the team around in another wide turn. The end result had the horses standing between the gun and limber, effectively protecting their ammunition and the men handling it with an open lid from enemy fire with their bodies. Apo, Kini Hau, and Billy Randall—his Numbers Five and Seven men—were already pulling equipment from the chest when Hanny trotted forward past them and cried, "Take implements!" Mac and Hahessy unclasped the worm and rammer staffs from under the cannon trail and off the implement hooks hanging from the front of the cheek irons. Private Ricken, still the Number Three man, disengaged the heavy wooden handspike from the right cheek and moved to insert it in the socket at the back of the trail. In less than a minute, the Number Two gun was ready for action and the Number One gun wasn't far behind.

"Shall we load, Lieutenant?" Hanny asked Barca, who'd moved over between the guns on his horse. Rangers were still collecting brush and dead trees, even huge bones—all sorts of things that had washed down during the last flood—to build a hasty breastwork.

Barca looked at his watch, a gift from Colonel Ruberdeau De Russy. "There should be some time yet, but we may as well. Load canister and hold. Don't prime."

"Gun Number Two! Load canister!" Hanny shouted, echoed by Corporal Dodd. Kini Hau walked briskly forward from the ammunition chest, large leather haversack looped over his shoulder and hanging at his side. Pausing by Hanny, he raised the flap so Hanny could peer inside to ensure he'd brought what he'd called for. Nodding him ahead, Kini went to stand on the outside of the left wheel. Mac had stepped inside, between the wheel and tube, and after handing Kini the worm staff, reached over the wheel and down in the haversack to pull out the fixed round of ammunition. It was a long cylinder, now soldered brass instead of paper-thin, tinned iron, containing ninety .69 caliber lead musket balls on top of a wooden sabot. Tied to the bottom was a cloth bag made of mixed wool and linen with a pound and a quarter of the best Uxmal gunpowder inside. Mac brought this up under the barrel and inserted it at the muzzle. Hahessy was waiting with his rammer staff and effortlessly shoved the whole thing down to the breech. There was no point in aiming yet, and they hadn't been ordered to prime, so Ricken merely inserted the priming wire in the vent to pierce the charge—and hold it in place if they had to move the gun. This technique was *not* in the manual, but it worked. Sometimes they *had* to move a gun after it was loaded, and this was safer than requiring the Number One man to re-ram a charge that might've shifted down the barrel. *Much* safer than re-ramming it after a primer failed to ignite it and the powder bag might be smoldering, waiting to go off any second. The manual taught them to flood the vent with water, then pour more down the barrel to kill the powder charge so the useless load could be drawn out with the worm. There wasn't time for that in battle.

"Gun Number Two is ready, sir," Hanny told Barca, a moment before Dodd proclaimed Number One ready as well.

"Fine," Barca said, glancing at his watch again. "Nicely done."

Hanny looked around. "Where's Major Anson, if you don't mind me asking? Looks like we're only supported by about a hundred of his men."

"That's about right, Corporal Cox," Barca agreed. "Major Anson and most of the rest of the Rangers are up there." He nodded at the rim of the arroyo.

"An' our bloody Mr. Boogerbear is off bein' the bait, I shouldn't wonder," Hahessy said with grudging admiration. The big Ranger, and possibly Sergeant O'Roddy, were probably the only men in the world who physically intimidated him.

Barca nodded. "That leaves me in command here. Does that pose a dilemma for you, Private Hahessy?" he challenged mildly.

Hahessy just shook his head. "Not in the least, Mr. Barca," he said very formally. "Besides, it struck me not long ago: despite yer airs, you ain't no more a 'gentleman' than I am—an' I mean no offense! Why, there ain't half a dozen gentlemen o' the sort I despise in this whole bloody army, an' almost none on the sharp, bloody tip. Colonel Reed an' Colonel Cayce are gentlemen, but they're a different sort. *Earned* the distinction, they have." He chuckled. "An' neither one's 'gentle' in a fight." He shrugged. "That said, once we get started, I likely won't *hear* any commands but Corp'ral Hanny's." He actually threw a grin up at their new officer. "So it wouldn't much bother me—even if it bothered me, Mr. Barca!"

Barca sent a curious glance at Hanny. Hanny could only shrug.

Boogerbear stuffed a big wad of the strong, sharp-tasting tobacco leaves in his mouth. Just like habitual pipe smokers (nearly everybody, including women), who cut the stuff with pleasant-tasting herbs, he'd flavored it with honey. That helped until he chewed it all out. Then it tasted like . . . well, he'd never actually *tasted* horse shit, so that wasn't really a fair comparison. *Better than nothin'*, he decided philosophically. "I hear horses clatterin' up the draw, yonder," he said, pointing east. The six Ocelomeh Rangers with him nodded. They'd heard it too. So far, so good. They already knew there was a small screen out front of the main body of lancers. They not only had to make this look like a chance encounter, they had to sting the screen before they ran. *Punch 'em in the nose an' hope we've already got 'em mad an' frustrated enough to light out after us without thinkin' too much about it*, he mentally summarized his own plan. It was a simple little plan that almost always worked against any enemy. Once.

"Let's go, fellas," he said, spurring his horse, Dodger, toward the noise they wouldn't hear over their own horse's hooves in the loose streambed shale. Rounding a gentle bend, they found themselves face-to-face with a rough double column of an equal number of Dom lancers, their once brightly polished breastplates now tarnished, the colorful sprays of feathers sprouting from equally dull brass helmets now tattered and drooping. With surprise on the faces of the enemy and for a calculated instant on Boogerbear's part, they all just stared at one another. Then Boogerbear patted Dodger on the neck and shouted, "At 'em!"

The Rangers crashed into the lancers before the enemy could bring their long weapons down. Horses fell and rolled, screeching in fear or pain as legs broke. Carbines fired, unusually loud in the confines of the old riverbed, and men screamed as big lead balls punched even bigger holes in brass breastplates. An officer had drawn a long, heavy saber, outreaching the long knives the Rangers carried. (They didn't have "Bowie swords" yet and had to make do with captured sabers or refashioned plug bayonets.) The officer had skill, slashing about him and hacking a couple of Rangers down before

Boogerbear shot him in the cheek with a Paterson Colt. Teeth and blood sprayed out the other side of his face, and he dropped his saber and fled. Other lancers turned to run, and a couple more were dropped as they did so, hit in the back by more flashing carbine shots. Boogerbear was impressed to see one lancer's brass backplate turn a respectable number of the teardrop-shaped "drop shot" that suddenly left a bright, dimpled pattern across it. A couple punched through, and the man whimpered as he continued on. For an instant, the fight was over.

"I thought lancers didn't run!" cried one Ranger triumphantly, forgetting their purpose for an instant.

"Not runnin', just rejoinin'. Them that can," Boogerbear corrected as the leading edge of the full column of lancers came pounding around a bend in the wash, drawn by the ruckus they'd raised. He was gratified to see a couple of flankers spilling down the sides from above, intent on joining their comrades. "Time to go." Pulling Dodger's head around, he led his surviving Rangers in a desperate retreat—real enough, despite the plan. Thus far foiled at every turn to catch the elusive Rangers and expecting these to lead them to more, the lancers would be anxious for revenge and probably confident they'd get it. The native horses most Rangers rode were tough and hardy animals, capable of running long distances and eating nearly anything, but even Boogerbear's larger-than-average Dodger couldn't compete for speed in a sprint or charge with the Dom animals. They were either direct descendants or hybrids of European/Arabian horses that arrived with the Spanish long ago. The Allied Army had captured quite a few, and Boogerbear could've had one himself, but Dodger had earned his respect and his curious, extremely focused species of affection.

"How far?" gasped one of the Rangers bolting along almost beside him, throwing dust and flat, sharp chunks of shingle from hammering hooves.

"Not far," Boogerbear replied.

"Section! Aim for the center of the arroyo, elevation for one hundred yards, as high as a man on a horse, then prime and come to the ready!" shouted Lieutenant Barca. Judging by how close the sharp little action had sounded and how quickly the echoing rumble of horses grew, there'd be no time to carefully aim the guns after all. "Rangers, make ready!" he called to the hundred or so dismounted horsemen on either side of his guns. His wasn't exactly an independent command, but this was the first time he'd been in charge of a separated detachment and was glad his voice hadn't betrayed how nervous he was. And he'd almost made a humiliating mistake. He considered his Ranger support "infantry" at the moment, and almost called them that—or riflemen. The first would've made them resent him, and the second would've been simply ridiculous since there wasn't a rifle among them. All were armed with shortened Dom muskets. Smoothbores. At least he'd reminded them to load with ball since—he hoped—their first shots, however inaccurate, would be fired beyond the lethal range of the drop-shot they preferred.

He watched as the heavy brass hammers on the Hidden's locks, lanyards already attached, were laid over to the left on the breech of each gun, priming wires (or "pricks") removed and primers put in place by the Number Three men on the right. Then the Number Four men gently stepped to the left, stretching the lanyards, while the Three men held the hammer back. As long as the Threes did that, there was no way the gun could accidentally fire even if the Four man tripped and inadvertently pulled the lanyard. When the Fours were in position outside the wheels, the Threes stepped out and signaled Corporals Cox and Dodd that their weapons were ready to fire. They, in turn, signaled Barca.

Just in time.

Boogerbear and four Rangers exploded around the bend of the steep-sided draw. Seeing the reception in front of them, they kicked their horses into a final burst of effort, clearing the confining space and darting to the right, out of the line of fire. Almost immediately, the hanging dust they left was colored by dull brass, dingy yellow uniforms, and a flowing forest of swaying, upright lances topped with needle points and red pennants still bright enough to reflect the sun. The leading edge of the racing column actually cleared the confines of the arroyo as well before its leaders saw what waited and began to pull up.

It was a natural reaction under the circumstances. Being suddenly confronted by a hundred large-bore carbines aiming right at you, not to mention the 3.67-inch muzzles of two 6pdrs, would give most anyone pause. The only "right" thing to do—charge straight ahead without thought—was practically suicidal. Barca doubted he could do it, but knew several people who would. Boogerbear, of course, and Major Anson. Almost certainly Leonor, Captain Lara, even Coryon Burton. Oddly, Colonel Cayce—and probably Varaa-Choon—would *seem* to do the same, but would probably consider and reject a dozen options in an instant. Barca suspected he'd do the same as this Dom commander—though he'd probably say a much different prayer.

The column was crashing to a jumbled halt behind its stunned and horrified leaders, injuring and possibly killing dozens of horses and men in the process as those behind slammed into the press ahead. A long moment passed while Barca knew nothing about what was happening elsewhere, but assumed the tail of the column must've sensed something at last and started to slow its mad dash, pulling up, pausing, starting to mill about.

And get shot.

A fusillade erupted a fair distance away as Major Anson opened fire. His men, over two hundred Rangers, would be firing straight down at very close range, probably with dangerously heavy loads of drop shot. Squealing screams of horses and men came to Barca's ears, and he reacted to "the signal."

"Fire!" he yelled.

Both 6pdrs roared simultaneously, leaping back and spewing a total of one hundred eighty .69 caliber balls shrouded in the billowing yellowish-white smoke that always accompanied canister. Dust started kicking up three-quarters of the way to the milling mass of Doms, but on this dry, hard surface, even projectiles that initially struck low would skate up into the target. Some went high, but were already dropping quickly enough to fall among Doms behind those in front. Most hit somewhere in the middle, a space tightly packed with men and animals. *Everyone* in the very front went down, often smashed by multiple, even dozens of, balls apiece. Horses simply crumpled, legs and bodies destroyed, and men were shredded in the fog of blood gusting around them.

Barca barely heard these closer screams begin because the Rangers around the guns opened fire as well.

"Sir?" Hanny shouted the question back.

Barca gulped. "Commence independent fire," he managed to cry with authority even as his stomach turned and bile rose in his throat. He was almost shocked by the casual, matter-of-fact wave the young, sensitive—he believed—Hanny Cox threw back before roaring for his crew to reload. The gleeful chortling of Daniel Hahessy was expected while they did bloody murder. Sheer, simple murder. Not a single ball from an enemy carbine warbled back toward them. He felt sick, like this was all a terrible mistake.

Then he heard the cries of the Ocelomeh Rangers as they fired. Almost all was in Spanya, but he understood it well enough. The things they shouted reflected sentiments like, "Come to murder *our* families, will you? Enslave *us*? How does it feel to *take* it for a change?" And most commonly, "Remember Los Arboles! Remember Agua Ancha! Remember Valle Escondido!"

That's when he remembered they hadn't chosen this war. Oh, they'd chosen to *fight* at last, when given the means, but the *dread* of war with so much at stake had been upon them for generations, torturing their souls if not yet their bodies. Even the skirmishing with Holcanos had been part of that—as the Holcanos themselves now knew. Despite their barely suppressed savagery, Barca actually pitied the Holcanos. Only the arrival of the Americans (imperfect "heroes" as they were)—witness men like Hahessy and too many like him—and then the Battle of the Washboard had shown them they had a chance, that they *didn't* have to just take it when the Doms came for them. Barca vaguely knew how that felt. He'd chosen not to take it himself, hadn't he? Instead of accepting whatever role might've been expected of him, he'd forged a place for *himself* among heroes. Now he must earn it.

They *weren't* doing murder here. They were destroying enemies who'd treat them unspeakably if they could. As they *would* if they weren't killed. These particular Doms may not be Blood Priests and hadn't massacred the villages along the Usuma River, but they were part of a system, a creed, that gave rise to creatures who could.

Poom! Poom! roared Barca's guns. And they *were* his guns.

Boogerbear galloped up on his horse, so lathered with sweat that the stripes were invisible. Barca crisply saluted him.

Boogerbear waved it away with a grin. "I b'leve you can cease firin', for the present," he said cheerfully. "A few are leakin' back the way they came, but you've built too big a heap in front of you to jump. Stay where you are, but hold off awhile. I'll send somebody back d'rectly." He gazed at the blackened guns for a moment while men sponged them out with black water. "Was I ever glad ta see *them*," he said. "Scary as hell ridin' into 'em, in case somebody got itchy," he confessed, "but I wasn't worried." He pointed back at the arroyo with the revolver still in his hand. "More worried about them boogers behind us. Ol' Dodger ain't a racin' horse, an' they were gettin' close." With another jaunty wave, he turned his tired animal back the way he came and urged him into a slow trot.

Barca turned back to his guns. "Section! Cease firing, secure your pieces!"

"Cease firing, secure the piece," echoed Cox and Dodd.

Barca shifted in his saddle and noticed First Sergeant Petty standing by with a musket on his shoulder. The artillerymen still kept muskets in the battery wagon for guard duty, foraging, and "just in case."

"I haven't seen you since we unlimbered, First Sergeant. Where have you been?" Barca asked.

Petty waved vaguely around. "With just two guns, nothin' much for me to do." He tugged on his sling. "Figured I'd stand around with this, case them devils got close enough to need it." He shrugged. "They didn't, an' you didn't need me." He came as close as he was probably capable to a smile. "You did fine, Lieutenant."

Barca took a long breath. "Thank you, First Sergeant. I appreciate that."

CHAPTER 24

ARMY OF GOD'S VENGEANCE

With an east, southeast wind and the land as dry as could be, the shroud of choking, swirling dust created by an army of more than twenty thousand men marching west with all their guns, animals, and wagons stalked and blanketed the entire column, including General Agon and his staff at the front, where dust wasn't usually a problem. It was hot too, and the chalky tan dust stuck to sweaty skin and sweat-dampened uniforms. Capitan Arevalo had attempted to shield his general from most of it with a broad, somewhat flimsy parasol, but the wind made it batter the general, replacing whatever dust it knocked off him with more it collected and deposited. Agon finally snatched it away and cast it angrily on the ground. A glance from Arevalo at a servant caused the man to retrieve the device. Who knew when it might rain?

"I never thought I'd miss the forest!" Agon exclaimed. "Just as dusty, I suppose, but rarely so windy." He frowned. "Rarely a breeze at all, in fact, and all the air as dense and hot and reeking . . ." He sighed. "But one could at least breathe it."

Arevalo looked around. There were still trees, quite a few, dotting the rolling, wash-cracked savanna in disorderly clumps, but most were quite stunted compared to the titans in the Yucatán. There were mountains far to the south (beyond view at present with all the dust), and there'd be another forest ahead, on the other side of the narrow bridge of land at Gran Lago, but the countryside would be more pleasant there, with more little villages and more people between what were considered the "old" and "new frontiers." They'd probably crossed the unseen but very real line designating the latter and the beginning of La Tierra de Sangre a day or two before.

"I don't miss any part of it," Arevalo said simply, and both knew why. This was *his* third "retreat" from Nautla and beyond. The first time he'd been desperately wounded, shot by the strange but beautiful daughter of the terrible Ranger named Anson. He probably should've died. If grace truly came from suffering, he'd already accumulated more than enough for passage into paradise.

"Yes. Well. I expect we've seen the last of that particularly disagreeable expanse of forest for a while. Who knows when we'll be at liberty to resume our work in the Yucatán?" What Agon left unsaid was that they'd probably have to win a civil war first.

A squadron of lancers clattered up alongside the plodding column, throwing more dust in the air and causing General Agon to hold a handkerchief over his mouth and nose and close his eyes. "I assume that's Coronel Uza, come to report?" he asked.

"Yes, my general," Arevalo replied.

"Well, Coronel, did you find what you were looking for?" Agon asked, squinting over the cloth as Uza slowed his horse beside his own and a gust of wind cleared the air a bit.

Uza hesitated a little too long, even uncharacteristically avoiding Agon's gaze.

"Well, speak up!" Agon demanded.

"Yes, my general," he finally replied, tone subdued. "Yesterday, we discovered a heavily used trail in an arroyo to the southeast." He gestured loosely to the left. "To the south now, I should think. You've marched farther than I expected since then. That's why we rejoined from the east, after a . . . delay." He pressed on. "As I suspected, the heretics *have* been using depressions such as that to move undetected, and the evidence indicated the trail had been made by a force roughly equal to my own, surely the bulk of the heretic raiders, apparently intent on outpacing your column and harassing it again at some point. That's what I thought. . . ." he added somewhat lamely, then straightened in his saddle. "In any event, as you commanded, I did not endanger myself"—that statement sounded almost like an accusation—"when I stayed back with this squadron behind me and dispatched the greater part of my battalion in pursuit."

Uza took a deep, bleak breath. "It was a trap. Shortly after we separated, I heard heavy gunfire some distance ahead. It was muffled and badly distorted by convoluted terrain, but I'm sure I heard at least two cannon as well."

Agon looked shocked. "We heard no cannon here. How far was this?"

"Less than two *leguas*, no more."

"It wasn't as windy yesterday, but it came from the same direction," Arevalo jumped in. "Combined with the noise of our army, and if this . . . trap occurred in a depression, it's entirely possible we wouldn't have heard."

"It wasn't just a depression, it was a pit of death!" Uzo snarled, control slipping. "I only got the details from the few survivors as I rushed forward myself . . ."

"Few survivors?" Agon breathed, glancing back at the lancers. There were less than a hundred, and many were wounded.

". . . and finally saw what happened," Uzo relentlessly continued. "That . . . *ese diablo llamado* Anson deliberately baited my men to their doom, like pouring ants into a cup and setting it on a fire! They had no chance at all. Worse, we rode as fast as we could, but by the time we reached"—he covered his eyes with his hand, and his voice broke—"that open grave of mangled flesh, the Diablos who dug it for almost *three hundred* of my men were already gone! Every one! There wasn't even a heretic *corpse*." He shuddered. "It was as if they were never there!"

"But there were other survivors?" Arevalo urged gently.

Uza wiped his face, smearing damp dust like mud. "Yes. More wounded than I counted. Some—and all the damaged horses—had their throats efficiently cut, but"—his tone changed to what might have held grudging appreciation—"it appeared only those who couldn't have lived were treated so. The rest were even left with water." He sounded like he could hardly imagine that.

Agon grimly nodded, contemplating what he'd heard and remembering when Coronel Itzam had proposed a truce to retrieve the wounded around Nautla. He personally believed Anson *was* a devil, of a sort, but this might've been the first time a credible senior officer openly called him and all his men "Los Diablos" out loud where everyone could hear. The whole army would be calling them that by nightfall, probably inclusive of all the heretics, and he didn't know if that would frighten them or strengthen their resolve. Conversely, what might *weaken* it was the mercy shown to the wounded. Mercy, or "misericordia," was a rarely used word in the Holy Dominion, and few would recognize it if they heard it. Many ordinary people practiced it among themselves, no doubt, but the Blood Priests would burn and crucify and impale the very notion out of existence. Of course, it wasn't as if the Dominion army was known for "mercy" either, and Agon's version in the same circumstances Coronel Uza had observed would've been to swiftly kill all the enemy wounded. *Who then truly is the devil in this contest?* whispered a quiet, careful voice in his soul. Don Hurac had decided the Blood Priests were the ultimate enemy, and Agon concurred. *Does that make them devils? How can it when they're merely rabid versions of ourselves?* As always, he grew very confused when he thought about such things.

All other confusion was gone entirely, however, and he spoke abruptly; "Detail whatever escort you can manage to fetch your wounded with however many wagons you need, Coronel Uza," he said. "Most of our wagons are quite empty at present, you know."

"Thank you, my general," Uza said, "but I should go myself."

"No. I said 'whatever you can manage'—*after* you send messengers to bring the rest of your lancers back up from behind us. I want you out front, scouting the way to Gran Lago. Fetch me General Tun!" he commanded one of his own messengers, then looked back at Uza. "Have you wondered *why* you were trapped so thoroughly here, now"—he snorted—"when 'Los Diablos' could've done it at virtually any point since *they* forced us to consolidate nearly all our mounted troops into a tidy package?"

"Because they could?" Uza answered bitterly.

"Of course, but there's more to the *timing*. We're getting very close to Gran Lago, which is as fine a choke point or 'cup' as your men found themselves in, and this entire army is now no better equipped to sniff out a trap than you were. To shamefully mix my metaphors, we're blind. As far as we know, Coronel Cayce continues to plod along the Camino Militar safely behind us, drawing no closer despite the delay caused by the raid on our camp. Why?"

He thought about that hard and barely noticed when General Tun rode up to join them. Finally acknowledging his friend, he said, "For the second time, I'm as sure as I can possibly be that Coronel Cayce is *not* where we think he is."

"Indeed? Then where is he?" Tun asked incredulously.

Agon pointed south. "Out there, somewhere, *alongside* us. Stalking us."

"You're mad," Tun huffed. "How? Why?"

"I believe—I'm certain—he's trying to get around us, to Gran Lago. That's what he's been doing all along! He *never was* at Nautla. At first he was probably just trying to get behind us and smash us between his force and Coronel Itzam's. It would've been *most* convenient if he caught us, bled white, in front of Nautla. . . ." He clenched his fist as realization came; how close he'd been to complete destruction. "But we left," he said, carefully controlling his voice. "Now—I don't know how—he's spent all these months contriving to do it *again*, and Gran Lago is the perfect place! We must hurry the column forward. Leave everything and everyone who can't make it behind."

In spite of his sudden, almost desperate intensity, Agon appeared almost giddy. Tun lifted an eyebrow at him. "Why so excited? Cayce's no longer our chief concern. A battle now can only hurt us, even if we win."

"True," Agon agreed. "But I've so craved another meeting with Colonel Cayce—without that fool Don Frutos on my back."

"'That fool,' and his puppet masters, will be on *all* our backs forever if we can't stop him. We must avoid a major action with Coronel Cayce if we can. We can't fritter our army away as we did at the Washboard, in point-less frontal assaults—even if he does reach Gran Lago before us."

Agon nodded wistfully. "I know that as well, but I'm . . . pleased that I divined Cayce's plan, so bold that it almost eluded me—again. But this time it didn't, and if we reach Gran Lago first, Cayce will have to come to *us*. He *must* if he truly means to march all the way to Vera Cruz." He made a moue. "I'm still not certain of that. It seems unbelievable that he'd try it, regard-less how tempting. But if he does, we'll have him!" Agon delighted in the prospect a few moments more before finally conceding, "We'd get hurt, no question about it, but then we'd have only the Blood Priests and Don Frutos to deal with, and half the Dominion in which to rebuild our strength on the way to Vera Cruz to rescue Don Hurac. From there, we march on the Holy

City and restore the Dominion to its proper path!" He lowered his voice. "Our fraternity of warriors will finally be appreciated and respected again."

"Wonderful, all of it," Tun agreed, then held up a finger. "*If.*"

"'If' what?"

"*If* we defeat or avoid Coronel Cayce. *If* there are any troops left to be had between Gran Lago and Vera Cruz—Don Frutos will have already passed through there, remember? *If* we defeat him before he murders Don Hurac. Who would we raise as Supreme Holiness in his place? And finally, *if* Don Julio hasn't already recalled the Gran Cruzada and sworn it to serve him. I've no idea how large it was when it finally departed, but don't forget the Blood Priests were involved in its creation from beginning to end, and it took *years* to build. We'd never raise an army to match it."

"No," Agon conceded. "But even if Don Julio—I *won't* call him 'His Supreme Holiness'—does recall the Gran Cruzada—most difficult without appearing weak—it will require months for so large a force to grind to a halt, turn around, and march all the way back to the center of the empire." He shrugged. "We have a long way to go as well and can only do what we can do, but all the more reason to hurry. Pass the word to all brigade commanders: we pick up the pace!"

As it turned out, General Agon didn't win the race to Gran Lago; nor did Lewis Cayce or "El Diablo" Anson. It was Capitan Ramon Lara and his 1st Yucatán Lancers, joined on his sweeping, end-around push by Coryon Burton's 3rd US dragoons and Dukane's battery of 12pdr howitzers, who got there first, groping about in the trackless, foggy, predawn dark. They would've bumbled around even longer without Alcaldesa Consela to guide them as best she could remember. She'd been born in the town of Gran Lago but fled the increasing religious intolerance of the Dominion with her family as a child, more than thirty years before. They hadn't been alone, and that exodus resulted in the foundation of several now-shattered villages along the Usuma River. Interestingly, her memory was aided by Father Orno who, along with his friend and colleague Reverend Harkin (still with Lewis Cayce), had worked together to compile the best possible maps from their own and captured sources before joining the army, and continued to update them as they advanced. Just as important, their shared passion for understanding the natural world God created gave them certain advantages when it came to interpreting the conditions as well.

"The fog is likely generated by offshore currents. We get the same at Uxmal in certain seasons," Orno had explained to Lara, Burton, and Consela as they rode. "And El Gran Lago is a very *big* lake, as its name implies, fed by the Grijalva River and cool freshwater runoff from the mountains to the south. Reverend Harkin and I have speculated that the narrow land bridge separating it from the sea might've been created over time by those very ocean currents opposing the silt deposits brought by the river." He'd smiled. "Or the ground might have moved, thrusting those deposits upward. Like the dams made by forest monsters to preserve their pools when the rainy season passes." He'd shrugged. "Only God knows, but it's quite thrilling when one *thinks* he has come to some understanding of God's design!"

Consela regarded him. "I was taught it was because the water on the south side of the lake is fresh and on the north it is salty. Storms sometimes blow the sea across the bridge, even through the town," she'd explained. "And there are different kinds of fish in different parts of the lake."

"How fascinating!" Orno exclaimed. "I wonder what keeps the different waters from mingling. One would think they eventually would."

Regardless what caused it, the fog was a problem, and the two mounted regiments (combined into 'Lara's brigade' for the present), had struck the lakeshore south of town and worked their way along it. Fortunately, the fog seemed to interfere with the senses of the beasts they encountered, and most were as surprised as they were and promptly fled, thrashing away in the gloom. They began to stumble upon stockaded homesteads and the occasional darkened villa. Scouts brought in frightened slaves who didn't understand what was happening. They couldn't imagine enemies of the Dominion could be *here* and were most afraid of what their owners would do to them for abandoning the flocks they watched. A few finally grasped the situation, that these were the very "heretics" troops from Gran Lago itself had been called to suppress in the Yucatán—wherever that was—and they understood what *that* meant: if heretics took control of Gan Lago, they'd all be destroyed by the wrath of the Dominion. Those captives promptly refused to provide any information at all.

"Don't they understand we're here to *liberate* them?" Lara had asked out loud, in frustration.

"They do not," Orno replied gravely.

Word must've spread ahead of them somehow, and as the fog began to brighten they found more and more dwellings already hastily abandoned.

"I'd thought we'd be welcomed as liberators too, even friends," Coryon Burton said, somewhat aggrieved.

"These people have no friends," Consela said sadly. "They know they can't fight you—whoever you are—so all they can do is flee."

"Will that save them?"

"I don't know," she confessed. "They'll be blamed for letting us capture their city, but they can't oppose us if they aren't here. Nor can they be blamed—they hope—for fleeing the very presence of heretics. That's the most terrible thing: failing to oppose heretics they've *seen* or been touched by in any way, as if they'll be infected by us and carry the sickness to others."

"Well, since that's rather what we hope will happen, I guess it makes a kind of sense," Lara murmured.

The fog burnt off as the morning progressed, and soon they could see all around them. The city was about the size of Uxmal and even resembled it slightly in form, with a riot of adobe, thatched-roof dwellings surrounding a low wall enclosing the inner city. The larger buildings inside the wall were made of painted stucco on baked bricks instead of ages-old shaped stone, but the architecture wasn't dissimilar—long rectangles two stories high at most, their roofs supported by columns. And there was the apparently obligatory stepped pyramid in a courtyard at the center of town, the eastern stairway—toward them as they viewed it—grotesquely darkened by splashed blood. The place was a madhouse. As empty of people as the approaches might be, a steady, chaotic stream of thousands was spilling out the western gate and flooding up the Camino Militar.

"I never expected this," Lara said somberly. "I hate that they're afraid of us."

"Don't forget what Alcaldesa Consela said," Orno reminded. "They're not as afraid of us as they are what will happen to them when the Dominion comes to punish us, and whoever was here to 'allow' us into the city. They've never seen us—never expected to, and don't know anything about us. They *can't* know we've already defeated an entire Dom army and bloodied and outmaneuvered another." He nodded at the distant panic. "Those people won't 'know' us either, but they *will* know we've come, and *that* word will spread. As we continue to advance, it'll finally occur to more and more that the Dominion can't stop us. Even more important, they'll realize it can't hurt *them* anymore. More will stay in their homes when we come. As they get to know us, they'll join us," he added with a pious certainty.

"I hope you're right," Burton said, looking farther afield, first at the sparkling sea to the north. Gran Lago was a seaport, but there wasn't a harbor to speak of, and only a couple of ships rode at anchor offshore. *Typical Dom merchantmen*, he thought, wishing Captain Holland's little navy had snapped them up. He glanced back at the fleeing horde. *Not that it matters now. The word of our whereabouts is finally out.* Turning, he gazed at the huge lake that seemed as big as the sea, yet lay still and flat in the increasingly hot, breezeless morning. The only place he could see across it was off to the west, in the direction the refugees fled, where he discerned the blue-gray line of yet another forest. He looked at Lara. "What're we going to do? Just move into the city and defend the walls?"

Lara was shaking his head. "Not only might we still have to fight to get in—I can't believe *everybody* will leave—it's too big. And there are all those buildings right up around it. No fields of fire. The enemy could work their way up under the walls and just swarm over them."

"Not if we burn the city outside the walls," Emmel Dukane suggested, riding up to join them. That gained him a harsh look from Orno, but he held up a hand, grinning between the wild side whiskers his high, stiff collar pushed out from his face. "Not really suggesting it. I doubt there are emplacements ready-made for my guns behind the wall in any event. And we'll need my guns," he assured them. They all looked back the way they'd come, just a few hundred yards toward a narrower gap between the lake and the sea. There was a knobby hill on the lake side, topped by an impressive villa, probably owned by some local *patricio*. There was nothing but a brushy mound on the seaside. The Camino Militar went right down the center, flanked by a few buildings. There was little beyond but more *jacales*. "Down there's the best bet," Dukane suggested. "Tear down the *jacales* and throw up a breastwork with a clear field of fire."

"It's still too wide," Lara objected. "There's a front of half a mile, at least."

"We can incorporate those larger buildings into the line," Burton said, pointing. "Put a section of Dukane's guns on the hill by the villa, the rest on the line—and we can move men side to side to reinforce as needed." He paused. "And we won't be alone for long."

"We *hope*," Lara emphasized.

"We hope," Burton agreed.

"I don't understand how you mean to fight," Consela tentatively said, "but I saw you make lines of men at Los Arboles. Is that what you'll do?"

"Essentially, yes," Lara told her.

"I remember a wide marshy place on the other side of town. The road even uses a bridge to cross it."

"That sounds promising," Burton told her and conceded, "we might have to fall back to there. But we have to *try* to hold this side of the city if we're to have a position our friends can join us in. Once we're pushed back, General Agon can reoccupy the city and cut us off. Just as bad, Colonel Cayce will have to assault him there—there's no getting around it—and Agon has more than enough men to defend it. We'll all be stuck here."

"But surely, once Colonel Cayce is joined by Colonel Itzam, his army will almost equal General Agon's. Wouldn't that be enough?"

"Not to attack a fixed position," Burton denied, glancing at Orno, "and Agon will burn or otherwise clear the buildings from around the wall. Even if Colonel Cayce won." He frowned. "Not a very appropriate word. I'm afraid our army would be spent. We could go no farther, and we'd be lucky to keep Gran Lago."

"I see there's much I don't understand about this kind of war," Consela said sadly.

"It's not really so different from the kind your warriors fought against the terrible monsters menacing your village," Father Orno told her. "They'd attack with overwhelming numbers, would they not? And couldn't sustain too many losses, or there'd be no one to rid you of the next one."

"I suppose that makes more sense," Consela agreed, "though the 'numbers' we're talking about here . . . I can't even imagine a battle such as you're preparing for."

"Well," Lara said, "we know General Agon can, now. Let's hope most of his men can't either." He sighed. "All right. Captain Dukane, I understand in your service artillerymen study engineering more than infantry"—he smiled slightly at Burton—"or dragoons. Please supervise the emplacement of your guns, the destruction of the *jacales*, and the construction of our defenses. My lancers will be at your disposal for labor." He turned to Burton. "Scouts, if you please. Some to observe the enemy, and others to make contact with the rest of our forces."

CHAPTER 25

GRAN LAGO

Coryon Burton's dragoon scouts didn't have far to look for Anson's Rangers. They came with the late afternoon, blue uniforms and sweat-foamy animals caked in dust after a long, grueling ride. Anson was glad to see Lara's brigade, of course, but pretended to be put out. "I'd hoped to beat you here," he told Lara and Burton with a tired smile as he bivouacked his men and horses behind one of the large buildings. It was a warehouse they'd found, to their delight, apparently dedicated to the collection and storage of agricultural "taxes" from farms and ranches on the east side of the lake. Many of the animals had been driven away at Lara's approach, but there was plenty of grain for exhausted horses and food for tired, hungry men. Not that there were a great many of those. The entire force "defending" the city of Gran Lago now constituted twenty-three hundred troopers from the three mounted regiments, six 12pdr howitzers in Dukane's battery, and Lieutenant Barca's two-gun section of 6pdrs—which were moved to replace Dukane's two guns on the heights because of their greater range. That kept Dukane's battery "together," even though it was spread along the line. Barca's section was used to being independent.

"I kind of hoped you'd beat us here too, sir," Burton replied with a grin. "Would've saved us a lot of work on the breastworks."

Anson was looking at those. "You chose right, puttin' 'em where you did," he confirmed. "As long as we can hold 'em. Best estimate of the ene-my's still about twenty-four, twenty-five thousand."

"And Colonel Cayce has?" Lara prompted.

"'Bout nine-thousand-odd in First an' Second Divisions, maybe . . ." Anson hesitated. "Two or three days behind us. I think he means to skin his scouts down to nearly nothin' an' send the rest of his rangers, dragoons, and Meder's riflemen ahead. Could get here tonight or tomorrow, another fifteen hundred or so, all told."

"Not much," Burton said.

"Not enough to win," Anson agreed. "Maybe enough to hold this nar-row front, since the Doms won't be able to maneuver. An' Colonel Itzam's scramblin' hell for leather up behind Agon now, with all o' Third Division except what's left at Nautla an' Campeche. Another eight or nine thousand, I expect." He turned to look behind them. "You sent anybody up to the city yet, to see what's what?" The flood of refugees they'd watched earlier in the day had slowed to a trickle.

"No sir," Lara said, "but we haven't seen any Dom soldiers on the walls." He frowned. "The slaves that we . . . took into custody—more than two hun-dred by the time we reached here"—he gestured toward the big storehouse where they were being kept—"seemed to agree, when we could get them to say anything, that most if not all the troops in Gran Lago had long ago marched to join General Agon." He paused. "On the other hand, as sus-pected, Don Frutos and Tranquilo came back through, more than a week ago, with about three thousand troops and Blood Priests. No one knows how many local freemen and even slaves they conscripted. Quite a few. I'll wager they emptied the city armories and hauled off any artillery as well."

"Don't believe I'll take that bet," Anson said. "Even if they found more weapons than they could pull or carry, they probably destroyed or hid the rest." His lips twisted with disgust. "Folks here are just lucky they didn't treat 'em like the villagers up the Usuma River. Still . . ." He looked over at Boogerbear. "Take a dozen men on fresh horses an' have a look at the city. Get in if you can, an' see what's left. Skedaddle if you take any fire you can't sort out."

Even the mighty Boogerbear looked worn down and older, the dust in his huge black beard turning it gray, but he merely nodded and whistled piercingly at some of his men who'd made the mistake of coming close enough to listen. "You fellas heard the man. Throw yer saddles on some likely lookin' critters an' be ready in ten minutes." Looking back at Lara, he pointed offshore and asked, "What's the story on them ships? You'd think they would'a sailed an' got out, like the locals."

Lara seemed to flush, though it didn't show on his reddish-brown face. "We don't know that either, and frankly haven't paid them much attention," he confessed. "Not knowing how far the enemy is, my first priority was to establish a defensive position and await relief. I'm surprised the ships remained, but they appear only lightly armed and haven't harassed us. Perhaps their crews were ashore and fled on foot with the rest."

"Don't think so," Anson said with a grin, studying the vessels through his glass. "Have another look at 'em."

Lara, Burton, and Dukane all looked. No one knew when, but at some point a pair of large, new-made American flags had broken to stream from the topmasts of the awkward-looking ships (of all the flags of the Allied city-states, the Stars and Stripes was the most distinctive from a distance), and a boat was rowing ashore through quickening, rising tide surf.

"That's interestin'," Anson said, then observed the labor under way at the breastworks. It was going too slow. "See if you can get the slaves you liberated to help with this work, Mr. Lara. *Ask* 'em to—they ain't slaves anymore, far as I'm concerned." He pointed up at the villa on the hill. "Send some to help Mr. Barca dig his guns in as well. He ain't gonna have much room to shift 'em around up there."

"The locals don't seem much inclined to help," Lara objected wryly.

Anson snorted frustration. "Alcaldesa Consela, have a word with 'em, will you? Tell 'em what happened to you, an' remind 'em that, at this point, they're likely dead if we lose." He nodded at the shore where the boat was being dragged up on the beach, aided by a squad of lancers. "I'm goin' down to see what our sailor friends have to say. Come with me, Mr. Burton."

Giles Anson might've been slightly more surprised to see Sam Houston walking toward him up the sandy beach than he was to find his old friend Sal Hernandez among the cluster of approaching men, but not much. "I'll be damned, am I glad to see you!" he said, swinging down from Colonel Fannin's saddle and vigorously shaking Sal's hand.

"Me too, Cap'n—I mean 'Major.'" Sal grinned under his huge mustache. "*Hola*, Coryon," he told the dragoon, then looked back at Anson. "Though I ain't too excited about the fix you're in. You *do* know there's a helluva Dom army slitherin' up from the east, right?"

"Yeah," Anson said.

"Yeah," Sal agreed, then lamented, "seems we're all gettin' cut off an' surrounded these days."

"I heard that crazy Cap'n Holland wants to stick at Vera Cruz," Anson said, eyes rolling heavenward as if in prayer, "like Travis at the damned Alamo!"

"I hope it ain't that bad," Sal hedged, then introduced the men with him.

Anson appraised the short, rather round one Sal called "Cap'n Razine." "I heard o' you. You're the ex-Dom skipper o' one o' those ships."

"*Roble Fuerte* is mine," Razine answered with great dignity. "I not only command her; she is my property. Her *free* crew and I have wholeheartedly joined your cause."

"Well. Good to know *some* Doms ain't crazy, an' think for themselves." He tilted his head back over his shoulder. "We had a whole city run off from us. God knows how many'll starve or get ate in the wild. Boogerbear's goin' to see who all's left."

"They are afraid, Major Anson," Razine explained.

"Sure, an' I know why," agreed Anson, "but you musta been scared too."

"I remain so," Razine assured him, "but rational men appealed to my reason, over time. The people here have had no time. Let me go with yours to talk with the ones still here."

Anson considered that. "Sure. Mr. Burton, tell Boogerbear to bring another horse an' come get Cap'n Razine." When Burton galloped away, Anson turned back to Sal and the rest. "So, yeah, we know Agon's comin', but so's Lewis. Colonel Itzam too. If we can hold till they get here, we'll rope Agon into a fair-size dispute. That's the plan, anyway. But what're you doin' here?"

"We came lookin' for you, amigo," Sal said with a lopsided grin. "It took a while, with this strange easterly wind, but we beat far out in the gulf, then slanted down toward Campeche before followin' the coast with the wind behind us. We found Colonel Itzam and spoke to him five days ago—and he *is* swiftly gainin' on Agon—but then we saw Agon's force. They signaled us but we ignored them." He chuckled before turning serious once more. "We anchored here only yesterday, but the city was already in turmoil. Perhaps they knew you were coming."

"Maybe," Anson said, "or were still stirred up after Don Frutos an' Tranquilo came through. Don't matter. How far do you reckon Agon is?"

Sal scratched his upper lip through his mustache, then swept the whiskers back into place with his palm. "If he keeps pressing as hard as it seemed he was . . ." He paused, thinking. "He could be here tomorrow afternoon? Evening? I doubt he'd rush straight into battle. His men'll be exhausted. But he could attack by the following day."

Anson mashed his own wild, dusty whiskers against his chin. "Well, that'll give us more time to get ready, I guess. An' more time for Lewis to get here."

"Unless the armies find each other first," Sal observed darkly.

Anson grinned. "Oh, I guarantee Lewis knows where Agon is—an' Agon prob'ly *suspects* where he is too, but can't do much about it." The grin turned wicked. "Seems Agon misplaced nearly all his scouts a while back. The only way he can effectively fight is right out in the open, where he can see."

"Like here," Sal said with a raised brow.

"Well, yeah . . . but why were you lookin' for us anyway?" Anson backtracked.

Sal glanced at the other men with him: an Ocelomeh Ranger NCO, an Uxmalo infantry lieutenant, and what looked like a couple of civilian types. "Honestly, we came lookin' for help. More veterans to help train an' stiffen the spines of our recruits at Vera Cruz. Colonel Cayce sent orders for Itzam to ship us some, but then he got busy chasin' Agon." He waved around. "Now this."

Anson laughed. "Yeah, I guess everybody's got their own chore to finish before they can spare anybody for Holland's adventure." He held up a hand, forestalling objections from Sal's companions. "After we're done here, we'll see. I figure it's a good idea, myself. Pretty sure Lewis will too."

Sal nodded. "In that case, I'd be proud to help you 'get done'—if you'll give me a horse. I *hate* walkin' in this damned sand. An' I bet we can bring a hundred or so armed men off the ships."

"Every little bit helps," Anson agreed.

Sal was suddenly looking around. "Say? Where's little Leonor at?"

"Where do you think? Still doggin' Lewis."

"I swear. I never thought anybody'd pry her away from you."

"Me either," Anson confessed a little sadly. "Not even sure I'd mind that much if I was sure he returned her feelin's. I *think* he does, mind you, but he won't encourage her while there's this war to focus on."

"Like you an' Mistress Samantha?" Sal teased.

Anson turned to remount his horse. "That's different. She came out to join the army at Cayal—I guess you didn't know that. She's with Colonel Cayce an' the rest o' the army. But I 'encouraged' her to wait till the war's done so she'd quit pesterin' me now."

"How's that workin'?" Sal asked with a chuckle.

"So far, so good. But if we ever *do* finish this war, I won't have a choice but to marry her."

"*Pobrecita*," Sal mocked him.

Settling in his saddle, Anson grinned at his friend. "Yeah."

———

As Sal Hernandez predicted, General Agon's Army of God's Vengeance began to arrive the following afternoon, almost dangerously on the heels of the roughly fifteen hundred remaining lancers, dragoons, and Mounted Rifles Anson said Lewis had promised. Not that the Doms could catch them with the meager mounted element in front of their long, fat column, but if they'd come half a day earlier, they could've kept the reinforcements from breaking through. The rest of the few Dom lancers were doubtless out on Agon's left, hunting Colonel Cayce, but just enough Rangers were left to fend them off. Nonetheless, the reinforcements were cheered enthusiastically as they came dragging in on blown horses, the animals tended by their rested comrades and the men fed where they practically dropped. Felix Meder of the Mounted Rifles reported to Anson and told him about where Colonel Cayce was.

"I wouldn't mind goin' for a ride," Sal offered. "The colonel needs ta know what's what here. Besides, I been mighty cooped up at Vera Cruz, an' then aboard ship."

Anson looked at his friend. "You think you can find him? You've never been over this country. There's some *really* big critters too."

Sal snorted disdain. "You forget who yer talkin' to?"

Anson shrugged. "Sorry. I've missed you, amigo."

"I'll go with him," volunteered Lieutenant Fisher of the dragoons. "Not that Captain Hernandez *needs* me," he hastily added, "but my observations of . . . local conditions might be convenient." He'd spent the day with Boogerbear, in the city and beyond, scouting extensively.

"Well . . . sure. But pick some good, fast horses, both of you."

"Any message for Señorita Wilde, if I see her?" Sal asked solemnly.

It wasn't possible to see a blush under Anson's sweaty, gray-streaked beard or sun-darkened skin, so it couldn't undermine his severe expression. "Yeah, you ol' bandit. 'Respects,' of course."

The lancers and dragoons rejoined the command of Lara and Burton, and Felix Meder's riflemen were sent to the hill to support Barca's section of artillery. Not only did he need the support, the riflemen would finally be able to use their weapons as intended: to kill the enemy beyond the range of their ability to effectively hit back. At least individually. And by the time the Doms began to shake out of their column into a brigade-strength defensive line about twenty-five hundred yards away, their dingy uniforms but freshly polished brass and bloodred flags brightly lit by the setting sun while the rest of their army began erecting a marching camp, Anson's defenses were nearing completion. The feeble breastworks had been reinforced by a gravelly earthen mound thrown up from trenches on both sides by the troops—and roughly three thousand locals Alcaldesa Consela and Captain Razine persuaded to help. The locals had even been armed with pikes (there were lots of those in the city), and enough had been brought out for everyone since, with the exception of the riflemen who'd had bayonets adapted to their rifles and the artillerymen who'd kept their muskets, no one had bayonets for their short carbines. Almost everyone had sabers or short swords now, even the Rangers who'd had more opportunities to take them from Doms—along with a fair number of pistols—but pikes might make the difference if things got close.

Little was expected of the locals in battle, of course, but if it was true that any who stayed would be killed whether they resisted or not, at least they could fight for their lives if they had to. Interestingly, Boogerbear and Captain Razine found a cache of other arms that Don Frutos missed: obsolete matchlock arquebuses of the sort replaced by the army and once traded to the Holcanos. Kisin and his personal guards had already acquired Dom flintlocks, but Alcaldesa Consela's small company and a few of the local freemen and hidalgos with army experience knew how to use the old-style weapons. If they showed proficiency and a desire to do so, they were allowed to join Lara's lancers on the battle line. Most had no idea, however, and there wasn't time to train them.

"Lord above, but there's a swarm o' the devils," Preacher Mac proclaimed, tiredly leaning his shovel against the left hub of the Number Two gun up on the hill after helping level the piece. Now he quickly unbuttoned his sun-faded jacket (it was starting to look more purple than blue) so the cool evening breeze could flood his sweat-soaked shirt. The rest of the men were doing the same, stripping to shirtsleeves to refresh themselves after heaping up as much protection for the guns as they could. Now they were staring out at the enemy camp taking shape about a mile and a half away.

"Quite a few," Hanny Cox agreed nervously, "but the word is, there's not as many as there was at the Washboard."

"Nor as many o' us neither. Not by a long shot," Hahessy pointed out.

"*Looks* like more, from up here," Kini Hau said.

"You weren't even at the Washboard," Apo Tuin reminded, but thought about it for a moment. "You're right, though. It looks like more."

"That's only 'cause, up high like this, you can see more of 'em at once," declared First Sergeant Petty. He was right, but even at the peak of the hill they were barely a hundred feet above the plain. "An' put yer goddamn jackets back on! What'll them riflemen think?" he barked, cutting his eyes in the direction Felix Meder's men still worked, extending the breastworks from where the 3rd Dragoons ended on the flank of the hill and into a sa-lient semicircle around the brick and stucco villa. "You look like a buncha prisoners on a goddamn chain gang, or worse—sailors!"

Stepping up behind him, Barca started to object out of compassion, but decided the worst thing he could do was countermand an order by Petty. He was the highest-ranking NCO and had much more experience than he. Besides . . . "He's right, fellows. You'll catch cold, or have a cramp."

"I'm crampin' already," Hahessy griped, "an' if it felt this fine, I could catch cold an' die right now, I could," he added wistfully, but did retrieve his soggy jacket and stuff an arm in the sleeve.

Captain Meder strode purposefully toward them, and Barca saluted. Meder returned it and said, "Damn you, First Sergeant, I was about to tell *my* lads to shuck their jackets! Can't do it now, and have you fellows show us up." He shot Petty and the other artillerymen a quick grin, then looked back at Barca. "What do you think, Lieutenant? You've been here longer than us, and as soon as I reported, Major Anson just pointed this way and said, 'Go.' I've no idea what's happening."

Barca explained as much as he could. Having arrived with the second "trickle" of troops, as it were, he didn't know much beyond the obvious. "We're here, of course, with Mr. Burton's dragoons on our left. As a strong-point on high ground, the enemy may give us more attention than we want, and the dragoons can support us with their rapid-fire Hall carbines." Barca pointed. "Beyond the dragoons is the first section of Dukane's battery and Mr. Lara's dismounted lancer regiment. Their carbines, or 'musketoons,' load almost as quickly as Halls but aren't as accurate. Dukane's second section is next, right in the middle of the line, and Major Anson's Rangers, actually our largest element, with over a thousand men—and keeping their horses near on the beach, I might add—are on the left flank by the sea. Dukane's first section is there, and I understand Captain Razine's ships will try to give us some covering fire with their few guns as well." He paused. "It appears that Razine and Alcaldesa Consela have secured some cooperation from the locals. I've seen them working on the fortifications below, but none have come up here. I'd prefer more obstacles and entanglements in front of us." He pursed his lips. "That's all I know about our disposition, as obvious to you as to me, and apparently just as thin as it looks."

"Hmm," Meder responded noncommittally, before gazing out at the enemy. "It seems 'old Agon' learned a lesson or two the last time we met. He's making camp just out of range of your roundshot."

"Oh, we could roll a few through his tents from here, Captain," Apo gamely assured, "but it would be falling so sharply it would lose too much power when it struck to carry on and do any real harm."

"We've got the last of the exploding case shot left in the world—until they learn to make more," Barca said quietly, "and I expect we'll use it all. On the other hand, as hard and dry as the ground is, roundshot will bound along nicely and should be just as effective as case when the enemy comes closer. What's the range of your rifles?"

Meder pointed downslope and a surprising distance out on the grassy flat, where blue-jacketed men were driving bright wooden stakes into the ground as range markers. "Any of my lads can kill a man at two hundred yards. That's roughly from here to the base of the hill, as you see. No one's accepted in the Rifles if they can't do that. It's the minimum requirement, but honestly the best that most can consistently do. On the other hand, about half of our weapons came from a Deringer contract equipped with an ingenious long-range sight, and about a quarter of the men can shoot to three hundred rather easily. I even have a . . . talented minority who can usually hit a man at *five* hundred yards, but the lethality of the ball is somewhat limited at that distance." He chuckled. "It'll still wound, though. Gives the enemy something to think about, and my lads something to do."

Standing aside, Hanny Cox was amused to hear Felix Meder talk about his "lads" because he and the young officer were about the same age. Hanny had just turned nineteen and figured Meder was twenty or twenty-one. But just as Hanny had matured into his own lesser authority, Meder was well suited to command the Rifles. Elijah Hudgens, Hanny's nominal battery commander (though the section had spent little time under his authority of late), thought the world of Meder, and both had been privates when they came to this world. *Everyone in the army has grown,* he decided. *The American troops—of whatever original nationality—have grown closer together and shouldered a heavy load. The Uxmalos and other city folk, once content to let others do their fighting, have become real soldiers—and the Ocelomeh have done the same, while accepting a new discipline they'd never imagined before. All for the same worthy cause.* He snorted as he contemplated what might've been his own greatest accomplishment: the still meager but apparent rehabilitation of Daniel Hahessy. *Even he seems resigned to becoming part of something bigger than himself.* Looking down at the spreading, blossoming tents and lights and kindling campfires of the massive enemy camp as the sky in the west went purple and stars flickered to life behind the rising, smoky haze, he feared they'd run up against something bigger than they could handle.

CHAPTER 26

ARMY OF GOD'S VENGEANCE / GRAN LAGO

"We nearly *destroyed* this army on the last grueling segment of our march, and the enemy *still* got here first!" General Agon almost raged, standing outside his just erected command marquee, peering at the sunset-silhouetted emplacements stretching from the hill on the south side of the narrow land bridge to the sea.

"It's only their mounted troops," General Tun consoled, though his tone was just as grumpy. "There can't be more than three or four thousand, and only eight guns have been seen. We can handle them easily."

"Easily," Agon snapped sarcastically. "A meager four thousand. 'Only' eight guns! I doubt we actually engaged more than that at Nautla, and they slammed us to a bloody halt."

"Engaged, yes," Arevalo agreed, "but they had many more in reserve to fill any gaps. The enemy has no such luxury here. And the defenses are nothing like those at Nautla."

"They're similar enough that we can't maneuver and have no choice but to approach directly. And the power we face is quite sufficient to inflict similar losses to those we suffered at Nautla. At least!"

"More than likely, my general," Arevalo confessed.

Agon was shaking his head. "We can't afford it, don't you see? This army is all we have between the Dominion we've always known—that God Himself created and charged us to defend—and the . . . heretical, abominable rule the Blood Priests would inflict on us, grinding what honor our profession retains in the dust, and—quite ironically—severing forever the blood ties of our rulers to the founders! We can't risk its destruction."

"Four thousand men and a few guns *can't* destroy this army," General Tun objected dismissively.

"They can hurt it badly enough for *Colonel Cayce* to destroy it!" Agon roared in reply. He stood a moment, breathing hard, regaining control. When he spoke again, his tone was mild once more. "But here we are, aren't we? We don't have a choice. We *must* go forward. If we got here first and had that position"—he pointed—"I'm confident we could've at least shattered Colonel Cayce's pursuit. I was—and am—prepared to lose *half* this army to do that. Ten thousand men, these *hardened* men, are enough to complete our campaign of restoration before the enemies of God decisively gather in the Holy City." He gestured helplessly. "So tomorrow we must carry the enemy works regardless of cost. If we have enough left to stop the main heretic army while preserving that essential minimum, we'll do so. Otherwise, we press on to the marshes beyond the city. There, even a relatively tiny force can hold the elevated road and bridge. They can destroy it if they must. The land between the city and the forest will keep the heretics back."

General Tun remained unhappy. He understood Agon's frustration, but his old friend had never spoken so harshly to him before. "Then we attack at dawn?" he asked.

Agon rubbed his chin whiskers in thought. "Yes, but don't forget the fog here. It will come again tomorrow. We can use it to advance under cover, but that's one thing we've never trained for. We could be asking for hopeless and costly confusion—whole regiments marching straight into the lake instead of the enemy! But the opportunity is too great to pass." His expression firmed. "We'll begin a bombardment as soon as our artillery can see the vaguest target—we do at least have a small advantage in artillery this time, and the enemy can't maneuver either. We'll pound them for a while, then advance all along the line under the cover of smoke and fog. I want the men to move swiftly and we'll land the heaviest blow on the left, against that inconvenient hill. Once that's overrun, we can roll the enemy up and push them into the sea!"

1ST AND 2ND DIVISIONS / SOUTHEAST OF GRAN LAGO

Lieutenant Fisher, 3rd Dragoons, and, to everyone's surprise, Sal Hernandez, of all people, swept down out of the burning sunset glaring off the apparently endless lake to the west. Their horses, fine former Dom mounts, were hopelessly blown, and the riders didn't look much better when they came to a halt beside Lewis Cayce and his eclectic staff. His personal companions were Varaa-Choon, Leonor Anson, and Corporal Willis as always, but King Har-Kaaska, Colonel Reed, Reverend Harkin, Dr. Newlin, Consul Koaar-Taak of the 1st Ocelomeh, Marvin Beck of the 1st US, and George Wagley of the 2nd Uxmal were there as well. And Captain Olayne had escorted Samantha Wilde forward to hear the news when the first cry of "messengers comin'!" was raised. She'd continued her excellent logistical work alongside Dr. Newlin (they headed the field quartermaster's department in all but name together now), and she'd borne up well and cheerfully under the hardships of the campaign. No one begrudged her presence, particularly since she hadn't seen Major Anson for but a short while when the forces briefly converged at Valle Escondido. She was understandably worried about him.

They all moved aside so the tired troops could keep marching on without altering their grueling, metronomic pace. Fisher saluted. "Beg . . ." He coughed and took a mouthful of water from his canteen, swished it around and spat away from everyone. "Pardon me, sirs, mistress," he said, mortified, then looked even more embarrassed when he realized he hadn't addressed Varaa as anything. She laughed and waved him on. Nodding his thanks, he started again. "Beg to report: all mounted forces are deployed and dug in east of the town of Gran Lago. Most of the populace has fled the city, but a few came over to our side. Unfortunately, the lead elements of General Agon's army were arriving and going into camp as we left. Major Anson estimates the enemy at twenty-odd thousand, as observed before, and expects a general assault in the morning."

"Thank you, Mr. Fisher. A fine report," Lewis said, turning his attention to Sal. "I assume you were . . . found at Gran Lago?"

"Yes sir. Down from Vera Cruz with a couple ships." He shrugged. "Lookin for you, sir." He winked at Leonor, then quickly removed his hat and addressed Samantha. "I also bear the sweet, longin' words an' lovin' regard for you, *señorita*, from the noble heart of the courageous Ranger Anson!"

Samantha fluttered her fan and flushed. "Did he really tell you to say that?"

Sal laughed. "Of course not! I said all that was from his heart. Bein' his friend for twenty years, I know what's in there better than he does."

"I expect he's right about that," Leonor said, lips ticking upward.

"But why were you looking for us?" asked Colonel Reed.

"To take troops back to Vera Cruz," Sal replied with exaggerated patience. "I understand there's another matter to decide first."

"Too true," said Dr. Newlin.

"You just came directly from Gran Lago," said Major Beck. "*Exactly* how many more miles is it now?"

"I'd say *almost* 'exactly' nine," Sal replied, still a little sarcastic. He couldn't help it.

Lewis puffed his cheeks and glanced at Varaa, who was whispering urgently with King Har-Kaaska. "Another four or five hours at this pace, and that just for the lead elements," he murmured grimly. "And the men are already *so* tired."

"We have to press on," Varaa insisted. "March all night if we must."

"I know," Lewis said.

"If it comes to that, half the troops won't make it," Dr. Newlin warned. "And half that do won't be fit to fight."

"I'm aware of that," Lewis said, teeth set.

"So what's the point?" asked Colonel Reed.

"Sirs, if I may," interjected Lieutenant Fisher. He continued when he saw nods. "I personally don't think Major Anson's combined force can withstand a determined assault. The numbers . . ." He shrugged. "He'll try, but he'll fail, and all those men—virtually all the mounted troops in this army—will die. The worst part is, they'll have died for nothing, because even if they badly damage the enemy, there's an almost impassable marsh west of the city the Doms can cross and effectively block behind them forever. I scouted it myself, along with a company of Rangers under Mr. Beeryman, shortly after we arrived. I hate to presume to offer a suggestion—"

"What he's sayin'," Sal interrupted, proud of the young lieutenant for speaking up, but suspecting his word might carry more weight with some—certainly Leonor, and therefore Colonel Cayce—"is there's only two real choices. Either *get* there somehow an' *save* the blocking force, or send us back—we'd be obliged for fresh horses—to tell Major Anson to pull out tonight an' open the road. The campaign'll be effectively over, though Gran Lago'll be a good place for a new frontier defense, but it'll be over anyway if Major Anson gets wiped out."

"What if my fath—I mean, Major Anson," Leonor corrected herself sharply, "pulls back to the crossing on the marsh himself? Blocks the enemy there?"

Sal was shaking his head. "Then the Doms would have the city an' you can't get past without attackin' it, which would be a bloody nightmare. An' the mounted troopers'd be cut off."

"Why doesn't Anson just pull back into the city himself, then?" Reed asked.

"He considered defending there at first," Lieutenant Fisher confirmed, "but the perimeter's simply too big. If he only had to defend one wall, he'd be fine, but the enemy could envelop him and attack multiple walls at once. The defensive position he's in now is actually better in most respects."

"I see," Lewis said, noting for the first time that Samantha and Leonor were both watching him closely.

Varaa cleared her throat, and they looked at her, blinking and whipping her tail. "It's no secret that King Har-Kaaska had . . . doubts about this alliance, about its ability to even protect the cities on the Yucatán, much less actually beat the Doms." She looked at Lewis. "It did both those things, then defeated and incorporated the Holcanos, and has now chased another large Dom army halfway across a continent." She glanced at Har-Kaaska. "After getting . . . a little excited at Cayal, he's reluctant to put himself forward during discussions like this, but I'm not—and I feel the same way he does. We want to *beat* the Doms, not just chase them away! They'll be back someday, worse than ever with the Blood Priests in control." She flipped her tail and glared at Colonel Reed. "If you want to stop and rest the night, fine, but Har-Kaaska and I will lead the First and Second Ocelomeh Regiments onward tonight. They, at least, will be in position to support Major Anson in the morning."

"But . . ." Reed sputtered. "You can't just *leave!*"

"Actually, they can," Lewis said gravely. "All the Ocelomeh can. Despite my urging and the good faith efforts by most, a true union of all the city-states and people in the alliance has yet to be agreed upon. Absent such an agreement, I'll remind you that Har-Kaaska warned at the very beginning that the time may come when he'd reassert control over his Ocelomeh. They're *his* people."

"But he can't just *go off* with them!" Reed insisted.

"He's not," Varaa denied. "*We're* not. We're going to fight the common enemy."

Sal suddenly snapped his fingers. "Wait a minute! Look, there's no need to split anybody up. Not even much need to rush. Sure, nobody'll get any sleep, but those nine miles ain't the roughest country, and if you can keep to a couple miles an hour, that'll have you in position by midnight or thereabouts. You can throw down and sleep then, for a while."

"We can't just *collapse* in the face of the enemy!" Reed exclaimed, sounding indignant, and Sal wondered why he was being like this. He'd always been a careful soldier, but not hesitant. Maybe the fact they were so far out on a limb finally had him spooked. Sal shook it off. "They'll never know you're there. See, I almost forgot; up where we'll be—an' Lieutenant Fisher an' I will lead you—there's this *really* thick fog in the mornings. . . ."

CHAPTER 27

GRAN LAGO

Major Anson," came a whisper, jerking him instantly awake. The form leaning over where he'd sat down "for a moment" against the rocky, raw earthen berm near Dukane's center section of guns was indeterminate in the darkness. "It's me, sir. Lieutenant Barca. Captain Meder sent me to ask if you had any special instructions for us, up on the hill."

Anson blinked gummy eyes and looked where lanterns still lit men placing entanglements in front of Barca's and Meder's defenses. The dragoons were dug in almost to the top, but there was a gap where it got steep. *It does look a little lonely up there*, he reflected.

"Still, I wouldn't have disturbed your rest if we hadn't seen that," Barca continued, gesturing out to the front. Anson now realized there were several men standing over him. One was obviously Boogerbear. The other two became clear when Dukane's voice identified them.

"Lieutenant Lara and Captain Dukane, sir. Lara's fellows spotted the activity first, and we came looking for you. Since then, well, see for yourself. Should we stand to?"

Boogerbear reached down and hauled Anson to his feet, turning him to look out at the space between the breastworks and the enemy camp. More lanterns had been arranged and lit in a circle about three hundred yards out, and several shadowy figures stood within it. "I'll be damned," Anson said. "Looks like Agon wants to talk again. He's become a fiend for that, an' I heard he had a long palaver with Colonel Itzam at Nautla. Devil's gettin' downright sociable. No, Captain Dukane, don't rouse the men. Let 'em rest. If I'm right, talkin' tonight means straight to fightin' in the mornin'." He pulled out his watch and tilted it so the distant gleam illuminated the face. "Barely nine o'clock. I'd thought it was the middle o' the night an' ol' Agon was bein' rude." He looked apologetically at Dukane. "Didn't mean to drift off."

"You need rest as much as anyone. More," Dukane scoffed.

"Hmm," Anson replied noncommittally. "Looks like four of 'em out there. No tellin' who they are from here. Boogerbear, pick a couple fellas an' ride out to see who they are an' what they want."

"Want me to kill 'em?" the big Ranger asked casually.

"Not yet," Anson replied, equally mild.

In minutes, Boogerbear and two other Rangers had retrieved horses and pounded out to investigate. They came straight back. "A lieutenant an' some other sacrificial lambs," Boogerbear reported. "Said Colonel Itzam had 'em do it this way at Nautla an' it made sense. If you wanna talk, I'll ride back an' give 'em the word. They'll go tell Agon everything's set, an' you an' two others can go meet him an' two others." He hesitated. "Why not kill *them* when they come?"

Anson chuckled and sighed. "Ain't sportin'. An' Lewis wouldn't approve." He looked around. "Mr. Lara, you an' Mr. Barca, come with me."

GENERAL AGON APPEARED largely as Anson remembered him: short, stocky, dark, and perhaps a bit more menacing in the meager light of a dozen candle lanterns. His yellow uniform and knee-high boots seemed less immaculate than before, the silver lace dull and tarnished against the faded black cuffs and facings of his coat. Even his large, silver-trimmed tricorn was more gray than black and had lost its crisp shape. His companions looked the same: worn down by a long, grueling march, and Anson thought he recognized them from a previous meeting. He definitely remembered the tall aide, the first "Dom" he'd ever seen—and the one Leonor once shot with a Paterson Colt. The other was a taller, thinner version of Agon, but could've otherwise been his brother. He was eventually introduced, after a long staring session, as "General Tun." The enemy leaders had met Lara before as well, but not Barca. Anson was a bit surprised that they showed no curiosity regarding his race. Then again, it seemed there were many very dark, indeed quite black, inhabitants of the area around Gran Lago, and not all of them were slaves. Anson was equally surprised and glad that fact had gone virtually unremarked upon by his own troops. Father Orno, and certainly Reverend Harkin, would have theories about it, no doubt, but now wasn't the time to speculate.

"So, we meet again," Agon finally said rather awkwardly, addressing Anson directly.

"I reckon we been 'meetin'' for the last couple hundred miles," Anson reminded. "I don't know off the top o' my head how many *leguas* that is."

Agon frowned. "Quite so, and congratulations, I suppose. Dominion lancers have been the finest horsemen on the continent ever since they were formed, yet you essentially exterminated ours." Tun grunted sharply, and Agon continued, "I give nothing away by acknowledging that."

"No sir, you don't," Anson agreed. "An' if they were the best around . . . well, I hate to speak ill o' the dead, but that ain't sayin' much. Comanches would'a ate 'em alive even quicker." It was difficult to tell in such meager light, but Anson would almost swear he'd seen surprise and concern cross Agon's face at the mention of Comanches. Or maybe he just feared there might be another group he didn't know, like mounted Holcanos, who literally ate people?

Anson let it pass, but General Tun bristled. "Not saying much indeed, it seems," he spat at Anson, "but you, their betters, will soon be just as extinct. You've surrendered your mobility and trapped yourselves!"

"I guess that's what we're here to talk about, ain't it? Your usual demand for me to march my fellas out to be burnt alive, impaled an' crucified? No thanks. We seen enough o' that—a bunch of Tranquilo's Blood Priests went on a spree in some villages we passed on the way here. They're all dead now, by the way," he stated simply, "along with most o' their soldier escorts. Wounded an' surrendered troops were well treated—at least them that were just bein' soldiers." His tone turned harsh. "Those that were seen by survivors to be carryin' on just like Blood Priests while they *impaled* innocent people, or *nailed women an' children to crosses* an' then *burnt 'em alive* . . . Well, they were still soldiers of a sort, so they were shot. We gave the Blood Priests to the villagers we rescued for *proper* justice," he added with satisfaction, then took a deep breath and cocked his head to the side. "Now we're here to sort *you* out."

Agon nodded slightly. "Even outnumbered ten to one, I've no doubt you'll try. But what if I told you I *applaud* your actions in the villages and we now *share* the same chief enemy—that it's Don Frutos and Tranquilo's Blood Priests I'm after, not you?"

"I'd say we pretty much guessed that. Some sort o' power play or coup by the Blood Priests. Word from Vera Cruz—which I'm sure you know we hold with the *aid* o' locals—bears that out."

"Then you understand why I'd be content to allow you to march out of your works, but not to your doom. I simply want you to . . ." He paused and waved. "Go away. I don't *want* to fight you. Not now. I only want to pursue and destroy the same rabid Tranquilo whom you also despise."

"Are you implying we're now on the *same side* in some way?" Lara asked incredulously.

"Of course not!" General Tun almost exploded. "You're still only vile, savage heretics, and we'll come for you again one day. At the moment, however, you pose a less immediate threat to the Dominion as a whole than the despicable and despotic Blood Priests. For now, we'll lend you your miserable lives if you give us the road!"

"If I may, Major," Barca asked, and Anson nodded. "I'm afraid I'm confused," he told General Agon. "You originally came against us under the *command* of Don Frutos, with Blood Priests in your midst, professing the same hate and either performing or enabling the same atrocities. We defeated you badly at the Washboard and drove you away. Now you've had a break with the Blood Priests even as you resumed your offensive against us . . ." He paused. ". . . and Colonel Itzam stopped you at Nautla."

General Tun was simmering, Captain Arevalo looked thoughtful, and Agon showed no expression at all.

"My point is," Barca continued, "as depraved as we find the Blood Priests—and believe me when I say that appraisal's recently been fortified," he added darkly, glaring at General Tun. "In our eyes, there's no appreciable difference between you and them, and your threats only reinforce that conviction. If you're somehow different, you must explain how. What makes them worse than you, to us, and why should we care? Give us a *reason* not to oppose you with every last drop of our blood."

Anson gave Barca an approving nod. "Well said," he told him.

"You should 'care' because we'll let you live, for now. They wouldn't," Tun huffed.

"You wouldn't either, while they were in your midst," Lara restated patiently.

Tun was fashioning another scathing retort when Agon held up a hand. "He's right, you know," he told his friend, then looked back at Anson. "Our understanding of God and His requirements is different from yours. I know little of the world you—perhaps we as well—originally came from, but my impression is that it's a somewhat . . . gentler place in some respects. It's therefore understandable that you, and quite probably many of our own ancestors, imagined the god we share—oh yes, I believe He *is* the same god—to be somewhat gentler as well. But others of our ancestors native to this world, or deposited here much earlier, had their own, harsher understanding of God. Considering the nature of this world, it should be easy for you to grasp why some of their beliefs rang more clearly to our ancestors and were so widely embraced and comingled to form a more perfect truth. . . ."

"And to quickly, cynically attract the broadest base of support from the locals, by incorporating the more terrible—and perversely more popular—pagan rituals into the new 'combined' faith," Lara seethed.

Tun started to object, but Agon restrained him once more. "That may be," he confessed. "But that which is most widely believed by the greatest number is doubtless closer to the truth, is it not?"

Anson could only shake his head. "No, it ain't," he said. "Especially if what's 'most widely believed' is horseshit to begin with, religious or not, an' enforced by murderin' anybody who don't agree. That ain't just your Blood Priests"—he tilted his head at General Tun—"that's what your whole setup is built on. Well, 'gentler' world or not, when it comes to the kind of boogers runnin' around on it, I think you've learned we came from a place rough enough to make pretty good soldiers—while still generally keepin' faith with a 'gentler' God. So your 'don't blame us, we had it rougher than you' shit ain't gonna wash, an' there's *no way in hell* I'll leave my defenses so you can swoop down an' catch my men in the open." He shook his head. "No way."

Capitan Arevalo suddenly spoke up. "It seems we're all constrained by a complete lack of trust, and not just as individuals, but as representatives of inflexible beliefs. One thing you might be unaware of—though it was mentioned in passing when we last met—is that General Agon, in fact all the senior officers of this army, handpicked by him, possess a rather unique flexibility that is, ironically, rooted in the inflexibility of honor. We're among the very last members of an increasingly secret, even persecuted, military fraternity known as the Knights of Calatrava.

Anson blinked and looked at Lara, who shrugged, but Barca actually nodded and explained: "If I remember correctly, the order was somewhat like the Templars and coexisted with them, but was most involved in the reconquest of Spain from the Moors. Unlike the Templars, it still exists in a toothless, diminished condition"—he shook his head—"existed, where we came from." He hesitated, suddenly self-conscious. "I had frequent access to one of the finest libraries in New Orleans during my . . . former life." Turning his gaze on Agon, however, he glared. "But after helping drive the Moors out of Spain, the order became *less* militant and its purpose turned more to the protection of the *Catholic* Christian Church, and certain specific principles in particular. You've warped or forsaken every tenet of the order you claim to represent."

General Tun pursed his lips and shifted uncomfortably.

"Largely true," Capitan Arevalo agreed, surprising Anson, "and the name was deliberately misleading since the fraternity, while militantly protective of our faith, also adopted certain aspects of even older organizations, even 'cults,' one might say, to become a military association open to warriors of every type. Theoretically, as originally envisioned, any of *you* could be members and enjoy friendly comradeship on the very eve of desperate battle, when all those so cordially united the night before would try their best to kill one another—with no hard feelings, of course. But throughout the history of the Dominion, we never met a military peer to invite into the brotherhood. It therefore became a closed society, with only our own as members. Then, of course, its exclusive and secret membership drew critics, particularly from priests and Blood Cardinals who, not ordinarily being warriors, weren't invited to join. The society has gone almost extinct with the rise of the Blood Priests. None of *them* have ever been allowed membership and are sure we're a pack of heretics."

"Aren't you?" Lara demanded. "You certainly are to us," he added, almost mumbling.

"No," Agon denied. "Just . . . perhaps more open-minded than they, and sensible to the fact that, worship aside, no human undertaking is more consequential, more . . . extravagant than war on the scale we've engaged in with you. Despite our differences"—he sent a scolding glance at Tun—"we respect you, even honor you, and, heretics or not, would preserve you as colleagues, even adversaries for the future."

"You people are so weird." Anson sighed. "Now I learn you've got secret societies, like militant Freemasons, or somethin'—though I guess even those 'Anti-Masonic Party' whippoorwills weren't a patch to your Blood Priests," he added absently while fingering the tiny gold square and compass dangling from his watch chain. He'd noted Captain Holland had a similar fob and idly wondered how many more Masons were stranded on this world. A fair number, most likely. He knew of four others for sure, and hadn't even been looking. He shook the irrelevant thought away. "Well, sorry I can't oblige you. We're stayin' put. Come on over an' fight when you're ready."

Suddenly, he chuckled, surprising everyone, when he realized his mind had been wandering for a reason. The always annoying and even sometimes violent Anti-Masons had had their run. Some still cooked up conspiracy theories to justify vilifying or persecuting prominent masons, but the largely single-issue political party had been absorbed and diluted to nothing by the Whigs. "I got an idea," he said. "How about a little wager? An' let's try this with some rules."

"What kind of rules?" Agon asked, intrigued. "What manner of wager?"

"Simple," Anson replied. "We won't kill your wounded if you don't hurt ours, an' if you break through our line, we'll stop fightin' an' let you through. Then you honor the offer you already made; we leave, you go on."

"Preposterous!" Tun exclaimed. "Why should we then not simply annihilate you?"

"Because you can't. Even if you break the line, we'll pull back to secondary positions, re-form, an' keep the fight goin'. You'll get most of us eventually, but we'll kill a lot more of you before we take to our horses an' keep after you on the march. Keep bleedin' you white. Not a good way to start chasin' Don Frutos an' Tranquilo."

Agon frowned. "I'll consider it. But what is the wager?"

Anson grinned wickedly. "Just this: if you *don't* break us, if we stop you, you surrender to *us*."

"Why should we ever do that?" Agon snapped.

"Because you'll be stuck here, bloody meat for Colonel Cayce when he comes, an' he'll leave nothin' but shattered bones bleachin' in the sun where your army used to be," Anson said matter-of-factly. "An' if you do surrender, I'll try to see that you get to keep after Don Frutos. Your men still armed, no officers imprisoned, an' you still commandin' 'em—under Colonel Cayce's command, o' course."

"What? Impossible! Even you said—one of you said—we could never be on the same side."

"Well, we wouldn't have to be, would we? Separate logistics, no common camp, just two armies headin' the same direction an' only joinin'—loosely—to fight by Colonel Cayce's plan. Not allies—not friends, for damn sure—but both goin' after our own chief enemy at the same time."

"Why Cayce in command?"

"Part o' the wager—an' he's better than you," Anson said simply. "Though I expect he'll use up a *lot* of your troops. But you'll learn a bunch, won't you? Not just bein' on the dyin' an' losin' end for a while." He chuckled again. "An' Los Diablos'll leave off pesterin' you while we go after nastier buggers."

Agon looked at a speechless Tun and a thoughtful Arevalo. Of course, Arevalo was always thoughtful. "General Tun?" Agon asked.

"Madness," he said, but sounding uncharacteristically thoughtful as well. "Madness," he repeated, "and yet . . . we must crush the Blood Priests entirely or the effort will almost certainly be in vain—and if the Gran Cruzada does return before we reach the Holy City . . ." He glared intently at Anson. "You have the authority to make an agreement of this magnitude?"

"Not really. Well, not the authority, but probably the influence. I'm pretty sure I can get Lewis to agree. Others might be harder," he confessed, thinking of Varaa, Har-Kaaska, Consul Koaar, Sira Periz . . .

"Then, just for the sake of the intellectual exercise, since I can't imagine it for a moment, let's say you do manage to hold us back and we commence . . . operating in proximity to one another, our *ultimate* war aims are entirely different! We mean only to install Don Hurac as Supreme Holiness of the Dominion and return things to the way they were. You want to bring the Dominion down!"

"As it *is*, yes," Anson agreed, "though from what I hear, we may not have a problem with you ploppin' Don Hurac on the throne—or whatever—since he may surprise you with his notion of puttin' things back together. Either way, after we beat the Blood Priests, we can go back to beatin' on each other again, if we want."

General Agon was silent a very long moment. So far, and for as long as he could remember, it seemed his army had been dying to no purpose. And now he was "trapped" up against a determined adversary that would, at the very least, cost him a great many more men. To no other purpose than that the battle he'd craved for so long was at hand—a battle he could *win*, to expiate the shame of that previous meeting. Of course, if he slaughtered Los Diablos, he'd have to face an enraged Colonel Cayce—combined with Colonel Itzam into a near-equal force, no doubt—and he wasn't at all confident he could defeat them from within the city walls, or even after crossing beyond the marshes. Cayce would find a way to stay after him, he was sure. And all the while, the most pressing enemy of his people, the very foundation and fabric of the empire he was sworn to defend, was getting farther away. "I will consider it," he finally said again.

———

"Whew!" Lara said as they rode slowly back toward their lines. "Do you think they'll take the wager?"

Anson shrugged. "Who knows? If they crack our line, I guess we'll find out. Spread the word—especially to my Ocelomeh Rangers—that I don't want any holdin' back, but there'll be no deliberate killin' of Dom wounded—unless they're underfoot, still fightin', o' course. Huh. Don't even know why I made that part of the bet. Doms generally kill their *own* wounded if they ain't fit to move themselves."

"Do you think Colonel Cayce will agree to your deal?" asked Barca.

Anson chuckled. "Well, if they kill us all, I damn sure hope not. If we stop 'em?" He shrugged again. "Who knows? Could be interestin'. They might think *we're* Los Diablos, but they don't know Lewis like I do. We're both pragmatic, but in different ways. My way—probably Varaa's too, come to think on it—is more straightforward. I've gotten to where I actually kinda like Kisin an' those Holcanos with him, for example, now they've quit eatin' folks, but personally, without Lewis lookin' over my shoulder, I would'a just wiped 'em all out. An' I'd kill every Dom who stood up to us, Blood Priest or not, given the chance. Maybe that makes me more like 'em than I prefer to admit, but I prob'ly understand 'em better than Lewis. Kill 'em all, an' *that* problem, at least, is solved.

"Thing is, while 'pragmatic' means somethin' different to Lewis, he's the *real* Gran Jefe Diablo, an' he *hates* Doms on a whole different level." He glanced at Lara. "Probably more like Leonor used to feel about Mexican soldiers . . . for what a handful of 'em did to her, an' for a weirdly similar reason too. Lewis don't hate Holcanos, or even those lizard-like fellas they fought with for a while, because they were savages. He didn't like 'em, an' hated what they did, but they were just doin' what they do because they didn't know better. I guess he kinda figures we whipped 'em an' 'cured' 'em. *I* think that's nonsensical, but it seems to be workin' so far.

"But he hates the Doms because, as savage as they act, they ain't just savages as he'd define the term. They're a real threat to the survival of all the people he's taken responsibility for, an' not just the Americans that came here with us, but everybody who wants to live free, an' put their trust in him. Maybe worst of all, they personify human evil, don't seem to know what honor is—with a few weird exceptions—an' violate every feature of what he thinks it means to be 'civilized.' He hates the Blood Priests the most, of course, but the Doms as a whole ain't much better an' they're the roots under the bull nettles—if you get what I mean."

"I understand that, but what does the rest of it mean?" Lara asked.

"I think I know," Barca said as they reached some entanglements men were still working to emplace. A lancer sargento directed them to a gap, and they urged their horses through and up over the mounded earth and rubble breastworks.

"Go on, then," Anson told him.

Barca nodded. "I think Major Anson's assessment is essentially correct, quite astute, in fact, both in regard to Colonel Cayce and himself." His white teeth glared in the darkness as he grinned. "I think he's also more comfortable in his role of a devil to his enemies than Colonel Cayce, who I know for a fact at least strives to be a better, perhaps even godlier man than he is. I'm not sure about the latter because, though I've heard him express strong confidence in the existence of God, he isn't particularly religious. Perhaps he wants to be?" He shook his head. "Regardless, that also influences *his* variety of 'pragmatism.'"

"But what does it mean?" Lara repeated, exasperated. "What's the difference?

"Simply that if he's given the chance, Colonel Cayce will probably accept the deal Major Anson offered and try to cooperate with General Agon—to a point. He'll use whatever tools are at hand to complete the mission he's set himself, to advance the cause of those he's taken responsibility for. If he thinks joining with General Agon will aid in accomplishing that and result in less effort and bloodshed, he'll do it. He'll even give Agon the opportunity for a fair fight if and when the war aims eventually diverge, as General Tun suggested." He paused. "But God help them all if Colonel Cayce detects treachery in the meantime."

Stopping at last to hand off their horses to be taken to cover behind the line, Anson wasn't surprised to find a very tired Sal Hernandez and Lieutenant Fisher waiting. "Good to see you fellas back. Get somethin' to eat?"

"We just did," said Sal.

"You saw Colonel Cayce?"

Sal nodded.

Anson realized then that he was nervous as a cat. "Well? What did he say? When's he gettin' here?"

Sal slowly smiled. "He wasn't in much of a rush. The infantry's beat down an' just draggin' along. Damn, I *hate* walkin'! When we told him the situation, Colonel Reed wanted to order us out an' let Agon through. Gran Lago's far enough from our frontier. Let the Doms have at one another an' we'll pick up the pieces."

"Stupid," Anson simmered. "We can forget Vera Cruz, an' they got at least one city, Nueva Frontera, a couple hundred miles south of here. After they get their little disagreement settled, an' it might take 'em a while, but they'll get around us eventually an' we'll have to pull back to Campeche, at least. Practically back where we started."

Sal puffed out his chest. "That's what I told 'em, an' swore we'd bravely hold the Doms in front of Gran Lago until *el día del juicio*! We'll give 'em another Alamo an' be remembered forever! I only asked that, when they finally do arrive, they'll dig down beneath the pile of Dom corpses heaped atop each of us and give us suitable, *individual* burials," he added modestly. "No mass grave. I don't want to spend eternity spoonin' with you."

Anson took a deep breath and rolled his eyes. "Horseshit. Tell me the truth."

"I did," Sal protested indignantly, and Lieutenant Fisher coughed into his hand. "But I may have . . . understated Colonel Cayce's determination not to have to dig so many holes. I don't know what Colonel Reed's problem is—maybe he feels too exposed—but Varaa an' Har-Kaaska, others too, figure they can get most of the men in First an' Second Divisions up while it's still dark in the morning. Especially after I told 'em about the fog. Their biggest concern was gettin' jumped while they were strung out an' exhausted."

"So we stay," Anson said with satisfaction.

"*You* stay," Sal stressed, "an' *hope* I was just foolin' about becomin' famous. Lieutenant Fisher an' me have to go back an' lead the colonel in."

Anson took off his wheel hat and rubbed his eyes. The horsehair padding in the top had deteriorated badly and become oppressively hot, so like most of his men he'd pulled it out, leaving the hat somewhat shapeless and floppy. Dukane, Burton, and even Felix Meder had gathered around. "Then that's the plan. Colonel Cayce'll come with the fog—an' that's about when I expect Agon to hit us too."

"We're all about as ready as we can be," Dukane agreed. "My guns'll be shooting blind, most likely, but so will theirs. And we can adjust elevation by reports from observers out forward with the pickets, or even by how far it *sounds* the enemy is."

Anson nodded. "Best we can do," he said, then raised his voice. "All those not on watch, better get some shut-eye."

CHAPTER 28

Even with Sal Hernandez and Lieutenant Fisher back to lead them, it took much longer than hoped to assemble the bulk of 1st and 2nd Division just south of the Dom position. They still weren't exactly sure of their placement because, although there was a faint glow of firelight from the Dom camp seeping through the growing fog, there was no such light from the mixed division Anson commanded. They largely had to guess, groping to the left until they secured that flank with the lake, but the right flank was hanging in the increasingly opaque air. Even worse, the divisions were confused and intermingled after the long, brutally exhausting march in the darkness, on the heels of the grueling pace Lewis set for his entire army over the last week or so. For the very first time, men had started to straggle. It wasn't their fault, and it wasn't just the "city boys." Even some Ocelomeh fell out, and Lewis dispatched a few of his precious remaining mounted men to at least try to keep the stragglers in groups to protect them from predators. Fortunately, no one was lost like that. Apparently, potential prey and therefore predators were generally inactive while the local fog prevailed, but the army made no lights either, and whole companies got separated and lost while trying to deploy. Most eventually found someplace to be on the developing, generally north-facing line, but sometimes it was far enough away from the rest of their regiment that they were told to just stay where they were for the time.

"It's a mess, all right," Leonor said as if agreeing with an assessment Lewis was thinking. No command tent had been erected and all the senior officers had gathered near the center of the army, still mounted, behind where the 1st US and 1st Itzincab were sorting themselves out. And it was a mess. A lot of the men in all the regiments had simply dropped on the ground where they stopped and fallen fast asleep. That was fine with Lewis since they'd probably only have a couple of hours before things started happening. 1st Division, consisting of the 1st Ocelomeh, 3rd Pennsylvania, 1st Uxmal and 1st US was on the left, in roughly that order, under the nominal command of Colonel Reed. 2nd Division, led once more by Har-Kaaska, extended to the right but had the 2nd Uxmal and 1st Techon stacked up behind the 1st Itzincab and 2nd Ocelomeh.

"It'll get better when visibility improves," Lewis said with more certainty than he felt.

"Of course it will!" Samantha Wilde agreed brightly, accompanied at the moment by Reverend Harkin.

"Where should I put my guns?" asked Captain Olayne, almost pleading. He was essentially in charge of all their artillery now, but without being able to see the ground or the enemy, Lewis didn't know what to tell him.

"Probably best to keep them separate, for reasons of supply. At least for now, your battery of six and twelve pounders will remain in support of First Division on the left, and the two batteries of captured Dom eight pounders will support Har-Kaaska on the right." He tried to smile. "Don't worry about it until we can see what they'll be shooting at."

"How long do you think, until then?" Varaa asked, controlling her excitement. The Washboard had been the biggest battle she'd ever seen, or, frankly, imagined. This encounter promised to be even bigger and, if all went well, far more decisive.

Lewis took the pipe out of her mouth and held the glowing coal in the bowl near his watch. A lot of the men were smoking, and he would've prohibited it if the visibility was better. It was a quarter after four. Night marches were hard and confusing enough, but there'd been no moon, or even a road to follow. Add the thickening fog and it was practically miraculous they'd maintained as much organization as they had. All that ate into the time he'd hoped the men would have to rest, of course, but there was nothing for it. Handing the pipe back, he answered. "I expect the Doms will have improved considerably since our last meeting and Agon will commence firing his artillery before he can actually see his target. He knows the range, I'm sure."

"Then we need to be ready to return his fire," said Olayne. "We'll certainly see the muzzle flashes of his guns!"

"No," Lewis said. "Not unless he's shooting at us, which will mean he's aware of our presence and surprise is lost. I fervently hope we spend the first part of this battle as spectators."

"While the mounted troopers take it on the chin?" Reed declared more than asked. Lewis tried to see his expression in the gloom. "I'm afraid so. Major Anson will appreciate our restraint when the time is right."

"Oh, he might not 'appreciate' it, but he'll understand it," Leonor agreed.

"He'll appreciate whatever it takes to win," said Sal Hernandez. Fisher had rejoined the small detachment of dragoons who'd serve as messengers during the coming battle, but Sal remained by Leonor.

"So the Doms'll start shooting in an hour or so," Varaa mused. "But it could be two or more before *we* do anything." She yawned hugely, long canines almost as bright as her pipe. "I'm going to take a nap." She grinned. "Wake me when the battle starts."

"I hope Father Orno isn't injured," said Reverend Harkin, tugging on his still-baggy coat. Lewis noted the preacher had an M1817 rifle slung over his shoulder once more. "I'd like to assemble the troops for a prayer, just a company at a time, of course," he assured Lewis, "and I believe I've gotten better at keeping my prayers more . . . agreeable to all concerned, but I'd like to let the lads rest a bit more myself, and it'll be difficult to visit each company before the fighting begins. Father Orno would've been a great help with that."

"I'll stay with you, Reverend," Samantha said. "At least until the fighting starts," she quickly added for Lewis's benefit. He'd insisted she move to the rear when that happened and seek the security of their baggage train as it moved up to join them.

Lewis nodded appreciatively, then regarded Harkin a moment. Not only was he sure the preacher was actually worried about the little Uxmalo priest, he was surprised again by the increasing . . . elasticity of his sermons and prayers. The religious schism he'd once feared would shatter the alliance no longer much concerned him. "I'm sure Father Orno will be fine," he assured, "and he's got his own 'flock' to attend." He hesitated. "But perhaps you'd be good enough to share a quick prayer for us while we're gathered here. That way you won't risk missing us later."

Harkin beamed. "Perhaps a hymn?" he suggested, then pursed his lips at the less-than-enthusiastic response.

"Sir, the enemy might hear," Olayne reminded. The fog muffled a great deal, but it probably wouldn't cover that.

"Oh. Yes, of course. Perhaps something from Ephesians, then." He glanced ruefully at Leonor. "If I might be forgiven for tuning a word or two here and there to make a prayer of an admonition?" This was an old argument of theirs, but Leonor grinned and nodded. Harkin cleared his throat.

"Let us be strong in the Lord and in His mighty power, putting on all His armor so we may stand firm against all the strategies of the Devil. For we are not fighting against flesh and blood enemies only, but against evil rulers and authorities of the unseen world, against mighty powers of darkness and evil spirits in the heavenly places. I pray we shall stand our ground wearing the belt of truth and the body armor of God's righteousness, holding the shield of faith to stop the fiery arrows of the devil, protected by the helmet of salvation and wielding the sword of the Spirit, which is the Word of God!" He paused. "Amen."

"Amen," chorused most around him.

"Not much of a 'please don't let me die' prayer, Reverend," Leonor teased, "but all the better for it. An' as for the 'tuning,' you didn't leave quite half of it out, an' only changed a couple words."

"Well! With that glowing endorsement, I shall use it as the basis for my prayer with the troops!" Harkin exclaimed.

"That'll be fine," Lewis said, gazing around and then lifting his face to the sky, feeling the fog moisture on his cheeks. It would be condensing on everything soon, particularly weapons, and that would cause misfires. "Might should've added something about keeping our powder dry. Everyone pass the word to your men; most should know better by now, but they're to keep their muskets covered, and no one loads until told. Those with weapons already loaded"—pickets and troops on watch—"will draw the loads and clean and dry their weapons."

The fog seemed to be thickening, but brightening ever so slightly when General Agon, already dressed in his best and mounted on his black charger, leaned over to Arevalo and said, "Quietly pass the word to the brigade commanders to dispense ammunition and—again very quietly—have their men load their arms."

Arevalo frowned worriedly. "But the *humedad*," he objected with a glance at the sky.

"Will not be a factor," Agon assured. "These troops are better than any we've led, but the artillery will soon begin its work, and many of the men who haven't been near it when it fires in earnest will become nervous and load their weapons improperly, regardless. I've seen it. Besides, if this fog holds, our men will be quite close to the enemy before they're seen. The front ranks will fire one volley, fix bayonets, and charge, overwhelming the meager defenses with ferocity and numbers. If some of their weapons don't fire, it'll be of little consequence at that point." Agon sighed. "I do envy the enemy's bayonets, ingeniously mounted offset from the muzzle so they may continue loading and firing with them in place, but as much as our tactics have changed of necessity, there's no time for loading when armies come to grips, and the bayonet will always remain the primary weapon—our plug type that inserts into the muzzle, or theirs. Ours may even be better at that point: longer, with broader, double-edged blades."

"Perhaps," Arevalo hedged, "but the long, narrow, triangular shape they've adopted makes a gruesome wound not easily staunched. And the men who'll strike the primary objective—where the enemy defense is thinnest on the slope of the hill—may be under fire for some time before they can 'come to grips,' as you say."

"True," Agon agreed, "but they have only two great guns on the hill. They can fire down on our assault against other points, but none of the other guns can effectively support *them*. And the troops on their left are dragoons. Armed only with carbines and without bayonets of their own."

Arevalo was honored that the general allowed him the liberty to express his opinions. He even claimed that he desired him to do so, in private. But he knew when Agon's mind was set—and he could be right. He only hoped his general recalled the nature of the carbines the dragoons were equipped with. They'd never captured one, but it was obvious they could fire more rapidly than ordinary weapons. His hand absently touched his upper chest, just under the collarbone. He couldn't feel the scar through his uniform, but the dull ache remained. Especially on days like this. It was a constant reminder that the enemy had a variety of rapid-firing weapons.

"See that my orders are obeyed," Agon reminded gently. "We must begin soon so we can smash this little blockage and continue with our bigger business." His tone turned sad. "Not long ago, this would've been quite 'big' enough to satisfy me, and having taken the enemy's position, I'd welcome the later contest with Coronel Cayce. Alas, because of Tranquilo and his filthy ilk, all has been turned upside down! I must flee a worthy, honest enemy, deserving of my attention, in order to save my country from poisonous *arañas* in its bed! Now go, Capitan Arevalo!"

"Yes, my general!" Arevalo said and saluted.

Lieutenant Barca was back behind his guns, leaning against the low wall surrounding the somewhat classically shaped, whitewashed villa atop the hill and talking lowly with Captain Felix Meder. Of all the junior American officers in the army, Meder—and possibly Elijah Hudgens—behaved as if they hadn't the slightest notion he was a black man, or different from them in any way, in fact. Of course, both of them had started as private soldiers on this world, even lower on the social ladder than he in a sense, as he'd been perceived to be Colonel De Russy's personal servant. There'd been no overt racialism from any other officer, and Barca was sure Colonel Cayce would've crushed it if he heard. He wouldn't see any difference between disrespect toward him and any of the rising "native" officers. He'd made it clear there was no place for bigotry of any sort in his army, and men of any race or origin would rise on merit and capability. A very few might resent that, but the vast majority loved him for it (among other reasons) and would rather die than lose *his* respect. Still, Barca couldn't help but notice the occasional appraising, even slightly confused comment or glance. He was a black man, a former slave, and some must've felt his commission was just as strange as this world they'd found themselves on. Meder wasn't one of those, and Barca had begun to consider him a friend.

"I doubt we have much longer to wait," Meder said, pulling his pipe from his mouth and looking distastefully into the bowl. "This stuff isn't bad, compared to other tobacco I've tasted, but that doesn't mean I like it."

Barca was startled by the non sequitur. He'd been thinking along Meder's previous lines himself. The fog was brightening perceptibly, but that didn't mean visibility was improving much beyond a dozen yards or so. It only meant he could see more fog.

"I chewed a little tobacco as a youngster because all my friends did," Meder confessed. "Made me sick at first, then dizzy all the time," he chuckled. "Smoking it isn't as bad in that respect, but it tastes foul."

Barca was confused. "Then why do it?"

"Because I'm the youngest captain in the army," he replied as if that should be obvious. "Many of the men in the Rifles, under my command, are old enough to be my father. A couple could be my *grandfather* if they started young enough. I've got to do *something* to prove I'm not a child!"

It dawned on Barca then that he wasn't the only one who worried that others might be skeptical about him. "We're about the same age, I think," he offered.

"Yes, but you're a lieutenant." Meder grinned. "They're supposed to be wet behind the ears. Captains are older, more mature. Why, Colonel Cayce was just a captain when we came here, and he's *old*, almost *forty*!"

Barca chuckled. "About thirty-eight, I believe, and he doesn't act 'old' in battle. And aside from being the best shot in the Rifles, you've certainly proved yourself in action."

Meder waved that away with a grimace at the pipe in his hand. "Still, some of the older fellows—the best shots, damn them—tease me about my youth."

"In what way?"

Meder considered that. "Oh, they'll say things like, 'Just think how well you'll be able to shoot with a couple more decades of practice—if your eyes last that long.'"

"Sounds like rather complimentary teasing, to me." Thinking about Hahessy—the way Hahessy had been before—he continued, "Are they difficult to handle? Do they slack off, or avoid duties or chores? Fail to salute when they should, or exaggerate salutes when it seems inappropriate?"

Meder shook his head. "No, I don't think so."

"Then don't worry about it. I'd say you're that rarest of creatures—that this army has a surprising number of, in fact." Barca smiled. "Without seeking to be one to the detriment of your men, you're a 'popular officer' that your men *trust* enough to tease, on occasion. They might even tease you for your pipe smoking behind your back, but only because they know you do it to be accepted by them and it endears you to them even more."

"Really?" Meder asked, looking at him strangely. "How do you know all this? You're just as green as I am."

Barca shrugged. "I read a lot. Or I did. And I've made something of a study of leadership. Just now, Horace springs to mind: 'Mix a little foolishness with your serious plans. It is lovely to be silly at the right moment.'"

"So I should caper about, acting silly all the time?" Meder scoffed.

"Of course not. Only 'at the right moment,' it won't hurt to tease the men back, from time to time, and a captain has the perfect rank for it. Lieutenants are often too 'wet behind the ears' to be taken seriously and risk being seen to curry favor in the ranks. Generals—or Colonel Cayce—must seem to be above such things, serious and thinking *nearly* all the time, though a well-delivered joke to break the tension can be helpful. But a captain, while maintaining discipline, can be 'silly' more often without damaging the impression he's a serious man. At least that's been what I've seen here—and I observed almost every officer and unit before choosing to join the artillery. That opportunity Colonel Cayce gave me was probably unique in military history, at least in an army where you can't choose a unit and buy a place in it, and I appreciate it more than I can say."

"You may be right. I know a few captains who joke with their men in passing, yet ignore the lieutenants and NCOs who snap at them to be silent and straighten up afterward." He snorted. "Of course, some merely spew profanity, but that amuses the men as well. I don't think I could do that." He immediately contradicted himself when he exclaimed, "Shit!"

Barca turned his head to look where Meder had been staring as he talked and saw a dull orange ball flare and fade in the distant thickness of the fog. It was quickly followed by another, and another in quick succession, a total of ten before the booming rumble of guns finally reached them. A tearing-sheet shriek passed close overhead, a gout of rocky earth exploded upward from the slope of the hill, and a gravelly crash came from behind them as something heavy slammed into a wall of the villa and sent shards of dusty stucco and underlying brick in all directions. A muted bugle sounded to the left and men started running to their positions. Barca stuck out his hand, and Meder grasped it tightly.

"Good luck, Lieutenant Barca!" Meder said.

"God bless, Captain Meder!" Barca raced to his section. "Cannoneers, post!" he shouted. The artillerymen on both guns had already taken their implements as the sky began to lighten and were in the general vicinity of their positions. "Load solid shot! Corporal Cox, what do you make the range?"

Hanny shook his head. There was good visibility in their immediate surroundings. Everything was gray, of course, but now they could see almost everything on the top of the hill. Unfortunately, they already knew the fog would linger down low, possibly even getting thicker for a time before the sun burnt it off. "Maybe a thousand yards?" Hanny guessed. "They must've moved their guns forward. They'd never reach us this high from where they were without digging holes for the trails, and the shot wouldn't have hit as hard as it did even then."

"Very well," Barca said. "Elevate to three degrees and aim for the muzzle flashes. Commence independent fire!"

Dodd's Number One gun roared and rolled back first, but Hanny waited, crouched over the trail, face resting on his left hand clutching the cascabel. As soon as he saw another distant flash, he tapped the trail with his right hand until Private Ricken shifted it with the handspike. When Hanny was satisfied the front sight was centered in the rear notch on the pendulum hausse, already set at three degrees, generally where he'd seen the fuzzy orange flower, he stepped back and raised his clenched fists to indicate the gun was on target. Ricken pierced the charge through the vent and primed the gun. The Number Four man, Andrew Morris, stretched the lanyard while Ricken tended the lock. When the lanyard was tight, Ricken stepped out from behind the right wheel and shouted, "Ready!"

Hanny roared, "Fire!" Morris briskly pulled the lanyard and the Number Two gun bellowed and bucked, the roundshot shrieking louder than usual with all the moisture in the air.

The Battle of Gran Lago had begun.

CHAPTER 29

E ight-pound roundshot whipped in out of the morning fog, practically invisible until the instant before it struck, sending up rocky debris and choking dust all along Anson's line. A few hit the breastworks and added jagged splinters to the mix. Men were starting to get hurt and killed, and piercing screams rose above the distant roar of guns and the thumping crash of cannonballs.

"At least it's only solid shot and they don't have exploding case," Captain Dukane calmly remarked to Anson as they strode between the two center section guns. They were still quiet. "Still, much better practice than before, and they can't even *see* us," Dukane added with grudging respect. The 6pdrs on the hill to the right, virtually invisible from the flat, went *Poom! Poom!*, marking their positions with dull jets of flame, reports somehow louder than usual, while oddly muffled as well.

Fog does strange things to sound, Anson thought. "A helluva lot better. Faster too," he groused aloud as another strike showered them with gravel and clumps of soil. The shot bounded up over the berm and struck a horse behind them square in the belly. It squealed piteously as loops of shattered intestines uncoiled on the ground and it fell on top of them, kicking. "Why the hell aren't you shooting back? You've got *twelve pounders*, for Christ's sake."

Dukane nodded patiently. "Yes, but unlike Barca's six pounders on the hill and the two twelve pounder field guns in the rest of Mr. Olayne's battery—sadly not yet arrived—my entire battery is composed of lightweight field *howitzers*. Fine weapons for firing shell or case, and canister at close range, but never designed to throw solid shot. They have chambered breeches, you see," he explained, "smaller diameter than the bores, requiring lighter charges." He shook his head as if mystified by Anson's ignorance. "Even if I had some of the solid-shot ammunition for Olayne's twelve pounders, my gunners would likely be unable to force the larger diameter charges to the breechface to be pierced—I've never tried it, and I'm sure *I* don't know," he added primly. "Even if they could, the heavier charge and shot would cause sufficient recoil to shake the carriages apart and damage the tubes."

"I know all that. You *have* some case shot. Shoot it," Anson countered with a scowl, wondering why some professional artillerymen felt compelled to explain everything with a treatise. *Lewis ain't like that—but he's even worse, in a way*, he suddenly realized. *Just assumes anyone he respects for their intelligence already knows everything he does."*

Dukane looked stubborn. "I have *some* exploding case," he agreed, "but not much. When it's gone, there may be no more. The last pickets who came in said the enemy artillery is about a thousand yards out. Right at the *limit* of my effective range. I can't just wildly throw the last of my case shot about at targets I can barely reach and can't see."

Anson sighed and nodded. "Good point. It's just . . . It's hard on the men—me too—to sit an' take a beatin' without shootin' back. An' I expect the Doms'll be sendin' infantry through their guns pretty soon."

Barca's guns fired again, and Dukane nodded up in their direction. "We *are* shooting back, and using the proper tools. Don't worry, my howitzers will come into their own at closer range. And whether we see it or not, the enemy will have to cease firing for a time when they advance their infantry. I'll send a few rounds of case their way when they do. That way, we should catch *somebody*, even if our fuses run fast. Something they're notorious for, I'm afraid."

"Well, at least somebody's thinkin'," Anson complimented. "I'm too used to the cut an' slash, lunge an' bolt of my Rangers. Probably should'a put you in charge o' this part."

Dukane shook his head. "Oh, no sir. I'm only pretending to be calm. I can manage my battery, but I'd be useless in command of us all!"

"How do you think I feel?" Anson murmured, but only to himself. That's when they heard a blare of horns and the deep rolling thunder of kettle drums. Anson had heard those before, but the horns had only blared short sequences of notes like bugle calls passing orders. This was different. Even while the roundshot continued raining down, the horns commenced a harsh, menacing melody. It was jarringly repetitive, with the same series of notes played several times before they changed to a different sequence. Anson had heard that Santa Anna ordered the "Deguello" played every evening by his forces besieging the Alamo. It was an ancient Moorish piece that essentially meant "no quarter," and the Doms could've easily brought it to this world. He had no idea what it sounded like, but it could be the same. It certainly had a singularly foreboding feel to it. But what would be the point of playing it? The only prisoners Doms took were for slaves or sacrifice.

The barrage began to lift, and Dukane told his center section to make ready. The sections on the right and left would follow his lead.

"Commence firing!" he shouted. The howitzers boomed and jerked back, brake chains and implement hooks clattering before breeches dropped back on elevation screws with *clangs* like broken bells. Dark spheres arced out of the smoke, jetting fuses tumbling before they were lost in the fog. Seconds later came bright snapping flashes in the gloom in the air above where they hoped the enemy infantry had advanced a little beyond the guns. The right section fired, both guns together, then the left two boomed as well. Barca's 6pdrs fired, the shots a deeper, louder crack.

"I feel better already, Mr. Dukane," Anson said loudly so all around could hear. "Keep it up."

———

"This is startin' to *look* like a battle," Hahessy boomed as he rammed another fixed charge down the throat of the Number Two gun, giving it a couple taps for emphasis when it met the resistance of the breech. "Aye, a damned strange-lookin' battle it is, an' no mistake, but a battle nonetheless— with shots besides ours goin' *both* ways for the now."

It was very strange. The fog was still dense, but lower and shallower, thickening yet burning off under the full golden light of the rising sun. Those on the hill were almost entirely above it and had a fine view. After pausing for a while to the east, no doubt while the first wave of infantry passed through the guns, the artillery duel resumed with even greater fury as case shot exploded and the whole world seemed to pulse and flash with cloud-to-cloud lightning. The odd music the Doms were playing only added to the surrealism of the scene. Barca wished they could have music of their own to counter it, but the only mounted troops dedicated to an instrument were buglers. Others were fine musicians, but none would've traded a weapon for an instrument, at present.

A rider galloped to the top of the hill, seeming to materialize out of nothingness before looking around. Barca recognized Kisin, of all people, quickly followed by several more of his "guards." Kisin saw him and trotted over behind riflemen crouched behind cover until he stopped beside Barca. His followers quickly caught up.

"What're you doing here?" Barca asked.

"Looking for a place to hide, I bet," said Apo Tuin, behind the Number Two gun limber as he placed another round in Billy Randall's heavy leather haversack and motioned him forward.

"Foolish Uxmalo!" Kisin snarled. "Holcanos do not *hide* from a fight— as you city dwellers once hid behind your walls from Holcanos!" He looked back at Barca. "I come from the Anson to ask if you can see the enemy advance from up here, and judge its distance. I see for myself you cannot, as yet."

"No," Barca agreed. "It's rather inconvenient. We're fairly certain their infantry are coming, but don't know how many or where they're aimed. I suspect a large percentage are coming for us here, and every three shots, my gunners lower their elevation. Even if our shot falls short, it should bound into the enemy. Perhaps we'll . . . hear the results of that when it does and gain a better idea where they are."

"A fine idea!" Kisin enthused. "The . . . howitzers do the same, firing closer all the time, but will soon be out of their marvelous bomb shot. The Anson says Doms must have runners to go back to their guns and tell them when to stop shooting. When they do, even if we can't see them, they should be in range of the canister I so admire"—he chuckled—"now that I'm on *this* side of it! Your way of war is very noisy, but exciting."

"It'll soon more closely resemble your way of war, when the enemy's very close, but it'll still be noisy."

"I know!" Kisin exclaimed enthusiastically. "Where is your Capitan Meder? I will fight with him, on foot, when the time comes."

"Don't you need to report back to Major Anson?"

"I have nothing to report," Kisin said, brows narrowing, "and he told me to wait until I did."

In other words, he wanted rid of you too, Barca thought, then somewhat reluctantly, pointed toward the right of the line where Felix Meder was striding behind his riflemen. "You'll find Captain Meder over there," Barca said, then grinned. "Give him my respects—and apologies."

"Apologies?" Kisin asked, already moving away.

"He'll understand," Barca shouted over the roar of the Number Two gun. The *sheeesh* of the shot was much shorter now, and they clearly heard muted screams when it stopped. "What's your range?" Barca demanded.

"A touch under one degree of elevation," Hanny shouted back, "so . . . six hundred yards or so. Maybe a bit more since we're shooting down."

"There's something for you to report," Barca called after Kisin.

Then, suddenly, Barca *could* see the enemy—at least the indistinct yellow and black lines of them through the thinner overhead fog as the rising sun did its work. Despite the sun, he felt a chill when he not only saw how *many* lines there were, but how close the first ones were. Hanny's last shot had likely hit two or three lines back, skating through the fourth and fifth. . . .

"You see them?" he called to Hanny and Dodd.

"Yes sir," they chorused.

"Engage the first rank, then. They're not *quite* in canister range." He whirled back to Kisin. "Major Anson still may not see them. There's too much fog between him and them, but even if you hurry—and you better— the enemy'll be in canister range when you reach him. Go!"

"I don't take orders from you!" Kisin said haughtily.

Barca fumbled for the single shot pistol thrust in his belt. Colonel De Russy had given it to him, and it was a fine piece. He'd never fired it, but certainly knew how. "You'll take *that* order, you arrogant savage, or I'll blow you off your horse!"

"I will complain to the Anson." Kisin sniffed.

"Fine," Barca snapped. "If you tell him *why* I threatened you, he'll probably shoot you himself. Now go, or we're all dead. You too!"

With a final glance at the enemy, Kisin must've decided Barca was right and yanked his horse's head around and pounded down the slope, his followers close behind.

"Good on ya, *Mr.* Barca! Can we get back ta business, then?" Hahessy shouted cheerfully, actually calming Barca's stress-enhanced fury. A Dom roundshot slammed the slope just in front of the gun and sprayed dirt and shards of stone on Hahessy and Preacher Mac. "Heathen *bastards!*" Mac hissed, shaking his bleeding hand. "I'm fine," he assured Hanny, and Hahessy laughed.

"Keep firing as fast as you can," Barca told them. "How many rounds of canister are in that chest?" he asked Apo.

"Ten, sir."

"We'll need more than that," Barca said grimly.

"One of the chests on the caisson has nothing but canister in it," Apo reminded. "We can bring it up."

The problem with that, of course, was that each full chest weighed close to six hundred pounds, and it took time and considerable effort to change them out.

"No. We'll refill your empty slots by hand. Section!" he called louder. "Send your Number Five men to the caissons and form details from the replacements to bring canister forward. Use as many men as you can find haversacks for!" That was so they wouldn't be running around in the open with vulnerable cloth bags filled with a pound and a quarter of powder in their hands. All it would take was a spark.

"They're almost in canister range *now*, Lieutenant," Dodd shouted.

"Already are," Hanny countered, voice with an edge. Barca had been right, and it looked like the ranks angling for their position were deeper than others. Captain Meder was shouting, and perhaps a quarter of his men rested their M1817 rifles rested on the breastworks and started firing. Barca never would've said so, but he'd believed Meder had boasted a little about the skill of his riflemen. Not so. Even as he watched, fog-fuzzy shapes collapsed under their fire, and mounted men—likely officers—tumbled from horses as far away as four hundred yards. Barca was deeply impressed.

"Load canister!" Hanny yelled. Apo dropped a canister round in Billy Randall's haversack while Kini Hau raced to the rear with his own haversack flapping.

Rifles were crackling continuously now, and Barca raised his small telescope (another gift from De Russy). He could see a lot better now, the riflemen taking an increasing toll, but the broader view reinforced his inner horror. It looked like Agon was only sending half his men—a large, hazy block remained back where the enemy guns had been the night before and was moving very slowly if at all. But the "half" already committed to the assault, along with most of the enemy cannon being laboriously pushed forward by hand, outnumbered Anson's whole blocking force three or four to one.

"Fire!" Hanny cried, and the Number Two gun vomited the curiously yellowish smoke only canister produced. Barca watched a broad pattern of dust clouds erupt around the center of the closest Doms, and a dozen or more went down. *Poom-poom, poom-poom, poom-poom!* went the three, two-gun sections of Dukane's battery and Barca looked to his left. The fog was vanishing fast, and he was surprised how the visibility had improved. Aiming his glass at the enemy in front of the "main" line, he saw more dozens hacked out of the leading ranks as if by three big bites, yet the rest continued relentlessly on, a few clearly wounded staggering along to keep up.

"Fire!" roared Corporal Dodd, his pattern of .69 caliber balls nearly equaling an infantry company volley squalling downrange and sweeping away another eight or ten yellow-clad men. When the enemy was closer, even the balls that missed would be lethal when they bounced up from the hard ground.

We have to keep chewing on them, Barca thought, *nibble them down before they get in range of our men with carbines—because by then, we'll nearly be in range of their bayonets.* He took a long breath. He'd been in battle before and fought bravely enough to be widely noticed. That was just the thing, however; he'd "only" been fighting desperately for his very life, but that was all he'd had to worry about. He'd never been *in charge* of anyone but himself in battle, and it looked increasingly like his and Meder's defense of the hill might decide whether any of Anson's force survived. *And, God in heaven,* he thought with another icy spike of horror, *there are so many of them! We'll never stop them.*

Something hot and wet sprayed him just as it seemed a terrible gust of wind slammed him back against the Number Two limber. The horse on the right, just in front of the splinter bar, collapsed with a terrified shriek, but dropped utterly bonelessly, gasping on the ground, blood spewing from its nostrils. A solid shot had blown through the animal's withers, pulverizing its spine, before passing close enough for displaced air to physically move him. It cracked heavily into a wall of the villa and rolled slowly back in his direction. *Copper shot, just like we've begun to use,* he thought dazedly. *Very bright where it struck.*

"You all right, Lieutenant?" Apo Tuin asked, peering at him over the limber chest lid he'd just closed. The young Uxmalo sounded concerned, and it dawned on Barca he'd been drenched by horse blood. He was lucky none of the bone hit him. The horse had already shuddered and died, and he felt terribly sorry for it—and equally sorry for himself. Then he heard Hanny, one of *his* men, scream, "Load canister!"

He shook himself as if clearing another type of fog from his mind. "Fine," he replied to Apo, standing straight and tugging the bottom of his jacket down. "The enemy artillerymen are *very* much improved. Unhitch that poor animal from the traces and move the limber twenty yards to the left. We'll shift the guns to their secondary positions in a moment."

Hahessy was *laughing* as he slammed another round down the barrel, and Mac was just as loudly cursing the "damned idjit Irishman." Everyone on both crews except Hanny and Dodd had tossed their jackets and rolled their sweaty red shirtsleeves up. Barca cleared his throat. "Fire one more round, then shift the guns." Their secondary positions were only a short distance to the right and left. As tight as things were, it was the best they could do. It would give them better separation and require the enemy to shift their aim. When they started getting close again—if they hadn't ceased firing to prevent hitting their own troops by then—Barca would move his guns back where they started.

Each spewed out another yellow cloud and even before they stopped rolling back, the Numbers Three and Four men had snatched up the heavy trails by the handles. Kini Hau and Dodd's Number Five grabbed the sponge buckets and took the rammer and worm staffs from the Ones and Twos, who grabbed the spokes. Hanny shouted, "Trail left! And Ricken and Morris heaved the trail that direction until Hanny said, "Halt! To the rear!" Everyone heaved straight back, toward where Apo was positioning the limber with the help of several men from the caisson who'd already dropped more canister in the ammunition chest. When the huffing men had rolled the gun almost back to the foremost horses hitched to the limber, Hanny, pushing on spokes alongside Mac, loudly gasped, "Halt! Trail right! Halt! To the front!" The extra men rushed to help and both guns were soon in position, Ricken back at the handspike roughly straightening Number Two.

"Load canister!" Hanny yelled, voice getting rough.

Barca was impressed—and proud. It hadn't been a "parade ground" evolution by any means, and Hanny used less than a quarter of the commands required by the manual, even altering or abbreviating the ones he had, but it was accomplished in seconds to the shrieking and thumping accompaniment of enemy solid shot starting to churn the place they'd been. Now he was already loading, resuming what Barca had heard Colonel Cayce call the "dance of death," when each crew member performed his intricate steps in a precise sequence without another word from the gunner so they could all, together, as a team, smash more enemies than any could possibly manage by himself. It was ironic that Barca couldn't imagine anything so beautiful at the moment, any endeavor requiring such close, coordinated cooperation from disparate individuals, and all for such a destructive purpose.

Dodd's gun had moved almost as quickly on the right, and he looked to the front. It was still very hazy—the humidity was miserable, and his shirt felt like a slimy, fresh animal hide under his jacket—but the fog was almost gone, and only a little remained to the south, possibly blowing off the lake. That was the direction help would come from, and he strained his eyes at a fuzzy dark line, hoping it was already here. *It can't be*, he decided. *Colonel Cayce had too far to come. All I'm seeing are trees along a creek bed or the shadow of the fog.* He turned back to the front. The Dom ranks were bunching up at the base of the hill, and all the riflemen were firing. Now willing to bet they were as good as Meder claimed, Barca expected they were hitting men with virtually every shot. He hoped so. The dragoons to his left fired a volley with their Hall carbines, then another very quickly. Dukane's howitzers thundered, hidden under a pall of their own yellowish smoke, and Doms fell by the score, maybe hundreds, the front rank shattered and the rest stacking around and behind it at about two hundred yards. Even Razine's ships in the harbor were firing. With the advancing Doms in enfilade, they should've reaped a terrible harvest, but the range was too great for Razine's inexperienced gunners, and Barca couldn't tell if they were having any effect. Still, only the lancers and Rangers were quiet at the moment, holding fire until their smoothbore carbines would be most devastating.

Poom! Poom! rang Barca's section, *mulching* the mass of men below. But there were more. "Keep it up, boys!" First Sergeant Petty barked. "Hammer away. They're fish in a barrel!"

So were the men on the hill. The Dom artillery could no longer engage Dukane's battery without tearing into their own troops from behind (and the fact they didn't shoot anyway was further proof General Agon had full command of his army this time, and actually valued the lives of his men), but the hill remained in plain view above the Doms trying to attack it, and all ten guns shifted their fire there.

―――――――

"Well, hell. The hill's catchin' it now," Boogerbear remarked, his tone probably infuriatingly casual to some. Then again, he was always like that, especially in action. Almost . . . serene. *An' Sal Hernandez is the same*, Anson thought, *he just jokes more. An' God help me, Leonor's a lot like that too, though I don't know how she really* feels. Anson worried about his daughter, but not the battle, even now, when it looked like they might be overrun. He'd seen a lot of action, big fights and small for a very long time, and, well . . . he kind of liked it. Fighting, that is. Boogerbear was different in that respect, at least, since he didn't seem to care one way or the other. When Felix Meder sent a messenger to report that the entire Dom front was shifting away from the sea and would land all their weight to the right of the Rangers and Dukane's 3rd Section—basically on top of Lara's lancers, the dragoons and the hill—Anson summoned Boogerbear and a battalion of Rangers from the left to stand ready to reinforce the dragoons on the right. Boogerbear acted as if he'd been given a choice between corn and flour tortillas.

I guess we've been around each other so long, we get it from each other. Anson wondered about that, thinking of someone else. *Where does Lewis get it? "Serene" ain't exactly the right word for him, though. "Resolute" is prob'ly better, an' he doesn't second-guess himself after the shootin' starts; he just flows with it, focused on executin' his plan—then reactin' to what the enemy does in response quick enough that it seems like it was part of his plan from the start.* Anson snorted. *An' maybe it was.* If that was the case, he'd never seen anything like it. He thought plans were wonderful things, until they shattered into chaos. Lewis was the only leader he'd ever known who seemed able to mold chaos into a plan. *I don't know if he's smarter than me, but he thinks a lot deeper. Quicker too. Then there's those . . . spells he has, like he ain't really there anymore. . . .*

Anson shook his head, looking up at the hill, now completely visible. It was wreathed in smoke and billowing dust as all the enemy cannon rained shot on it. Something was burning. The villa had tile shingles, but the stable and outbuildings had wooden roofs. "Yeah," he finally agreed with Boogerbear. "Given how few options Agon has for maneuverin', he's actin' mighty wiggly. I *told* Lewis we taught him too much last time." He looked around. "Where's that damn Kisin? I haven't seen him since he came down. Must've been an hour ago."

"I am here!" Kisin proclaimed, behind Anson and Boogerbear. The Rangers were passing behind him, leading their horses. There was no telling if they'd *need* horses, but Anson hoped they might. Besides, the animals would be better protected on the back flank of the hill.

"What're you doin', sneakin' around?" Boogerbear asked.

"I'm not sneaking anywhere! Holcanos do not . . ." He stopped. Of course they did. His tone turned aggrieved. "I was watching Barca's great guns, and he sent me away. I watched Captain Dukane's, and he told me to leave. I tried to talk to Teniente Lara and Alcaldesa Consela—that is a *woman!*" he inserted enthusiastically. "And they said they were busy, though clearly they weren't. Everyone is so *rude*—after I've been such a faithful ally!"

Dukane's center section fired, pounding them with pressure while canister shrieked out to heap more Doms barely a hundred and fifty yards away. They'd slowed their advance, and it was costing them terribly, but they'd be shooting back soon. *Surprised they haven't already*, Anson thought, then glared at Kisin, startling himself with a sudden laugh. "Kisin, they ain't *tryin'* to be rude. You just don't know when to leave folks be. You're war leader of all the Holcanos now, sure, but there ain't two score of you here." He forestalled Kisin's objection. "I know that ain't your fault. You *could* do somethin about bein' the most puffed-up ol' toad I ever knew. An' you *smell*," he added, not particularly harshly, but as an indisputable fact. "It puts people off."

Kisin looked incredulous. "*Everybody* smells!"

"Not as bad as you," Boogerbear stated, with a meaningful glance at Kisin's animal skin breechclout. It was known that Holcanos tanned hides with urine, but some joked that Kisin was *still* tanning his.

A messenger from Lara ran up, visibly stopping himself from saluting. "Sir, the enemy has halted—is dressing ranks!"

"Here it comes," Anson said. "Stick with us, if you want," he told Kisin. "Plenty o' the lads'll be pissin' themselves soon enough. We won't even notice you." He raised his voice to shout, "Animals to the rear!" then pushed in among the defenders to join Ramon Lara.

Rifle and cannon fire slashed down from the hill as swarms of Doms crept relentlessly up and the dragoons' Hall breechloaders slaughtered men in front of them. The Doms had rattled off a pair of heavy, roaring volleys themselves, then fixed bayonets and charged. Many were now actually crawling up the slope while men in the rear ranks kept firing at defenders as incoming artillery fire dwindled. Here, for the moment, it was eerily quiet. Dukane's guns were being reloaded at once, and none of the troopers had been given leave to fire. The Doms were ordering their ranks as best they could amid jumbled corpses. Shouts of officers and NCOs rang clear and loud.

"*Lista tus armas! Aputén!*"

"Everybody down!" Anson and Lara roared.

"*Fuego!*"

Almost four thousand men of two Dom regiments had thickened and doubled the ranks in front of a quarter of the Rangers, all the lancers, and maybe a quarter of the dragoons not already in the thick of it on the right. Probably not quite a thousand men, including Consela's people and the odds and ends who'd joined them from the city. They'd been waiting for this, and dropped down as quickly as they could, but the blizzard of three-quarter-inch lead balls caught quite a few regardless, or smashed through the brush and timber atop the earthen berm and struck people who thought they were protected. Men fell screaming and writhing amid sleeting splinters and shattered stone, or tumbled back with chunks of their heads blown away. One of Consela's guards no longer had a lower jaw and made the most horrible sounds.

As brutal as the volley had been, Boogerbear was probably the only one who seemed to take heart. "Only about half their muskets fired," he said, so yes, it could've been twice as bad. "Silly buggers must've loaded 'em wet with the dew. Now they'll never get 'em ta shoot."

"Another lesson they've learned," Anson said, "now we drive it home." The Rangers with Boogerbear shoved their way through to join the line and he, Anson, and Lara all shouted, "Commence firing! Fire at will!"

The first roar of carbine fire might as well have been a deliberate volley, and Doms who stood loading in the open fell quickly despite the long range. The dismounted troopers conscientiously *aimed* their inaccurate weapons, just as they'd been taught, instead of merely pointing them in a general direction as Doms still did, and adjusted for elevation since it was almost impossible to miss *someone* in such tightly packed ranks. Still, their primary interest was in shooting fast and throwing as many deadly spheres at the enemy as they could, as quickly as possible. When Dukane's howitzers rejoined them, spewing even more lead, the difference in numbers was effectively reduced.

"We've got this for the moment, Boogerbear," Anson told his big friend. "Keep moving to the right with your battalion and join Mr. Burton." Things were looking desperate over there. Of course, the Doms had more fresh regiments there than here, still protected by the savaged troops in front of them.

Another ragged volley came from the Doms, butchering more defenders than Anson would've expected. *Maybe these damn Doms* have *learned to aim*, he thought grimly, momentarily tempted to keep Boogerbear's men after all, but he waved the man on.

"They're fixing bayonets!" Lara told him.

Anson nodded. "Right, lads!" he bellowed, drawing a Walker Colt in each hand. "They're comin' with their stickers. Keep yer pikes handy, but when they get close enough you only have one shot left, pour a handful o' drop shot down your carbines. Hammer 'em with that, an' there won't be a man left in their front rank fit to fight when they get here!"

A chorus of yells mounted, and there was every conceivable note and tone, from terror to fury, but soon there was some sort of shout in every throat, and the cumulative effect was awesome—and terrifying. The Doms had been ordered forward, two-foot-long, double-edged blades inserted in the muzzles of five-foot-long muskets bristling frightfully before them. It was a sight that had cleared every field on this continent for the better part of two centuries. At least until the Washboard. And now, when that once-unstoppable machine of shiny, rippling death—yellow uniforms sprayed and torn by blood and shattered bone as carbines thumped and cannon boomed—heard the thunder of defiance . . . and wavered.

"*Cargarlos!*" came a rising cry, and the Dom line stiffened, then somewhat falteringly, charged. It was met at a dozen paces by a searing fusillade of carbines packed with dozens of teardrop-shaped pieces of lead and nearly every pistol anyone had. Men fell screaming, horribly wounded by concentrated swarms of shot that pulped chests, guts, limbs, faces. Some were only struck by a few pieces, but they saw blood, felt pain and fear, and knew they were wounded. They didn't know how badly, but they naturally faltered, and the sharp, leading edge of the charge began to crumble. Anson fired his Walker Colts, taking his time, aiming carefully, killing officers and NCO when he could, or pretty much anyone intent on pressing forward. The enemies in front of him might've broken then, but literally couldn't stop or fall back as they were physically swept along, bleeding and screaming, by the ranks behind them. Some simply dropped to be trampled and most remained of little use except to stop projectiles, but before more than a few defenders could reload, a rush of fresh Doms broke through their mangled comrades to crest the berm.

"Pikes and lances!" Lara roared, and others took up the call. Men with heavy, cumbersome seven-foot spears that their muskets and bayonets had become were met by lighter, quicker, razor-sharp lances *nine* feet long, which took them in the belly, throat, eyes, crotch, under raised arms, all driving deep before pulling back. Then there were the actual pikes—sturdier, shorter, but still lighter than muskets that could be used by men trained with the bayonet. They waded into the ditch under the lances and started bashing Dom weapons aside, stabbing low. A howitzer boomed and blasted a steaming, mewling gap of shattered flesh in the attackers, but the Doms didn't hesitate to fill it and press through. The gun pulled back, its crew fighting with implements and short swords.

Anson's Walkers were empty, and he shoved them in the finely tooled holsters on his belt. Before he could draw his Paterson Colts from holsters under his arms, a bayonet almost speared him, and he whipped out the heavy dragoon saber he usually hung on his horse. He'd had little training with it—some pointers from Coryon Burton—but sheer savagery can make up for a lack of skill in a pinch, especially when one's opponent is no better at defending against a blade that's already inside his own. Anson hacked down, chop-slicing deep in the man's chest from the top of his shoulder by his neck. Blood fountained back in his face. "Save that gun!" he bellowed, pulling his saber from the corpse with his right hand while drawing a Paterson with his left. The howitzer's Number One man, an unusually tall Uxmalo, smacked a Dom in the face with the end of his rammer staff, but screamed when a yellow-coated officer thrust a sword in his belly. Anson shot the officer in the back of the head. "Re-form the line in front of this gun, damn you!" He shot another Dom in the face. "Pikes, fight through!"

He knew, in the old world, nothing did more killing on the battlefield or raised the spirits of men around it as artillery—and nothing shamed or demoralized men as badly as *losing* a gun under their protection. This gun and its sister in the section were right in the middle of the line. If the Doms overran them . . .

Lara was there with his sword, twisting past lunging bayonets to strike with his blade. His right arm would probably never fully heal from a wound he'd taken at the Washboard, but Anson couldn't tell that he was at any disadvantage. Some of his men were quickly beside him, as was Alcaldesa Consela, launching arrow after arrow with her bow. Anson figured she was close to fifty but didn't act it in a fight. And after what happened to her village, she had plenty of incentive. Still, she was almost overwhelmed before that ridiculous Kisin, powerful arms bulging as he swung his favorite club with one hand while jabbing with a shortened spear in the other, pounded and stabbed his way in beside her and gave her room to use her bow again. Anson was hacking and shooting his own way through, and no more shouts would be heard over the terrible rattling, screeching, rumbling din of two desperate armies at each other's throats. He saw a wild-eyed Dom pierce Teniente Espinoza with a bayonet, then try to give him another quick stab that seemed to be part of their training as the lancer officer fell back. Anson shot the Dom in the temple with his Paterson. Grabbing Espinoza's collar, he dragged him closer to the blackened muzzle of the gun.

"Load this thing!" he roared back at the surviving artillerymen. Someone scooped up the Number One's rammer staff and hurled it back behind the axle.

"They're really bunching up in front of us!" Lara gasped, suddenly beside him, checking Espinoza with a glance. The two were close friends and Espinoza was one of only a tiny handful of Mexicans from their old world left. The wound the man was clutching was bloody, but wasn't in a "no hope" place. Artillery replacements from the caisson were dragging him under the axle to the rear.

"They smell a hole openin' up," Anson agreed, shooting another Dom. He had one five-shot Paterson left before he'd be down to his saber alone, or have to reload. He'd left his rifle with Colonel Fannin, not that it would be much use in such close quarters. A shout filtered through behind him: "Load double canister!" It sounded like Dukane. Espinoza was gone, and a man crawled up under the axle and took the rammer staff another man handed back over it. Leaning it there, he next took a cylinder of canister with its tapered wood sabot and smaller-diameter powder charge, and shoved it in the muzzle. Anson furiously hacked at a pair of Doms, driving them back, before he saw the man push another cylinder with only a sabot in on top of the first.

"I need a little room, sir," the artilleryman yelled apologetically.

"Push 'em back!" Anson ordered, and the protective screen that had formed in front of the gun stabbed and shot and heaved. Anson emptied his revolver.

The man on the rammer staff heaved the heavier-than-usual load down the barrel, then ducked down between the wheels like a rabbit.

"Ready! Stand clear!" came a near-frantic scream that might've been Dukane again. Anson looked to the front. The gap, less than a dozen paces ahead, spread wider by the second, packing with hundreds of Doms and what looked like a thousand more, queueing up to pass through. They were still dying, still taking fire, even more so as they let up elsewhere to make for the breach. "Stand clear to the side!" Anson bellowed, voice cracking, grabbing Lara, who had Consela by the arm. They smashed their way to the right where a clump of lancers and dragoons pulled them on. Anson thought *most* of the defenders managed to get clear before the 12pdr field howitzer shook him with a harsher, deeper report than he'd ever heard as it leaped violently back from the huge, billowing, yellowish cloud. Almost immediately, the other gun in the section, more easily loaded, was heaved forward, trail dropped with a clank, lanyard stretched—*Poooom!*

"Moment" is such a subjective word, open to countless interpretations, and depending on the perspective of those caught in one, it might last an instant, half a minute, or the rest of their lives. In battle, an amazing amount of horror can be packed into a moment. The bulge in the mounted trooper's line at Gran Lago began to disintegrate in what might objectively be called an "instant," because scores were killed within the very second that the first load of double canister swept into their midst from a range well inside the technical definition of "point-blank." That instant lingered a few seconds more for those just realizing they were wounded or killed, but that's when the second howitzer churned the mob. In the "moment" including the instant and the short time to come, a stunning number of the enemy, and an unfortunate few lancers, were shredded into a dead, dying, badly wounded, or just emotionally and mentally ravaged heap, and those still standing near, even miraculously in the middle of it all, abruptly turned and fled.

The "moment" for most, alive or dead, was over, but it would linger in the present for many of the living who saw it—on both sides—for the rest of their lives.

This wasn't Don Frutos's Dom army, however, and it didn't break. General Agon had rebuilt it of sterner stuff even before the long campaign hardened it. The rest fought on, still hand to hand along the line and grinding up the slope. They were shaken badly when *all* the American guns started doubling their canister loads, but they weren't so concentrated anywhere else. The carnage was terrible, but they took it. On the other hand, double loading canister is hard on cannon, particularly the carriages, and might even crack a trunnion and ruin a tube. It's hard on crews as well, not to mention ammunition reserves. But the blocking force was fighting for *now*, not later, and there'd be plenty of "later" to rest and replenish ammunition and repair their guns—if they lived.

"*Madre de* Dios," Ramon Lara gasped, staring at the trembling, squirming, crawling expanse of tangled limbs and broken flesh while absently loading a carbine he'd picked up. Consela had picked one up as well and seemed either entirely unfazed or in some kind of functional shock. Kisin, of all people, was very gently showing her how to load it.

"Yeah," Anson agreed. "Helluva thing. Well done, Dukane," he shouted over his shoulder at the artillery captain who was focused on reorganizing the center section's crews and didn't hear him over the firing. The Doms right here started disengaging, pulling back a bit, troops and NCOs knocking bayonets out of barrels. Unable to sweep over the breastworks, they seemed prepared to trade fire—while bringing their own cannon up. Anson frowned, looking to the right, up the hill. The Doms weren't pulling back there, at least not on purpose. A second (or was it a third?) assault had been repulsed by Barca's meager section, the riflemen and dragoons, but a fresh regiment of two thousand men was starting up the slope. *It's really gonna get tough up there, an' if the Doms take the hill, we've had it.* "Messenger!" Anson shouted, and Kisin reached him first. "You? Really?"

"I want to *do* something!"

Anson realized it was true. "You *been* doin' stuff, but all right. Go get *all* the Rangers still down on the left an' hightail it up the hill. Stop an' get Boogerbear on the way. He's in charge."

"That'll leave us open on the left," Lara warned.

"I know, but the Doms are committed. They might bring up the second *half* of their army, an' do whatever they want with it, but I get the feelin' Agon's savin' it back—an' we've already got plenty to worry about." He refocused back on the immediate problem. "If they shift, we can put mounted men back in front of 'em before they hit us, but the *right's* about to go. If they overrun the hill . . . all we have left is to run like hell."

"You don't think Agon will just move on if he breaks through?" Lara was obviously thinking about the proposals made the night before.

Anson seemed confused for a moment, then remembered. He laughed. "Hell no!" He looked at Kisin. "Go!"

CHAPTER 30

Colonel Lewis Cayce had developed a quiet pride in his improving tactical, even strategic talent, but though the grand plan of this campaign—to widely maneuver around General Agon and catch him between various forces—had largely worked (despite all the unexpected events and difficulties), Lewis was vaguely mortified by the final execution of the plan, particularly the slapdash, willy-nilly movement to contact. He could only take pride in the troops who'd accomplished it regardless, and wouldn't be surprised to learn he had the honor of commanding the finest army on this entire mysterious globe. Now the regiments were all deployed and largely sorted out: 1st Division under Colonel Reed on the left, roughly eight hundred yards due south of the Dom assault on Anson's position, 2nd Division under Har-Kaaska on the right, probably less than a thousand yards south, southwest of Agon's large reserve, possibly his main body, slowly moving toward the fighting. All three of Olayne's batteries had unlimbered two hundred yards to the front.

What astonished Lewis now, even angered him somewhat, was that after all this army had been through, it still managed to achieve a menacing position, in clear view of the enemy now that the fog was largely gone, and no one even seemed to notice. To make matters worse, Lewis *wanted* to be noticed, to take pressure off Anson.

Varaa was still with him—she'd rejoin Har-Kaaska when the action commenced—and seemed to be thinking along the same lines, even more put out. "The fog has been gone for ages," she growled. "There's just a little haze. Are those fools so focused in front of them, they can't be troubled to look about?"

"Look behind us," Leonor suggested with amusement. Varaa did. The grassland here was rockier than along the Usuma River, but still interspersed with clumps of low, scrubby trees that reminded Lewis of live oaks, or some kind of dense-limbed elm. With all the long-necked creatures eating their leaves, trees had to produce an overabundance of them to survive. None of those creatures were in view, and except for a few very large, unseen . . . things that thundered down to the water and splashed away in the dark, they hadn't met any either. The battle started before they could even see, and that must've pushed most of them back or kept them hiding below bluffs along the shore.

But those clumps of trees thickened along myriad little creeks and mostly dry streams that fed the great, glistening lake to the west. Now, perhaps only Leonor had connected the fact that one of those streams was right behind where they'd deployed, and the remaining haze, combined with the dense blue-green leaves covering the trees and the dark shadows underneath, had rendered the largely sky-blue-clad infantry practically invisible from a distance.

"Oh my," exclaimed Samantha Wilde, drawing Lewis's attention, along with a frown. He'd already told her to withdraw to the baggage wagons on the other side of the wooded creek. "I don't suppose we could've hidden from sight more effectively if we'd tried."

Reverend Harkin put his hand on his breast and straightened. "Hide me in the shadow of your wings from the wicked who are out to destroy me, from my mortal enemies who surround me!" he quoted, then glanced triumphantly at Leonor. For once, he hadn't changed a thing.

"Well said, Reverend," Leonor granted, "an' if we'd known we could sneak up behind that tree line, we coulda' rested more on the way. Now it's kinda' defeatin' the purpose."

Lewis offered her a familiar, even affectionate smile, but then spoke in a determined tone. "It's simple enough to get their attention. Uncase the colors!" he shouted. "Captain Olayne, you may commence firing your battalion. The left battery will focus on the assaulting troops, the right two batteries will concentrate on the enemy reserve."

"Case shot, sir?" Olayne asked.

Lewis shook his head. "We have little enough for your six and twelve pounders, and the enemy's unengaged ranks on the left are in defilade. Solid shot will have greater effect, I think. And we don't have any case shot for the eight pounders at all. Battery fire for effect, at first, then turn your gunners loose."

"Sir!" Olayne replied enthusiastically and spurred his mount to gallop forward.

———

"We must send more men!" demanded General Juaron, controlling his spirited stallion with difficulty. With General Tun forward, the rather intense General Juaron was next in seniority among General Agon's staff. "The enemy has left his position by the sea almost utterly empty, and the pitiful fire from those ships offshore is nothing to fear. Send *my brigado*. I will lead!" he exclaimed.

Agon took a deep breath and sighed. "They might reoccupy the position before you close. We're still more than six hundred paces away, and they'll see what we're attempting at once."

"If they had troops to send, they wouldn't have taken them in the first place!" Juaron almost shouted in frustration.

"Remember who you're speaking to, my general," Capitan Arevalo warned lowly, polite but firm, hand moving close to the buttcap of his fine, brass-barreled pistol.

Agon reached over and put a hand on Arevalo's arm. Juaron wasn't ordinarily insubordinate and probably wasn't deliberately now. He couldn't have Arevalo shooting his senior officers just because they grew a bit rash. It was nice to have such a loyal aide, however. "I've told you—and *told* you—I've committed as much of this army as I intend to. As much as I can afford to lose," he added bleakly. "Twelve thousand remain, and there's no margin left if we're to have the slightest chance of saving our country from the Blood Priests! No margin at all." He gestured to the south without looking. He'd spent enough time staring in that direction to be noticed and was afraid he'd betray his nervousness. "And don't forget that Coronel Cayce is out there, somewhere. We must get through the city and the marshes beyond before he brings us to battle. If he does, even if we beat him, our 'margin' will vanish and we'll lose in the end." The men are doing well and the enemy can't hold much longer. We *will* get a breakthrough."

"Do you think that alone will end it?" Juaron asked almost scornfully. "Just because El Diablo Anson said he *might* stop fighting if we force a path?" He shook his head. "Even if he was so inclined, the fighting has been too bitter. His men can't just *stop* now, any more than ours could."

"Nevertheless," Agon pressed on, "if he does manage it, we *will* let him. General Tun is aware of my decision and will obey. Any troops who don't will be crucified. It *is* unnatural," he conceded, "but we've bigger business at present." He sighed again, nodding forward, trying to push his men up and over the nondescript little hill they'd spilled so much blood for by sheer force of will. The yellow-coated figures carpeting the slope looked more numerous than those still fighting. "Besides, it looks more and more like we'll have to kill them all before they give us the road."

He gave in to his impulse and glanced to the south again, seeing the same hazy, indistinct, purple-gray line of distant trees that had given him such a start when he first noticed it. Only with the sun now high overhead, clouds scudding away, and the lingering haze only making things fuzzy did he begin to note it wasn't the "same" at all. The color was brighter on the tops of the trees, making the leaves a lighter shade of green, and now he saw what looked like a sea of glittering flashes of reflected light as if the great lake had somehow flooded out into a long, narrow tributary just since the night before. *Impossible, of course.* Then, with a mental crash, he suddenly recognized the brilliant silver of polished musket barrels, bayonets, saber scabbards . . . The sun-bright golden glow of equally polished brass beltplates, buttons, breastplates on—yes, he saw them now—soiled but still white crossbelts. Other details resolved themselves, and he heard gasps and exclamations from his staff as flags were uncased, unrolled, and shaken out before being hoisted up high. He recognized some at once: the dreaded red, white, and blue ones, all jumbled with stars and stripes. There were several of those, one right by the solid blue one with a scene he couldn't see or remember painted on it. There were new yellow-gold flags with crossed cannons and red banners floating over the batteries— yes, he could see those quite clearly too, now—and the various city-state flags he remembered, with blue or red or other-colored saltires. There were more flags he'd never seen, *which only makes sense*, he thought dully, though how they could fight so well under so many different banners still mystified him.

"It's just as I feared," he said forcefully, his tone implying he wasn't just as surprised as everyone else. "Colonel Cayce is here and we must counter him. Sound the horns. Direct the regiments to wheel to the left into line." That was something they'd worked very hard on, and there'd be little confusion since each regiment was already assembled in blocked combat ranks that could fight as they were or double and extend. "Messenger to General Tun," he added. "He's to shift his entire force, including artillery, to the left as well."

"What about the hill?" Arevalo pressed, and Agon considered for an instant.

"General Tun will reinforce that assault only. The rest of us must hold Cayce back. Tun can *still* break through to the city, and we can withdraw behind its walls. Cayce's army must be exhausted. He can't possibly attack us there immediately—and we won't give him the chance. We'll abandon the city and cross the marshes as planned, leaving sufficient forces to hold the crossings. We can *still* prevail," he confidently predicted, though in truth he doubted the numbers he'd have left would justify the "victory."

Across the field, all three exposed batteries—*The heretics have six guns to a battery compared to our five,* Agon mused—fired as one, the great, billowing white cloud the twelve guns coughed out completely blanketing the enemy. He steeled himself for what was coming.

"Here they come again!" cried Apo Tuin, doing his best to crouch behind the Number Two gun while thumbing the vent, and Hahessy rammed another round of canister down the barrel. Apo had rushed forward to replace Private Ricken when an eight-pound solid shot smashed through the top spokes of the left wheel (spraying Preacher Mac with splinters) and tore poor Ricken's head completely off. He'd been standing exactly where Apo was now, and blood was still spattered everywhere. Apo's warning meant little. The Doms hadn't actually gone away, nor had their 6pdr ever stopped firing. The gun tube was too hot to touch without the protective leather thumbstall Apo used to stop the vent, but the enemy was making another concerted push for the top.

The reason was obvious. As the day wore on, those atop the hill had an increasingly panoramic view of the spectacle all around (it was a stunning sight—so many men and so many things happening within just a few square miles), and they'd distinguished Colonel Cayce's force arrayed to the south before the Doms did. Now they could see the enemy reaction and a report was duly sent to Major Anson. *His* front was clearing, but Cayce's appearance hadn't made any difference to the men on the hill—except to make things worse.

Some things. The concentrated artillery barrage had lifted, at least, as the enemy began shifting their guns to bear on the new threat, and Ricken, and most of the crew of the Number One gun, were killed by some of the very last shots fired in their direction. First Sergeant Petty replaced a wounded Dodd, and replacements came forward to fill out the rest of the undamaged gun's crew. Sergeant O'Roddy had rushed forward with more replacements for Mac (who loudly refused despite several bloody wounds), and Andy Morris, who had some big splinters in his face, by his eye. And some tools to make hasty repairs to the damaged wheel. He did his best but declared it couldn't hold for long.

"We'll bring the spare wheel from the caisson," O'Roddy had suggested doubtfully, since Hanny—who had a bright piece of a spoke sticking in his left bicep—never stopped shooting, even while O'Roddy worked.

"No time," Hanny snapped back. Something had . . . shifted in him when Ricken was killed. The older man wasn't a friend, precisely, but he'd been a good man. More important, he was part of Hanny's crew, *his* responsibility, *his* little "family," and the Doms had destroyed him and hurt some others. He'd slipped into a different reality where the enemy sweeping toward them weren't people anymore, just targets, like a swarm of ants he had to keep back. He wasn't even really aiming the gun anymore. He didn't have to. He'd already taken Ricken's place at the handspike, heaving the trail from side to side to "point" it by eye after each shot, and it was rolled back into battery. Occasionally, he'd lunge forward and give the elevation screw a turn. Other than that, he just stood in the open, gauging the effect of his canister and hoarsely shouting for his hurt and exhausted men to "Load" and "Fire!"

O'Roddy had looked to the front and knew Hanny was right. The riflemen were dwindling, their fire slower and less accurate as barrels choked up with fouling. Few had the time—or spit—to moisten a cleaning patch to swab their barrels. Most clearly expected it to come to the bayonet and had already affixed the wicked blades adapted to their rifles. The two overworked guns and their brutal fans of shot were all that kept the Doms off the hill. Even if the spare wheel was already at hand, it would take half a minute to change it. Half a minute while countless musket balls saturated the space around a tightly packed detail of men holding a one-ton gun up on one wheel. If any were hit, the whole thing could crash down on the rest. And half a minute was two or three shots . . . Sergeant O'Roddy had shrugged and taken Apo's place at the limber.

Now Apo was catching hell of another sort.

"Thumb that vent, god damn ye!" Hahessy roared as he quickly withdrew the rammer and stepped back around the right wheel. A musket ball struck the iron tire and sprayed him with sharp lead fragments that washed his left forearm in blood. He never noticed.

"I *am*," Apo screamed at the much larger man.

"Thumb it harder, then, could ye? Heard a hiss from the vent, I did. If a spark lights a charge an' blows me arm off, I'll beat ye ta death with it, I will!"

Stepping up by Hanny, Barca wondered how the big Irishman heard *anything* after the beating his ears had taken. He could hardly imagine how they all stood any of it: the noise, loss of friends, the terror . . . His every instinct screeched for him to crouch and avoid the incoming fire. He'd thought the fight on the beach with the Holcanos and . . . lizard people, after they first arrived on this world, was the worst thing he'd ever experience. This was much worse, and for many more reasons he couldn't even define. The sheer scope of it all was horrifying, even more than the Washboard had been. That was largely illusion, of course, since the numbers engaged were fairly close, but he could see more of everything, and it *looked* incomparably vast. He didn't just want to crouch, he wanted to run back to the shot-bashed villa and hide. But Hahessy and Mac were the most exposed, in front of the gun, and they *couldn't* crouch. Hanny wouldn't, so neither could Barca. Of course, young Corporal Hannibal Cox didn't seem to know Barca was even there.

Besides, even though the personal stakes hadn't much changed—he discounted the strange conversation between Major Anson and General Agon and knew in his heart they'd win or die—the purpose behind the war had changed monumentally. That still eluded quite a few, no doubt, but regardless how elusive a true political union of the Yucatán still proved to be, Sira Periz, Colonel De Russy, Lewis Cayce, Har-Kaaska, Reverend Harkin, Father Orno—many more—were strongly united in what they saw as a sacred cause, and Barca particularly embraced the fact that the war had turned from simple survival and defense to a struggle against evil and a crusade of liberation. The latter could be harder. The people on the Yucatán—Ocelomeh, Uxmalos, virtually all the rest, even Holcanos—knew what freedom was. But the Doms—even their slaves—didn't know any other way and change is never welcome. Sometimes even when it's for the best. Convincing *them* might be the hardest part of all.

But Barca felt this battle was worse for another reason: his cause was threatened by a more capable and determined enemy with a real cause of their own, beyond expansion and subjugation for their own sakes. Agon and his army were fighting them to defend *their* country against the inarguably greater evil of the Blood Priests. A difference of degrees, perhaps, but a big difference to them.

2nd Division had marched straight out against the main Dom reserve while 1st Division, maintaining a tentative connection, advanced on the re-forming remnant of the attack on Anson's blocking force. *Of course a lot of those Doms are coming here now*, Barca could see. Volleys erupted from long, thick lines of blue stretching to either side of colorful flags, facing return volleys from yellow-clad men under red flags and jagged gold crosses. It all looked so . . . conventional, and the plain was quickly shrouded with gunsmoke as thick as the earlier fog. *But the great battle unfolding below is only secondary to what happens here*, Barca knew. *And I and these men on this hill are standing between the enemy and their cause as surely as they're assailing ours.* It was already bloodier than anything Barca had seen. It was going to get worse.

"Fire!" Hanny almost croaked. The damaged gun bucked back, lead canister balls deformed by their own stacking and sudden contact with the harder metal of the copper cylinder and bronze bore whistled when they flew. It couldn't be said the attackers were charging, exactly, since they were just as exhausted as anyone and struggling, even crawling up the steepest slope of the hill, where many were actually under the guns—too close and too low to target. Most weren't, and it really was like shooting ants—with a shotgun—and a great oval of dust and cut grass drifted downwind, leaving dozens of dead and scores of writhing, screaming wounded.

"Reload!" Hanny grated again, guiding the gun forward with the hand-spike, shifting it to point a little more to the left as Hahessy and Mac gingerly heaved on the wheels.

Barca finally spoke as Hanny stepped back. "The repair won't hold for long."

"Doesn't have to," Hanny replied, voice very old. "Canister chest on the caisson's cleaned out. We only have five or six rounds left."

"What about the other chests? Barca asked, berating himself. He should've found the answer already instead of just standing here, philosophizing. "Each should have ten rounds, standard," he added.

"Already burnt through 'em," Hanny replied, watching Andy's replacement, a kid from Pidra Blanca they all called "Ricky," stretch the lanyard and nod nervously at Apo. Apo shouted, "Ready!" when he saw everyone clear of the gun.

"Fire!" croaked Hanny.

Poom!

"Thumb that god damn vent!" Hahessy bellowed at Apo.

"I *am*, you great, fat . . . slash toad!" Apo almost squealed with fury. Hahessy laughed.

A young, red-eyed, powder-smudged rifleman ran up to Barca and saluted.

"Don't do that here!" Hanny rasped at the kid. "I don't know if Doms salute each other, but I suspect they do—and know what it means. You want to draw extra fire at our officers?"

"Yes, Corporal . . . I mean, no, Corporal! Lieutenant Barca, Captain Meder's compliments, sir, and could you join him briefly by the wall around the villa?"

"Of course," Barca said. He looked at Hanny and hesitated, worried about him on multiple levels, but all he could say was, "Carry on. You're doing very well. I'll be back in a moment." Hanny waved.

Captain Felix Meder was strolling back and forth in front of a rubbled portion of the wall where enemy shot flying over the embattled section of guns had smashed it again and again. Musket balls whizzed and warbled thickly as they dropped even here, out of direct view of the ascending enemy, but Meder took no heed. He was swiping back and forth at flowery puffballs on top of tall weeds with the brass-tipped iron ramrod of the 1817 rifle slung over his shoulder when Barca joined him. Meder looked up, a half smile on his grimy, sweaty, boyish face. "We're holding them," he said by way of greeting. "God knows how they take it, but they do. And just keep coming." He whacked savagely at another colorful puffball. "*We* can't take it much longer, though. I've lost half my fellows, killed and hurt, and we're short of ammunition."

"We're down to the last few rounds of canister," Barca agreed. "Still a fair amount of solid shot and a few rounds of case we can cut fuses for muzzle bursts." He shrugged and held his hands out at his sides.

"I suspected as much," Meder said, pointing at the gap in the wall with his rammer. "Think you can pass your guns through here? If we don't get support damned quick—I've been sending runners, begging—we'll have to pull back to a more defensible position before we're overrun. The villa isn't *much* more defensible," he conceded, looking at the once picturesque main building, almost as battered as the wall around it, great gaping holes in the tile roof, "but it might give us a chance." He turned back to the front when the guns roared again, eyes sweeping the bloody crescent to either side, taking in his riflemen, ramrods flashing in the sun as they pounded stubborn balls down their barrels, jets of fire and smoke from others, aiming over the breastworks. They'd suffered so much to get here and now fought so brilliantly, he couldn't accept it was all for nothing just because, after all their long separate journeys, Agon got here a *single* day quicker with his army than Colonel Cayce with his.

Meder destroyed another puffball, belying his calm façade. "The hard part will be disengaging, of course, but the *shameful* part is that we'll essentially be surrendering possession of the hill. Anson'll have to pull back as well. I suspect the enemy only wants past us, so they might not linger to murder us all. Colonel Cayce will win the battle down there"—he gestured at the plain below with supreme confidence—"but if Agon escapes with the bulk of his army, we'll lose the campaign."

Barca rubbed his chin, agreeing with Meder's assessment, but what could they do? Surely it was best to save what they could. No matter how the day turned out, the veterans who'd fought so long and well *would* be needed again. He focused on how to save them. With its damaged wheel, he wasn't sure the Number Two gun could be moved any distance at all. He didn't know how it stood where it was, much less managed the recoil. He'd seen Preacher Mac do his best to make sure it stood on the soundest spokes when they rolled it back into battery. "They'll *fit* through, certainly, with plenty of men clearing the bigger stones and debris, but . . ."

"*But,*" Meder concurred, already knowing Barca's objection. "The enemy will tear us up no matter what we do. If we move quickly, practically *flee* from our current position, the Doms'll chase us and slaughter us from behind. If we go slowly, they'll feel it and rush us. And as soon as we pull your guns—we can't leave them for last and risk them being taken—the Doms'll rush us anyway, and all my riflemen left to slow them will die. I . . . I'm not *really* an officer, and I just . . . *don't know how to do this!*" he almost exploded in frustration.

Barca could sympathize. He felt much the same. *And at least he's conscious of the importance of my guns,* he reflected. There'd been growing concern over situations like this. In addition to the obvious effect on morale that so motivated Anson earlier, the American guns, and particularly their carriages, were so superior to the enemy's that they *couldn't* let them have one to study and copy. The versatility, practicality, and especially mobility the American artillery *system* gave them, the design of guns, limbers, caissons . . . everything, was the greatest material advantage they enjoyed. American muskets were better quality than their Dom counterparts, but the principle was the same, and they weren't that much more lethal. Hall carbines, when they worked, effectively doubled, even tripled the firepower of dragoons, and rifles could kill at longer range but loaded more slowly. There was always a trade-off. The revolvers a few of them had might've made a big difference if they had more, or could make them, but that just wasn't possible. There wasn't the necessary steel, tools, or probably knowledge among the Americans themselves. The most revolutionary contributions the Americans brought to the battlefield on this world were training, based on instruction and experience, and an artillery system incorporating the freshest cream of such thought from all over the world they came from. It was a *century* ahead of the enemy's.

Agon's army was catching up on training and experience. If he fielded the same kind of guns—and the allies had already proven Dom tubes were good enough to make the transition—the cause Barca fought for could take a fatal blow. *Is that Meder's primary concern? Even above his men?* Barca wondered. *To get my guns behind the wall and protect them from the enemy?* Knowing young Meder the way he did, he suspected that was the case—and the sacrifice could break him.

Then they heard a different rumbling and looked at the Villa. Beyond it was the winding road leading down to the plain and distant city. It was also the semiprotected route they'd used to send messages to Major Anson, and they recognized the distinctive thunder of hooves. Lots of them. Further undermining his façade of calm, Felix Meder almost collapsed with relief when he saw the huge form and wild beard of Captain Bandy "Boogerbear" Beeryman appear around the villa, leading a dense cluster of Rangers. And as they kept coming past Boogerbear, who stopped in front of Meder and Barca, they swirled around to the right side of Barca's guns and started dismounting, horse holders pulling animals through another gap in the wall around the villa while men with carbines and pikes rushed to join the exhausted, faltering riflemen and gunners.

"Thank God," Meder murmured, stiffening his stance as more and more Rangers galloped past. Boogerbear had brought them all. The first battalion was considerably diminished and looked hard-used, but after a section of howitzers rattled and pulverized gravel under spinning wheels up behind them and started unlimbering on either side of Barca's 6pdrs, a stronger, fresher battalion of Rangers brought up the rear and began reinforcing the line to the left. The volume of fire the defenders poured out quickly increased.

Boogerbear still sat on Dodger, calmly fishing a honey-sticky wad of local tobacco from a painted leather pouch before stuffing it in his cheek. Wiping his fingers on his dingy but still recognizably sky-blue trousers, he rumbled through the leaves in his mouth, "Sorry it took so long, fellas. 'Spect you were gettin' anxious. Would'a got here quicker, but the dragoons'a been takin' it hard too. Had ta lend a hand shovin' them yella' devils back before we could get all the way here." He was looking around as he spoke. "Lordy, what a view! Colonel Cayce's got the whole rest o' the Dom army tangled up on the flat." He spat a stream of brown juice and looked back at Barca and Meder. "Half o' the *first* half still seems most in'trested in us, though. Shiftin' this way at you an' the dragoons." He shrugged. "So Cap'n—I mean Major Anson's slidin' up this way hisself, backin' the dragoons with lancers as he comes. Ever'thin's gettin' mighty sqwozed, an' if Cayce hadn't showed, ol' Agon coulda' just marched on past by the sea." He spat again. "What do you need?"

"Your men are already falling in on the line where we need them," Meder stated, relief still clear in his voice. Barca suspected the relief came mostly from having the decision he'd dreaded taken from him.

"Ammunition," Barca said.

Boogerbear shook his head. "Ain't got none for yer six pounders, but them howitzers were on the far left an' have mostly full chests. They ought'a take up the slack. Their caissons are comin', an' Dukane might still bring the center section up. Can't place it on the slope."

"Rifle ammunition," Meder abruptly added.

"On the way from the supply wagons," Boogerbear assured. "You got water here, right?"

"Yes sir. Several cisterns, some cleaner than others. There's no well."

"But enough for the men an' animals for a couple days?"

Meder considered the increased numbers and quality of water in the cisterns he'd seen. "Probably," he conceded guardedly, clear he expected this all to be settled before then, one way or another. "There's only one source I'd consider safe for men. If they have to drink from others, they may be . . . haunted with internal discomforts."

Boogerbear finally stepped down from his horse and handed him off to a waiting youngster before waving away Meder's concern. "Most'll get over that. They won't get over dyin' o' thirst." Looking at the gap in the wall, he added, "I know what you were discussin' back here, but it won't come to that. It *can't*," he stressed, drawing his revolvers and inspecting them. "Now let's get back in the fight."

In spite of the reinforcements, or possibly because of them, even in the face of renewed, withering, small arms fire, canister coughing from the howitzers and the final rounds from the 6pdrs—all of which strewed the slope with screeching wounded and dead, the ground actually *muddy* with blood—the Doms charged.

"Muskets, damn it! I want our muskets!" Hanny Cox shouted back at Sergeant O'Roddy. The Number Two gun was teetering badly now, the sound spokes no longer directly under the axle (it was hard to ensure that since the gun actually jumped up an inch or so each time it leaped back). The spokes were rarely in the same place when rolled back into battery. They'd made do by stopping a little short or long of their initial mark when Mac shouted that they were "good." The Number One gun kept firing solid shot with handfuls of gravel on top (First Sergeant Petty must understand how desperate they were to countenance scratching the gun's beautiful new bore), but Number Two wouldn't stand another shot. Most of its crew had once been infantry, however, and brought their Springfields with them. They weren't supposed to, but Sergeant Visser in the 3rd Pennsylvania had been discreet. It was just as well. O'Roddy had already called the men forward from the caissons and forge wagon, bringing the weapons stored there, and they quickly handed them out, along with full cartridge boxes.

"Fer what we're about tae receive," Mac grumbled, ramming a ball down his musket and affixing the bayonet."

"Aye, back ta smellin' their breath, it is," Hahessy agreed, already loaded and running his thumb along the edge of the flint to test it. Originally in the 1st US Infantry himself, he knew what to do. He hadn't been given a musket to "keep" before, but had Ricken's weapon now. Hanny was loading and peering down the hill at the surging, yelling horde when Barca and Boogerbear joined him.

"Not sure whether ta use this gun for cover or pull back an' hope it falls on the enemy," Boogerbear quipped. The left wheel wasn't the only damage. Many of the right wheel spokes were damaged as well, struck by musket balls. Even the axle was splintered in places. It was a miracle Hahessy and Mac were still alive.

"She's covered *all* of us for quite a while," Hanny snapped at the Ranger. Barca felt a surge of annoyance at Boogerbear's casual disparagement himself. He was right, of course, but even Barca, much newer to artillery than the men around him, already felt protective of the guns in his section. It was often said "every cannoneer loves his gun, even if the bitch doesn't love him back," but this gun and its sister had saved their lives so far.

"No offense, fellas," Boogerbear said mildly. "Just watch yourselves." Aiming a Paterson at a wild-eyed Dom struggling upward toward him, he fired. Mac and Hahessy weren't far behind him, then Hanny fired, and their different reloading drill began at a furious pace.

CHAPTER 31

T his ain't how you wanted it to go, is it?" Leonor asked Lewis Cayce, mounted beside him as always. Her short, dun-and-black-striped Sparky next to his tall, powerful, chestnut Arete made a contrasting but amiable pair. The battle was growing beyond anything she'd seen. Even if the numbers were similar to those at the Washboard, Agon hadn't stacked his regiments like Don Frutos did, and many more troops were actually in action at once. The scope of it all, and the crashing volleys and chest-thumping cannon fire was awesome and terrible. At the same time, she watched Lewis closely as well because, though he seemed excited by the battle to a degree, she could also tell he was deeply troubled. His army, tired as it was, had maneuvered to contact almost flawlessly, keeping near-perfect alignment despite robust fences designed to keep large beasts from destroying outlying crops and a kind of stunted orchard of what looked like plum trees that would've badly scattered less-disciplined troops. He had to be proud, and the sight was indeed stirring, but the bulk of the fighting was now under way upon that very rarest of things: a plain practically made for a battle.

"No," he confessed. "I wanted to get here first, of course, and force the enemy to attack a prepared position." He gestured at the hill and line of mounted troops to the northwest. "Not just your father and his much smaller force. I'm afraid they'll have suffered terribly. Still are." He sighed. "And the *last* thing I wanted was a stand-up fight in the open, where the enemy's numbers might still mean more than our better tactics and training. They can see everything we do, and any surprises will be difficult to create. So no matter what happens here today, it's going to be bloody for everyone." He paused. "There's one thing your father might do," he corrected, "that would kick a leg out from under Agon's chair. *If* he sees it and is able," he amended. "I'm sure he'll see the opportunity when it comes," he said with growing confidence, "I just don't know if he'll have the power to do anything about it."

Leonor didn't know what Lewis was talking about, but was certain her father would. She refused to finish that thought with the inevitable qualification: if he was still alive.

Har-Kaaska's 2nd Division was still in four regimental blocks, two deep and two abreast, the 1st Itzincab and 2nd Ocelomeh in the lead, trading volleys with the heavier Dom regiments opposite them while both batteries of 8pdrs advanced with the infantry, slashing the enemy ranks with canister. Strangely, the Doms hadn't extended their line to the east, which is what the 2nd Uxmal and 1st Techon remained in reserve to counter. It was as if Agon was still only thinking about matching Lewis's movements and deployments instead of forcing or preventing them. That left 2nd Division's reserve brigade a real reserve for the rest of the line, and another possible way to break the Doms. The 1st Uzmal and 1st US extended the line to the left, delivering searing, professional volleys as well. The 1st Ocelomeh and 3rd Pennsylvania were only lightly engaged at the moment, pushing hard against the re-forming regiments that had been assaulting Anson. A large percentage of those were still attacking the hill and its top was wreathed in smoke.

Seeing the "whole battle" was an unusual phenomenon and sensation; they hadn't even been able to do that at the Washboard because of the convoluted ground. This was how Leonor always imagined it must've been like at Waterloo, even though the various accounts her father made her read about it—or any battle—always made them seem "flatter" and more classically laid out than they could've been. Hindsight, even influencing participants' accounts, added to that. But here, now, it was really that way, and she could see it all from Sparky's saddle. So could the enemy. She suspected Agon himself was in a large mounted cluster behind the center of his army, surrounded by a cloud of red flags with crooked gold crosses on them. *I bet he's looking for Lewis*, she thought. But Lewis's small entourage shifted back and forth, and its members changed depending on where on the line he was. Only herself, Sal Hernandez, Reverend Harkin, Corporal Willis, and Dr. Newlin were "permanent" members, along with a large number of messengers. *That doesn't count Mistress Wilde, of course*, Leonor mused. The Englishwoman hadn't retreated to the baggage wagons as told, and now made herself scarce, fluttering around the periphery and trying to avoid Lewis's notice. As focused as Lewis often got in battle, she might've even succeeded. Leonor thought not.

Then again . . . A dusty, exhausted messenger had been passed through the ring, dressed like a dragoon but with greasy hair braided down the sides of his head in the Pidra Blanca style. *Not many Pidros with us*, Leonor thought as the kid said something to Lewis, who grinned and nodded. "Fall back on the baggage wagons, get something to eat and a fresh mount. Try to make it back if you can, and hurry them along." When the young man was gone, Lewis only said, "Colonel Itzam's Third Division is less than eight miles away." That's when Leonor saw, all of a sudden, Lewis's eyes flitting back and forth in that remote way he had when he became *part* of the battle, seeing, even *feeling* it all, as if it were unfolding in the palm of his hand. The missing piece of his puzzle was now in hand as well, and he could finally *plan*.

He couldn't just summon that state of mind, and it usually came on him unaware. He'd hated it once and tried to fight how detached he became, thinking he was a monster. Now he vaguely feared it wouldn't come when he needed it and he couldn't do what he must without it. He'd never admit that, would consider it a weakness, but Leonor knew it bothered him, and the longer "it" took to come over him, the more he worried.

Now his jaw worked as he raised his glass and evaluated the enemy, looking at their faces to see how they *felt*, watched whether they loaded their weapons with firm or trembling hands, considered and rejected a dozen actions at once, or built on them and went down some very twisty "what if" trails. *Injins prob'ly do that when they're huntin'*, Leonor thought. *Knowin' all the habits of their prey in general, they instinctively note the ground, wind direction, age of a track, an' whether the critter was runnin' or just amblin' along. Then they get in the head of the particular critter they're after: Is it goin' to food or bed? Does it know somethin's after it? Will it double back? Go high or low, an' why?* There were thousands of variables they probably never consciously calculated. They just knew. *That's how Lewis gets,* Leonor thought, and was proud of her sudden insight.

"Marvin!" Lewis shouted after another somewhat extended volley by the First US as he urged Arete toward the regiment's mounted commander, Major Marvin Beck. Beck's aide, Lieutenant Malcom Harris, ducked a little when a Dom roundshot shrieked past, one of the first directed at them, and Beck gave him a look.

"Sir?" he replied to Lewis in the momentary near-quiet that followed. The Dom line was about seventy-five yards away and were loading at present as well, standing in a hedge of yellow-and-black-clad corpses. Lewis flinched visibly at the similar, if thankfully lesser, number of blue-clad forms lying around Beck's men. *This is already costing too much, and it's killing him,* Leonor thought grimly. But Lewis was "in" the battle now and didn't let his feelings touch his voice when he said, "Enough of this foolishness. Time to move forward and get on with our business, don't you think?" Pressing the enemy would be costly, but no more than this drawn-out, formalized butchery.

Beck grinned relief. "I do indeed, sir."

"Messengers," Lewis called behind him. "General advance, signaled from here. Har-Kaaska will extend his line with the First Techon on the march, while detaching the Second Uxmal under Warmaster Varaa to the far left at the double time. I'll join her as she passes, and Major Beck will command here after that." Beck looked surprised but didn't interrupt. "The enemy may try to match Har-Kaaska's movement," Lewis continued, "but will just as likely shy toward their center or try to refuse the flank. Either way, the First Itzincab and Second Ocelomeh will make the most of the confusion and *charge* while the First Techon performs a left wheel to smash that flank. Understood?"

"Sir!" cried an Itzincabo messenger.

"Very well," Lewis said, then gestured for him to go. Pulling the striped, wide-eyed horse's head around, the Itzincabo galloped off to the right.

"And we're to just keep grinding forward?" Beck asked.

"Sorry, yes," Lewis agreed. "The First US, Third Pennsylvania, and First Uxmal. Messengers to Major Ulrich and Major Manley," he instructed. When two more riders raced off, he said, "I'll signal you when we, meaning Varaa and the Second Uxmal, join Consul Koaar and the First Ocelomeh.

When you sound the general advance and commence the assault, we'll smash through the Doms on the left that remain in disarray and attempt to relieve Major Anson's forces on the hill."

"And we'll have the Doms in a sack," Beck mused.

"A weak, fraying sack by then, I fear," Lewis warned, "but a sack after all, which can't instill confidence. Agon's no fool, and he knows Colonel Itzam and Third Division must be drawing near, which they are," he assured, then snorted. "I expect another opportunity to talk to Agon, about then."

"Understood," Beck said.

"Good." Lewis grinned. "Then let's have some music to fight to! I recommend 'The Old 1812.' Agon will remember that."

Drums thundered and fifes skirled, and the popular tune commenced and spread. The fighting continued, Doms still suffering the worst by far as massed musketry and canister swept into them, but seeming almost content to continue like this until the matter was resolved. Perhaps they were, or Agon was, imagining this the "proper" form a battle should take. Lewis wasn't content at all and was relieved when Varaa arrived at the head of the Second Uxmal, trotting in column. He nodded a greeting at his Mi-Anakka friend, then turned Arete to the left. "Follow me," he called. Leonor, Sal, and Corporal Willis did as a matter of course, but so did Reverend Harkin and Dr. Newlin. Samantha Wilde as well, though she held back by Varaa, who blinked questioningly at her.

"Shush, Varaa," she said sternly. "If he hasn't noticed I'm here, I shan't take it well if you tell him."

"Not me," Varaa said, blinking and flipping her tail, arched up over her saddle cantle. "My perspective is different from most, even in my homeland, but I don't believe anyone should be prevented from fighting a battle they believe in, certainly not simply because they're female. Do you have a weapon?"

Samantha patted tooled and brass-accented pommel holsters. "A brace of captured Dom pistols. Quite nice ones, in fact, and carefully loaded just this morning," she said with a touch of pride. "They were an engagement present of sorts from Major Anson," she explained with an ironic smile.

"Good," Varaa replied lowly. "Idiots get those around them killed. I'd consider you one if you hadn't armed yourself."

Leonor caught that exchange. So did Reverend Harkin, who didn't tattle, but frowned very deep disapproval. Dr. Newlin pretended ignorance, and Willis, already unhappier than usual over the unprecedented amount of time he'd spent in a saddle, just said, "Shit," likely expecting it would fall to him to protect her. It was possible Lewis, farther ahead, might still be unaware of Samantha. Or perhaps, having accepted Leonor's status as a combatant as a matter of course, rather shared Varaa's philosophy now. Either way, he had a new vision for the battle and nothing would distract him but changes in the battle itself. That was confirmed by the fact that, at some point during their ride around to the left flank of the army, he'd drawn his M1840 artillery saber without even seeming to realize it. Another sure sign he had, or was about to, set everything he thought necessary to victory in motion. *There'll be no keeping him out of it either,* Leonor reflected resignedly. In truth, she was more than ready to join the fight herself.

The 1st Ocelomeh was already pressing hard when Lewis and Varaa brought the 2nd Uxmal in behind. The bloodied, exhausted opposition had never properly coalesced, and was still weakened by the loss of battalions assaulting the hill. Dom fire was desultory as the Ocelomeh—all dressed as regular infantry now—savaged them with disciplined volleys.

"Colonel Cayce!" Consul Koaar greeted happily as Lewis and Leonor joined him, outpacing the rest.

"Consul." Lewis smiled in return. "Captain Gomez." He nodded at Koaar's aide. "It seems you've prepared the enemy well for what we're about to do."

"I certainly hope so," Koaar agreed. "What *are* we about to do?"

Lewis chuckled. "Warmaster Varaa is bringing the Second Uxmal up, and I've sent for Captain Olayne's battery as well. It was . . . underutilized against the Dom center, and we can make better use of it. As soon as he arrives and the Uxmalos catch their breath, we'll signal Major Beck, who'll sound a 'general advance.' We'll be part of that, but our objective is more ambitious than just pushing the enemy back."

Koaar grinned, exposing wicked canines, tail whipping in anticipation.

━━━━━

"I can't see *anything* for the smoke!" General Agon complained, straining to stand as high in his stirrups as he could and waving ineffectually at the dense, white, sulfurous cloud enveloping everything. It was as bad as the fog had been—except the fog hadn't been thick with deadly, shrieking projectiles. It was also more localized. Capitan Ead Arevalo knew the capricious wind had pushed more smoke from the fighting on the hill and their own artillery down on them, and the visibility was actually better than he liked just a short distance to the front. He'd just returned from there—and it might be just as well his general couldn't see what was happening. Agon had come to love the army he'd built, and desperately relied on it to save his country from the usurper Don Julio and the Blood Priests. He hadn't sought this battle and would've avoided it if he could—the very idea of avoiding battle with *heretics* was proof of his dedication to his greater cause—but Arevalo's short inspection showed him that cause was doomed. He had no doubt that Agon's army was the best-trained, most highly disciplined (not only by fear) force the Holy Dominion had ever placed in the field, but he'd seen in a moment that it was slowly dying, like a stupendous *serpiente*, bristling with a thousand arrows. The men were standing firm, dealing death as they took it, but they simply couldn't *advance*. That boiled down to the bitter fact that the enemy was better yet, man to man, and their sheer volume of fire had destroyed every effort to close with them. Attacks started well enough, the men still willing, but their cohesion shattered almost at once, often by *artillery* that just appeared in front of them out of the smoke as if by magic, and all the strength and coordination of the attack was lost. Those who could limped back to the line and kept fighting, but it was the best they could do. This he'd reluctantly reported to his general.

"We'll wear them down eventually," Arevalo consoled. "We still have the numbers."

"But they're killing us at *least* two to one," Agon seethed back. "At that rate, they'll soon have the 'numbers' to swamp *us*." He gestured vaguely to the east. "Particularly when their other force arrives! No, our only chance is a concerted attack by everything we have all at once, up and down the line! Their demon-crewed artillery is moving to meet attacks they see building, but they don't have enough guns to put them everywhere!" He clutched his ears in furious frustration. "And I want that damnable music *stopped*!"

The enemy had begun serenading them with the same jaunty tune they'd defeated them to at the Washboard and Agon had been enraged, remembering it all too well. No doubt many of the veterans in the ranks recalled it also. Other tunes followed, all bizarrely cheerful in some inexpressible way, yet undeniably martial at the same time. The thundering drums accompanying the squealing flutelike instruments saw to that. It reminded Arevalo of the irreverent dance music enjoyed by the lower classes, not appropriate for the solemnity of a battlefield at all, and he had a very strange thought: *Battle is like a dance to them, even more than us. But our "proper" dances are very solemn, with carefully choreographed, ritualized, even religiously significant steps. Their . . . livelier music lends itself better to improvisation, even . . . spontaneity.* He started to point that out to his general, abruptly sure it was significant, but he didn't have time. A bugle sounded over the roar, echoed by others, and all the guns facing them flared in the smoke, pummeling their chests with pressure and ravaging horses or tossing men from saddles even here. A massive volley, thousands of smaller, duller flashes, swept down from the right, followed by screams of pain. It flowed right across in front of them and continued on to the left, but the thumping crackle of musketry was immediately joined by a growing roar, expectant, terrified, exultant, and savage.

Arevalo turned to Agon in horror but saw his general was down, leg pinned under his writhing black horse, face set in a grimace.

"My general!" he cried, leaping off his own animal and pulling a pistol from his sword belt. Drawing the hammer to full cock, he touched the wounded horse's head behind its eye with the muzzle and squeezed the trigger. The pan flashed, and for an instant he thought the too-long-loaded weapon had misfired, but then it *banged* and jumped in his hand and the horse went stiff and quivered. Thrusting the smoking pistol back in his belt, he dragged General Agon clear. "Help me!" he roared at other stunned staff and messengers.

"I'm fine, the leg's not broken," Agon declared with a hiss. It might not be broken, but it clearly hurt. "Fetch me a fresh mount!" he shouted, then looked up at Arevalo and said, barely audible over the crashing surf of screaming and desperate fighting, growing quickly closer. "They beat us to it, didn't they? That *demonio* Cayce *beat me to it* and charged his whole army at *us!*"

"I'm afraid so, my general," Arevalo agreed as the first spurt of wounded, bewildered, or just terrified men started running past in the smoke. Most had no weapons.

All it took was a single musket ball shattering one more spoke and the Number Two gun started to fall with a snapping, crackling sound as loud as the fighting. The gun itself was no longer firing, and it wouldn't have mattered if the wheel failed now, except for two things: First, they'd never move it if they had to pull back and it might still fall into enemy hands. Second, quite a few men were using it for cover as they fired their muskets, and in just the space of a breath, it was sure to collapse right on top of Preacher Mac and Hanny Cox, killing or maiming them both.

Barca saw it happening as if time had slowed to a crawl in one way, while leaving no time to even shout a warning. All he could do was drop the wounded Ranger's carbine he'd been using and lace his fingers under the hub and heave with all the strength in his legs and back. He hadn't even thought about it. Now he did. *The last spokes are giving way. I'm too small and not nearly strong enough. Now the gun will crush me as well.* That's when he saw something he was even less prepared for. At the same instant he'd acted, the hulking Private Hahessy dropped his own musket and grabbed the top of the opposite wheel, heaving back with all his might. Corded muscles bulged through tattered and bloody shirtsleeves and vessels popped out on his reddening neck, his face a rictus of impossible effort. He didn't have the right leverage, simply wasn't *heavy* enough to counterweight nearly half of an unsupported ton, but between his effort and Barca's, they slowed the inevitable long enough for others to shout warnings (neither could talk), and Apo to snatch the handspike from the trail and pass it under the axle. Another man took it, then another, then Kini Hau joined Apo on his end. Hanny and Mac scurried clear, as did Barca and Hahessy, finally relieved after several eternal seconds, and Apo shouted, "Let fall!" The four men on the handspike jumped clear, and the gun crashed down.

"Thank God!" Mac hissed, pulling his and Hanny's muskets out from under the wreck. Neither was damaged, but anything the size of a man would've been smashed.

"What about me, damn ye?" gasped Hahessy in a surly tone retrieving his own weapon and resuming reloading it.

"Aye, an' you too, ye mad, poxy Irishman!"

"Thank you both," Hanny said. "Thank you all," he added to Apo and the others, already rejoining the fight. Oddly, his tone sounded more like the "old" Hanny now. He seemed to notice it himself, and shook his head as if coming out of a daze.

Barca still stood with hands on knees, trying to catch his breath. "I didn't know I had it in me." He tried to laugh, but couldn't.

"Me neither," Hahessy said sharply, raising his musket to fire. After he did, he looked briefly back. "Seems there's more to the both of us than either thought o' the other, Lieutenant Barca," he said roughly, "er even ourselves, come ta that," he added before pulling another cartridge from the black leather box at his side and tearing the paper with his teeth. Priming his musket, he dumped the rest of the powder down the barrel, followed by the paper-wrapped ball, and rammed it all down. Raising the weapon, he quickly fired again. "Jus' gonna stand congratulatin' yourselves the rest o' the day, are ye?" he demanded harshly. "The godless bastards're nearly on us, an' I'll not stop 'em by me'self!"

He was right. Hundreds of Doms were within pistol shot now, coming on with a grim new intensity. They knew the hill had been reinforced, and Boogerbear's Rangers had already helped throw them back once, but there were more Doms as well, probably everyone not involved in the fight on the plain, and they fought like they knew this was *it*. *This* time, they'd sweep over the defenders and take the hill, or they'd never summon the strength and courage to try again. They were using it all up in one final effort. So were the men on the hill. The howitzers slammed out a final murderous spread of canister before their crews took up fallen weapons and fought from the cover of their guns like Barca's section was already doing. Carbines thumped and boomed dully but continuously while riflemen dropped naked balls down fouling-choked barrels and fired without patches. Their excellent, deadly weapons were actually *less* accurate than muskets when used that way, and they'd have hell cleaning lead out of rifling, but they had to shoot faster to earn time for that later.

The wreck of the Number Two gun was near the center of the defensive crescent and drawing the most attention, so that's where Boogerbear and Felix Meder both gravitated, Meder's rifle still choosing Dom leaders when possible, Boogerbear's pistols firing at screaming shapes clawing over the breastworks. The fighting was more intimate for the rest. *Hanny, Apo, and Mac make a good team*, Barca thought, *two always jabbing or thrusting bayonets while one reloads and shoots their most troublesome opponent*. That might not work if the Doms could reload as well, but most who'd reached the breastworks had inserted their plug bayonets—wicked weapons in their own right, but now their muskets were little more than spears. Barca whipped his "found" carbine to his shoulder and shot a smoke-shrouded figure poised to stab Hanny. The man's black tricorn tumbled away in a spray of blood and bone as the Dom sprawled back on his comrades. Hanny sent him a quick, thankful nod before returning to his work. *Damn*, Barca thought, already reloading. *I aimed as his chest.*

Hahessy fought differently, roaring and cursing, stabbing and battering, brutally ripping bodies open with his bayonet or bashing out brains with the buttplate of his musket. His antics drew a crowd of enemies, as he no doubt intended, but he wasn't fighting alone. Even as Barca reloaded his carbine, he noted little Kini Hau crouching behind Hahessy, stabbing at men who sought openings between the much larger man's extravagant blows. They never practiced that, Barca knew. It just . . . happened. It dawned on him then that, after everything, Hahessy had found a home. Not only did someone—and it could've been anyone on this gun crew, at least—care enough about the unpleasant man to watch his back, Hahessy trusted them to do it. *Well, he's slowly proven he can be trusted, and especially so today*, Barca mused.

With only a carbine and no pike, like many of the Rangers had brought, Barca stayed a little back from the main point of contact. Not all the Doms had plugged their muskets, and plenty of balls still whizzed through the smoky air around him. Glancing to the side, he saw Captain Meder standing calmly upright beside Boogerbear as if they hadn't a care in the world. The big Ranger acted like he always did: no shouting, no gesturing, only telling breathless messengers what to tell someone else and sending them on their way, all while firing his revolvers or double-barrel shotgun at whatever target drew his eye. Sometimes he'd talk to Felix while they both reloaded.

Felix tried to act the same, but did occasionally shout encouragement to his men. *He's not a "proper" officer, any more than I am, but he knows how to act like one*, Barca thought.

"Ah, Lieutenant Barca! Good shot a moment ago!" Felix exclaimed loudly enough for some of those fighting to hear. High praise, coming from him, since Felix was probably the best marksman in the world with his rifle. His tone was cheerful enough, but just as brittle as Barca's when he replied, "Thank you, sir. Hard to miss at that range." Of course, he *had* missed what he aimed at, but that didn't matter. He'd figuratively stepped up on the theater stage with the other actors, performing for the men. He appraised Boogerbear for an instant. *No, Felix and I are the only actors here.* He spoke again, as quietly as he could. "I've read quite a lot and know it's often done. I've *seen* Colonel Cayce do it, but does it really help to stand in the open like this? Like targets?" To his surprise, Boogerbear answered.

"Sure. You catch fellas lookin' back now an' then, prob'ly thinkin' we're crazy, but also that we ain't scared. Steadies 'em. Can't exactly lead from the front, right now. Mixed up on the line, nobody'd see us. So we lead from behind, as it were, but up close where we're sharin' the risk, see?"

"But what *good* does it do?" Felix asked.

Boogerbear seemed to consider that. "Once the metal starts flyin', nobody's fightin' for the cause no more. That's what brings 'em *to* the fight, but they forget it when the shootin' starts. Country too. Even their homes an' fam'lies. They might think o' their poor, aged ma when they're hurt, but they ain't fightin' for her. The good ones ain't even fightin' for themselves anymore, but for their pals around 'em. That's their only real fam'ly in battle; fellas they respect, an' want respect from. They won't skedaddle with those fellas watchin', nor us neither if they respect *us*. They ain't as scared o' the enemy, even o' dyin', as they are their pals—or us—thinkin' they're yella."

"That's why the Doms are fighting harder this time," Barca deduced. "It's not just fear of what'll happen to them if they don't. Not anymore. They're fighting for their army, for each other as well."

"Right."

"What makes *you* fight, Captain Beeryman?" Felix asked.

Boogerbear shrugged. "Respect o' my pals comes into it. Cap'n Anson, Leonor, Sal . . . even you fellas. But mostly, I'm good at it . . . an' it's kinda excitin', ain't it?" He confessed the last with the closest thing to bashfulness either had ever seen in him.

An explosion of blue wool fuzz and blood vapor sprayed Barca's face, and Felix Meder was hurled to the ground. Boogerbear and Barca crouched by him, tearing his jacket open, launching brass buttons. Blood was quickly soaking his white shirt, and Boogerbear ripped that as well.

"Jesus, I'm shot!" Meder hissed.

"Yep," Boogerbear agreed. "Ain't too bad, though. Straight through, under the skin in yer side. Might'a nicked a short rib." He tore more of the shirt apart and started packing it around the wound.

"I'll live?"

"Prob'ly," Boogerbear answered, matter-of-fact. "Seen lotsa fellas live through worse, even without the better medicine our healers got here."

"Then help me up," Meder gasped, starting to refasten his few remaining buttons.

"Felix!" Barca objected, "you should go to the rear!" He started to wave for stretcher bearers to approach from behind the villa wall, where they'd been collecting the wounded.

"No, I'm staying, and I'm standing. If Captain Beeryman's right, my men at least will respect me more for it!"

Perhaps they did. Maybe everyone did, because the battle on the hill suddenly redoubled, the defenders fighting even harder, yelling louder. The riflemen had bayonets too, but as long as they could still shoot at all, they'd been less anxious to use them than the Rangers with their pikes, or the cluster of artillerymen with infantry experience. Now they charged forward, bayonets bristling and quickly turning red, Doms reeling back in surprise or agony.

"Let them have it!" Hanny Cox roared, voice cracking and breaking. Riflemen and Rangers around the howitzers pushed the enemy back far enough for the left gun's crew to load it. Yellowish smoke exploded outward for the first time in a while, and there came the terrible, rapid *whopping* sound of dozens of balls striking flesh all at once. Doms screamed and moaned, some bellowed frustration—especially when they saw more exhausted, reeling, filthy reinforcements filing in from the left. Barca blinked in surprise to see the dragoons, Hall carbines dripping black water as someone—Coryon Burton!—ladled it on them as they passed by a bucket someone brought from a cistern. Firing grew as dragoons used their shirts to wipe soupy black crud off their breechblocks, cocked up at an angle, and dry them on shirttails hanging down past their jackets. Popping a couple of loud Uxmal caps to dry their weapons further, they loaded and rejoined the fight.

Burton handed the ladle to another man and came over by Barca. He looked positively ghastly. Red-eyed and covered in black fouling and blood, he resembled Barca's artillerymen more than any dragoon he'd ever seen. "You all right, Felix?" Burton asked Meder. "You've got a new hole in you, and seem a tad pale."

"Just disappointed. I thought my survival had raised the men's spirits. I might've known it was the arrival of our dashing dragoons instead."

"Not very dashing at present," Burton denied, "and I doubt it was us." He gestured forward. "See for yourself."

As quickly as the firing had intensified, it was already falling off. The Doms weren't exactly running away, but they were edging back, and as Burton, Barca, Meder, and Boogerbear moved up behind Hanny Cox and the rest of the gasping crew of the Number Two gun, they saw the enemy didn't really have anywhere to go. The howitzers and Rangers had probably made taking the hill impossible, but the arrival of the dragoons only reinforced the futility of further attempts. To make matters worse, there was suddenly *sky-blue-clad infantry with white crossbelts* at the bottom of the hill, and the Doms were cut off. A line of that unexpected infantry was facing up at them now, not shooting, but three other lines were pouring volleys into a collapsing, disorganized mob trying to pull back to the east to rejoin the larger mass of Dom troops. And the other two sections of Hudgens's battery were down there as well, quickly unlimbering. Hanny, Mac, Rini and Apo, even Hahessy, raised cracking voices in cheers as "their" other two 6pdrs and two 12pdrs added their weight to the argument.

More than that, though it was hard to be sure through the haze of smoke, it appeared the Doms on the other side, a couple of miles away, were peeling back to the center as well. *Yes!* Barca saw the new flags of 1st Techon and Second Ocelomeh hemming them in.

"Oh my," Felix Meder whispered.

Barca thought he'd collapse against the wrecked gun carriage in relief, but something caught his eye. "What's that?" he cried, pointing to their right where the hill curved back toward the lake. A dozen or so riders were galloping up, staying clear of retreating Dom infantry but exchanging a few shots all the same. All wore dark blue jackets and wheel hats so no one on the hill fired at them. Moments later, Colonel Cayce's magnificent horse leaped over the breastworks between the Number Two gun and the howitzer to its left and trotted in an anxious circle, blowing hard.

"Well done! Well done, by God! You held them just long enough," Lewis shouted for all to hear, saber still in his hand. It looked like it had seen some use. "It's my fault it took us so long to arrive, and I'm very, very sorry. I should've known . . . but I *did* know you'd hold! You're the best soldiers on this Godforsaken world, and I couldn't be prouder of you all. . . ." He seemed close to tears. Leonor's Sparky jumped the breastworks next, followed by Varaa, Sal Hernandez, Willis, several outrageously clean dragoons, Reverend Harkin, more dragoons . . . Barca—and Major Anson—would later learn Dr. Newlin had originally accompanied Colonel Cayce, but remained with Koaar as much to help with wounded as to *force* Samantha Wilde to stay with the larger force. The Englishwoman was popular with the army, and her attachment to Anson was well-known. That she'd tried to join him in the heat of battle only raised her stature, as did—amusingly—the argument Reverend Harkin finally used to prevail upon her: "My dear," he'd said with perfect sincerity, gesturing sadly at the modest but fashionable day dress she wore, "I'm afraid you simply aren't dressed for it."

In any event, in spite of their suffering and misery and all they'd endured, in spite of Lewis's confession (true or not, nobody cared), he hadn't forgotten his mounted force at all, he'd come as fast as he could, saved them in grand fashion—and ridden right up a hill under fire to greet them himself. They cheered.

"Y'see?" Boogerbear said lowly to Barca. "He cares about 'em an' respects 'em, so they care about him back. Even better, he gives 'em victories. They *love* him for that. Damned if they wouldn't march through hell for him." He shrugged. "I guess they kinda have." Raising his voice, he called, "Hidy, Sal. Glad you made it." Looking at Leonor, he beamed through the grime on his face and in his tangled beard.

"Who's in charge, here?" Lewis asked.

"Could be me or Meder or Burton," Boogerbear said, then tilted his head slightly to the side. Neither of those young men would give him an order and pretending otherwise was ridiculous. "Me, I guess."

"Are you well, Captain Meder?"

"Yes sir. Just a scrape."

"Glad to hear it. Where's Major Anson?" Lewis asked anxiously. Leonor's expression never changed, but Boogerbear knew she was worried.

"He's down with Mr. Lara's lancers," Burton supplied. "Probably getting them mounted by now and bringing the rest of our horses up." He grinned. "He *knew* you'd come, sir, and knew you'd want us mounted when you did."

Lewis looked at Sal, who nodded back and galloped off in search of his friend. "I do," Lewis told Burton. "All who can ride."

Word was spreading that they were going to mount up and "finish the Doms," and men were gulping water, feverishly cleaning weapons and generally rushing about. Reverend Harkin rode among them, praising them for their valor and getting in the way, but the men didn't seem to mind. Hahessy was cleaning his own musket by the simple expedient of spitting water down the barrel and squirting it through the vent with his rammer head wrapped with a piece of his shirt. When the greasy black stream dribbled to a stop, he ran the rammer up and down a few times, then drew it out and removed the now jet-black piece of wet cloth, which he used to wipe fouling out of the pan and off the lock. Tearing off more shirt, he proceeded to dry everything in a similar way, but caught Lewis's eye while he did so.

"Private Hahessy," Lewis acknowledged neutrally. Of course he remembered the big man. He was quite distinctive, and he'd once nearly had him hanged. "You seem to have made yourself of use, at last."

Hahessy frowned, but Barca spoke up. "He did, sir. Quite valiantly." He looked at Hanny and the others. "All my men did, and losses were severe on the Number One gun. This one's out of action, but only until we replace the wheel. Speaking of which . . ." He turned to see Sergeant O'Roddy and another man rolling the spare up behind them. First Sergeant Petty and several more men had come over from the Number One gun to help mount it. Barca grinned. "Speaking of which, never mind."

Hahessy laughed. "Colonel Cayce, if ye please, I've a small complaint ta report." Mac and Hanny glowered at him, but he ignored them. "It's my understandin', sir, that our section o' Mr. Hudgens's battery is the only unit in the army that didn't elect its own officer."

Lewis was frowning now as well, and Leonor looked furious. Varaa was grinning hugely and blinking something no one could read. "Untrue," Lewis said sharply. "We've had to appoint quite a few officers, for their experience, to some of the newer units."

"Aye," Hahessy amiably agreed, "but we ain't one o' *them*, now are we? No." He looked hard at Barca, then back at Lewis. "I think it's only proper for us so'jers ta exercise the rights ye granted us, an' I want it on record that I, Daniel Hahessy, nominate *Mr. Barca* for our Lieutenant." He glared around. "Vote 'aye,' damn ye all, or I'll choke the life out o' ye, I will!"

The rising tension around him shattered, and men exploded in laughter and a chorus of "ayes." Barca felt stunned, looking around at the battered, bloody men, all grinning at him. *I haven't done anything, really*, he thought, *but they've accepted me anyway. Even* him. He loved them for it. Probably like Hahessy in another respect, he had a home for the first time as well.

Varaa was nodding. She'd seen it, somehow, and even Colonel Cayce was smiling now. "I'll take it under advisement," he said dryly to another round of laughter.

"What the hell? We ain't got time for foolin' around!" Anson bellowed, riding up beside Ramon Lara, whose arm was in a bloody sling again. The same arm as before. About four hundred tired, scruffy lancers were strung out behind them. At least their horses were fresh. Anson looked around disgustedly. "What a sorry, worn-out-lookin' bunch. Busted guns, half-dead troops—ain't fit ta shoo flies off a turd." His severe expression broke. "But I bet there's *two thousand* dead Doms on the slope o' this hill, an' I think we can summon the gumption ta add some more!"

"It's good to see you too, Major Anson," Lewis said ironically. Leonor didn't go to her father but was smiling with relief.

"Sal's bringin' the rest of the horse-holders up," Anson continued more seriously. "Dukane's wounded an' his two sections of howitzers still down below are shot out. I figured to leave 'em in place with support as a deterrent." He gestured down the hill at the milling Dom soldiers. No one was shooting at them now, but they weren't shooting either. "We need to leave some troops here too. Walkin' wounded who can still fight, at least, so how many saddles can we fill?"

Meder and Burton quickly conferred with Boogerbear. "'Tween the Rangers an' rifles an' dragoons who just joined us, we can mount a thousand," Boogerbear said.

"We need four horses," Barca said abruptly, earning a nod from O'Roddy. "We lost that many, shot down in the traces."

"We've already unhooked 'em," O'Roddy reported. "Four more for the howitzers. An' they lost their officer," he added with a look at Barca.

"Fine," Barca said, effectively accepting command of a short battery. He looked challengingly at Lewis. The Number Two gun's shattered wheel had been replaced while they talked, but the whole carriage was shot to pieces and whiskered with splinters from musket balls. The Number One gun would be just as bad, and Barca realized he needed to spend time with its crew, now. Especially since most were replacements. The howitzer crew to the left was watching.

"Have you any ammunition left at all?" Lewis asked gently.

"Solid shot," Barca answered at once. They still had quite a lot of that in the chests on the caissons. He looked questioningly at the howitzer crew, and the gunner stepped over the trail to stand before him. "We have six rounds of canister and six exploding case. I expect the other twelve pounder has about the same. They can't shoot any faster than us," he added proudly.

Barca looked back at Lewis, who was nodding. "That's enough to be useful, and the Doms won't know any better." He scrutinized the young gunner. "The question is, are you game for more?"

The kid—he really was just a kid, like Hanny—glanced at Barca. *Just like me too*, Barca acknowledged. The gunner nodded. "Hell yes . . . sir. We want to *whip* them this time, not just run them off."

Lewis arched a brow. "Very well. That's the idea, and this is what we're going to do. . . ."

―――――

It couldn't really be said that General Agon was "behind" the lines of his army now, because those lines had grown hopelessly entangled as both flanks peeled back upon him. He was at the rear, however, because what was left of the Army of God's Vengeance now stood between him and the enemy on three sides, and the only thing behind him and his diminished staff was the beach and the sea. Even back there, he was exposed, remounted beneath his cluster of flags for all to see on another shiny black stallion. By some miracle, he hadn't been wounded beyond the wrenched and painful leg, but he was in agony nevertheless, his heart torn to shreds as his army died around him. He'd never poured so much of himself into anything as he had this army, and as it died and contracted inward, he felt his soul do the same. "And now we're effectively surrounded," he remarked with despair.

"As thinly as if by the shell of an egg. We still have more men than they do," General Tun rasped, arms firmly crossed over his chest as if holding his ribs in place. He'd been carried back from the collapsing right after his horse fell and rolled on him. His teeth were pink with blood, and he spat it out constantly. Agon was sure he had internal injuries, broken ribs at least, but Tun had demanded another horse and now faced the storm beside him.

"Not for long," Agon replied miserably. He couldn't see it through the gunsmoke himself, but it had been reported that a heavy cloud of dust was rising in the east. That would be Coronel Itzam and the fresh division that had followed them all the way down from Nautla.

"Then we must break through *now*," Tun pressed.

Agon just looked at him. "How?" he demanded. "This army has been battered into the shape of a *ball*. It's a desperate *mob*, with every regiment intermingled. As it is, it still fights—by firing in all directions—but if I tell the . . . western half to attack toward Gran Lago while the eastern half holds the forces to our east and south, what do you think will happen?"

"The . . . eastern half will break through to the city!" Tun declared.

"I think so as well," Agon agreed, "with barely five or six thousand men fit to fight, no artillery, and little ammunition," he countered relentlessly. "It will be of no use at all in catching and defeating Tranquilo and stopping the Blood Priests. In the meantime, the 'eastern half,' no longer supported from behind, will panic and be slaughtered." Agon blinked and looked at his hands. "I formed this army as well as I could, with the finest material left to us. But what 'formed' me as a general? High status due to an accident of birth, a little experience with savages on the frontier, and a *single* meeting with *properly shaped* officers led by an imaginative and flexible commander I continue to underestimate—even as I *scream* at myself not to! I thought I'd learned from him—and I did, a few things—but nowhere near everything Coronel Cayce had to teach." He laughed bitterly. "The worst of it is, we even deduced his strategy, and he *still* outmaneuvered us because he has men like El Diablo Anson—and who knows how many more?—who can move independently of him. Could probably *replace* him if they had to! Who do I have besides you, General Tun, who could even complete my own modest schemes?" He looked thoughtfully at Capitan Arevalo, sitting silently on his nervous horse while cannon boomed and musketry crackled, and the ball shrank ever smaller. He shook his head. It didn't matter.

"God will grant us victory, when we suffer enough to earn it," Tun declared, but he sounded less than certain.

Agon snorted. "Don't be absurd. You sound like Tranquilo yourself! God has *abandoned* us because we abandoned *Him* long ago!" He gestured around. "There is abundant proof. The enemy still worships the very same God as those who brought The Blood to this world in the first place! Even if our leaders, and certainly those such as Tranquilo, have forgotten this, those in our order of soldiers know it's true." His eyes went wide. "Cayce, the enemy, all of them . . . they're the *true* instruments of the *one* God our people have forgotten, sent to destroy those who serve . . ." He covered his face with his hands. "Oh no," he murmured. "All who've died here today for God, for decades, for almost *two centuries* of Dominion rule, have instead died for a usurper far worse than Don Julio!"

Arevalo looked very troubled indeed. "Either you speak blasphemy, my general, or . . ." He paused, expression torn by a mounting horror beyond anything he'd seen that day. "Or our cause, all along, has been that of *el verdadero* Diablo. The *true* Devil," he almost whispered.

Can it all be that remarkably, hideously simple? Agon silently begged of himself, and a God he was suddenly certain wasn't listening to him at all. *Of course, the God of the Dominion never* hears, *does He? He only* watches *and glories in suffering and pain and death like some demented, voyeuristic . . .*

"My general!" cried Coronel Uza, bashing his horse through stunned and milling infantry who didn't know where to go. Agon looked at him, disassociated for a moment, utterly adrift, deserving to die.

Apparently at a loss for words himself, Coronel Uza could only point behind them with his saber. At the sea. Bugles were blaring and a long line of horsemen was clearing the grassy dunes by the shoreline, surging up from the beach. A beach touching the nearly unmolested left of the blocking force's fortifications, and which couldn't be seen from the battle plain. *Of course,* Agon thought dispassionately, then turned to the west and gazed at Anson's line once more. There were still heads peering over the breastworks and a few guns here and there, but nothing like there'd been. *They've emptied their line, possibly all the way up the hill.* Not that it mattered now. More enemy infantry and artillery were moving to interpose themselves. Some were turning his own abandoned cannon against him.

"That will be El Diablo Anson himself, I shouldn't wonder," Agon said without inflection, looking back at the advancing horsemen. "More than a thousand mounted men, aimed directly at our utterly distracted and unprepared rear. And look!" he said, something bizarrely almost like enthusiasm creeping into his tone. "They've even brought a battery of guns! How do they *move* them like that? So rapidly, so much like . . . quicksilver flowing across the palm of one's hand!"

The milling infantry started to panic, pushing, shoving, voices rising. The terror would quickly spread. Even men on the firing line would soon be distracted, try to pull back. They'd been through too much—*and for nothing!* Agon suddenly knew. Wincing at the pain in his leg, he stood as high in his stirrups as he could and tried to shout over the roar of battle and growing bedlam.

"Cease firing! Cease firing!" He looked at the red flags with jagged gold crosses fluttering around him. "Throw those down!" he shouted at the men holding them.

General Tun said nothing. Arevalo looked shocked, but was beginning to nod understanding.

Coronel Uza's eyes bulged. "What are you doing? You can't do this! Better to die for God than surrender to heretics!"

Agon looked at him. "Yes!" he cried, "I'll fight to the death for God, for this army, but I'll spill no more blood to amuse the Devil, and that's all we've ever done! God, the *real* God, is *not* on our side, and I don't say that just because we've lost. *We* are the heretics! Surely that should be clear to you now. This entire campaign has been cursed from the start, just as the one before it. We attacked the only people left in this land who worship a God who doesn't enjoy their misery and were repulsed at Nautla, marched through hell and were harried by El Diablo all the way here. Your lancers were *annihilated*." He waved at the disaster unfolding around them. "Now this! *We* have been the playthings of the Devil and done his bidding far too long."

"Blasphemy!" Uza shrieked, pulling his long, brass-barreled pistol from his sash. It shone like dull gold in the sun as he pointed it.

Looking down the large, dark hole, Agon was disappointed. Uza had believed in the cause of stopping the Blood Priests, but he was a lancer. Lancers, by and large, were the most devout troops in the army. He'd opposed the Blood Priests because they meant to subvert the *obispos*, "stack" the Blood Cardinalship with their own, and change his religion. Agon had just denounced it outright. *At least I won't live to see my army die for such a terrible cause*, Agon thought. He heard a shot, but felt no pain. No new pain, anyway. He hadn't realized he'd closed his eyes, and now opened them to see Uza slide off his horse and fall with a thud in the tall, dusty grass, his head a bloody, mostly hollow gourd.

Capitan Ead Arevalo grimaced slightly and thrust his own smoking pistol into his saber belt. He'd rather liked Coronel Uza. "You heard the general!" he shouted at the flag bearers. "Throw those down at once! They're bloody, perverted *lies* and no longer stand for this army!"

General Tun spat more blood and looked at Agon with a strange expression. Finally, he nodded. "I thought someday it would come to this with you." That could've meant anything, but Tun joined with Arevalo in calling for the men to stop shooting and cast down the Dominion flag. With the guns of the enemy battery already unlimbering less than three hundred paces away and the mounted men pausing to dress their lines before they struck, Agon could only hope they'd grasp the significance of what he'd done. "General Panti, are you with me?" he asked the commander of the closest and most intact brigade. Panti looked frightened, and not of the enemy. Even if they lived through the day, the army's mission had very suddenly gone beyond merely stopping the Blood Priests and anointing Don Hurac as Supreme Holiness. Of course, aimed where it was, even the relatively small mounted force would scatter them. If they didn't do something quickly, the army would have no mission because it would cease to exist.

"Yes," General Panti tentatively replied, then his voice firmed. "I am *with* you, my general!"

"Then take charge here. *Stop the fighting, however you must!*" Agon looked at Tun. "Come, General, if you're able." His voice filled with irony. "We ride out and speak with El Diablo Anson once more. Join us, Capitan Arevalo. I don't think he'll shoot just the three of us. Really," he added absently, "I do wish we'd established some means to signal we wanted to talk."

"My apologies. I never thought we'd meet them . . . socially again, but I should've mentioned that their Capitan Lara told me a white flag is customary," Arevalo supplied as they urged their horses into the open and set a quick but careful pace that wouldn't cause Tun more discomfort than necessary.

"Indeed?" Tun hissed, spitting blood. "That would've been good to know."

CHAPTER 32

Lewis, Anson, Leonor, Varaa, and a grumbling Corporal Willis galloped up behind Barca's short battery of combat-ravaged guns and men as their limbers completed wide turns to the rear and gunners shouted, "Load!" The guns looked much like the men: battered, blackened, and covered with blood, little wounds showing all over them. Even their once-glistening bronze tubes were dull and lightly dented under contrastingly bright lead smears. Three of the four had replaced a wheel, and two were still missing at least one spoke. But they'd sent runners to secure shot-torn battery flags from Captains Hudgens and Dukane and the sections stood under the flapping gold banners, ready and willing for more. Barca had remained mounted on Dukane's own horse in the center of the battery, slightly back, posture stiff, but apparently confident.

He has every reason to be, Lewis thought, glad he'd allowed the young man to choose what he *wanted* to do, instead of just putting him somewhere—or worse, keeping him on his staff as he'd personally preferred. It was clear that Barca could do anything he set his mind to, and as fine an addition as he would've been to Lewis's staff, he would've been wasted there.

"Look who I found!" Reverend Harkin exclaimed happily, trotting up to join them with Father Orno on the horse behind him. Orno had been on the line with the lancers, helping healers as best he could, and was left behind when the lancers pulled out. "Little fellow was desperate to come, but nearly missed the boat!" Harkin continued. It was obvious he'd worried about his spiritual colleague and had missed him more than he'd admit.

"For some reason, I was drawn to be here. I . . . can't explain why," Orno confessed.

"Are you sure Reverend Harkin didn't snatch you up an' 'draw' you along against your will?" Leonor asked, her face very pretty as it always was when she smiled, in spite of the sweat-streaked grime.

"Quite sure," Orno declared.

"I know how you feel," Varaa said lowly, tail whipping, blue eyes wide and unblinking. The roar of battle remained intense ahead, but the rising breeze dulled it somewhat. "I should've returned to the Second Uxmal long since, but Consul Koaar can manage without me." She didn't need to remind them that, as Warmaster of the Ocelomeh, she was still technically Koaar's superior in battle. She'd only been delivering the 2nd Uxmal to him, and it didn't really need her. Lewis might. She did blink then, in a pattern Lewis had learned meant something like wary certainty. "Every action we took today had a decisive effect, but *this* is where the *decision* will be. I'm compelled to be part of it."

Lewis nodded understanding and glanced to the sides where the mounted men waited. Turning to Barca, he started to tell him to commence firing when Anson suddenly shouted, "Wait! Look at that! I'll be damned!"

"My God!" Harkin exclaimed. "They're throwing down their flags!"

Anson had summarized the proposals he and Agon had exchanged while they raced down to the beach to get in position, but Lewis hadn't given them credence. Neither had Anson. "I *will* be damned," he said now. "Shootin's easin' off, an' there's riders comin' out. Three of 'em."

It was true, and Lewis couldn't believe it either.

"It's another goddamn Dom trick," Willis blurted.

Lewis shook his head and looked at Leonor. "No," he said softly. "I don't think so. Captain Burton," he shouted. "Have your buglers sound 'cease firing' and keep them at it until the troops under Colonel Reed and King Har-Kaaska respond." He looked around and nodded forward. "Who's going with me?"

"I am," Leonor stated flatly, eyes challenging. "I'll always be with you, wherever you are."

Lewis smiled, a little sadly, it seemed. "I know."

As romantic interludes went, it was very subtle, but coming from the two of them, they might as well have shouted it to the heavens, and everyone caught it. Willis rolled his eyes and muttered, "Oh God!" The rest reacted as well, but only replied to Lewis's question. Harkin beamed and said, "Father Orno and I, of course." Varaa whipped her tail triumphantly but kept her tone serious when she simply said, "Me." Anson frowned, but then shrugged. "I'm comin', an' so are Boogerbear, Sal, an' a company of Burton's dragoons. This *ain't* a parley; they want to quit—they're throwin' down their flags! We don't have to worry about scarin' 'em off."

"Very well," Lewis agreed, urging Arete forward as the bugles blared. Leonor gently spurred Sparky and matched Lewis's pace, exactly at his side.

"They're good for each other. They need each other," Varaa told Anson as they followed. "And it's not like anything has *changed*. They already belonged together."

"They said it out loud, right in front of ever'body, damn it. That changes a *lot*," Anson grumbled. "I hope it don't get 'em killed."

Moments later, they all slowed to a stop and faced three now familiar enemies once more. They heard answering bugle calls from beyond the Dom . . . "formation" wasn't really the word anymore . . . and the shooting was beginning to slack at last. Lewis noted a few shots in the vicinity of Dom flags still defiantly waving before they also went down.

"Seems like, here lately, I've talked to you fellas more often than people I *like*," Anson snapped.

"It does," General Agon agreed, tone subdued for the first time they'd seen. He looked at Lewis. "I'm gratified—and somehow not surprised to find you where I least expected. I'd imagined you were in command of the larger forces to our . . . front." He gestured behind.

"He is," Varaa said simply. "We went for a ride."

"Extraordinary," Agon murmured, shaking his head. "I was right."

"About what?"

Agon shrugged. "A great many things. But wrong about the most important of all."

Lewis spoke up. "I assume we're here to discuss your surrender?" He was still a little shaken by that. Doms didn't surrender. But what else could it mean when they cast down their flags? He continued, "I recall the last time we spoke, you were looking forward to another meeting. A test of faith as much as arms, I believe you implied. Your god against ours, or something like that." Lewis's lip twisted in sudden fury. "Well, I'm not particularly religious." He gestured sharply at Harkin and Orno. "These men advise me on things like that. But I think it's clear 'our' god has beaten yours, and I only hope you've spilled enough blood to satisfy the evil bastard and nobody else has to die today."

"I hope that as well," Agon said, looking down. Raising his gaze, he continued: "What I mean is, I hope the fighting between us can end. Not that any bloodthirsty god is appeased. But instead of surrender, I'd offer an alliance. . . ."

"What?" Leonor blurted, amazed. "We *beat* you an' you still want things your way? You *lost!*"

"Yes!" Agon retorted bitterly. "I lost a battle. I also lost a large part of my army—which means more to me than I can express. Above even that, I've lost any lingering faith in the 'bloodthirsty god' I once served!" He looked at Orno and Harkin. "He isn't a *god*, He's the Devil himself! *You* already knew that, but it took me all my life to see it." He looked back at Lewis. "And yes, it took a defeat like this; like being shaken awake after a lifelong nightmare. Disarm us, enslave us. Do whatever you will! I'll serve *you* in whatever capacity you desire if you spare my troops, but never again *Him*, the usurper, in any fashion, for any reason." He pointed at Anson. "As I told him, we have a common foe in the Blood Priests, and I was already willing to work with you against them, to a degree." He snorted. "At least postpone our own disagreement. Now?" He shook his head, eyes wide with something like desperation. "I still want that, but I don't want to use you to further *my* cause, I want to join *yours!* Our 'common foe' now includes the terrible god of the 'Holy' Dominion itself, and I want *Him* cast down as much as you." He took a deep breath and closed his eyes. "I only wish I'd realized that sooner. You can't *imagine* how much I wish that!"

Taken aback, Lewis looked at Orno and Harkin, just as wide-eyed as Agon had been. "My God, I believe him," Harkin said softly.

"Possibly," Varaa unwillingly hedged, "but even if he speaks the truth, how many of his army feel the same?"

"Not all," confessed Capitan Arevalo. "Perhaps not even most." He glanced at Harkin and Orno. "They might help with that, and we'll need as many as are willing. I fear, after today . . ." He rubbed his sweaty brow. "Even all of us together might not be enough for what we must do. Neither of us could remake or bring down the Dominion alone." He gave Leonor a slight bow. "As for me, I believe I have *you* to thank for a wound that nearly shut my eyes forever, but also began to open them."

"You're welcome," Leonor said wryly, lifting a brow.

"As far back as that?" Agon asked him, surprised.

Lewis waved his hand impatiently. "All that can wait. I can even wait to be convinced of your sincerity. And I'll *have* to be convinced," he added darkly. "But at the moment, our people are still suffering and dying." The shooting had almost stopped, but there'd be a sea of hurt and badly wounded. "We'll pull back to a defensive posture, but you'll *immediately* begin to disarm," he told Agon. "Mr. Burton!"

"Sir!" replied the dragoon.

"Assemble all your men out here at once. Mr. Barca's battery as well."

Agon realized with a start that this was the closest he'd ever been to the enemy artillery, just a little over a hundred paces, and he tried to pick out what made the guns special. The carriages seemed oddly lightly built, with spoked wheels instead of solid, of course, and the ammunition carts rode very high, with the same wheels as the guns. But even at this distance, it was the men around them that struck him most different of all. He'd heard from Coronel Wicklow, a captive they'd taken off *Isidra* and held until just before the Battle of the Washboard, that Lewis Cayce was once part of an elite artillery unit, used to demonstrate the latest tactics on parade before being called to battle in his old war on that other world. *No parade ground artilleros, these, however,* he considered as he studied the exhausted men, practically lounging at their posts, even leaning on the wheels of their guns. But they'd amply proven they were good at what they did—all the enemy had—and the cannoneers in particular, even burdened by such big, heavy weapons, looked at him now with the calculating but bored expressions of a pack of sated predators. He shivered slightly and returned his attention to Coronel Cayce.

"Your men will form single-file lines leading to mine—*not* abreast—and start stacking arms. The first couple of companies to do so will stand aside while the rest are escorted toward the city by Mr. Anson's Rangers and Mr. Lara's lancers. I'll get infantry relief for you as fast as I can," he told Anson aside, "and we'll establish other collection points as quickly as messengers inform Colonel Reed. No wagons," he added to Agon, "and leave your wounded. We'll bring them into the city ourselves with the help of those first men of yours."

General Tun was frowning deeply, lips still rimmed with blood. Agon saw and frowned as well. "I suppose they *must* disarm us," he told him, "before they decide whether to arm us again."

"That's right," said Lewis grimly, "and anyone caught concealing a weapon will be shot where he stands. No exceptions." His expression lightened ever so slightly. "Except for your swords, and those of other officers you trust. You may need them to defend yourselves from your own men." He suddenly looked around. "Where's Kisin? Is he alive?" he asked whoever might know.

"I saw him with Mr. Lara at the breastworks. I think he stayed there with Alcaldesa Consela when we pulled out," offered Father Orno.

"Put him in charge of checking the prisoners. He might enjoy that." Lewis glanced once more at Agon. "He'll offer them no undue indignities, however. Prisoners will be searched and passed through"—he shrugged—"or shot. But they won't be abused."

"Treated with dignity or killed," Agon mused.

"Yes," Lewis said. "Better than we could've hoped for from you."

Agon shook his head. "In the past, yes. But even before my . . . epiphany, I'd decided to simply ignore Major Anson, as proposed, after we broke through his defense. Once through the city of Gran Lago, I could've ignored you as well, Coronel Cayce." He looked at Anson with something like astonishment. "I never thought you could stop us."

"Neither did I," Anson confessed. "But you couldn't've ignored me, an' I'd've dogged your ass from then on."

Agon looked troubled. "Still El Diablo of a sort, then. I suppose it's fortunate for both of us that things turned out as they did."

"We'll see," Lewis said, still skeptical and having trouble finding anything "fortunate" about the loss of so many troops. He refrained from pointing out that Agon couldn't have ignored the rest of the army either. Besides, he'd been just as concerned that Anson couldn't hold, and another way to get back in front of Agon had already occurred to him. He might still use it, to cut off Tranquilo and the force Agon was chasing. In the meantime . . . "Give the order, General. Now. Give the order for your men to disarm, or we'll finish our battle once and for all."

Agon looked at Tun and Arevalo. Finally, he sighed. "Very well."

"I MEANT WHAT I said," Leonor told Lewis as they rode back in the direction of Barca's battery, just the two of them for the moment.

"I know," Lewis replied.

"Did . . . did you mean what *you* said?"

Lewis smiled. "I don't recall saying much of anything, beyond acknowledging a much-appreciated fact. I know you've saved my life more often than I've even noticed."

"That's not what I meant, an' you know it!" Leonor insisted.

"Yes," Lewis relented, stopping Arete and turning to gaze at her now, an expression of something like wonder on his face. "You're a remarkable woman, Leonor. Very beautiful when you want to be, and even more so *to me* when you give it no thought at all, soaked in sweat and utterly deadly. That's a quality I appreciate more than most in a woman and haven't encountered before," he said with an ironic smile. Leonor absently touched her greasy, shoulder-length, blue-black hair in disbelief, and Lewis continued. "Nor have I often found your honesty, competence, and general intelligence . . ."

"Me? Smart?" She snorted. "Not like you. An' I sure don't *talk* very smart."

"*How* people talk means nothing," Lewis said dismissively, with a touch of impatience, perhaps even anger. "It only reflects where and how they're raised. I'll never be mistaken for a professor of grammar or rhetoric, and my Latin is appalling even compared to your father's, to my surprise." He snorted. "We'd all likely be amazed how many *private soldiers* in our army have at least a little Latin, but I doubt anyone understands the ancient Greek spoken in three fifty BC, so we'd all think Plato was a jabbering fool if we met him on the road." He shook his head emphatically. "It's *what* you say that matters, and you're *much* smarter than I am in many practical ways I admire and rely on."

He sighed and managed a smile. "So yes, I want you by me, now and always. Now as the fine soldier and trusted confidant, even protector I too often need. In the future . . ." He looked away. "As a great deal more I'm afraid to even plan for." He shifted his gaze back to her and smiled very gently. "But I do very much enjoy thinking about it."

Even under Leonor's dark, grimy skin, she managed to blush, but her tone was light, even slightly mocking, when she replied, "You? Afraid to plan? Far as I can tell, that's all you ever do. So . . ." She grinned. "Does this mean we're engaged? Like Father an' Mistress Samantha?"

At that moment, the woman in question, along with Dr. Newlin and Consul Koaar, galloped up with a tired but fresh-looking company of dragoons from the right, near the base of the hill where all was now quiet. Samantha stopped in front of Anson and started berating him as an "inconsiderate ruffian" and for "abandoning" her to "go off on his silly adventures" as Koaar and his escort peeled off toward Lewis.

"Most assuredly *not* like them," Lewis stated flatly, then lowered his voice. "But certainly . . . connected, if you wish."

Leonor chuckled, then said very solemnly, "Well, then I guess you can kiss me, if you want."

Lewis chuckled back, but affected an expression of horror. "Here? Now? In front of the army? In front of *General Agon*? I think not!"

He hauled on Arete's reins just short of the resurrected Number Two gun and allowed Koaar to catch him. They exchanged grinning salutes while the battered artillerymen traded less respectful greetings with the relatively clean dragoons. Lewis recognized Colonel Itzam's Itzincabo aide, Captain Raul Uo, leading the escort. Looking east, he knew where he and his men had come from. 3rd Division was no longer just a cloud of dust on the horizon, but a long, fat column of dusty men in blue with skirmishers out front. Glancing back at Agon, still where he'd left him (attended by Sal and Boogerbear while Dr. Newlin adjusted his spectacles and began to examine General Tun), Lewis had strongly mixed feelings. He'd respected Agon as an adversary in much the same way he would a venomous serpent. Even after learning there was a distinction between him and the Blood Priests, he'd considered it insignificant and wanted to destroy him. But doing so now was like cutting a rattlesnake's head off with a knife while it was biting you. *You'll certainly live longer, and I guess that's a "victory," but you still might die.* And the true difference between Doms like Agon and the direction the Dominion was heading was greater than he'd imagined. With Agon possibly "converted" . . . He didn't know if they could cooperate or not, but if they could, even accounting for losses, they'd effectively doubled Lewis's strength. *With hundreds of miles still to go, through the dark, bloody heart of the Dominion—and with the probable intervention of a huge enemy force that's certain to be recalled to stop us both—I think we better try very hard to get along.*

EPILOGUE

==

C aptain Eric Holland stood on a high promontory west of Vera Cruz with Captain Ixtla and Lieutenant Hayne and half a dozen guards and runners, along with Don Hurac, Capitan "Don" Roderigo, and an equal number of militia guards for the Blood Cardinal. Squalls were lashing Vera Cruz with intermittent downpours, visible for miles as they marched toward shore, and Zyon, Don Hurac's . . . woman? Wife? Slave?— her actual status remained uncomfortably unclear to Holland—was holding a broad parasol over her husband/master to protect him from occasional sheets of rain. Everyone else, including Zyon, was sopping wet, viewing the progress of the defensive works the townsfolk had been laboring on. Work was ongoing, even in the rain—except in the deep pit surrounding the works encompassing the portion of the city they had to defend. It was starting to look like a flooded moat.

Earlier that day, they'd seen one of the prize merchant galleons (immediately identified by the Stars and Stripes that broke out at the masthead) driving into port on the leading edge of a squall. *Isidra*, now fully functional and armed with a pair of 36pdrs retrieved from one of the fire-damaged warehouses and mounted on pivoting gun carriages that could fire to either side, steamed over to investigate before she dropped anchor. Second Lieutenant Randall Sessions, *Isidra*'s half-black former privateersman skipper, must've been convinced of her innocence, because she was allowed to proceed. A boat was quickly hoisted out and rowed toward shore. *Tiger* was still on patrol, out at sea. Despite her age and the weight of her own new armament (several more 36pdrs had been mounted on her hastily reinforced gun deck), *Tiger* remained the fastest, most seaworthy, most powerful ship they had. The weight of metal she could throw was still a far cry from her glory days as a fifty-gun ship, but with a total of ten 36pdrs added to the 12pdrs and 6pdrs she already had, even Don Hurac—who still maintained they'd written off the Dom navy prematurely—conceded she outgunned anything he knew she might ever meet.

"Shouldn't we go down ta meet 'em, sur?" Hayne asked as they watched the progress of the longboat toward the dock. "They're bound ta bear news."

Holland shook his head and growled, "Aye, an' they can 'bear' it a bit further, if it's urgent. Ever'body knows where we are. We're already soaked, none of us is the horseman you are, an' it took us half the mornin' ta get up here." He sighed. "I ain't a soldier. Most of us ain't, not really, so I want everyone to *stare* at that damned city, all its defenses an' possible lines of approach, until you could paint it from the picture in yer head."

"I never was much good with paints," Don Hurac murmured apologetically. "But I've an excellent memory for images—and I've lived here most of my life."

"I can paint a picture for you, Your Holiness," offered Don Roderigo.

Holland rolled his eyes. "It was a figure o' speech—though, come to that, a picture ain't a bad idea. Most of us *ain't* been here long."

More rain came, loud enough they couldn't talk, and they moved under the meager protection of some trees, where they discussed the various directions Don Frutos and Tranquilo might come from. Ixtla asked Don Hurac to speculate on the numbers they'd be looking at by then, and Hayne proposed harassing attacks with increasing enthusiasm. Holland honestly didn't know *what* to do and simply kept silent while they talked. He'd done all right in "command" of the raid, he supposed, but had no business commanding the defense of a city. Once again, he was strongly tempted to evacuate everyone who wanted to go by sea to Uxmal and just abandon the place. That line of thought was swept away when four mounted figures trotted up the switchback slope in their direction. The rain was tapering off again, and one, the least capable on horseback by far, was dressed like he was—as a "naval officer"—in a long, blue, unornamented frock coat. Holland guessed it was Capitan Razine. No guessing was required to determine who his companions were. One was the Ranger, Sal Hernandez—easily the *best* horseman Holland knew—and another tall man had to be Reverend Harkin, though there was only about half as much of him as Holland remembered. The last, furry, drowned-rat form, tail whipping sprays of water, could only be Warmaster Varaa-Choon. Relief flooded through Holland when he saw her. He didn't know *why* she was here, or what happened to allow her to come, but it was a given he was off the hook and she'd take operational command in his place. He grinned for the first time since . . . he didn't know when.

"You might've come down to meet us," Varaa accused as she drew near and led her companions in dismounting. Her features were even more feline than usual when she was wet, including the apparent inherent misery all wet cats endured as a matter of course.

Hayne looked scoldingly at Holland, who said, "We didn't know it was you. Could'a just been Razine comin' in with another request for a refit." Razine's ship, *Roble Fuerte*, was his own property, and he was happy to accept the care being lavished on all the ships in the tiny Allied fleet at Vera Cruz. Razine bristled, but Holland cut him off. "Glad to see you all. Don Hurac (Holland had begun to like the Blood Cardinal in spite of himself but was damned if he'd call him "Your Holiness"), you've met Sal Hernandez and Capitan Razine, but I'd like to present the Reverend Samuel Harkin, of Pennsylvania, and Warmaster Varaa-Choon of the Ocelomeh."

To everyone's surprise, Don Hurac bowed very low. "I'm honored to meet a priest of God from another world," he told Harkin. "I believe we have a lot to talk about." He looked at Varaa. "I've never seen your kind, but you've been described to me by others, from a time when several were . . . guests in the Holy City."

"Captives," Varaa said lowly. "Tortured. Two died, two escaped. I helped with that."

"Indeed?" gushed Don Hurac. "Within the very heart of the Dominion, looking . . . as you do? Extraordinary."

"It wasn't 'in the heart,' but just outside. They were freaks on tour," she added with disgust. "One of those two is now dead," Varaa continued, "killed by the Holcanos—who *were* puppets of the Dominion. The other is Har-Kaaska, king of all the Ocelomeh and second in command of a division in our army."

"I dare say he's a vengeful sort," Capitan Roderigo mulled.

"He is, by nature," Varaa agreed.

"Quite understandable. I was 'on tour' myself during that period," Roderigo explained obliquely, "and not only viewed the captives but remember the uproar around their escape. Your king might be mollified to learn that a great many of his captors received considerably more painful and permanent treatment."

"He might," Varaa allowed. "He concurred when Colonel Cayce let the surviving Holcanos live . . . after we destroyed them as a threat to the Yucatán forever."

"Did we, by God!" Hayne exclaimed. That was apparently news, and Don Hurac and Don Roderigo looked at each other.

Sal Hernandez coughed. "As you might imagine, we have other news." Looking at the sky as if to see if the rain had stopped long enough to deliver it, he fished in his vest and brought out an oilcloth packet. He started to hand it over to Holland, but gave it to Varaa instead. Varaa held it a moment. "I don't know exactly what your . . . arrangement is here. Only what Mr. Hernandez reported." She blinked at Don Hurac. "I've heard our people have chosen to help defend the inhabitants of Vera Cruz from extermination *by their own people*, and in exchange for our use of the port and city in aid of our campaign against the Blood Priests. Is that essentially the case?"

Don Hurac pursed his lips. "Yes . . . essentially, and I'm ashamed the protection is necessary. I can't even blame the Blood Priests for that, since the tradition of leaving no witnesses to the success of other cultures ruled by different beliefs at our expense began long ago. I understand the populations of any number of frontier towns were entirely replaced by those who expelled the natives that overran them. That served two purposes: leaving no one to remember life under different laws and rulers, as well as providing a loot incentive for 'liberators' of territory already claimed by the Dominion." He spread his hands at his sides. "One of many flaws in our national administration that Don Datu and I had hoped to change after his elevation." He looked away. "I believe now, looking back, even as we discussed that and other things, I subconsciously suspected there *was* no repairing all the Dominion's ills—short of replacement. Now? With Don Datu likely murdered and Don Julio as Supreme Holiness, the system *will* change—for the worse." He shook his head and returned his gaze to match Varaa's. "As to your use of Vera Cruz and the extent of our cooperation in general, that determination has been awaiting details from the southeast. From you and General Agon, in point of fact. I tried to imply—and 'imply' was all I could do—that the General should seek a similar understanding with Coronel Cayce before they destroyed each other. You understand I couldn't *tell* him to do so without risking losing his support. Or if not his, then his army's." He shrugged. "One might *think* one knows another man's mind, but when they're afraid to come right out and tell you . . ." He shrugged again.

"They met. There was a battle," Varaa said simply, then finally handed the packet to Holland. Also glancing at the sky, Holland unwrapped the oilcloth and began reading the pages they protected. After several moments of deep concentration, he suddenly snorted incredulously and looked up. "This is some kinda goddamn joke," he accused with complete conviction and glared at Varaa and Harkin. "Says Agon was 'decisively' defeated at a place called Gran Lago"—he raised a brushy brow at Razine—"where we sent *you* to watch." Flicking his eyes back to Varaa, he continued sarcastically, "Which is great to hear. Huzza! But then you made all this other shit up, just ta burst my brain."

"What the devil are ye talkin' about?" Hayne asked.

Holland shook the page. "According to *this*, after as bloody a fight as you can imagine, Agon came over to the side of goodness an' light. We're all friends now, an' jointly engaged in a war against the evil Blood Priests! Agon and most o' his army have *joined* ours and will be comin' here directly." He glanced dubiously back at the page. "How, it don't say. But on top o' that, that little Papist Orno—no offense to your pal," Holland assured Harkin with a wave, "preached a sermon ta the Doms an' converted 'em by the bushel!" He blinked. "He's been asked to *baptize* General Agon in the lake by the city!"

"It's true," Harkin practically whispered, recalling it all with a sense of wonder. "I helped with the first troops to convert. Father Orno and I baptized *hundreds* of Dom soldiers in Gran Lago. I never expected to live to see such a thing. So many souls, so *hungry* for salvation!"

"Anxious not to get shot or hanged," Sal muttered to Varaa, who shushed him impatiently.

"What did you say?" Don Hurac asked.

"Blood Priests found lurking in the city of Gran Lago were hanged," Varaa confirmed louder, blinking something a few had learned to recognize as a mixture of horror and fury. "After the atrocities we watched them perform, that's a . . . tradition we've initiated. None were found in the ranks of Agon's army, but a few of his soldiers were shot. More were confined in Gran Lago and will remain so until the war is over. The city is now under the same threat of extermination as Vera Cruz, I presume, so the remaining populace quite willingly joined our cause. In any event, after he declared he'd be baptized—not in blood, this time," Vara added sharply, even challengingly, for Don Hurac's benefit, "General Agon proclaimed that his army would be a *Christian* army, following the original faith of his warrior society and the first founders of the Dominion."

"Indeed," Harkin enthused, also specifically addressing Don Hurac. "Apparently, having been beaten by an army largely accepting Jesus Christ as its *savior* instead of a distorted example of the suffering required to enter paradise, so he's broken entirely with the foundational faith—that you represent—of those now in power in the Dominion, albeit doubly perverted by the Blood Priests, whom you claim to oppose. The troops *Agon* had shot all agreed to the general's . . . new direction, as it were, yet attempted to subvert him from within and make a mutiny. As Warmaster Varaa said, those who simply chose not to convert will be prisoners of war."

Holland was looking at Don Hurac. "I wonder where that leaves you. You might be at odds with 'em, but as a Blood Cardinal, you might be included in Agon's definition of 'those now in power.'"

Seeming oddly amused, Don Hurac shook his head and reached over and grasped Zyon's hand. "Under sentence of death myself, with Don Frutos and Tranquilo marching to destroy me and all the people who look to me for protection, I doubt I could be considered 'in power' by anyone's definition. Besides, I was struggling with my faith much like General Agon must've been on the very night you raided Vera Cruz. *Before* it all began," he stressed. "Bear in mind, I'd just returned from the Holy City and seen the direction of things." Glancing at Harkin, he continued, "I find I have a yearning for the older beliefs myself, and once my people here fully accept how badly *they've* been betrayed by their faith, I might ask you to perform yet another baptism."

"God damn me!" Holland exclaimed, glaring at Harkin. "You old gospel shark. You finally got your way at last. With part o' the Doms on our side, it'll be a 'holy war' after all."

Harkin was shaking his head, exasperated. "Don't be absurd. It's *always* been a 'holy war.' Not of the sort we're used to—Christians versus Mohommadans, Protestants against Catholics or everyone against the Jews. Certainly not of the sort I once waged, over comparatively minor disputes between denominations. This is a war to determine what 'holy' *means* on this world!" He narrowed his eyes at the sailor. "Whether or not you even believe in God, in fact. We must fight to ensure this continent, possibly the world, will be ruled by 'goodness and light,' as you put it; justice, tolerance, equality—all the 'inalienable rights' and virtues of the Constitution Colonel Cayce so rightly reveres, and not be forever subject to the foul, bloody-minded reign of the Devil. "Evil" is part of the Devil's name, after all, and the Blood Priests personify the Beast whether you believe he's real or not. I think he is, of course," Harkin ended with a prim grimness.

Holland waved his hand as it started to rain again. "Oh, so do I, preacher. God knows I seen enough o' his works. But even if God brought us to this world like you say, to save the Uxmalos from the 'Devil-Doms' or whatever, I don't think he really expected us ta whip the Devil for good an' end evil forever. I ain't seen any sign o' that happenin' back home. As for helpin' save the Uxmalos an' Itzincabos an' the rest, ain't we already done that? I mean, we've whipped the Holcanos an' run the Doms out of the Yucatán. Agon could come here an' hold Vera Cruz forever, if we helped him with the defenses an' kept him supplied by sea." He waved again. "Other than that, we just . . . go home. Back to Uxmal. I *like* it there. The Doms'll have their civil war that'll last for years. Even if the Blood Priests win, it'll be a generation before they pester us again."

Don Hurac looked suddenly very surprised, as if he'd finally discovered the root of some profound misunderstanding. He started to speak, but Varaa beat him to it.

"One of the problems with that approach is we can never win," she said hotly. "I want to *win*, and as Lewis always says—has strongly convinced Sira Periz and the other *alcaldes* of the Yucatán—the strongest defense only postpones defeat. Sometimes it postpones it long enough for the enemy to collapse, or lose his will and simply leave the defender alone, but there can never be a decisive, threat-eliminating victory except by attacking the enemy until he *knows* he's beaten. We can't do that by going home."

"There's another problem with that," Don Hurac informed them somberly, turning to face Holland. "Why are you so confident the Dominion navy is no threat to you? I know you have armed your few ships quite heavily, but they're still very few. I've repeatedly told you the Dominion navy is larger than you realize, but you've paid me no heed. I assumed that meant you had some sort of plan to neutralize it. But simply 'going home' won't do."

Holland scratched his stubbly chin. "Aye," he agreed. "We'll have to build up our navy a bit. It'll take time, but we should have it. Even you admit we've knocked out all but two or three warships in the Atlantic, an' they're probably laid up in Cuba. Only the fleet in the Pacific would worry me, an' it's busy supplyin' the big army o' the Gran Cruzada on its way to the Californias, er watchin' for Imperial ships o' the New Britain Isles that might harass those supplies. So?"

"So, Don Julio *will* recall the Gran Cruzada to solidify his position, if he hasn't already. Some of those forces may take ship. How long do you think it'll take them to get here? To reach *Uxmal*?"

Holland looked confused. "Better part of a year, to sail around the whole damned world in the tubs you have. No offense, Razine," he hastily added. Then glanced at Varaa. "*You* said any passage south around the horn was too choked by ice ta use."

"That's right," Varaa confirmed, also wondering what had Don Hurac so suddenly concerned.

"Oh dear," said Don Hurac, measuring Capitan Razine. "Being a private shipowner, I doubt you've been engaged to sail to the Pacific? Never south of fifteen degrees of northern latitude, in fact?"

"Never," Razine confessed, now totally confused as well. He'd seen drawings of the known world and been particularly impressed by the great embroidered atlas in the *alcalde*'s audience hall at Uxmal, but despite its precision, its scope was limited. He'd seen no other proper charts of any region besides that which he regularly plied, primarily between Vera Cruz, Tampico, and several Caribbean isles. Varaa was suddenly blinking something like dread, and Holland remembered she'd once told him of an area where her own long-ago survey of the coast had been interrupted.

"Therefore you, who have been our friends' principal advisor on nautical matters, haven't heard of El Paso del Fuego," Don Hurac said flatly. It wasn't a question.

"I've . . . heard the term," Razine hedged a little reluctantly, knowing whatever, *wherever*, it was, it was a closely guarded secret he shouldn't have even known about.

Don Hurac faced the others. "El Paso del Fuego is a treacherous but quite navigable passage between the Atlantic and Pacific oceans, roughly three hundred *leguas*, or a thousand miles, to the southeast of here. We know it didn't exist on the world we originally came from and assume it was carved over the ages by vigorous volcanic activity. Judging by your expressions, I now see you had no such place where you came from either. The problem remains, however, that you haven't nearly as much time as you thought and can't simply go home and let a civil war in the Dominion run its course. Those who oppose the Blood Priests must *win*"—he nodded at Varaa—"and do so quickly, before the weight of the Gran Cruzada descends upon us all, and there's no home for any of us to return to. Anywhere."

ACKNOWLEDGMENTS

As always, I'd like to thank my agent, Russel Galen, and my incredibly supportive editor, Anne Sowards.